GALE FORCE

★

COUNT FIVE AND DIE

★

THE BIG BITE

GALE FORCE

Elleston Trevor

★

COUNT FIVE AND DIE

Barry Wynne

★

THE BIG BITE

Charles Williams

★

also two short stories from

ALFRED HITCHCOCK PRESENTS

The October Game

by Ray Bradbury

The Most Dangerous Game

by Richard Connell

ODHAMS PRESS LIMITED

LONG ACRE, LONDON

S.1158.1R.PQ.G.

MADE AND PRINTED IN
GREAT BRITAIN BY ODHAMS (WATFORD) LTD.
WATFORD, HERTS

CONTENTS

GALE FORCE

Elleston Trevor

"Gale Force" is published by
William Heinemann Ltd.

The Author

Elleston Trevor, who served in the Royal Air Force during the Second World War, is the author of *The Big Pick-up, Squadron Airborne, The Killing Ground* and numerous short stories and other novels, which have placed him in the best-seller class. He met his wife, Jonquil, during the war, and they married in 1947. They now live with their small son at Brighton. Elleston Trevor's chief interest is motor-racing. He owns a new Rolls-Royce and recently toured Luxembourg in it. Among his other interests are playing tennis and reading modern fiction.

CHAPTER ONE

At midnight the *Atlantic Whipper* was two hundred-odd miles from Land's End, steaming north-east and homeward through a quiet sea. She was a deep-water merchantman on voyage from Buenos Aires, with four thousand tons of grain and ten passengers. She was bound for Avonmouth. Above her to the north there was a sick half moon; beneath her the sea was black. The only sounds were her wash and the low drone of the rigging, tuned by the wind of her own passage. There were few lights burning in this, the graveyard, watch; the ship was as dark almost as her element, and as quiet. Her size, shrunk to a pin-point by the vastness of sea and sky, allowed of no surprise that a mass of six thousand tons with forty men in the crew could make so little disturbance in the night. For all her great dead weight of thick cold steel and the tonnage of cargo in her holds, she was her true size here between the far horizons, a drifting mote.

On the bridge the watch was quiet, part of a slow hypnotic rhythm that seemed motionless. The second mate took two more paces to his left, and stopped, and balanced on his heels, and turned, and paced again slowly to his right, and stopped again, and came back, his tread monotonous and measured as if he were waiting for something. Ten paces to the left, ten to the right, and then back again, and back again. He had walked miles here, and got nowhere.

He stopped and stood at the binnacle, looking at the compass card. He said in a casual grunt:

"Where the bloody hell are you going?"

"Ay, ay, sir," said the helmsman, and put the wheel down a spoke, watching the indicator and the card. The officer paced off again. They were both glad of the sound their voices had made in the quiet wheelhouse; the spell of the night had been broken for a while by the unnecessary question and the ready answer. Tug Wilson was a good enough helmsman to steer through a needle's eye, and Beggs a good enough officer to let him alone at the wheel; but the respite from silence in the graveyard watch was a little relief.

Beggs went out to the port wing of the bridge. The look-out was still as a stanchion.

"See anything, Mounsey?"

The white of his face turned in the gloom. "No, sir." They listened to the bow-wave and the rigging's drone. "I'd say she's freshening, sir."

Beggs sniffed the wind. The glass had fallen, hours ago, and before midnight there had been gale warnings on the radio. He said, "She'll freshen all right, don't you worry." But ahead of the *Whipper* the sea looked flat, a flinty black waste with not a chip of white in it anywhere. When he turned and looked astern he could see where the breeze was coming from, up from the South Atlantic. It would follow the *Whipper* home.

From the wheel Tug Wilson glanced up and had a glimpse of the second mate's back through the door of the wheelhouse; he looked down again at the compass card, thinking of Mr. Beggs, and the bit of a scrap there'd been in Buenos Aires the night before the *Atlantic Whipper* had sailed for home.

Wilson hadn't been in Mickey Green's when the scrap had started, but Mounsey had told him about it, grinning like a long monkey with his white teeth fanning out in the delight of it—"It was a couple o' cowsons o' drunken Scowegians, first go off. They come bargin' into Mickey Green's lookin' for trouble, an' by God, they got it, see, 'cause the place was stuffed to the ceilin' with dagos, Yankees, Scots, Irish, Liverpool-Irish, Geordies, Lascars an' bloody Chinks. Not to mention a mob o' Canadians."

"Oh gor bli'," Wilson said.

"These Scowegians have a pint, see, an' then turn their mugs upside-down on the bar—you know. They didn't have time to see who was goin' to 'ave a go—they was down on the floor before you could look round, hollerin' out for daylight."

"What were you doing?" asked Tug Wilson.

Mounsey's grin cracked his face. "Me? What the 'ell d'you think I was doin'? I was trying to find the door, quick. Then some clot smashed the lamps, so I got under a table for the duration. After a bit, in comes Jimmy Beggs."

"How did you know it was him?" asked Wilson. He knew Mounsey never embroidered his stories, keen though he was on telling them in all their detail; Wilson just wanted to know how he'd recognized Jim Beggs from underneath a table in the dark.

"I knew by 'is voice, mate. The door come open an' there 'e was, hollerin' out, 'Who's from the *Whipper*? Who's from the *Whipper*?' One or two blokes answered 'im from above the din, an' went outside, but I stayed where I was."

"Why?" asked Tug Wilson. You had to keep asking Mounsey questions, to keep his steam up, when he was telling a story. He liked to know you were listening.

"Well, there was some bastard got 'is teeth sunk into my ankle, an' I was tryin' to get a grip on a bottle to 'it 'is 'ead with an' make 'im stop. In the end I had to break it over 'im before he'd give over." He dragged his sock down and showed Wilson. "You can see I'm tellin' you gospel, mate."

Tug looked at the three red marks on Mounsey's ankle.

"Gor bli'," he said, "it looks like a rat."

" 'E was a rat, all right." He pulled his sock up and grinned again as his memory delighted him anew. "An' then someone gets a lamp goin' again, see, an' Jimmy Beggs starts in. From where I was I could see the bosun, stood on top o' the bar with a chair-leg in 'is fist, waitin' for customers, an' there was poor little Tich Copley bein' torn apart by one o' the Irish——"

"Poor little Tich," said Tug Wilson.

"I know." He lit a cigarette. "Where was I, mate?"

"Under the table."

"I mean what was I sayin'?"

"About Jimmy Beggs——"

"Christ yes, old Jimmy. Well, 'e got started in, soon as the lamp was goin' again. You should'a *seen* 'im! It was bloody murder, honest to God it was!"

"Well, what did he do?" asked Wilson.

"Well, 'e weighs sixteen stone, don't 'e, an' 'e come in at a run for the Irishman who was tryin' to stuff poor little Tich Copley's face with one o' the walls——"

"Why wasn't you helping him, then?"

"Who, Tich? Christ, by the time I'd'a got across to 'im from where I was, 'e'd've been dead, mate, an' so would I." He spread his hands out, worried by Tug's reproach. "A shortarse like Tich ought to keep out o' places like Mickey Green's on a Saturday night. Christ, any sixteen-year-old sawn-off pixie ought to keep clear o' places like Mickey Green's on a Saturday——"

"Go on, then," said Tug Wilson. "What did Jimmy do to the Irishman?"

"I couldn't've 'elped poor little Tich, honest, not from where I was, mate." He spread his hands wider. "It would've been——"

"'Course you couldn't," said Tug Wilson. "I can see that. Now what did Jimmy do?"

The sun of Mounsey's grin came out again and he said, "What did 'e do? It was a treat. A treat, mate. There was nothin' rough, see—that ain't Jimmy's way. 'E just bent down an' picked up the Irish's feet. He come down with a wallop on 'is face, hollerin' out something cruel an' tryin' to kick Jimmy through the roof, but o' course Jimmy wasn't 'avin' any, so 'e goes on holding the Irish with 'is 'ead down until Tich gets out. Then, when the Irish gets a grip on someone an' swings 'is arm round at Jimmy, Jimmy just kicks 'im in the face till 'e stops." His grin exploded into a chuckle, and he blew out smoke from the cigarette in a luxury of delight.

"I see," nodded Tug Wilson, "nothing rough."

Mounsey spread his hands again in defence of the second mate. "Well, 'e had to look after himself, didn't 'e?"

"'Course he did," said Wilson. "What happened after that?"

"He drops the Irish, who's out cold, an' starts on a couple of gits that are tryin' to get the bosun off the bar. I found a bit o' space, just then, so I got out an' dived through the door, see, just as some bastard lobs a bottle. It catches the door, right by my 'ead, just as I'm divin' through." He turned his head and leaned towards Wilson, to show him the scars. They were just healing, but still looked messy. "You can see I'm tellin' you gospel, mate."

"You were lucky," said Wilson.

"I'll say I was lucky. I stopped outside to have a look, an' there's Jimmy Beggs still in there, hollerin' for the rest o' the *Whipper* boys to get out. I seen him pick up a Lascar an' throw 'im through that door so fast that 'e fetched up in the dock!"

"From Mickey's?" Wilson frowned. Mounsey tapped him solemnly on the knee.

"From Mickey's, into the dock."

"Ber-*li'*," said Wilson.

"Then I found poor little Tich Copley, bent down double over 'imself, winded——"

"Poor little Tich," said Wilson.

"I know. I picked 'im up an' carried 'im to where it was quiet. The coppers'd come up by then, an' someone was tryin' to get the Lascar out o' the dock, an' there was a Yankee hollerin' out that he was dyin', every time they went to pick 'im up. It'd come on to rain a bit, too, so I got 'old of poor little Tich and carried 'im on board."

"Before he got wet," nodded Wilson.

"Eh?" Mounsey dropped his cigarette and stubbed it out. "But you should just've seen Jimmy Beggs, mate."

Standing at the wheel, Tug Wilson looked now at the second mate, catching a glimpse of his back before he looked down again at the compass card. Beggs was all of sixteen stone, with a head like a boulder on which thin hair grew like seaweed, and a face like an ageless rock that the storms have weathered to a stony crag; yet he was a quiet man, with a small high voice that piped from the button-mouth that was lost somewhere between the hook of the nose and the butt of the chin. He was a slow-moving man with gentle eyes—alert enough and alive enough, but gentle—and his big hands, clasped behind him as he paced his ten paces to the left and ten to the right, had seemed to have come together for a prayer. Watching him with a brief glance at long intervals, Wilson found shelter in the man. If he were in bad trouble, he would like to be somewhere near Beggs.

As for Mounsey's story, it had made him shudder to the heart of him. He had seen dockside fights himself, one of them fatal and with no more cause than a laugh from a coloured whore; and they had always scared him. He was strong, and not much under six feet tall, and didn't mind heights or depths, or snakes, or dentists, but a big fight among drunk seamen would frighten him, perhaps because they usually sprang from nothing, and achieved nothing. He'd seen half a bottle of liquor make a monster of a quiet Scot and send him at the nearest throat with a will to murder, and for nothing; he'd seen a kid of a Greek dragging one broken leg along behind him, out of a Marseilles bar, too sick to scream with his pain, for the sake of an argument about a girl—you could say, for nothing. He had seen men behave worse than beasts, with less dignity and far less cause than beasts—men who were his own shipmates with a mother somewhere and clean collars at home. A fight had to be about something important, and then Tug Wilson could be counted in; but these senseless brawls made him sick to think about.

Beggs stopped by the binnacle and slapped it gently with a big hand.

Wilson brought the wheel up a spoke. "Ay, ay, sir."

The *Whipper* ran on through forty-seven north, seven west, north-east to England with her grain and passengers in the quiet of the middle watch. The lookout on the fo'c'sle thought he could smell the Channel, and thought of his home. Soon, when smoke began drawing down across the bows thickly as if the *Whipper*'s hair were tangled over her eyes, he turned for a quick look at the sea in the south. The smoke was billowing down from the funnel, and on each side of it he could see the white chips in the black flint sea. He remembered what the bosun had said last evening, when the sea had been glass-calm and the sky clear as a girl's eyes. "There's a breeze o' wind down south'ards," Art Starley had said. And here it was, true enough, coming up astern and chopping the water, touching the ship and darting away, to swoop back and tug the smoke from the stack and pull it down across her bows; it sang in the rigging, the soft song rising and falling, lifting to a thin high drone and dying away as if far distant suddenly; it came back and banged a door, and slapped the Red Duster at the mainmast; it fled up, the wind, and dived in little gusts at the sea, cuffing and curling it. A breeze o' wind down south'ards, and now it was here. The bosun knew his weather and that was a fact.

The lookout stood with his back to the wind and watched the shift of smoke going away in the dark ahead of the *Whipper*. It made his work more difficult. A ship's light could come up through that veil of smoke and not be seen until the last few minutes when the two masses in their thousands of tons drew together in the night at thirty knots or maybe forty, and the shouts would go up and the bells ring and the wheels spin hard to break a collision-course.

Then the smoke thinned as the coal brightened in the furnaces, and his mind was eased. Towards the end of the graveyard watch a man on the fo'c'sle was prey to all the fancies of the night, and stood there jostled by the crowd of his superstitions until his very reason was sore at the elbows, pushing them away. In less than an hour the light would come and the day break, and he would go off watch. Roll on, the bells.

CHAPTER TWO

A QUARTERMASTER woke the first mate at ten minutes to four. Turnbull was alert within seconds.

"What's that sea doing?"

"Gettin' up, sir."

The first mate got out of his bunk and looked through the scuttle. It was still dark, but no longer night. In the darkness there were the fragile tints of the coming day, a small cloud very high, touched with first light, and a softness to the east horizon too feeble to define; but they were there. At this time, when a day was born, he often felt that it was touch and go with so delicate a birth: you could smudge out the small high cloud and draw the dark of your hand across the horizon and the day would die in the womb. It would not matter to Turnbull.

He washed in cold water and shaved deftly, watching his face afterwards in the oblong glass with his mouth tight and eyes unfriendly, for he was a vain man and over-critical of himself at this time of the day. Towards evening with a drink or two in him he could relax and admit to himself that here was a rare man, well-knit and superior to most in many things. He would turn in at night, satisfied; but each new day was a challenge to his faith in himself, and he knew it, and was ready with a quick temper if anyone tried to cross him.

He went on deck, and was hit by the morning's hand, by the gusty wind and the light sharpening against his eyes, the clip of the waves as the *Whipper* met them and broke them along her sides. He could hear crying, under the sky, and looked up. There were sea-gulls, out from England. He went into the wheelhouse.

"Good morning, Mr. Beggs." A tight mouth, formal.

"'Morning, sir."

"Where's the relief quartermaster?"

Able-seaman Robins was behind him. "Sir?"

"Very good." He stood at the binnacle. "Course?"

Beggs said, "North forty-one east, sir." He stood with his back to the windows, waiting for the chief officer to get his eyes. He was not worried by Turnbull's brusque formality. He was rather fond of Turnbull, because he was a man with a worse weakness than most, and it must be hard to bear with, alone. Turnbull had a master's certificate and had skippered the *Sea Lord II* for Watson and Blount three years ago in the Pacific; but these days there were more masters than ships, because a sailor was born quicker than a ship was built, and only one master for each.

"Take over."

"Sir."

The wheel changed hands. Wilson looked neither at Beggs nor Turnbull as he went below. It was dead funny to see the two of them in the wheelhouse together, Jimmy and Old Bull, with all that parade-ground blarney flying about as if the owners themselves were there to watch the business. Mounsey had said, two days after the chief officer had got this berth, "We're goin' to have trouble with that one, you see if we don't." But there hadn't been much trouble from Turnbull. He'd go barking about the place with his eyes everywhere and pull you up for nothing, but when you stood your ground and stared him out he'd suddenly go under, and you'd know it. All he wanted was a lot of quick seamanlike ay-ay-sirs to show him you knew your place, and he was satisfied.

There was something inside the first mate that was as soft as a rotten apple, cowardice maybe, or kindness gone bad. Some said he was scared of something, but he wasn't scared of the sea, and that was enough for Tug Wilson. He'd been through a fog collision with Chief Officer Turnbull, off the Dogger, and he was all right. Whatever it was that had gone soft inside him, or had been born inside him, it wasn't the fear of the sea or of anything the sea could do to a ship or a man. To Wilson, who had crawled about in the scuppers in his nappies on board his father's trawler more than twenty years ago, Turnbull was a reckonable sailor, and he was satisfied. But it was dead funny to see him in the wheelhouse with a man like Jimmy Beggs, twice his size and twice as quiet.

At the wheel, Able-seaman Robins checked the course at north forty-one degrees east and put the midships spoke down a bit, feeling the slight beam-sea. The first mate said to Beggs:

"Have we had more warnings?"

"Yes. Southerly gales. She's force four now, near enough." A minute passed, and Turnbull said:

"All right, I've got my eyes."

For the benefit of the helmsman, Beggs said cheerfully, "All's well, lights a-bright!" He went below to turn in. Robins waited for the nonsense to start. They had told him, shipping out of Buenos Aires, "You'll be in the mate's watch," and he had cursed his luck. There was nothing much wrong with Old Bull except that he couldn't keep his mouth shut. Looking as thin and as tight as that mouth did, you'd never think it'd ever come open, but you were wrong.

The relief lookout on the wing sang out in the same moment as the telephone buzzed from the fo'c'sle—"Steamer lights two points on the starb'd bow!"

The first mate went out to the starboard wing. In the faint light of the dawn he could see the outline of the other ship as well as her red port lamp. She was long and low in the water, her midships freeboard lost in a smother of foam. She'd be down from the Irish Sea. Mr. Turnbull watched her, fine on the bow, and judged her distance and her speed and the speed of the *Whipper,* the run of the tide and the lie of the wind. He came back into the wheelhouse.

"Steer five degrees to starb'd."

Robins moved his hands. "Steer five degrees to starb'd, sir!" The sea came round from her quarter and followed astern.

You'd never hit that tanker, thought Robins, if you kept your course and drove at her full ahead. You could go five points west, at this speed, and still miss her by a mile. But the Old Bull was on the bridge, so he had to talk, and chuck the ship about, or things wouldn't be right. The nonsense had started. Not that Robins minded. He'd as soon put the *Whipper* in circles as leave her be, for she was a well-found ship and fine to handle. Turn her round on a dinner plate if you had to. He'd taken her through the Needles, once, when the Skip had been on the spree; and two or three times up the Thames, in ballast and with a force ten wind and half the North Sea shipping coming in for shelter. She was all of a ship, all of a woman, and nothing she wouldn't do for you, if you loved her. But you had to do that.

"Steer five degrees to port."

"Steer five degrees to port, sir!"

The tanker went slipping through the dawn, clearing their course. She was flashing her Aldis lamp, and Turnbull stood on the port wing of the bridge, reading.

Penny for the guy?

Turnbull said to the lookout, "What the hell does he mean?"

"Fifth o' November today, sir."

"Fifth of November, is it?" He went back into the fug of the wheelhouse and took out the lamp. He sent:

Will you dive for it?

The tanker dropped away to port under the lightening sky. Up there, mares' tails were beginning to fly from the south-west. He was not worried. Already there were a few big Cornish gulls escorting the *Whipper* home.

Just after seven o'clock he went and stood in the doorway of the wireless-room, where Mr. Bond was tuned in to London. *There are gale warnings in operation sea areas Rockall, Hebrides, Irish Sea, Fastnet, Biscay, Bristol Channel, Plymouth and Dover.*

"Well, the next watch can have it," said Turnbull.

Bond glanced up. He had a round pink face and the eyes of a man who normally wears spectacles, though his sight was perfect. He gave a quick nervous grin.

"It'll get it."

"There's no need to look so bloody cheerful."

"I always look bloody cheerful, sir. It conceals a sad heart."

There was Morse coming through on the trawler band. He corrected the signal. Turnbull stood there for another half minute, listening.

"All they can think about is stinking fish," said Bond. He looked up, but the first mate had gone back into the wheelhouse. Alone again, Bond relaxed in his swing chair, listening to the trawlers and thinking of his wife. Alone, he didn't look cheerful; there was no need for the quick nervous grin. He found himself staring at the photograph on the bulkhead, as often he found himself doing through the long hours on watch. She was young-looking and pretty, the sort of stranger a man would want to meet in the flesh, if this were a good likeness. It was a good likeness, but she wasn't a stranger to him, and he would meet her again only because he had to. A ship must make landfall, and a man must come home; it was the order of things.

She might, of course, not be there. The last letter had said she was all right, and that she was sorry about 'all that'. But that was three weeks ago and in three weeks a lot could happen to change Thelma's mind. It could change overnight, and she could wake up feeling 'different'. She would tell him she had been thinking about 'things', and that she had decided there must be an end to 'all this'. She had a label for everything that was past. The long mounting crisis between them was 'this business', but it was not yet past. What, in plain words, did he call this crisis himself? He could never give it a name; it was not a positive thing but negative, and all the clues to it went springing away whenever he tried to slam his hands down on them and hold them still for inspection; all the complicated moral structure of it collapsed and rebuilt itself unrecognizably as soon as he cleared his mind to view it objectively. Nothing positive, but negative; they were breaking up because they couldn't get on; she wasn't ill, but she was unwell; he had sympathy, but couldn't understand. There was, when he thought about it, nothing wrong . . . but there was nothing right.

The photograph smiled down. *Love, Thelma.* Love from Thelma, her love to him. The love of the young-looking pretty girl to him, her husband. This photograph, here, to remind him of her when the long voyages blurred her image and name and form, dissolving the memories. And now, at last, no love.

He felt the movement of the ship about him. The sea was short and she was lively. He longed, perhaps without fully realizing it, for the *Whipper* to turn about, and steer from home, and go on steaming to anywhere else in the world or to nowhere, just go on steaming. He had felt like this at school, at the end of the term in the summer when his mother had died. They had sent him home for two days, because she had not died there but in Wales, two hundred miles away. His father had talked to him at home, trying to ease the shock to the young schoolboy mind, to explain that everything had been done to prevent this terrible thing and that nothing more could be done now, nor tears help. But of course tears helped and his pillow was soaked by morning, and came springing hot again as the hateful day began. He went back to his school, where he would be busy among his friends and not idle in a saddened house; and slowly through the rest of the term the first throat-filling ache diminished, and whole minutes came when he had no time to think of his dead mother, and then one whole hour when there was a vital match with a visiting team. And there were treats planned and promised in his father's letters, and even the terrible relief that the funeral was over without him there —"she'll know that it's not out of any disrespect, Anthony, and you must believe me when I say that she'd rather you stayed with your friends and just remembered her as she was, pottering about the garden with her flower-scissors and calling for help when she came across a worm, and then laughing at herself afterwards when she'd brought us all running, remember?"

It had been wrong, writing that. It had brought it all back, and the pillow was blotchy again because he would never hear that comical little scream from among the rose-trees, and never say again, "Hello, Mummy's found a worm!" But there were other wrong things in his father's letters, all of them meant for kindness, and he learned to cry less about them and one day was shocked by his first unselfish startling thought that his father must feel this, too. There were, towards the end of that term, the dreadful moments when he caught himself enjoying the drama that surrounded him; when he walked by himself along the trees by the pavilion, playing the part of the boy who'd lost his mother. 'What's up with Bond, d'you know? Haven't you heard? Is that why they sent him home?' He walked in his short-lived grief, hero of his dreadful situation, and then hated himself for it, and then forgot about her again for another hour; and finally he reached the end of a term that should have been impossible for him to live through, unthinkable, a nightmare that would never let him go. He reached the holidays, and got into the train; and then, minute by minute, he dropped out of the noisy chatter and sat watching the trees go by, and suddenly began wishing the train would never stop, but go on through his station and go on and on to anywhere in the world or to nowhere, just keep on going.

This was the feeling that was on him now, so similar that he recognized it, and remembered the train and his school-friends and even the stained corner of his attaché-case where Smithy had spilled some acid, larking about in the chemy-lab. The house at the end of the journey was not the same as the one he had left; he didn't want to go back to it. Thelma wasn't dead, but her love was, and that was much the same.

Making in to Brixham . . . a poor catch . . . it's blowing hard. . . . We passed Willow Girl . . . She's staying out. . . .

He switched wave-lengths and heard Niton. The distress metres were blank, and he picked up a coaster reporting a patch of timber south of Fastnet. It was ten minutes now to the end of his watch, and he could soon go below and take his time to think.

The movement about him developed a rhythm; the seas were growing longer as the wind built them up from the south, gathering small short waves into one green ridge and blowing the froth off. He could watch the sea from in here without even looking at it. He knew by the rhythm, because it was the same rhythm and the same sea that had rocked him through that part of his life from school until this day. A fortnight ago he had turned thirty-one.

He felt old, not because of his age but because he would have to begin again, any time now. There had been years wasted. Had he been forty he would probably have realized that he was still young and had plenty of time; but at thirty-one a man feels that half his life has gone.

The ship's movement calmed him as she ran into the bright morning with the sea astern. When he went off watch at eight bells he paused on the wing of the bridge and drew the air in deeply. Oh God, how clean the sea was, with the soft wind sweeping it and building the blue-green water into serried trough and ridge, then frosting it with crisp white caps and touching spindrift off; how clean the gulls' wings overhead and astern above the wake, cutting the pale sky and wheeling, bearing a mournful cry aloft, sharp in the sad morning; and clean the astringent tang of the salt, the raw slap of it against the skin, the cold of it against the eyes as he stared across the curve of the world and was lost again, over the horizon where he should have stayed for ever.

"Hello, Cock."

He turned and saw Costain, up for the forenoon watch.

Bond gave him a quick grin. "How's Little Audrey?"

Costain kept a tight face, only his eyes amused. He was very much alive, this thin dark boy, a third officer in his early twenties with a straight future mapped out for himself and a quick heart to get him through it.

"I wouldn't know," he said. He stood with his hands stuck into his jacket pockets, his eyes going to slits as the wind slapped, then widening as he watched the sea.

"I said she'd let you, didn't I?" said Bond. He was interested in other people's affairs, because they were less dreary than his own; and he envied Costain, who was young, and had no house to go to. Costain said, watching the sea:

"It's none of your bloody business."

"It certainly is. We've got a bet on." He studied the third mate's face. He had laid him five shillings that Ann Brown, the only unaccompanied woman passenger, would leave her door ajar in the middle watch. This was usually the time, within a day or two of landfall, when campaigns were concluded; though Costain, with his thin good looks, worked faster than most.

He moved his hands suddenly and found a half-crown and a florin among the coppers. "I'll have to owe you threepence."

Bond grinned again quickly and took the money. "Keep it for luck. Was she nice?"

Costain said slowly, "I think you're just a lecherous old pimp."

"I'll bet she was a honey."

"No more bets. I'm broke as it is."

Bond made a great show of licking a finger and wiping it down the windbreaker, marking another one up for Costain.

"*Vive le sport,*" he said, and left him. Costain looked up at the sky. It had been a high dawn, with clouds on the horizon below the sun; and now the mares' tails had merged to form oily-looking banks, sharp-edged below a steel-blue sky. One or two gulls were dropping ahead of the ship and flying straight, leaving her for the land. There wouldn't be much of a muster for lunch today among the passengers. He turned and went into the wheelhouse, and looked in at the doorway of the wireless-room.

"What's on the met.?"

"Dirt."

He wandered across to the binnacle, checking the course and compass. The *Atlantic Whipper*'s E.T.A. at Avonmouth was two o'clock the next morning. The weather would get there first, at this rate.

Pacing along the windows, turning and pacing with his hands

in his side-pockets, stopping and turning, pacing and coming back, he thought of Ann Brown. He still didn't know who she was. He knew she was a teacher in some kind of school, and knew her name and where she lived . . . "with a blank wall a yard from the window and a sooty windowsill, and that damned bus depot right opposite —that's why I can't keep away from this porthole, because of all that glorious space out there . . ." but he didn't really know who she was. Not married, he imagined. A teacher in a school of some odd kind (sitting on the bed, sharing her cigarette in the faint glow of the pilot-lights defining the port-holes, it hadn't been easy to listen to what she was telling him, as close to him as that, her promise already obvious or he wouldn't have been there at all), a school for the deaf, he remembered now—"You mean deaf children?"

"Yes."

"All of them?"

"Yes." She took the cigarette and drew on it, and passed it back, touching his hand but not feeling it. "We try to teach them how to speak."

He didn't want to talk about deaf children, because that was a sad enough subject, God only knew, and this would be the last whole night at sea and it was nearly two o'clock. But he said, "It's very difficult?"

"Yes. They were all born deaf, and so they've never heard anyone speak."

He looked at her silhouette, a slight profile with the lips moving, a gleam of light reflecting in her eye on this side under short spiky lashes. In the silence, his wrist-watch ticked. He began smiling in the darkness at himself. Here he was, alone with her, sitting on her bed . . . talking about deaf children. Poor little wretches, granted, but it was no good letting yourself start worrying about things like that or you'd spend your whole life weeping for beggars and polio cases and the blind. At any moment, anyone in the world could become one of them, and then regret the selfishness that had gone before. Misery was a thing you had to help when you could, and forget for the rest of the time.

"Poor little devils," he said.

"They're wonderfully happy."

"They're what?"

She turned her face to him and he saw she was smiling. "They don't know what they've missed—I mean things like music and birds—so they've nothing to long for, and I suppose we're kinder to them than in ordinary schools." He gave her the cigarette and she said, "It's burning rather short."

"I'll put it out." He leaned over to the ashtray, and in the silence the pull of his sleeve made a great deal of noise. He could hear her swallowing. She said:

"I'm a washout, you see."

He leaned back, not wanting to take her hand. He wanted to go. They had started this meeting on the wrong tack, and now they were well adrift.

"Are you?" He tried to get interest into his tone.

"At this kind of thing."

Feeling suddenly very annoyed he wanted to ask, 'What kind of thing, for God's sake?' If he were to get up and go, saying good-night, would she be hurt? Did she even realize there was a man in her cabin, in the dark? She was different, so absolutely different, from the person she had been when they'd danced together in the saloon after dinner. It must have been the wine. That had happened before. He had nearly been thrown off his ship once, when he'd shown up in a cabin during the middle watch, fully confident after a warm invitation, and had his face slapped and the door slammed in it. She had threatened to tell the captain in the morning. Now this was another one. A glass of wine and she'd melt in your arms, dancing, and whisper heaven and earth in your ear; an hour later she'd whinny for help if you picked up her handkerchief. The Canadians had a word for them.

She said quietly, "You're furious, Peter."

"Why?" If she wanted innuendoes she could have them. It was dead easy. All you had to do was ask a lot of silly questions that couldn't possibly be answered except with another silly question. Women were great conversationalists.

She touched his hand, and found it limp. "How old are you?" she asked.

"Twenty-three."

"That's young."

He thought bitterly, 'All right, call me Sonny.'

"But very experienced, I should imagine."

"I've had my ticket two years."

She was laughing suddenly and softly, startling him because for nearly half a minute she couldn't stop. He said, "I don't see it."

"I'm sorry." She got a handkerchief and sniffed into it, and he wondered why people always had to make a gesture of apology after a good laugh. "How many does your ticket entitle you to?"

She put her handkerchief away. He felt thoroughly fed up, and sorry for those poor little bastards. But they were happy, she'd said, so he could forget them.

"Anyway, please try not to be furious, Peter." She waited, but he just said something about his not being anything of the sort. It was very difficult. She had stopped talking about her job, because she had realized it was wrong, but they couldn't sit in silence holding hands. Shouldn't he do something? She had read that it was the man who set the pace, but was that wrong?

He found his cigarette-case and opened it for her.

"No, thank you."

He took a cigarette and put it between his lips, but while he was getting a match she said, "I've told you I'm a washout. That really meant you don't have to stay, just out of politeness." She held his hand firmly, the one that had the box of matches in it. She was terrified now, but didn't know whether it was by the thought of his going or staying.

As kindly as he could he said, "I know when I'm being kicked out." He stood up and dropped the fresh cigarette into the ashtray. Bitterly he thought she might see it there when she woke in the morning, and be sorry. "Good night, Ann."

Before he reached the door she was sobbing, loudly because she was trying to stifle it. He came back, bewildered.

"What have I done?" he asked, but she was too busy with her handkerchief to hear. He knelt by the bed, without thinking, and touched her. He was young, and tears from a stranger could move him. And it might be his fault, so he had to find out before he left her, and if necessary apologize.

She got a grip on herself and said almost without a tremor, "I'm not attractive enough."

"You're madly attractive." His tone made the cliché sound sincere. He really meant it. She was damned attractive and he wished to God he'd never met her.

"I thought you—you wanted me."

He said, "I did. I mean, I do." He was still sincere. "What the hell are you crying about, Ann?"

She brought her face down and kissed his brow, trembling. She said in a small voice, "I don't know what I've got to do."

"Oh, Ann . . ."

Pacing, turning, pacing back, hands in his pockets, past the binnacle and back again, he went on cursing his stupidity. Certainly he had slept with only five women since his unthinkably clumsy initiation at the age of nineteen, but that should have given him enough experience to steer him through last night with more pleasure and less humiliation for Ann. He had behaved like a callow adolescent awaiting the attack of a full-blown seductress, instead of realizing her sensitivity and her unfamiliarity with the situation. The others, before, had all been the same sort, who made love between gins and forgot about it by breakfast-time.

Poor little Ann.

"Ship three points on the starb'd quarter!"

He wandered moodily to the wing and looked across the sea. A liner, Southampton-bound, yawing a lot in the hard swell. He answered the lookout and went back into the wheelhouse.

He'd make it up to her, if they ever met again. She couldn't be having much of a life, shut up first in that room with a blank wall a yard from the windows and the bus depot opposite, then in a schoolroom full of poor little deaf mutes. No husband: he was certain of that. Then what did she do for sex? She wasn't used to it, to judge from her constraint last night (hell, he could talk!), yet she'd enjoyed it enormously. When she was back in England, what then? The cramped room, the school, and the short journey between, and nothing else?

It was the first time he had felt sorry for a woman he had slept with, and it worried him. A gin, the bed, another gin and then thanks for the memory—the routine had changed last night. Standing here by the binnacle, automatically checking the course, he was seized with an incredible thought: was there something more to making love than that?

He'd have to be careful, damned careful in future. This thing had the smell of dynamite.

"Mr. Costain."

"Yes?" The second wireless-operator was in the doorway.

"The owners are asking for confirmation of E.T.A. Any change?"

"No, but remind 'em we've had gale warnings and that we're still sixteen hours outside. What the hell are they worried about?"

"I don't think they're actually worried." He went back to send the signal, wondering what was up with Pete this morning. He sounded more like Turnbull.

Costain went out to the port wing, and caught a wind-gust; he clamped his cap on and looked at the sea. The water was a wicked green, topped with white crests. Half the south sky was clouded, and the clear blue that had been in the north was hazing over.

The last gull had gone. The wind was alive in the rigging, and a halyard was crackling somewhere, quivering against timber. Ahead the sea was a flat of white spindrift, but when he looked astern he could see the true shape of it. There were waves racing in ranks with hundred-yard troughs between. The horizon was lost.

His feet swayed to the broken rhythm of the ship as she yawed to the following sea, plunging uneasily and lifting, sometimes bringing her screw clear and shaking it, sending the vibration through the deck beneath him. For'ard of the bridge the bosun had some men out along the hatch-coamings, checking on the covers. They had put oilskins on. A wave broke and came over white, with the spindrift curling back in the wind. The bosun's team worked more quickly, tapping the wedges, testing them, moving along the coamings like bent black beetles as the long foredeck shuddered and was still, shuddered again as the next sea came and broke along the sides.

The owners, he thought, had better have another signal. It was a pity they didn't pay more attention to the met. reports themselves. They knew where the ship was and they knew what the weather was: why waste Sparks's time?

He clamped his cap down again and turned back into the wheelhouse.

"Good morning, Mr. Costain."

The captain was up.

"Good morning, sir."

"It looks like a nice fresh morning."

"Yes, sir."

CHAPTER THREE

Ron Mounsey counted the rivets above his head. He lay flat in his bunk, staring up at them and making patterns: those three rusty ones where the paint had chipped off were almost equidistant, and made a fair triangle. There was a fly on one rivet, and every time it moved he was able to make a new pattern, with the rivet the fly was on and the three rusty ones. Sometimes the fly landed between them and he watched it sourly until it chose another rivet. It had been in no-man's-land for half a minute now, and didn't look like going on with the game.

"Get up, you bastard," said Mounsey, his face dark.

Across the cabin, Tug Wilson dropped his guitar tutor and picked it up, and began using the plectrum again with the confident emphasis of the true novice.

"Get up, sod you," growled Mounsey.

Wilson got his tongue in and rested his guitar. He looked across at Mounsey.

"What are you griping about?"

"That bloody fly."

"Is that who you're talkin' to?"

"Ay. He won't shift."

Tug watched him for a moment. "P'r'aps he's a Frenchie, and don't know your lingo."

Mounsey's sense of humour was simple. He grinned. "Don't give me that. I'll make the little cowson shift in a minute if he don't move 'isself."

Tug plucked again at the guitar. It was a beauty, with mother-of-pearl decorations and the maker's name inside the sound-box. He'd had to trade in quite a lump of ship's chandlery for this.

Ron's fly had gone off, out of sight. He cursed it and turned his idle attention upon Tug. "You don't get any better, y'know."

"I'm trying," said Tug mildly.

"What you want to play that thing for, then?"

"Can't you shut up?"

Mounsey hitched himself on to one elbow. "Well, look who's talkin'!" He listened for a while to Tug's careful search for the right note, and then his patience wore thin. "Can't you go an' practise that in the wheel'ouse or somewhere?"

Tug lowered his beautiful guitar and said casually:

"Teresa said she'll marry me when I can play it."

"Don't give me that, mate."

"She says a Spanish girl can't marry a man who can't even serenade her with a guitar." He studied the tutor again.

Ron Mounsey gave a laugh like a window breaking. "She's not any Spanish girl, mate, she's a bloody Mexican-Peruvian with a touch o' Chinese-Irish about 'er. Don't you know Teresa yet?"

Tug did not answer. He plucked again, listening enraptured to the twang of the strings. He was getting on like a house on fire. He could hear himself improving every day. He'd got a real talent for this, and no mistake.

"Teresa . . ." grinned Mounsey. "The las' time I was in Buenos Aires she was callin' herself Lula. Ask me, I'd say she was christened Fanny."

Tug struck a chord, in self-congratulation. "Stow it, mate. She's a nice girl."

"Are you serious?" Mounsey's deep voice was pinched into a squeak of disbelief.

"'Course I'm serious."

"Then you're crackers, mate. Real crackers, you are. I can tell you a thing or two about your little Teresa that'd make your short-hairs curl. If she——"

"Then don't."

He played three slow notes, almost perfectly. Ron leaned towards him from his bunk.

"Are you honest-to-God *serious,* Tug?"

"Much as I'm fond of this expensive instrument," said Wilson slowly, "I'll crown you with it if you don't let up."

Mounsey fell silent, not because of the threat but out of respect for his shipmate's feelings. If poor old Tug was off his loaf about that half-breed little dockside judy, it was his business. But it made you laugh, all right.

He rolled a black shag cigarette and threw it across to Wilson. "There y'are, Don Juan, set your mustachios on fire wi' that." He began rolling another one for himself. The cabin gave a lurch, making him spill some leaf. "Jeese, she's pipin' up a bit, isn't she?"

Tug lit his cigarette. "We've got more to come. Didn't you hear what the bose said? Force-ten gales comin' up from the south."

"Garn, what's a force-ten gale to the *Whipper*? Now if we was on some lousy packet full o' cockers with a dead-beat skipper, that'd be diff'rent. Christ, where did they get this shag from, out of a brewer's dray 'orse?"

The ship took another sea on the quarter. Mounsey's locker door swung open and hit the bulkhead with a bang. Wilson just saved his guitar.

"Here it comes," he said.

"Well, let it come, we're 'omeward bound, mate."

Sea-boots crashed down a companionway and the bosun's mate poked his head in. "Put up the deadlights an' secure. Where's Stubbs?"

"'Aven't seen 'im. What's this about deadlights?"

"Just get 'em up, an' look lively." He left them. A door banged, somewhere topsides. Mounsey swung himself out of his bunk with a grin.

"Be a bit o' caviar left over from lunch today, from what I know about passengers. Make a nice tuck-in for the likes of us."

Tug Wilson put his guitar away carefully, and then saw green water go sliding over a porthole. A tin mug clanged down from a locker; a book slid off a sea-bag and fell spread-eagled.

"Let's get them deadlights up," he said.

* * *

The bosun had his team and the chippies on the after-deck, working steadily along the battens of number three and four hatches. Above them the whine of the shrouds and aerial had become a constant song and they no longer heard it. Spray exploded across the bulwarks at intervals and white water drained through the wash-doors, banging them and making percussion for the high wind's drone.

"Stubbs! Where the hell've you been?"

The man leaned on the wind towards the bosun.

"I've not been feelin' so good, Bose."

They stood together for a moment while the seamen worked on.

"Listen to me, Stubbs. You've not been feelin' so good since we started out. You've had a loggin' from the skipper once, an' you're workin' up for another, quick. What the hell's up with you, man?"

"There's nothin' up wi' me." Their faces stared at each other, framed by the black oilskins and the green sea beyond. They were having to shout into the wind. "There's nothin' up wi' me that your good riddance won't cure."

Art Starley waited for a couple of seconds. He didn't want to say a wrong word. He wanted to tell Stubbs exactly where he stood, with no misunderstandings. "What's your complaint? I want to hear it. If it's justified we'll get somethin' done about it, double-quick. If not, you'd better pipe down about it, for good. Come on now?"

"I got no complaint—why should I have? I get all the bloody jobs while Wilson an' Smithers an' Harris an' that lot take it nice an' easy on their bloody arses." Spray came over the side and slashed them; they turned against its white sting but did not look away from each other. "Some on us are expected to work like blacks," Stubbs shouted against the wind, "an' the rest can hang on the slack, for all you care." He stared into the dark round face of Art Starley and hated it and hated all bosuns and all officers and masters and owners, superior snotty-nosed bastards full of their bloody class-consciousness because they went about with a lot of brass crap on their sleeves and called each other Mister. The hate was in his voice. "You call yourself a bosun, do you? Eh? Call yourself a bloody ship's bosun?"

Starley didn't hit him. There was a big sea running and a lot of work to do. He shot out his hand and gripped the seaman's arm, and Stubbs jerked his muscles instinctively to ward off a blow and give it back. He didn't shake the bosun's grip from his arm but his hands were squeezed white at the knuckle. They stood together with their stance shifting for balance as the deck tilted, their heads turned away from the side where the sea broke and the wind rushed. They stood a degree below fighting-point.

"Listen, Stubbs. Wilson an' those other two are among the best men I've got on board an' they pull their weight. It's no good you thinkin' you can make 'em out to be bosun's favourites. It's men like them I can leave alone, an' they'll go on working. You? You're a bloody free passenger in this ship. Soon as we're through on this job, we'll see the skipper, you an' me. You've got ten minutes to think out what you're goin' to tell him."

He released Stubbs's arm and turned away to help two men who were stowing deck-rope before it fouled the wash-doors. Starley didn't like a following sea. A ship was designed to take her punishment on the nose, where she could see it coming, and meet it and deal with it, shaking the last sea from her head before the next one came. This gale was southerly and it had come stalking up behind the *Whipper* and she couldn't turn, but had to run on where her course lay, chivvied and harassed by the stern seas where there were no sharp bow-plates to cut at them as they came.

"Watch it—here comes a dipper!"

The men heard him and dodged for what cover they could, or clutched at the nearest stanchion while the water hit them, the white salt spray bursting over them with tatters of green flying between the rails. They were working again within a moment. carrying on until the next wave came. The bosun watched the length of the swell and judged its height. If this wind strengthened according to forecast, the sea would start pooping.

Watching him from the port wing of the bridge, Captain Harkness stood with his hands buried in his coat. The bosun did a job handily; such men were good to watch. He turned to face for'ard. and a few minutes later went back into the wheelhouse and said to Costain:

"Get the lookout up from the fo'c'sle."

"Ay, ay, sir." The third mate unhooked the phone. The shipmaster stood at one of the windows, a short big-shouldered man whose strength was expressed more in his stillness than his movements. He listened to the tick of the echo-sounder by the chart-room door and watched the sea ahead, his thoughts faster than his ship but on the same exact course, to England. The *Atlantic Whipper* was due for a refit, and he was due for leave. He was not excited by the immediate future. He would spend the next few weeks in the perfect comfort of his home, where his slightest wish would be met by dear Margaret. He knew that she was living impatiently through this day, working without any trace of anxiety that their house would not please him in the smallest respect. The doorstep would be a glow of red tiles, the knocker shine, the windows glitter, admitting clear light to gleam on the polished wood and burnished ornaments. The fire would be bright and the scuttle filled. (Did she really dust the coals? He believed she did.) The place would be perfect.

He thought, standing with his feet balancing his short strong body as the ship moved in the swell, that in the long list of imperfections with which a man must live, perfection came somewhere about the middle.

The fo'c'sle lookout came up to the bridge with water still draining from his oilskins. He took up his station, shielded in part by the windbreakers. He watched with pleasure the ship's head dropping, bringing up water and shipping it across the rails and winches on the fo'c'sle head, where he had been standing before. Mr. Beggs, coming up the companionway, said to him cheerfully, "Getting soft, are you, Phillips?"

The man grinned with a wet face. "Orders, sir."

Beggs came into the wheelhouse and fetched the sextant.

"Taking sights, sir, before the sun's gone."

"Good, Mr. Beggs."

The sun was a hazed blob; in half an hour it would be lost above the cloud-packs, well before noon. He worked with the sextant and went into the chart-room to mark their position and course. While he was in there the bosun came up to the bridge and asked to see the captain.

Harkness went out to the wing. Starley said:

"I'm sorry to trouble you, sir. I want to report one of the hands." There was a mist of salt clinging to his heavy eyebrows, and a drip on his nose. The ship lurched and they both leaned to the movement.

"I'll see him in fifteen minutes, in my room."

"Thank you, sir."

"Is everything secured, Mr. Starley?"

"Yes, sir."

"Very good."

Harkness returned to the wheelhouse. Beggs was out of the chart-room. Costain was watching the compass card. Beggs had told him the drift, and he was worried by the skipper's presence. In a few months he would be sitting for first mate's ticket, and he wanted a good recommend.

"Starb'd ten," he said carefully.

"Starb'd ten, sir."

They could feel the sea coming stronger on the beam.

"Meet her."

"Ay, ay, sir, meet her."

Costain checked the new course and stood back from the binnacle. Harkness was gazing through the window. The sun was being absorbed by the clouds' fringe; it threw down a last ragged light and then the sea darkened, and took on the colour and heaviness of lead. The spindrift lost its ice-white sparkle as the wind-gusts whipped it from the crests; between the crests, the troughs were scooped out and ran in shadows. The last of the blue had gone from the sky, the last of the green from the sea. The ship rode in a world of monochrome greys with the tinting harsh and metallic. In the foreground of the captain's vision, out at the edge, the bright red of the fire-extinguisher glowed in contrast with the rest.

"Meet her."

"Meet her, sir."

The telegraph showed Full. With the seas quickening, the screw was losing thrust. Costain counted the minutes. At noon he could hand over to Jim Beggs and have a drink and thank the Lord. He had no liking for a rough passage, keeping watch with the Skip up here.

A few days ashore, Beggs was thinking, and he could fish the old Aston Martin out and run up to London, caning her all the way and drifting the bends, with a bit of a welcome from the boys at the Hub Club when he got there.

His clothes would be ready for him, thought Harkness, perfectly pressed, his shoes perfectly polished; and there would be nothing out of its place; and Margaret's devotion would minister to him without fuss; and he would wait in patience for these comfortable weeks to pass, and feel the excitement rising in him on the last evening, when his thoughts would leave home ahead of him, and go to the ship and the sea and the demands they would make on him, and the happiness they could give him that Margaret never could.

Costain thought, 'The small cramped room, and the school, and the short journey between, and nothing more? Poor Ann.'

Eight bells were rung and their thoughts fled away in the clangour and the call to movement. Beggs took over the watch. Costain went below. The wheel changed hands. The captain moved away from the windows, and with the sight of the rising seas in his mind and the feel of the ship's uneasiness beneath his feet he said:

"I'll be in my cabin, if you want me."

CHAPTER FOUR

THE bosun had taken off his oilskins and stood with his cap tucked under his arm. Already the atmosphere of this sacred cabin was making him regret having reported Stubbs; but the threat had been made and it couldn't be withdrawn.

He should have hit the man and got it over with. Stubbs would have understood a thing like that, and it would have saved all this palaver within a few hours of the crew paying off at the end of the trip.

"Yes, Mr. Starley?"

The captain was sitting. Stubbs stood on the bosun's left. The cabin was warm, and quiet, and full of the smell of pipe-smoke. Starley said:

"This man is giving me constant——"

"This seaman, Mr. Starley." The captain's face was bland, his pale blue eyes almost sleepy. His voice was gentle.

The bosun swallowed bitterly, and began his rehearsed speech again. "This seaman, sir," and he made the tone of the word sound as much like 'bastard' as he could, "is giving me constant trouble on deck—when I can find him, which isn't often. He is a malingerer, and insubordinate."

It wasn't a bad speech, he thought. It was short, and couldn't be misunderstood.

Captain Harkness turned his bland face to Stubbs, the expression unchanged. It was an amiable stare that he might be giving two of his closest friends, or two cockroaches he was about to crush underfoot. An impartial man, he had an impartial face. He had corrected the bosun just now with no thought in mind of taking him down a peg in front of Stubbs. It was simply that Stubbs, on board as a member of the crew and with his book and rating all in order, was a seaman, and must be allowed the right of that title in a formal interview.

His quiet, ordinary question had all the force of a long silence behind it.

"Well, Stubbs?"

The seaman met the master's eyes with a directness that was out of character for an insubordinate malingerer.

"I'm not satisfied." It was said with firmness.

The captain's stare was bright and his voice still gentle. "You will address me as 'sir'."

Stubbs looked down. Starley gazed at the curtain over the scuttle. He began counting the seconds as they crept nervously by through this silence. It was the kind of silence that brought sweat out on you the longer it went on, until you began praying that you wouldn't have the ghastly misfortune to burp, or cough, or give any audible sign that you were still here in this unbearable, unbreakable trap of soundlessness that went on and on, until you were certain that when someone dropped a pin your feet would clear the floor with the shock.

Stubbs brought his head up, and looked at Harkness. Harkness was still gazing at him, bright of eye. Starley was sweating. Stubbs had brought his head up with the effort of a man dragging a rock to a mountain-top. A neck muscle creaked.

"Sir."

Starley collapsed inside himself. Where had the Skip learned to do things like that, for Christ's sake? It was murder.

Gently, "You're not satisfied——" a slight pause—"with what?"

"With this ship." Starley tensed again. The silence had begun. If it went on he was going to blow up or fall apart or—"Sir." He went slack with relief. He was a good bosun. He could work. He knew the sea and ships and men. He could fight, and draw bad blood in a good cause if necessary. But he wasn't built to stand this kind of war, when a mere syllable went clipping through the air like a bullet. He should have just thrown Stubbs overboard. Hanging was better than this.

Captain Harkness was speaking. It was all right, thought the bosun, so long as people spoke. The devil's own voice would be sweet music compared with the kind of silence the Skip could conjure up.

"You are not satisfied with my ship. I am anxious to know in what particular respect we have failed you." He thought Stubbs was being absurd. Nearly two hundred miles out in the ocean, this ship was the world, and he was saying he wasn't satisfied with the world. Who was?

"The bosun picks on me, sir. Ever since that last time he's 'ad 'is hooks into me."

"What last time?"

Stubbs began talking more quickly, more easily. You couldn't make sense to anyone if you had to stare them out and refuse to address them properly. The thing was to put your case, and make it sound better than the other one. The Skip had got sense, you could see that. It was this cowson of a bosun he was up against.

"When you logged me, sir. I reckon I deserved it, that time. But this——" he jerked his right hand—"but the bosun won't forget it. He's been chasin' me ever since, while some o' the others can take it easy, go as they please. It's not good enough, is it, sir?"

Captain Harkness had listened attentively, had looked once at the bosun and then back to Stubbs. There was a lot of sincerity in the seaman's voice. Harkness believed him, in part. It was probably true that the bosun had been chasing him; it was probably untrue that some of the hands were allowed to take it easy. He said slowly:

"You said you weren't satisfied with the ship. Let us hear about that."

Stubbs moved a mouth muscle, shrugging. "I reckon I meant the bosun, sir."

Harkness sat farther back in his chair and stared for a while at the middle distance. Looking at him, you would not know whether his mind were a blank, or deeply occupied, whether he was calm or in a controlled rage. You didn't know where you were. "You 'reckon' you meant the bosun. Can we for the sake of saving our time be quite *sure* you meant the bosun, and not the ship?"

Stubbs said, reluctantly, as if he were making a late attempt not to appear unfair in actually accusing the bosun:

"Yes, sir."

Harkness looked at Starley. "Have you been chasing Stubbs, Mr. Starley?"

"Yes, sir."

"Why?"

"You've got to, sir. He won't work otherwise."

"Are some of the other hands allowed to go as they please, and take it easy?"

"You'd know it, sir, if the ship was bein' run like that."

"I'm not asking you what I know or don't know. Shall I repeat the exact question?"

Starley's head had begun aching. This wasn't the idea at all. He'd meant to shoot Stubbs into this cabin so the Skip could boot him out again with orders to pull his weight. This was a sight worse than the Old Bailey.

"No, sir. Every man in this ship's got a job and he does it. Except for Stubbs. I have to chase him, an' it makes my own job a deal harder. I don't do it just because I've got nothin' else to do."

There was silence; this was an impressive one, to the bosun, and it didn't worry him.

"You mentioned your last logging, Stubbs, just now. You say you reckon you deserved it. I remember at the time you reckoned nothing of the kind. You left my cabin feeling very hard done by." He gazed bright-eyed at Stubbs, waiting.

"Well, it's natural, sir, isn't it? At the time you always feel you're gettin' a bad break."

"It is very natural, yes. You are feeling it now. But later, are you going to 'reckon' you deserved it?"

"All I know is that I'm bein' chased about, an' I'm fed up, sir. Fed up."

"So is the bosun. This is very sad." He turned his stare upon Starley. "Have you anything you'd like to add to your accusations, Mr. Starley?"

"No, sir."

"Then you can go back on deck.'

"Ay, ay, sir."

Starley shut the door firmly behind him. He didn't know what was going to happen about Stubbs, and he didn't give a curse. There was work to do, with a gale coming. All he knew was that the next time Stubbs gave him any trouble he'd knock him across the scuppers and call it a day.

In the quiet of the cabin, Harkness said gently:

"You hate his guts, don't you?"

Stubbs was surprised into a rueful grin. "I reckon we don't get on, sir."

"It may well be," said the captain sadly, "that he hates your guts too. It sometimes happens, in the close confinement of shipboard." He got up, and tucked his hands behind him, going to the scuttle and looking out at the sea. After a moment he said, with his back to Stubbs, "We have a gale forecast. We shall need to work well to run through it with the minimum possible discomfort to the passengers and ourselves, and the least possible damage to the cargo that is in our charge." He turned slowly to stare at Stubbs. "Your record is not the best. You must realize that, once off this ship, you'll not be signed on again, so long as Mr. Starley is bosun. You're prepared to accept that. There are many other ships. But at the moment you are serving in this one, and have certain obligations not only to me but to every other soul on board."

The deck gave a tilt, and Stubbs watched the gold-coloured curtain behind the captain hang away from the scuttle by a degree, two degrees, three, until it hung motionless. He waited for it to swing back, as it must. It hung without moving. The blurred white horizon did not appear. He felt the vibration of the engines under him, and heard timber creak as it lay strained to the angle. He must watch the curtain swing back. It hung where it was. Without knowing that he was going to speak, he said:

"She's listing, sir."

The curtain moved, a degree, two degrees, three, and swung back to lie against the edge of the scuttle. The vibration grew worse, then eased. The timber creaked again, then was silent.

Sweat pricked his scalp.

The captain said, gazing at Stubbs's cold face, "So that I am going to demand of you that until we reach port and you are paid off, you will work hard, as befits your responsibilities as a seaman on passage." Slowly Stubbs drew his eyes down from the curtain to the captain's face. "If you fail to carry out that order, I shall personally see to it that you are never given a berth again at sea as long as you live."

Stubbs had nothing in his mind to let him make an answer. He had been scared by the curtain. You always knew that when the ship rolled she'd go back; but you waited for it to happen, and sometimes waited for so long that it broke you down, slowly. On deck you could watch the sea and the ship, and sometimes see the crest that she was mounted on, and work out how many seconds it would be before she ran clear and righted. But here in the cabin, with the quiet stare of this shipmaster on him, his nerve had broken quickly, so that he had believed that it wasn't a roll but a list, and he had been forced by his nerves to tell someone, to shift some of his fear on to another man and make him share it. Vaguely he was now aware that this man could share nothing he could give him, least of all fear.

"That is perfectly understood, Stubbs?"

"Yes, sir." He just wanted to go, get out of here. "Yes, sir."

"Then get on deck, and work."

When Stubbs had gone, Harkness lit a pipe, feeling the next uneasy roll of the ship and waiting for her to right. She was a good weatherly ship, neither stiff nor tender; she would be all right. But if the gale was a big one, a full force twelve, they would have to work hard into Avonmouth with all safe and the cargo sound.

When he had levelled the ash on his pipe and put the tobacco jar safely in the drawer he went on deck, meeting his boy in the alleyway and telling him to make things secure in his cabin. On the bridge the second mate was in his reefer, standing on the wing and watching the stern.

Harkness stood beside Beggs, shielding his pipe from the wind. The swell had drawn out farther, leaving fifty-yard troughs. The south sky was black. Above, there was dirty cloud-scum topping the milky haze that was brought up flying from the sea. Astern of the ship the waves rose twenty feet high, some of them broken by the stern before they were full-grown, others reaching their height and falling across the wake. When one of those waves timed it right, the *Whipper* would be pooped.

"What's our position, Jim?"

"Five minutes ago it was forty-nine north, fourteen twenty-one minutes west, sir. Course north seventy-two east." They watched the next sea coming. It looked taller than the rest, a big curler, maybe a seventh wave. This one had timed it right. It swelled, lifting strongly until the wind tore at the crest and ripped white streamers from it; then it curled, and hung its great dark hook against the ship's taffrail; then it fell, exploding against the stern and blotting the poop-deck from sight until the welter went tiding across to the hatch-covers and leaping high against the side of the companionway, to fall again and join the main rush of water to the scuppers where the wash-doors banged. Number four hatch had taken it solid; the tarpaulins gleamed black as the last foam drained.

"She's pooped, sir!"

Harkness nodded. They felt the *Whipper* heaving bows to wind as the quartermaster held her back to the course. She yawed heavily and her mainmast shivered, the stays tautening on the one side and slackening on the other as the wind sang through. A knot of deck-hands were pressed round the port stanchion below the samson post; now they broke away and trotted round the coamings, making for the shelter aft of the bridge.

Harkness went into the wheelhouse and through into the chart-room to study the markings. When he came out he lit his pipe again and stood for a few minutes at one of the wheelhouse windows, to watch the sea and the sky. Turnbull came up and went into the wireless-room, then came and stood a few feet away from the captain, face to the window. He had put a reefer on. Harkness looked round.

"Mr. Beggs."

"Sir?" The big second mate came in from the wing.

"Find out our position."

"Ay, ay, sir."

Mr. Turnbull said, "The *Valenca*'s in trouble in Biscay, sir."

"*Valenca*? That's timber."

"Yes, sir. She's sent out a call, distress wavelength."

"Any reply?"

"*Abeille IV* is within an hour's steaming-distance. She's making there."

"Then she'll be all right." The *Abeille IV* was a deep-sea tug, the answer to a sailor's prayer.

"Yes, sir. This is pretty widespread. There's colliers making in along the west coast."

Beggs came out with his dead-reckoning. Harkness knocked the ash out of his pipe, bracing himself against the bulkhead as the ship gave a lurch. Vibration started as the screw came clear. There were shouts from below, and a distant tinkle of something breaking, crockery or glass. Ahead of the ship the sea was lost in haze that went flying above the troughs, veiling them. The open doors at each end of the wheelhouse were oblongs of black sky. The long-awaited gale was force eight or nine, and it was strengthening. A smaller ship, or a ship this size in ballast, would have turned about before now, to lie hove-to.

Beggs and Turnbull were waiting, already obeying in detail the order that must soon come. The helmsman worked steadily at the wheel, finding the seas and meeting them, waiting for the next and judging it and meeting it, keeping his stance on the grating as the *Whipper* rolled, yawing and planing as the sea crept to the quarter and sent the wheel alive.

"Mr. Turnbull, is all secure?"

The first mate answered almost before the question was out. "All secure, sir. I went round after the bosun."

"Very good." Harkness went over to the telephone and got through to the engine-room. "Chief? We're going to come about and heave-to for a bit. I shall want two or three minutes' full speed as soon as you're ready. Yes. Thank you, Chief." He hooked the telephone back and looked round for the third mate. Costain was here; he had not seen him come. Costain, he thought, was reliable for his age. He said to him, "Tell the chief steward to go round the passengers. We are turning about in a few minutes, so that we can ride quiet until the gale passes. Absolutely no cause for alarm, but things will be a bit noisy."

"Ay, ay, sir." Costain left the bridge.

"Mr. Turnbull, we'd better shut all watertight doors. Chief won't be ready for a few minutes."

Turnbull went below. The captain stood by a window again, reaching there in time to see spindrift racing in a white cloud past the bridge and foremast from a shipped sea aft.

"Mr. Beggs, have a signal sent to the owners. We are heaving-to until the gale abates. Ship in good trim and all happy aboard."

"Ay, ay, sir."

A metal door clanged below the fo'c'sle head; the sound was whipped away. Timber was straining under his feet and behind him; it was a contenting sound, the easy give-and-take of flexible structure dealing with a stress that would break a more rigid design. There was very little welding in this ship; she was built with rivet and joint and would give the seas best as they came for her, but only to a degree, enough to weaken their force and leave her own strength untouched. He had all faith in her and in her crew.

A minute passed and she was pooped again, and he watched the rush of white past the starboard door. As it died away and merged with the haze ahead a telephone rang and he picked it up.

"Engine-room, sir. Ready when you are."

"Thank you, Chief." He hung up and crossed to the binnacle, watching the card and lifting his eyes to watch the sea. He said to the quartermaster, "Wilson, stand by to come about to starb'd."

"Stand by to come about to starb'd, sir!"

Harkness watched the waves and felt a seventh hit the stern, a big one that lifted the screw out and sent a blizzard of spindrift past the bridge. When the wave was rolling ahead clear of the bows he reached his hand to the telegraph and gave a double ring Full Ahead.

They felt the rise of the engines in the deck, and the stern go slowly down to the screw's thrust. A minute passed, and he said to the helmsman:

"Hard a-starboard."

"Hard a-starb'd, sir!"

The *Whipper* began to turn. The sea came round to her starboard beam and slowed her, and she leaned to port, and shook herself. A wave took her and she leaned badly, then came back and began wallowing half-way through the turn with the sea full on the beam. Her speed had been drawn down as she began struggling to bring her bows into the face of the gale.

The helmsman worked hard, giving a spoke and taking it back. The captain watched the compass bowl, the glow of its light on his quiet face as his ship was made to fight from the worst position, beam-on and broached-to, with the seas coming hard.

"Ease her."

"Ease her, sir."

She leaned again as a sea came, pounding her plates; then she wallowed with the helm slack in her mouth until Harkness said, "Bring her back to starb'd."

"Bring her back to starb'd, sir!"

She found her shoulder against the seas and held it there until she took a big one on the flare of her bow. It struck at full height and was sent climbing in a hard white fountain across the fo'c'sle head before the wind took it and broke it away into haze. In the moment of the impact a sharp sound came from below for'ard, a cracking of timber that was loud even in the wheelhouse.

Captain Harkness looked up from the compass bowl and saw Turnbull staring at him.

CHAPTER FIVE

In the engine-room the chief engineer heard the crack and looked at the Third, who stared back at him. Their expressions were very different. Mr. Brewer was close on thirty but still a boy to look at, perhaps because he was below average height and brushed his putty-yellow hair straight across from the parting and had nothing of the sophistication of his age in his appearance. He was a chief engineer-officer of the new kind that was finding its way to ships and to the sea: educated boys, some of them from universities, their heads packed with theory and their hands inexperienced. Many went back to the land; those who stayed were among the best of them.

"Christ!" said Brewer. "What was that?" He had given a brief explosive laugh when the noise had sounded above the high sweet run of the Kincaird engines. It was the sort of laugh anyone would give when his best friend became merry and suddenly took his trousers off to amuse the company: a laugh of shocked amusement tempered by the thought that he must shortly get out of here, or his trouserless friend might claim him in front of everyone. Brewer, for a man who was certainly no prig, had a sense of the rightness of things. Sudden disorder shocked and amused him. He had given this familiar laugh of his a few weeks ago when a dockside crane had dropped a four-hundredweight crate of glassware into the dock. He had enjoyed the noise and been impressed by the comment of the boss stevedore who had been standing beside him; but his real shock derived from the disorderliness of this event.

His third engineer, Gyorgy János, was unable to understand this peculiar sense of humour. He stared at his chief with his thoughts almost visibly written in his eyes. Brewer stood listening, his hands stuck into the belt of his white overalls. The sound might come again, and give a clue to its direction. He thought it was from for'ard somewhere. It had been a very disorderly sound, the kind to alarm a less confident man.

The Third said something in Hungarian. They both waited. János was watching a rag tied to a rail; one of the greasers had knotted it there, so that he would find it easily. It was hanging away from the vertical by ten or fifteen degrees. The ship was broached-to and still trying to go full round and finish up head-to-sea. János became slowly fascinated by the hang of the greaser's rag.

Mr. Brewer put his hand on the telephone, but decided against calling the bridge. They would be busy up there, trying to bring the ship round; he must not interrupt a manœuvre that in this sea was difficult. They would have heard the noise; he was certain of that.

János watched the rag with a child's serious interest. He was much bigger than the chief, with a massive head and fine features; he expressed much with his eyes. They sparked as the telephone rang and he watched Brewer pick it up.

It sounded like Peter.

"You all right down there, Chief?"

"I'm fine. How are you?"

"Did you hear that crack?"

"Not half. What was it?"

Costain said, "We don't know."

"Well, it wasn't the mainshaft. It came from well for'ard of here, I'd say."

"We'll find out. We're still turning."

"I know. We're standing on the bulkheads down here. Can we do anything to help?"

"Keep steam up."

"Naturally." He put the telephone back on to its hook. János was still watching him. Brewer shrugged. The bridge didn't know. They could feel the ship fighting to get her head round, with the helmsman giving her a bit and then taking it back; the rag moved a degree and moved out again from the vertical. They watched the gauges and listened to the beat of the pistons. The sinews of the ship were alive about them as she fought to complete her turn. János looked deeply unhappy, his quick imagination trying to riot and unnerve him. Brewer did not move away from the telegraph. He expected it to ring. They both looked now and then at the greaser's rag. It had hung out like that for a long time.

Above them and for'ard the chief steward was trying to push a tray-stack back on to its shelf, so that he could fix the movable ledge and lock it. He was poised on the balls of his feet, his arms out straight, his hands braced against the trays, so that when the roll of the ship corrected he could push them in and fix the ledge. He had stood like this for half a minute now, and had begun sweating. He had begun trying to push the ship back straight, as well as the trays. He didn't like this. They were playing a fine bloody game up there on the bridge.

An assistant steward looked in, his face a muddy white.

"Stack o' crocks gone, Jack."

"I heard. Give a hand with this lot."

The assistant steward lent his weight. Jack Persham could feel the aura of fear about the man. They both pushed at the heavy steel trays and shifted them back. Persham snapped the ledge up and flipped the end-bolts. He stood away and wiped his face, looking at Dodds, giving him a cigarette.

"Why aren't you in your bunk, mate?"

"I couldn't sleep, with this lot." They lit up, but Dodds wouldn't meet his eyes. "What was that noise, Jack?"

"God knows."

"It wasn't the crocks."

"Bose has been through, checkin' up." They had turned to look at the porthole, but they could see nothing outside except flying white spray. The deck under them was still on the tilt. It must be a full minute now. Persham smoked nervously, his anxiety deepened by the colour of Dodds's face. It had been an awful crack, and this was a nasty list. The ship was out of hand. He took another lungful of smoke and nipped the cigarette out, dropping it neatly into the top pocket of his jacket. "I better go an' calm the passengers."

The chief steward left him, limping down the alleyway as if one leg had become shorter than the other. It was a list, all right. She wasn't going back. They'd all be in a state, the passengers. He was in quite a state, himself.

He found Mr. and Mrs. Jocelyn standing in the main doorway to the promenade deck, on the lee side.

"I'll have to shut those doors I'm afraid, sir."

"All right." Jocelyn gave him a hand with the vertical bolts while his wife stood back and watched them. She lit a new cigarette from the butt of the last. She said when the steward straightened up:

"What's all the excitement?"

"No excitement, madam. We're jus' comin' about."

Jocelyn looked at Persham with a smooth bland face. "We got the message about that, but no one's told us what the noise was." He stood with his hands in the pockets of his uncreased gaberdine slacks, looking like a gentleman-beachcomber in his shirt and cotton scarf. "I mean that cracking noise."

Persham darted to the scuttle along the bulkhead, calling over his shoulder, "Noise, sir?" He slammed the scuttle and fixed the catch, hoping as he swung round to see something else that needed immediate securing, before they could question him more fully. He didn't know what the noise had been. He thought that if it was nothing worse than the foremast splitting in half they were all lucky.

Penny Jocelyn, a small pert woman with lovely eyes and a catlike grip on life, said to her husband, "Are you really a good swimmer, Pooch?"

He watched Persham dodging round the tables in the saloon, checking on their chains. "M'm?"

"I mean, have you done life-saving and everything?"

He smiled suddenly, and his fresh round face went amiable again. "Balls. Let's go and get a little drinkie. Someone might know something." He thought for a moment that under his feet he could feel the ship righting herself, but he couldn't be sure. This was the first time he'd been on the sea, except for fishing.

boats round the coast, and his inexperience gave him nothing to go on. Was this a bad angle for the ship to take? What had that breaking noise been? Someone had said it was crockery smashing, but he knew that wasn't right. Why were the stewards lying? He preferred going in aeroplanes. Next time he'd take a nice clean aeroplane; one good meal and you were there.

His wife took his hand and they edged along the port side of the saloon towards the bar. At the bar was little Papasian, sitting as upright as he could. They had never seen him at the bar before; he was usually glimpsed for a couple of seconds, darting into the toilets or across to the rail with short delicate steps and a green face, hurrying as unobtrusively as it was possible to any haven where he could privately deliver himself of his misery.

"Would you like to join me in a drink?" He managed a smile, hopping off the stool and waiting until Mrs. Jocelyn had sat down, then hopping up again, the gold tooth winking its welcome as he smiled, the yellow brief-case tucked beneath his arm. The only thing they knew about him was that he was an Armenian.

"On us," said Jocelyn, feeling for money. Tonio, behind the bar, was looking pleased with them. He liked passengers who made for the bar in time of uneasiness. He hoped, when he grew old enough to be tired of keeping young, that he would be giving such passengers as these their last drink when the siren sounded abandon ship.

"Please no," said Dr. Papasian, and put down a note, nearly toppling from the stool because his left arm was permanently incapacitated by the yellow brief-case. Jocelyn steadied him.

"Well," he said politely, "thank you, sir." He looked at his wife. "We'd love a Scotch."

"For me," Dr. Papasian said as Tonio got a brandy glass, "cognac."

"Cognac, Doctor. Two Scotch."

Everything suddenly shook: the counter, the bottles, glasses, mirrors, artificial flowers, the stools under them. Then it was over.

Tonio had paused, so that he should not spill the brandy. He set the glass down so close to Dr. Papasian and so near the edge of the bar that he must pick it up at once. It would be safer in his hand.

"Cheers," said the Jocelyns when they had their drinks.

"Cheeri-ho," said the little man. His idiom was too studied, but this was almost the only imperfection in his English. Alan Jocelyn was trying to think how the man was able to come here and have a drink when the ship was roughing it; throughout the earlier smooth crossing he had been plagued by sickness. Or had he made up his mind to get quickly sloshed, and thus anæsthetize himself?

"For you," Dr. Papasian was saying. Tonio thanked him with pleased surprise, perfectly simulated, and reached for the bottle of Valdepeñas that he kept behind him in a corner. As a child he had gone up the hillside every autumn to help his family pluck at the vines, and had mastered the family *porrón* before he was ten, trickling the light young wine expertly into his throat with his eyes closed against the burning turquoise sky and his sister Maria's voice in his ears, for she was always singing and had sung until she died of the tubercle. Now he drank from the round plain glass, his head first inclined in thanks to the doctor, his feet braced to the angle of the deck, his eyes open to watch the flying horizon beyond the windows, but with these old memories on his tongue; for this was the same wine, perhaps even from the same hillside.

The vibration came again, and he thought of mentioning it, saying it was just the screw coming out of the sea and meant nothing at all bad; but the little doctor was perched with his nose buried in the fumy glass and the English couple were turned to watch the windows and the sea. They were not interested in the vibration, so Tonio did not mention it.

In her cabin, Miss Brown filled another blue-tinted page, still rather proud of the monogram in the top corner with the ship's name below it. For a few more precious hours her address would be this tiny moving island somewhere in the Atlantic. Miss A. K. Brown, on board the *Atlantic Whipper,* at sea. It should go on like this for always, always, with the bright veneered woodwork and rich curtains and the rose-shaded lamp, and outside the clean wide world of the sea and sky, enormous enough to be lost in and never found, never brought back, never called Brownie again nor requested not to water the window-box so carelessly that drips went down into the area, nor warned that the milkman had called three times this week for his money and would stop leaving her any on Saturday, nor asked to be firmer with Tommy Watson who was badly in need of discipline. . . . Poor Tommy, was he still there beyond the horizon with his red face and squint and steel-rimmed spectacles, kicking at the girls, at the teachers, at the table-legs if there were nothing better handy?

This breathless winging life could not go on for very long, even if she could afford to give up her work and to travel where she chose; because of Tommy. He needed her ankle to kick when his miniature rage sought the only relief within reach and his eyes were red with watching the laughter—the silent unhearable and unbearable laughter of small cruel mouths—when the others felt the need of an easy clown to make their fun with. She would go back tomorrow (tomorrow was as sad a word as yesterday), and be careful not to let the water drip, and not to forget the milkman's money; but she would not be firmer with Tommy. She must make a resolution for the small new year of her landfall; and it would be that.

She wrote again. *It has been utterly perfect, and if it is the last real holiday I ever take, I shall always remember it. It probably will be, too! I had no idea how much the little extras would come to—but I mustn't start regretting the expense. It has been worth it, every single penny.* She looked up from the paper. It would be her last chance of even mentioning his name. Once on the land again this heady champagne mood would go, and she would never tell a soul, even his name. This would be the last chance of leaking just a little of the miracle away, before she drowned in it. There was no need to say much. *By the way, I have been . . .* been what? Dancing . . . *dancing with an awfully nice young officer on board, and he's . . .* and he's what? Wonderful—can't put wonderful, shouldn't have started this at all. Tear up the page and begin again? Why should I be frightened, spinsterly and naïve and scared of even mentioning his name? He's magnificent, and kind, and in a way very boyish, though his eyes are like young eagles' eyes when he watches the sea—he must love the sea; no one could not love it, and he's so obviously at home with the sea and the ship . . . *been telling me all about the ship. His name is Peter.*

Peter Costain.

I expect I shall see you before this letter reaches you, so I suppose it's rather absurd.

Absurd to be going back, or absurd to have come away, half the world away? She wrote: *with love,* and signed the letter, uncrossing her legs and leaning back along the padded seat, to think about him and try to see his thin young face and the way his eyes changed when he looked at the sea, and changed again when he looked at her. Peter Costain. Would it be very long before she could hear that name spoken by chance, and not remember, not feel her heart go tight and her breath catch? How many years? When the year came, bringing so great a forgetfulness, she would be old, very old. There would not be another Peter, because . . .

one knew these things, one felt them. There wouldn't be any more impulsive trips to South America, costing the last penny of her savings; and at home there was too much to do and think about, too little time to let herself become interested in—in anything like that, and besides . . . besides nothing—she didn't have to explain to herself why there wouldn't be another Peter. So, when she was old, and someone said his name, she wouldn't remember.

She wouldn't remember anyone called Peter Costain. After tomorrow she'd never see him again, and by this time next year would have forgotten what he looked like and the sound of his voice; another year and her memory would play tricks by sly degrees and change him little by little so that the fine dark hair would perhaps lighten, and the shape of his chin alter, his whole face change so that she would be thinking of a face that was not his nor anyone's, only a dream face with a dream voice masquerading in his name because she had to remember Peter (more and more desperately as the years went by) and what he looked like. But she would be looking at the ghost-face of someone who had never existed. The time would come when by chance she might catch a glimpse of the real face, Peter Costain's face, and not recognize it because the face in her mind, recomposed by a failing memory, would be utterly different. In a few years. . . . She tried to think of fresh tortures for her mind to purge itself with. This bitterness must be got over before she reached home. There mustn't be any quiet shutting of the door, and the dusty embrace of the old familiar loneliness, and then the thoughts of Peter whom she would never see again. No sudden pangs, no tears and no self-pity, up in that small high room; because up there she would not be able to bear with it. She must get it over now.

These tears were not deliberate. She wanted to cry, to be rid of them; but she could not have manufactured this suddenly blinding misery that took hold of her now and left her crumpled on the padded seat with her slight body shaking and her breath fast as if she drowned.

The knock at the cabin door was quick and brusque; the door was opened before she could call out, and for an instant she was scandalized by the violation of her privacy as she flicked a hand to her face, brushing away tears and covering her mouth to still the tremulous breathing.

Peter was astonished, and closed the door, coming to her quickly. "Darling . . . it's all right." He was crouching in front of her, taking her wet cold hands; she knew he was watching her face and thinking how ugly the sobbing had made it; and this thought, together with his presence and immediate sympathy out of the blue, brought the tears freely again, and she tore her hands away from his so that she could cover her red ugly face.

He held her shoulders. "Darling, it's honestly all right, honestly. We're only turning about, because of the weather." He must make her understand; she mustn't be as frightened as this. He remembered the Skip's phrase, and used it to persuade her. "There's absolutely no cause for alarm. We're all perfectly safe, darling. Please, Ann . . . please."

She wriggled away from him, nearly falling as she crossed the cabin, forgetting the angle of the floor. She found a handkerchief; to Costain it looked as though a whole white-laced cloud of them came blossoming out of the drawer. She snivelled and tried to pick some of them up, and he helped her. "Gosh, what a lot of handkerchiefs."

She blew her nose. "I seem to need them, don't I? A permanent waterworks." They both stood up, with most of the handkerchiefs back in their drawer. She was smiling.

He said gently, "It's perfectly all right, darling. I know it's noisy, and we're tilting over a bit, but it's honestly quite safe."

She smiled again, bravely, and let him hold her.

"Honestly, Peter?"

"Of course. But I know how you feel. As a matter of fact the Skip sent me down to let everyone know there's nothing to worry about."

"Then—then that's all right. That's fine." She gave a last snivel and tucked the hanky away. He could scarcely bear his pity for her, for this slender body that still trembled a little in his arms, for this small hot face with the tears wet on it. He had never been so sorry for anyone in his whole life, and this was an attractive girl who only last night had let him . . . it was almost unbearable. He stroked her soft brown hair.

"Poor darling little Ann, poor darling heart."

She began laughing. "I'm laughing at myself, Peter." The laughter made her body tremble again, and he held her closer. Oh God, if only the ship weren't in trouble, with the captain on the bridge and orders flying about . . . if only there were a few minutes, now. . . . "Darling, darling Ann."

She made him let her go. "Peter, you mustn't stay. You're on duty."

He had to make the effort; she was right. If anyone found him here—Turnbull, perhaps!—with a passenger in his arms at a time like this when the ship was . . . Could say she'd broken down when he was reassuring her . . . only obeying orders, calming the passengers . . . this one was very frightened, and . . .

"You must go, Peter. Please. I'm all right now, honestly." She went to the door. "You mustn't get into trouble." He moved and stood with her for a moment, making her kiss him. The feel of her hot mouth and the salt of her tears sent him dizzy again with pity and with love. She pushed him away.

"I'll get into trouble too, for keeping you here." He nodded, not able to speak. When he put his hand on the door-catch she caught him again suddenly and rubbed the back of her hand against his mouth, laughing softly again. "Lip-stick . . . they'd murder you!"

"Oh, my Lord!"

"It's all right now."

He opened the door, touching her hand quickly. "Listen, darling. The ship's perfectly safe. If there's a lot of noise, or anything, just remember. There's absolutely no cause for alarm."

Quickly she said, "I'll remember. I'm not frightened now."

He left her, shutting the door and hurrying along the alleyway, padding one hand along the bulkhead to steady himself, listening to a sound that must be Ann laughing aloud in her cabin, alone there and laughing . . . giving in to relief, it must be, now that he had told her it was all right and there was no danger . . . always crying or laughing, sometimes both at once, until you didn't know where the hell you were or what you'd done or what she was going to do next . . . poor darling Ann. . . . His hand went padding along, hitting the bulkhead. Gosh, were they all like that, when you got to know them, or was it only the marvellous ones like Ann who could let themselves go and make you feel . . . oh gosh! The others hadn't been like that, before. This was dynamite, but he didn't want to be careful any more. He was ready for blasting.

"Dodds!" The steward was coming along from the pantry, with a sick-looking face. "Knock at number nine, and ask if Miss Brown would like a drink brought. Brandy, or something."

"Nine, sir?"

"She's worried. Ask her if she'd like anything."

He went on past the steward and shot up the companionway, making back to the bridge. Thank God the Skip had sent him to reassure the passengers. She would have been so lost, crying alone in there. Poor darling Ann. It had made him feel very strong, suddenly. A man. In love. God, what a time to fall in love, with the ship broached-to in a heavy gale and a noise like the crack of doom down for'ard somewhere.

He climbed to the bridge, pushed aloft by the gusts of wind that were sending water along the decks in a stiff fluttering cloud that stung his neck as he clambered on to the bridge-end where the lookout stood huddled and alert.

He tugged the door open and slammed it behind him. The wheelhouse was quiet, the Skip and Beggs and the quartermaster all standing quietly, engrossed in their work. He wiped the spray from his neck and tried to compose himself and fit into this haven of calm.

"Ease her."

"Ease her, sir."

Timber creaked. The deck shifted under them. Spray hit the glass panel of the door. The captain watched the sea.

"Mr. Costain."

"Sir?"

"How do you find the passengers?"

"Fine, sir. Not worried."

"Very good."

The deck shifted under them. A thin cackle of Morse came from the doorway of the wireless-room. Outside, the gale sang in the shrouds. They could feel the ship meeting each sea and slowly overcoming it, wallowing to meet the next and overcoming it, until the quartermaster felt the great strain go out of the wheel as the bows began cutting into the waves and breaking their force. The sea was no longer pounding at the flat plates along the starboard side but was being brought obliquely across the bows; and the bows dipped and rose and ploughed the big waters and shipped them, tossed them and dropped them across the fo'c'sle and sent them washing into the scuppers and away.

"Ease her."

"Ease her, sir."

The light from the compass bowl cast a sick blue sheen on the captain's face as he watched the card. Mr. Beggs stood near the windows, judging the sea. Costain was by the door to the starboard wing, his excitement gone, replaced by a calm contemplation of this scene in here. The Skip was good to watch: he stood quite still and yet it seemed he was moving strongly with his ship and with the sea that was their enemy. Beggs loomed beyond him, with not a hint of movement in his big body; but when he looked once across at Costain, the third mate could see the thoughts there in the steady eyes of the man. Wide open and intelligent, they were reviewing the entire situation with an appraisal as primitive as an animal's. The sea had become a hunter and this brain was finely tuned to meet the threat.

"Midships."

"Midships, sir."

A wave caught the flare of her bow and she yawed to it.

"Wheel's amidships, sir!"

The *Whipper* was round, her head to the sea and the gale. The fo'c'sle was already lost in a smother of white.

"Steady . . ."

"Steady, sir." The midships spoke came up. "Course, sir! South, thirty-one degrees west."

Harkness stared into the compass bowl with a fortune-teller's concentration. In a few seconds he brought his head up and looked at the sea.

"Steer south thirty-five west."

"Steer south thirty-five west, sir." The quartermaster put the wheel down starboard. The captain watched the sea and the lie of it. "Course south thirty-five degrees west, sir!"

"Very good."

He moved to the telegraph and rang Half Ahead to keep steerage-way. It was no longer quiet in here. The gale hit the windows and they became semi-opaque under the hail of spindrift.

The second mate had moved away from the windows and stood watching the inclinometer. For a moment Harkness joined him. The list was fifteen degrees. Harkness said above the noise, "See how Mr. Turnbull is getting on."

"Ay, ay, sir." Beggs braced the door open against the wind's force and banged it shut behind him. Turnbull would be on deck for'ard with the bosun's team and all spare hands. That was where the crack had come from.

Harkness went into the wireless-room and said to Bond:

"To owners: *Position forty-nine ten minutes north, thirteen fifty minutes west. Am hove-to in south-westerly gale.*" He went to the doorway into the wheelhouse as the first mate came up. Turnbull's black oilskins were astream with water. He was breathing hard and there was a red gash on his hand.

"Shifting-boards gone in number two, sir. The grain's shifted. We're doing what we can to trim it now."

Harkness stood listening to the slam of the wind against the superstructure.

"What was the condition of the shifting-boards in Buenos Aires?"

"Good condition, sir."

"You checked them yourself, Mr. Turnbull?"

"Yes, sir."

Harkness watched the windows. The spray flew against them, bursting. "Do what you can."

"Ay, ay, sir."

When he had gone, Harkness turned back and said to Bond:

"Add to that message: *Cargo shifted. List fifteen degrees. No anxiety.*"

He watched the wireless operator working. When he had finished, Harkness said, "Send the same complete message to P.O. for distribution."

Bond's hand went to the dials. "Require assistance, sir?"

"No. All we want is some shovels, Mr. Bond."

The captain went into the wheelhouse and said to Costain:

"It's close on tea-time. I'm going below, to take some tea with the passengers, should you want me."

"Ay, ay, sir." Costain watched him walk down the tilt of the deck to the wheelhouse door. Before he opened it he turned his head and looked at the third mate.

"I'll send a steward up. Tea or cocoa?"

It sounded important. Costain's face lost its strain as he smiled. "Cocoa please, sir."

The captain nodded, and pushed open the door.

CHAPTER SIX

The bosun had twenty-four men with him on the foredeck where the seas were coming in white-peaked mountains that shattered as the ship ran into them. As they shattered the wind tore the fragments away and drove them stinging across the deck so that the men would hunch and take the water on their backs and then work on again until the next wave crashed over the bows and the salt-blast struck at them and they stood with their feet braced in whirling water; then they worked on again until the next wave came, and the next, while the bows of the *Whipper* went into them and clove them and shipped them boiling white across the fo'c'sle head. The wind drove low, pressing the funnel smoke down to the lifting crests and howling through the shrouds and stays and aerials so that the ship was loud with hellish music as she wallowed head to weather, keeping her steerage-way and letting the seas come, and meeting them, sometimes lifting her bows above a wave as the last one ran astern and left a trough, sometimes butting her bows down and cleaving a wave at the base so that water came green against the winches and broke there in a burst of spume that could hardly rise before the wind struck and drove it across the foredeck and hatches and bridge.

Art Starley worked his men at the after end of number two hatch, above the hold where the grain had shifted. They had loosed the battens and drawn half the tarpaulin back, rigging it as best they could at an angle to protect the others as they worked in the narrow gap between the boards and the after coaming. When the bosun had piped them on deck they had fought their way against the wind to the forestore for shovels; now they were out of the wind, shielded by the rigged tarpaulin that took the main force of each ragged gust as it flung white water flat against it with a percussion that numbed the ears.

The men who worked w th the shovels waded knee-deep in the grain, driving the shovel-biades down and turning them, shifting the grain from the port side to the starboard, digging and sending it flying in the half-light of the dying afternoon, digging and bringing it up and sending it scattering through the gloom until their boots sank deeper and they must drag them out and stand on the shifting surface and then slowly sink again as their shovels dug, and drove, and flung, dug, and drove, and flung the grain aside while their muscles burned and the sweat ran stinging in their eyes.

They were standing on top of a thousand tons of grain, ants in a sugar-bowl. Only now, after thirty minutes' toil, were they beginning to realize that this was a fortnight's job under their feet.

Starley clambered over the coaming and picked on two spare hands. "Go an' ask the chief engineer if we can have two shovels from the stokehold!" He watched them dart away, dodging through spindrift, then turned and shouted to Wilson and Copley; but water exploded against the tarpaulin and his mouth moved in silence.

"You two! *You two!*" They looked up, their faces bright with sweat and their chests heaving. He pointed to Mounsey and Smithers, who were braced with their backs to the edge of the tarpaulin, their hands dragging down on the ropes. "Change places, you lot!"

Copley, a five-foot-nothing deck-hand on his first trip deep-sea, stuck his shovel into the grain and scrambled out, catching his sea-boot and going down spread-eagled as another man brought his shovel back with a swing and deflected the blade in time. "Christ, I thought you was a beetle, boy!"

"Jump to it, Copley!"

His feet scattered the grain. Someone gave him a hand as Smithers dropped and took up his shovel. The tarpaulin above them cracked as the wind struck it; a rope skinned through a man's hand; he cried out in pain and grabbed the slack, lashing it round the crook of his elbow; the shovels hit the grain and lifted it in dull gold showers.

Copley clung to his rope, feeling the wind trying to take the tarpaulin. Was it strong enough, the wind, to rip the corner away and take him with it on the rope? The rope jerked in his hands; he took another bight when it slackened for an instant; if the lot went up he must go up with it, and that was that. He had to hang on, and bring his slight weight down when the wind tugged, and keep the rope like a live thing trembling in his arms, and feel it trying to lift him bodily and drag him upwards into the great strong flight of the wind and flick him into the sea. The bosun had given him the job and he'd have to do it, and when he'd done it he'd go below and sick up all the fright that was in him now.

He saw the banners of spray go flying against the superstructure and breaking to a mist that came sucking back as the gust blew out; he shut his eyes and took the sting of the water in his face; he clenched up his face like a knuckle and clung to the rope, and dragged on it, and felt it lift him, and dragged again while the spent spray went trickling down his neck, chilling him under the oilskin. He got his breath and opened his eyes, re-establishing himself in this vast explosive world of wind that could whirl him aloft, taking the tarpaulin, the rope and this whippet-thin boy before he could free himself. He felt it happening, time after time as the wind whipped and the rope went tight; and he wanted to be sick at the thought, and thus get rid of it. If the wind took him, the sea would kill him; but if he didn't hang on, the bosun would.

"Smithers! *Smithers!* Get back 'ere to the coamin' before that shovel brains you! Keep over this way, you stupid git!"

The shovels went in, and lifted, slinging the grain aside while the ship wallowed and shifted it back. The men swore at the grain and the wind and the sea, and dug their shovels in, and turned the blades, and sent the grain to starboard while the ship took water along her side and shifted the grain to port.

"Let's see you bloody well work, then! Where's yer spunk, you bunch o' bleedin' sparrers?"

But Starley was working with them, harder than most; and they knew it, and drove themselves, with the tune and their own pet words to it running through their heads. . . . 'Starley is a bar-stid, a bar-stid, a bar-stid . . .' while they dug their shovels in and slung the grain aside, and the ship rolled, and slung it back.

They had worked for an hour. Two shovels were broken and a seaman had been dragged out of the hold unconscious, blood streaming from his head where it had caught the edge of the coaming as he had lost his balance on the shifting grain. Under a thick scud of cloud the light was fading. Water had been taken in as a wind-gust veered and sent a wash of it below the tarpaulin and into the hold.

Starley groped his way to where the first mate was braced against a samson post, and cupped his hands.

"We're not gettin' anywhere, sir!"

Turnbull jerked his head away as a drift of white spume smothered them. The water ran from their faces. He would have liked to tell the bosun to keep the hands working until the grain was back and the ship was eased from her list, even if they worked till their hearts burst and they dropped; but this hardness in him was not from any spite. In times like these Turnbull was at his best, and the ship was his only concern, and the men in her, even if they must work till they fell in order that she would be helped in her struggle with the sea.

"We'll never shift it, sir, in this weather!"

Turnbull opened the slit of his mouth. "Get them out. Get the tarpaulin back and batten down."

"Ay, ay, sir!"

They came out, bringing their shovels, exhausted as much by their knowledge that they had accomplished nothing as by the jading pace at which they had worked.

"Those two shovels, back to the stokehold. The rest in the fore-store. Copley, what's the matter with you?"

"Nothing, sir." He was huddled over his stomach, a bundle of creased oilskins with a pinched white face.

"Get below." He swung round and saw the carpenters. "Take these two an' mend 'em, lively. We'll want 'em again, any time." He gave them the broken shovels. "Wilson!"

Wilson dodged towards him. Starley jerked a hand in young Copley's direction. "Take the kid below an' see he's all right."

"Yes, bose."

"Rest of you on the tarpaulin—lively, now!"

Against the wind and the torn water that was driving across the foredeck they worked while the daylight faded about them, putting the boards back and dragging the tarpaulin over them, slinging the battens down and making them fast. The wooden chocks were swollen with water, and would hardly budge.

From the bridge, Beggs and Costain saw the men finish the work and struggle in a group for the shelter of the companionway. Beggs turned from the windows and looked at the inclinometer. The mean reading was still fifteen degrees.

* * *

Captain Harkness had left his coat in his room before going along to the saloon for tea. He had also brushed his hair and corrected his tie. Along the alleyway he had filled his pipe and lit it, so that when he entered the saloon he was looking spruce and unworried. Persham, the chief steward, was handy to receive him formally.

"Tea, sir?"

"If you please."

But there was a bleakness about the saloon. There were only four people here: Mr. and Mrs. Jocelyn, Dr. Papasian and Major Draycott. The movement of the deck was not too bad, but the list was noticeable. Major Draycott, a thin yellow-faced man whose Army days had ended a long time ago, was sitting alone at the foremost table on the port side, reading a battered book. The Jocelyns were more at their ease, talking to the little Armenian, and when Harkness came in, Alan Jocelyn got up and met him amiably.

"Are you going to join us, sir?"

"If I may, Mr. Jocelyn."

Dr. Papasian stood up as they reached the table, his gold tooth winking its welcome. It was quite extraordinary, Jocelyn thought, how the rough weather had seemed to cure him of his sea-sickness. He had drunk three brandies and was ready for tea.

"Hello, Captain." Penny Jocelyn put a lot into it, making it sound as if she had said Cap, or Skipper. She liked Harkness; she considered him a really wonderful hunk of a male. He had a face like a slightly crumpled balloon and a figure that was dead square whichever way you looked at it; but there was so much strength in the man that it shone out of his pale blue eyes—not just muscle-power, but a bigness of will and spirit that was evident in his very calm. "Come and sit down," she said, and made it sound like Come and Sit with Me.

He turned a bland smile on her. "Thank you."

"What's it like on top?" asked Jocelyn. It was the first of the questions that Harkness was down here to answer. He was ready for them all.

"Windy." He left his bland smile on; it was correct wear for a captain taking tea with worried passengers. "Rather windy."

Penny Jocelyn said from beside him, "I'll bet it's a real whizzer, on deck."

He appeared to consider the word. "That would be a very fair description, Mrs. Jocelyn. A whizzer."

Two stewards brought trays and set them out. "I wonder," said Harkness, "if we should ask Major Draycott if he'd care to join us? He seems rather lonely."

The chief steward was ready to take the message, balanced on one foot; but Mrs. Jocelyn was slipping out of her chair. "I'll get him." The angle of the deck didn't seem to trouble her. Alan Jocelyn watched her lean both hands on the Major's table so that she could look directly and appealingly at him with their faces on the same level. From where he sat, Jocelyn admired the taut angle of her body as she leaned on her hands. She really was a lavish little wench; she used it on everybody, young and old, provided they were trousered. He watched the Major take his horn-rimmed glasses off and struggle to his feet; the book dropped, and she quickly stooped and laid it on the table still open. The poor old boy looked disturbed, as if his quiet reading had been interrupted, however pleasantly; except that Jocelyn knew that in the past half an hour he hadn't turned a page. Had his fine-boned face looked as yellow as that, before the gale had come? It was difficult to remember an exact shade of yellow.

When Draycott had sat down with them he seemed as lonely as he had been before, and less at ease. Penny said to him:

"The Captain's turned us round, Major. Back to the South American sunshine, since the weather's so filthy in England."

It was a silly enough remark but she had thrown it to him as a small lifeboat in his loneliness; he would have to think of an answer, and then she could pull him in. But the silence became awkward; he didn't seem to realize at once that he was being saved. He had clearly heard, for he was looking at her; but no faint change came to the yellow skin, no hint of a smile.

"You're not very well-informed, Mrs. Jocelyn." She relaxed. His voice was gentle, though it seemed a slight effort for him to use it. "According to the latest reports there were bright patches in Manchester, yesterday morning."

He blinked to the slight shock of the laughter that went round; his eyes had the defensive look of a man who shies from attention.

"Then we shall certainly turn about again," said Harkness, "as soon as we can. That shouldn't be very long, perhaps a few hours. I'm sorry, though, that we're meeting with this delay. The wireless-room is ready to send any messages to friends ashore, if anyone is being met at the dockside."

"I've always longed," said Penny, "to cultivate the kind of friend who'd wait for me on a dockside in winter at two in the morning." She crooked her hands in front of her dramatically. "Maybe it's because I don't *give* enough of myself."

Jocelyn murmured, "Oh, surely not." She gave him a quick fierce grimace. Major Draycott said:

"I assume the cargo has shifted?"

Captain Harkness turned his mild gaze on the man. He judged Draycott to be sixty, though long illness had aged him early. He looked a typical case of a man who serves his government either in or out of uniform, prodigally throwing down the vital years as the price of his promotion, quitting his own country and sweating the middle years away with a ration of gin and quinine, and returning withered by the black man's sun and by the first searing anger that he had nursed in silence against the petty shifts and subterfuge of white man's lordly government—an anger long since burned away and buried with its secret epitaph, *It wouldn't have Paid*. But a major now, and back to England with all honour. A job well done, and no trick left untried. A major, among the minors and sub-minors and the other majors and super-majors jockeying for their rightful position: at the top. But, failing the top, the prize. The pay-off and the pension, the yellow skin, and all the time in the world for self-pity and the search for friends, or, failing friends, people who would listen, or failing those, just people, any people wherever they could be found and pinned down, in the club, in a bar, in a ship. Listen to my gallant past, and throw me the biggest biscuit of them all, and call me Major.

Almost typical, this man Draycott, except in one respect: he didn't want anyone to listen. He had kept intact his humility through all those regretted years; he needed his title only to show that he had not always been a sick old man with an unread battered book.

"That's quite correct, Major." The captain bowed his head in a careful nod. "The cargo has shifted. Not all of it, of course. The trouble is in number two hold—that's the one just forward of the bridge. The men are working on it now."

Mrs. Jocelyn said in a pleased voice, "And will the floor be straight when they've finished?"

"Until the gale drops, the floor will lie at all angles, according to the ancient traditions of the sea." He turned his head as he heard voices. The Sennetts were coming in, unobtrusively; their voices grew quiet as they chose a table, but before they had sat down Penny Jocelyn was hailing them.

"Captain's conference. Disciplinary action will be waived, in this instance, for late arrivals."

Unobserved by the rest, Major Draycott's face had warmed to a wintry smile as he sat watching Penny. She reminded him of a girl he had known, a long time ago, before he had gone out to Kenya. But he could not quite remember her name.

Persham, the steward, was slipping the chains of two chairs and moving them to the table where the captain sat. Dr. Papasian was bobbing up as Mrs. Sennett neared. Harkness rose, moving his chair to make room. Jocelyn was slower. Major Draycott made every gesture of rising, except that of actually leaving his chair, delaying the moment until it was too late and Mrs. Sennett was putting her hand lightly on his shoulder—"Please don't disturb yourselves." She slipped quickly into her chair next to the Major. He was much relieved. Throughout this never-ending voyage he had carried the last words spoken to him on the shore, "And remember, no exertion." He would have wished for a more romantic farewell.

"We didn't know there was a conference on," said Sennett. He sat with his stiff left leg in front of him, his gloved left hand on his lap.

Harkness said, "In actual fact it's just a tea-party, but I expect you'll realize that Mrs. Jocelyn's flair for the dramatic has charged the occasion with solemnity."

Jocelyn beamed at the Sennetts. "You were going to be piped into the saloon, but Mrs. Jocelyn's psychiatrist has confiscated her mouth-organ."

Major Draycott's faint smile had gone, except perhaps from his eyes. He looked younger. Sennett noticed this. He also noticed that the banter seemed to be skating nervously across a very thin surface. The captain wouldn't be down here drinking tea for the want of something to do. Sennett thought there was probably a great deal to be done, on the bridge. He said when the moment was right, "I'm glad we've turned about. It was beginning to feel rough." His glance moved by degrees to Harkness.

"There's no indication," Harkness said easily, "that this weather's going to fine down before noon tomorrow, even if then. We shall be delayed, obviously. As I was saying before you came in, messages can be sent to England to that effect, if there's anyone likely to worry." He swallowed some tea and pushed the cup away, keeping his finger-tips on it while the saloon tilted, and tilted back. Then he got up. "If you'll excuse me. I'll look forward to seeing you all at dinner."

When he had gone, the conversation stopped skating. Major Draycott was already asking a steward for a message-pad.

"What's the report?" asked Mrs. Sennett over-casually.

"Cargo's shifted," said Jocelyn. He looked at his wife. "You owe me five bob on that."

"I'll pay you in kind."

Mrs. Sennett said something quietly to her husband. Penny was watching them. They fascinated her. The girl was almost beautiful, with a long pale face that was so inanimate as to be uninteresting, until she spoke. She spoke with a sad timbre that was always there in her voice; even when she laughed there was a hint of wistfulness. Most marked was her devotion to Sennett, and her adoration of him. It would have been easy to conclude, at first sight of them, that because he was striking in his looks she adored him for his gold hair and brilliant ice-blue eyes and the chiselled fineness of his bone-structure, the firm set of his mouth and the sculpted shape of his head. When Penny Jocelyn had first seen him she had murmured to Alan in a deep velvet key, "Adonis, in person. It's not possible." Jocelyn had agreed. The least vain man would envy Sennett his looks. It would have been as easy to conclude, at first sight of these two people, that the girl was devoted to him because he was an object of pity, with his stiff leg and gloved hand, however much these injuries could lend a grim romantic air to his appearance. There was glamour, even at serious levels of thought, about a man who had suffered and emerged less whole.

No one on board the ship knew whether such first-sight conclusions were right; they had to settle for the obvious. It was assumed, understandably, that Sennett had come down in a blazing bomber; nothing less heroic could fit such a face; no other picture of his past was even sought for; but he gave no hint, even by the unconscious use of R.A.F. slang in his conversation. Nor was any light thrown by his wife. Most of their conversation was reserved for themselves; even in the throng of an after-dinner dance on board, when the full muster of passengers and officers seemed to crowd the small saloon, the Sennetts kept together, and danced together, admired for the picture they made of a couple in perfect love, and for the dexterity his practice and her harmony brought to their steps. The result of this withdrawal from other people was that they had become the immediate focus of conjecture and discussion during a long sea voyage. Penny Jocelyn had summed up the whole thing on the first evening:

"Well, obviously he's been through a bad time, and she's more in love with him than ever because she can now take over all the duties every woman yearns for—of wife, lover, mother, sister, protector and watchdog. She's obviously delirious about it."

"And penitent," Jocelyn had said.

"Penitent? What about?"

"Him. In some way. And he's up to his neck in self-pity."

"Well, he doesn't show it."

Jocelyn had shrugged. It was quite true—there had been no signs of self-pity in Sennett. He let her help him into his rain-proof coat when they went on deck, and find a cigarette for him when he began tapping his pockets, and sometimes light it for him; but these courtesies were returned. One almost began to feel it would be rather refreshing if one of them suddenly slapped the other one's face.

"Did the captain actually say that?" asked Sennett now.

"What?"

"That the cargo's shifted."

Dr. Papasian entered the conversation for the first time. "Oh, yes, Mr. Sennett. He did not like telling us."

Jocelyn grunted amiably. "And we did not like being told."

"We shall trust in our good ship," said Penny. "We shall face the future with strong hearts and quiet fortitude, so that with the help of the Lord we shall prevail."

It fell completely flat. She lit a new cigarette from the butt of the last, and started to tap her teeth with her thumb-nail. Too late to help her, but cutting the silence short, Alan Jocelyn said:

"Well, as long as they keep the bar open we shan't come to much harm. I'm saving the empties and putting the corks back. Lashed together they'll make an excellent life-raft."

"I imagine," said Major Draycott cautiously, " that if the cargo has shifted, we'll have signalled someone for assistance?" By the tone of his voice he imagined no such thing; he simply hoped.

"In this weather, yes." Sennett sat comfortably beside his wife. Whenever he spoke she turned her head to watch him, as to hear an oracle. "The cargo's mainly grain, which is treated as liquid. The only way to get rid of it would be to pump it out with special gear, which the ship doesn't carry. It's strictly a dockside operation." He spoke to no one in particular, though he was answering the Major's question. "So we shall finish the voyage with a fifteen-degree list. That's not awfully serious."

Penny said, "Is it fifteen degrees?"

"Approximately." His steady gaze was friendly but she couldn't meet it for long. It was difficult to look at Sennett without losing grip on the libido. She said quickly:

"Have you spies on the bridge?"

His smile was charming. "Oh, no. We drew a circle on a piece of paper and then split it up into seventy-two segments." He looked, still smiling, at his wife. "It took half an hour before we'd got it right. Then we held it against a bulkhead, as near to the fore-and-aft line as we could judge." He was looking at Penny again. "If you like, I'll take over your five-bob bet with Mr. Jocelyn."

Alan said straight away, "That it's fifteen degrees?"

"Well, we had to draw the segments freehand. I'll lay you it's nearer fifteen than ten or twenty."

"Taken. Where's the bit of paper?"

"I think we left it in——"

"I'll go." Mrs. Sennett was getting up. Alan said:

"Oh, no, don't worry about it now. Bring it when we meet at dinner——"

"It's no trouble."

"It'll give us something to play with," Sennett said when she had gone, "if the weather keeps us out here for a day or two."

Major Draycott's face had lost the last vestige of amusement. He looked old again. "You think it will?"

Sennett shrugged easily. "It's a comfortable ship, and very well run. I should think the worst we'll have to put up with is boredom."

CHAPTER SEVEN

WIRELESS-OFFICER BOND had sent the messages off. The chief steward had brought them to him in a batch soon after the captain had come up from tea.

To Mrs. Draycott, 14 Pembury Crescent, Tunbridge Wells, Kent. Will be delayed. No cause for worry. Tom.

To C.M.O. St. Peter's Hospital, Weyland Street, Hampstead, London. Ship delayed. Do not know for how long. Will contact again soon as possible. Apologies. Good wishes. Papasian.

To Mrs. Timsett, Flat 5, Courtney Lodge, Bournemouth, Hants. Delayed. Will phone when landed. Please tell Mr. Sennett and Paul's firm. Lovely trip. Our love. Moira.

To K. Jones, 1 South Street, Kensington, London. See under ships overdue. Have borrowed galoshes. Don't flog furniture till executors say. S.W.A.L.K. Alpenny.

The first message given to the chief steward by the Jocelyns had read, *Ship sunk. Drunk as a skunk in funk in bunk. Gugnunk.* But Persham had suggested to Mr. Jocelyn that the information contained in the message concerning the ship was untrue, and that the wireless-officer, being an employee of the shipping company, would decline to accept such a mistruth for putting out on the air.

A message from Miss Brown had reached the wireless-room before tea-time, and had gone off. *To Miss Pierglover, Principal, Suretidge School, The High, Croydon, Surrey. Terribly sorry. Delayed. Will phone. Brownie.*

She had questioned Dodds, the steward, whom Peter Costain had sent to her cabin. "Is this what you'd call a bad gale?"

Dodds had issued himself with a tot of rum and had crept back to the fringe of courage. Orders had been sent from the bridge that passengers must be reassured.

"Bad, miss? Bless your heart, no! Bit choppy, I'd say."

"But we've turned the ship round."

"Well, it's best." He grew confidential, screwing half his plump face into a wink. "We could've risked goin' on, see, an' ten to one we'd've done no worse'n break a bit o' crockery. But Captain

'Arkness, 'e's not a man to go 'an take risks, for 'isself nor anyone else. 'E's the bravest man I've met in me life, but 'e plays safe." He screwed his face up another wrinkle and sank his voice still lower. "'E plays safe, miss." There was a wistfulness in his face and voice to think of so brave a man, playing so safe. It was a Thought for the Day.

"That's nice to know." She was conscious of her red-rimmed eyes; their hot feeling reminded her that she was meant to be very frightened about the gale. "I feel much safer, now."

"Of course you do, miss. There's nothin' to fret about, you mark my words. It'd take a sight more'n a bit o' wind to send *this* ship to the bottom." That should reassure her.

"Well, that's—that's fine. I won't give it another moment's thought."

"That's right, miss. Now what can I get for you? Somethin' to drink, p'r'aps?"

"Well, no——"

"It 'elps, you know. It 'elps somethin' magical."

"I—I expect so, but I won't, just now. You've restored every bit of my confidence. But if we're facing the wrong way, it means we shall be late getting to England, won't it?"

Dodds shrugged off the thought as absurdly unimportant. "P'r'aps a few hours, p'r'aps a day, miss." So small a point. England could wait.

"Then I'd better send a message, by wireless. I can do that, can't I?"

"Why, cert'nly you can. I'll get the chief steward for you, an' 'e'll take your message to the bridge." He opened the door. "An' you won't have just one little . . . ?" He held up a finger and thumb enticingly. She smiled and shook her head.

"Not just now." It would cost as much as the message, and the message was more important.

Mr. Bond, sitting in the wireless-room, had dealt with the signals from the passengers and some of the crew. Should he send one to Thelma? She was expecting him home. Early tomorrow morning he should be going up Beaker Street, Bristol, his case in his hand, a present for her inside. How would he find 'things' when he got home? She was sorry about 'all that', her letter had said. She was all right now. For how long? She might run to the gate to meet him when she heard it open; or she might manage no more than a weary smile in the hall; he did not know and could not guess. Almost he would prefer her to leave him in peace, and ignore him while he was in the house; at least he could get on with the work on the new V.H.F. set he was building, without any pleas to go dancing at the Regency or to spend an evening with the Macrowans. Couldn't she get all the fun she wanted while he was at sea, and let him work in peace on his few days ashore?

She might, of course, have gone into his den and broken up the half-finished V.H.F. It had happened before, when he'd forgotten some friends were coming and had shut himself away with his beloved equipment. He awoke that night and heard it being smashed. He had not gone in to see what was happening; he knew what was happening. He should have changed his clothes, the evening before, and made sure the drinks were ready and the log-basket filled—"the simple duties of a good host," she had called it, standing there after they had gone, her hair shining in the light of the standard-lamp, her eyes brilliant with anger, her voice rough with it. "I know you're a genius, Tony, and that God made Adam, and then Eve, and then a wireless-set; but couldn't you for once act like a human being and get your feet on the ground and have some fun before we're both too withered with age to enjoy ourselves in even the simplest ways? I know you can't stand the Regency—all right, it's fairly crummy and full of yobs; and you don't care for the Macrowans because Bill always gets a bit tight when we have drinks together—all right, he is a bore when he's tight and he doesn't know the first thing about valves or wavelengths and that sort of technical stuff; and the pictures bore you stiff because the acoustics want redesigning and most of the films are about mush and murder anyway——" And he had watched the light on her hair as she flung it about, and the flash of her eyes and the white of her teeth as she had gone on and on, her hands flying out, flying up to her hair, spreading and clenching as she stood in the dark blue dress she liked so much, the one he hadn't noticed when she had put it on for the first time . . . but she had so many. He had stood watching her and listening, just wishing it would stop.

"But for God's sake, Tony, give me a break sometimes! Just one week in a year, when we could do something for its own sake, for the fun of it—even a few days' fishing in the country by a river, or a night in London for a show or something—anything, *anything* except letting me sit here twiddling my thumbs while you shut yourself away upstairs and twiddle with knobs—Tony, can't you understand even a fraction of what I'm saying?"

She had stopped. He had understood a fraction. After a long minute had crept by, shy of the lamplight and her brilliant cold eyes, he said:

"I'm dull."

Her hands flew again, as if she were conducting the rhythm of the words she said, though they tumbled out erratically in passionate fits and starts. "Not dull, Tony, because you're kind and have a really clever mind, and ——" she searched desperately for another quality, but had to call in a vague generality—"you're a good husband and all that." She shook her head. He thought how pretty she was. "But you just don't see. Do you?"

"Of course I see. We'll go out somewhere. Now."

She looked at the clock. "But it's gone eleven."

"Tomorrow, then. Shopping, or—or something, in the morning."

They had gone shopping and she had spent seven pounds, five of them on things she didn't want. In the evening they went round to the Stapletons, who never got tight; but Thelma had put on her most extravagant off-the-shoulder dress and looked rather absurd beside Jean Stapleton's comfortable twin-set; and this time it was Thelma who suddenly wanted to get tight and managed to do it on the meagre supply of South African sherry they kept for Christmas and what they slyly called High Jinx. She was taken home from an atmosphere of gathering shock, and had been defiant and contrite in turn, cursing the stuffed-up suburbanity of the Stapletons and being sorry for smashing his wonderful gadgets last night after he'd promised to take her shopping. ("But I think it was the thought of shopping that hit me in the night, Tony—it was such a bloody let-down, really, and I couldn't sleep and I wanted to—to hurt you badly, and there wasn't a better way of doing it.")

The next day she showed no more defiance. She left him alone, and took lunch up to his den with hardly a word. Later, she said she had been thinking about 'things', and had decided they must 'finish all this'. He had never bothered to ask how, or why, because his ship was due for sailing and he left early, to 'pick up some things'.

He was prepared for anything when he went home next. Late tomorrow, with any luck. The scenes would be the same, and they would be glad to say good-bye again. Yet what was wrong? 'Tony, you've a terribly limited imagination.' But surely his job alone required imagination?

He was staring up at the photograph. Love from Thelma. He looked down. The chair creaked under him as the ship heeled, and paused, and righted. There was less movement now that the *Whipper* was head-to-sea. She was turned away from land. Perhaps, with any luck, she'd never get there. There was a sulky triumph in the thought; but he was not so childish as to think vengefully how sorry she would be. He knew quite well that she would not be sorry at all.

* * *

"What happened?"

"You got knocked out, mate."

Persham snipped the lint strip and pinned it.

"Show me th' bastard, then! Who was it?" Harris tried to sit up.

"Lie quiet and let me finish what I'm doing!" Persham had a first-class proficiency certificate, and he was glad of a chance to practise.

"Who was it, then? Eh?"

"Oh, for Chris' sake shuddup, Harris. You knocked yourself out—that's the sort of prat you are. Now keep still."

Harris looked up at the chief steward, his eyes trying to focus; but they were deeply sunk into the white face, and he couldn't keep them open for long. He lay back as Persham swabbed the rest of the congealed blood from the side of his neck.

"Knocked meself out?" It was hardly audible. He watched Persham's fringe of red hair moving against the background of plates and rivets above his head. "Down in the grain?"

Persham said nothing. The swab in his hand was now pale crimson, and he took a new one from his kit. If only there'd been enough money. Christ, if only there *had* been. He could have finished his training by now; this year he would have been qualified, and working in a wonderful clean operating-theatre on a complicated case instead of down here in a sweaty cabin in a lousy cargo-packet with nothing more important than a stupid git of a seaman's flea-bitten head to patch up.

"Down on the grain, was it?"

"Yes. Now give over and keep still."

Harris remembered the grain now, and the bright flying of the shovels and the hailing of the grain in the half-dark while the wind howled past the tarpaulin and bloody Starley yelling his bloody head off at them to keep on shovelling, when any half-witted clot could see they'd never shift that much grain if they worked all their lives, when the ship was pitching it back again as fast as she could go. Jesus, what a passage this had turned out to be, with the mate a tight-mouthed bastard and the bosun a bone-headed git, and the seas up and the cargo shifted and the gale getting worse! And not even a doctor on board, only this bloody longshore waiter who knew all there was to know about first-aid. First-aid? He couldn't stuff a duck.

His head throbbed to the rhythm of the engines. His brain was going to shake itself off its bearings. Men ran somewhere on deck, their boots thudding above the cabin, thundering across the top of his head. He felt chilled from his tongue to his bowels, and the cabin lifted and dropped, tilted and swung, and he was afraid.

"They'll never shift it," he said, not clearly enough for Persham to understand. He went on mumbling. Persham dropped the last swab and used the towel. There'd be no thanks for this. Harris wouldn't thank him, nor anyone else. No fee, and no thanks. But it didn't worry him. He could say it himself, 'That's a tidy job, Jack boy. Dr. Kildare couldn't have done neater than that.'

He packed his kit deftly. Money wasn't evil. You had to have it. People didn't realize. His father didn't. "I've talked to the matron at the hospital, Jack, an' she knows all there is about it. It's no go, boy. It'd cost a mint o' money. Even with the scholarships, you got to keep yourself, and nothin' comin' in to the house, no matter how hard you'd work. Not a penny. So you'd best forget it, Jack. There's plenty of other ways to make a good livin'."

"It's not a question of makin' a livin', Dad. It's a question of bein' a doctor." The gas-lamp flared above them. His father shrugged.

"We can't all be doctors, y' know. Rest of us has got to be the patients." He smiled. "Eh?" The smile died slowly.

"Yes, Dad."

He had not turned up for instruction at the St. John's depot, the evening after; but a friend of his, who worked at the hospital, persuaded him to finish the course; and he got his certificate, and showed it to his father, but—"It's no go, Jack. I realize you've got the ability. It's a question o' the money, see?" He had tapped the certificate. "If that were a hundred-poun' note, we could start talkin'."

Jack had torn up the certificate and dropped it down the

lavatory pan; there had been a sour pleasure in pulling the chain on it. Before that year was out, he was at sea.

"They'll never shift it." The deck tilted to a roll, and tilted back. "See what I mean? You could work a month o' Sundays down that bloody hold, an' finish up where you started."

Jack Persham fetched a cup of water. Harris was still mumbling, his eyes open. ". . . just as well try an' empty th' ocean wi' a shovel." He laughed with slack lips; a bubble of saliva rose and burst.

"Take these, mate."

The eyes moved to look. "What're they, then?"

"Only aspirin."

"I don't want bloody aspirin."

"Come on. I've got some work to do."

"I don't take orders from a bloody steward."

The deck tilted, paused, tilted back. Voices shouted from above; one sounded like the bosun's. "That bastard."

"Come on, take these. I'm tryin' to help you, aren't I?" He had one arm round Harris's shoulders, lifting him so that he could drink. He was holding the cup near Harris's mouth. "Come on, mate. They'll stop a temp'rature, an' give you some sleep."

The smell of the blood and the antiseptic was sickly in the air. The water shivered in the cup as he tried to keep it steady. His arm was aching under Harris's weight. It was an ignorant, obdurate weight.

"Come on, it's not askin' much."

"You think asp'rins're goin' to help when there's a thous'n' tons o' grain down in number two?"

"Look, what've you got against me, mate? Aren't I trying to help you feel better?"

Harris managed another grunt, meant for a laugh. "All right, Doc."

Persham got the tablets into his mouth and held the cup while he drank; then he drew his arm away gently. When he had rinsed the cup and picked up his kit he took a last look at Harris, who had closed his eyes. Going out of the cabin, Persham was thinking, 'It's no good getting ideas, Jack, just because he called you Doc. He called you a bloody steward, too, and that's what you bloody well are.'

Art Starley had been down to see Harris, and Persham had told him he'd be all right in a couple of days. A couple of days were no use to the bosun because in the next forty-eight hours he was going to need every man's strength. Blast that sailor's eyes for his clumsiness at a time like this. He was just as useful now as if he was dead.

Someone knocked on the door of his room. He didn't answer. The bitch, the real bitch, was the grain. It was foxy tackle, once it took charge. If the seas got smaller they might shift the grain back with shovels, and rig a jury shifting-board to keep it there while the *Whipper* steamed for home. But the seas were going to get bigger. The forecasts said so. This lot was all over everywhere, from Hebrides to Biscay, and the *Whipper* wouldn't run through it with the grain like that. She could get home if the wind dropped to half, with the list that was on her now; she could get home in this full gale if the grain was trimmed; but until the wind dropped or they could find a way of trimming it they must stop out here in the deep water with the ship's eyes to the south, keeping steerage-way and meeting the seas, come as they might.

He felt jaded, sitting here in his own sweat with grain in his boots and salt on his face. He felt impotent. Stubbs was dead right. Call himself a bloody ship's bosun, did he? But there was nothing he could do until the weather gave him a break. Then he'd have them down in that hold and shifting the grain by the ton.

The knock at the door came again. His voice was sharp in the tiny cluttered room. "Well?"

When the door was wide open, there was no space for a man to pass between it and the bench, which was long and massive and buried beneath timber and paint and glue and ship's chandlery and tackle, with a space pushed clear for the bosun's paper-work.

Tich Copley said, "Can I see you, sir?"

"If you can't, you're blind." They stared at each other.

Copley was trying to shut the door, and Starley watched him. There was a rack of tools on the left of the door, with long handles sticking out so that they could be grabbed easily with no messing. With the door wide open at ninety degrees, as it was now, a man could stand here, just inside the room, as Copley was standing; but he couldn't go forward because of the bench, nor sideways to his right because of the door, nor sideways to his left because of the tools in the rack. He could go backwards, pulling the door after him, but there was no angle of less than ninety degrees at which the door gave room for a man to squeeze through; and the tools were stacked from the floor upwards, so that it wasn't possible to crawl under them and come up on the other side of the door.

Copley turned round, and tried to close it, fetching up sharp against the tools. A file dropped; he picked it up, and saw where it had come from; he slid it into the pigeon-hole and turned back and opened the door again, looking down at the bosun, who sat behind the bench.

"Shut that bloody door," said Art Starley.

"Ay, ay, sir."

Copley had broken out in a sweat. He backed, bringing the door after him until it was almost shut, so that he could try squeezing through the gap where the tool-racks gave more room. The bosun was watching a narrow strip of Copley, who was more outside the cabin than in it.

"Where the bloody hell are you goin'?"

The deckie pushed the door open wider and ignored everything: the door, the tools, the bench, the bosun. He just pushed his way onwards towards the bench; but he didn't get through. A mallet-handle struck him in the stomach and three or four spare timbers jammed the door as he knocked into them. He slid them back, and turned sideways, and sidled carefully into the gap until there was timber pressing against his buttocks and the door-handle was lodged in his groin. He breathed now with difficulty, saying over and over again to himself, 'God, why did I come here? God, why did I come here?' The physical energy he was using would have been enough to fight a bull off; the nervous strain of trying to outwit the door and the tools and the bench was making his head pound.

He did not look at the bosun any more. He had his back to him now, and faced out of the room, pulling the door an inch towards him and then edging sideways between it and the bench. It was successful up to a point, the point where his body was squeezed so tightly in the gap that it forced the door wider again, until it pinned him as hard as a wedge.

"I can't think," Starley said, "what'd happen if anything man-sized came in here." He lit an American cigarette, and leaned back in his chair.

The smoke crept past Copley's face; he breathed it in. His scalp was hot and he was still saying the same thing in his mind, asking God why he had come here, but now he was stringing the question out with terrible other words, mixing them up with names for the bosun and his door. He freed himself, and turned round slowly, leaving the door wide open at right-angles to the bench; then he stood facing the bosun with his legs at ease and hands tucked behind him. He looked down at the bosun with his jaw tilted and his eyes gazing steadily into Starley's. There was no expression on his white pinched face, for the mouth was set and the eyes had gone like stones; but the bosun knew that Tich Copley was telling him carefully, 'I've tried all ways, and can't do it, so now I'm going to leave the door open, and you can stuff yourself.'

Starley's voice was quiet, but it came resonant from a big chest that made a magnificent sound-box for the lower register. He said, "That's how I feel about the grain."

Copley's face stayed set but his eyes lost their look of stones, and sparked with intelligence. He said nothing.

"Now you just give the door a shove, boy."

Copley pushed it. It swung away from him and banged flat against the bulkhead, leaving enough room for a man to row a boat through.

"Now come on in."

Copley turned and walked past the front of the long bench, keeping his shoulders pulled back.

"Now swing it shut."

He swung it in one slow movement. It banged shut. The bosun said, "I keep the hinges oiled. That's why it's so easy."

Copley stood facing him again, balanced with his feet apart as the ship rolled; he bent his knees and waited; the roll stopped, and began again the other way. He straightened his knees. The bosun dropped the packet of Fifth Avenue towards him along the bench. "Have a fag, Copley."

"No, thank you, sir."

Starley grinned pleasantly. "Go on, son. You can do with it. Don't deny yourself just because I'm a bastard." He watched Copley take a cigarette from the packet and light it. "Now what d'you want to see me for?"

"I've forgotten which accident boat I'm in."

The bosun widened his stare. "You goin' to have an accident, then?"

"No, sir."

Starley's tone was reasonable. "Jesus, you can't come in here at the end of a two weeks' trip an' say you've forgotten which accident boat you're in! How many times have you done boat-drill in this ship?"

"I can't remember."

Starley tried to find a hint in the kid's expression that he'd gone mad. Copley said resolutely, "It's a lapse of memory, sir."

After a moment the bosun got up and leaned against the timber-racks. "What makes you think I won't murder you, for comin' in here with this bloody tale?"

Copley said nothing. He had smoked half the cigarette already, pulling at it hard. He had needed it; he needed it still. The bosun said, "What's on your mind, kid?"

"Nothing, sir. I've just forgotten, that's all."

"You've jus' forgotten." He studied the boy carefully. He had a jockey's body, made of ribs and wire and knuckles and marrow bone; a gristly boy with a tousled head and a face nearly all chin, a body nearly all elbows and knees. All the vitality and expression was centred in the eyes: they could light up or dance or burn with anger or struggle to understand; they could go shut, without shutting. The bosun had known Copley three months, maybe less; but he knew what kind of boy he was. The good Lord had chosen gut for this one, thick gut for the sinews and fine for the nerves, and had afterwards tuned the instrument beyond the point of its ever going slack again. It rather frightened Starley to be in the presence of so much tension.

"You're a liar," he said.

Tich Copley did not answer. He was not interested. All he wanted to know was his accident boat station.

The bosun said, "Why didn't you ask your mates? They'd know."

"I didn't want to look silly, sir."

"But you don't mind lookin' silly in front o' me? You know I oughter sling you out of here for wastin' my time, Copley?"

The eyes went shut, without shutting. "I'd best go and ask my mates, then."

Art Starley was having a day of it. First in the Skip's room, with him and Stubbs stalking each other like cats round a chimney-pot; now in here with this kid. This kid was worse than the Skip, in some ways. You could pick him up and toss him through the porthole if you wanted to—but, flying through the air, he'd win. You'd be left like a fool, knowing it wasn't the answer. Shifting grain was a picnic, compared with this.

"Look here, kid. You often lose your memory?"

"No, sir."

"When did it happen the las' time?'

"I can't remember. I don't think I ever have, before."

The bosun said, "Are you scared?" Fright could do it.

"I don't think so."

"Aren't you certain?"

"I'm always sick when I'm scared."

"Most of us are." He stared at Copley as if he could see through his skull and read the bright worried mind. "How long've you been at sea?"

"Three years, sir."

"Then you've been in storms?"

"Yes, sir."

"Did they scare you?"

"Yes, sir."

"Well, you're normal, thank God. But what's so important about this accident boat? Why come here an' ask me *now*?"

"The cargo's shifted. If we've got to take to boats, I'll have to know."

"You think we'll have to leave the *Whipper* just because she's got a bit of a list?"

"I want to know, that's all. So I can be ready, like the rest."

"You're sick-scared, aren't you?"

"No, sir."

They held their feet to the next roll. It was a big one. A glue-pot shifted on the bench and Starley had to grab it. They waited, feeling the shudder of the engines as the screw came out. Timber was straining, as slowly as the creak of a footstep on the stair. The wind fluttered in the ventilator. The screw went back and the shuddering stopped. The angle eased suddenly as the ship came back from her roll. Starley took his hand away from the glue-pot.

"You're in starb'd, aft. Don't forget again."

"Starb'd aft, sir."

The bosun dropped his dog-end and stood on it; the last smoke floated round his face; he squinted through it at Copley. "You did right, to come an' ask me."

Copley opened the door, drew it right back, got on to the other side of it, and said, "Ay, ay, sir."

The bosun grinned. "Sod off."

When Copley had gone, Starley looked through the porthole. The sea was racing by in a long white parade of waves that boiled at the crests as the wind curled them over. A big one went by and broke astern of the ship as she lay wallowing in the trough. That was a seventh. He was awed by the sight of its breaking, by the white tumult as the wind knocked it down and smothered it in its own foam, big as it was. He'd seen waves sixty feet high—

three times the size of that one. You get a seventh wave in a sea as big as that and you've got a killer. There were waves that nobody ever came back to tell of, yet you knew they were there, out there over this horizon or the next, by day or in the dark; giants, they were, standing up green and black and towering above you, coming for you, while you stood and watched them with their shadows coming over you and over your ship like the shadows of mountains over the land below, and you had to watch them come against the sky, leaning with the wind against their backs and scooped out dark underneath, until you tried to cry out and couldn't, and your bowels opened and you couldn't stop them; and underneath you was the deep, where you were going now, buried under the big killer when it dropped.

"Fester," he said softly, turning away from the porthole, "fester." What did that stupid short-arse want to come here and talk about accident boats for? He should've skinned him alive.

CHAPTER EIGHT

DARKNESS had come down three hours ago; the sea and sky were black, with no stars to glint upon water, and no moon. It was a simmering dark, full of sound, covering the sea but leaving it alive; the wind clove through the dark, driving the sea and tormenting it so that its waters rose as if against the wind, to be whipped and sent down again with the waves' backs broken and their strength spilled in a flurry of foam, while others rose up and met the wind and were whipped down by it and scattered, while others rose, and others, in their tens of millions across the sweep of the South Atlantic; they ran their rising, falling race across the deeps below, where the wind could not go but where the big currents moved against the ocean's floor across the reefs and the ledges of sand and wreck and weed, journeyed through by the winter fish whose dark ways ran fathoms below the storm, and were not touched by it. The ocean worked its tides in quietness, only its surface in a rage.

The Breton fishermen have a prayer, as old as the sea it speaks to, "You are so mighty, and my ship is so small. Have mercy."

A ship is a mote in the sea. Be it a great ship with a royal name and a master strong and as one with the will of God, with huge dimensions and of a shape considered perfect by designers who have lavished their genius on its making, it is a mote in the sea. The sea is so mighty, and a ship is so small.

In this sea that was harried by the gale, Harkness kept his ship against the elements. He was a man of some faith in God, as a man must be if he leaves the safety of the land; but he had no faith in the mercy of the sea. It could not know of the things that died in it, nor wish for their death; it could only bury them quiet in its deeps. It was an insensate element, and it was absurd to speak of the sea as a cunning enemy; nor was the wind a friend if it filled your sails or a foe if it stripped them from you. But in any struggle between a man and some insensate thing the issue becomes personal, so that he will shout at it and curse it and give it foul humiliating names while he is fighting it; and sometimes it seems that the thing—be it the sea or the wind or flood or forest fire—has awareness of him and of his cunning, and answers with cunning of its own.

There was no cunning in the sea, this night. It came for the *Whipper* in her face, and pounded her as she lifted and shook the water down her sides, her sharp bows turned to face the sea and cut into it when she could. Her list had not worsened, but there could be no work in the hold where the grain had shifted until the sea grew less. Twice the bosun had taken men there, and the clusters had been lit from the deck-plugs so that in the blaze of light they could inspect the scene, and try to find a way of trimming the cargo.

From the wheelhouse Costain had watched the foredeck, a pool of light in which stood the shadows of the mast and samson posts and the rigging's web. As the seas met the bows, white explosions bloomed enormously against the dark, and spindrift came in a blizzard from the fo'c'sle head, driving white across the deck and blotting out the scene below the high lamp-clusters so that in a moment all was lost—the deck, stanchions, posts, hatch-covers and moving men as the blizzard swept over them and reached the bridge and burst against the wheelhouse windows with a rattle as of flying stones. Costain, keeping the first watch of the night, did not pity the men down there; they were seamen and there was the sea and this was their work; he was simply glad he was not one of them.

He could hear Tony Bond at work in the wireless-room; signals were pippling the closed-in silence here, as the frail communications were kept up from ship to ship and from sea to shore. Captain Harkness was in there with Bond, after making a token appearance in the saloon for dinner. He had not been at ease; the passengers were worried and anxious to deceive him; he had been glad to leave them. He said to Bond:

"How's the *Valenca* faring, have you heard?"

"The tug's still searching, sir. She's not answered for the last hour, but she sounded cheerful enough when she gave a call just before eight. As I work it out, the *Abeille*'s nearly closed her, twice."

Harkness knew the *Valenca,* a German-built ship with Greek owners; she had a beautiful sheer and a long counter, and slipped through the seas like a fish. He could picture her now, with a deck-cargo of pit-props or perhaps soft timber, the uprights leaning out from the bulwarks under the pressure of the shifting cargo. She'd have a list on; maybe as much as the *Whipper,* maybe more, for a timber-ship was buoyant and could lean hard against the sea without alarm. But the hundreds of logs would be a worry by now, or she wouldn't have sent an S O S. Harkness knew her master, who was a Greek with a finger gone, and he was a man to keep his cargo on board until the ship was down. No carrier lightly jettisons his goods, any more than a tug deserts a tow. Socrates Nakonis would be watching his cargo at this minute, ready to give the order to knock off the slips and let the timber go; but his ship would have to lie over almost on her side before he was forced to do it.

Harkness did not know the *Abeille IV,* but like most of the deep-sea tugs she had a reputation talked about from Southampton to Sydney. She'd turn out in the face of a hurricane and bring back a cork in the dark if you threw it for her. Let her once find the *Valenca,* and she'd be safe. That was the only danger: that the two ships would not find each other in the tempestuous night. For all the radios and direction-finders and radar systems that filled wheelhouse and chart-room with their magical presence in every fair-sized vessel afloat, the search by one ship for another was no foregone conclusion in the vastness of the deep and the dark. A ship was a mote in the sea.

"Trawler, sir."

The captain looked down at Bond. The voice on the radio-telephone was faint, the words fluttering through static.

'Willow', 'Willow', 'Willow'. 'Flasher', 'Flasher', 'Flasher'. Can you get us? Come back on the 138. Over.

Bond said, "*Flasher*'s been silent for a long time now, sir. I've been trying to find out if——"

Hello 'Flasher' to 'Willow Girl', 'Flasher', 'Flasher'. Are you staying out? Over.

Bond stared at the dials, his eyes dreaming. One of his lost sheep was back. The *Flasher* was still sending.

'Willow', 'Willow', 'Willow'. No, we are making in now, making in now. It's not worth it, Georgie. Keep wiggin'. Gone.

Harkness said, "Who'd be in a trawler on a night like this?"

"It's the stink of the fish I couldn't stand, sir."

They listened again as a signal came through in code from a cruiser to Commander-in-Chief, Plymouth. Behind him Harkness heard the third mate giving an order to the helm. He left the warmth of the wireless-room. Costain had been joined by Turnbull, who was standing by one of the windows. Harkness glanced at the inclinometer and saw that the mean reading had increased a little. There was less rolling now that the ship was head-to-sea but she was putting her bows down heavily as the gale sent water rising for her.

He had been down to the engine-room and talked to the chief. The engine was turning at revs for nine knots but she wasn't making more than four through the water, keeping her steerage-way and burning coal and getting nowhere. The met. reports gave no hope of the gale fining down tonight nor even tomorrow before noon. They couldn't turn about and run for home; even if they could bring the ship round safely the list would remain and she'd be pooped by the following sea until her stern was smashed. Nor could they stay here much longer burning up coal until there was none left to turn the engines. Without engines in this sea they would be lost, with the steering gone and the ship broaching to and taking the seas on her side until they turned her over.

These thoughts were not only the captain's. Turnbull, at the wheelhouse window, was burdened with them. Costain's nerves were on edge as he stood by the binnacle, checking and re-checking the quartermaster's course as the seas thundered against the starboard flare and then the port and then the starboard again, while Wilson brought the wheel a spoke down, a spoke up, watching his lubber-line and waiting for the third mate to say it again.

"Meet her."

"Ay, ay, sir, meet her!"

"Steady . . ."

"Steady, sir."

As Captain Harkness came and stood beside him, Turnbull said:

"We've had it green, sir, over the fo'c'sle."

Harkness gazed through the window without answering. Spray came against the glass in a peppering of small white bursts; then the glass ran and cleared, giving them a hazy view of the next wave that was running towards them. They watched it gain height, a soft flurry in the gloom beyond the foremast steaming-light; then it hit, and was clove by the bows; it fountained on both sides, and the wind took it and the foredeck was a-smother. The explosions came again on the windows and they went blank. Under their feet they still felt the shock of the impact of wave and ship.

"I'm thinking about number one hatch, sir."

Harkness gave another nod. He was thinking about number one hatch, numbers two, three and four hatches, the bow-plates, the stern, the derricks, bridge, winches, ventilators and samson posts; he was thinking about four thousand tons of grain and ten passengers and forty crew.

The next wave was shipped green and they saw the black wall of it come up out of the dark and stand there and stagger in the gale until the ship drove into it with her head down and the screw coming out. They saw the fo'c'sle head vanish and then the hatch-covers and foremast and derricks and then the two big samson posts, and then they saw nothing, for the toughened glass of the windows was hammered as the water hit it and flattened so that the ship seemed suddenly to be deep in a drift of snow. She was still shuddering from the wave's brunt; the wheelhouse was loud with the din of the windows as they were smothered in the spray. Costain was shouting something to the helmsman and the helmsman made an answer. The faces of the captain and mate were a sick white in the glow reflected from the windows. They drained slowly.

Turnbull said nothing more to the captain; the captain was not in a talking mood; but Turnbull had a master's certificate, and he was thinking that if he were master of this ship he would have sent a signal by now, not informing the owners that their precious cargo was shifting but telling anyone who was within listening-range that the *Atlantic Whipper* was in need of help. The message was simple enough: *Save our souls.*

It irked the mate to be standing here, unable even to speak and get an answer, when he would have wished to go into the wireless-room and have a signal sent and at least know that he had taken what care he could, and in good time. He felt far out on a limb, his last touch lost with security. A signal would reassure him. It would do no harm. It could, if the gale worsened, save all their lives. These winter gales in the Western Approaches were as bad as any round the Horn; more ships had foundered in these waters than in the Pacific.

Harkness was leaving it late. It wasn't an easy thought, standing here and watching the big seas come, dropping their tons of weight across the hatches down there. There was grain in the holds below, and if water reached it each single pip would swell to twice its size and the ship would need the cubic space to take eight thousand tons of it instead of four. She would be split like a nut.

"Meet her."

"Meet her, sir!"

The wave struck. The bows vanished into dark water. Turnbull stood waiting for the shock to reach the bridge. The wind brought the water still black at the base with half the big wave still standing astride the foredeck as its top broke up into spray. The shock came, shuddering through the deck under their feet. The wave was only now dying, torn slowly apart by the wind; if it had done damage, the sound would have been lost in the tumult; it would not have been possible to know.

The windows went white as the water reached them and rattled with a crackling fusillade that numbed the ears.

"Steady." Costain's voice piped thinly above the din.

"Steady, sir!"

The ship staggered, falling into the trough and wallowing there. Through the clearing windows Turnbull and Harkness saw the foremast appear, and then the fo'c'sle head. White water was still draining across the scuppers. Below, a man shouted. They could not hear what he said.

Harkness had not moved. The feel of the ship under him was all the movement he wanted to ease his mind; there was strength in her, and he could feel it as she trembled; she was alive, responding to the helm and to the sea. But he must send a signal soon, because that was only one big wave that had struck her just now. There were more coming, in hundreds, a dark pack of them driven by the gale; and the *Whipper* must meet them all, one by one as they came for her. But she could not meet them for ever; she could wait here with her head to them so long as she had coal left. At this speed she could keep steerage for another thirty hours. The gale could last a week.

Costain, being the officer of the watch, answered the telephone when it rang. Turnbull had moved his head to look at him. Harkness was still gazing through the window. Costain spoke into the phone, nodding. His face had gone white but when he turned to the captain there was nothing wrong with his voice.

"Bosun from fo'c'sle, sir! Number one hatch-cover's been stove-in by seas."

Turnbull dragged up the hood of his reefer and put his shoulder against the door to the bridge-end, pressing it open against the gale. As it slammed behind him a shower of spray came into the wheelhouse and spattered across the planks, flying against the captain's shoes as he went into the wireless-room and said to Bond:

"Signal."

"Sir?"

"S O S. 'Atlantic Whipper' lying hove-to approximately forty-nine-fifty north, twelve-forty west. Cargo shifted, slight list, number one hatch-cover stove-in by heavy seas and taking water." When Bond had transmitted, Harkness said, "Send a Mayday call to all ships and let me know immediately we have an answer."

He went back into the wheelhouse. White spray was blanking the windows, and when the rattle of it died away there was left the sharp ripple of Morse from the wireless-room.

"Thank you, Mr. Costain. I'll take over."

CHAPTER NINE

ACROSS Cornwall the gale hammered at windows and sent slates whirling away from roofs that were exposed to the direct onslaught of it. The gale drove across dark wastes of heather and rock and field, striking the walls of barns and farmsteads, wrecking a hut and taking the splinters with it until a gust died and they fell scattering along a road where a man walked with his torch shielded with his hand as rain came, stinging his face. Lights were uneasy, shining from late windows, and doors banged, shaking the houses as the wind rushed in and then was shut outside by the nervy, rattling latch. It was as dark overland as on the sea; but lights were more frequent. Sleep would be late coming, tonight.

Where the sea met the land along the Cornish coast there was a long smother of white as the waves staggered home with their backs bent; they pitched headlong against the rocks and were flung up in fountains that drove across the shore and became mist, joining the soft salt haze that drenched the wind over the land beyond. Before darkness, rain squalls had driven people into their houses; now the night was soaked and cobbles gleamed in the light of fitful lamps. Paper went whirling from dustbins the wind had overturned, and fluttered past windows where a candle burned and a child tried to sleep; in the narrow streets of Hayle and Helston and St. Mawes people had to shout to be heard, though they walked together side by side with their bodies bent against the gale.

Along the coastline many of the land people thought of the sea, for only a few of them had nothing to do with the sea and the fish and the ships. There was worry for the small boats that lay on the beaches, and for the trawlers in the bays towards Brixham. Down here in the foot of England the sea had claimed the land in subtle ways, exacting from whole families their lifelong dedication, giving them fish for a living and taking their sons away. On this night the sea was a hard bargainer, out for its price. But the people were safe, here on land. The wind might blow an old one over, and break windowpanes and send a bicycle sprawling from its perch on to the pavement; but the houses were safe; they would stand through this wild night as they had stood through others and worse; they could not overturn and drown in the deeps, taking their people with them; they were not ships.

But the people thought of the ships. Even those few who had no son nor brother nor friend who lived his life on the sea were thinking tonight of the trawlers up in the bay, and the traffic through the Downs and across the Irish Channel, and the *Valenca* in Biscay that Captain Tremayne had told them about when he had come home from the wireless station to look to his young wife, who had a five-day child in her arms that had not yet screamed shrill enough with its puny lungs to take the love-light from her eyes. "You howl," she had been saying to the child, "and let the wind howl, an' we'll all fall down an' call it a miracle."

Captain Tremayne was back at the radio station by nine o'clock this evening, with food in him and warm clothes on, for he expected to be here all night. He was in the station when at 9.23 p.m. another signal came in from the sea, from a ship two hundred miles away in the southern reaches of the storm.

The W/T operator shifted his log book an inch towards him and wrote steadily as he listened to the Morse.

SOS . . . SOS . . . SOS . . . DE GBAC/Atlantic Whipper . . .

He reached for a message-form and copied the signal, then

passed it to the R/T operator beside him, who began speaking quickly but with careful emphasis into the mouthpiece of the radio-telephone:

"Mayday . . . Mayday . . . Mayday! From steamship 'Atlantic Whipper'—'Atlantic Whipper' . . ."

When he had finished speaking he got up and went into the next room and put the message into the teleprinter, and set off the automatic alarm system with twelve four-second dashes and the A.S. The alarm-bells began ringing at 9.26 p.m. on board the liner *Iberian Princess,* at anchor in the Solent, the motor-ship *Tribernum,* moving up-Channel beyond Portsmouth, the destroyer *Brindle,* steaming due north in the Irish Sea past Mizen Head in search of a crippled trawler, and the steamer *Angeles,* ploughing doggedly through big seas a hundred and thirty miles north-west of the stricken *Valenca.*

The Commander-in-Chief Plymouth had the message at 9.27 p.m. or a few seconds after, by land-line. The problem for him was whether to despatch a ship from Plymouth or to order H.M.S. *Brindle* to give up her search for the trawler and steam south to the position given by the *Atlantic Whipper.* The trawler had last signalled her propeller gone; she was in a critical condition. If the destroyer were called off the search for her, would she have sufficient help from other ships in her vicinity? She was in worse shape than the merchantman, which was still under command: but the trawler was nearer shelter than the steamer, and closer in touch with the emergency services.

The Naval Officer-in-Charge set himself to solve this problem with the least possible delay. Meanwhile a request went out to shipping that radio silence be maintained during the first fifteen minutes of every hour except for distress calls.

Lloyd's of London picked up the Mayday alarm call as it was put out by Land's End Radio. The Watson and Blount Sea-Trading and Navigation Company's London offices had a message by land-line informing them of the position and condition of their steamship the *Atlantic Whipper.*

At 9.35 p.m. Watson and Blount were in touch by telephone with the Southern Salvage and Long-distance Towing Company, which had three tugs; but only two were equipped with deep-sea towing-gear and both were engaged already with casualties: the *Salvado* was closing the trawler in the Irish Sea and hoped to reach her within an hour, while the *Sea Horse* was in the narrow reaches of the Channel towards Dieppe, answering a call from a

Swedish cargo ship that was in danger ten miles from the coast, her engines dead of a burst steam-pipe. The nearest available tug would be the *Abeille IV,* if she could soon take the *Valenca* to harbour and sail again for the *Atlantic Whipper.* The French company thought it unlikely that the *Abeille* could deal with her present casualty quickly enough to be of any help to the *Atlantic Whipper* before noon in two days' time at the earliest. Much would depend on the state of the weather in the meantime, and on how well the *Valenca* would handle in tow.

Watson and Blount sent a message via P.O. to their ship, saying that all available resources would be tapped. It did not add that there were no known resources available at the present time.

At approximately 9.30 p.m. the duty officer in the control-room at R.A.F. Redmoor, Cornwall, took a message from G.L.D. and within a few seconds the Tannoys were sounding in the airfield buildings—*Dinghy . . . Dinghy . . . Dinghy! Air-crew to briefing!*

Thirteen minutes after the master-pilot had taken his orders from Control, the stand-by machine was airborne and making south-west into the dark street of the gale carrying rescue-gear, flares, inflatable dinghies, life-rafts and hermetically-sealed food and comforts. The navigator passed the course to his pilot, according to the last-reported position of the S.S. *Atlantic Whipper.* It was unlikely that one aircraft, flying in bad weather and by night, could be of much use to a six-thousand-ton cargo ship still under command; but it was another link between sea and shore, between the danger-zone and a haven. If the chances had been a thousand to one against the possibility that the aircraft could help the ship, it would still have flown course 221 towards ship in distress 49.50 north, 12.40 west. The link must be made, however slender.

In the coastguard lookout huts between Land's End and Plymouth the duty wireless-operators were sending Z-series calls to establish the latest distress signal. There was nothing for them to do but keep watch at their radios and pass on information to land stations that others might have missed. Reception was poor. The network was by its own nature fragile, with its trembling web of aerial wires festooned in the dark above radio masts sent whipping by the gale; but many channels were duplicated, and there were many stations: civil, maritime, Naval and R.A.F. A breakdown of any size was hardly possible, though the gale shook even the buildings where the operators listened and replied. The call from the

Atlantic Whipper had been established throughout the immediate network before 9.45 p.m., and acknowledgments were coming in from ships.

Tribernum judged herself to be too far up the Channel to help; but if no other ship were within shorter steaming-distance of the *Whipper* she would at once turn about and make for that position. *Sea Horse* was closing the Swedish timber-ship and must deal with this casualty first. *Salvado* had not yet located the crippled trawler in the Irish Sea but felt certain she was close and could help her. The tug was in contact with the destroyer *Brindle,* who was also trying to reach the trawler *Minniscoe.* There had been no orders from C.-in-C., Plymouth, for the destroyer to break her search and turn south for the *Whipper.* There was no immediate acknowledgment from the *Abeille IV,* who had now reached the *Valenca* in Biscay. Anchored in the Solent with a full complement of passengers, the *Iberian Princess* could offer no assistance.

But there was one call, a faint one whose message picked its way through the static and the tangle of other signals, that gave hope. *'Angeles'—'Angeles'—'Angeles' to 'Atlantic Whipper'. Am steaming for you. Position about* 47.50 *N.,* 8.40 *W. Will help you quick. A vous.*

It was the first comic note struck in the discord of signals this night: a message that started formally, lapsed into bad grammar and finished in French. It was from a Spanish ship. Such a man as Manuelo Lopez de las Castillas would send such a signal at such a time. His ship was an old one, as ugly to look at as a worn-out shoe, and he was already putting her into seas that had sent the crew praying hours ago for the salvation of all their souls and the eternal damnation of Manuelo Lopez de las Castillas for having brought them to these regions of Cain in a ship that bucked like a mule and shook like a jellyfish and stank like the summertime armpits of a Barcelona dustman. Yet their captain had received the message from the merchantman, and had sent the only reply that was possible. He was coming. He would help quick.

Those who listened, in the wireless cabins of ships and in safe warm rooms of the land radio stations, at once began to measure the chances. Much of their calculation was necessarily guesswork: they judged optimistically that the ancient *Angeles* could make perhaps nine or ten knots through a storm such as this, and with luck cover the two hundred miles to the *Atlantic Whipper* in less than twenty hours. They could not hope to judge the direction or distance of drift that would be made by the distressed ship during those twenty hours, nor how long her radio would hold out as a guide to the *Angeles*. They dared not judge whether it was possible at all for the Spaniard to take his ship across an almost beam sea at force-ten strength. By logic the journey could not be made and could not even be dreamed of except by a fool. Only a few of the men who listened had personal knowledge of Manuelo, and knew the two things about him that at this moment counted most. He had no logic in him, but he was no fool. But this did not mean they believed he could get his ship to the *Whipper*. Their calculations supported the findings of all the other men who had no personal knowledge of Manuelo. They had set out to measure the chances, but now knew there were none.

If Manuelo had known these findings he would have gone on scratching his belly beneath the white silk shirt he wore. People, he would have said, were entitled to their opinions, but they must not ask him to be interested in them. He had many opinions of his own (he would have said), and they ranged from the convictions he had about flea-circuses and soya sauce and the laxative properties of liquorice root to his bright high faith in the teachings of his Church; but he did not ask people to be interested in them. Likewise the opinions of others did not affect him. He could scratch his own belly and sail his own ship, and neither task could be accomplished better by any other man. It was a simple order of things so obvious as to be beyond argument, so that when one of his crew suggested that he was taking these many good men to their death without so much as consulting them he replied in rich Castilian that if he were a horse-knacker he would hardly consult the horses before cutting off their testicles.

Turning his ship westwards, he felt the seas coming to meet her a-beam and had to brace himself to keep his feet. There was shouting from below decks. He could hear things pitching and smashing and hoped that his servant had put away the big photograph of his family and also the hand-tinted photograph of the Christ in the Iglesia Parroquial de Santa Maya, before their glass was broken by their falling. Everything else could smash, and the sooner the better, for the *Angeles* would pitch and roll like this for the next twenty hours, and a thing could only smash once and leave peace afterwards.

Amid the noise of the shouting and smashing he thought of the people who were on board the vessel who had called for help. They would be frightened, perhaps, as many times he himself had been frightened by the sea. They must be comforted. He staggered across the wheelhouse to the wireless-room and let his big hand fall like a blessing upon the shoulder of the operator.

"Para *'Atlantic Whipper': No tiene miedo. Vamos rapidamente con Dios.*"

A cry came from somewhere below as the *Angeles* fell against a wave and shuddered as if sick, and as he lurched back to the wheelhouse he swore in his mind at a man who could cry out because he was merely uncomfortable. A man must make a noise like that, a donkey-bray, at respectable times when his mother died or his house burned down or his wife dropped a pitcher of wine; such a dismal trumpeting must be reserved for important times, and not spent on matters of discomfort. His ship and all in her must go like this through the night, and into the day, and through the day and into the dark again before they would come to the one they were to save. It was too early yet for twittering aloud like so many palsied pups of flea-bitten baboons.

At a minute to ten o'clock the *Atlantic Whipper* received the signal from the *Angeles*: *Have no fear. We are coming speedily, with God.*

Towards midnight a message flickered through the network of land-based aerials, from the destroyer *Brindle*. The trawler *Minniscoe* had been overwhelmed off the Irish coast. One survivor and two bodies had been picked up. The tug *Salvado* was still searching the area. Orders were requested from Plymouth.

Arrangements were made along the land-lines. Brief questions were asked and answered by the Admiralty, Watson and Blount, and the Southern Salvage Company, while in the windy dark the search went on for another bobbing head, an upturned face among the heaving trough and crest of the Irish Sea. It was perfectly simple, on paper. The destroyer was to attend rescue until relieved by the lifeboat now putting out from Wicklow, and then turn south for position 49.50 north, 12.40 west if she judged her remaining fuel to be sufficient. The tug was to leave the scene immediately and steam for the *Atlantic Whipper*.

On board the *Whipper,* Anthony Bond intercepted these several messages and passed them to the captain. They were reassuring; but they could not, even with the confidence expressed in their formality, more strongly sustain the heart of Captain Harkness than the signal he had been given earlier. *We are coming speedily, with God.* Now a crumpled ball of paper, it was still in his hand, buried in his pocket as he watched the white spray breaking on the windows of the wheelhouse. He knew what kind of a ship was the little *Angeles,* and he knew her position and course. Even with God, she would not reach the *Whipper*. Therein lay the strength of the message in his pocket, and its reassurance. On his behalf, a man was attempting the impossible.

CHAPTER TEN

THE three people in the lounge of the *Atlantic Whipper* had been silent for so long that it seemed deserted, and five minutes ago a steward had turned the lights out, not even troubling to look round the place. There were now only the smouldering points of light from the pilot bulbs to keep darkness away. In this faint glow their faces seemed to float in shadow and their hands to flutter up as softly as doves when they moved them to hide a yawn or light a cigarette. The glow did not define the unreflecting fabric of their clothes but only the pale skin of hands and faces, and the gold of Dr. Papasian's wrist-watch, and Major Draycott's horn-rimmed glasses, which he had not taken off although it was too dim in here now even to pretend to read his battered-looking book. Ann Brown was turning a small turquoise ring on her finger, slipping it round and round as she sat with her head back against the padded banquette, thinking of Peter. For a little while the Major had been watching the soft glint of the lamps on the ring as she turned it. He was becoming hypnotized.

She thought, 'Dearest Peter,' and felt the touch of him again and recounted the host of quiet intimacies, certain that she remembered each smallest one of them, and certain she always would.

The dim light gleamed again, again on the turning ring as her fingers moved, and the old man in the chair nearby dozed off, his waking worries turning to worried dreams.

Dr. Papasian took the handkerchief from the breastpocket of his coat and as quietly as he could blew his nose. He was cold, but there was nowhere else to go. His mind was very alert; there could be no question of sleep; if he had wanted to sleep he would not have used the drug. He put the handkerchief back, and sat for a long time without moving. The floor trembled under his feet but the small pilot lamps burned steadily, reminding him of the lamps that glowed in the early hours along hospital corridors. He would be there again, in St. Peter's, going along the corridors and into the wards and theatres, busy with work. There was nothing to worry about; he would soon be there again.

The floor trembled. The lamps glowed steadily. Draycott slept. Ann Brown's fingers moved, turning the thoughts round with the ring, turning them back, and round again, to gleam in the quiet of her mind.

Anthony Bond had sent a message to his wife, as soon as he had realized that the chance of sending private messages was thinning fast. He had simply said, *Will be delayed. Love. Tony.*

Love, Thelma, said the photograph. *Love, Tony,* said the telegram. The most abused dog-eared word in the language, used on Christmas cards by people who had nothing in common, certainly not love for each other; used on the telephone when the left ear ached to escape the pressure of the hard black bakelite and the monotony of the distant intimate voice—'Well, I've really got to dash now—remember me to Beatrice, and give her my love'; used as a quick paying-off when the pen neared the bottom of the notepaper with sudden relief. 'Affectionately' would be too personal a word, an obvious lie; but 'love' would be all right; it could be used for anything—disinterest, duty, habit, even hate.

But now he had forgotten about sending the message. There had been others since, much more important ones from Watson and Blount, and G.L.D. Land's End, and the *Angeles.* A few minutes ago there had been another:

'Salvado'—'Salvado'—'Salvado' to 'Atlantic Whipper'. Am making for you now. Please give position accurate as possible.

He had given the tug their position from the precise figures that Beggs had written down for him. He had asked Beggs:

"What's it like up for'ard?"

"Dodgy."

Beggs went back into the chart-room. In the wheelhouse Captain Harkness was by the binnacle again. The mean list on the inclinometer was still less than twenty degrees. The list was not so important now as the trouble in number one hold; but if Turnbull and the bosun and the men down there failed to check the water, the list would grow, and the small thin needle on the indicator would move hour by hour into the danger section. It was no good breaking the glass and putting a finger in and pushing the little needle round to zero. The ship would have to be moved round the needle. A cycle had started when the hatch-cover had been stove-in. Riding head to sea, the ship was taking water over her bows and it was flooding into the hold; in the hold it was surging forward every time the bows went down to a trough, so that, every time, the bows went deeper and shipped more water than before. Soon it would flood across to number two hatch where the barley had shifted, and if number two hatch were stove-in the list would increase and there would be no stopping it.

That was the black side. Harkness had assessed it and dismissed it. On the other side there was only a pattern of chance, but it was based on realities. The gale could drop: if only it dropped to force seven or eight they could weather it until help came. The *Salvado* could reach them in a day and a half, and she was built for these seas; they were her natural element. The *Angeles* would never get here unless the storm died, and if it died there would be no need of her; but she was the nearest ship and even her presence gave comfort.

Harkness had answered her second signal by saying, *We are all right. You should resume your course. We shall not expect you but send our thanks for your offer.*

He had never met the master of the *Angeles* but he had met his kind. Manuelo Lopez de las Castillas would be very indignant at the reply from the *Whipper*. Spanish conceit would be sorely pricked. So the captain of the British ship considered the *Angeles* too old and feeble for the task of saving him? He would be shown that it is better to be saved by even a drifting hulk with a crew of leprous rubbish-pickers mustered from the stinking garbage-heaps of hell than to wait for a smart new tug that would arrive to find him sunk.

You should resume your course. No message could drive Manuelo more urgently to heap his coal on. But had Harkness said, *Thank you, we shall expect you,* the *Angeles* would have steamed precisely in this same direction at full speed. There were no words a radio-transmitter could ever send that would alter Manuelo from his course or purpose; but for the record and his conscience, Harkness had tried.

Spray hit the windows and they went white in the glare of the lamps. Afterwards there was silence, a deep uncanny silence that would have led a landsman to believe the gale had dropped suddenly and completely to leave a perfect calm. The ship was canted forward and for this halcyon moment seemed transfixed in the sea and the silence. Harkness went to the port wheelhouse door and opened it. A moment ago it could not have been opened without a man's shoulder against it. Now it swung easily and he went out to the bridge-end. A soft breeze whispered past his face, rich with salt. Above him there was a mist flying past the lamps, racing along below the greater dark; spangles of it were caught by the angular tableau of the direction-finder and aerials on the monkey island above him; their pattern was frosted by the mist that clung where the light fell. He looked down, across the foredeck to where the lamps shone and the men worked. He pitied them. They were working against hopelessness more than against the sea itself.

Reluctantly he raised his head, and looked at the sea. The ship was listed to port, so that standing level here he was looking down at the water. It was black and a man would think he could walk on it. This was the bottom of the trough between the last wave and the next and the silence would go on until that next came. It would be high. He could make out its height already. It formed a ridge as solid-looking as a mountain-ridge against the white salt sky. It was higher than the ship. He watched it coming. There was still only the soft fanning of air against his face, and there was still the silence. Standing here like this in the midst of a violent gale you could believe in anything, in God or ghosts or poltergeists; you could see a flight of angels go overhead or a flock of bats sent by the devil to take your soul to hell; you could believe that these were your last few seconds of life, eked out by your quiet watching of the wave that was coming for you and your ship and all in her.

Matthew Harkness had seen waves like this, coming for him through the years of his life; he was not afraid of them; but he was awed by them, and by the bigness of the sea. He never forgot how big it was, or what it could do if you turned your eye away or mishandled your ship. Those who forgot died early. Those who were afraid had reason to be, for a man in fear has lost nine-tenths of the fight; they were afraid of the sea, but their worst enemy was within. The deadliest fear of all was the fear a man had of himself, of his own weakness and of his inability to meet danger and shout it down and deal with it. Turnbull, he thought, was not afraid of the sea, but he had no faith in himself. He would be afraid of not acquitting himself in the sight of others. Only a vain man could have this worst of all the fears, a man easily slighted. Turnbull was down there now, with the bosun and the men, working with them and urging them on, and urging himself on, committed to the absolute necessity of proving himself and outlasting them in strength and breath and courage, so that they should never find out. That was the paradox. Only a coward could be braver than the others, having to deal with his fear as well as with the danger;

he would lead them to the exposed hill-top where the enemy guns were trained and waiting, or take them into the jungle where the night was stealthy, or urge them to the task of saving their ship from the deep when the hurricane raged. The coward was the bravest of them all, when his vanity drove him to prove it.

The wave neared, rising taller and beginning to stoop as the wind pressed against its back and tore away thin water from its top. The white spray was flung out and began falling, pattering on to the superstructure as Harkness turned for the door and opened it. He knew how to time a wetting. He was in the wheelhouse with the door slammed tight when the wave broke against the bows of the ship and its white wreckage came spilling and boiling over the fo'c'sle head. The night exploded and it seemed there could never have been such a thing as the silence that had gone before. The windows shuddered as the water hit them and in the wheelhouse the sick radiance shone, the white spray reflecting the lamplight and draining colour away as snow will do beneath the window of a room.

Harkness thought of the men for'ard; they would have run for the fo'c'sle shelters before the wave broke. They would be waiting now to dodge back to their work while the ship laboured into the trough and gave them another chance. Turnbull would be there, shouting obscenities against the sea and helping the men. There would be no time for prayers; a quick black oath worked wonders when the heart was sick.

Bond came out of the wireless-room. Pitching his voice above the dying tumult he said, "Main aerial's gone, sir!"

Harkness looked at Bond. His face was crumpled and he looked lost. His big toy had broken.

"Can you rig a jury?"

It was as if Bond had never thought of it. In the despair of this terrible thing he had not been able to project his mind even to the next obvious step. His face brightened and his voice was eager.

"Oh. Yes, sir!" He ran to the door. Harkness looked at the brass clock on the bulkhead. It was nearing two a.m. From two until two-fifteen, shipping would maintain radio silence and await calls from the *Atlantic Whipper*; now there would be none.

The door opened again and Harkness thought it was Bond coming back, but when he turned he saw the mate. Water fell from his oilskins on to the dark patch of boards by the door. He wrenched off his sou'wester and stood with it in his hand. The gash on his hand had opened again and it bled brightly. He stood getting his breath. He had run aft from the fo'c'sle while the ship was in the trough. Harkness waited.

"Two pumps are going, sir." He took another breath. "We've got timber across number one but we can't rig a tarpaulin because there's——" then the next wave came and he stood shouting silently to the captain while the snow-light bloomed in the wheelhouse and the windows trembled. When he could be heard, Harkness stood close to Turnbull and said:

"What's number two hatch like?"

"All right so far. We're going to reinforce it after we've finished the other." He breathed deeply again, standing erect in the belled-out oilskins. Water was still running from his sea-boots and a rivulet had formed and was tracing its way towards the echo-sounder stand on the port side.

"There's help coming," Harkness said. "The *Salvado*'s on her way. Tell the men."

Turnbull tightened his face in case it should show relief. He said, "We can get home without a tug." He was prepared to play this the way the captain wanted it. If he had been here as master he would have sent a distress signal earlier than Harkness had; the *Salvado* would now have been closer. But Harkness had waited, maybe out of pride. Turnbull could be proud, too, prouder than Harkness, than anyone. He had to be. Most vital of all, he had to show it. He had been in a rage with Harkness when he had left the wheelhouse in answer to the call from the fo'c'sle that had reported the stove-in hatch. He had cursed him aloud in the welter of the wind as he had dodged from shelter to shelter across the foredeck, because Harkness had committed him to courage, out of pride. His rage had hardened him, and he was ready for the challenge, as always he had been ready throughout his life, forced to meet the little and the big challenges that had been thrown to him by kids at his kindergarten and by the puffed-up gang of hoodlums in his street, by his father, and his family, and the war. He had met them all, from the threat of a thick ear in the playground when the girls had been watching and cat-calling their derision, to the threat of a German U-boat's torpedo that had riven his ship and spread its wreckage on the water where he swam among bodies and red unrecognizable shapes. Now he had grown weary of challenge, and must steel himself harder against it and whip up his nerves to meet it, calling upon reserves that must one day run out and leave him naked, no braver than the others. Somehow he must arm himself even against that day, and be ready when it came. Unless, by luck, death gave him no time, and there was no one there to see.

Harkness said to him, "Yes, we might get home without a tug, but only a fool would try. The important thing is to tell the men there's help coming. Have you got any of the electricians down there?"

"I've mustered all hands, sir."

"Send the electricians up here. The main aerial's gone and Bond's rigging a jury."

The wheelhouse suddenly swayed. They shot their hands out for support and Turnbull's sea-boot slipped on the wet planks. Harkness caught his arm and checked the fall as he skinned his head across the door. The quartermaster had called something but no one heard him as the spray came at the windows and burst there. He dragged at the wheel, but the ship had taken the slack and was wallowing with a crest under her until she slid to the trough, half buried in water at her stem.

"Meet her!"

Harkness shouted it. The mate was against the bulkhead, his hands pressed against the graze on his scalp. Harkness left him and staggered to the wheel, bringing his weight to bear with the helmsman's on the spokes. The card swung in the compass. Something fell to the planks from the first-aid shelf. Turnbull was upright, hands down from his head; he shook his head slowly like a dazed boxer.

The wheel came round. Vibration ran through the ship in a wave and then stilled. Beggs appeared from the chart-room, saw Turnbull, and went over to him, but Turnbull put a hand up in a queer gesture of defence as if Beggs were attacking him. He went on moving his head while the second mate held him. A bandage-canister rolled down the planks and stopped against Beggs's foot. Turnbull said in the noise, "Leave me alone."

Beggs picked up the canister and took it to the first-aid shelf. When he came back, Harkness was with Turnbull, examining his head. Turnbull was saying, ". . . to get back down there, they'll——"

Harkness said to Beggs, "Jim, go for'ard and look to the men."

"Ay, ay, sir."

Turnbull tried to reach the door first, throwing one hand out like a toppling drunk. Harkness held him back as Beggs pushed the door open against the gale and went out to the bridge-end.

"It's my place down there, it's my place," Turnbull said with a thick tongue, petulantly. The captain shouted for the lookout. Smithers came in, a pink face propped up by stiff black oilskins. Harkness told him:

"Help Mr. Turnbull below."

When they had gone he rang down to the chief steward and said that the mate was going below with a head wound. Persham was good with medicine.

"Are we okay, sir?"

"Just a big wave. Look to the passengers and make sure no one was knocked over." He was thinking chiefly of Major Draycott. He had to repeat it as the ship ran into the next swell but Persham understood and said he would see to everything.

Harkness went back to the binnacle.

"Starb'd ten."

"Starb'd ten, sir."

He watched the compass card with its glow on his face. The illuminated figures meant little; he was judging the course they needed by feel and instinct as the deck trembled under his feet.

"Midships."

"Midships, sir."

When he was satisfied he moved to the windows and waited. It was half an hour before Beggs came up to the bridge.

"Well?"

Beggs was a shapeless hump in his drenched reefer. "Number one's stove in again, sir. Two men hurt, not bad." Water trickled down his strong blunt face as he waited for Harkness to speak. The windows thundered and whitened. After they had cleared Harkness said:

"I take it there's no point in working any more on the hatch."

"It'd be dangerous, sir."

"Are the pumps still working?"

"Yes, two of them."

"Tell the bosun to get the hands below. Take some of them to help Sparks rig the new aerial. Where's Peter?"

"In his bunk, sir."

"Let him sleep. While you're below, ask Dr. Papasian if he'd mind looking in at the sick bay. Persham's there with Steve. See how Harris is. Tell any passengers who ask about that noise that the gale's as bad as it can be, and it can only get better after this. You're not a good liar but make it sound convincing."

Beggs nodded. "Anything you want sent up, sir?"

Harkness looked at the water collecting messily against the port side bulkhead. "A man with a mop."

Beggs left him. Harkness returned to the binnacle. He did not like seeing water in the wheelhouse; it was untidy, even dangerous —as Steve Turnbull had found out. And dear Margaret would be dreadfully self-satisfied if she could see these messy planks. She had set out, eleven years ago, to show him that a gentleman's life was on the land in a clean safe house, and that she could keep a finer home than a ship could ever make. She had not spared herself in her pathetic competition with the sea for the comfort of his company through these eleven years, blindly unconvinced that he would never leave the sea until he was too old or died with it; but he felt he must at least compete in his turn with her, even when she could not know. He had asked for a man with a mop.

He checked the helmsman, mentally reviewing his position. There could be no more work on number one hatch; in a sea like this a man could go overboard without a cry, or spill his brains against an obstacle. The two pumps must clear what water they could from the hold. The list would now increase. The grain in number two hold could not be shifted back. If the gale held at this force, number two hatch would be stove-in unless the ship could keep her head up with slack water below. The engines were using coal, burning it away at half speed to do no more than keep steerage. She was moving no nearer the land.

The *Whipper* lay perilously beset. His duty, at this moment of his admission, was changed. The cargo had no value now; if he could, he would jettison it to lighten ship, enough to bring her head up. His task was not to deliver his cargo and passengers to harbour, but to forget the cargo and ensure the safety of the ship and those on board. If the *Salvado* or some other ship arrived in time he must consider the step of ordering his passengers to the boats, and the three injured men and possibly Steve Turnbull as well, if Dr. Papasian advised it. The tug would take them on board and they would be safe. If by that time the sea was too bad for the boats to be launched, or the list too severe, the passengers must jump into the water with their life-jackets on and be picked up by the tug.

He hoped it would not come to that. They had their trust in him; to have to order them overboard into a violent sea would humiliate him; it was the least gallant way of saving life. But they would suffer no more than the soaking and the shock; in a few hours they would emerge from their blankets on board the *Salvado*, warm from the brandy and relieved of this nagging fear that must be in some of them now. But he would not let it come to that, if he could help it.

He crossed the slope of the deck and called the engine-room on the telephone. He was answered by János, the third engineer. Harkness asked him:

"Are you all right down there?" He could visualize the Hungarian nodding his big handsome head.

"We are all fine, sir, yes."

"Have you had water on the skylight?"

There was a pause. János thought slowly, double-checking his reply before making it, as a chess-player deliberates on his next move. "There was some water, sir. Then we covered the skylight."

"I see. Has the Chief turned in?"

There was another pause, then Brewer's voice. "Chief here, sir."

"János says you're all right."

"We'd rather be down here than up there." He knew what the captain had telephoned for. "I thought you'd want the latest figures on consumption, sir."

"I should."

"We'll steam twenty-three hours at this speed. If you could drop one knot we could make nearly thirty."

The gale was worse now than an hour ago. "We can't risk it, Chief, unless she pipes down a bit."

"It's twenty-three hours, then, conservative."

Before Harkness had rung off he had run the simple calculation through his head. The *Salvado* would take thirty-six hours to get here. So far as he knew, there was no ship nearer than the tug except the *Angeles,* who would never reach this far in this sea without foundering. So there would be thirteen hours for the *Whipper* to spend here alone in the gale, her bunkers empty and engines dead. She could not do it. The moment the propeller stopped turning her steerage would go, and she would swing slowly round and broach-to. The first wave against her side would fill number one hold and smash the after hatches. The second or third would find her with a dangerous list and within minutes she would lie on her beam-ends.

Mathematics was a wonderful science. You could divine the future with it. At fifteen minutes to two tomorrow night the engines would stop and the ship would move into immediate danger. She could perhaps last another hour, lying broached-to and receiving the seas as they chose to come at her, pounding her and filling her until she foundered. So that by fifteen minutes to three the seascape in longitude 49.50 north, latitude 12.40 west, would be unbroken by the *Whipper*'s shape.

The gap of thirteen hours was no better than a gap of thirty. The vital hour would be that which followed the dying of the engines when the coal ran out. In one hour the sea could easily obliterate this mote.

The deck tilted.

"Meet her!"

"Meet her, sir!"

The thunder came, the burst of water against the bridge. White drifts of it went whirling by. Then there came the trough, and the wallowing, and the unearthly silence.

Thirteen hours; but if they could be narrowed to a few, and the gale eased a little . . . there was a chance. You had to weigh it all up. You had to conjure with unknown figures, and turn your mind against unreasonable hope. If you were experienced, and judged things right, you could save this ship, twenty-three hours in advance. And, knowing this, you must bear the appalling weight of the decision. There was no one to help you. The officers and the engineers could give you information, and help you carry out the decision once it was made; but only you could make it. You were supreme here, and alone.

The storm burst at the windows. He could see his reflection in the whitened glass. He stood like a faded photograph, a hump of dark and a peaked cap and a white face. He thanked God he was not Turnbull. Had Steve been standing here, that would be the enemy he would have to fight, the man there in the glass. The windows cleared and the silence came. In the silence of the deep troughs he could think better. There was only one thought worth considering at this moment. If he were to order the engine-room to slow, he would imperil the ship, leaving her less headway to meet the seas with; but the danger would not be certain. The danger would be certain if her present speed were maintained. It would strike at fifteen minutes to two tomorrow night. If the thirteen-hour gap could be narrowed there was a chance, involving a change in the gale that could only be prayed for; but with less speed and less headway than this, the seas could come at the ship more strongly, and a big wave could fill her decks and send her down at any hour—tonight, or at dawn, tomorrow noon, or evening.

The scales were level. Chance was heavy on both sides. There had to be the decision. He stood near the binnacle, watching it, for a few seconds prolonging the luxury of leaving all this to God. The wheelhouse door was pulled open on the port side and a seaman came in; he slammed the door and gave a cheerful grin to the captain and then began pounding his mop across the planks.

Harkness watched him for a moment and then went to the telephone and rang the engine-room. When Brewer came through he told him, "Chief, you can have your knot."

"Ease speed one knot, sir. Ay, ay."

He hooked the receiver back. The gap was closed from thirteen hours to six.

CHAPTER ELEVEN

COSTAIN came along the passage at a half-run and as the deck tilted he caught his shoulder on a fire-extinguisher bracket and span round under the impact. There were only the pilot-lamps burning and his eyes were still slow from sleep. He went on again and came to cabin nine, and knocked. There was no answer, so he knocked again very briefly and opened the door. It was dark inside. "Ann." He put his head out again so that he could take a look along the passage, both ways. This was very irregular. He looked into the cabin again. "*Ann . . .*"

The ship yawed and the door tried to swing away from his hand. He found the light-switch and flipped it and the light burst against his eyes, showing him an aching golden scene whose furniture took shape by painful degrees. The bed was empty and tidy; none of her clothes were about. He switched off the light and drew back into the passage, shutting the door. When he turned round he looked directly into Dodds's face. The shock of seeing his white face and white jacket floating there in the gloom was a fair one; on top of it, Costain shouldn't be coming out of a woman passenger's cabin in the middle watch.

His heart pumped badly but his tone was authoritative. He might have to slip the man a pound for this, but that must settle it. They were still officer and steward. "Is Miss Brown all right, Dodds?"

The white face and jacket swayed and hit the bulkhead but didn't fall. The small bloodshot eyes wavered with a kind of bodiless independence as they searched the gloom for the voice.

"Damn you, is she all right?" He was angry with Dodds for

being drunk and finding him here and not answering. There mightn't be any blackmail, now. Or would it be worse? The man might go shouting about, broadcasting with bawdy gusto the story of the Third Mate and the Frightened Lady. Costain was sweating.

"We'll all go down . . ." Dodds said suddenly and very loudly—"All go down . . . the bloody ship an' all, we will!"

Costain slapped his face hard and he stopped, and drooped against the bulkhead, shivering noisily. "You'd better go and put your head under a tap, Dodds. If the mate finds you like this you'll be slung overboard." He stepped past the man, angry at the delay. The big wave had wakened him and he had turned out half-asleep. He wasn't on watch but he ought to be on the bridge. The watch-rota had been shelved but they must all help. He had to find Ann first, though, and tell her not to be frightened. She would be very frightened by now, and probably crying again. He began trotting along the passage.

The smoking-room was dark but he put the main lights on in case she had fallen asleep in a chair. There was no one here. He heard footsteps and turned and saw two men staggering together along the passage from the for'ard companionway. Christ, was the whole crew drunk? He caught them up. From the twin lurching bundle of oilskins a face turned as he called to them. Smithers said, "The mate's hurt, sir."

"Who the hell's that?" Turnbull lurched on, not looking round.

"Where are you taking him, Smithers?"

"Sick bay, sir."

"Can you manage?"

"Of course he can bloody well manage," said the mate bitterly. "Where are you going, Mr. Costain?"

They kept together in a shambling group along the narrow passage. "Bridge, sir."

"Well, this isn't the way, don't y' know that?"

Costain turned back without answering. At the end of the athwartships alleyway he stopped and found the door of the lounge bolted open. He switched on the lights and saw three people sitting in the corner. Ann was one of them. He took a step inside, then turned back and switched off the lights. It would be better. He hit a chair, going forward again in the total darkness that followed the glare. Slowly the three faces became visible in the glow of the pilot-lamps. Someone asked what time it was. It sounded like Major Draycott; his voice was bewildered, as if he had been woken up. Costain had automatically checked his watch when he had turned out.

"Two o'clock, sir." He stood at a loss. He had to talk to Ann, but not in front of Draycott and Dr. Papasian. He could not imagine ever being able to talk to Ann again in front of anyone else.

"There's a message for you, Miss Brown." He said it quietly, bending over the chair near where she sat on the banquette.

"A message?"

"Two o'clock, what day?" asked Draycott from the gloom. He sounded worried.

Peter Costain said quietly, "It's been sent to your cabin."

"Tuesday," said Papasian.

More quietly still, Costain said, "Ann . . ." Surely she'd understand and come with him?

Papasian said alertly, "What was that sway?"

She had to come. He must get up on the bridge as soon as he could. He said, "Sway?"

The alert voice nodded. There was the gleam of a gold tooth. "The lurch. The ship lurched."

Ann was moving. He said, "We hit a wave, Doctor, that's all."

"Tuesday morning," the Major said loudly to no one. "Tuesday *morning.*" He coughed to clear phlegm that had gathered in sleep. "It's not Tuesday *night*?"

Peter stood back and shifted the chair as Ann got up; the chair would not move more than a couple of inches because it was chained. He put a hand out and guided her between the chair and the banquette.

"Has anything happened?" she asked.

"No." He went with her to the port-side doorway. She was cramped and lurched against him on the tilted floor and he steadied her, thinking, 'There's not time to go to the cabin.'

"Nothing's happened at all," he said when they were in the passage. The main lights were not burning and they were out of sight of the lounge doorway now. Her face looked very pale but she did not sound frightened.

"What message is it, Peter?"

"There isn't one. It's from me. I had to talk to you. You're not frightened?" He held both her hands.

"Why should I be?" Her hands were not cold. He didn't understand this. She had been so frightened, before, that he had found her sobbing in her cabin. The gale was worse now and there had been that terrific lurch.

"I—I just thought you might be worried." He wanted to kiss her, but it would be irrelevant and could lead nowhere. He had to be on the bridge.

"I'm perfectly all right," she said.

He was oddly disappointed. He had been ready to protect her and she did not want protecting. He should have been glad she wasn't frightened.

"I'm glad," he said rather bleakly. "You were scared, before."

"When?" She was still trying to talk like a passenger to a ship's officer but it wasn't going to work. "Oh, in my cabin." She smiled suddenly. "I wasn't scared, Peter."

"But you were crying. You said——"

"I was only sad about growing old."

He could think of nothing to say. She began laughing softly. There she went again. Why couldn't he ever see anything funny, when she was tickled to death? He had spent all that energy in reassuring her, trying every trick he knew that would stop her being scared of the way the deck was tilting after that hideous crack of the shifting-boards, and she'd been crying because she was sad about growing old. And she had humoured him, pretending she was being comforted.

"My God," he said, "what a damn' fool I must have looked!"

She stopped laughing. "Dear Peter."

As an afterthought he said, "But you're only twenty-eight!"

"Then I must have been sad about being twenty-nine. Did you come here to comfort me again, Peter?"

"Yes, but I'll know better in future."

"Don't be angry with me."

"I'm not angry with *you*!"

"Then who?"

"God knows! It's—it's just that I've got no sense of humour, or something." He must go. "Anyway, I shan't have it on my mind that you're worried. The ship's all right. As soon as we reach port we can really talk, and—and see each other." Still angry that she had made a fool of him, not angry with her but with—with whom? Himself, he supposed—and conscious that he must hurry away, and that the gale was worse and that damned steward was drunk and the mate was injured, he said urgently and not graciously at all, "Oh Lord, Ann, I'm in love with you, up to my neck." Ashamed of the way he had said it, he took his hands away from hers. "I've got to go now."

He wanted her to say something before he ran. There had to be an answer of some sort. Or would she just laugh softly? If she did, he'd have to ask her this time what was funny. He wasn't going to be left out of every joke.

"You mustn't be in love with me, Peter."

He heard someone coming. "It's just one of those things you can't stop." He turned away and saw the second mate looming along the passage. Ann whispered:

"Thank you for coming, Peter. You're wonderful."

Jim Beggs reached them and said, "You seen Dr. Papasian?"

"In there. What's up, Jim?"

Beggs passed them and went into the lounge, snapping the lights on. Peter said to Ann, "Sorry." He hurried off along the passage. There must be a clause in the book about officers canoodling with women passengers when the skipper was on the bridge and the ship was hove-to in a gale. It was unthinkable. That was what she did to him. This was love, and, God help him, he was in it.

Persham was dropping down a companionway as he reached the end of the passage, with a box and some scissors.

"Pershy!"

He stopped and looked up from the bottom of the steps. Costain said, "That man Dodds is drunk. You'd better——"

"I've fixed him. He's got it all up."

"How's the mate?"

"Contusions, nothin' bad." He looked like a busy doctor itching to get away from a visiting director of the board.

Behind Costain, Beggs and Dr. Papasian were hurrying along from the lounge.

"Someone's going to tell me what's happened," Costain said furiously, but Beggs and the little Armenian went bobbing down the companionway and he was left unanswered.

He got a rich oath out and went on deck into one of the silences as the ship lay wallowing in a trough. Before he had reached the wing of the bridge the next wave came and he arrived in the wheelhouse drenched. Captain Harkness looked at him idly, and said:

"The deck has just been mopped, Mr. Costain."

He looked down at the pool of water forming round his feet. He squelched towards dry planking. "Sorry, sir."

"That mop has been left here for our use."

Costain took up the mop and pushed it over the wet planks. How the hell could he come in here with his feet dry when the sea was breaking green over the decks? He opened the door when there was a chance and wrung out the mop, coming back and propping it head-up in the corner of the wheelhouse. His feet squelched in his boots as he came across to the captain.

"Is there anything I can do, sir?"

Harkness remained in the grip of his thoughts, gazing at the windows as the spray came and turned the glass opaque. His face went dirty white in the back-glare. Obliquely Costain was watching him. Would he ever come to look as experienced as this master, as resolute, with a face as lined? Surely there was nothing in the world that this man hadn't seen.

After the wave's sound had died, Harkness looked at the third mate. "Have you just turned out, Peter?"

"Yes, sir."

The boy's face looked so young; but it looked an intelligent face, an honest one. It wouldn't be a bad face to see, later, when the crisis was on them all. He realized that for the last few hours he had been studying the men who were with him on this mote in the sea. He must try to know what pressure could be put on this man or that, so that when the time came he could pick the best of them for the most vital work. This one was reliable. He said:

"Do you know the general situation?"

"No, sir."

"I'll bring you up to date. Number one hatch-cover's been stove-in again and we've stopped work on it, leaving two pumps going. Two hands are injured, and the mate. The main aerial's been carried away and Sparks is trying to rig a jury. Until he does, we shall remain cut off from signals."

The next wave came. He waited, watching the big smother of it blot out the fo'c'sle and foredeck. When he could be heard again he said, "We expect the tug *Salvado* alongside in thirty-six hours. Our coal will last us thirty, as we've reduced speed one knot. We'll do what we can about the six-hour gap when there's a chance. That is the present situation."

They bent their knees as the deck swung. Peter had the sudden dreadful vision of Ann floating in her life-jacket. Oh Lord, what a time to fall in love!

"Are the hands hurt badly, sir?"

"No, but I don't expect they'll be much use to us."

The next wave broke. He listened for the cracking of timber as the water fell across the deck. With every wave he listened like this, as the water dropped by the ton across number two hatch-cover. If it were stove-in, the six-hour gap would lose its importance; with both for'ard holds filling, the *Whipper* would not ride another thirty hours; there would be coal left in her bunkers when she sank.

The silence of the next trough came. "Dr. Papasian has been asked to look at their injuries. We're lucky to have him aboard."

"Persham's busy, too. I passed him as I came on deck."

"Yes." He thought of the chief steward; he was one of those he could rely upon. "Didn't he want to be a doctor?"

"I've heard him talk about it, sir. I don't think he could afford the training."

"What a stupid waste."

The next wave thundered out of the night. When the windows drained clear he said, "Get the Aldis. After each wave, turn the beam on number two hatch and let me know how it looks."

"Ay, ay, sir." He fetched the lamp.

Dr. Papasian straightened up. "Now you should rest."

The smell of medicines was heavy in the air, a smell to make ill even the fit. Turnbull hated it and was afraid of it. The Seaman's Hospital at Greenwich had smelt like this for seven months and he remembered only the pain and not their kindness. He said:

"I can't rest, Doctor." He stood up. Someone had a hand under his elbow to steady him. Persham's. He shook it off. He couldn't feel the bandage round his head; he could feel only the aching rhythmic beat of the dying-away pain. The Armenian shrugged.

"You will make the damage worse."

Turnbull walked carefully down the slope of the deck. He must get outside before the smell made him retch. Papasian grimaced, turning away to wash his hands. When they came to you for healing you knew better than they did; when you had healed them they knew better than you.

Persham had the tap running, and waited near the basin with a clean towel ready. Papasian bent over the basin. The water swirled to the vortex tinged with red. As the sick bay lurched, Persham put a hand out and steadied the doctor.

"Thank you. The gale is worse?"

"It'll blow itself out, Doctor."

He took the towel and dried his hands, glancing once at the steward. "You have worked in a hospital?"

"No, Doctor." He felt proud, and bitter.

Papasian gave him the towel. "There is nothing serious," he said, looking round at the bunks. "Let them rest. That was the first officer, who went out?"

"Yes, Doctor."

"He will be back, I expect. Send for me."

"Is there any sign of concussion, Doctor?"

"No. Just stupidity." He gave a quick gold smile and Persham laughed. It was heady to discuss a case like this, and share a joke about the mate's stupidity. It made up for a lot. "The way out is up those stairs?"

"I'll show you, Doctor."

From his bunk Harris watched them. The bloody steward creep-arsing the little medico; it made you sick. But it was too true what they said about the mate: he was a sore-headed bastard now, all right.

When Papasian had gone up the companionway, Harris called out to Persham, "Come on, Flossie Nightingale, my nose wants wipin'!"

Persham came along to his bunk. "Why don't you shut up? The other blokes need their sleep, don't you know that?"

"I'm goin' to turn out, mate. I've 'ad enough o' this."

"You'll keep where you are. You don't know when you're well off."

"Well off? Down 'ere in this stinkin' butcher's-shop?"

"You're feelin' better, I can see that."

"Go on, you mus' be psychic, mate. Now 'elp me out."

"Listen, I've asked the doctor about you, an' he says you got to rest." He turned as someone came down the companionway. It was Stubbs.

"Look out," said Harris, " 'ere comes the fairy queen."

Stubbs walked carefully down the slope of the planks. His eyes were bloodshot and a mist of spray clung to the stubble on his face. His reefer dripped water. Persham's instincts rebelled at the sight of anything so unhygienic coming into his sick bay. "What do you want, Stubbs?"

"I don' feel so good."

"You wanter tonic?" Harris grinned from the bunk. "Go an' take a look at the Ole Bull with 'is 'ead done up like a puddin'!"

"Look," Persham said, "these blokes have got to sleep. Now get off out of it."

Stubbs looked down at Harris and said, "All nice an' cushy, eh? Bosun's bleedin' darlin', all tucked up in bed!"

"Now don't get on my tits," Harris said. Persham left them, to tidy the medical kit on the table. He couldn't handle men like Stubbs. They were just animals. You couldn't make them see sense when it was staring them in the face.

Harris asked Stubbs, "You got that grain shifted?"

The pale stubbly face lost the last of its colour and the beard showed up a dirty grey. "Would she be lyin' over like this if we 'ad? You don't know much, do you, down 'ere out of the way? You should see number one hatch, boy, fillin' up quick an' nothing to stop it." He looked directly into Harris's face, speaking urgently, persuasively. "She's down by the head an' she won't come up again. You know what that means. I don't 'ave to tell you."

Harris frowned. "Number one got stove-in, then?" He had been awake only a little while, he still felt light-headed. He called to Persham, "Hey, did I lose much blood?"

Persham came over and said, "What sort of selfish bastard are you? If you don't shut your row an' let these blokes sleep, you can just clear out of here. They've been hurt a sight worse'n you. Don't forget, now. One more shout, an' you'll get out, and don't come back with your head split open, because I won't be interested." He left them. Harris said:

"What's the time, Stubby?"

"I got no watch. It's night." He put a hand on Harris's shoulder. "You want to know what I think? This lot's due for the bottom." Harris realized at last what was bothering Stubbs. He was scared sick. "Listen," Stubbs said. "We sent an S O S a long time afore midnight, because there was a plane over us, tryin' to find us. You don't send for bloody aeroplanes unless you're in bad trouble. That was hours ago. Now she's goin' down by the head. I tell you we got no chance, an' the bloody afterguard knows it, an' won't even warn the passengers."

"Well, what d'you think I can do, for Chris' sake?"

Stubbs lowered his voice. "Tell the Skip we want to abandon ship an' take to the boats."

"Who, me?"

"You an' me an' Dodds—he'll go with us. I been talkin' to 'im."

Harris leaned back on his pillow. He had used up his

few reserves of energy. "What's this, then—a bloody mutiny?"

Drops of water fell from Stubbs's reefer. The lamplight touched his face; it looked dirty and afraid. "It's every man for 'imself, soon. Who d'you think's goin' to look after you, when she starts going down? Eh?"

Harris closed his eyes. "You talk a lot o' bull."

"Bull, is it? You don' know what's goin' on up there. You bin asleep. I s'ppose you know the aerial's gone, an' we can't get no signals out, or receive any?"

Persham was standing beside him, looking at Harris. Harris was spent. Persham told Stubbs, "Get out."

"What's the matter with you lot?" Stubbs said. "Don't you know when you're in a sinkin' ship?"

Persham was shivering and his eyes were bright. "Get out, Stubbs. This is a sick bay."

"Sick bay, is it? You'll be wantin' a sick bay when——"

"*Get out!*"

Stubbs stood over Persham, who was a small man. "Quite the little doctor, aren't you? Considerin' you're just a bleedin' flunkey——"

Persham had brought the scissors with him because Stubbs was twice his weight, and he jabbed with them because he must get Stubbs out of here, and because Stubbs had called him a flunkey, and it was right. He jabbed at the wrist and blood came quickly as Stubbs jerked back and stared at the blood and then at Persham. He made an animal noise of surprise.

"Now get out."

Harris had opened his eyes at the sound of the steward's voice. He said, "Jesus."

Stubbs held his wrist and looked at Persham. As if he had just thought of a good idea and was still surprised at the simplicity of it he said slowly, "I'm goin' to kill you."

Harris got on to one elbow and said, "Leave the kid alone. He's told you to get out, an' he means it."

The air fluttered in the ventilators and vibration ran through the deck as a squall rose. The tilt increased but Stubbs was no longer frightened. He came towards Persham very deliberately and Harris said quickly, "Leave 'im alone, you fool."

Persham did not back away. He held the scissors in front of him. "You'll get it again," he said, shivering. He hated the man in front of him, for his dirt, and stupidity, and ugliness, and for his being in here.

The tilt stopped and then came back almost at once as if the ship were stiff. Stubbs took his hand off his wrist and attacked, swinging a blow sideways because of the scissors. They leapt like a bright fish and Stubbs screamed, falling across the slope, holding his arm. A hiss of breath came from Harris. Persham's face was sickly as he watched Stubbs crouched over the wound in his arm. The wrist was bright with blood and it fascinated him, horrified him. Someone should pity him, even his enemy. "I'm hurt bad," he said.

"Get out." Oh God, he shouldn't have done this, shouldn't have done this. It wasn't the way.

"You got to do something." It was a whimper. Persham knew he hadn't struck the artery; the floor would be smothered by now if he had.

"He'll bleed to death," Harris said. He wanted to rest and shut his eyes and wait for the throbbing in his head to stop. He must not feel weak like this when the ship was going down. Was it going down? That was Stubbs's tale. Stubbs was going to bleed to death. The scissors were red and Persham's face looked dead; but his eyes were bright; he must be mad; he must do something to stop the blood; this was a sick bay; the kid had said it; it had sounded as if he was saying it was a church; the kid was mad; the blood dripped; his head beat and beat and his stomach was cold, suddenly cold, and sweat was crawling over his face as he watched the bright blood and the big man crouched there with the kid over him and the scissors red.

Persham heard Harris vomiting.

"Help me," Stubbs said.

The smell of the vomit came into the air. Persham looked away from Stubbs for the first time, down at the scissors. He would do anything not to have done that. Against the boards, the vomit crept down the slope of the deck, coming to the blood-spots and covering them. He looked at Harris; he was lying back again with his eyes shut; his face was wet.

He wanted to move and wash the scissors, but movement would make him aware of himself and he would be at the mercy of the self-contempt that was waiting to swamp him. The scissors seemed stuck to his hand as though he must carry them for life so that people should know what he had done.

He was standing like that when the bosun came down the companionway. He didn't ask a question but flicked a glance at Stubbs, at the steward, and back to Stubbs. Persham moved at last, taking the scissors to the basin and turning the tap on.

"Stubbs, get up." Starley stood at the bottom of the companion-way. Persham got a mop and began clearing the mess from the deck, taking the mop to the bucket-hanger and rinsing it, coming back with it. Starley said, "What's the matter with him?"

"He's bleeding."

The bosun came across to Stubbs and took his collar in one hand, yanking him up. His arm flew out and flecks of blood spattered the bosun's face.

"What are you doin' down here, Stubbs?"

"I'm hurt, bad."

"What was it about, the fight?"

"He come at me, with scissors——"

"You could've eaten him, otherwise, couldn't you? What did you come down here for?"

"I'm bleedin', bad. You can see."

"Get up on deck."

Stubbs looked bewildered. They didn't understand. He was losing blood and his arm had gone numb. There were tears of frustration in his eyes. "I been hurt, damn you, *damn your bloody eyes!*"

Starley said, "Get up on deck."

Persham wrung out the mop and came over to them. "I'd better see to him."

Art Starley was smiling. He shook his head. "No, Pershy. I've got a job for him. He's been down here before, hasn't he? I've told him what'd happen if I found him down here again." He turned his bright smile on Stubbs. "I told you, didn't I?"

Stubbs had a sob in his breath. "Christ, can't you see I been hurt?" He thrust his bloodied wrist in front of the bosun's face.

"That's nothin', mate. I've not started yet. Get on deck."

Persham took the bad arm and raised it. "Keep it above your head, high as you can reach."

"You got to do somethin' for me."

Starley told the steward, "You're wasting your time. I'm taking him with me."

"But he wants attention, Arthur. He'll lose blood."

"He'll lose blood all right. Stubbs, I'm counting three."

Stubbs kept his arm as high as he could. The numbness was worse. His hand was white.

"One."

Persham said, "He's not fit to work, Arthur. You're not daft."

"Two."

Stubbs began backing away. "You can't," he said, "you can't."

"Three."

"Arthur," Persham said, "for Christ's sake give him a chance and——"

Starley hit Stubbs and he fell. "You're soft, Stubbs. Get up. You're goin' on deck."

"You'll kill him," said Persham. There was nothing he could do now. Even scissors wouldn't help. They hadn't helped before; they'd brought things to this. He turned away and soaked a swab, and wiped Harris's face. Some of his colour was back but he was still unconscious.

"All right," the bosun said, "I'll kill him."

Stubbs was in a heap, looking up at Starley. "Haven't you got no mercy?"

"Not for lice." He pitied the man but was resolved. "This time it's a beating-up. You've had enough warning. If I took you to the captain again he'd murder me. They've got quite enough to do on the bridge. I don't put up with a parasite, even in good weather. Time like this they're a menace. Get up. You're bigger than I am."

Stubbs was holding his wrist and his face was grey. He looked old. Pity was nagging at Starley, so he got hold of the man again and dragged him to his feet and hit him down again. "Get on deck before I lose my temper." Stubbs was whimpering like a child and the bosun was furious with him for awakening his pity. Stubbs was a danger in this ship, adding to the danger of the sea. He had been trying to spread panic among the hands ever since the hatch was stove-in, and he had probably come down here to work on Persham. He would be best overboard; but that was murder.

Stubbs went on whimpering. How bad was he? The bosun had no medical knowledge. He had seen men looking a sight worse than this in a dockside shindy. Poor little Copley had been worse than this, outside Mickey Green's in B.A. Tich Copley was worth ten of this bastard. Starley knew he was strong enough to lug him up the companionway and sling him on deck; but he wouldn't work, he'd pass out first. It wouldn't be the best thing. He'd have to be strong enough to leave Stubbs down here and forget him. He looked round the sick bay. There were two empty bunks. He stooped again and knocked the man's hand away as he tried to shield his face. He hit his face hard, and heard Persham behind him saying, "Don't, don't." Then he got a grip on Stubbs and dragged him across the sloping deck to the nearest bunk.

"He's out cold, Pershy. Gimme a hand."

They lifted him and got him into the bunk. Persham was very quiet. It had been a terrible thing to do, with the scissors, and terrible not to have stopped the bosun hitting Stubbs. He was in charge of the sick bay, but had no authority. It was terrible to have no authority, even enough to match his small responsibilities here.

"I'm sorry he's on your hands, Pershy, but he'll be no bloody good to me on deck. If he gives any more trouble, bash him."

When the bosun had gone, the chief steward made a bandage-sling and tied Stubbs's arm to the rail above, then cleaned the two stab-cuts and dressed them. Afterwards he got the mop again and cleaned the deck. When he rinsed it in the bucket-hanger the water was tinged with red, as it had been in the basin when Dr. Papasian had washed his hands. He went over to Harris and counted his pulse, and wiped the sweat from his face again. Then, when there was nothing more he could do for the moment, he sat on the stool near the basins and held his face in his cupped hands.

This had to be got over, but as he reviled himself he offered his own excuse, his voice trembling among the other uneasy sounds in the sick bay: the fluttering of the ventilators, the strain of timber, the bright tingling of a spoon in a glass, the open-mouthed breathing of sick men asleep. "I've got no authority . . . I've got no authority . . ."

He said it again and again with his eyes hot and shut, his face imprisoned in his hands with the guilt and the excuse.

Major Draycott had sat alone for ten minutes after Miss Brown had left the lounge with the young third officer and Dr. Papasian had been summoned by Mr. Beggs. The Major had not talked to them when they had been sitting near him in the gloom, nor they to him or even to each other; but when they had gone he had missed their company. The lounge was a place of shadows; even his own presence did nothing to keep away the feeling that it was now utterly deserted; he was a ghost sitting here, and if anyone came they would not see him.

He had come from the lounge to his cabin; it was smaller, and the lamp beside the bed was cheerful; he was still alone but the loneliness seemed less huge to him.

He read his book for a little while, and then, because he had read it so many times before, he shut it again, imagining the dust that would be clouding out from between the pre-war pages. He had become increasingly conscious of dust over the past few years; he could smell it, or seemed to smell it, when he opened the door of his room, and when he took his shoes from beneath the bed where his uniform and souvenirs were stored in the shallow sagging trunk, and when he opened the glass doors of the cabinet to touch his ivory miniatures that turned more yellow as each year came, bringing its dust and its gathering army of regrets that had been on the march since his mind had stopped looking forward and begun looking back to find the missed turning and the signpost that was now too far away to read. There was dust in his books and on his shoes; of late, it had begun powdering silently over his heart.

His brother had said it was unwise of him to have made the long trip to South America just to see him for a matter of days; but there was no other relative to see, and he was not sorry he had gone. There had been no sunshine, and the sands were not as golden as he had pictured them; but he had gone to see Clive, and Clive was well and prospering; he had shared for a few days in a life that had gone right all the way along, and his nature had little envy in it to sharpen the regrets.

But this storm was very troubling. Even the others were worried by it, even those whose luggage was free of the solemn advice for daily use: there must be no exertion. The words had gathered dust already but he must not ignore them.

He went to the cupboard beside the porthole after shutting his book, and took down his medicine bottle, and shook it as directed on the label, where the stuff had run down from the neck and stained it. The cabin swung again, and this time it was much worse than the other times, so that he reached quickly behind him for the small arm-chair and sat down in it with the bottle in his hand. The floor tilted very badly and his left hand gripped the arm of the chair; the chair was shaking to the vibration. Then there came the dreadful noise from outside—more than just water falling. The floor was a dangerous slope; the chair pulled at its securing-chain as he crouched deeper into it. The book slid off the bed-table, but he did not notice it in the midst of the dreadful smashing sound that was still going on outside.

CHAPTER TWELVE

At daybreak, Tuesday, gusts of ninety miles an hour were recorded at coastguard stations along the Cornish coast. With the wind there was rain. Windows were still lit long after dawn, for it was a grey watery light that seeped from the tempestuous sky.

Land's End Radio was still calling. *GLD—GLD—GLD to S.S. 'Atlantic Whipper' to 'Atlantic Whipper'. Can you hear? Can you hear?* It had been calling at one minute past each hour since two o'clock in the morning, when the *Atlantic Whipper* had failed to send. She had been silent now for seven hours. At Lloyd's, members were conscious of the familiar pattern formed by the signals that had come from this ship, as it had formed many times before. At 4.17 p.m. yesterday the *Whipper* had sent: *We are heaving-to until the gale abates. Ship in good trim and all happy aboard.* At 4.26 p.m. the signal came, *Am hove-to in south-westerly gale.* It was a confident, reassuring message—the master had said that he was going to heave-to, and now he had completed the planned manœuvre. But three minutes later there was the unexpected addition to the last signal, *Cargo shifted. List fifteen degrees. No anxiety.* Still confident, still reassuring. For nearly five hours the owners and Lloyd's were able to comfort themselves with the old saw that no news is good news. Captain Harkness was on the spot; his ship was listing to shifted cargo in a south-westerly gale, but if he said there was no anxiety, then there should be none felt by those with their feet firmly on land. The five hours ended at 9.23 p.m. last evening. *S O S. 'Atlantic Whipper' lying hove-to approximately forty-nine-fifty north, twelve-forty west. Cargo shifted, slight list, number one hatch-cover stove-in by heavy seas and taking water.*

Confidence ran out, suddenly. Signals such as these had led so many times to disaster. When the markets opened this morning, Tuesday, rumours immediately circulated in the City among insurance companies and marine underwriting syndicates. The first reinsurance rate quoted was ten guineas per cent. It was widely believed that a total of half a million pounds liability was spread over several insurance interests. Cargo value was estimated at a hundred and twenty-five thousand pounds. The early quotation of ten guineas per cent was not due to the gravity of the last signal sent out by the *Atlantic Whipper,* but to the long silence that followed it. No news was not good news when a ship lay in this critical condition.

Lloyd's issued a brief report to the Press, simply repeating the S O S and giving the estimated time of arrival of the tug *Salvado* alongside the distressed ship. This was given as 2 p.m. tomorrow, Wednesday. News that the Spanish steamer *Angeles* was much nearer the position than the *Salvado* gave rise to hopes; but not in all quarters. There were those who from their personal knowledge of the sea were ready to declare positively that the *Angeles* would never reach the position, steaming at ninety degrees across the path of the gale as she must.

The first of the day's B.B.C. bulletins gave no indication that the winds would moderate before evening. No mention was made of the *Atlantic Whipper*. Her name, however, appeared in the stop press of a few papers: she was reported in trouble, and a tug was going to meet her. It was quite simple; and on the breakfast-tables where these few papers were propped the bacon was getting cold.

In the big towns of England the wind was a nuisance, blowing dust into people's faces and scattering paper through the streets. In London a crowd collected when a chimney-pot blew down and landed near a bus-stop without hurting anyone. It was the talk of the day for those who had seen it. A flag-mast in Manchester was broken, and hung across its wires until a fire-engine was sent for: another small crowd had dramatic news for those at home this evening. When the rain came, umbrellas went up and a few blew inside-out. The wind was a nuisance across the land—even dangerous, as the chimney-pot had proved.

The steamship with forty-three Englishmen on board had now been silent for nine hours. This was hardly news, so that there was no mention of it in the noon editions. The Englishman, the son of the island race that is said by foreigners to have the sea in its blood, is not half-hearted about his insularity. Anything over the horizon is out of his sight.

Only among those whose lives were directly linked with the ship was there any concern: they were the families of the crew and passengers, the owners, the interested parties of the insurance companies, and the officers of coastal radio stations and coastguard headquarters and other services devoted to the safety of shipping.

The telegram was delivered in Beaker Street, Bristol, with the first post. Thelma Bond was still in her dressing-gown, and the telegram was in her hand when she came back to the bedroom.

"Is it trouble?" her friend asked. She shook her head.

"He's going to be delayed. That's all it says."

He laced his shoes and stood up, lighting a cigarette.

"Probably the gale."

"Probably." She looked at him critically, without meaning to. Behind him the bed was in a mess, with the bedclothes spilled half on to the floor; there were cigarette-stubs in the ashtray. His eyes were a little pink-rimmed, and she supposed hers must be. They had slept no longer than an hour or two, kept fitfully awake by the wind and the passion. Had there really been much passion? He wasn't very attractive. She felt no peace in her mind or body, no lingering after-glow. She just felt unwashed in the bleak windy light of the morning.

"Is there a smut on my nose?"

She said, "What?"

"You're staring rather hard."

She managed to smile. "I was miles away. Sorry."

"Are you worried about him?"

It occurred to her that she might be, subconsciously. "I don't know, really. It's not a very worrying message." She thought it must be the sense of guilt, the degrading sight of the bedclothes, the long creases in the under-sheet where they had lain, the memory of the unfamaliar smell of his hair-oil beside her face in the dark. Tony had such a pink washed-looking face and clear eyes, and he didn't use anything on his hair. If only he weren't such a single-minded specialist with his nice head full of valves and soldered wires, she wouldn't have brought herself to this.

"There might be something in the paper," he said. "About the ship."

"You think so?"

"I wish to God you didn't look so wonderful, even at this unearthly hour. Women don't usually, however pretty they are."

Why did he have to make a set speech? Did he always make it, between lacing his shoes and putting his coat on? A sort of gentlemanly farewell address? 'Women don't, usually, however pretty they are.' As if he were explaining the habits of the green-tailed parakeet. 'Their plumage turns mud-brown in the morning.'

"I'll get the paper," she said. She escaped from the scent of the hair-oil. There was nothing about the ship in her paper; it was one of those that didn't carry the few lines in the stop press; but as she was dropping it still open into the chair the telephone rang; and she was worried.

"It's Jean," the caller said. Jean Stapleton. "Have you seen the paper?"

"Is there something about Tony's ship?"

"Hang on a minute, dear." She waited, hating the drama in Jean's tone, and the taste in her own mouth of the night's lechery, and the way he talked about women as if he were making a mildly curious study of their habits. "Thelma?"

"Yes."

"It's in the stop press. Are you listening?"

She felt drained even of impatience. "Yes, Jean."

"This is it. 'Cargo ship *Atlantic Whipper* reported in trouble two hundred miles south-west of Land's End. Salvage tug *Salvado* on way to meet her.' Did you get that, dear?"

"Yes."

The voice sounded slightly indignant that she was not bursting into tears. "Well, I do hope Tony's all right. It's a pretty bad gale, you know."

"There was a wire from him, a few minutes ago. It just says he'll be delayed."

"A *tele*gram . . ." Her tone was ominous. "Would you like me to pop over and see you, my dear?"

It would be almost worth a laugh, to see Jean's face when she arrived here, to find she was—how would she put it, in euphemistic surburbanese?—*not alone*. But it wouldn't really be funny; it would just be part of the whole sordid pattern.

"No, I'm not worrying. They'll be all right with a tug standing by."

"But, Thelma, how can we know that? It might be very serious." The tone changed key to the motherly. "I don't expect you're wide awake yet. Give me a ring after breakfast, and if you feel like talking to someone about it, I'll pop across on my way to the shops."

She sensed him standing near her; or it was the faint oily smell. She turned her head. He was looking at his watch, pointedly.

"All right, Jean. Thank you for phoning."

"My dear, I wouldn't not have. Now don't go worrying, will you?"

"No, I won't."

He was pacing with studied quietness up and down the narrow draughty hall. He looked exactly like every other small-time successful seducer, neatly dressed and with a homburg that had a brim just a fraction too wide.

". . . been through so many storms at sea," the voice chirped persistently, "that I'm sure he'll know what to do for the best."

"Yes. Good-bye, Jean."

"Good-bye—and don't forget, if you feel like talking to someone—"

"Good-bye." Only the receiver could stop it. He took off the homburg with pointed politeness; she was certain he'd put it on just so that he could go through the little act of remembering his manners, despite the urgent problems that were on his mind at the beginning of a hard business day.

She returned his kiss coldly.

"You were splendid," he said, with the generous overtone afforded by the imminence of their parting. "Splendid, Thelma."

She said that it was nice of him to have come. Lovers not in love must find words for good-bye, to round it all off for the sake of propriety.

The wind tore at the door as he opened it, and she stood back where she couldn't be seen from the street; though it hardly mattered. In the draughty reaches of dejection the worst catastrophe looked small.

The stray bitter thought that was in her mind as she went upstairs to run the bath was that instead of telling her she had been splendid, he might have said he hoped the ship would be all right.

The day's light began lowering early in the afternoon. The rain was coming inland from the sea in long squalls that broke across the rocky coast of Cornwall and were gathered up by the higher wind that raced from the south. Visibility was bad wherever a man was, for if he were behind a window the glass was distorted by the rain and if he were in the open he must screw his eyes up against its sting.

The ether was charged with electricity that crackled among the signals criss-crossing the land and the sea, distorting them, blotting out a word and groups of words as men spoke into the radio-telephones. Silence was no longer requested of general shipping during the first fifteen minutes of each hour. GLD was still calling.

Land's End Radio—Land's End Radio—Land's End Radio to 'Atlantic Whipper', Atlantic Whipper'. Come in, please.

There had been no answer for fourteen hours.

Captain Tremayne said that she must have gone down. One big sea could overwhelm her if she were listing and the for'ard hold were filled with free surface-water. He had been quiet, during the snatched hour at his home where the five-day-old child still shouted at the storm in puling rage. His wife had asked about the ship and he had been glum, and she had said it was sad, but they must not take it so to heart. He had hardly glanced at the child, and she had been glad to be rid of him when he had put on his big coat and gone back to the radio station. Since the first cockleshell had been fashioned by barbarians, women had been jealous of ships, quick to see how men came to love the ugly things and give them girls' names—it was all 'she' this and 'she' that, as if they talked of another woman; and it was worse than another woman, for you couldn't scratch the eyes out of anything so big and cold.

Tremayne was back on duty a tired man; his ears ached for an answer from the sea, just a word to show him that the *Whipper* was not deep in the dark, deaf for ever to the quick tapping hand, *GLD—GLD—GLD—to 'Atlantic Whipper'. Can you receive me? Can you receive me?*

There was no comfort in the other signals that were threading through the tangle of the static.

'Salvado' to Land's End Radio. Position 51 *north,* 7.20 *west. Speed thirteen knots. Heavy seas. Any signal from 'Atlantic Whipper? Any signal yet? Cannot raise her.*

'Angeles'—'Angeles'—'Angeles'. Position 49.30 *north,* 11 *west. Where is 'Atlantic Whipper'? We must be near. We must be near. Wind bad. No visibility. Does anyone know where is 'Whipper'?*

Nobody knew. She might be anywhere on the surface, or under the waves. It would have been heartening to realize how well the Spanish steamer had kept her course, how fast she had made through this bitter storm, but for the knowledge that even if she came within a mile of the distressed ship they would be blind to each other. The light of the bleak day was drawing down, and the rain cast a veil across the waves, merging with the spindrift that was torn from their tops to lay a screen from one horizon to the other. The *Angeles* carried no radar. Her signal was strong but she must have an answer from the region of 49.50 north, 12.40 west. How big a region was it by now? The *Whipper* could be drifting a long way north-east, her engines unable to give her headway in the sea. Already the *Angeles* could be steaming away from where she lay, and so could the *Salvado,* and the destroyer *Brindle*. Their reports to land stations gave their radar-screens as blank, still blank: *Still nothing, still nothing, cannot raise her, cannot receive her*. Part of the fragile network had broken down, the most vital part. There was a gap of silence, two hundred miles south-west of Land's End, the geographical point in the ocean that had now been extended northwards and eastwards to cover a half-circle. The ship was anywhere in that area. She would not be south nor west of the geographical point 49.50 north 12.40 west, for the wind had not changed its direction. The drift would be north and east, towards the land, towards the barrier of rocks where the spume boiled and spilled flotsam into the caves and creeks—old shoes and fishermen's corks, split-open rancid oranges and the splintered skeleton of a deck-chair down from its summer in Torquay, and the remains of a broken ship that had gone down last year off the Lizard. If the *Whipper* were drifting, it would be towards this coast.

When night came, some gave up hope. There was a fuller report in the evening papers: some of them devoted nearly a dozen lines to the vague story of the ship that was in trouble. The news varied; you could believe which version you wanted to. Most of it was plain information: the *Atlantic Whipper* (or *Atlantic Whippet*) was a cargo ship of six thousand tons (or nine thousand five hundred and twenty-two, to quote a journal well-known for its insistence upon precise figures) and was carrying grain and other goods (or bales) from Buenos Aires to Avonmouth (or Liverpool). She had a crew of forty (and this was the only figure on which all were agreed) and ten (or a dozen) passengers among whom was Dr. Papasian (the name had five variations, for he was a foreigner and no one would know), until two years ago personal surgeon to the President of Brazil. From this general information the reports slipped freely into speculation, but no paper committed itself to facts, since no facts were known of the ship's whereabouts. She had sent no signal for 'some few hours' (since noon today, since midnight last night), and it was feared she had been overwhelmed.

This final item of speculation was innocent of any cruelty. It must have been clear to editors that among their readers would be friends and relatives of the crew and passengers, reading and re-reading every brief report they could find in any paper they could come by, pinning their hopes to a single word of good news if one were offered them. But the news must go through; the public was owed a solemn duty by the Press; so that if a junior editor who had spent six months at sea before being put ashore for reasons of chronic sea-sickness or hopeless incompetence now declared that he believed, from his personal experience of the sea, that the *Atlantic Whipper* must have foundered, the opinion must go into print. For the want of facts, a chance remark will have to suffice. The truth would not suffer for being printed in more formal language: 'I'd say she's had it, myself,' meant precisely the same as: 'It is feared she has been overwhelmed.'

It was not known, nor was it considered important to guess, how many people read reports such as this in the evening papers of today, Tuesday. There were fifty on board the imperilled ship. Even a friendless man with no more permanent home than the ports of the ocean has seldom fewer than two other people on the earth who love him; the average would be nearer six. So that there were some hundreds on this anxious night who were denied their sleep for thought of a friend's or son's or brother's death in the violent seas that were pounding this ship where she lay helpless or nursing her wreckage a score of fathoms down. Some telephoned the offices of the newspapers (for if they didn't know the facts, who did?); some made enquiries at the Admiralty, the radio stations and coastguard headquarters and harbour authorities. Someone must know. But there was no news.

Official reports carried negative information. Twice during the day an aircraft had taken off from R.A.F. Redmoor to search the area where it was judged the *Whipper* must lie; but the sea had no visible surface anywhere. Through the rain-distorted observation-panels and the rain-haze itself there could be seen nothing more than a desert of spindrift and the occasional white upthrust of a wave-crest that became mist a moment afterwards. The aircraft had flown low, driving with flimsy strength against the gale, turning and drifting, flying always outside the limit beyond which an aircraft could not be expected to return to base without the extra reserve of skill and courage that danger brings to a pilot and his crew. It had come home, with no news.

The tug *Salvado,* at nightfall within a hundred miles of the point 49.50 north, 12.40 west, called up Land's End repeatedly for a bearing. There was none to give her. She altered course slightly to eastwards, her master certain that if the *Atlantic Whipper* still floated she must have drifted to north and east of her last reported position. The tug, within a hundred miles of that position, could be within fifty of the *Whipper* if she had a two-knots drift on her, northwards and east. In a few more hours there would be the danger of coming upon her in the dark and the blinding rain, with no warning of her presence until the collision came.

The *Angeles* signalled soon after dark that she was hove-to in position approximately 50 north, 11 west. Manuelo de las Castillas informed Land's End that he would conserve his coal until day-break; meanwhile he would signal hourly to the *Whipper*. With naïve confidence he had ended, *We must be close to her, and she must answer soon.* There was the suggestion in these words that it was God's will. He was answered formally by Land's End; but from the destroyer *Brindle* there came the message: *You have done magnificently to have reached your present position. Have you cornered the market in miracles?*

It was two hours before Manuelo, in worried consultation with radio officers and those on board who could muster a word of English, could make anything of the idiomatic signal from *Brindle*. There was nothing helpful in the phrase-books about cornered markets. It was decided finally that a corn-market must be alluded to, and the word 'miracles' suggested a biblical connotation. But none among the crew could remember a miracle involving corn especially. Did the British naval ship mean: had the *Angeles* as many miracles as there are grains of corn in a market? It was very worrying, this, for Manuelo, because the message from the *Brindle* was full of praise and kindness, and she must be thanked for it, and aptly. There must be a little joke, for cheerfulness.

Towards ten o'clock the radio officer in *Brindle* picked up a signal from *Angeles*. *Thank you. It was nothing. We have a cargo of marbles.* The Spanish letter 'v', virtually interchangeable with 'b' in both speech and writing, was responsible for the perplexity on the bridge of H.M.S. *Brindle*. Commander Lawson held the message-slip at arm's length, in case physical perspective might render the words more clear. "Marbles? What extraordinary merchandise some of these boys carry."

Half an hour later the *Angeles* received a signal. *Excellent. We'll give you a game when we meet.*

Manuelo Lopez de las Castillas hurried into consultation again with the more scholarly members of his crew.

It might have seemed they had forgotten why they had brought their ships here to this violent region where the wind and the waves attacked them again and again as they sent their little jokes to each other to pass the hours. The destroyer bore steadily south, nearing the area of search. The *Angeles* lay with steerage-way on her, wallowing, her ancient timbers with the ague in them as the sea pitched, and the ship pitched, and the sea fell away, and she fell away too, until a man rolled from his bunk below and cursed Manuelo, just as he had been cursing him in his dreams. From the north came the *Salvado,* so near the *Brindle* that they had each other on their radar-screens. Soon they would pick up the Spanish steamer, and at daybreak the search could begin. If the *Atlantic Whipper* could last the night they would find her to-morrow: but had she lasted even through the day?

There were no more aircraft despatched from Redmoor by dark. It would have been pointless. There were no fresh orders from C.-in-C., Plymouth, to *Brindle;* her course would bring her to the search area almost together with the *Salvado,* a little after noon tomorrow, or if the distressed ship had drifted more north than east they might come upon her as soon as it was light. There were these simple reckonings and these trumped up hopes to sustain them through the night. It was not known what Manuelo thought of the chances. Commander Lawson seemed confident that something could be done; but if he were asked on oath for the truth in his mind he would have said he was looking for wreckage and survivors. Captain Howes, master of the deep-sea tug *Salvado,* was of like opinion in the privacy of his own counsel. It was almost twenty-four hours since the casualty had signalled that she was listing and taking seas into her for'ard hold. In this gale her condition would not have improved. Had she been able to signal, what would she have sent? *List increasing. Number two hatch stove-in. Steampipe fractured. Engines dead and steering gone and men injured.* A dozen shades of darkening tragedy could have blotted her slowly out. The last signal, had she been able to send it, would have been: *Am sinking.*

Howes, like Lawson, would be looking for survivors when first light came, for wreckage, an oil-patch, a huddle of half-drowned figures in a boat. There had not been one spark of hope to brighten the long exchange of signals through the day and half the night. In the late evening the Admiralty had requested radio amateurs to listen for signals from the distressed ship and to report anything they picked up, however faint. There had been no reports from these wavelengths.

As eight bells were rung at midnight and in these three ships the graveyard watch began, hope had run out. In these first hours of a new day the heart of any wakeful man is at its lowest ebb, even on the land. In this cold heaving waste there was nothing to help Lawson or Howes or Manuelo to believe that anything good could come to this night, not even one grain of a miracle. But soon after two in the morning the gale began dying, and by three it was dead, and the sea quiet.

CHAPTER THIRTEEN

THE sea was inert. There were yellow scum-patches where the waves had brought up seaweed; in the pale starlight you could believe they were patches of sand, small low islands in the water. A flight of stormy petrels traced through the faint milky light, haunting the night to the north; and not far from their passage the ship lay.

She was dark. There was a gentle movement on her, a look of exhaustion about her as a low wave crept and lifted her bows and let them fall again, easefully. All the anger and passion had gone away from the sea and the ship; like lovers they lay quietly, saddened and exhausted by the orgasm. Soft light went rippling along her side when a wave stronger than the others broke a froth of bubbles in the shadows and the starlight caught them and lit them. Their sound was stonily musical, less easily heard than the stronger steamy sound of the water that fell to the sea from the two pumps that were still working in the for'ard hold. Where these two jets of water reached the sea a lacework of bubbles went spreading in a slow circle through the black.

Sometimes a flicker of light sparked from the darkened shape as a man worked; there were figures along the foredeck and in the tangle of rail and wire and cable above the monkey island.

An hour ago, when the ship had been wallowing in great seas—listing badly and refusing for the last time to take a mortal wave, refusing again for the last time, each time seeming to have no strength left to deal with one more wave and yet refusing again, always for the last time—the lookout had come in from the bridge-end, his voice full of wonder.

"She's piping down, sir. She's piping down!"

Captain Harkness had looked at the man. The man was mad or mistaken; his wet face looked exalted as he stared at the captain. But behind him the door was not smashed shut as the ship staggered to the next crest and the wind came, and there was no blizzard of spindrift. Water burst lazily over the fo'c'sle head and fell away to the port scuppers with the angle draining it fast. The door slammed, but only as an angry man would slam it, and not a tempest in a rage.

For a few seconds Harkness did not answer. From the lookout's oilskins water trickled to the deck and ran down the slope, puddling in the corner that was already filled with water that had burst in through the smashed window. Since it had been smashed and then boarded up, water had sprung between the boards whenever a big sea broke at the bows; but none came through there now. The lookout, Mounsey, the tall man with the white grin, stood waiting, watching Harkness. The Skip must say something; something had to be voiced, about this thing that had happened to them all. He must say God had saved them, or must tell him he was wrong, tell him to get out of here before he was kicked out for coming away from his station with this bloody tale.

But he couldn't be wrong. It wasn't only that he had felt the drop of the gale against his crouched body, the sudden astonished relief when the next wave fell short of the bridge and didn't drench him. You could tell it was true: the windows were clear; the noise was less; the ship wasn't plunging into this trough with her head down and her whole length shuddering; she was wallowing into it with her screw still thrusting underwater. But the Skip must say something. Silence couldn't contain this moment. He'd come in here to tell the Skip the gale was piping down, after forty hours, and there'd have to be an answer from someone, from another human voice to comfort his nerves after the loneliness out there on the wing between the black water and the black sky with nothing on his mind but the thought of death.

Harkness said, "Yes."

The deck tilted as the *Whipper* rose to the next wave; it was a smaller wave, pathetic after the others; it could hardly spill itself on to the fo'c'sle head. The screw came out this time, and the shudder came to the wheelhouse. They braced their legs and waited; the ship settled in the rough sea where the waves rose ten feet high and the wind tore the white from their crests: yet in comparison with the storm that had been here minutes ago it seemed they sailed through calm.

The second mate was near Harkness. Mounsey looked at him to see if he were going to say anything. Beggs was standing with his head lowered and his hands held loosely in front of him. Mounsey was embarrassed to see a man as big as the second mate praying. He turned away and opened the door when the ship began sliding into the next trough. Standing on the wing, alone again, he had the feeling of anticlimax, as when the surgeon comes past you in the corridor with his mask off and his hands pulling at the tapes of his gown, saying casually in answer to your frozen half-sick question, 'Oh, yes, she's out of danger now.'

The *Whipper* was still afloat, and the gale was dropping. Why had the Skip said nothing more than 'yes'?

Now the gale was gone. Under a soft breeze the sea had a swell across it, if you could call it a swell after watching the sixty-foot waves that had come at you like mountains in the dark. The men were working at the for'ard hatches, and up on the boat-deck where cables lay twisted and severed. The two lifeboats had been filled, smashed and carried away some little time after two o'clock, and the dreadful sound of their going had brought the passengers from their cabins; there had been a clamour of white-faced questions and one of the women had been crying and saying something about children; but there were no children in the ship. Some of them had asked why nothing could have been done to save the two lifeboats, yet no man in the crew had sworn at them. They were gathered in the smoking-room, most of them at the bar, where Tonio was serving drinks, and the woman who had cried before was crying again because the gale was over.

The passengers could not sit at the stools; and it was difficult to stand. The Sennetts' tattered piece of paper—named recently by Alan Jocelyn as the Longshoreman's List-indicator—now showed the angle of the ship as thirty degrees. Behind the bar, Tonio the Spaniard had stacked his bottles and glasses into corners to secure them; he still trod broken glass whenever he moved his feet. But he was very happy. It was startling to see his face, his smile, to hear him laughing as he spoke. He was the happiest man on board, because in the midst of the terrible storm he had been told by the third mate, who had come down here to look to the passengers, that a ship was coming to help them, that she was already nearer them than any other, and that the name of her brave captain was Manuelo Lopez de las Castillas.

For a long time Major Draycott had been crouched in the chair by the door, watching Tonio as a galley-slave in his chains would watch a sea-bird perched on the prow. Because of the storm and the condition of the ship, Draycott was chained to his fear as his chair was chained to the deck; but Tonio was free. His face was full of smiles. Only a few of his thoughts were in this ship; the rest were in the other, the *Angeles*. Manuelo—it was a good name;

his own grandfather's name was that. He would be seeing his grandfather again; now he knew it. The gale was over and the *Angeles* was close. Soon he would be home; already he could smell the sunshine in this bleak swaying saloon where the passengers had come together for comfort. They were so white-looking and miserable; he was sorry for them; it was a sin to feel as happy as he did.

"I suppose he's been drinking," Paul Sennett had told his wife.

"He doesn't seem drunk, darling."

"I think he's drunk." Sennett had lost his golden colouring and the blaze of the blue eyes had dulled. He had passed the point when he cared whether the others saw that he was afraid or not.

"How do you feel, darling?"

He said, "Splendid. Why shouldn't I? There's nothing on my mind, except the thought that we're all going down."

His mouth had a twist when he spoke like that; she looked away from it. "But the gale's over, Paul. We'll be all right now." She must never be angry with him; not again.

"That's wonderful. It must be reassuring, having two good legs to swim with."

However much he reminded her, she must never be anything but tolerant; she could never atone. "We shan't have to swim," she said.

"Have you had confidential information about that?" He leaned his head forward; even in his fear he tried to talk sense. "The port boats have been washed away. We can't lower the other two, at this angle. When she goes down there'll be only a few bits of timber to hang on to—those of us who don't get sucked under."

She was chilled by his tone; fear gave it vibrance, as if he were only just in control of a passionate conviction. Perhaps he was: the conviction that he was going to die. It might be true. She might have only a few more hours left in which to atone. It wasn't long enough; it was unfair.

"Don't worry, darling. We'll be all right."

He leaned his head back, and did not answer.

Another glass fell from the bar as the ship lurched; but Tonio laughed ruefully and did nothing about it. A shout had sounded from above, from somewhere on deck, as if the noise of the glass had called for comment. A few minutes after, a seaman went at a jog-trot past the open doors. Any sound, any sign of excitement now played on the fears of them all. A ship could go down within a few minutes: if you had never experienced it, you had read about it or been told by someone. You could be trapped below deck without a chance. A final lurch as slack water shifted in the holds, then the plunge. You would have a minute to watch the others who were with you. They would not look pleasant; you would try not to panic when the bulkheads reared and the furniture went smashing against them and the water came in from the blackness outside, bringing the blackness in here.

The lights here had come on half an hour ago; they could flicker out again as they had before. You watched the bulbs, and the faces of the others, and the man running past the doors. Whatever happened you would not panic.

The seaman had climbed the companionway and joined the others who worked on the foredeck, now by the light of the Aldis lamp. There was a great comfort in the light, after the darkness before. The men worked steadily, slinging new timber across number one hatch. High above them Tich Copley came down the mast, monkey-quick and out of breath. Another man followed, looking down so that he should not put his boots on Copley's hands as they plucked at the rungs, one below one below one until he could jump. The two electricians stood by; they looked like dead men, with their eyes hollow in white faces; they had spent too many hours on their task to feel any elation now that it was finished. They had worked through the daylight yesterday, and much of the night; they and the others had rigged a new aerial three times in the last twenty hours and three times it had been torn away from their hands and the masts by the violence of the gale. Two men had been sent below for Persham and Dr. Papasian to deal with; one had been knocked unconscious, the other ripped across the face and shoulders when a taut cable had parted and whipped him with its torn metal end; he had been lucky, they all said, not to be killed or blinded.

When the gale had died they had rigged the aerial for the fourth time, and there was no wind to snatch it away before they could secure it. It was up there now, singing. There was no triumph in them; they wanted to go below and sleep or be sick or get drunk or just sit in the dark with a cigarette. There was no excitement in the knowledge that a signal would go out now, for the first time in twenty-four hours. Much good might it do to send a signal now with the ship lying in the sea like a half-dead fish and her crew sick with strain.

They were sent below and given rum. They went, some of them, into the sick bay to ask how their friends were feeling; but there was no comfort in there; their friends were feeling bad, worse than they were; it didn't console them.

Mr. Bond had come down from the monkey island to the wing of the bridge, and made his way up the thirty-degree slope of the deck in the wheelhouse. Turnbull was with him, his face pinched and bitter and his head throbbing under the bandage: he had worked with the men, driving himself, making them see that he could do it; and some of them had been convinced that he worked like this for the sake of rigging the aerial and saving the ship.

Captain Harkness looked at Bond as he went into the wireless-room. He did not ask if they could now send a signal; Bond would tell him. He must wait, composing the message in his mind.

It was a quarter past three when the call was picked up by the major land-stations, twenty or thirty coastguard lookout huts, the Admiralty, the R.A.F., the *Salvado, Angeles, Brindle,* and close on a hundred and sixty amateur radio-fans tuned in to the distress wavelengths. In the quiet of the night, while surprise was still in men's minds that the gale had abated, the signal had the force of an electric shock.

DE GBAC—'Atlantic Whipper'. DE GBAC—'Atlantic Whipper'.

The quiet of the night had gone. Under the bright lamp-bulbs the operators reached for their message-pads, turning their heads to alert the others in the wireless-rooms, giving a quick word as their fingers touched the dials to strengthen the magic that was coming.

"Whipper!"

"What?"

"She's calling . . ."

DE GBAC—'Atlantic Whipper'—do you receive me?

The Morse picked through static.

"Quick—phone Tremayne."

"You certain?"

On board the *Angeles—"Capitano! Escuche! Escuche! El Wheeper!"*

"No es verdad!"

"Es verdad! Venga—escuche!"

DE GBAC—'Atlantic Whipper'—do you receive me, please?

In the high attics, the cluttered basements, the amateurs sat startled and could not call out to their families who were fast asleep—many of them had been told to go to bed, hours ago, because of school tomorrow or the early train to work. Some were half-asleep, sitting with an eiderdown drawn round them, sitting alone in the dark in defiance of the orders of a family that had never understood this unreasonable preoccupation with wires and valves and dials; but this was the moment, the grand justification. They were in touch with a miracle.

'Whipper'—'Whipper'—'Whipper' to Land's End Radio . . . Do you hear me, please? Over.

At Plymouth, Staff Operations was given a message-form from the Main Wireless Office. H.M.S. *Brindle* had been on the R/T hourly since dark had come, and the message-forms made a little pile on his desk. Now the name was not *Brindle,* but *Whipper.* The operator left his office and hurried to the radio-room.

The owners were informed by land-line. A signal was picked up from the tug *Salvado* to her company. At R.A.F. Redmoor the duty pilot was called to the briefing room; on the tarmac an aircraft was warming-up.

DE GBAC—'Atlantic Whipper'—do you hear me?

Many heard; many answered. At Land's End, Plymouth and Niton the operators were busy trying to clear channels. The ether was jammed for twelve minutes.

At 3.27 a.m. the first clear message was picked up by Land's End. It was the message that before dawn would be recorded in the offices of Watson and Blount, Lloyd's of London and the half-dozen major national newspapers with their headquarters in Fleet Street. This would be served tomorrow with the bacon and eggs. It was not headlines, but it was front page.

'Atlantic Whipper'—'Atlantic Whipper' to Land's End Radio. Approximate position 49.30 north, 10.35 west. Moderate breeze, slight sea. Number one hold filled to coamings, one pump still working. Number two hatch stove-in, pumps operating. Two boats washed away port side. Six hands injured, one badly, but doctor on board. Water in generators now cleared, jury aerial rigged. List to port now thirty degrees and ship down by the head. Will not withstand further heavy seas. Would not be able to lower starboard boats. Need met.-report and new E.T.A. of 'Salvado', please. Over.

Jim Beggs took star sights again as a double check while Bond was receiving from Land's End. Captain Harkness was in the chart-room. On Beggs's reckoning the ship had resisted the northward force of the gale and had even made headway a few miles south, but had drifted eastwards over a hundred miles, with the wind against her higher starboard side.

"Got a call from the *Angeles,* sir."

Harkness straightened up from the chart-table. Bond gave him the message-slip. He had almost forgotten the Spanish steamer; the *Whipper* had been out of touch with land and shipping for twenty-five hours. "So she's still afloat, is she?"

"Bit more than just afloat, sir."

Harkness read the message. *'Angeles' to 'Atlantico Whipper'. I am* 49.20 *north,* 11.10 *west. I am near you. I will see you. Your ship is brave.* The message was signed in full. Harkness looked up at Tony Bond.

"Is it possible?"

Bond said with his quick smile, "It's a strong signal, sir. I'd say they're close."

Harkness bent over the charts again, and said in a moment, "Forty to fifty miles." He looked at Bond again. "If that position's accurate, we were drifting a matter of ten miles north of them during the night."

Bond grinned again with his red-eyed sleepless face.

"Land's End gives the E.T.A. of *Salvado* and *Brindle* as eleven o'clock this morning, with the better speed they can make our new position, now the weather's okay. But the *Angeles* can reach us by eight or nine."

It was a matter for pleased surprise, but Harkness went on looking at Bond as if it were tragic news. His voice was low. "But how did she get through that gale?"

Bond shrugged. "Manuelo Etcetera said he would. I suppose he knew he could do it."

"But it should have sunk her!" He put out a hand as the slight swell moved the ship but he went on looking at Bond. "And he tells us our ship is brave!"

A signal began pipping and Bond turned away to get it. Harkness did not move for a moment. The lamp glared painfully across his eyes. He had reached the stage where a man knows that he is tired, where he feels the stubble on his face without touching it and sees the redness of his eyes without a mirror, the early stage through which he will pass to the much longer period when he will forget he was tired, and no longer think about sleep; but his brain was electrically alert as it considered this news from the *Angeles.* She could not be as near as this. There was a mistake.

Something to do with her radio officer's lack of accurate English, or her navigation officer's reckoning.

He moved suddenly down the sloping planks and went into the wheelhouse. "Mr. Beggs."

"Sir?"

"Your bearing was accurate." His tone didn't lift it to a question, though it was a question.

"I double-checked it, sir." There was no indignation in the second mate's voice.

"Of course." Harkness turned sideways into the wireless-room and said to Bond, "To *Angeles.* Please repeat your position."

"Ay, ay, sir." He moved the dials, thinking, 'Is Thelma asleep now? Did the telegram mean anything to her? Would she be glad if we didn't make it, apart from the sadness of so many dying?' *'Atlantic Whipper'—'Whipper' to 'Angeles', 'Angeles'. Over.*

Harkness went back into the wheelhouse. Turnbull had come up, a clean bandage on his head. Below it his face aroused pity in Harkness.

"Get below, Steve."

"Air's fresher up here, sir."

"It's mutiny."

"Then string me up, sir."

Was there anything of amusement in those hard scared eyes? Harkness looked for it. Triumph, perhaps. What would happen if he made it an order, and sent Turnbull below? He'd go. And would never forgive him. Harkness told him:

"The *Angeles* reports she's close, south'ard of us."

Turnbull said, "She can't be."

"We're asking her to repeat."

"How close, sir?"

"Forty to fifty miles."

"Someone's slipped, then."

"Yes," said Harkness, "I think so." They braced themselves against the windows, watching the play of starlight on the rolling backs of the swell. In a little while Harkness said, "You're weighing up the chances, I imagine."

Turnbull watched the swell. "Of turning about, sir?"

"And running for home."

The slight wave reached the bows, a sinuous rolling of black water that was slowly pewtered by the stars; the ship moved gently; it was an easy movement with nothing of the shock and shudder that the waves had brought when they were hitting her mightily, driven on to her by the gale; but there was in this movement a heaviness, a dullness. Along the port bulwarks the water ran between the rails however slight the waves, because of the dangerous angle at which she lay. The two men felt the heaviness under their feet. The *Whipper* was lolling in the sea. She was no longer sensitive to its movement; she responded only with a slack movement of her own. Until the pumps could draw the free surface water from the two for'ard holds she would lie like this, carrying the extra thousand tons of dangerous cargo as painfully as a great fish about to spawn.

An extra thousand tons would not affect her trim, if it were well stowed and balanced; as it was she had left Buenos Aires with less than full cargo. But this cargo was water, and it was not well stowed. It had burst in through the hatch-covers and now it was free down there to slop about, its huge liquid weight exaggerating every movement she made: if a wave came under her high starboard bow it would lift her and lift the water in her and the water would surge against the port bulkheads and double the force of the wave. With a big wave, raised by even a force-seven wind, she would be in danger of rolling slowly on to her beam ends and staying there. The slack water in her was as dangerous as explosives.

Turnbull could see it, the dark water that surged below as each wave came and touched her lazily; he could feel how dull she was, how heavy. He said:

"It'd be a risk, sir."

"There'll be a risk, whatever we decide on."

In his mind, Harkness could see beyond the water in the holds. It could not all be cleared. Even if the pumps could draw up all the free water that was there, they would leave the grain behind; and the grain had been waterlogged for twenty-four hours; it was swelling, every peck of it, locking the water in; the pumps could not get at it, ever. So that if he decided against the risk of turning the ship about and taking a wave on her side that could roll her over, he must accept the other risk and let her lie here until help reached her. But it must reach her before the weather broke again, before the grain swelled and split her plates open to the inrush of the sea. There was no hope of making an estimate, in terms of hours. You knew how much coal you had and how much you would burn at a given speed; you could not know how fast the grain was swelling, how fast the pumps were drawing the water out, how fast the ship was settling by the head as more water was taken in across the sharp angle of the foredeck and between the cracks of the timber that was battened over the holds. You couldn't know when the wind would come again.

They would rather have stood here with their feet braced against the quicker movement of a stiffer ship, and feel her respond to the sea, than feel this dreadful sloth in her, this wallowing.

"We can last as long as the weather," Turnbull said.

"That won't be long. The met. gives a bad outlook."

"If we could get the passengers off . . ."

"Could we get those boats clear?"

"Starley's tried every trick he knows, sir. For all the good they are, we can say we've no boats."

The ship moved slowly as a swell rolled under her. A soft rush of water ran along the port rails and left a scum in the starlight. Both men automatically judged the height of the swell and its speed and its distance from the next one, and imagined a swell of this height and speed meeting the ship beam-on if she lay with her starboard side exposed as she tried to turn about. Their findings were much the same. If she had been turning about when that wave had reached her she would have been in worse danger than she had been when the storm was at its height. Turn her to starboard, and a wave could surge over the port-side bulwarks and cover the makeshift timbers on the for'ard hatches, and some of it get through. Turn her to port, and a wave could roll against her high starboard side and send her over to lie capsized in the sea.

If a ship reached the *Whipper* before the next wind rose she stood a chance of putting off her passengers and crew before she sank.

In the glass of the window Turnbull's reflected face looked back at him. He thought to Harkness, 'How proud are you now?'

A scuffle sounded behind them and when they turned they saw Bond fetching up against the echo-sounder stand. He grinned quickly, embarrassed. Harkness said to Turnbull:

"You see why you shouldn't be on deck, Steve."

Turnbull's head began throbbing badly as he watched Bond stand upright again on the thirty-degree slope of the planking.

"He wants to learn to walk," he said with his mouth tight.

"*Angeles,* sir," said Bond. "She's confirmed her position." He gave Harkness the slip of paper.

"Then there's no question."

"It isn't natural," said Turnbull.

Harkness stood with the piece of paper in his hand. Less than fifty miles on their port bow must be the Spanish steamer, making for them through the dark. Manuelo had said he was coming with God. Surely he could never have come alone.

"Tony, repeat our position to the *Angeles*. Make quite certain she understands. And say——" what could possibly be put into words? Nothing of what he felt could be attempted in a radio message. "—And say that we shall be delighted for her to join us."

The Spaniard would consider the message stiff and formal, typically English. Well then, he must.

He told the first mate, "If she can hold her speed she should be within sight of us at eight, or not long after."

Turnbull said nothing. Watching the glint of starlight on the black water, watching it through the reflection of his face and the pale bandages, he wanted to lean his head forward two inches, and rest it against the cool glass, and let his eyes close. That was why he stood with his feet braced hard and his head up, well clear of the window. Harkness thought, 'Why don't you give in? I wouldn't think any worse of you.'

Sometimes as they watched the swell they could see a ruffle of wind cross the slow rollers, chipping a fleck of white from their backs; but it was only a little wind. If it grew no bigger they would be here when the *Angeles* broke the horizon. But it might grow; it could grow in much less than four hours. Harkness had been in the North Sea on convoy in a dead calm and the calm had changed to a hundred-mile-an-hour blizzard within ten minutes, with the seas flying across the deck in iced fragments.

The *Whipper* could not take any more. A wind could rise and come for her and find her helpless and send her down and there would be nothing that anyone could do.

He turned his head to the door of the port bridge-end and called, "Lookout!"

Mounsey came in. "Sir?"

"A steamer will rendezvous with us at about eight o'clock. She should appear on the port bow. Be sure to pass it on to your relief."

"Ay, ay, sir."

Harkness turned away and telephoned the fo'c'sle, and then the chief steward. "My shaving things, and a tray of coffee. My compliments to Mr. Costain. Would he report to the bridge."

He moved close to Turnbull, so that they could talk without the helmsman hearing. "Steve, we might have to leave the ship at any time in the next four hours. You'll need your strength then. There's nothing for you to do now. Get below and sleep if you can."

"I might be needed."

"If so, you'll be sent for."

Turnbull would not look at him. His head had begun bumping with anger. Harkness said, "You're released."

The words came with difficulty from so hard a mouth.

"I'd prefer to stay on the bridge, sir."

The ship moved with her dreadful weight as the swell rolled under her; then she lolled easy.

"You are ordered off watch, Mr. Turnbull." He moved away from him to stand by the binnacle. He was checking the compass when the first mate went out and the door shut behind him. Costain came up a minute later. Harkness noticed the boy had shaved.

"Yes, sir?"

"How are things below, Peter?"

"Bit tilted over, but everyone's cheerful, sir."

"How is Dukes?" Dukes was the man who had been ripped by the parting cable.

"The Doc's got him under a drug, sir. He says there's a good chance."

"Does he need any supplies?"

"He didn't ask for anything. He's got a bag with him."

The movement came. They braced their feet. It ceased. They relaxed. "Listen, Peter. If this weather holds, we should have the *Angeles* alongside in four hours. If the sea gets up, we shall be in difficulties. I need Jim Beggs with me up here and I've sent Mr. Turnbull below to get rest. I want you to look after the passengers and also to co-operate with the bosun. He is lashing up life-rafts. Your job is to keep everyone down there in good spirits. If you can get them to match your own, that's all I ask. Some of the passengers are knowledgeable; they'll know the critical condition we are in, so make a great deal of the *Angeles*. She's steaming for us at full speed and is now less than fifty miles away."

The door banged open and a steward came in. Costain grabbed one end of the tray as the man slithered on the steep deck.

The man cursed quietly and then said, "Could do with one leg shorter 'n the other, sir, eh?" The coffee had spilled from the jug, a little of it, enough to make the tray look messy in this messy wheelhouse that Margaret would be disgusted to see, and triumphant. He mustn't hate her. He watched the steward put the tray down, propping it level with a box from the first-aid shelf. When he had gone he said to Costain:

"As soon as you've told the passengers about the *Angeles,* give them routine life-drill."

He felt the ship moved again by the swell. She felt heavy, so heavy. He said, "See they do it well."

CHAPTER FOURTEEN

BEFORE a ship sinks, she seems to die. The life and warmth goes out of her, even though people are still on board. There are draughts everywhere; there is wet, and cold. There is no more comfort in familiar things; at the sight of them there is a taste in the mouth; they seemed so important, before now, so treasured—a handbag, a pair of skin shoes, a favourite pipe, a photograph—but now there is no more comfort in them because you are cut off from the continuing sequence of your life and your place in it is lost. They become symbols, these prized possessions, for the comfortable orderliness that was your link with the world. Now they are not yours, nor anyone's; they are shapes drifting away from you until you stand naked of them; you don't want to touch them again because you know the feel of them will not be the same. You do not expect to touch a dead friend and feel him warm.

With the draughts and the cold there are the noises; and they are different; there is no more comfort in them either. They are unnatural sounds; you would rather not hear them but they go on; they are the sounds of a ship, sinking. There is wet, almost everywhere. Water is dripping from a skylight on to the fragments of glass where the rich carpeting has darkened and has a sheen made by the water; there are puddles gathering in corners; trickles and rivulets creep down the slope of the deck; somewhere there is the bleak drip of a leak in a tin bowl, a deserted sound, the sound of rain soaking into a derelict house from which everyone has gone. Only you are left behind; you go into a cabin or the smoking-room and find people and talk to them, but you know by the sickness inside you that only you have been left behind; these others are strangers, and you never knew them.

The cold is the worst. It is partly the draughts, partly the wet; mostly it is fear. Along with the fear, discomfort. The discomfort confirms the fear in little ways. You feel sweat on you but there's no time to bath; your shoes are damp because you walked through a patch of water in the dark, but there's no time to change them; there is a bruise, possibly a gash—tingling, going septic?—on your leg because you lurched into the table when the floor swung, but there's no time to look at it, and nobody would care; your face has a slight stubble on it that is itching, and your nails feel dirty and teeth furred and eyes sticky but there's no *time*. You won't shave or sleep or clean your teeth again because they are on the list of the last things, a remembered list of a thousand daily actions that won't be made again. Like the treasured possessions, these life-long habits are drifting away, becoming symbols, showing you what you used to be, not what you are: dying.

There is no comfort, and no charity. The seamen have no civility left for passengers—passengers become a dangerous nuisance when a ship is sinking. The passengers have no respect left for a crew that has let this disaster come upon them all.

One constant is left, and that is the authority of the captain. Every man on board will leap to his slightest word. Whether they love him or think he is a bastard or a stupid fool or a gutless pimp they will obey him faithfully; because he is the only one in the ship who can save their skins.

Dodds the steward had said with his head buried in the grease-smelling curtain of the slop-chest scuttle, "We could've got in the boats, the bloody boats, while there was bloody time, instead of this . . . instead of this . . ." His breath trembled as he talked to himself and tightened his muscles to stop his water coming.

Stubbs had told Harris, "If we get out o' this lot, an' there's an enquiry, I'll be there, boy, I'll be there. I'll see this sod of a ship-master don't get himself another ship, nor the soddin' bosun neither. Didn't I tell you? We could've taken to the boats, long before this." Braver than the steward, his fear was turning to anger and revenge as he sat on the bunk in the sick bay, short of blood.

Persham was not listening. He had been silent for a long time, moving busily about, collecting medicines and equipment, putting them into boxes, wrapping them in the green waterproof silk. He worked with devotion. Dr. Papasian had been down here, his eyes strangely bright. "I am told there are two rafts being made. We shall put these people on one of them, and look after them as best we can. I shall need your assistance. You will be in sole charge of them. I cannot be expected to do all this alone. I will come down again as soon as I have collected my things."

Persham worked steadily. He was in charge here. He had been given authority. He worked with devotion—not to Dr. Papasian but to a concept of humanity that he could never have grasped mentally, nor would ever have believed was in him, because of what he had done with the scissors.

"I'll see they scrag that stuck-up sod for this . . ."

Persham did not hear what Stubbs was saying. The patient was light-headed, short of blood. Soon he would be quiet, because Persham had got him to drink some 'water'. Stubbs had looked up at him with steady red eyes. "If this don't do me some good, I'll drown you when we're in the water, son. For what you did to me." He drank the sedative. "An' never swing."

Harris was talking again, but he and Stubbs kept their voices low because of Dukes in the end bunk. That kid had Harkness to thank for what had happened to him. If Dukes died, there'd be something to say at the enquiry. Dukes had signed up under Harkness, had worked in the bosun's team and was now in the care of Persham. Those three had it coming to them if that kid died.

Harris looked up and said to Persham as he passed, "How's the boy-o, Jack?"

Persham did not answer; he was going carefully across the tilting deck with a glass jar. Stubbs told Harris gently, "He won't last, the kid won't." He looked down the tilted length of the sick bay to the hump in the end bunk. Dukes wouldn't have anything of a face left, even if he lived. It'd be worth him going. "He won't last, you'll see if I ain't right."

Harris pressed his hands to his face, bored with Stubbs and the smell in here and the thoughts of drowning. "You don't 'ave to sound so bloody pleased," he said into his hands.

A draught was coming through the sick bay, fluttering at the hanging edges of linen, touching Harris's hands. He shivered to it.

The bosun's mate came in to talk to Persham about the rafts, and moving the sick. He had changed into his number one rig, looking all wrong with his strained unshaven face and sleepless eyes below the neat blue cap; but these were the only clothes he'd get ashore with and they might as well be his best. Many of the seamen had put on their shore-going rig, slipping away from the work to tear the stiff stained trousers off and drag the smart ones on, punching their fists through the sleeves of the jacket and buttoning it with sore fingers clumsy with haste. Going back on deck they did not feel spruce in their creases and shiny buttons; there was none of the shore-leave feeling; the shore was a tidy way off and they might have to swim every mile. But they were practical men and had done a practical thing, and felt a little satisfaction in the midst of their anxieties.

Starley the bosun had not changed; there'd been no time. The two rafts were finished; he wasn't pleased with them; already they looked like wreckage—a trellis of lashed timber with empty drums beneath. They'd float awash when they were loaded.

"Christ alive," he said, "they're rough enough."

"They'll float, Bose. They'll float."

The men stood round him in the light of a deck-cluster. The ropes had ripped their hands and one man was crouched by the companionway, ruptured when his sea-boot had slipped on the planking. His face was bloodless but he talked to the others as if he were resting: "Launch 'em with a bottle o' lemonade, Bose, launch 'em proper!"

"You better get down to the sick bay, Robins."

"Not likely! Look what 'appened to Stubbs!"

"You get down there. You're for a raft, mate—you can't swim with your guts half-out."

A man stood over Robins. "Come on, Rob, I'll give you 'and." Another came, ready to help.

"I don' wanter move. Lea' me alone. I'll move when I got to."

Starley came across to him. Robins had his hands driven hard against his groin. A voice as strong as this shouldn't come from a face so white. "You better leave him, then," said Starley to the others. "Put 'im on the sick-raft when we go. You want a drink o' water, mate?"

"If I see any more water I'll die o' mildew."

The bosun turned away and saw Copley climbing over the tangle of cable below the boat-davits. "Hey, Tich! You find him, did you?"

"Yes, Bose. He's comin'."

The ship moved and all the voices that had been audible a second ago were now silent as the throng of men felt the ship move and waited for her to stop. There was the distant rushing of the pumps and a soft whine of wind in the shrouds, but no other sound from anywhere. The water came quietly up from the sea as the ship wallowed with her port bulwarks leaning lower, lower into the quiet wave that ran through the rail stanchions and the tangle of cable just below where the men stood. They watched it. The sea was coming for them quietly, to play about their feet and swirl among the torn cables it had ripped apart when it had been angry. Now it was languid, reaching along the great hurt body of the ship as if to heal it with a soothing touch. The men knew better. The sea was coming quietly for them, creeping with the blind foul stealth of a fatal disease.

The ship stopped moving and lay for nearly a minute like this, with no strength in her to swing to starboard and send the water away through her wash-ports. She had passed the point where she could steady herself; she lay without dignity, wallowing in the sea. The wind stayed in the shrouds and aerial, a constant whine. One or two of the men looked up, as if they could answer the enemy by looking at it; but the wind was invisible.

The ship swung to starboard now, slowly, as the sea on her starboard beam fell away and let her fall there. She moved with an obedience that sickened the men; she was passive in the sea and it could do what it liked with her.

Starley looked at Copley. "What?"

"He's comin', Bose."

"Comin', is he?" The bosun's anger with the ship must vent itself on anyone, anything near him. "Where is he, eh?"

"Lamp-locker."

"Fetch him. Mac an' Yorky. Fetch him!"

The two big men left the group. They'd no stomach for the mission. Fred Sackett was a stupid bastard, drunk on a sinking ship. Better that he should drown when the lamp-locker filled and know nothing about it than meet the bosun again in this life.

They trod through water in the thwartships alleyway. Potatoes were tumbling down from the door of the galley and then bobbing as they reached the trapped water.

"We'll say we can't find him, Mac."

"The Bose'll tear our giblets out."

"I got no more use for mine, once this lot goes."

They stumbled on the potatoes and cursed the cook and the bosun and Fred Sackett and the wind that had started in the shrouds.

The wind touched the face of the lookout on the bridge-end and he could see it on the water below the steep starboard side of the ship. It was coming from the west; he could feel with his face where it was coming from; sometimes it shifted and he turned his head to keep with it; it would swing from sou'-west through west to nor'-west and then steady, moving about the night-sea with the stealth of a prowling cat, never going away—the cold soft music in the shrouds played a constant note. This wind would not pipe down; it had not awoken for nothing; it was here to try its strength. All this the lookout knew, and felt on his face; he had lived his life with the wind and tonight hoped not to die with it.

Near him in the wheelhouse they knew about the wind. They had watched the white coming to the top of the swell as each swell rolled quietly to meet the ship and move her. Harkness had a phrase in his mind now, all the time, a few words that made a statement and not a plea. *She won't stand any more.* It would be useless to say it to the wind or the dark or the sea or even to God; he said it to himself, to convince himself that what he was going to do would be right.

"Peter."

"Sir?"

"The bosun has the rafts ready?"

"Yes, sir."

A minute passed, while the ship was moved and they stood awkwardly, waiting, holding their nerves in a tight ball. She was so heavy.

"There's rough weather coming," said Harkness slowly. "It'll be here before the *Angeles.*" Costain waited and said nothing. He would see that nothing happened to Ann. It was most important, almost all he thought about; it was dreadful to stand here close to the Skip and keep this secret: that he was thinking more about Ann than about the rest, about the *Whipper.* "I expect you can understand," Harkness said, "how difficult it is to abandon ship before we're forced to—I mean difficult to decide on doing it—like ducking before anyone lifts a hand. But we're going to do that. There's a gale coming, and the ship won't stand any more. In the shape she's in, she could go down very suddenly, and there wouldn't be time——" he turned and looked at Costain. "I'm telling you this because you'll be in charge of the rafts. Mr. Turnbull is sick and he'll be treated as a sick-bay case; I'll need Jim with me up here. You'll get plenty of questions. There won't be any trouble from the hands, of course, but you'll have to satisfy the passengers that we know what we're doing. If you don't, they'll make things difficult for you. Your job is to save life and you won't want any opposition."

Rain came against the windows, softly. They looked at the mottled glass. Rain would make no difference, really; but it wouldn't help to lift depression. "A reminder of home, Peter. You'll have to think of things like that. Down there you'll be a reassurance salesman. We'll all be home soon; meanwhile, salt water's wonderfully antiseptic and has tonic properties, and the fresh air's much healthier than stuffy cabins. Try to keep it cheerful. Actually it won't be so bad. Have you done it before?"

The rain pattered now at the windows but it did not bring a sense of cosiness in here, as it can to a house.

"I've never been in charge before, sir, but I've done a bit of swimming."

Harkness nodded. "I've complete confidence in you. That's all you'll need." He realized he was trying to think of something more to say; it was a weakness, this hesitancy; there was no room for it. "You can start organizing things now. Muster the passengers on the port shelter deck. They can take small personal possessions but no cases or trunks. Give them fifteen minutes in the baggage-room if they want to take anything small from their luggage. You will require absolute obedience, as this is an emergency. The stewards will help you serve out the life-jackets. A few minutes before the order is given to abandon ship I'll come down and have a word with everyone." The rain spattered, driven by the rising gusts. "That's all, Peter."

"Ay, ay, sir."

When Costain left the bridge the brass chronometer in the wheelhouse said eleven minutes to five. Harkness looked at it and realized vaguely that the gap was still too big. The gap had been thirteen hours, estimated by taking the number of hours the coal would last from the number of hours the *Salvado* would take to reach here. Then he had eased speed by one knot, closing the gap to six. The *Angeles* had thrown these simple mathematics aside as soon as the wireless aerial had been rigged and the *Whipper* could be told how near she was. Now the gap had narrowed from six hours to three or four: the *Angeles* was expected here by eight or nine o'clock. There was the unknown factor: how long could the *Whipper* stay on the surface during the storm that was coming? Not four hours, nor three. Two?

Perhaps two. From now until seven o'clock. That left the gap narrowed to one hour. From thirteen down to one. It was still too big. Any gap was too big: even a gap of one second between the going down of the ship and the arrival of help. Help must come before she foundered, if all were still on board.

"It's no go." He said it to Jim Beggs, who had come out of the chart-room. He had to say it to someone. He was still not convinced he was right, for all his mental repetition of *she won't stand any more*.

"What's that, sir?"

He looked at Beggs. Beggs seemed larger than ever, his great hard rock-like face expressionless. You would have said he was witless. Even the eyes were quiet. Harkness thought 'I'm going to miss you.' He said, "I've been working it out. She's got to stay afloat for three hours, perhaps four."

Their spines crept as the sea answered; it was as if he had called to the sea: *Are you going to give us three hours more before you sink us?* The deck was tilting slowly. A wave had flowed strongly against the starboard side and the ship was lolling to port. In the two for'ard holds the free surface water was surging and building against the port bulkheads and helping the sea to drive her over. The inclinometer moved from thirty to thirty-five degrees, to forty, forty-five. It took nearly a full minute. They heard the helmsman say something. A tin box came off the after bulkhead shelves and burst open on the planking. Below the port bridge-end there was water rushing against the base of the superstructure. It had not come so far inboard before. They listened to it. Then the starboard door came open and the lookout was shouting.

"She's going! She's going, sir!"

A flutter of wind came through the open door. Harkness felt it against his neck. His feet were about to slide; he could do nothing to stop them. Beggs put a hand out to the binnacle. He had stopped watching the inclinometer. A few drops of rain came flying through the doorway, spitting against his back. Vibration began as the screw came out. Everything tramped—the planking, door-jambs, window-frames, stanchions. Something smashed in the chart-room.

A faint chorus of voices came on the wind. It sounded like a cheer, just as a moan of pain can sound like a moan of ecstasy. The bosun and his team, trying to save the rafts—or a man had gone overboard or was being crushed as deck-gear shifted. The sound was gone now.

The lookout said quietly, awed, "She's going over, sir."

Harkness had pain in his right hand; he was gripping the window-strap. "Get back to your station, lookout."

They heard him forcing the door upwards; he had almost to climb out of the wheelhouse; then the door slammed. The rain stopped pattering against Beggs's back. When the ship steadied he said, "That's all, sir."

"Yes."

She must start going back now, if she could. Harkness decided to give her one full minute. If she stayed at this angle he would use the whistle for abandon ship. His head was tilted to watch the brass chronometer. The vibration grew worse and then the deck began coming up, easing the strain on their feet. From the narrow puddle of water against the port bulkhead little waves crept, shivering to the vibration and spreading back. The needle of the list-indicator moved from forty-five to forty, to thirty-five; it stayed there. The vibration stopped.

Jim Beggs said, "List increased by five degrees, sir."

Harkness let go of the window-strap. "I've sent Peter to muster the passengers and get them ready for the rafts. Some may prefer to swim in their belts and leave more room for the women and the sick cases. Get down there and help him. I want to have every man off as soon as possible, before the lights go out or she rolls too far. Please hurry."

Beggs nodded. As he went out of the wheelhouse Harkness moved awkwardly against the tilt, reaching the telephones. He rang the engine-room. Brewer answered.

"Chief, you've got another ten minutes down there before we abandon ship. I want you to leave enough steam for the auxiliaries and pumps, after we've finished with engines. Have you got that?"

"Leave ninety pounds, sir. I wish we could stay, though. We're okay down here, dry as a bone."

"You felt that last roll, and there's a gale coming. She won't stand any more——"

"It's a bloody shame. She's only young."

Harkness grew impatient. Did the chief think he liked doing this? "She'll be old before daylight. Just leave me ninety pounds, and when I ring Finished with Engines get your men out to the port shelter deck. Then over the side. You'll be the last to leave."

"That'll be something, then." He swore with the three most apt words he could use about the wind, and the calmness of his voice made the curse sound more vicious than had he shouted it. Then he said, "All right, sir. Understood."

Harkness leaned one shoulder against the bulkhead as a slight sea moved the *Whipper*. "There may not be time to see you, Chief. If not, good luck."

When he had put the telephone back he went down the slope to the wireless-room. Bond had a trickle of blood still oozing from the left side of his face; he had opened his cheek. He saw Harkness looking at the blood and said, "I slipped, sir." He gave the quick smile from habit.

"Wants some plaster on it."

"No, it'll heal all right. We're still in touch, sir, but there's nothing new."

Harkness felt confidence in here. You could be in touch with land, here, and other ships. You felt less sinkable. But it was an illusion. He mustn't go back to weighing the chances; he'd been doing that when the wave had come just now. There weren't any chances left.

"You're finished in here, Tony. We're going. Pick up what you want from your cabin and get along to the port shelter deck."

Bond wiped his bloodied handkerchief carefully along his jaw, below the gash. "I won't be in your way, sir, till you go. We might get a message."

"There isn't any message that would help."

Bond stood in front of him thinking of something to say, something to persuade Harkness to let him stay on for a while. This was the best home he had; there was no one who would feel any pain if it were his last.

"I can't swim," he said with the quick hopeful smile.

"You won't have to. The *Angeles* is coming. You'll float until then." He turned away from Bond. "Report to the shelter deck."

When he left the wireless-room, Bond was shrugging into his reefer. Half a minute later he came through the wheelhouse. "Shall I see you down there, sir?"

Harkness was at the binnacle. "Yes."

There was only one wave, bigger than the rest, before Turnbull came up to the bridge. The wave put the list-indicator down to forty-five degrees; it returned to thirty-five. He had kept his balance by holding on to the binnacle. The quartermaster had spun the wheel, held it and spun it back. There had been an odd intimacy between the two men while they waited, an affinity that three would not have felt. Neither had looked at the other, nor spoken, but they had thought about each other clearly and consciously. They were the last two survivors of a wreck that hadn't happened yet, and they would have to spend the rest of their lives together, the whole of their ten-minute lifetime that was left.

Turnbull must have been outside on the bridge-end or on the companion when the wave had sent the ship listing; he came into the wheelhouse as soon as she had righted. The door swung shut behind him with the force of its own weight. He grabbed the storm-rail before the angle of the deck could take him down at a run.

"I'm all right now, sir."

His eyes were narrow with pain. Harkness climbed the slope from the binnacle. He knew Turnbull would force him to say something that shouldn't be said in front of the helmsman. Did these things matter at a time like this? More, he thought, than normally. "We're leaving her, Steve. You'll be on the sick bay raft."

Turnbull looked past Harkness to the helmsman, to the echo-sounder, the big brass clock, the telephones. Harkness knew he was thinking, 'We can't leave all this.'

"They said orders were to give me a knock-out drop, down there. Was that right, sir?"

Harkness felt impatient, as he had been with Brewer. "Not my orders, no. I expect discipline without resort to drugs." But he couldn't hurt this man more than he must. If the ship had had a face it would be as full of pain as this one. Steve couldn't stand any more. It wasn't only the wound on his head; he was knotted up; he'd been born with a cruel tightening-mechanism inside him and it had been stretching his nerves through the years.

"What do you want to do, Steve? Stay in the ship?"

"You're going to. Why shouldn't I?"

"Who said I was going to?"

"I don't need telling." The way he spoke, he might have hated Matthew.

"I'm not going down with her, Steve. The tradition's not practised any more."

A rattle of rain drove against the windows. Turnbull said: "Whatever you're going to do, you'll want help."

"Yes. But you're not giving me any. There's not much time left and you're wasting it."

Turnbull began breaking. His mouth lost its tightness. No man can plead stiffly. "I don't want to leave her till she goes. I don't want to. Not like a rat."

It was an effort for Harkness to keep himself from wrenching the mate's hand from the storm-rail and pitching him out of the wheelhouse. This was why Turnbull had lost his command of a ship and why he was a bad first officer. He had more to deal with than his situation; there was the twist in him that he must straighten out, as well; and he wasn't big enough for both when they had to be dealt with together.

"Not till she goes, for God's sake." He was unused to pleading and the words wouldn't fit his voice, his voice wouldn't fit his face. Yet he was bitterly sincere. "You can't ask me to do this."

"Listen, Steve. I've sent Jim and young Costain down there to save lives. I don't consider they're rats. I couldn't do this without their help, but I can do it without yours. If you haven't got the guts to obey my orders and co-operate, then you can stay. But not on the bridge." He turned away from him. What had made him concede so much? Pity, he supposed. It didn't make any difference. There were only the two things, the ship and the sea. The sea was coming for the ship. Before it happened, life had to be safeguarded.

The door to the starboard bridge-end slammed. Turnbull had gone. 'But not on the bridge.' Had there been enough pride in him, then, to be pricked by that?

CHAPTER FIFTEEN

Tonio the barman was not smiling any more. He worked deftly, dispensing drinks, and was very civil towards the passengers; but he did not smile any more because they had come to resent it and to show him they resented it. He understood. Their grandfather's name was not Manuelo, and they had no trust at all in their own captain. They were ignorant, but then all passengers were that. It did not matter. Soon the *Angeles* would come. Meanwhile he reaped a little harvest; the passengers did not worry about change when they paid for their drinks; their eyes were haunted by the future.

"Gin."

He poured it with a gesture. He could be generous too. Soon there would only be fish gliding here in the deep sea gloom among the bottles; the beautiful labels would come off because of the water and no one would know what was in them, and the fish would not care.

"That's all right."

"Thank you, sir." He must be careful. He had nearly smiled.

Sennett was in a chair, facing starboard so that he was pressed back into it. He had not spoken for a long time. His wife had left him, and talked to Penny Jocelyn, who was a little drunk. She was alone now, leaning with her back to the curtain on the port side. Dr. Papasian had gone away half an hour ago and had not come back. They said a man had died in the sick bay.

Ann Brown was talking to the Major. They were not drinking. "Said I mustn't exert myself, you see."

"You won't have to. We'll look after you."

But he said that he'd had a premonition of this, before he had come on board.

Sennett was sitting and looking with hatred at his wife, who still leaned with her back to the curtain, alone. The two young Mexican boys who had boarded the ship at Buenos Aires were nowhere to be seen; but then they had not been seen very often, except at meal-times. They were conspirators of some kind, people said.

"Even climbing a couple of stairs is an exertion, you see."

"We'll lift you." 'Lift' sounded better, somehow, than 'carry'. You lifted a child, carried the dead.

Jocelyn was also a little drunk, but he and his wife were quiet about it; it was obviously no new sensation and they were neither boastful nor obtrusive.

"He looks as though he hates the sight of her."

"He probably does," she said.

"Are you cold?"

"Yes. Alcohol lowers the temperature."

"I'll get you something else to put on."

"No." She touched his hand. She didn't want him to leave her. They mustn't be separated if anything happened. "I've been talking to her, Pooch."

"Moira?"

"M'm." Her glass was empty again but she didn't want any more. This was exactly the right state to be in. Paul should have got himself exactly like this, but they'd tried to make him drink with them and it was no good. "You know you said you believe she's penitent, not just sorry for him?"

He looked into his glass. How many more gins to the end of his life? Two? A thousand? There was always the last drink, the last cigarette, the last shave; very often you didn't know you should be savouring the taste, the smoke, the tingle, at this of all times, the last; but if you knew, the taste would turn in your month and the smoke choke you and the blade cut your face. But how many more gins for him? Should he be savouring this one?

"What?" he said.

"Never mind, Pooch. You just dream."

With slow amiable impatience he said, "What were you saying? Something about someone being penitent. Who?"

"Oh God! Moira Sennett. Skip it. Another drinkie?"

"Listen. What about her?"

"You look like an owl when you're cut. What do I look like when I am?"

Working it out carefully as he went along he said, "I'm not cut enough to not to want to know what you're talking about." He ended rather triumphantly, and beamed.

"Was that in Morse?"

"So I'm listening."

"Is it really going to be worth it, Pooch?" She looked past him, to Paul Sennett. "With a face like his I suppose any man would have trouble with women. Anyway, she said she drove a car at him."

Alan swung his head instinctively to look at Sennett, but caught it in time and gazed at the Major, who was talking to Ann. "Christ!"

"He was in the back of their garage and they'd had a pretty bad row again about his women. This was after they were married. She'd had some drinks because of being so bloody miserable and apparently it turned to anger. He'd blamed her for scratching the wing of the car or something, and that was the last straw. She didn't even do it just to frighten him."

After a moment he said, "She must've been very rocky."

"Living with a face like that and not having it to yourself exclusively would probably send you round the bend about it after a time."

"Poor little bitch."

She looked at him as if at a revelation. "I still don't ever know what you're going to say."

He frowned heavily, his gestures exaggerated. "Aren't you sorry for her, then?"

"I suppose so."

He moved his head again. Moira Sennett had gone away from the curtain; she was sitting in a chair beside Paul, talking to him. He was not looking at her. There was no sign that he was listening. Alan thought she was rather lovely, the long pale face and wistful smile. The man had been lucky, to get off with a hand and a leg. There was no need for her to be a slave for the rest of her life—worse than a slave, a penitent.

"What a perfectly revolting set-up."

Penny said, "I believe he rather flung them in her face. The women."

"What made her tell you?"

"She didn't. I just gathered——"

"No, I mean the whole thing."

"I think she wanted someone to hear it, in case anything happens."

"D'you still want to sleep with him?"

"You still want to sleep with her?"

Ann Brown had stood up and was looking at someone coming in. Costain, and a steward. He looked very white, coming awkwardly across the tilting floor, stopping, wondering which one to speak to first. Major Draycott was nearest.

". . . Anything in your luggage . . . nothing big though . . ."

"What?" Alan said.

"We'd better go and listen."

"Every passenger will have two seamen with him," Beggs said. They stood like dummies in their life-jackets. The low wind moved Moira Sennett's hair. The rain was not reaching them here on the shelter deck but they could hear it hissing into the sea. The water ran by in the lights with a ruffle of white foam breaking where the rail-stanchions stuck up. They could smell it.

Jim Beggs looked enormous, standing with his back to the sea and the dark. They had heard him laughing a few minutes ago, a great-chested laugh very unlike his squeak of a voice. A seaman, a tiny man with a brooding face, had gone past the end of the shelter deck with an enormous sombrero on his head. Everyone was going to take something over the side with him: small presents for wives, children, sisters; small possessions they would never part with; packets of waterproof-wrapped cigarettes, cigars; a small flat box fastened to a man's groin with sticky tape because you could get ten years for this much heroin; and the tiny man with the brooding face was taking this with him, perhaps for his wife, this enormous sombrero. Hearing the second mate's laughter he cast him a dark indignant look, which made him funnier still. He had gone bobbing off like a busy candle-extinguisher.

What could be wrong with the barman and the second officer? Their laughter had been heard in this ship during the last hour. What sort of people were they that could laugh in a sinking ship?

They resented Beggs's laughter; yet there was undeniable comfort in it.

"Your life-jackets," he said to them, "will keep you afloat indefinitely. In actual fact you'll be in the water less than sixty minutes. The *Angeles* will be making for us not long after dawn."

They looked beyond him. There was no light in the sky. Dawn might have been hours away. Something would have to happen. A radio message would reach the ship and they would all be saved.

If only the second officer would laugh again; but he did not laugh.

A steward checked Mr. Sennett's tapes, making sure they were not too tight.

A few minutes ago in the confusion of people coming on to the shelter deck Peter Costain had spoken to Ann. He found she was not afraid. But she should be afraid. He didn't understand her. "I'll look after you, Ann."

"You'll have a lot to do. I'm going to look after the Major."

"He'll be on the sick-raft. I've fixed it. Ann, you'll be all right."

"Of course." The wind raced round the superstructure and cuffed their faces; drops of rain were torn from the paintwork and came flying on the gust.

"I want to marry you, Ann."

Men shouted, for'ard. Something splashed into the sea, a line of some kind. She turned her head back to look up at him. "Oh, my darling . . . no."

She mustn't laugh at his dear frowning face; he would be more hurt by that than by her answer. But he looked so very intense. He could think of nothing to say. She said, "Do you always propose on a sinking ship? It's like you. To hell with the weather, you've your own splendid directions." She felt a laugh coming, because she was a nearing-middle-aged teacher of deaf children who lived in a high mousey box among the chimney-smoke, and he was a ship's officer with all the world in his arms, and to stop the laugh coming she buried her brow against him and held on to him tightly.

"Ann. I love you. I've never wanted to marry anyone before. I'll give up the sea. If that's worrying you, I'll do it."

"This is a shipboard romance, Peter." Her voice was muffled, her face pressed against him. Past his rough sleeve in near focus she could see the dark water go rushing by.

"It's not. I've had them." There was no time to choose roundabout words. "Give me a reason. You don't love me?"

"Yes, I love you."

"Then . . ."

There was so little time. If she didn't convince him now, he would want to meet her in England. The dark water turned white as foam swept against the rail-stanchions.

"I'm married," she said.

"You can't be."

"I call myself Miss Brown because—I suppose I want to forget I'm married. But it doesn't change anything."

"Why did you leave him?"

"He left me."

"He must have been mad."

"You must help the others," she said.

Two seamen went clumping past towards the doors. Peter felt a slow fever mounting. There was no time to do anything now. But she had to promise.

"We'll talk about it later," he said. "I've got your address."

"Don't come there; it's a dreary place."

"I'll write and we'll meet. Promise."

Someone was near them; they sensed it. He turned his head. Major Draycott was making his way towards them over the tilted planking, one stiff white hand sliding along the rail.

"Ann. Meet me. Promise."

"There's nothing to talk about, darling." She moved away from him. She was chilled, now. It would be dreadful if they were to meet again, in cold blood, because they had said they would.

"*Promise.*"

The Major was saying something to her. For a moment she couldn't look away from Peter. It would be so easy to get this business off his mind and let him help the others.

"They've told me I must get on a raft." Draycott was appealing to her, oblivious of Costain. She had said she would look after him, and now he was lost.

"I'm coming, Major." She tried to turn towards him but Peter put his arm across; she heard his hand smack flat against the buttress beside her.

"*Promise.*" She was shocked by his urgency.

"I'll meet you again," she said. The chill rose in her body. Draycott was saying something again.

Peter said quite calmly, "It'll be all right. Nothing more than a wetting. We've got everything organized." He turned and looked at Draycott; he looked dead. He looked lost, and deserted. Costain felt a sudden anger against old people who clung on, who expected the whole world to rally to them because they had grown too feeble and selfish to help themselves.

He took the Major's arm. "You're on the sick-raft, sir. I'll show you where. Every modern comfort—you should see what they've rigged up."

Draycott walked between them for two or three paces along the dangerous slope and then shook them off with sudden impatience. "I only want to know where to go. I'm not injured. I don't want to go on the sick-raft."

They stopped. He looked less dead, less deserted. But there was no time to let him remember he was a soldier. The performance would take too long and be unbearable to watch.

"That's all right, Major. There's plenty of room, and you can help look after the others." *I'll look after you, Ann. I'm going to look after the Major. You can help look after the others.* But there wouldn't be much they could do, except look after themselves. There was a gale rising and the sea was deep, and sometimes a woman floated upright, trapped in the silent passages of the tomb on the sands, gliding from the lounge to the smoking room on a gentle current, upright because of the air in her breasts, seeming alive because of her hair moving behind her.

"Williams!"

"Sir?"

"Help the Major. Sick-raft."

They picked their way among ropes. *These are my best green shoes.*

"My doctor says I mustn't exert myself, you see."

"Ann, I'll be back."

"Yes."

"You two, this lady's in your charge."

"Ay, ay, sir."

The water rose along the bulwarks and sent a smother of foam that was carried away in a dirty froth by a gust of wind that had gathered along the foredeck. There was the smell of seaweed, the childhood seaside smell. The bosun was clambering over one of the rafts—"Mac! *Mac!* Douse him with water. Get him sober!"

The long boxes in their row along the shelter deck were all empty now. There was no one without a life-jacket on. A man was moaning, sitting on the rough timbers of the sick-raft. Persham was with him. "You're okay, mate. We got you."

"I'm bad."

"We'll have you in bed, soon as we land. I'm going to look after you, see?"

Mac and Yorky held Fred Sackett by his legs and pushed his head into the next long roll of water as it came rushing over the bulwarks. "Poor bleeder. 'E'll be drinkin' quite enough o' this without our 'elp."

"Get that bastard sober!"

The rain hissed into the sea.

Persham held his patient. "You'll be okay, mate." He was in authority. He could heal a hundred men like this. Beside him someone was laughing, head on his knees. "You know something, Jack? I've bequeathed my body to a hospital. Couple of years back."

"Easy, mate. Don't worry about anythin'."

With the persistent obstinacy of the light-headed the voice went on. "How're they going to find the thing, twenty fathoms down?"

"That's enough—he'll do!"

Mac and Yorky pulled Fred Sackett up the slope of the deck. He was shouting at them, cold sober and full of rage. They let him roll over and sick up the salt water, doubled on his knees.

Robins kept his head down, nursing the big pain in his groin. Persham had fixed him a truss, but he couldn't move. Christ, if anyone tripped and fell on him, what would he do?

"You feelin' easier, Rob?"

"Yep. Easier." The breath hissed through his teeth.

"A-way raft!"

Turnbull was on deck. Bloody Turnbull. They said he'd died in the sick bay. Wishful thinking. They must have meant Dukes.

There was a scream of timber as men moved, heaving. A line snaked across the planking and nobody picked it up.

"And again—*heave*!"

If they move me, I'm done.

A tin drum came away from the spars, wrenched free as the raft went up and was steadied and then was let fall. It caught and hung half in the water.

"Clear that line, some o' you!"

The deck-lights flickered and they were silent; the lights came on again. A man stood waist-deep in foam, hacking at the fouled line and parting it.

The rain hissed into the sea.

The second officer reported to the bridge and said the rafts were over the side and waiting. The passengers and the sick were in good care. Emergency equipment had been stowed.

Dukes?

Dr. Papasian was with him and would stay with him.

Where was the first mate?

On deck, in charge.

The helmsman listened. *Let's get off this ship. Just let's get off this bloody ship before she goes.*

His legs ached, keeping him balanced on the thirty-degree tilt of the platform.

All hands to be mustered excepting the engine-room. Get all away. And good luck.

At a few minutes after six o'clock Captain Harkness telephoned the chief engineer and asked him to keep his men on duty, ignoring the signal to abandon ship. A minute later the whistle sounded a series of quick short blasts and the sound flew away in the wind above the heads of the people who were clustered together on the port decks.

The last order to the wing lookout had been to hoist the daysign from the foremast: Vessel not Under Command. In the rain-haze that was turned a pale gold by the deck-clusters below, Harkness could see the daysign. In an hour, when daylight came, its message would be correct, if the ship were still on the sea.

He had been down to the shelter deck and talked to the passengers and crew. He had not stayed long, nor been consoled by the signs of first-class seamanlike organization that were obvious to him. He did not believe he had let them suspect his humiliation. He did not apologize. There was nothing to be anxious about. They were in good hands. The rescue ship was due in these waters in sixty minutes.

They were in the water now, drifting astern of the ship. He had seen the dark shapes from the bridge-end. The *Angeles* would not be over the horizon yet, but every chance must be taken of guiding help towards the rafts and the swimming men. He sent up three Schermuly rockets from the starboard wing of the bridge, and for a few moments watched their red diffusion staining the scum of cloud. Then he came back into the wheelhouse and telephoned the engine-room.

It was warm down here among the machinery. The wind was hardly audible and the sea was out of sight. The beat of the

Kincairds was steady. If they beat on, all would be well; when they stopped, all lost.

But there was no comfort in this sinking ship, even down here where it was warm. This place was a trap. You were in the bowels, here, already below the waterline. When she went down, filling and blowing, you would go down with her because there wouldn't be time to get up the ladders. You'd try, and that would make it worse. You were out of the wind and the cold, and the sight of the sea, but you were nearer the deep than the others, and you knew it. The place was a trap.

Water slopped below the metal walkways; you could hear it. She would turn on her side like a great dying fish and the sea would come in up there through the smashed skylight and the stove-in doors, solid water, black, filling this place and killing you slowly, giving you time to see it coming, time to shout and try to get clear of the deluge, knocked spinning and then up again drenched, frightened (*mother, mother!*) and the black water icy, freezing after the close air in here, and the air blowing out, escaping while you were cut off and had to fight your way to the metal rungs and climb through the downrush of the water until its cold dark weight tore your hands away and you went down with it! and if your back broke across the metal rails it would be merciful.

The whistle was piping, faint and urgent.

"That's for abandon, sir!"

"We're to hang on," said Brewer.

A bewildered face, oily, shining under the naked lamps. "Hang on, is it? For why? That's for abandon!"

"Rats first, then the Taffies. Aren't you proud to be in the Merchant Service?"

János came walking like a big bear along the rails, swinging against them to keep upright. "Ninety," he said. Brewer looked up at the gauges, and went to the telephone.

The water slopped below the metal walkways. A steam-valve whispered, high up the bulkhead in the gloom. The gauges were steady. The pumps were still cut in and the diesel hummed; but the Kincairds were silent. The men had gone. The telegraph stood at Finished with Engines.

In the lounge the main lights were out. Behind the bar a bottle rolled, hitting the leg of the stool and rolling back, hitting the leg again until it turned in line with the tilt and rolled to the other end of the bar and struck and broke. Along the passages the pilot-lamps glowed, shining against water that had gathered along the wainscoting; it rippled back and forth to the rhythm of the ship. A cabin door hung open; inside, a small lamp was overturned; its shade lay on the carpet; the heavy base was still suspended by the wire flex, and swung to the bulkhead and back, and swung again, tapping at the woodwork.

A box of pills was scattered in the passage; one of them that had rolled into a puddle of water had begun dissolving, to leave a powder-scum on the surface. A woman's glove lay at the intersection of two passages, fingers curled upwards. The door of the little library was open. Three books had come off a shelf and had fetched up fanwise. A deadlight banged on the ship's side as the water reached it. The sound echoed along the passage where the potatoes had rolled from the galley. They were now collected in the lowest corner, and jostled together; the water lapped at them.

Soon after the engine-room crew had been ordered over the side the helmsman was sent down from the bridge. He had been the last man to leave.

Not long before dawn a signal was picked up from the *Atlantic Whipper*.

Have abandoned ship, except master.

CHAPTER SIXTEEN

THERE was the smell of antiseptics but the room did not sway. There was no sound of the wind or the sea. Grey light came in at a window and outlined the high white ceiling. He knew what this place was. He'd been in one before, at Greenwich.

"Where's this place?"

A pulse began beating through his head until he could feel it throbbing on the pillow. The same smell and the same silence.

"Where's this place?"

The same kind of voice, motherly, admonishing. "You mustn't shout." Footsteps. They always wore thick ugly rubber heels and had strong capable bodies and smelt like everything else in these places.

His head rocked on the pillow so that the room seemed to be swaying. But there was no sound of the wind or the sea.

"Where's this place?"

"Plymouth." A cool hand.

"Hospital, eh?"

"Yes. How d'you feel, Mr. Turnbull?"

"What day?"

"Friday."

He tried to think back, but couldn't. "Where's Captain Harkness?"

"Still out there."

He closed his eyes. He couldn't stand motherly faces. He had to meet everything in life alone, and these people could just keep out of it.

"Now don't talk, and don't worry. I'm going to get you a drink."

"Out where, for Christ's sake?"

"You mustn't shout."

"Out where, then?"

"On the ship."

"What ship?"

"Yours. The *Atlantic Whipper*."

"He can't be. What day is it?"

"I've told you. Friday."

"When did I come into this place?"

"Yesterday." The pillow rocked. The bed rocked. He opened his eyes. A motherly face.

"When did she go down?" he asked through a tight mouth.

"Now you mustn't talk——"

"Listen to me. If you work in a seaman's hospital you ought to know what seamen are like. I want to know when my bloody ship went down."

The quiet voice went stiff. "The *Atlantic Whipper* is still afloat and Captain Harkness is on board her."

"She can't be. He can't be."

"Now please stop talking. You'll disturb the others."

He found the cool hand and gripped it hard. "Still afloat, is she? When did you hear that one?"

"You'll be in trouble if you don't behave." A mother's word, 'behave'.

"Who told you?" He had to shut his eyes again to stop everything rocking; but now the dark rocked.

"It's in the papers. They've taken the ship in tow."

The dark rocked and his nerves felt the water clamping his body. He was going down again, rising again as his numbed hand gripped the line that was lashed round the edge of the timbers.

Someone on the raft was crying out; a woman; they could never be quiet, women. He was going down again, rising again with his cold hand like a hook. If he loosened it he'd go down and not rise again. Someone was prising his fingers open gently. He gripped harder.

"Don't worry. I'll get you a drink."

He gripped harder but his hand was too weak. The water rose over his head again and he clamped his mouth shut. His hand was forced open and he went down, and down.

The newspaper was on his knees. He had read it three times, just the report about the ship; and the news was stale. He would telephone again, in an hour, if he could keep his patience that long.

Thelma said, "Does it hurt?"

"No." She had brought more coffee for him. He looked up at her. She wasn't much like the photograph. "You look prettier," he said.

She turned away. His face felt stiff. He could feel the opened cheek healing, as if a benign current of electricity were flowing into it. He remembered hearing Peter saying to a passenger, 'Salt water's got wonderful tonic properties, you know.' Had he said 'tonic' or 'antiseptic'? It didn't matter. Thelma said:

"This is the kind of time when——"

He read it again, TUG REACHES CRIPPLED SHIP. He looked up and said, "What?"

"I don't feel very pretty, that's all." She was standing with her back to him.

He must be still rather light-headed, because he was saying things that would normally remain well battened down.

"When I came up the road, I had a job not to turn back and just disappear." There were raindrops on the window, and her hair looked as if it were surrounded by stars. "I was pretty certain you'd been hoping I'd be lost." But there had to be kindness even in cold truth. "Maybe not actually hoping—I mean just neutral about it. If I went down with her, it wouldn't be your fault. I mean you wouldn't have been exactly sorry."

Her shoulders were shaking, and her head went lower. She was holding her hands up to it. He wished she'd turn round.

"Are you crying, Thel?"

How many years since he had called her Thel? She wasn't making any noise about it. That was like her. He felt perfectly unemotional, saying, "Cheer up. This is just a bit of sick-leave.

nothing permanent. You'll hardly know I'm here, and as soon——"

"*Stop it!*" She swung round. Her dark hair span against the raindrops. They stared at each other. The cup of coffee tilted on the arm of the chair and slopped into the saucer. He saved it, and looked up at her again. She said, "That was an appalling thing to think." She really looked appalled, with wide scared eyes. With the force of an accusation she said, "I *want* to know you're here. I *want* you here."

She wasn't lying, he knew that. She was just conscience-stricken. "Thelma——" because 'Thel' had just slipped out, and mustn't be used again—"I don't regard myself as a shipwrecked sailor. It all went very smoothly, thanks to the Skip. Don't think it makes any difference. I shan't trade on it, and I don't expect you to treat me as—well, someone you nearly lost. I suppose it reminds one of the good points in people, when you nearly lose them; but it doesn't last long."

He felt bleak and a little sick. There wasn't any 'nearly' about it. He was going to lose her, soon. He shouldn't have come home at all.

Very quietly she said, "I'm not sorry for you because you've been through a bad time." She denied herself the relief of looking away from him as she cut the matter to the bone. "I didn't hope you'd be drowned. I didn't hope you wouldn't come back. But I spent a lot of time thinking about it—about losing you."

When he could say it steadily he said, "Any conclusions?"

"No." It was a relief for both of them to speak the perfect truth; the only difficulty was in knowing what it was. "But when I saw you, I was glad."

He stirred the film on the top of his coffee, and drank some. There was no sugar in it. "Glad I was alive," he nodded carefully.

"Glad you'd come home." It was odd, she thought, that one of the nicest things about him was that he didn't use hair-oil. "Jean Stapleton rang up, quite a lot—I mean after we knew what was happening to the ship. I don't think I've loathed anyone's voice so much in my life."

"You wanted to think things out, by yourself."

"Yes."

And suddenly the whole subject appeared to be closed, as if they'd reached some agreement. He knew agreement wasn't the right word. Understanding. He said, "I'm going to phone them again."

He finished the cup of cold unsweetened coffee. She must have been watching his face very closely, because she asked, "Was that horrid, Tony?"

"Was what?"

"The coffee."

"It was all right. I was only worried it might come out again through the hole in my cheek." Whenever he tried to give his quick smile it turned into a wince.

"I'll make some more," she said, and took the cup from the arm of the chair.

"Not unless you want some yourself, Thel."

"Yes, I do."

"You did very well, boy."

They stood at the bottom of the steps. Light rain came down from a thin mean sky. They breathed the air in deeply.

"I don't do anything very well," Copley said.

"Where d'you get that idea?" The bosun had his blue mackintosh on, and looked smart, a smart seaman on leave. There was no sign about him that he had just come off a sinking ship, or out of a hospital ward.

"I'm too bloody small," said Copley.

Starley looked down at him. "Napoleon never thought 'e was too bloody small."

"An' look where he finished up."

"Listen, Tich. You can't expect to paddle about in a bad sea savin' everyone's life as if you'd been trained for it. We all got to do what we can, and leave the rest to someone else."

"You did all right, anyway."

"I was lucky."

"You'll get yourself a medal, Bose."

The rain pattered about them. An ambulance came in and turned; the rear doors swung open. Absently the bosun said, "Nurses don't get prettier, y' know. It must be somethin' to do with the food. Listen, the last time I fell in the water they gave me the M.B.E. I s'ppose it's all right—you got an excuse for a bit of a piss-up at 'ome, an'——"

"They gave you the what?" Copley stood stiffly in his new brown gloves, his face awed.

"But where's it get you, boy? What's it for, eh? It makes your kids proud but they cheek you jus' the same an' you can never find any empty bloody chair to sit in. It doesn't get you extra money—but who wants extra money for savin' somebody's life? How would they ever work it out? Tanner for a tich your size an' a couple o' quid for a big 'un?"

He hit Copley in the stomach and nearly doubled him up. "Come on, I'm goin' to stand you a drink. You did very well—a sight better'n some other blokes bigger'n you are."

They watched a stretcher come out of the hospital into the ambulance. When the doors had closed, Starley said, "Anyhow, we all got through it, even Phil Dukes. That was a marvel, that was." They began walking down the short driveway to the road where the buses went past. Puddles were gathering. "You live in London, don't you, Tich?"

"Yes." The M.B.E. What did it feel like?

"You goin' home, then?"

"Not till they get the Skip off."

"You stayin' at the Mission, then?"

"Yes."

"So'm I."

They hesitated at the bus-stop, then walked on. The rain became steady, and the sweet fresh smell rose from the pavement. They walked for quite a time in silence like two old friends, content with each other's company.

"You think the *Whipper*'ll get in, Bose?"

A girl looked at them, hurrying past through the rain.

"If anyone can bring her in, the Skip can." He turned his head, and gave Tich Copley a nudge that nearly knocked him over. "Wouldn't mind a day at the races with that one, eh?"

Copley stepped right into a puddle and felt the water trickling down his ankle into his shoe. "What races?" he said.

"And how long were you in the water, Major Draycott?"

"About an hour, I think."

"It must have been a terrible experience."

The pencil waited. The bored young head was tilted. The curtains had a smell in this place, of old age and comfort and stale cigar smoke. Mrs. Draycott sat opposite. There were some muffins on the little table but the young man had shaken his head.

"Yes, I suppose it was."

"You must be feeling very relieved——" he turned his head automatically—"and you, Mrs. Draycott. Sometimes it's even worse, waiting for news."

She had a dry hard voice that seemed to call down a voice-pipe to a servant in the basement. "We're sueing the company, of course."

The young man's pencil did not move.

"'They speak highly of the captain," he said, and waited. Major Draycott gazed abstractedly at the muffins. Their butter had melted and run on to the plate and hardened. Where had he seen that girl, Mrs. Jocelyn, before? Or someone like her. It had been years ago, when he was a young man, so it must have been someone who looked like her. India? Ireland? The same rather mischievous eyes.

"If the captain could remain on board," said Mrs. Draycott, "I don't really see why the passengers had to suffer the severe ordeal they were subjected to. After all, the ship is now being towed in quite safely. We shall expect to be granted appropriate compensation."

Draycott was looking at her. She was attempting her social smile on the young reporter, quite certain he was in agreement with her point of view. He had a rather well shaped head and looked intelligent.

"I see," the young man said. He put his pencil away and folded the notebook.

She arranged her fur wrap. "You must have some more tea." Business over, her tone was arch. The young man thought, 'She must have talked like this on the croquet lawns, hundreds of years ago.' He must get away from the smell of these curtains.

"I wish I had time, Mrs. Draycott, but thanks just the same."

She folded her long pale hands. "Well, I'm very disappointed in you," she said.

Watching her, Major Draycott saw the faded vestige of mischief light her eyes as she studied the young man. He had only just realized how long a lifetime could be.

The reporter stood up, buttoning his coat. Draycott was still watching his wife. Not Ireland, but India. The Mountridge Club. Christmas Eve. Out of the dusk, the soft blue mischievous eyes and then the dance.

She held up a long white hand. "We shall be here for a few days, until my husband feels fit again." She left it as a vague invitation.

Sennett held his left leg in front of him. His voice was crisp, his face fresh. The young man was made to be interested in the story by the sheer conciseness of its delivery. He wrote in shorthand, sitting forward on the edge of the chair.

"The whole manœuvre had the stamp of a military exercise. I had the impression of being in the hands of experts, and so my wife and I were never at any time seriously worried. The captain and crew inspired enormous confidence in us by the way they went about their work."

She stood sideways to the bar, watching him and the young reporter in turn. 'Save me, save me,' he had cried out to her when the raft had pitched them into the narrow waters between it and the side of the *Angeles*. 'I can't swim, you know I can't swim.' His hand had felt like a claw on her wrist and she had been afraid he would panic finally, and drag her down. The raft had smashed against the side of the steamer and there had been a moment when she knew she was going to die. 'Save me,' he had called, and she remembered how his face had looked.

". . . The bosun, I believe. Some of the others must have seen him do it. I don't know how many of us owe our lives to him, but the others might be able to give you a clearer picture. He behaved magnificently."

His face had looked two-dimensional against the background of the terrible wave, a white cut-out mask staring at her, choking; yet he was floating well enough.

". . . Although I can't vouch for that personally. My wife's not a very strong swimmer and I didn't have much chance of helping anyone else."

The pencil stopped. The young man said, "You don't feel there was any negligence, then, of any sort? One or two words have been dropped, on that subject."

Sennett appeared to consider it very carefully. The pencil waited. The girl took up her drink and lifted it. "I imagine there'll be an enquiry. If I'm asked to give evidence I shall say that both my wife and I are proud to have been present in a crisis where heroism, discipline and devotion to duty were the paramount features." He looked at the girl. "I can speak for both of us, can't I?"

She looked at the reporter, amused by something. "Yes."

The young man wrote and then put away his things and buttoned his coat. "You er—you were handicapped, Mr. Sennett, in the water. You did pretty well. The war, was it?"

The clean-cut golden head was bowed an inch: he studied the

fingers of his gloved hand. It was Moira who spoke, very lightly and with nothing of the sad lilt in her voice.

"No, a woman did that to him. In the past they used to scratch, but these days they're tougher." She finished her drink and gave the reporter a quick smile. He was looking as if he had stepped on a rake.

"I've got no complaints."

"But you said you'd put the skids under 'im."

"That was a while ago."

Harris shrugged. "I'm easy."

They lit up another cigarette. "What changed your mind, then?"

Stubbs said, "Nothing. I'm glad to get out of it alive, that's all. An' I'm not signing on again, not even in the *Queens*."

Harris grinned. The cigarette-paper stuck to his top lip and he pulled it away. "You think they'd have you in the *Queens*?"

"All I'm sayin' is they can stuff the sea. I'm done with it."

The rain tapped at the windows of the rest-room. Someone was making tea behind the hatchway, clattering about. Harris got up and flexed his shoulders. "Well, Stubby, look after yerself."

"I'll do that, all right."

Harris grinned again. He stuck his hands into the pockets of his mackintosh. "We'll meet again, in the sweet bye an' bye."

"I tell you I'm done with it."

"That's right, Stubby." He went to the doors and pushed the bar. "That's what they all say."

The doors clattered shut.

On the telephone Jocelyn said, "You can knock it into shape later. No one panicked. Who? No. There's something in the book about that—wait a minute. If a master is in difficulty and reasonable apprehension, his first task is to safeguard life. You'd better check on the exact wording. It's a good bit to put in, because Harkness certainly did just that. We had several sick-cases and one old boy with a dicky heart, and the lot came through. No, I'm sticking here till they bring in the *Whipper*. You got my number? Leave a message if I'm out."

When he came back into the hotel lounge, Penny was waiting for him. She had bought a pair of slacks and a duffle-jacket yesterday; the clothes she had worn in the sea were finished.

"You look rather delightful," he said.

She dug her hands into the duffle-coat pockets. "I've just met a man who told me I looked *very* delightful." She still had the feeling that this was a holiday, a planned one, not the miserable tag-end of a sea-trip. The new clothes, perhaps, and a strange hotel in a town she had never expected to be in. And there was the blessing of still being here, being anywhere. "How's Barney?" she asked.

"Quite excited. We're front-page news. I've also been down to a local editor here and offered him my exclusive story." He beamed smugly. She asked:

"How much?"

"Well, I suggested a couple of thousand but he said his paper was very poor, and he only ran it because Plymouth was a place that deserved a newspaper like the *Argus*, and, after all, this was a heroic story and Plymouth had historic associations with the sea—he reminded me about Drake—and he was quite sure I wouldn't want to make profit from a story that was shining with the highest examples of——"

"How much?"

"A tenner."

"Well, it'll pay the bill here."

They found themselves drifting towards the bar. When they were perched on the stools she said, "Is there any point in staying on, Pooch?"

"I think so. The weather report's very mucky. There's a nice big story here, whether he brings her in or not." His bland face was turned to gaze at the rain on the windows. "The thing's this. There'll be a whole gaggle of blokes on the quay-side with offers for the story, and only one of them will be able to go up to Harkness and talk to him before the press conference. Al Jocelyn."

"Don't hug yourself so hard or you'll bring on blood-pressure. Barney can't compete with the big Londons."

"He's told me to go to a thousand."

"The big ones'll make it twenty."

He shrugged. "I've got an ace."

She said in a sing-song tone, " 'I Was On Board'—story of heroic courage at sea by Ace Jocelyn."

He gazed at the windows for a moment more and said, "Of course this local chap was right, even though he wasn't there. D'you remember that bosun?"

She nodded. "And the boy on the *Angeles*, the one who jumped in." She picked up her drink a little impatiently. "Isn't it lousy to have to cash in on a thing like this?"

"You shouldn't have married a journalist."

It was still raining when dark fell, and the wind was rising across the town. In the evening papers there was a picture of Captain Harkness and another of the *Atlantic Whipper* showing her in the Mersey after fitting out, five years ago.

Many of the crew had left Plymouth by train—Brewer the chief engineer, some of the cooks, most of the seamen who lived in London, Birmingham and Cardiff. The second mate, Beggs, was drifting the bends through Dorset in his Aston Martin which he had picked up in Avonmouth. A few more were still in hospital beds: Dukes, Robins, Smithers. Steve Turnbull was on his feet but not yet discharged.

Two representatives of Watson and Blount, the owners, had arrived in the town. Mrs. Harkness had been offered a car by a London newspaper and was driven down by a chauffeur to the Metropole, where one of the best rooms had been booked for her.

Tony Bond had gone home. Peter Costain was still in the town, trying to reach Miss Brown by telephone at the Suretidge School for Deaf Children, Croydon.

Wilson had been discharged from the Seamen's Hospital during the afternoon and had joined the steward, Tonio, on board the Spanish steamer *Angeles,* now lying in the South Dockyard. He had taken his guitar and was a hero among the crew for having nursed his precious instrument in a waterproof parcel through the terrible sea. One of the Spaniards had an uncle who had met the mistress of the man who had made this very guitar—see, here was his signature inside it—and several of them had met Teresa in Buenos Aires, and were overjoyed to learn that such a brave Englishman was to marry her and save her from the life she was leading now. Wilson became rather subdued after this reference to Teresa, and passed out before midnight from the effects of strong Malaga wine and depression.

The wind rose to half a gale during the early hours of Saturday and gusts of sixty miles an hour were recorded by coastguard stations along the Cornish shore.

Only a few of these people heard the news when it came in by radio. They were the owners' representatives, Mrs. Harkness, Tony Bond—who had telephoned the radio station hourly since dusk last evening—and Manuelo de las Castillas, who had awakened from a long sleep to conduct the celebrations on board his ship in the South Dockyard and was now sitting in his cabin with his own radio tuned in to the shipping wavelength.

The others would not hear the news until they read the morning papers or were told by word of mouth.

The signal came from the tug *Salvado,* reporting strong gale conditions and heavy seas. The tow had parted and the *Atlantic Whipper* was lying over at sixty degrees with her port-side main-deck awash. She was drifting north-eastwards without lights or radio. The tug and the destroyer, still standing by, were trying to make contact with the casualty by radio and signal-lamps, but so far there had been no response.

The last message from the *Atlantic Whipper* had been flashed by Aldis lamp two hours ago, soon after midnight. Since then there had been no sign that Captain Harkness was still on board her.

CHAPTER SEVENTEEN

PAIN woke Harkness. He was lying face-down in the dark, and could smell salt water. It was washing in the angle between the deck and bulkhead, trapped water that surged and lapped against his chest. His face was close to it and so its smell was strong. The pain was in his face and head, in the cheekbone and brow—mostly the pain of pressure, for when he lifted his head it was eased. He listened, and the sounds were similar to those he had heard before he had pitched down, felled by the final onset of sleep that he had been fighting off for days. There was the wash of water, inside the ship, and the rush of it along her side, and the banging of a metal door, far away, as it swung on its hinges, and banged, and swung again as the sea moved the ship; and the smaller and more dangerous sound of a timber straining, a wire singing towards breaking-point, a loose piece of deck-gear sliding across the planks, ripping their soaked surface—he could visualize the wet dark wood torn slowly into fibres as the sea moved the ship and the gear slid again, grinding over the deck.

He could feel that his eyes were open but he blinked them to make certain. It was totally dark. His tongue was clogging his mouth. He felt unclean and humiliated, and the humiliation grew as he lay sprawled in the corner of the wheelhouse with his memory flying back—the helmsman perched on the wrecked boat-davits, staring up at him before he dived into the sea. *Has every man left her?* The white face staring up from the tortoise-like bulk of the life-jacket. *Every man's left her, sir!* And he had dived.

The humiliation was worse than the bruises on his face and head, worse than the taste in his mouth and the chill of his soaked body. They had all looked to him for their welfare, and he had ordered them into the sea.

He lifted himself until he was sitting cradled between deck and bulkhead. The *Whipper* was lolling badly. What did the list-indicator show, across there in the dark? Sixty? More? The sounds were going on all the time; it was like listening at the doorway of a torture-house as the sea worked on the ship. Water surged below-deck, hammering dully, and metal tore as rivets were sheared by the great slow weight of the sea. The sounds that unnerved him were those he couldn't identify—that one, now, was a strange one, a new one. The coal had shifted in the bunkers a long time ago, and just before he had sent the last signal with failing batteries there had come a hideous musical sound that had sent him below to find its cause, for he had to know everything that was happening in his ship. It had been a great crash, with splintering, and then the strange dream-like music echoing away and making him doubt his sanity. It had taken him a quarter of an hour to find the smashed piano in the smoking-lounge.

This one, now, had no music in it; but he couldn't identify it. It worsened his humiliation: something was happening in his ship that he didn't know about; it was like listening to unfriendly voices saying something about him in words he couldn't catch.

The humiliation itself was a danger, clogging his mind. He must be practical, and work, and not sit here in the dark with his sores. There were antidotes to his depression, very potent ones: the signal from H.M.S. *Brindle* that had come in the evening——*Plymouth reports every man safely landed by 'Angeles'*. He had ordered them into the sea but they were safe. Was that not merciful? And his situation at this moment: the ship was still afloat. She could have gone down while he slept and in his exhaustion he could not have roused his brain to save himself. Was it not merciful that he was still alive?

She could have gone down with all on board her, and there would have been heavy loss of life, but—*every man safely landed*. The seas could have come for her while he was unconscious, trapping him in here and taking him down (how much water now, Mr. Beggs? Forty fathoms, sir), taking him forty fathoms down to the sands where she would lie, keeping him with her until he was another skeleton captain with his crew gone and his engines cold and his bones picked clean by fish. Or would there have been air trapped in her? There were ships in the sea that never reached the bottom when they sank, but were left half-buoyant by air or cargo; and the deep-sea currents moved them across the ocean floor, great slow shadows with no direction of their own, their steering fouled and charts obliterated, the compass rusted in the bowl and the long aerial wires picking up nothing but the shreds of weeds . . . but still moving with the slow grace that a big ship has when the light is on her, moving down there with no fixed course and every harbour closed to her for always. When she went down, would she . . . ?

Morbidity. From pain to humiliation to morbidity. It was the lack of sleep: he had slept for long enough to let his brain register the pain in his face and head, so that he had woken to the warning. A few minutes of sleep, after how many days and nights? What night was it now, what hour?

He got to his feet and stood with his shoulder against an upright. His head swam; he waited until it cleared. His shoulder was hard against a flat surface, so that he knew he was leaning heavily and must judge the angle by his sense of balance alone, for he could not see the water. The flat surface was rough under his hand. His brain was shocked as it was forced to assess the ship's angle and he breathed quickly and deeply for minutes, steadying slowly. His feet were on the bulkhead, and he was leaning against the deck. She was nearly on her beam-ends.

When he moved his feet he kicked at rubbish—empty tins, a bottle, some loose candles. They fitted into place in his memory. And the signals that had crossed the mile of water, two nights ago (that was to say, last night—but which night was this one?) —*What do you need most?* He had answered, *Food, milk, candles.* And then the long hand-skinning business of catching the messenger-lines without losing his grip on the tilting rails. Two hours, perhaps more, before he could hack open the first tin of soup and drink it cold from the tin, cutting his mouth as the ship had rolled and sent him pitching against the bulkhead with the tin splashing away. Dear Margaret, with your elegant damask tablecloths and embroidered napkins, the gleam of the soup spoons under the gentle lights, where would you draw the line between sorrow for me and triumph for your perfectly ordered home?

The rubbish clattered as he worked his way towards the windows. One was broken: where was the wind, then? The other way, piling against the starboard side. He could hear it go whistling past. Now he could see the water surrounding the ship, a faint white haze lying like a scum on the dark shape of her.

There were lights suddenly to port, quite close. A ship had topped the swell and he could see her clearly, standing off to leeward. The *Brindle*. A lamp was flashing. He braced himself against the deck and watched. Sometimes the lamp dipped and was lost—for minutes he thought it was going out, breaking off in the middle of the message; then he realized the destroyer was vanishing into a trough. The swell was higher than he had thought. A—R—and then darkness—O—U—and a break and then—O—K—it made AROU break OK. They began again—A—R—E—and he got it. He had to think where his hand-torch was, had to climb back through his memory over obstacles (the batteries had failed and the Aldis no use—how had he signalled before he had been pitched into sleep?) until he could remember the hand-torch; and then he had to remember where it was. It was in his pocket. He pulled it out and even before he moved the switch he could feel the thing was smashed.

—O—U—break—O—K—and they began again. How long had they been keeping it up? He let the torch drop and it clattered about tinnily before it rang among the rubbish. Water slopped against his ankles and suddenly he was aware that one of his shoes was off. The foot was coming back to life, tingling. It was bruised. The shoe must have been wrenched off when he had fallen, when his brain had thrown the switch arbitrarily, blowing the fuse before worse happened.

He bent down and rummaged among the rubbish, finding a candle from the few that had spilled from the box. It had broken in many places but the wick held it together. Matches?

Back over the obstacles to find the matches among the memories of the rocket-line that had cleared the ship but fouled on the aerial, the net of supplies that had come down out of the dark, hitting his shoulder and nearly sending him down the slope of the deck to the smashed rails and the water, the rip of skin as his arm had grazed down the stanchion—back to find the matches. Had there been any? Where were they now?

—R—E—break—Y—O—U—

The flashing lamp sent a pale light into the wheelhouse, persistently flickering. The matches were in his pocket, like the torch; like the torch, useless, soaked. He struck a dozen and there wasn't a spark between them. He flung the box away with a jerk of his hand and then thought, 'Patience. Step by step.' Anger was a new emotion to him; it was rising to do battle with the humiliation: you could not feel humbled and angry; you had to win. But there was danger in anger; with the humiliation, reason went too. Step by step. Find the matches, light the candle, signal the destroyer, wait for daylight, rig a new tow and get home, get home out of this sick dark waste where murder was being done to his ship.

He had found the matches but they were damp. There must be more, somewhere.

He searched for an hour. At the end of his search he had not found matches, but knew every aspect of the wheelhouse, chartroom and wireless-room. The *Whipper* was rolling through eighty degrees and the sea was rising to the superstructure at minute intervals. He watched black water coming, on the other side of the port wheelhouse door where the glass panel was cracked but not shattered. The water turned white as it boiled against the bridge-end and he heard the great hissing of it and smelt the rotten tang of weed.

He put one foot—the one with the shoe on—against the glass panel of the door and broke it, and stamped the fragments clear of the frame; otherwise he might step on the glass and not realize it, thinking it to be solid. The water lay below it.

—K—and a break—A—R—E—break—Y—O—

When his hand felt the cigarette-lighter in his pocket he was warned again of danger—the danger of not thinking properly. He should have thought of the lighter, long before this. An hour searching for matches, with no alternative in his mind . . . it was dangerous not to think properly. No batteries and therefore no Aldis lamp. The torch, then. Broken? A candle, then. Matches damp? Find more, then. But his brain had got tired. It hadn't thought of the cigarette-lighter. His brain mustn't get tired again.

He worked his thumb at the lighter and it sparked, and in a moment a flame lit, dazzling him with its light and its unexpectedness. The first sight of remembered things: soaked planking, the thick white-painted stand of the echo-sounder, blood on his hand, the glitter of broken glass and the wink of light on tins among the rubbish.

He could not show the candle from the wheelhouse door, because it was below his feet. The windows were taking the gale past them and he would have to hold the candle through the broken one for its light to be seen by the destroyer; but the wind would blow it out. The top of the wheelhouse was now a wall, tilted at twenty degrees from the vertical; and there were two small skylights, one at each end.

It took him half an hour to climb on to the echo-sounder, because the first attempt had knocked the lighter from his fingers and it had landed among the rubbish; he had searched by touch, thinking the word aloud, 'Patience'. When he had established his perch on the echo-sounder there had been the awkward business of staying there, gripping the candle under his arm and lighting it and then taking it out before he dropped the lighter again or fell off his perch.

The skylight in the port side of the wheelhouse deckhead was now at arm's length above him. It faced to leeward, towards the destroyer. It was hardly worth the effort. The outside of the glass would be thick with salt, and if in reaching up he fell from the echo-sounder he would pitch down through the door panel and hit the sea.

—U—break—O—K—break—A—R—E—

He could not see the lamp, from here, but only its flickering reflection in the windows below him. He must make the effort.

He leaned his back against the deck, and slid his body upwards, inching it slowly by straightening his legs. The round metal stand was hard under the arch of his bare foot and he had to come down again, and move his foot at an angle, and then push himself up again, slowly, stopping when the sea came under the starboard side and sent the ship rolling, pushing upwards again when she steadied. Then he raised his arm, and felt the hot wax dripping from the candle down his wrist. He moved the flame higher until it reached the little skylight, and lowered it, and raised it, and lowered it, working steadily until the wax was caking his wrist and his whole body was shaking with the need for relief. He gave it no relief until the *Atlantic Whipper* had completed the first signal she had sent since midnight, five hours ago.

* * *

The lamps in the lounge of the Metropole Hotel were still burning, two hours from dawn. The main entrance doors had not been locked all night. Sometimes a car had pulled up outside; people had come into the hotel or left it, hurrying down the staircase with a coat half on, cigarette-ash dropping, or hurrying in through the main doors and glancing quickly about them in search of the face they had come to see.

"I'm Scott. The Elk sent me . . ."

"You're welcome. Nothing's happened. What'll you drink?"

The big doors brought a draught in. The chandelier in the domed ceiling was faintly trembling to air currents that were never still as the young, thin-faced, badly-dressed men went out, came in.

"Where's Henry?"

"For Christ's sake, I don't know."

"This is nothing to do with Christ. Harkness is the name of the century, just for this week. You want me to spell it?"

"I haven't seen Henry. Try the Gents."

The brilliants of the chandelier trembled in the ceiling. A telephone rang and was answered at once because there were very strict orders that the Residents must not have their Rest Disturbed by the comings and goings of the Gentlemen of the Press. The atmosphere of traditional quiet must be maintained in the Hotel Metropole.

"Hey, Mac! There's a wire from London, says he's been drowned."

The doors swung shut. The chandelier sent sparks of light reflecting across the dome.

"Please, gentlemen," the night-porter called, "I keep on telling you there's residents trying to sleep——"

"They're lucky they've got beds, old sport——"

"It's a phoney, I'd say. How does anyone know?"

"You might at least lower your voices——"

"They're lucky they're not out there on the *Whipper*. You can remind 'em of that."

The doors opened. A car sped away from the pavement outside.

"Where the hell is Henry?"

In the far corner where the wall-lamps were out sat the slim woman in tweeds, alone, watching the doors, the glimmer of light in the dome, the pale faces of the hurrying young men. The early arrivals knew she was here, and had not bothered to tell the others. They'd had her statement ("You call that a statement, Henry? What's the Elk goin' to print it on—bus tickets?") and had decided to leave her in peace until some news broke. When some news broke, they said, she'd have to talk. Even a woman like this one would have to *express* something sooner or later if only to keep her face pliant.

Her face was calm as she sat watching the doors and the lights and the men. There was detachment in the angle of her head, the stillness of her folded hands, the neatly crossed ankles.

"Quite a dish."

"Too strong and silent for me."

"I mean in a regal way."

"I like them alive, myself."

The doors opened, swung shut. Cool air touched her face. The thing she expressed so clearly in her eyes and face and whole body as she sat here alone had no news-value for them; it was detachment.

"Call that a statement? You'll have to blow it up twice the size to rate a single in the Agony."

"Forget it. It's her old man that's news, not her."

"But the human angle, the anxious wife who——"

"Human? Her?"

She watched them. Had there been a tank of tropical fish let into the wall she would have watched them as steadily.

Possibly they resented her attitude less because it had no news in it than because it had dignity. They had not tried very hard to melt her; they knew by their long experience when they were striking rock.

"You must be counting the minutes, Mrs. Harkness."

She had lit a cigarette.

"I mean, it's going to be a race against time and tide."

She had asked pleasantly in her low hard voice, "Isn't that what they call a cliché?"

None of the four had answered that question. They had their own kind of dignity, comparable with the retreat of a hermit-crab into its shell. Like the hermit-crab, they stole out again, warily.

"At least you must be thankful they were all landed safely. That news must have cheered you in your anxiety, Mrs. Harkness."

"Of course."

"Did you go to see any of them? I mean the passengers?"

The tendril of smoke rose from her cigarette, exquisitely detached. "Why should I?"

Henry was looking nettled, the other three noticed. A private car and chauffeur at her disposal, one of the best rooms in the hotel. She didn't seem to recognize any of the rules.

"Anyway we're glad to have you here, Mrs. Harkness, right in the front row, so to speak. We shan't ever regret asking you to come all the way to the coast—we knew it was what you wished for."

The silence was awkward. They were all back tight in their shells, even Henry. Should he have said that? To hell.

"I was told there was no obligation. Has there been a change of policy?"

They had counted five before Henry stood up and excused himself.

Without Henry, maybe a little diplomacy might take a trick or two. In a frank open-hearted way, of course.

"Now, Mrs. Harkness, we don't pretend we did you anything of a service. Possibly it might have been more convenient for you to accept the little we offered than to take a train and book a room for yourself, but we hardly feel we've helped you as much as we could, by affording you mere convenience. What we regret is that there's nothing really valuable we can do for you, when you're going through an anxious time like this, waiting and wondering, hoping and praying . . ."

Mac was no better than Henry. Just losing himself in his own diplomacy and coming up against the old-fashioned sob-angle before he had the sense to go round it.

She had said nothing. Vosper tried:

"Mrs. Harkness, you're too intelligent a woman——" he was in his fifties, old enough to have been her father, and only he among them could try this kind of approach—"to mistake this situation. Whether the Captain brings his ship home safely or not, he's already endeared himself to the nation not only by making the terrible decision of ordering those people off his stricken ship into a bad sea, but by remaining on board himself. In brief, he is a hero. His countrymen want to know more about him, more about his background, his home, his wife—about you. Now is that wrong? Is that surprising?"

Pause. Don't spoil it. But she said nothing. He leaned forward. "At any moment we might hear that the *Atlantic Whipper* has gone down. We might hear that she has been taken in tow again and stands a chance of getting home. We might hear——"

"I'm not interested in the ship."

Just a detached remark.

"I don't quite see what you mean," said Vosper. He wished he were alone with her. There was a story here that went down deep; not necessarily one he could ever print; but it would be interesting. He was constantly having to make a distinction between what could and could not be printed. He passed news to his editor and kept back the real stuff for his own reading and re-reading. People were his life. When he found out what went on in them it made him feel sick, or cheered, or warmed or frozen stiff with astonishment or horror or cold fright. Mostly, sad.

"It's just your husband that's on your mind—what might be happening to him."

She said casually, making his seriousness seem like an act, "What does it matter if a ship sinks, as long as there's nobody on it?"

He had forgotten he must look for news. He was now looking for Margaret Harkness. Even the tiniest clues had value: for instance she called a ship 'it'.

"The Captain wouldn't agree with you," he said.

"No."

If the other two were called away, he could talk to this embittered woman, and make her talk to him. She was dying to talk to someone. To tell them what?

He listened for the telephone, the noise of a car, the doors. Wouldn't something happen to call the others off?

She watched him thinking, and knew he resented the two younger men being here. What was this man Vosper really like, when he wasn't raking his nose along in the gutters for the little victories and failures and indecent secrets and plain honest-to-goodness human weaknesses that could be twisted into Human Interest? He looked middle-aged and had the hard stamp of the news-hawk on him yet something told her that he had kept a part of him clean, over the years of muck-spreading in the great Sundays.

Mac said quickly, "Your only concern is for your husband. My God, that's natural enough, Mrs. Harkness!"

"But scarcely news."

Vosper waited impatiently.

"And you're confident he'll make it," said Mac.

She saw it in print, *My only concern is for my husband, but I'm confident he'll make it.* That brave little woman, chin up, faith steady in the man she loved.

"No," she said.

"No?"

Vosper wanted to smile. Mac sat back, giving it up. She said, "He's out there on a sinking ship and there's a gale blowing——" and Mac leaned forward again as if she had drawn him on a string—"and the nearest ship is a mile away. Why do you want me to say I'm confident he'll make it? I think the chances are that he won't, but you won't print that. You won't print anything I can tell you. It wouldn't have—what's the word?—an angle."

Her eyes, Vosper noticed, were green. Had he failed to observe this before, or were they now lit with anger?

"Come now, Mrs. Harkness," Mac said. Silence would have had as much meaning.

"Please get one thing clear, gentlemen. If you misquote me by one word, I shall sue. My friendly advice to you is to go and find someone with the right angle. Otherwise you'll be in real danger of printing something straight."

Two of them just got up and walked away. Vosper stayed where he was.

After a minute passed he said conversationally, "You don't like newspapers."

It was extraordinary how she could keep that beautiful dignity and yet say things like, "I think they're appreciated wrapped round fish and chips but I doubt if they keep the stuff any cleaner."

She said it with no animosity, no contempt. It was a detached remark. That was how she did it, kept the dignity.

With a tone of detachment that matched hers Vosper looked at his nails and said, "Newspapers, and ships."

Behind them the doors opened. Someone came in. If it were anyone to see him, he could blow. He'd got his baby alone now.

"Also," she said, "break-back mouse-traps, race distinction, garlic sausages, television parlour-games and burst pipes. I could extend the list but it wouldn't be news."

As if she hadn't spoken he murmured, "Especially this one. The *Whipper*."

"Naturally."

"Because?"

"It's liable to cost him his life. So many thousand tons of rusty iron lying waterlogged out there, and any minute it can sink, and take him down too. He could have been safe on land now, with the others."

Vosper let another minute go by, and selected his answer from the half-dozen that occurred. "There's nothing I can say, is there? I mean, apart from the obvious things."

"You don't seem a very obvious man. Try something."

"All right. It's difficult not to over-simplify, but it'll be a start. You look as though you might be going to lose the fight, after all these years. How's that?"

"Wouldn't it be a laugh if you went and printed it?"

"No. People would understand."

"Then print it."

"But it's not the kind of thing they *want* to understand." They were both leaning slightly forward now and spoke more quietly. The press interview was over and they were just two people putting in time until the news broke. "It's like that cancer-of-the-lung scare, you see. Most people understood the situation. About two per cent of all cigarette-smokers gave up smoking. The rest argued the point, because it wasn't the kind of thing they *wanted* to understand. We were glad to stop printing the facts and opinions. Bad news is no news." He shrugged.

She said nothing. He moved the ashtray towards her and she put her stub into it and leaned back into the chair, and he knew the interview was over.

"It's been nice talking to you, Mrs. Harkness." He stood up, straightening his worn double-breasted jacket. "And I hope you win."

That had been hours ago. She stared at the ceiling now, and sometimes caught a glimpse of Vosper going through the lounge or talking to the others. From this distance he looked a very tired man, tired with a long-term beaten-down fatigue, not just with the long night's waiting here.

The wall-clock said five. Her eyes felt heavy. Vosper had spoken to her again, for half a minute, coming over and giving his worn grey smile. "There's nothing come in yet, but when it does, I'll let you know. If you're upstairs asleep, I'll phone."

"I shan't leave here."

He had shrugged, and gone away again.

In the absence of news there were rumours. The only facts were figures: the force of the wind out there, the height of the waves, the angle of the ship, the number of hours and minutes that had gone by since there had been a signal from the *Atlantic Whipper*. Four hours, fifty-two minutes. The hand on the wall-clock moved. Fifty-three.

The rumours contradicted one another. A body had been picked up, believed to be Harkness. He had left the ship and swum for the *Salvado*. He had signalled that he intended to go down with his ship. The *Atlantic Whipper* was still in complete darkness. A light had been seen on board her.

Margaret Harkness watched the clock on the wall, the light in the dome of the ceiling, the doors and the young men who came and went, bringing a new rumour and scotching the last.

If the rumour were right, the one about a body being picked up, it could only have been Matthew's. How long ago? When had the clock stopped, for her? She did not look at it again, but concentrated on the talk of the journalists, catching a word here and there, building them into sentences. Rumours were still coming in; you could take your choice.

God, bring him home. Never mind the ship, bring Matthew. Let me see him again.

"Hey, Mac!"

"Quiet, will you? People're trying to sleep."

"There's something come in."

"From where? Delphi?"

The doors swung shut. Cool air moved against her face. The one called Henry, the huffy one, was driving the night-porter behind the reception desk where the switchboard was.

Vosper and two others had turned their heads. They watched the porter plugging in the leads, saying something to Henry. She didn't have to lip-read to know he was saying that he didn't like newspapermen. Suddenly she felt sorry for them all.

A car pulled up outside and a door slammed. A young man came in with a girl in a duffle-jacket. Someone waved a casual hand. "Over there."

Henry was talking into one of the telephones, very quietly with his body crouched over the receiver like a monkey with a big special nut. She couldn't hear one clear word.

The young man and the girl were coming between the chairs, picking their way to the unlighted corner of the room.

Without meaning to she looked at the big gilt clock. It was ten minutes past five.

"Mrs. Harkness?"

"Yes."

"My name's Jocelyn. This is my wife. We were passengers on the *Atlantic Whipper*." He spoke like a silenced machine-gun. "This message has just come in by radio. It's authentic."

He gave her a slip of buff paper and she turned it to catch the glow of the main lights. He clicked his cigarette-lighter and held it near the paper. "Thank you," she murmured.

To C.-in-C. Plymouth from 'Brindle'. Signal received by flashing light from 'Atlantic Whipper'. Begins: Sorry, fell asleep. Ends. Time of origin 05.01.

CHAPTER EIGHTEEN

AT the Hub Club, London, S.W.7, Jim Beggs had eaten a good lunch but passed the next few hours in the grip of indigestion. On his table there had been four noon editions of London papers, still neatly folded because he was interested only in the front page. At four o'clock he was sitting in his Aston Martin half-way along Buckingham Palace Road. Newspapers were on the seat beside him and on the floor below his legs. Two others had been blown whirling out of the car as he had driven hard along Kensington High Street. His destination lay south. He had telephoned his parents, saying he would be with them in the evening, and he had telephoned a girl in Mitcham saying he would collect her tomorrow morning, Sunday. Now he was parked in Buckingham Palace Road. This was as far as he could go, southwards, and he knew it. He left the car, found a telephone-box, cancelled his appointments and went back to the car, turning it towards Hyde Park Corner and heading west out of London.

He felt happier: the decision had been made. Through Kensington again he slowed only to pick up the wording on newspaper placards with a glance. At lunch-time they had read variously: *Tug has 'Whipper' in Tow—100 Miles to Plymouth—He Says he can Make It!*

As the Aston shot along through the west-bound traffic he became practised in picking out the white placards and getting their gist. *Still in Tow—Keep Your Fingers Crossed!—Seventy-five to Go.*

There was no other news on the placards. In the headlines of the popular papers there was no pretence of formality. A spiritual touch-line had been set up and the people of the country were crowding along it, ready to cheer. Jim Beggs had intended driving down to Plymouth tomorrow afternoon, but this was more than he could bear with.

He pulled up at a chemist's shop in Staines and asked for bismuth—yes, in a glass of water—and the girl couldn't get the cap off and turned indignant when he grabbed it in a great fist and dealt with it. She watched him obliquely as he drank the mixture—big men always ate like pigs and this would teach him a lesson. He picked up his change but left the bottle on the counter and was swerving away from the kerb when she came to the door and called out. She hoped she wouldn't see him again. There seemed little chance: the thin howl of the engine was already fading in the drizzle.

He took on petrol in Basingstoke and bought a paper.

Homeward Bound at Three Knots.

He drove on, now behind headlights.

Steve Turnbull had been down to the harbour three times during the day, walking slowly with his collar turned up against the rain. He had been on his own since he had left the hospital. He knew where Starley and Copley were, where Costain was staying, where Beggs had gone; but he did not go to see anyone among the crew. He wanted to be as alone as the man on board the *Whipper.*

It wasn't easy for Turnbull, but he was getting round to a grudging acceptance of what had happened to him. He had met his biggest challenge yet: he had been asked to play a minor part in a major affair, and he had come through it with the knowledge that he had at least obeyed orders.

There was only one rather bitter consolation. He said quietly through a tight mouth to the rain-squalls, "You wish to God you had me there with you now, bloody Matthew."

He knew what Harkness was having to do, single-handed. That new tow hadn't been rigged easily. The wind out there was force six and the sea was toppling. The tug and the casualty must have been hard put to it even to close each other. The first rocket-line wouldn't have landed right, nor the next nor the next. Matthew had had to fight for that line, and fight to hold it when he'd caught it, and fight to bring the thicker one aboard, and then the tow, sodden with water and twice its dry weight. But he'd got it round the bitts. There wouldn't be much skin on his hands by now but only God knew how proud bloody Matthew must be. He'd wish there was someone there with him—not to help him, just to see what he could do when he'd got his proud mind made up to do it.

The rain beat in Turnbull's eyes. Matthew had it coming to him; he was all right. They were putting flags out, in the harbour, and the Mayor and Corporation were going down there. They'd got bands practising, and you couldn't move along the pavements even now. Cameramen everywhere, and police to see no one got killed in the rush to welcome bloody Matthew home.

The rain was cool on his face as he stood alone watching the sea and the battered *Angeles* lying in for repairs. There was the hero, if you wanted one. Picked up fifty men from a murderous sea after steaming through a gale that had left her plates stove-in and her foremast splintered in two. If he had gone to see anyone, Steve Turnbull would have gone to see Manuelo de las Castillas, and the deck-hand who'd jumped into the water because he couldn't wait to get his hands on all those lives and save them. But you couldn't move on the pavements here, and they were standing with their backs to the *Angeles*. She wasn't all that much to look at and she was a foreigner anyway. *"We want the 'Whipper'. We want the 'Whipper'."*

They could bloody have her, and Matthew too.

But he was beginning to feel better. There wasn't the throb in his head. If his body mended by the time the ship came in, much of his morbid jealousy would perhaps be eased.

"Mid-day tomorrow," the bosun said. "That's if another gale don't come."

Tich Copley sat on the bench against the wall, jacket open, hands stuck into his trouser pockets. There was another pint in front of him—the third or fourth?—and he was going to have to drink it, or the Bose would grin and tell him he couldn't take his liquor, and give him a playful punch in the stomach, and that would bring the lot up, that would.

"It'll look a treat, Bose. A treat. Eh?"

Starley had a moustache of beer-froth. "You know what I heard? Goin' to be a message from the Queen read out to 'im by the Mayor, when he lands."

Tich looked away from his vast glass of beer, his spirits lifting at the thought. A message from the Queen. The *Queen*. What would it feel like?

"He'll get the Silver, too, boy. Automatic."

"What silver?"

"Lloyd's Silver Medal. Outstandin' courage an' devotion to duty, see?"

Tich belched carefully, letting the wind out as quietly as he could. He'd have to make room somehow. "He ought to get everything," he said. "Everything there ever was."

He lifted the glass. It must be a good six inches tall. And full.

Slopping over. Six foot to a fathom. Jesus, this was a twelfth of a fathom deep. You could drown yourself in this.

"'Ere's how, Bose."

"Mud'n yer eye, boy." When he had wiped the froth off, Art Starley said, "You never been in a ship that's in tow, have you?"

"Not yet."

"It's murder."

"You been in one, then?"

"Yeh. Sea was like it is now. You close to somethin' like a hundred feet, so you can fire the line, see? Then it's a bear-dance. One minute the tug's on a crest an' lookin' down the ship's funnel, nex' minute the ship's on a crest an' lookin' down the tug's. God, never again. Then you start towin'. You'd think she'd follow the tug like a bitch on a lead, wouldn't you? She don't, y'know. She starts sheerin', first port, then starb'd, right out, she goes. You think she's gone mad. You can't see the tow-rope—it's under water. By God, though, you can feel it. You think you've got a live whale on the end. You ever see a whale brought in to the fact'ry-ship?"

"Not yet. Have you?"

"I'll say. Twelve months down in the Antarctic, me, 'fore the war. Can't stomach even the memory. But that's what it's like, Tich. A live whale, fightin' to free itself."

Copley had taken an inch of beer off the top of his glass. Five more to go. He'd have to do it somehow. He said, "Were you in the tug, or the casualty, that time?"

"Me? In the tug. Deckie."

"God, it's special sailoring, tug-work!"

"I'll say."

"Where *haven't* you been, Bose?"

"Now come off it. I'm on'y tellin' you what it's like out there now, with the *Whipper* in tow an' the sea like it is. Murder. An' only the Skip on board. Christ alive, I wish I was out there with 'im."

"So do I." He belched again. "But I'm glad I'm not."

In the evening, Tony Bond made up his mind to go down to Plymouth. He had been out of the house for an hour, and when he came back he found Thelma on the landing.

She called down the stairs, "Did you get wet?"

"Not very." He stood in the dark little hall. "What's up?"

"Nothing."

"You look guilty."

She had a duster in her hand, and waved it casually against the door of his den. "I've been dusting. But I was careful."

"Dusting? In there?"

"It wasn't locked."

He thought it was stupid of him to feel like this, just because she'd been dusting his clobber. He managed his quick smile without hurting his cheek. "I'm going down to Plymouth," he said. "Tonight."

"Oh."

He could see a little way up her skirt as she stood on the top stair. He could remember thinking, a long time ago, that she had wonderful legs. God, what a waste! Surely there was a good shore job for him, in wireless?

"I'll find out the trains for you, Tony." She began coming down.

"I've hired a car. Small one."

"Oh."

He climbed the first few stairs. "There'll be a hotel, without booking."

"The town's filling up, Jean told me. Everyone's making for Plymouth. You'd better try booking."

"All right." There was one more stair between them. "Come down there with me, Thel."

"What for?"

"Oh, I dunno. The ride."

He knew that she was pleased at being asked. He mustn't expect her to show it, at once. The past was meant to be dead. (*For God's sake give me a break, sometimes, Tony. Stop burying us both in this place while you shut yourself up. Can't we go out somewhere, anywhere, just for a day even?*)

"The Wallaces are coming in for drinks, before lunch tomorrow." She didn't sound very excited.

"They can go to church instead."

"D'you honestly want me to come?"

He turned and went down the stairs. "I'll phone the Wallaces to put 'em off, and then book a room down there. Room with a view." He picked up the telephone and while he was waiting for the line to open he looked up at her through the banisters. It made him feel almost sinful to think he was going to be in a strange hotel-room with a girl like this. Oh God, she mustn't kick him out now. He'd considered spending the rest of his life married to Thelma, when he was in the water keeping his weight on the raft-ropes to help steady it, and listening to someone's hysterical voice calling 'Save me, save me!' He'd thought about his marriage, almost all the time until the tall bows of the steamship *Angeles* had cut their way through the mountainous seascape and they all knew they were going to live. If he were going to live he must think what to do with his life; and he had thought it out, bobbing in the water watching the others go up the rescue-nets of the ship's battered side.

I'm dull . . .

No, not dull, Tony . . .

He said, "The best room they've got."

The odd thing was that he wasn't doing this because he must force himself not to be dull. It was coming naturally. Would it last, this careless excited feeling? Lord, make it last, and don't let her kick me out.

Looking down at him, Thelma said without speaking, 'You've changed, haven't you? What made you change? Being nearly drowned? I suppose it would change most people. You look very boyish, standing there with your bandage on, enthusiastic about the trip—not a bit like . . . with his little black business-man's hat with the hair-oil patch inside the crown. He's a comical person, I can see that now. I don't want to think about him again. It was filthy and dreary and very dangerous. It'd be terrible if you ever found out, because you'd think there was a great deal to it, and there wasn't.'

Looking up at her, he thought, 'What's made this difference in me? Being shipwrecked? If so, everyone should do it, once in their life. It ought to be made compulsory.'

"I'll go and get ready," she said.

He felt a thrill in him. It was bloody silly, really. It was bloody magnificent.

Click. "Charles Wallace here."

"Hello, Charles. How are you?"

"Who's that?"

He wanted to say, 'The new Anthony Bond.'

Jim Beggs arrived in Plymouth at a quarter to twelve on this Saturday night with a thick mud-film on the Aston. He called at the hospital first to see how Dukes was getting on. Dukes had regained consciousness during the afternoon and was off the danger-list. Mr. Turnbull? No one had seen him since he had left here. Harris? Discharged. Robins? Still dopey after the operation: he could have visitors tomorrow.

Beggs phoned five hotels and drew blank. The town was full. He booked in at the Y.M.C.A.

Mr. and Mrs. Bond had arrived in the evening. Stored furniture had been moved out of a top room in the Beacon Hotel and Guest-house and a double bed moved in with three hot-water bottles to air it. They were sorry to give so much trouble. It was no trouble, bless them—anyone in the crew of the *Atlantic Whipper* could have the run of the Beacon Hotel and Guest-house, and welcome. Mrs. Bond must be very proud of her husband. Yes, she said, she was.

They could see the end of one of the jetties from the cracked patched window. They couldn't ask to be much nearer the centre of things than that. It wasn't very romantic, he said when the proprietor had left them. She said it was the most romantic place she'd ever been in, ever. But they forgot about the hot-water bottles and stung themselves, and hurriedly threw them out.

Starley the bosun and Tich Copley had found a wet hunched figure on the harbour wall. "You drunken son of a whore!" shouted Art Starley, making him spin round startled.

Fred Sackett grinned sheepishly. The three of them stood together in the rain by the harbour wall. They'd not see the *Whipper* tonight, but this was the nearest they could get to her.

At midnight there was no change in the news, except that H.M.S. *Brindle* had been relieved by the destroyer *Vixen*, which had been lying at Plymouth under immediate notice for steam since Friday morning. The *Atlantic Whipper* was still in tow at a steady three knots, listing badly and down more by the head; but if she could maintain her reserve of buoyancy for another twelve hours she would make Plymouth.

The weather report forecast gales.

In the town the streets were deserted. Earlier rumours that the three ships might be visible on the horizon before nightfall had been discounted, and the crowds had gone home early to bed. Alarm-clocks in a thousand rooms had been synchronized to ring at dawn. The telephone exchange had put two extra men on duty in the early morning shift to cope with the plague of requests for alarm calls at seven o'clock tomorrow.

In the docks, lights burned all night. The Southern Salvage Company had already arranged berthing facilities. A salvage vessel was standing by. Three divers had arrived in the town and would be ready with their equipment tomorrow morning.

At the closing of the markets the re-insurance rates had fallen to ten guineas per cent in the City, where prophecy cost money. There was no more practical a statement of hope in any quarter. The City thought Harkness could make it. So did Fleet Street and so did Plymouth, where decorations already hung limp in the rain from lamp-posts and flag-masts, windows, balconies and the rails along the jetties and quays in the South Docks. Most cheerful of all were the members of the Southern Salvage Company. The cost of maintaining a tug of the *Salvado's* type ran to something like five hundred pounds per week—when she was lying idle. Three times in the last month she had been out deep-sea, reaching the casualty's position too late to save her, or in such seas as disallowed the passing of the tow. But she was bringing the *Atlantic Whipper* home on the same no-cure-no-pay terms; and this time there was hope. The financial reward to the salvage company was estimated at between five and six hundred thousand pounds.

A message came in at one o'clock on Sunday morning from the *Salvado.* She had been in contact again with her tow. Captain Harkness was tired but confident. He wished to thank all concerned for their messages of good will. Captain Howes, master of the tug, sent a personal message to the Mayor of Plymouth. *We shall try to deliver the 'Atlantic Whipper' into Plymouth at some time tomorrow if conditions permit us to hold our present speed.*

This was the last signal received during the night, but the silence brought no anxiety. Had any trouble developed, the *Salvado* and the destroyer *Vixen* would have signalled shore.

The wind drove the rain through the empty streets, and sometimes a gust stirred the soaked bunting that hung along them. The policemen on the beat, looking up at their bleak fluttering, had the impression that the celebrations were already over, and not waiting upon the morning to begin.

CHAPTER NINETEEN

THE tug's course was roughly north-east and the wind was in the west, coming on to her port quarter and sending sea after sea across her towing-deck. A thousand yards astern of her was the *Whipper,* sheering to starboard of the *Salvado* as the seas drove her that way. Half a mile to windward of them the *Vixen* was steaming with her lights bright.

Towards dawn a lookout in the destroyer reported a light to the north; but it could not yet be landfall. There were other ships not far away, riding between here and the coast; but there would be no collisions. There was no ship in these waters that did not know her precise position and the position of the others. There were to be no errors now, for there was no margin for them.

The *Atlantic Whipper,* her head down under the weight of swollen cargo and slack water in her two for'ard holds, was under tow stern-first, so that Harkness could not see the lights of the tug from the wheelhouse. Sometimes he could see the destroyer when she rode a crest, and at these times he feasted on the sight of her glimmering lamps through the rain-haze, because his worst enemy was now loneliness.

It would have seemed impossible for a man to feel lonely within a thousand yards of two other ships, and with the knowledge in him that so many millions of people were thinking of him at this moment, praying that he should win this fight he had taken on with the sea. But in all his life Matthew Harkness had never felt so lonely as this, had never known that loneliness could be so terrible. He knew that to a great extent it was fatigue, a middle-watch morbidity spreading from his blood to his brain; but to know the cause of an illness is not to cure it.

He had not slept since the pain in his face and head had wakened him, earlier this night. He felt now that he could finish his whole life without sleep, but knew that he would prefer death to a lifetime of consciousness such as this. He was alone in the torture-house and in the dark, listening to the sounds that a ship made when she was breaking up.

Sometimes he found himself raging with helplessness, beating his hands, talking to the sea, to God, to the ship, begging and cursing and demanding that the sea should now leave his ship alone. She was in safe hands and she was going to harbour. The sea had tried to take her down but it had failed. Now let it abate.

These fancies—this logical view of the situation—ran through his mind until he could see nothing but black and white, right and wrong, good and evil. Possibly had this mood of his remained as it was now, he could have unseated the greatest judge in the kingdom. There was wisdom in him, and he seemed able to stand back and to see everything in perspective. There must be a natural law, somewhere in the cluttered archives of the universe, that would dictate that the sea be calm, now that the ship had refused to sink into the depths of it.

At intervals in this stream of wisdom he realized that he was thinking like a drunken Irish poet. He must get his mind clear. The job was not over. She could still go down. But God knew his ears were alert enough to this warning. There was no minute went by but it did not fill the wheelhouse with the sounds of the *Whipper's* dying; and Matthew could do nothing more to help her. A long time ago, when she had given up responding to the sea's movement, when she had lost all movement of her own, he had known that though she still floated she was alive no more. Now he had the feeling strong in him that he was to lose her soon. This great and still graceful shape on which a man looked like an ant was lying in agony, and soon would go, and be seen no more. The waves would close. A scum of débris would float and slowly disperse. When day came, the ship would not be here. There would be nothing in the world with the name of *Atlantic Whipper*. Her name would be struck off the books; her crew would forget her and find berths in other ships. They would forget how slim she looked and how clean her bows cut the sea and furrowed it white so that as she slipped horizonwards she left a milky wake; would forget her great engines with their steel strong and the copper gleaming, the brass bright; forget her white and gold paintwork below deck, the rich carpeting, the gentle movement of her as she left harbour with her lights tracing through the dark and voices quiet.

'This is senseless!' Aloud, or to himself? He didn't know. 'This is murderous, murderous! Leave her alone!' His voice became just another sound of agony in the darkness. 'God make this foul black bastard of a monster leave my ship alone!'

A plate screamed as the rivets went. Water rushed in, the sound of it sending him sick in his heart. He cursed again, shouting, beating.

At other times he was normal again, as an epileptic is eased after the terrible paroxysm. 'Dear Margaret, stop praying for her to sink. Keep on praying for me, but let me bring her home. I can do it. We can all do it. There's only you among all of us hating this ship.'

He knew his wife very well. He knew what she was doing at this moment. Poor Margaret. Her mother had told him of a conversation, years ago, because now it was too late for the truth to matter. Her mother had said to Margaret, 'You'll never make him give up the sea. You've married a sailor, and you'll have to accept that.' And Margaret had said, 'I can do it, in time. Give me five years, Mother.'

Longer than five years ago. Much more like ten. She had never understood the unspoken terms: love me, love my ship. At first she had been very confident, giving him freedom, pretending to be interested in the sea and often making long voyages with him as a passenger, delighting or seeming to delight in the strangeness of far places. But her father had warned Matthew, even before the marriage, 'She's a girl for home. A home's her element.'

Poor Margaret. The cost had been mostly hers. She had lost her only love, but he had kept the sea.

The water rushed below, to surge and hammer for escape against the weakening structures. It could do it, in time. Any ship could be attacked like this, and in time, however long, could be broken and taken below. Give it another day, for the *Whipper*.

Give me five years, Mother.

He hated her.

'Steady,' he said, 'steady. Patience. We're under tow. There's land coming, and daylight—daylight will help us all after this blindness of the dark. Patience.'

Often he found his body in a sweat and his hands shaking; but these bouts were understandable. He lacked sleep. His nerves were keeping his eyes open and his legs straight when his eyes tried to shut against the blood-red sparks and the whirl of images and his legs tried to buckle and pitch him down; at one time he had seen a snow-storm of flying white against the cracked windows of the wheelhouse, but the flakes had not settled and he had closed his eyes and then with enormous effort opened them again and the snow was gone.

A light flashed.

He answered with the hand-torch that had been sent across to him with the last batch of supplies: biscuits, chocolate, condensed milk, matches, cigarettes, and the hand-torch, a long black rubber one, waterproof and shock-proof, the best. He was grateful to them. He flashed the torch at the windows. *O—K . . . O—K . . . O—K . . .*

He mustn't fall asleep again.

A flood of white light suddenly bathed the ship and for an instant he was afraid his eyes were burning away and that blindness was going to be like this, a flare of white instead of darkness;

but it was the *Salvado's* searchlight. Captain Howes was checking on his tow, having a look at her. What did she look like, from a thousand yards ahead? Her stern would be high, her rudder clear. She would appear to be almost on her side, with the water rushing white past her superstructure. How confident was the master of the *Salvado* now? How confident is any man at sea, in this last hour before dawn?

After a long time the light went out and the night turned pitch. He was alone again, listening to the shrill tearing of metal as the sea hammered, pounding and surging back and charging again, little by little breaking up his ship. But he mustn't sleep, nor be angry. Keep patience and he would bring the *Whipper* to harbour, as that magnificent Spaniard would say, with God.

With the morning, the miracle. There was rain on the sea but the sea was dark, with no whiteness anywhere on its waves. There was a wind but it was low, and had no strength in it. This was a grey day, a dull one, with no character in the skies, a day you could forget about while you got on with your business.

'So much for your careful forecasts, gentlemen!'

Matthew was beyond the point where he could feel elation. He accepted the miracle with no marked feelings at all. His emotions had long ago become dulled and he did not see this peace upon the waters as anything strange. He merely observed a wind force two or three, sea smooth to slight, steady rainfall, visibility fair.

H.M.S. *Vixen* signalled: *Top o' the morning!*

He replied: *Thank God.* But he was not moved to any reverence in his mind. God had two faces, and this was the one with the smile.

When the daylight strengthened he clambered on to the starboard wing of the bridge, using the rope he had rigged there yesterday. Hoisting himself upwards he clung for a moment, staring across the rail, northwards. He could see the land. He said: "England." It meant nothing. He must get his ship to the land, and then it would be over. He must bring his ship to harbour safely, and then . . . and then nothing. For six days he had never thought beyond that point. "England," he said; but it meant nothing.

He slid down the rope. The palms of his hands were hard with dried torn skin; he was no longer troubled by their condition. *Salt water has antiseptic properties, Peter. Tell them that.*

The *Whipper* was well out on a sheer on the tug's starboard quarter with the tow-rope drawn taut and flinging up spray. The strain was in the region of forty tons and both ships felt it. He was reminded of his duties. He must drop from the bridge and make his way along the afterdeck, and inspect the shackle and tow, see that the terrific friction was not burning the rope away as the *Whipper* came back from her sheer and followed astern and then sheered off to port, wallowing through the sea. He must see to it that she made the land over there, before God showed His other face. Matthew did not trust God.

At fifteen minutes past ten on this Sunday morning the message came from H.M.S. *Vixen* to shore stations: *Wind force four, sea slight, rainfall, visibility fair. Tug and casualty appear well. Captain Harkness signals he is in good spirits.*

There had been no message from the *Salvado* since dawn, when she had reported her position, course and progress.

By eleven o'clock the tug, casualty and escort were reported to be fifteen miles from Plymouth. The rain had eased. The wind was rising in gusts and was backing south-west. The casualty's starboard plates were already exposed to the great blows of the waves and it seemed impossible for her to ride like this for another five minutes; yet she had been at this dangerous angle all through the night when the seas had been bigger than these. She had found a reserve of buoyancy and was trying to keep it.

On board the destroyer and the tug no one was anxious. Masters and crews felt they could bring the *Atlantic Whipper* through a hurricane, with land now less than fifteen miles away.

At noon: *Wind strengthening, sea slight to moderate.* But after the gale it seemed as if the water were almost calm.

A mile from the three ships was the Plymouth lifeboat, standing by to landward. A helicopter from Redmoor had been over twice, hovering within a dozen feet of the crippled ship. Harkness had waved, indicating that he was all right and certainly had no intention of being taken off his ship now that she was nearly home. Back at the R.A.F. station the crew of the helicopter reported Captain Harkness as 'looking just about all-in'.

The wind blustered but did not strengthen again. There was white on the wave-tops but there were no big curlers. The miracle, now with the shine off it, was nevertheless still operating: the ship was being given more chance than she could expect, with the barometer falling and the south sky dark.

At about one-thirty Matthew opened a tin of fruit-juice, squatting in the wheelhouse among the rubbish, holding the tin steady and waiting for the ship's movement to ease before he drank, for the cut on his mouth was festering and gave him pain. The noise came from for'ard, below deck, muffled at first and then thundering, and with it there came the vibration, a gigantic shuddering that knocked the tin of fruit-juice from his hand.

He began shouting in a kind of mad protest, his voice drowned in the din of metal being torn apart, of timber splintering. His body trembled with the ship and he shut his eyes, and shouted again, as if his voice were the voice of the *Whipper* in her pain.

When the shuddering stopped, silence did not come. There was the rush of big water, for'ard in the ship. He listened with his head couched on his doubled-up knees and his eyes still shut. He was muttering. A single shudder ran through the ship, and all strain was gone. The waters had met.

He pushed himself upright against the planking and then the ship lurched and threw him against the echo-sounder. Light flashed in his head and he caught at the stanchion and clung there until his brain could clear; then he moved, with his left shoulder numbed and the arm useless. The shoulder had taken the impact of his weight against the stanchion and he wanted to be sick, but there was no time. He knew that he must hurry now.

When he had raised himself enough to look through the salt-filmed window he saw the big fissure across the foredeck where the water had surged through. He felt for the grabbing-rope and climbed to the starboard bridge-end, his left arm dangling. The wind came fresh against his face. Twice in his journey aft from the wheelhouse he gave himself rest, gathering a little more strength. The second time it was difficult to lodge himself against the wreckage of the after derricks, for the ship was lurching with her head going lower. He took in deep breaths, watching the foam being left on the hatches and then being whipped away in the wind. A parted wire was swinging from the mainmast. As it passed near him he could hear it whining. Débris was falling down the steep angle of the deck and floating off. Watching it, taking the slow deep breaths that must give him the steadiness he needed, he saw a terrible thing.

One piece of the débris was moving strangely with a seeming motivation of its own. When it struggled clear he saw that it was a big brown rat. In a moment it had darted down towards the ruff of white water that was sluicing along the hatches; now it dropped into the sea, and for an instant he could make out the wet sheen on its fur as it began swimming.

He looked away, sickened.

At the stern of the ship, now higher above the water, the big towing-shackle was swinging and then drawn rigid as the tension eased and returned. He had left the steel mallet wedged inside the base of the winch, and had to sit down and brace his legs against the steel flanges before he could drag it free. He lifted it, rising to his feet by pressing upwards against the winch, and moved forward until he reached the shackle.

He had worked, yesterday and again during the night, to secure this shackle with the tow round the bitts. He had worked beyond the point when he knew he must fail, the point when the mind backs out of the job and the will has to take over. Two hours, the first time, with his hands raw at the finish. The second time much longer, because the seas had been worse and it would have been so easy to get his hand or leg trapped under the big steel shackle and lose it, and lose the tow, and lose the ship.

He made all fast, and had made all fast the second time after the first tow had parted. He had brought the ship to within sight of land, and the sea had calmed for him. But now the brown rat had dropped overboard, preferring the sea to the ship.

He lifted the mallet and brought its head against the quick-release pin of the shackle, and missed, and swung it up, and hit square, and swung again, and hit again, and the pin was driven out and the shackle rocketed away, smashing a path through the chocks.

Two minutes later the tug signalled the destroyer in surprise: *Tow's parted.*

H.M.S. *Vixen* was already swinging her bows to starboard and closing the casualty at full speed. She signalled the tug as she came:

'Whipper' sinking. Am going in for captain.

CHAPTER TWENTY

In the streets the rain had eased, and down by the docks people were closing their umbrellas. Educated in the cinema, they felt it was quite right that the rain should stop, now that the *Atlantic Whipper* was due to arrive among them. Rain would spoil the grand occasion; therefore it was easing off.

A brass band was waiting at the water's edge. It had been there for three hours and was now drenched. It looked forlorn, and people had been giving buns to the bandsmen, and someone had brought along a canteen thermos-flask of tea.

The Mayor was at the Town Hall, waiting for the news.

Two B.B.C. mobile transmitters were down in the harbour. A newsreel van with mounted camera was still crawling through the narrow ways, and every time a group in the crowd was photographed it cheered self-consciously.

Peter Costain was down at the South Docks with some of the *Whipper's* crew. He had made his fourth telephone call to Ann Brown and had pinned her down to a meeting. She had sounded reluctant. There was this marriage business, quite irrelevant as far as he could see. It had cost him fourteen shillings in small silver and a short fierce argument with an overworked operator to get the story from her in its raw details. She had been a nurse, and there'd been a man, this particular man, who had thought he was dying—which in fact he was, she said—dying of shrapnel wounds. And he had wanted her to marry him, so that there'd be a pretty girl to leave his money to, because he had nobody else at all, and when she tried to head him off it he got really scared and said it was as good as telling him he was done for ("But you said he knew that, anyway," Peter told her. "Oh, he *did,* but this made it look—all right." Peter said, "Just go on from there"), because no girl wanted to marry a dying man just because——

"He was terribly kind, you see, Peter."

"Yes."

"In the end I said I'd do it. We had a parson in."

Peter had to stop a bitter-sounding laugh. She said the man recovered in three weeks and was discharged, and wrote saying he'd torn up the will because 'he must have been a bit rocky in his mind, being so ill and all that,' and he was sorry he'd given her so much trouble.

"So I suppose it saved his life, Peter. I mean he thought he must have had a chance, if I was willing to marry him. I suppose it gave him the will to fight for himself."

"You don't really believe that, do you?"

Her voice had been bleak on the long-distance telephone. "No."

And there it was. Divorce was expensive. There was undeniable desertion, of course. He said he would fix it for her, find a lawyer, but—"It's not easy, Peter. I don't know where he lives."

He had wanted to put his fist through one of the glass panels in the telephone-box. They were very inviting, these small square panels, if you wanted to let off steam. Didn't the Postmaster General realize that a lot of highly frustrating conversations must go on in these little boxes, all over the country?

"I'll fix it somehow, Ann. When I see you, we'll talk about it, and I'll fix it."

She had said yes, reluctantly, and they had arranged when and where to meet.

He stood in the drizzle, fretting. Was it just an excuse of hers to get rid of him? But she'd said she loved him. Did she mean that? Did she know what love meant? Try to see her point of view: she was a responsible woman doing a rather wonderful job, when you thought about it, and he was just a wandering third mate with no home, kicking about the globe and getting little enough pay for doing it. Not much of a catch.

Why couldn't she just drop a hint, then?

The rain crept down inside his turned up collar. He listened to Art Starley profaning to someone. Either she loved him or she didn't, and if she did, it would be all right.

Wouldn't it?

"D'you know anything about women, Starley?"

"Yessir. They're p'ison."

The newsreel van crept on soft springs along the harbour wall. A constable kept the people back. An hour ago the horizon had come into view through the rain-haze; now it was possible to see the dark shapes, sometimes two, sometimes three; but no one could make out which ship was the *Atlantic Whipper*. From here they all looked the same.

They looked the same all over the world. Margaret Harkness was at the window of her room in the Metropole. She had been talking to the young man and his wife, the Jocelyns. He said he was a journalist but he seemed different from the others. But they were among the people who felt that a ship was something more than rivets and timber. They spoke about the *Atlantic Whipper* as if it were something unique. She would have asked to be left alone, except that they spoke, too, about Matthew Harkness. They were among the people, the strangers, whom she had sometimes met by chance and who had talked of her husband with a deep affection; and this outweighed their odd defect of the heart, this absurd devotion to rivets and timber. She had long ago ceased to ask them to explain it. Matthew had never been able to. It was as if she had asked someone to explain why they believed in God. They would have said: 'It's a thing you feel, and if you don't feel it for yourself, you'll never understand.'

She had let the Jocelyns stay with her, and no one else. How much had the young man engineered her tolerance of them? He was a journalist and had a job to do; but if he had partly persuaded her, it had been done very subtly in his bland-faced way (rather like Matthew, to look at, a young Matthew with his face as yet unlined—there were strange likenesses in the people you met, and surely it must influence your opinion of them when they reminded you of someone you liked, or didn't like).

"If I were in your place," the girl was saying, standing beside her looking like a pert child in the duffle-coat and slacks, "I'd be doing something awful now. Climbing up the curtains or blowing a trumpet or something. Just lack of poise, I suppose. I used to bite my nails, at this kind of time. Usually with my gloves still on."

She lit another cigarette. In a mild voice Alan Jocelyn said: "That was before she took up chain-smoking."

A little later, about noon, he said, "The rain's stopped."

The day took on a glare, shining across the pavements and the sea.

Down at the South Docks, Turnbull was standing in the crowd, not far from Costain and the others. They had seen him, but no one went up to him.

Bloody Matthew looked like doing it. Even if Steve had hated Matthew he would have come here to stand like this at the edge of the sea, urging him home with his ship. And he didn't hate him. Matthew was just a man he would have liked to be himself. There weren't many; but he was one.

The newsreel van was not moving any more. This seemed to be the best vantage-point. The band was a few yards away, and the platform well in focus. A lane was being kept clear by police, for the Mayor to drive through. Captain Harkness would get into the Mayor's car, after the preliminary speech of congratulation, and the newsreel van could turn and follow the procession to the Town Hall, and the boys inside take over with their cameras. It was a nice exclusive set-up, and even the rain had stopped.

A man was going through the crowd, selling postcards—actual photographs of the *Atlantic Whipper*. Where had he found them? He was a man of initiative. There was a small trade in autograph-books—your new autograph-book was a sure winner if the first name in it was Harkness.

A woman fainted and was taken out of the throng.

In a radio-van against which Starley the bosun and two seamen leaned, a short-wave set was tuned to 140 metres. People had lodged themselves near the open door at the back of it, but there'd been no signal since eleven-thirty when H.M.S. *Vixen* had passed on a message from Captain Harkness to the *Salvado*: *Slight chafing, have used last grease.* There had been no action taken: Captain Howes had decided the tow would last the trip.

That was over two hours ago, before the three ships had been sighted over the horizon. It was now possible to tell one from another by their size and position. The *Atlantic Whipper,* lying over at a steep angle, dominated the two smaller vessels. There was a shifting haze, getting a little thicker as the sea rose and the wind took spindrift from the crests. Sometimes only two of the ships were visible, but the third would reappear, relieving the nerves of the people who watched, their eyes hot and feet numbed as they stood in the puddles, hunched in chill mackintoshes and drenched overcoats. But it was going to be worth it. Nothing could make them leave here now.

A mobile canteen pulled up near the radio-van, claiming a few of the faithful. The others were too chilled to want to move, even for tea, even to find a sodden cigarette and try to light it. There was a spell on them.

It was broken by a sound that came from the sea. Some of them didn't hear it at first, and went on talking, and were hushed by others who were listening to the sad far-away sound.

The face of Steve Turnbull had drained white.

Someone asked: "Where's it coming from?" Another said: "The sea." It was like the war, a woman said, it gave you quite a shiver.

"Ships' sirens," Tich Copley said, not wanting to breathe. He could see nothing through the flying salt haze—a dark blob or two, nothing indentifiable. "Bose," he said. "Bose!"

Starley turned and pushed his way through the shoulders, trying to reach the open door of the radio-van. People moved back for him, surprised and frightened by the look on his face.

In a little while the far sound died away. Soon voices were heard from the pack of people round the radio-van. It sounded as if they were arguing, or protesting. Was someone drunk? Others pressed nearer, trying to hear what was being shouted, to see who was shouting.

It looked like a fight starting, because Art Starley had forced his way round to the open door of the van and was shouting at one of the men inside, one of the men with headphones on. The bosun reached inside and grabbed him by the collar.

"She can't have! You got it wrong! She can't have!"

The shout was full of anger. The people on the fringe of the crowd were certain it was a fight; a big man was trying to force his way into the van, and the men inside were trying to keep him out. The people swayed together, asking one another what was happening; but for a few minutes nobody seemed to know, until the news came through to them, passed as quickly as a ball tossed shoulder-high across the crowd, the few words flicked by the sudden turn of a head, and repeated, and repeated, until everyone had heard.

After they had heard, there was a strange low sound from them, flowing in a sad wave along the harbour wall. A small boy, jostled by the people about him, dropped his glossy postcard, and a shifting foot sent mud across it at the edge of a puddle, and the picture of the ship was blotted out.

An aircraft had been over the sea, flying very low and circling, probably taking the last photographs. Matthew had heard the drone of its engines above the destroyer's wash. He was not interested in the aeroplane, nor in anything at all.

He had been in the water less than ten minutes. He had jumped from the funnel, when the doors of the wheelhouse had blown out. The water had rushed in below-deck, compressing the air, and the doors had burst outwards. Then he had jumped, for a man must use his good sense at sea, though he will hold on longer than a rat.

He had floated in his life-jacket among the débris that was still dropping from the decks as the *Whipper* rolled on to her side. Water went rushing into the funnel, and the great length of her shuddered, again and again, until with his one good arm he turned his body in the water so that he need no longer look at her. She lay in the scum of flotsam and floating grain. After five days the slack water in number one hold had swelled the grain and she had been split open by its pressure. The grain floated, pale as vomit, and he denied that it could humiliate her, that a ship's death could look as ugly as a sick woman's. He began swimming away from her, driving his right arm and kicking with his legs, until a boat from the destroyer made towards him and picked him out of the sea.

When he was on board H.M.S. *Vixen,* her surgeon wanted him

to go below, because with his blood-red eyes and white face he looked in great need of attention; but he asked the captain if he might stay on the bridge for a few minutes. They fetched blankets and put them round his shoulders. The sea had been winter-cold and he did not cease trembling.

From the bridge of the destroyer he watched the *Whipper* go. Her stern was still above water when he first sighted her. She was nothing of a ship now, but just a dark stump above the waves, poking up through the débris with spray breaking against it. The rudder swung from side to side, freed by a broken gear. It flapped slowly like the fin of a dying fish.

When her time came she went quickly, for her size. The dark stump drew downwards and the waves rose about it; then the water rushed white, threshing into whirlpools with the débris tossing in the foam; then she was gone.

The tug sounded her siren, and the destroyer joined her in the salute. Matthew turned away and told the surgeon that he was sorry to have kept him waiting; he would go below with him now.

At nine minutes to two, H.M.S. *Vixen* sent a signal.

The 'Atlantic Whipper' has gone down. Her captain is safely on board with me.

Then the destroyer was turned in the short white sea and her stern went down as she began steaming for the land.

THE OCTOBER GAME

Ray Bradbury

"The October Game" from the book "Alfred Hitchcock Presents" published by Max Reinhardt Ltd. is reprinted by arrangement with the author and A. D. Peters

HE put the gun back into the bureau drawer and shut the drawer.

No, not that way. Louise wouldn't suffer that way. She would be dead and it would be over and she wouldn't suffer. It was very important that this thing have, above all, duration. Duration through imagination. How to prolong the suffering? How, first of all, to bring it about? Well.

The man standing before the bedroom mirror carefully fitted his cuff links together. He paused long enough to hear the children run by swiftly on the street below, outside this warm two-storey house; like so many grey mice the children, like so many leaves.

By the sound of the children you knew the calendar day. By their screams you knew what evening it was. You knew it was very late in the year. October. The last day of October, with white bone masks and cut pumpkins and the smell of dropped candle fat.

No. Things hadn't been right for some time. October didn't help any. If anything it made things worse. He adjusted his black bow-tie. If this were spring, he nodded slowly, quietly, emotionlessly, at his image in the mirror, then there might be a chance. But tonight all the world was burning down into ruin. There was no green of spring, none of the freshness, none of the promise.

There was a soft running in the hall. "That's Marion," he told himself. "My little one. All eight quiet years of her. Never a word. Just her luminous grey eyes and her wondering little mouth." His daughter had been in and out all evening, trying on various masks, asking him which was most terrifying, most horrible. They had both finally decided on the skeleton mask. It was "'just awful!" It would "scare the beans" from people!

Again he caught the long look of thought and deliberation he gave himself in the mirror. He had never liked October. Ever since he first lay in the autumn leaves before his grandmother's house many years ago and heard the wind and saw the empty trees. It had made him cry, without a reason. And a little of that sadness returned each year to him. It always went away with spring.

But it was different tonight. There was a feeling of autumn coming to last a million years.

There would be no spring.

He had been crying quietly all evening. It did not show, not a vestige of it, on his face. It was all somewhere hidden, but it wouldn't stop.

A rich syrupy smell of candy filled the bustling house. Louise had laid out apples in new skins of caramel, there were vast bowls of punch fresh mixed, stringed apples in each door, scooped, vented pumpkins peering triangularly from each cold window. There was a waiting water tub in the centre of the living room, waiting, with a sack of apples nearby, for bobbling to begin. All that was needed was the catalyst, the inpouring of children, to start the apples bobbling, the stringed apples to penduluming in the crowded doors, the candy to vanish, the halls to echo with fright or delight, it was all the same.

Now, the house was silent with preparation. And just a little more than that.

Louise had managed to be in every other room save the room he was in today. It was her very fine way of intimating, Oh, look, Mich, see how busy I am! So busy that when you walk into a room *I'm* in there's always something I need to do in *another* room! Just see how I dash about!

For a while he had played a little game with her, a nasty childish game. When she was in the kitchen then he came to the kitchen, saying, "I need a glass of water." After a moment, him standing, drinking water, she like a crystal witch over the caramel brew bubbling like a prehistoric mudpot on the stove, she said, "Oh, I must light the window pumpkins!" and she rushed to the living room to make the pumpkins smile with light. He came after her, smiling, "I must get my pipe." "Oh, the cider!" she had cried, running to the dining room. "I'll check the cider," he had said. But when he tried following she ran to the bathroom and locked the door.

He stood outside the bath door, laughing strangely and senselessly, his pipe gone cold in his mouth, and then, tired of the game, but stubborn, he waited another five minutes. There was not a sound from the bath. And lest she enjoy in any way knowing that he waited outside irritated, he suddenly jerked about and walked upstairs, whistling merrily.

At the top of the stairs he had waited. Finally he had heard the bath door unlatch and she had come out and life belowstairs had resumed, as life in a jungle must resume once a terror has passed on away and the antelope return to their spring.

Now, as he finished his bow-tie and put on his dark coat there was a mouse-rustle in the hall. Marion appeared in the door, all skeletonous in her disguise.

"How do I look, Papa?"

"Fine!"

From under the mask, blonde hair showed. From the skull sockets small blue eyes smiled. He sighed. Marion and Louise, the two silent denouncers of his virility, his dark power. What alchemy had there been in Louise that took the dark of a dark man and bleached and bleached the dark brown eyes and black black hair and washed and bleached the ingrown baby all during the period before birth until the child was born, Marion, blonde, blue-eyed, ruddy-cheeked? Sometimes he suspected that Louise had conceived the child as an idea, completely asexual, an immaculate conception of contemptuous mind and cell. As a firm rebuke to him she had produced a child in her *own* image, and, to top it, she had somehow *fixed* the doctor so he shook his head and said, "Sorry, Mr. Wilder, your wife will never have another child. This is the *last* one."

"And I wanted a boy," Mich had said, eight years ago.

He almost bent to take a hold of Marion now, in her skull mask. He felt an inexplicable rush of pity for her, because she had never had a father's love, only the crushing, holding love of a loveless mother. But most of all he pitied himself, that somehow he had not made the most of a bad birth, enjoyed his daughter for herself, regardless of her not being dark and a son and like himself. Somewhere he had missed out. Other things being equal, he would have loved the child. But Louise hadn't wanted a child, anyway, in the first place. She had been frightened of the idea of birth. He had forced the child on her, and from that night, all through the year until the agony of the birth itself, Louise had lived in another part of the house. She had expected to die with the forced child. It had been very easy for Louise to hate this husband who so wanted a son that he gave his only wife over to the mortuary.

But—Loüise had lived. And in triumph! Her eyes, the day he came to the hospital, were cold. I'm alive, they said. And I have a *blonde* daughter! Just look! And when he had put out a hand to touch, the mother had turned away to conspire with her new pink daughter-child—away from that dark forcing murderer. It had all been so beautifully ironic. His selfishness deserved it.

But now it was October again. There had been other Octobers and when he thought of the long winter he had been filled with horror year after year to think of the endless months mortared into the house by an insane fall of snow, trapped with a woman and child, neither of whom loved him, for months on end. During the eight years there had been respites. In spring and summer you got out, walked, picnicked; these were desperate solutions to the desperate problem of a hated man.

But, in winter, the hikes and picnics and escapes fell away with the leaves. Life, like a tree, stood empty, the fruit picked, the sap run to earth. Yes, you invited people in, but people were hard to get in winter with blizzards and all. Once he had been clever enough to save for a Florida trip. They had gone south. He had walked in the open.

But now, the eighth winter coming, he knew things were finally at an end. He simply could not wear this one through. There was an acid walled off in him that slowly had eaten through tissue and tissue over the years, and now, tonight, it would reach the wild explosive in him and all would be over!

There was a mad ringing of the bell below. In the hall, Louise went to see. Marion, without a word, ran down to greet the first arrivals. There were shouts and hilarity.

He walked to the top of the stairs.

Louise was below, taking wraps. She was tall and slender and blonde to the point of whiteness, laughing down upon the new children.

He hesitated. What was all this? The years? The boredom of living? Where had it gone wrong? Certainly not with the birth of the child alone. But it had been a symbol of all their tensions, he imagined. His jealousies and his business failures and all the rotten rest of it. Why didn't he just turn, pack a suitcase and leave? No. Not without hurting Louise as much as she had hurt him. It was simple as that. Divorce wouldn't hurt her at all. It would simply be an end to numb indecision. If he thought divorce would give her pleasure in any way he would stay married the rest of his life to her, for damned spite. No, he must hurt her. Figure some way, perhaps, to take Marion away from her, legally. Yes. That was it. That would hurt most of all. To take Marion away.

"Hallo down there!" He descended the stairs, beaming.

Louise didn't look up.

"Hi, Mr. Wilder!"

The children shouted, waved, as he came down.

By ten o'clock the doorbell had stopped ringing, the apples were bitten from stringed doors, the pink child faces were wiped dry from the apple bobbling, napkins were smeared with caramel and punch, and he, the husband, with pleasant efficiency had taken over. He took the party right out of Louise's hands. He ran about talking to the twenty children and the twelve parents who had come and were happy with the special spiked cider he had fixed them. He supervised PIN THE TAIL ON THE DONKEY, SPIN THE BOTTLE, MUSICAL CHAIRS and all the rest, midst fits of shouting laughter. Then, in the triangular-eyed pumpkin shine, all house lights out, he cried, "Hush! Follow me!" he said, tiptoeing towards the cellar.

The parents, on the outer periphery of the costumed riot, commented to each other, nodding at the clever husband, speaking to the lucky wife. How *well* he got on with children, they said.

The children crowded after the husband, squealing.

"The cellar!" he cried. "The tomb of the witch!"

More squealing. He made a mock shiver. "Abandon hope all ye who enter here!"

The parents chuckled.

One by one the children slid down a slide which Mich had fixed up from lengths of table-section, into the dark cellar. He hissed and shouted ghastly utterances after them. A wonderful wailing filled the dark pumpkin-lighted house. Everybody talked at once. Everybody but Marion. She had gone through all the party with a minimum of sound or talk; it was all inside her, all the excitement and joy. What a little troll, he thought. With a shut mouth and shiny eyes she had watched her own party, like so many serpentines, thrown before her.

Now, the parents. With laughing reluctance they slid down the short incline, uproarious, while little Marion stood by, always wanting to see it all, to be last. Louise went down without his help. He moved to aid her, but she was gone even before he bent.

The upper house was empty and silent in the candleshine.

Marion stood by the slide. "Here we go," he said, and picked her up.

They sat in a vast circle in the cellar. Warmth came from the distant bulk of the furnace. The chairs stood on a long line down each wall, twenty squealing children, twelve rustling relatives, alternately spaced, with Louise down at the far end. Mich up at this end, near the stairs. He peered but saw nothing. They had all groped to their chairs, catch-as-you-can in the blackness. The entire programme from here on was to be enacted in the dark, he as Mr. Interlocutor. There was a child scampering, a smell of damp cement, and the sound of the wind out in the October stars.

"Now!" cried the husband in the dark cellar. "Quiet!"

Everybody settled.

The room was black black. Not a light, not a shine, not a glint of an eye.

A scraping of crockery, a metal rattle.

"The witch is dead," intoned the husband.

"Eeeeeeeeeeee," said the children.

"The witch is dead, she has been killed, and here is the knife she was killed with."

He handed over the knife. It was passed from hand to hand, down and around the circle, with chuckles and little odd cries and comments from the adults.

"The witch is dead, and this is her head," whispered the husband, and handed an item to the nearest person.

"Oh, I know how this game is played," some child cried, happily, in the dark. "He gets some old chicken innards from the icebox and hands them around and says, 'These are her innards!' And he makes a clay head and passes it for her head, and passes a soup-bone for her arm. And he takes a marble and says, 'This is her eye!' And he takes some corn and says, 'This is her teeth!' And he takes a sack of plum pudding and gives that and says, 'This is her stomach!' I know how *this* is played!"

"Hush, you'll spoil everything," some girl said.

"The witch came to harm, and this is her arm," said Mich.

"Eeeee!"

The items were passed and passed, like hot potatoes, around the circle. Some children screamed, wouldn't touch them. Some ran from their chairs to stand in the centre of the cellar until the grisly items had passed.

"Aw, it's only chicken insides," scoffed a boy. "Come back, Helen!"

Shot from hand to hand, with small scream after scream, the items went down the line, down down, to be followed by another and another.

"The witch cut apart, and this is her heart," said the husband.

Six or seven items moving at once through the laughing, trembling dark.

Louise spoke up. "Marion, don't be afraid; it's only play."

Marion didn't say anything.

"Marion?" asked Louise. "Are you afraid?"

Marion didn't speak.

"She's all right," said the husband. "She's not afraid."

On and on the passing, the screams, the hilarity.

The autumn wind sighed about the house. And he, the husband, stood at the head of the dark cellar, intoning the words, handing out the items.

"Marion?" asked Louise again, from far across the cellar.

Everybody was talking.

"Marion?" called Louise.

Everybody quieted.

"Marion, answer me, are you afraid?"

Marion didn't answer.

The husband stood there, at the bottom of the cellar steps.

Louise called, "Marion, are you there?"

No answer. The room was silent.

"Where's Marion?" called Louise.

"She was here," said a boy.

"Maybe she's upstairs."

"Marion!"

No answer. It was quiet.

Louise cried out, "Marion, Marion!"

"Turn on the lights," said one of the adults.

The items stopped passing. The children and adults sat with the witches' items in their hands.

"No." Louise gasped. There was a scraping of her chair, wildly, in the dark. "No. Don't turn on the lights, don't turn on the lights, oh God, God, God, don't turn them on, please, please *don't* turn on the lights, *don't*!" Louise was shrieking now. The entire cellar froze with the scream.

Nobody moved.

Everyone sat in the dark cellar, suspended in the suddenly frozen task of this October game; the wind blew outside, banging the house, the smell of pumpkins and apples filled the room with the smell of the objects in their fingers while one boy cried, "I'll go upstairs and look!" and he ran upstairs hopefully and out around the house, four times around the house, calling, "Marion, Marion, Marion!" over and over and at last coming slowly down the stairs into the waiting, breathing cellar and saying to the darkness, "I can't find her."

Then . . . some idiot turned on the lights.

COUNT FIVE AND DIE

Barry Wynne

"Count Five and Die" is published by
Souvenir Press Ltd.

The Author

Barry Wynne, born 1929 in Eastcote, Middlesex, is married and has two children. During the Second World War, after serving for one year in the ranks, he obtained an infantry commission in the Devonshire Regiment. Sent out to the Far East, he arrived in the first week of the Malayan emergency and was immediately in action against Chinese guerrillas. Later he transferred to Special Air Services and became a paratrooper and small boat expert. After demobilization he decided not to pursue an early training in commerce and turned instead to writing plays, film scripts and articles.

FOREWORD

PROBABLY one of the most successful deceptions in military history was that of the Trojan Horse, but, alas, in modern warfare the opportunity to carry out such a simple subterfuge on your enemy is almost non-existent. For, although the originating conception may prove just as simple in its broadest aspects, yet it becomes in operation a complex exercise that has to be carried out with cunning, ingenuity and the utmost skill.

However, this story of a great D-Day deception was born, not in the mind of some brilliant military strategist, but, as is often the case, was conceived far from the scene of its final enactment by a set of circumstances which, in themselves, proved not only a personal failure for two unfortunate officers, but also, unhappily, resulted in the loss of many Allied lives.

It is one of the tragedies of war that individual men are called upon to face such stresses and strains as they might never meet in a lifetime of peaceful existence. But, by their actions at these critical times, so they are judged, and it is the corner-stone of this story that Operation Stampede might never have taken place had it not been for the carelessness of these two officers, at a time when they should have been most on their guard.

We tell it because, in the final analysis, it proved a triumph of success over initial failure and probably saved the lives of countless Allied soldiers, sailors and airmen in the bloody battles that later took place in the fields of Normandy.

This is a true account within the dictates of public security of a principally American operation to deceive the enemy in the three months prior to the landings in Normandy. It is based on material supplied by one of General Donovan's aides, Colonel William Eliscu, O.B.E., who took part in the operation.

In order to protect the true identities of those involved it has been felt advisable to change certain minor incidents and the names of the leading participants in this operation.

CHAPTER ONE

A SHORT, sparse little German, with a beak-like nose, bullet head and wearing rimless glasses, walked briskly along the Promenade du Prado in Marseilles, turned left and right a couple of times and soon found himself in the Rue Darsé.

He came to a tall, dilapidated house, with the paint peeling off the door, and rang the bell once, paused and then rang it twice again in quick succession. It was shortly opened and he disappeared inside.

On the top floor was a room freshly whitewashed and crammed to the ceiling with radio equipment. Two men rose to their feet and clicked their heels. A third sat at a chair in front of a powerful receiving and transmitting set, absorbed in his task of "listening-out".

"No contact yet, Herr Brenner," said a stout middle-aged man standing behind the operator.

For a few moments silence fell over the room, while the dials on the receiver were twisted and turned, searching diligently for any distant signal.

Brenner, as second in command of an Abwehr section in Toulon, was responsible for liaison with certain agents in North Africa. When he had reached his office that morning, a telephone call from his chief, who had been called to Berlin, had sent him scurrying over to Marseilles.

Apparently a report had just come through via Tangier and Spain requesting them to stand by for an important wireless message from an agent who had been operating in Algiers, but who had been out of contact for some time.

Suddenly the loudspeaker burst into life, spewing forth a staccato crackle of dots and dashes that made up the call sign.

This was quickly acknowledged and then the operator picked up a pencil which swept swiftly over his message pad. When decoded, the text read simply: "Excellent contact with Headquarters, 26th 77th American O.S.S. Stop Teams of one two and three men being dropped by parachute into South Italy Stop Invasion imminent Stop Will endeavour to obtain exact locations

Stop Suspect Sicily as well Stop Listen out each night between 22 and 23 hundred hours Stop Please contact Berlin."

Brenner could hardly contain his excitement.

"Send a message immediately," he exclaimed. "'Excellent work. Imperative you obtain details as outlined. Will contact Berlin.'"

So, at last, a German spy was gaining access to Allied Force Headquarters.

In those early days no one would have dreamt that, through this isolated instance of espionage, the first pawns had already been moved in what was to become one of the greatest bluffs perpetrated on the Germans in the Second World War.

The hot North African sun burned down with unremitting fierceness on the streets and alleys of French Algiers. The time was Spring 1943.

At the Hotel St. George, General Eisenhower had set up his Allied Force Headquarters and, with his staff, was working far into each night on the plans for the coming invasion of Sicily and Italy.

A few streets away, at 117 Rue Michelé, plans of a different order were being drawn up and vetted by one Stephen Martinelli, a cold calculating American of Italian descent, who bossed the Italian Special Intelligence Section, or S.I. as it was known, of the local unit of the O.S.S. (Office of Stategic Services).

This was the first occasion in the history of the United States of America that she had boasted of her own secret service or espionage agency.

Within hours of the first Japanese bombs descending on the unsuspecting American fleet at Pearl Harbour, President Roosevelt had sought out the one man in the American Army whom he thought capable of creating a functionary secret service. He was, of course, the First World War hero of Château Thierry, General William (Wild Bill) Donovan.

The 26th 77th Group of the O.S.S., working in Algiers, was one of their first operational units and had been modelled to a great extent on the British Intelligence Service, renowned throughout the world for its efficiency, reliability and success.

Martinelli's S.I. Section—a so-called Sensitive Unit—were engaged with the operating groups in gleaning information from behind the enemy lines, in order to ascertain if it were humanly possible the enemy's order of battle. As if this task were not sufficient in itself, he also endeavoured to keep his finger on the pulse of all the other espionage activities that made up the everyday scene in the stinking back alleys of the Casbah.

The German Secret Service had already been given ample opportunity to infiltrate their many spies into Algiers by using the excellent cover afforded by the German Armistice Commission, which was set up when Petain negotiated his separate peace with Hitler on behalf of the Vichy Government in 1940.

The Commission had taken over a large white-faced building at the bottom of the hill in the centre of the town and, with glorious multi-coloured posters, had proclaimed to the Arab world their desire for peace with their darker skinned brothers. Through the portals of this building, many a German spy returned hot-foot with information that he had gathered in the bazaars and cabarets where the hog-wash of the world's humanity eked out their everyday existence.

It may be wondered how any vital military information would ever find itself in such strange surroundings. But in the heavy stench-laden atmosphere which had suffered never a cool fresh breeze in a thousand centuries, news of any sort had a price and was a commodity which could readily be bought and sold if the pocket were willing. But for Martinelli the urgent matter in hand was the training and selection for various missions of men who had arrived fresh and keen from the Force's Headquarters in Washington.

Already the Allied war machine was poised expectantly for its first assault on the fortress of Europe and even before the first waves of infantry swept across the beaches of Sicily and Italy, O.S.S. and British agents would be paving the way by linking up with the Italian partisans, blowing up bridges, causing havoc and dislocation to the transport system, and, of course, gathering the vital information that is necessary for any army commander who is about to commit his main force to the battle.

For these men, waiting expectantly and with a trace of apprehension for their various assignments, the only relaxation that offered itself were the cabarets and restaurants which afforded, besides good black market food, the further alleviation of their hunger, in the form of women of every nationality. There were French, Belgian and Dutch refugees, who had taken wing before the thrusting fangs of Hitler's Panzer divisions, and, of course, there were the residents: girls from the Nile, girls from the arid desert, girls from the scattered islands of the Mediterranean.

Each of these fresh arrivals from the States had been screened by Martinelli's security men and warned of the pitfalls and dangers of too much vino rosso in the cellars of ill repute. But such is the nature of men that their appetites were only whetted the more, and so it came about that a certain lieutenant-colonel, who shall remain nameless, met and was captivated by a Dutch refugee girl of some 28 years, blonde, lissom and with the clear-cut beauty of her distant homeland. She was certainly no hell-cat from the grottos, but was rather a vivacious, intelligent creature, and a desirable guest at the many cocktail parties thrown by the officers of the O.S.S. at their Villa Magnol.

She had learned with consummate skill the talent, so highly prized by men, of being a good listener and for hours on end she would be bored to death with the descriptions of home life in Cincinnati or Mason City until, possibly in the early hours, a pearl would fall by the wayside and, gathering it up, she would lock it accurately and unfailingly in the innermost depths of her memory cells.

One morning, in the Rue Michelé, Steve, as he was affectionately known to his subordinates, called a hasty conference, and it was soon discernible to his audience that the boss was in a tricky mood. He spoke in a soft drawl and his bright eyes swept over the men gathered before him.

"When you boys arrived from the States, I made it a top priority that each of you should be warned of the vital necessity to maintain the strictest security, but right now I am in the unhappy position of having to tell you that we suspect some sort of leak. We don't know from where and it may not even concern anyone in this room. But a tip from one of our double agents has given me the gravest suspicion that information about our activities is becoming known to the other side. That would mean, in effect, that every one of our missions and every one of your lives is in danger. As you know, we have already dispatched half a dozen drops and the first major landings will take place at any time now. And so, for heaven's sake, keep a zipper on your mouths. . . ."

But already this warning had come too late. For, lying on a desk at No. 74 to 76 Tirpitzufer in Berlin, was a short typewritten document, and reading it was a man of some fifty odd years, with white hair and a benevolent countenance whose name was Admiral Wilhelm Canaris, head of the German Military Intelligence Service, or better known as the Abwehr.

Within hours, the German teleprinters had sent a signal to a certain divisional commander in the south of Italy who was being left in no doubt that, within the immediate future, his troops dotted around the Sicilian and Italian countryside, would be in the front line of battle.

Fortunately for the Allies, there was only sufficient time to send a few brief wireless messages, for already on the airfields in North Africa, giant troop-carrying planes were warming up their engines, whilst stick upon stick of highly trained parachutists were climbing uncomfortably into the fuselages, with all their paraphernalia of modern war.

In retrospect, it is a great comfort to know that, thanks to "The Man Who Never Was", at least two German divisions were not facing the first eager soldiers who were about to descend into the midst of their enemy.

But, however unpleasant the fact remains, it must be admitted that some of the invading troops had lost one of the cardinal principles of attack, that of surprise. For, as any infantryman well knows, his chances of success depend on three simple rules—speed, surprise and simplicity. Already one of these had been betrayed and a certain number of our assault troops had been subjected to a storm of withering fire.

For Martinelli, about to move his headquarters to Italy, there remained a vital job of work to be done. No matter at what the cost, the source of information to the enemy had to be found. His lawyer's background demanded immediate enquiry, a careful check of facts, a reappraisal of the evidence, and finally a close interrogation of his own men. Time was of vital importance, for the war was rapidly moving on, and an enemy agent who had proved so successful in the alerting of his superiors to the secret hour of attack would not be left in idleness for long.

CHAPTER TWO

THE 26th 77th Group of the O.S.S. moved forward into Italy, but it was decided to leave behind in Algiers a few selected personnel of the section called X-2, or counter-espionage.

Their immediate task was to check on two main groups of people. First, the double agents who might be prepared, for a price, to disclose the suspected spy working in our midst, and, secondly, the more tedious job of checking-up on all the casual acquaintances and close friends of those O.S.S. men who had now moved on to Italy.

Arrangements were also made with Washington to make yet further enquiries into some of the men's background histories, for the reasons that made them volunteer for special duties were not only varied and interesting but might provide an invaluable clue to any traitor, should one exist.*

Of the great majority, it can proudly be said that they were dedicated men. Often, their immediate past was closely linked with Europe for, of course, one of the obvious qualifications for a job of this nature was an aptitude for, or close knowledge of languages. Therefore, some of them were new citizens of the United States of America, anxious to serve the country of their adoption with loyalty and devotion, but often motivated with a merciless hatred for Hitler and the Nazis, who had hounded them from their homeland.

There were also those American-born citizens who had lived, for a variety of reasons, in Europe, possibly to study at the Continental universities, or purely to engage in the mundane activities of commerce.

Sometimes there were deeper personal motives—the unhappy home, the broken marriage, or the lost girl. But, by and large, these cases were in the minority and, therefore, a cross-section of the average O.S.S. unit revealed a conglomeration of nationalities, religion and background.

Although it was stated earlier that the American Secret Service was modelled on that of the British, yet there was one essential difference. The British had a code and standard of operation to which they closely adhered; on the other hand, the Americans also had a code and standard of operation, but to which they seldom conformed, preferring to rely on each set of circumstances to be dealt with in the way which they thought best at the time.

It is sometimes erroneously assumed that a spy earns tremendous remuneration for his activities, but this is not often the case.

The British had always considered that a man working for money alone can be too easily bought and sold, and had, therefore, made a point of paying them only a moderate salary.

In the O.S.S., for instance, the monthly pay cheque could be as

* In fact no "traitor" as such did exist.

low as 100 to 150 dollars, with the added security of a life insurance, taken out for the widow or mother for something in the region of 5,000 dollars. Then, of course, many of these men had been employed in other branches of the services and on these occasions were naturally paid in accordance with their rank.

The terms of contract for their employment were brief and to the point. "... The employer shall pay the employee the sum of ... dollars in the currency of the United States of America each month while said contract is in force.... And further that this contract is a voluntary act of employee undertaken without duress...."

To become an American spy was not just a simple matter of signing the aforementioned contract, but necessitated the undertaking of a gruelling and expensive training. The would-be agent had to spend weeks learning to master the radio transmitter and receiver. Further weeks on the intricacies of demolitions and explosives; hours and hours of concentrated study of codes and de-coding methods. The art of fighting and using whichever weapons came to hand; interrogation with all the niceties of operation. Geography and map reading; the gathering of useful military information and, finally, with the direst doubts as to whether he would survive, came the enrolment in a course at the Parachute School.

Back in Algiers things were beginning to hum. The surreptitious enquiries being conducted by the X-2 Section had revealed the very slimmest of clues.

John and André, two of the operators, had been checking and re-checking on a list of names supplied by Martinelli, as being the various acquaintances of his men. They had had to return to one particular house on several occasions, because it was found to be a clandestine meeting place of several nefarious groups of people deeply enmeshed in black marketeering activities.

This eating house or restaurant, near El Biar, looked innocent enough, with its white stuccoed front and steps leading up to the door. However, once inside, the atmosphere changed. The corridors and staircase were dimly lit with soft glowing wall lights and at the top of the main flight of stairs was a small hall with a little ornate desk in one corner. Behind this sat an attractive woman in her middle forties, obviously French and owner of the establishment.

Her dark, vivacious eyes scanned John and André as they mounted the last few steps and smiled a warm welcome.

"Ah c'est bien de vous voir. Comment allez-vous, mes chéris?"

André's face broke into a boyish grin. "Bien merci, et toi, Eliane?"

With an arm on John's shoulder, André steered him toward the little door leading into the restaurant proper with its soft lights, music and discreet little tables burdened with the finest black-market food that money could buy.

As he passed close to the desk, he leant down and whispered a question into her ear, little knowing that he was about to forge the first link in what was to become the great D-Day deception.

"Tell me, Eliane, will Hannie Herodsen be here this evening? I want to introduce her to John."

"But of course not. She left weeks ago—surely you knew."

André's eyebrows shot up in surprise and, grinning, he turned to John. "Now I shan't be able to introduce you to the most fascinating creature alive." His voice betrayed no hint of sarcasm, but there was a meaning look in his eyes.

Was this the end of the road? Had the name lying second from last on the list prepared by Martinelli turned out to be their elusive German spy?

"Always for me the luck of the devil. Tell me, when will she return?"

Eliane's mischievous eyes laughed teasingly: "Ah, mon pauvre, but I do not think she will ever return. She said she was going away for good."

Two hours later the radio at Martinelli's headquarters in Caserta received the following message in code:

"Enquiries almost complete. Only one possible clue. Check any personnel having contact with Hannie Herodsen who I remember was known to some of the boys. She was supposed to be Dutch and she's disappeared."

When the signaller brought the de-coded message to Martinelli his instinct told him that this was the lead they had been waiting for. He, himself, remembered the girl and his heart missed a beat when he realized with whom she had been so friendly, for it was none other than Colonel X, one of his own colleagues and a member of the O.S.S.

Martinelli sent for him, but there is no record of the conversation, except that it was heated and lasted for well over an hour.

In matters touching on the loyalty and efficiency of his group, Martinelli was a man-eater, mean and cruel. The former friendship was forgotten and never a punch was pulled. This, of course, would mean court-martial, return to the States and possibly prison.

It was not suggested, of course, that this colonel had willingly passed on any vital information, but the fact that he drank heavily and had probably in those unguarded moments fallen victim to the sensuous attraction of this "Dutch" girl did not relieve him of his responsibilities to his country.

To the sound of distant gunfire, rumbling in harmony with his thoughts, Martinelli wandered out into the warm, sultry night. The enormity of their first failure appalled him. He dared not think what Donovan would say, yet even in his moment of anger and frustration he could not but feel a tinge of pity for the man who now faced ruin.

The moon had not yet risen and the night was dark, lit only by a myriad twinkling stars. Occasionally, a flash swept across the far horizon, betraying the position where the Allied and Axis armies were locked in mortal combat.

His mind went back to two of the earliest missions which had so miserably failed. Had these been the fault of this woman spy?

He came to a little tufted hillock, where crickets sang in grand confusion. With his well-trained legal mind, Martinelli set about analysing the extent of their setback. Soon he had sunk into the depth of despair, and it was only with a conscious effort of self-discipline that he made himself remember that even in the midst of defeat there can be victory.

Even as this thought flashed across his brain, the process of constructive thinking gave birth to an idea, which, in its very simplicity, pleased him, making him feel like laughing aloud in the night.

The gunflashes around Monte Cassino lit the distant sky. True they had suffered a failure, but surely in the very tracking down of their own weakness they had forged a weapon which could be used with devilish effect upon the masters of this woman agent.

While it was true that the girl had now left Algiers, it was quite obvious that she would be used again, and the only question to answer was when and where? Another simple thought struck Martinelli as he clambered to his feet and started to wend his way home. Might not the Germans, believing her to be undetected, try and use her as a bait at Eisenhower's headquarters once more? Surely it would be the obvious thing to do. She already had numerous contacts, and the risk involved would be slight compared to the potential gain.

It was obvious, even to the Germans, that a second attack on the bastion of Europe could not be delayed for long, and it was equally obvious from whence the attack would come. Great Britain was being turned into a vast and powerful arsenal, with a build-up of military strength never before seen in the history of the world.

To this armed camp Eisenhower belonged, and it would be interesting indeed to see whether Hannie Herodsen would reach London too. What an opportunity this could afford. A known German agent, in touch with Berlin, a direct link with the Nazi High Command. What commutations could be worked out on this theme?

He smiled to himself in the darkness and quickened his pace, but for only a moment or two, for suddenly he came to a halt. The bright silver crown of the moon came rising over the summits of the nearby mountains, giving them a tenderness and enchantment never seen by the light of day. Martinelli continued walking home in a far happier mood.

The same moon that swung high above the mountains to the east of Caserta also cast radiance over a little sandy bay just outside the town of Bougie, some 200 miles to the east of Algiers. An Arab dhow was putting out to sea from around a little rocky headland and, as the dirty white sails caught the breath of the off-shore wind, she heeled over in silent ecstasy, tripping her way through the dancing waves and responding to the heave of the open sea.

Sitting perched atop the forehatch, with her eyes looking far away across the bows, was Hannie Herodsen, successful master spy.

For the first time in two years she felt happy and serene as she drank deep the fresh sea air, cleansing her lungs of the smell of spice and donkey dung, of mint tea and charcoal fires.

She had worked well for her Fatherland, but the fire of her patriotic fervour was now subdued, as she wistfully looked back across the years. She had given all that a woman can give for her country and now she felt soiled and a little afraid. Poor Bill, what an easy fool. But she'd had no feeling for him, for this, as the Fuehrer had so often said, was total war.

She glanced back toward the stern and saw one of the Arabs sweeping the sea with a pair of fine binoculars, probably filched from the body of one of her own dead comrades, she mused. They appeared more frightened than she of falling foul of the British and American warships carrying troops and supplies to Italy.

She changed the course of her thoughts and let her mind drift back to those carefree years when her parents had sent her to college in Holland. She remembered the day she had spent in the country with Piet, of their swimming and sailing, of their love and joy. She remembered the fire that he had made on the bank of the river, how the flames had created grotesque figures that danced and flashed on the surface of the stream. She remembered waking up when the dying embers glowed red, fanned by the late night breeze. Soon, if all went well, she would be back in Berlin and with luck would be granted some leave. She wanted to see her mother again, for in these days the future seemed so insecure.

The acrid smell of the Arabs cooking their evening meal brought her rudely back to the present.

For the past five minutes a bank of cloud had obscured the moon, but, even as she was wondering if they would give her anything to eat, the clouds sped away on their endless journey in space to reveal in the sudden moonlight the dark grey shape of a destroyer bearing down on them. At the same instant the Arabs must have seen it also, for they shouted a frenzied word of warning. Throwing herself from the hatch, Hannie was just scrambling down the fo'c'sle when the brilliant white glare of a searchlight stabbed the darkness and came to rest on the dhow, turning the night into day.

She bruised her knees and elbows severely as she hurled herself, head first, down the companionway, to land in a pathetic heap at the bottom of the steps. Although the breath had been knocked from her body, she quickly crawled into the false locker that had been created for just such a purpose and squeezed her way within.

Even as she struggled to close the door, she heard an English voice over the loud hailer—"Heave to." And a few seconds later, "Heave to, you bastards, I say."

Slowly, she felt the boat come on to an even keel as its bows were thrust into the wind. It seemed like an age, in her cramped and airless quarters, before she heard the tramp of hobnailed boots on the deck above. The Arabs, she knew, would be playing their part well. With violent exclamations of injured innocence they would explain from whence they came and whither they were bound.

Suddenly a couple of men clattered down the steps beside her, brushing past the false bulkhead not six inches from where she crouched in silent terror.

She need not have feared, for the inveterate smugglers of opium knew well the art of concealment, even to such prying eyes as those of a chief petty officer in the Royal Navy.

Having conducted their cursory examination, His Majesty's sailors felt satisfied, and after another brief interval, interjected with abusive language on both sides, the dhow was again left in silence.

She waited for a few more moments and then heard the soft shuffle of unshod feet as one of the crew made his way toward her.

He tapped lightly on the bulkhead and she released the catch inside, struggling to extricate her blood-starved limbs from out of their temporary coffin. A pair of strong brown arms grasped her round the shoulders and heaved her out into the passage. She noted that it was Shirez, one of the brothers who owned the dhow. And, grinning, he spat gleefully as an expressive gesture of his contempt for the British Navy.

When she scrambled back on deck, there was no sign of the enemy destroyer, and, having allowed a decent interval for its departure, the long tiller was thrust hard over to port and the flapping sails filled once again to the caressing breath of the cool night wind.

An hour later, after they had supped on the foulest dinner she could remember for many a day, she watched Shirez and his brother haul aloft a lantern, which swung gently on its halyard twenty feet above the deck. A second lamp was taken to the stern and attached tightly to a stay, while a third was taken amidships and attached to the gunwale on the starboard side.

The Arabs grew increasingly nervous as the long minutes slowly ticked by, and after they had sailed steadily for another three-quarters of an hour, a hasty conference was called.

The excited Arabic chatter had risen to a violent crescendo, when a shout from the for'ard lookout drew everyone's attention to the sea some hundred yards away. With water spuming and cascading off her glistening sides, one of the last of Hitler's Mediterranean U-boats came swiftly to the surface.

In an instant, men seemed to appear from nowhere, and, with the decks still awash, the gun crew leapt to their positions, swivelling the long barrel into the direction of the dhow.

Hannie's heart raced for the second time that evening, as she saw a light flash the pre-arranged signal from the conning-tower.

Ibrahim, the elder brother, answered with a powerful flashlight as other members of the crew hastened to lower the sails. Soon they were rocking in the gentle swell and she could hear the German captain shouting words of command. Slowly, and she thought beautifully, the U-boat nosed its way toward the side of the dhow. Members of the crew, in their dark trousers and white sweaters, stood at intervals along the outer casing, waiting to fend her off as the two boats came together.

Hannie interrupted Ibrahim as he was cursing one of the members of his crew:

"Yes, missy?" he enquired.

"Here is the balance of the money promised you now that we have made our rendezvous."

"Thank you, missy," he exclaimed in eager anticipation.

She handed him an envelope.

"Five hundred American dollars in ten-dollar bills. You'd better count them."

As he was doing so, a head suddenly appeared over the rail, and for the first time in many months she heard in her own tongue the familiar greeting—"Grüss Gott."

"Grüss Gott," she cried.

Briefly she said goodbye to her Arab friends and, handing her valise to one of the U-boat's crew, she struggled over the side. The operation of boarding the submarine was not as easy as she had expected. With little light, except for the moon, and with each craft rising and falling as much as four feet at a time, she could not find a footing, until a young authoritative voice from the conning-tower brought rescue with the aid of two or three men who helped her clamber up the slippery deck. Immediately she became conscious of the throb of heavy motors deep below the casing, and almost before she had time to get her breath, a volley of crisp commands had the men scurrying to their various posts as the *Kapitan* prepared to dive.

As she climbed down the steps of the conning-tower she was met by a blast of warm air. She felt almost at home and certainly safe among friends.

That evening, after an excellent meal prepared in her honour, the young U-boat captain handed her a sealed envelope with a message inside.

"We received this signal about four hours ago," he said. "Perhaps you would care to read it in my cabin."

It was terse and to the point:

"Immediately on arrival you will be flown to Berlin. Oberleutnant Heitel will meet you at the dockside and escort you to my headquarters. Signed: Kaltenbrunner."

She sat down in the chair. Kaltenbrunner—why was she not reporting to Admiral Canaris? Before she had time to speculate further, a klaxon sounded stridently in her ear and she could hear the sudden rush of men pounding to their stations.

As she jumped to her feet, the cabin door was opened and a junior officer said, smiling pleasantly and reassuringly:

"No need to worry. Just an alarm. There is a ship going to pass directly overhead. We'll just stop engines and wait and see."

With this he pulled the door to and, as the sound of the U-boat's engines gradually died away, she sat down again to ponder the significance of this summons to the office of the dreaded Kaltenbrunner. Surely she was not to be used again straight away? Before she could answer the question in her mind, the distant thud of approaching propellers drove all other thoughts from her head. Nearer and nearer they came until the whole U-boat seemed to vibrate with the noise of the screws and then suddenly they had passed overhead.

Hannie was just about to breathe again when a series of violent explosions hurled her to the floor. The U-boat seemed to buck and twist under the blast and suddenly the lights went out. She bit her lips, trying desperately not to scream, and expected any moment to feel the sea rushing in to engulf her. To her horror she heard the engines above rapidly approaching again, although this time they sounded slightly farther away. Again the ship was torn by blast as the depth-charges exploded in the sea all around, but this was as near as they came.

Although the attack was pressed home for a further quarter of an hour the worst was over and, finding her way to the bunk, which she could just see by the light of the emergency bulb, she buried her head in the pillow and burst into tears. All the pent-up strain of the last few years came tumbling out as she clutched the pillow in her hands.

Even for a top German agent there comes a limit, and Hannie Herodsen had reached it several months before.

CHAPTER THREE

By early March 1944, General Eisenhower had been long established in London, working and planning on the mounting of Operation Overlord.

Martinelli's forecast in Italy the year before was not far out and he was correct in yet another way for Hannie Herodsen had come to London. It was not until after the war that we learned how she had accomplished this difficult task.

Having been taken to Berlin, commended for her excellent work in Algiers, and given one month's leave, she returned to be briefed in detail by Kaltenbrunner himself.

She was unable to dispel her innate fear of the man. His personality was crude in the extreme and she wondered to herself how much he was responsible for the downfall of her previous chief, Admiral Canaris.

As she sat in a red leather chair, dressed in a neatly tailored suit, she felt distinctly apprehensive as Kaltenbrunner's eyes swept over her, with a hardly concealed look of animal lust.

In spite of the fact that it was only eleven o'clock in the morning, he went to a cabinet and took out a bottle of champagne.

On her polite refusal he suddenly erupted like an angry gorilla, crashing down a big stubby hand on the edge of the desk and storming: "You *will* join me." She felt very frightened. And as he brought round the glass she noticed his ill-conditioned teeth and a strong smell of alcohol.

However, his mood quickly changed and, sitting down, he looked across at her with his piggy brown eyes.

"I am about to entrust to you," he said, "the most important mission of the war. You have proved yourself most capable of handling American officers. . . ." With this he gave a lecherous smile. " . . . and consequently it has been decided to send you direct to London. It is quite obvious that the British and Americans must be preparing an attack which we believe will be launched soon. You must endeavour to obtain any information that you possibly can. You will be taken, by U-boat, and put ashore in England. After that your method of working will be entirely your own. With regard to further details I shall brief you again tomorrow afternoon."

With a perfunctory gesture, he dismissed her from the room

and, as she rose to leave the office, Hannie noticed Kaltenbrunner pouring himself another glass of champagne.

So, on one moonless night and feeling bitterly afraid, she was rowed ashore in a collapsible dinghy close to the little town of Winchelsea.

To her it seemed madness in the extreme to land on such an open piece of coast, but she needn't have worried, for the spot had been picked with admirable care. They were very lucky for the sea was calm for the time of year and Hannie was reminded of her nocturnal fishing trips in the Baltic before the war.

Now she could hear the waves breaking on the beach, although it was far too dark to see anything yet.

One sailor was rowing, the second was up in the bows waiting to step over the side and carry her on to dry land, for it wouldn't do to be found soaking wet from sea water if accosted by anyone.

As they pulled into the shallower water the waves started breaking and several times they almost capsized.

Then, quite without warning, the U-boat sailor leapt over the side and, turning the bows out to sea, he reached in and took Hannie into his arms. Fighting to keep his feet, pounded by the waves, the sailor gallantly struggled to get her ashore. The next moment, after a whispered farewell, she found herself dumped unceremoniously on fairly dry land.

Clutching her little valise, she struggled on the pebbles, fighting her way up the steeply sloping beach. Suddenly she slipped on a piece of seaweed and, as she fell in the darkness, she heard the sound of footsteps rapidly approaching. She fought to get her hand into her right overcoat pocket and withdrew the squat Mauser automatic. Suddenly the sound of the footsteps halted and she lay trembling and wet on the cold foreshore.

The night was so dark that she couldn't even see the shadow of the man that she knew must be within a few yards. Panic seized her and she had an overwhelming desire to jump to her feet, rush down the beach, plunge into the sea and swim to the distant U-boat, which was waiting impatiently for the return of their dinghy. But she never moved, hardly daring to breathe, until softly out of the night she heard an English voice enquire:

"It's a cold night for a swim."

And with a sense of the utmost joy she replied:

"But the water is warm."

In a second she was being helped to her feet by the man she

still couldn't see and, supported by his arms, she tottered up the beach and soon felt her feet on firm ground.

They walked briskly over some turf and came to a little country lane.

"It is becoming extremely difficult to move about down here," said her companion, "for all movement of civilians is being banned by the authorities. Anyway, don't worry, we've got it all arranged." After they had walked a further half a mile, they came to a little van pulled into the side of the road.

"If you give me your valise you can hop in the other side."

And still she didn't know to whom the voice belonged.

"By the way, perhaps I'd better introduce myself, my name's Jimmy Foster, I'm a commercial traveller as you'll see by the things in the back of the van, and I'm going to drive you straight through to London. I've managed to find you a little furnished flat in Maida Vale and, so far as the landlady is concerned, you are my fiancée. I understand you're supposed to be a Dutch refugee."

"That is quite correct," Hannie rejoined. "Thank you for all your assistance tonight. As you have probably heard from Berlin, both you, Baber and the others of the group are coming under my direct command. I have a most important job to do. But I will tell you about it later."

By many devious routes they proceeded toward London. On several occasions they passed long rumbling convoys of trucks moving forward in the cold light of early dawn. There seemed a lot of military activity in the area. And, as the light improved, they could see several aerodromes upon which there were every type of aircraft, from large heavy bombers and fighters down to tiny spotter planes.

In order to make the most of the journey, she started cross-questioning her companion on all the changes in English life that had taken place since the war. The intricacies of rationing, the procedure to be adopted when requested for one's identity card, the sort of food one might expect in a restaurant. All these were vital details with which she must become familiar in the shortest possible time, for Hannie hadn't been to London for just over five years and much must have changed.

She enquired as to the state of London and was most surprised to learn that, compared to Berlin, it was comparatively unscathed.

Soon they were driving through the outskirts and she felt a little dismayed, for she noticed as the workers hurried to their places of employ that they walked with a brisk and determined air. She turned to Foster:

"Are you English, by any chance?"

He laughed, a somewhat dry rattle in his throat: "Naughty, naughty! No, I am not English, I am Welsh, a Nationalist, you see."

Hannie felt a tinge of repulsion. What was it that made a man betray his own country, especially when it appeared to be on the winning side?

Shortly, they were driving down the Edgware Road and finally turned left to proceed along the side of a canal.

"This is what the residents optimistically describe as 'Little Venice', and you are about to become a Venetian," he smiled.

He turned the car sharp right and brought it to a halt under a lamp-post.

"This is Clifton Villas. Warwick Avenue tube station at the bottom of the road. Your flat on the left-hand side."

Foster led the way up a very short path and, taking a key from his pocket, unlocked the front door of a tall, nondescript house, one of twelve in a row.

They walked up three flights of stairs and Hannie was a little perturbed to see that none of the flats so far had its own front door, but when finally they came to the last flight, she was relieved to see that the top one had. Once inside, they seemed entirely remote from the outside world. On the immediate left was a small kitchen, fitted with a good gas stove. On the right a comfortably furnished, long sitting-room, at the end of which was a door leading into a tiny bedroom. It was a tall house and from the windows she looked out over the roofs of the surrounding area. But she liked the place, for it had a warm and friendly atmosphere.

"I expect you'd like to get a little sleep. Anyway, there are a few little jobs that I've got to do, so I will be back at five this evening. There is plenty of food in the larder, but one thing I forgot to mention is that the bathroom is on the floor below."

"Thank you once again," Hannie murmured.

And with that he turned and was gone.

Suddenly she felt unutterably tired and alone in this unfriendly city. Not a single person did she know outside, except, of course, Foster.

She took off her outer garments and lay down on the bed. Could he be trusted? Well, she would soon see.

Martinelli walked into General Donovan's office in Grosvenor Square.

"Good morning, Steve."

"Good morning, Bill."

"What's good today," murmured Donovan, as he thumbed through his mail.

Martinelli sat down.

"I've got some good news. That's why I thought I'd better pop over and see you.

"You remember two or three months ago I asked you to arrange with the British to give us any information on that German girl. Well, a report has just come in. I don't know where they've got their information from. But you know the British, they never say a thing. . . ."

Donovan smiled: "But you say you've got a report . . ."

"Yeah, but you know what I mean. They don't tell you how they found out. Anyway, she's supposed to have left Berlin seven days ago and she is due in London at any time. Can you beat it!"

"Well, that's great! It's just what you wanted, isn't it?"

"Yeah. By the way, at the bottom of the message it said: 'Source of information—Berlin.'"

"Well, that sounds pretty good to me. Now it's going to be a question of finding her when she arrives."

Steve looked at his feet and started pacing the room.

"Well, I figure it's not going to be too difficult. They must know that D-Day is getting pretty near and they certainly wouldn't waste time letting her bum around the lower echelons. So my guess is that she will somehow turn up around here. Don't ask me how."

"Well, I shouldn't worry too much, it may be a week or two before she puts in an appearance, but I think you'll find her, Stephen."

Martinelli turned to go.

"Well, perhaps I'd better have a word with the M.O. boys,* because we're going to have to think up a suitable bait," he grinned. "I think I'll have to make him high, wide and handsome!"

* Morale Operation Group.

Donovan smiled: "O.K. Let me know how you go and if you want any more help from the British just give me a buzz."

Back in Maida Vale, Hannie had slept spasmodically for several hours and now lay awake wondering what to do. The bathroom, Foster had said, was downstairs on the floor below. This presented something of a challenge. Should she meet the people from the flat beneath, what should she say? Was it the custom in England to introduce yourself, when sharing another's bathroom? Or did they retain their rigid self-control and choose to ignore you? Then, of course, they might be out at business, in which case this would be the ideal time. And so, without further hesitation, she grabbed a towel and warily descended the stairs. She need not have worried, for there was no one about. But, stepping inside the bathroom, she was confronted with yet another problem. The water was heated by gas from a geyser and underneath the basin there was an ugly black box which obviously required to be presented with money if it were to be called upon to provide hot water. To this there seemed no solution. Firstly, she hadn't any money of the coinage type; secondly, if she had, she wasn't sure which coins to use. So, hastily grabbing her towel again, she decided to retreat upstairs and explore the kitchen. The larder seemed to contain the bare essentials to sustain life, such as a tiny pat of butter, a vast sugar bowl with a couple of spoonfuls of sugar, a tin of something called Spam, another of corned beef, some breakfast foods, tea and, she noted with excitement, some real coffee.

In the middle of boiling herself an egg, the telephone rang. She made for the sitting-room and then stopped dead in her tracks. Who could it be? And what would she say if it weren't Foster? On second thoughts she decided to leave it alone. If it were Foster he would certainly understand. After a few more moments of stubborn persistence, the caller obviously gave up.

She sat down to enjoy her meal and, noticing a clean newspaper on one of the larder shelves, she decided to pull it out and read the British version of the news.

At that moment, she heard the key turn in the front door and Jimmy Foster walked in.

"Hallo there, so you're up already."

Hannie smiled: "Yes, I couldn't sleep."

He was carrying a large brown paper bag stuffed with food, which he put down on the kitchen table.

"Thought you might like a few luxuries. There is some extra sugar, butter and tea, some cold chicken and, believe it or not, a tiny piece of steak."

"How wonderful," Hannie replied. "By the way, the telephone rang. Was it you?"

"No, I didn't call."

"Then I wonder who it could be? Have you given anyone the number?" Hannie enquired crisply.

"Of course not. But I shouldn't worry. There must have been someone living here before—probably a call for them. All you've got to say, if it happens again, is that the previous occupants are no longer here."

"Very well," Hannie replied. "But I must have it clearly understood that this address and telephone number must never be disclosed to any of our other contacts. You will be the only one to know it. This is a top directive from Berlin."

Foster sat down. "That's O.K. by me."

"Now, I need to get in contact with the Americans again. Have you any suggestions?"

For the next few days there was considerable activity both by Scotland Yard C.I.D. and M.I.5, who, in their quiet, methodical way, started checking and cross-checking in their efforts to establish whether Hannie Herodsen had arrived in London.

During the war, possibly to some people's surprise, there were a number of enemy agents operating in London and various parts of the British Isles whom we permitted to continue functioning, working on the theory that the devil you know is better than the devil you don't know. By tapping their 'phones and keeping them under constant surveillance, they guided us to many spies who had, up to that moment, remained undetected.

When new German agents came to Britain they were virtually forced to contact one another, for, by and large, they could rely on almost nil co-operation from the populace and were therefore thrown upon their own resources to a far greater extent than Allied agents on the Continent.

But, as it happened, Jimmy Foster was unknown to M.I.5 or, in fact, the C.I.D. However, Hannie Herodsen was eventually traced, and very much as Donovan and Martinelli had foreseen.

For the first ten days or so, Hannie allowed Jimmy Foster to take her around, introducing her to various people in order that she could orientate herself to wartime life in London and gain her confidence.

It was an odd quirk of fate that one night, returning from a cinema in the West End, she and Jimmy Foster were almost killed by a flying bomb which landed 400 yards away.

Much remained to be done and there was very little time to do it in. It was imperative that Hannie obtain a job and this would involve the first use of her cover story, carefully prepared in Berlin.

It had been decided that she should try to obtain employment as a Dutch interpreter. But, when applying for the job, it was obvious that she would have to explain her background. It had therefore been decided to keep as close as possible to her cover story in Algiers. In other words, she had left Holland at the time of the German invasion, crossed to France, made her way down to Marseilles and had finally obtained a passage in one of the last boats sailing to Algiers.

Her new story was to the effect that she had been given a seat in a car going to Cape Town in exchange for her services as nanny to a French family with a young baby who were going to settle in South Africa. She was to say that she had remained in their employ for just under a year and had then decided that she wished to make her way to London. She, therefore, took passage in a Dutch ship, sailing from Cape Town to Liverpool, having obtained her fare by saving her wages for the previous year.

The great weakness in her story was the fact that she had never been to Cape Town. But, in order to supply the necessary material evidence, a German agent actually working on this particular ship had managed to get her name included on the passenger list that went forward to Liverpool. She had spent many hours learning the full cover story and had been thoroughly briefed by a German who knew Cape Town well. She had been shown pictures of the ship, had learnt by heart the names of all the officers on board and also the ports of call.

It was decided, after much deliberation, that she should apply for a job at a Ministry, rather than approach an official Netherlands organization. This she had managed to do with the utmost ease by calling at the local Labour Exchange, who were most sympathetic and attentive to her needs.

She had finally come out of the Labour Exchange with two introductions, one to the Dutch Red Cross and the second to one of the Ministries. She decided to try the latter first, and had made an appointment to see a Mr. Johnson the following afternoon at three.

Not a little apprehensive, she had gone down to an address in St. James's Square and, punctual to the minute, she presented herself for interview.

With memories of her briefing by Kaltenbrunner crowding her mind, she sat in a waiting-room, mentally checking over the pieces of her story. She wasn't kept waiting long, and, after being taken up in the lift and shown down a long passage with many doors, they came to room No. 641, with Mr. Johnson's name printed on a piece of paper outside.

Taking a final hold on her nerves, she walked briskly into the austere office. She need not have feared, for Mr. Johnson was approaching sixty and would, no doubt, but for the war, have since retired. He was a white-haired, benevolent gentleman with spectacles, and he quickly ushered her to a chair.

"So my dear young lady, you are from Holland."

"Yes, that's right," Hannie replied.

"Well now, there's a country I've always wanted to see. Unfortunately, although I've been to Switzerland and France, I've somehow missed the Low Countries. A great pity, but after the war perhaps I'll go."

Hannie smiled. Here was no Kaltenbrunner, but a nice old gentleman who had probably forgotten why she'd even come.

"Now then, let me see . . . Oh yes, I remember, you want a job as an interpreter. Do you by any chance speak any German?"

Hannie's eyes flickered. "Yes, a little," she replied.

"Ah well, that's excellent. I think you're just the girl we need. Anyway, I'll just telephone to Mrs. Wainwright who is in charge of our department dealing with Dutch nationals. Their office isn't very far, just off the Tottenham Court Road. Of course, the wages aren't very high, but I think we could offer you seven pounds ten a week."

Hannie could hardly believe her luck. She smiled demurely. "Oh that would do very well, thank you."

"Good. Well, let's fill up an application form," said Mr. Johnson.

He rummaged in the top drawer of his desk and, as he was searching for the necessary document, he enquired: "Have you many friends in London?"

"Oh no, not very many. I am quite alone."

Hannie Herodsen realized what a useful contact this might prove.

"Well, perhaps one of these evenings you might care to come down and have dinner with my wife and I."

"Oh, I should love to, Mr. Johnson, how very kind."

"My wife would be delighted," he replied. "We've got a son, you know, in the Air Force, but he's serving in Burma right now. What a pity he isn't at home." His eyes twinkled mischievously. "Now then, let's see . . . Full name and date of birth . . ."

Half an hour later she was standing in St. James's Square. She could hardly believe her good fortune. In the short space of less than an hour, she had managed to obtain a job as a Dutch and German interpreter, willing to translate as well. She had also received a pleasant invitation to dinner and she had managed to get through the details of her background without causing any suspicion at all. Now all that remained for her to do was to find her way to Tottenham Court Road.

That night, Jimmy Foster took Hannie out to dinner, and over tall glasses of lager they discussed the situation so far.

All seemed progressing well, if not with particular speed. She was now firmly established in London and had already made contact with Radmin, who would in future be responsible for sending her messages to Berlin. She had an excellent job and a possible friend in the English Civil Service. But her luck in contacting the Americans was slow in the extreme. It was true that she'd met one or two officers but they had been of no consequence, having been merely in London on leave and with only one idea in their minds.

She said goodnight to Jimmy and made her own way home. As she sat in the Tube train, she pondered over the best method of approach, for London was swarming with Allied officers and men.

But little did Hannie know that fate would shortly take a hand.

On returning to the flat, she decided to make herself a cup of coffee before going to bed, and had only just put the milk in the saucepan when the 'phone began to ring. She went across to it and, lifting it up, quietly said: "Hullo."

To her surprise she heard an American voice at the other end of the 'phone.

"Say, hullo, is that you, honey?" the American voice enquired.

Almost instinctively, Hannie's voice hardened:

"Who is it you wish to speak to?"

The voice faltered at the other end of the line. "Say, isn't that Jane?"

"No, I'm afraid there's some mistake. There is no one here of that name."

Even as she spoke, in a cool and rather offhand manner, an idea flashed into her head.

"I'm so sorry, but I have only just moved into this flat. Perhaps that was a girl that lived here before?"

"Oh, that's too bad. I was rather hoping she was in."

Hannie's voice changed subtly: "Oh, what a pity. I hope it wasn't urgent."

"No . . . er . . . not really. I've been out of town for a week or two and I was just going to invite her out for a bite of dinner tomorrow night."

Hannie laughed softly: "Oh, what a shame."

Into this brief phrase she poured a wealth of meaning.

"Say, I don't know who you are, but if you wouldn't think it impertinent of me . . ." His voice trailed away.

Hannie laughed mischievously again.

"Oh, so you want to make—how do you call it—a blind date?"

The American took her up immediately. "Say, why not? That's a whale of an idea. I don't know you and you don't know me. It could be lots of fun."

"But you don't even know what I look like."

"Sure, that's true. But I'll take a gamble on that slinky voice . . ."

"Then you'll have to wait and see. I'll meet you in the Cumberland Hotel at 6.30 tomorrow night. I'll be sitting on one of the back-to-back seats in the foyer. I am a Dutch girl." She hesitated a little. "I am blonde and I'll wear a red scarf."

The American also laughed at the other end.

"Why this sounds really great. By the way, my name's Mike O'Haloran. What's yours?"

"I'll tell you when I see you. Until tomorrow night then. Goodnight, Mike." With that, Hannie Herodsen put down the 'phone. She wasn't laughing, she wasn't even smiling. It was just a job that had to be done.

She took out a cigarette and lit it, and went through to the kitchen where the milk had boiled over.

Major Mike O'Haloran put down the 'phone in the Officers' Club in Gloucester Place. He lay back on the bed and let out a long, low wolf whistle. His brother-officers on the staff of General Eisenhower's Headquarters would really get a kick out of this story.

CHAPTER FOUR

THE first thing Hannie had to do the following day was to go shopping for clothes with Foster, and this was not an easy task in wartime England. However, having plenty of money at her disposal, she went from shop to shop, gradually gathering about her a sensible wardrobe to fit the rôle she was about to play.

At the end of the morning, Jimmy Foster jokingly said: "You know, the clothes cost almost as much as the coupons. You've used about four women's ration for a whole year."

They ate a hurried lunch in one of the stores and then took a taxi back to Maida Vale. On the way, Foster told the driver to stop by a public call box, and when he returned he whispered that Bruno Baber wanted to see her urgently, and had suggested that they should meet in an hour's time.

They arrived back at the flat and paid off the taxi. Upstairs, Foster explained his method of contact with Baber, which they had perfected over the years.

It was very simple. They had four regular rendezvous, two outside in the open and two indoors in case of bad weather. The first was near Baber's home and was a park bench which you reached by walking over the North Gate Bridge linking the Regent's Park Outer Circle with Prince Albert Road. If you turned right along the side of the canal, the first bench on the left was their meeting-place. If Baber was sitting at the left-hand edge of the seat, all was well, but if he was sitting at the right-hand edge Foster knew that he was not to be contacted. This was in the event that he was suspicious that either one of them had been followed.

The second meeting-place was also an outdoor seat, but was located in the gardens of Leicester Square. Here the rules were slightly different. If Baber were reading a newspaper, he was not to be contacted. If, on the other hand, his paper was folded on his lap, all was well.

The third meeting-place was a stand-up sandwich bar a short distance up Shaftesbury Avenue from Piccadilly Circus.

The fourth and last rendezvous was the foyer in the Regent Palace Hotel.

In order to make the necessary arrangements for a meeting, Foster would ring Baber from a public call box and would use a different Christian name each time. In his apparently innocent conversation, Foster would convey to Baber the suggested time and place of the meeting. No matter which day was indicated, it always referred to the day of the call. The rendezvous was made clear, simply by calling it either one, two, three or four.

An example of one of their telephone conversations might go something like this: "Hello, Bruno? Phillip here. I wondered if you'd like to pop over for a drink on the second at about six-thirty?" This conversation meant that the proposed meeting should be that day at the "second" rendezvous (Leicester Square) at six-thirty.

If this wasn't convenient for Baber, he might say: "Can't manage it on that day, I'm afraid, Phillip, but what about the day after?" So in other words the meeting would be tomorrow. Should Baber wish the meeting at one of the other places he would simply say: "Too difficult on the second, Phillip, but I'd very much like to on the fourth." So he preferred the Regent Palace to Leicester Square.

They had worked out many variants on the theme, Foster told her, and they seemed simple and effective.

For this particular afternoon, Baber had suggested the Regent's Park bench and they were due there in just over half an hour.

Hannie decided that it would be better if she went alone and had therefore asked Foster to take her part of the way in order that she should be certain of the exact location and then return to the flat and wait for her.

As time was short, they walked up Maida Vale and caught a taxi to Prince Albert Road. The sun was shining and the birds were singing on this warm afternoon in the first week of April. Here and there, some of the trees were becoming tinted with green.

"How lovely to have a flat overlooking the Park," said Hannie, as they strolled along in plenty of time.

"They are nearly all occupied by the Air Ministry," Jimmy Foster replied. "Look at Viceroy Court, a luxury block pre-war, in one of the most select areas that money could buy."

After a few minutes more, having carefully explained to Hannie that she should turn right at the next traffic lights, cross the bridge, turn right again and the first bench on the left-hand side should be the one that Baber was sitting on, he turned and retraced his steps toward the flat.

All went well for Hannie Herodsen, and there, sitting on the bench, was Bruno Baber, looking immaculate and very cheerful.

"Why, hello," he said. "Isn't it a lovely day?" And, rising to his feet, he tucked his arm into that of Hannie's and proceeded to walk her along the side of the canal. There was no one in sight and he was able to speak quite freely.

"I'd been hoping that Foster would ring and I've waited in all day. I spoke to Berlin in the early hours this morning and they are very anxious to know why there has been so much delay in your getting established. Of course I explained the difficulties, but apparently other agents are reporting tremendous military activity and they are obviously getting impatient for news."

It was a difficult situation, Bruno Baber agreed, for obviously a lot was expected of her.

Hannie explained that the meeting she was having that night was her only link with the Americans so far.

Baber suggested that he should report it to Berlin in order to keep them happy that all possible was being done at their end.

Finally, as they wandered back towards the bridge, she discussed Foster with him. Somehow she felt she could rely on Bruno, after all he was German born and had proved himself a most exceptional agent.

"Well to be honest, I've never quite made up my mind just how much I could trust him," Bruno declared. "He is a nice enough boy and I have got no cause for suspicion, but don't forget that the battle is beginning to go the other way."

"Are they paying him enough?" Hannie enquired.

"Oh yes," he laughed, "I took care of that. After all, he is very useful to me."

On this topic of conversation they finally parted company, and Hannie Herodsen wandered home in a pensive mood. It was quite obvious that she would have to act boldly if Berlin were so anxious for immediate news.

Anyway, it was comforting to be backed up by a man of Baber's calibre. His cover occupation was a supposed pharmaceutical business operating from the East End.

Bruno Baber's only other permanent espionage contact in London was a man by the name of Kurt Radmin, who since the early thirties had rented a consulting room in Wimpole Street. However, quite without either knowing about it, M.I.5 were aware of the latter's activities and preferred to let him continue. This in the end proved a most rewarding investment.

That evening, Hannie Herodsen prepared her make-up with extra care and decided to wear one of her prettiest new frocks. With a last-minute sprinkle of perfume, she dashed off and caught a train to Baker Street and from there she took a taxi.

The main entrance of the Cumberland Hotel, looking out on to Marble Arch, was already shut for the night and so she had to go round and enter by the side doors. She wondered, a little cynically, what the major would look like and even if he would actually be there. She need not have worried, for the combination of her telephone voice and the tantalizing mystery of a secret assignation had provided the perfect lure.

When she reached the seats in the foyer, she noticed that they were all occupied and in one of them sat an American major with slightly greying hair.

As she approached, O'Haloran's eyes watched her every move. She certainly looked Dutch, or she might possibly have been Scandinavian, but surely this couldn't be the girl? After all, this little number had a figure like an hour-glass . . .

"Good evening. Major O'Haloran?"

"Say, you quite took my breath away . . ." he stuttered.

"I am Hannie Herodsen from Amsterdam."

They shook hands and, feeling as if he were walking on air, Mike O'Haloran piloted her across the foyer and down to the bar. Over a couple of highballs, they soon began to get acquainted and he told her that he had got two tickets for a show.

Consequently it was not until later in the evening, when the candles on their little table in a Soho restaurant were burning low, that Hannie Herodsen began to make progress.

"As a matter of fact I have only shortly come over to England," she said. "But for a time I was living in Algiers and there I met quite a few fellows from your O.S.S."

This evoked an immediate reply. "Well, what d'you know, they've got offices in the building a couple of blocks from mine, but," he laughed quickly, "I'm not going to introduce you to those glamour boys. I want you all to myself, honey."

Hannie smiled in mock surprise. "You're a spoil-sport, but never mind, I'll probably meet them myself one day." She shrugged her shoulders coquettishly and then looked away.

"Oh now, wait a moment," Mike O'Haloran replied. "Don't

take it like that." He paused for a moment. "I tell you what I'll do. When I go in in the morning, I'll pop around and mention your name. And if any of them remember you, I'll promise to tell you next time we have a date."

Hannie smiled across the table. "That's kind. Now, why don't you ask me to dance?"

The following day at lunch time, one of the senior S.I. boys, Johnny Sutaro, who had trailed Hannie with André in Algiers, was having a sandwich in their canteen when Frank Jackson, a man who had always got an eye for the girls, passed by his table.

"Say, Johnny, guess what! I was sitting at my desk this morning when a guy bowls in and asked me if I remembered a Dutch dame we knew in Algiers."

Sutaro choked and almost swallowed his sandwich whole. "Did he tell you her name?"

"Sure," he replied, "Hannie Herodsen, the blonde doll with all the know-how, but never up for sale."

"Yeah, I recall. What's she doing over here?"

"Some sort of an interpreter," he said.

Johnny Sutaro, who was one of Martinelli's best men, thought very quickly, for although he was not aware of the latest developments he felt sure his chief would like to know that Hannie Herodsen was now in London. How could he find out more about her?

"Tell you what, Frank, we're throwing a party tomorrow night. Why don't you give this guy a call and tell him to bring her along?"

"Sure, why not? But on one condition though, that I'm invited too."

Sutaro smiled. "It's a deal."

With that, Jackson passed on to his table and it was all that Johnny could do to stop jumping up and rushing to ring Martinelli.

He finished his coffee, climbed slowly to his feet and, with an air of studied nonchalance, went outside.

He grabbed the nearest 'phone he could find and rang his chief.

So, at last, Hannie Herodsen was coming into the open.

Martinelli had already been in contact with General Donovan to give him the news and had been told to go ahead immediately to formulate a plan.

First they had to arrange the party for the following evening, but this was far more complicated than it might otherwise appear.

Martinelli had to choose the man he was going to use as his decoy. It meant setting him up as a guinea pig and it went very much against the grain.

As it was now obvious that Herodsen was out to crack the date and place of Operation Overlord, it would certainly be necessary to select a man in whom she could have perfect trust and confidence.

Martinelli sent for Johnny Sutaro.

"Come in, Johnny, take a seat. After what happened at lunch time, I've decided to use you on a vitally important job. You are one of only three men in London who knows that this girl, Hannie Herodsen, is in fact a top German agent. Let me put you in the picture."

He described in detail all the events that led up to the present position.

"Now, before I go any further, Johnny, I must make myself quite clear." Martinelli paused for a moment.

"No one must ever know the truth about Hannie Herodsen. You only know it because I used you in Algiers to catch up on her. For what I've got in mind, not a single soul must even suspect that she isn't just what she makes out to be—a Dutch patriot working as an interpreter in London. You will never, I repeat, never, discuss this with anyone but me. Is that absolutely clear?"

Sutaro replied immediately, "Sure, I understand."

"Good. Now we've got several jobs to do. First, we must introduce her to someone she thinks a pretty top guy. Second, we've got to convince her that he is what she thinks he is. Third, if the first two come off, we've got to think of some way to exploit the situation. I thought of it like this: she's been very successful before and the man she was after never knew. Now, I think we've got to find a boy she'll really go for in exactly the same way, but I don't think we'll ever dare tell him."

"What do you mean, Steve? Let her take him for a ride?"

"I'm afraid so. A man in the know would never be convincing enough. I've seen it too often. It's got to be someone she thinks she can trust; not a glamour pants or a death or glory boy. He'll have to have done several missions before. We may even have to send him on another one again, just to paint the scene and let her think she's really on to something. When all that's completed, then we can really go to town."

"How?" asked Sutaro.

"Well, I've given a good deal of thought to this. The Germans are quite aware of our probable area of attack. I dread to think what reports must be slipping through on the build-up of strength over here. Thank God they haven't got any air power left. Now it would seem to me the thing to do is to try and sow some seeds of doubt. Put yourself into Hitler and Rommel's position. They're being pressed hard on the Eastern front, their factories are being pounded to hell and they know we'll shortly attack. They've got one chance and one chance only, so far as I can see. If they could pin-point our area of landing before we arrived and concentrate all their efforts into throwing us into the sea, the military set-back would be such that it would prolong the war for several years and give them the breathing space they so desperately need. Now, they know that we know that the Atlantic Wall, as they call it, is heavily defended right the way up as far as Holland. Therefore, they must often wonder—and I bet it's their pet nightmare—if we will dare launch a frontal assault at a point where we know they are strongest. Consequently, they must always harbour at least a suspicion that we'll try and come in through the back door, or anyway a side entrance! Now, if we could only convince them that we were coming through somewhere like Holland, for instance, they would never dare leave it undefended—not that it's that even now. Instead they would have to leave sufficient forces in the area to be able to repel a full-scale seaborne and airborne invasion, and that would require thousands and thousands of valuable troops.

"Now, to come back to our problem, this girl is masquerading as being Dutch, hence my suggestion of Holland. It may somehow give us the excuse to use her, I don't know how, but if she's as successful with our new guy as she was with the last one, the news is bound to get back to Berlin."

Sutaro remained silent for a few moments.

"It's a long shot, but, my God, it's worth a try. I think it's a hell of an idea and I'm sure glad to be in on it, Steve."

"Don't forget, Johnny, there are many other deceptions. The point is we don't know which ones are having an effect. The British have got one worked out for the Pas de Calais and we might be able to link up ours with theirs, but, of course, Holland would be the ideal place. If we could get any troops tied up in there, it would take them a damn long time to pull 'em out, and, by then, it could be too late anyhow. We might even be able to bomb all the bridges and so prevent their armour from leaving.

"The point is that we've got a wonderful opportunity; a known German agent working apparently undetected and about to walk into our web of her own volition. We mustn't disappoint her."

"By the way, have you any idea of which chap you'll use?" Johnny asked.

"Well, I've got several lined up, but I'm not quite sure yet. After all, she may not fall for the first one. I was thinking of taking a chance on a man like Dan Russell. He's straight, he's sincere, he's intellectual and this girl's nobody's fool. He's also good looking. Dan's already done two or three missions and been very successful. As you know, he's working in 'Morale' and we'd have to arrange his release, but I've got a hunch he's my boy."

That night, Dan Russell had an invitation to go to the party and the following day poor Frank Jackson, who had not only been instrumental in leading them to Hannie Herodsen, but was also highly delighted at the prospect of meeting her again, received orders that he was posted temporarily to a U.S. Air Force base in Norfolk. They couldn't have too many men gunning for this woman. He was told it was in connection with a top priority mission, but before he left he called in on Johnny Sutaro to curse his luck and tell him that he'd heard from the major next door that he'd accepted the invitation to the party for himself and Hannie Herodsen.

So now the stage had to be set and the party to be prepared.

At a meeting later that day, Johnny asked Martinelli how they were going to introduce Russell to Herodsen.

"Well, I'm not sure, but I think perhaps you had better have a shot at introducing yourself to her first. After all, you did meet her a couple of times in Algiers.

"I think we've got to look upon this mission as being a ninety-nine per cent gamble. It's been a gamble so far and I think it will be a gamble right up to the end. It may not pay off, but if they do fall for all the tricks we could line up for them, it might have far-reaching results on D-Day. And of one thing I'm absolutely convinced, it's worth a try."

"I'm with you there," said Sutaro. "The only part I really don't like is setting Dan up for a stool pigeon. It's being damned unfair."

"It may save thousands of lives," Martinelli cut in.

"Is there no other way?"

"Not a chance."

"Very well, I'll take your word for it. We certainly can't miss an opportunity like this, it's heaven-sent."

Steve smiled: "It's partly Martinelli-sent."

They both laughed.

"Well, this is certainly one party I'm really looking forward to. I hope she turns up."

"Are you kidding? She knows she's going to get back on the bandwagon, right where she left off. She'll be there," said Martinelli confidently.

After Sutaro had left his office, Martinelli sat behind his desk for a full quarter of an hour, toying with his paper knife.

It was the details that counted in a thing like this. The whole operation had got to be smooth, so that neither the girl nor Russell ever had an inkling that they were merely pawns in the game. This could only be brought about by careful planning and looking ahead. For instance, if the contact tomorrow night was good, something would have to be arranged almost immediately in order to bolster up and confirm in Herodsen's eyes the standing of Captain Dan Russell. How could this be achieved? As far as Martinelli could see, there was only one method, and it was a dangerous one. Russell would have to be sent on a mission and dropped over the other side. It might waste a valuable week, but it would certainly add credence to the fact that he was a top American agent.

It was going to be an interesting study in psychology. Would Hannie Herodsen get any information out of Russell, who could hardly be described as a talkative guy?

The next thirty-six hours, to Martinelli, dragged by on leaden wings. There was nothing very much to do. It was quite a simple problem. Could he or Sutaro engineer the right sort of introduction to bring Russell and Herodsen together?

He picked up the telephone and asked for General Donovan. While the exchange was getting the number, he wandered over to the window. Spring was certainly well on the way. A couple of pigeons were making love outside on the balustrade.

The telephone rang.

"Martinelli. Ah—hello General. I've just been making the final arrangements for the party tomorrow night. I've decided to stick my neck out and use Russell." He paused, listening to Donovan. "Thanks anyway; I only hope this doesn't prove an awful waste of time. Goodbye."

So he had the General's approval. That was really great.

Martinelli wondered idly how Donovan could ever have been tagged with such an inappropriate nickname as "Wild Bill".

Nothing could have been so incorrect. Always prepared to listen, however far-fetched the scheme might appear; seldom if ever ruffled; always kind and considerate, he was a General indeed.

As sometimes happens when no special care is taken, the party turned out to be a good one. The waiters made certain that there were no empty glasses. There was stimulating company, and the music was soft and well chosen.

Herodsen was the first of the main characters to appear on the scene.

Martinelli and Johnny Sutaro were chatting with a small group of fellows in a far corner, carefully surveying the crowd, when Stephen noticed Hannie arrive on the arm of a major. Although they were quite a way away, he thought he could detect an air of tension about her. He noticed her eyes swiftly and methodically being cast over the room. He turned his head away when she looked in their direction. She was certainly a very attractive woman; he wouldn't have used the word beautiful, because she looked a trifle too hard. She had an excellent figure, lovely hair and a very good dress sense. Altogether an enviable target for an espionage affair.

He caught Johnny's eye and managed to whisper: "Let her settle for half an hour."

Anyway, Russell hadn't appeared yet, so Martinelli wandered off among his friends.

As for Sutaro, he was beginning to feel distinctly nervous and decided to get himself a nice stiff drink. When he made his approach, he would have to appear supremely confident. She might remember him from Algiers, but, on the other hand, she might not. Not only had he to introduce himself but also he had to try and drive a wedge between Hannie and the luckless major.

It would indeed be ironic if Hannie herself wished to be introduced to someone like Russell, yet their combined efforts be thwarted by this innocent bystander. Anyway, time would tell.

Sutaro suddenly had an idea. Making his way over to Martinelli he drew him aside and quickly explained his plan.

"Look, Steve, Russell hasn't arrived yet, but I'm afraid that major guy looks pretty close to her. I'm sure she'll drop him, although I've got a feeling that he won't want to drop her. So this is the way I think we'd better do it. I am going to go across and introduce myself, say I remember her from Algiers. When a suitable opportunity occurs, I'll ask her to dance. Directly you see us go on the floor, see if you can possibly nail the major and lead him right away. By that time I hope Russell will have turned up and I'll introduce them and leave it in the lap of the gods."

With that, they moved back into the middle of the room, which was now crowded with couples and small groups, all chatting animatedly and apparently thoroughly enjoying themselves.

Johnny Sutaro edged his way through the throng and found Herodsen and her major tucked away in a corner, but quite alone. Smiling broadly, like a schoolboy on Thanksgiving Day, he poked his head between them:

"Say, don't I remember you from Algiers?"

She looked up quickly, and he thought with a tinge of anxiousness, but it was gone in a moment.

"Why yes, that's right. I must say I seem to remember you, although I'm afraid I've forgotten the name."

Johnny laughed: "Johnny Sutaro, and the last time we met, if I recall, was at our Villa Magnol."

"Of course," Hannie replied. "How good to see you again. May I introduce you to Major O'Haloran."

They both shook hands. Sutaro immediately started making conversation, fearing that he might be given the cold shoulder.

"Say, what are you doing now?"

Her answers came, smooth as silk.

"I'm a Dutch interpreter, but I've not been over here very long."

"Well, you must come and see us again. Tell me, where did you go after Algiers?"

"Oh, I spent a year in South Africa before coming to London."

The music had just changed from a waltz to a quick-step and Johnny seized his chance.

"I say, Major, it's a long time since I last saw Miss Herodsen. I suppose you wouldn't mind if I asked her to dance?"

He obviously did. But Hannie herself didn't give him time to reply.

"How nice. I haven't danced yet this evening."

With a reassuring smile at O'Haloran, Hannie moved swiftly away and Johnny followed. "My God," he thought, "she knows what she's doing. Poor O'Haloran's right out in the cold. Still, she'd drop me flat if I were to introduce her to someone like Donovan." He couldn't help smiling to himself as he took her on to the floor.

She danced with graceful ease and he was really beginning to enjoy himself when he suddenly noticed Russell standing only a few feet away and quite alone. This was the perfect opportunity and he grabbed it, not one might say without a little reluctance.

He whispered quietly into Hannie's ear:

"Standing just over there is Dan Russell, one of the top boys in the O.S.S. Have you ever met him before?" He nodded in Russell's direction.

"No, I don't think so, but it is difficult to see with so many people in the way."

"Well then, let's go over. Come on."

He took her hand and led her through the milling crowd of couples.

"Say, Dan." He struggled to attract his attention. "Say, Dan, I'd like you to meet Miss Hannie Herodsen; she used to be with us out in Algiers."

Russell smiled a little distantly, and Sutaro's heart missed a beat.

"How do you do," he said, extending his hand.

But once again Hannie was taking a lead.

"I don't think I remember you in Algiers."

"Oh, I was only there for a very short time."

Sutaro laughed shortly: "We never quite know where Dan's going to be. But I'll tell you one thing, Dan, you're not going to ruin this dance. You'd better book Hannie for the next one, otherwise you'll never get a look in."

"Oh thanks, I'd like that," he said, slightly bemused.

"You're welcome," Hannie replied.

Johnny Sutaro was hoping that by making her a little hard to get, not only would it arouse a spark of interest in Russell, but would also make the whole meeting seem far more spontaneous. Back on the floor, he drew her close to him, just for the devil of it.

Hannie talked little, but moved with effortless ease in response to his every little pressure. All too soon the music came to an end and, looking round, he was relieved to see that Russell was still on his own and that there was no sign of the major. Full marks to Martinelli.

He led her back to where Russell was standing and he was just about to make a remark when another character passing by suddenly recognized Hannie.

"Why, it if isn't Hannie Herodsen," he exclaimed, and, forcing his way through the group, he extended his hand. "Do you remember me? Tony Delgado."

"Why, of course. Hello, Tony."

"Say, I've got a girl over the other side. I'll see you later. You're looking fine."

To Johnny Sutaro's relief he disappeared in the crowd. Why the hell couldn't Russell play that sort of a line? Anyway, Hannie was doing her piece very nicely, for, turning to Russell, she said:

"Aren't we going to dance?"

"Of course, I'd love to. Will you excuse us, Johnny?"

"Sure, go ahead."

Sutaro looked round to find Martinelli standing at his elbow. They exchanged glances but said nothing. Could they have been thinking the same thoughts, Johnny wondered. For there out on the floor dancing in each other's arms were Captain Dan Russell, top American agent, and Miss Hannie Herodsen, top German spy.

CHAPTER FIVE

For Martinelli and Sutaro, the rest of the dance had been a nerve-wracking affair. Would Russell clinch the deal? They knew they could rely on Hannie for her side, but, after all, it's the man that's supposed to make the running. They were a little reassured when they saw them dancing cheek to cheek.

Arrangements had already been made for Martinelli's men to follow Hannie when she left the party, for they were naturally most anxious to learn her address.

It was not very much later when they saw her leaving with O'Haloran, but when they looked round for Russell he wasn't in sight.

Johnny called "Goodbye" as they were going out, and she turned and smiled.

Although it was nearly eleven-thirty, Martinelli decided to go back to the office.

Had the bait been taken? Had the lure proved good? Now it was the old, old story of waiting. From now on, every move that Hannie Herodsen made would be reported and that of Russell too. They had to find out in the shortest space of time which way the land lay, and for Martinelli it proved an agony of suspense.

The following morning he read the report of her movements after the party. They were very simple and gave Martinelli every reason to hope that she was transferring her affections, for apparently she and O'Haloran had caught a taxi back to Clifton

Villas in Maida Vale and, although it had stayed two or three minutes outside one of the houses, she was the only one to alight. To Martinelli that could only mean one thing. For any guy to take a blonde home from a party and not get invited in could only mean that he was being left out in the cold. Obviously, Hannie Herodsen had bigger fish to fry.

The next morning, Martinelli sent over a report to Donovan. So far as he could tell, the operation had good possibilities of success, but they still needed definite confirmation. He suggested to the General that immediate application be made in official quarters for Hannie Herodsen's telephone line to be found and tapped.

This took some days to arrange and it wasn't until the following Friday, by which time Martinelli had been through every conceivable form of anxiety, that they were able to confirm that Russell and Hannie had, in fact, been in contact.

Apparently, at seven o'clock that Friday evening, Russell had arrived in a taxi and gone up to the flat. He had stayed there for about half an hour and then they had come out and taken the underground to the West End.

Unfortunately, the man following them had lost contact in the Piccadilly crowds, so it was not known where they had spent the evening.

However, Martinelli wasn't worried; in fact, he was overjoyed that all appeared to be going according to plan. There was very little time to lose. Although the actual date of Operation Overlord was not then known, yet it was almost sure to fall some time during the first two weeks of June, when the moon and tide phases were right.

There were now two very important steps to take and there had to be no delay. The first was to thoroughly establish Dan Russell as a top American agent in the eyes of Hannie, and second, to prove beyond any shadow of doubt that she was in touch with the German High Command.

Martinelli decided to go across and see Donovan.

"My problem is this, Bill. Although we know that Hannie Herodsen is a top German agent, we cannot be certain how much reliance they place on her. Obviously, she must stand fairly high in their estimation after her success in Algiers or they would never have sent her to London. But, so far, from the reports on her telephone tappings, it isn't even certain that she is in contact with any other agents in London. She must be, of course, but who it is we don't know. She's certainly very cautious on the telephone."

"What do you suggest, Stephen?"

"Well, I think there is only one way in which we can effectively achieve both objects. We'll have to send Russell on a mission. I think we should drop him into France on some pretext, to contact the various Maquis leaders."

Donovan thought for a moment or two.

"Of course this might establish another important point, namely whether Russell is talking to the girl. He may be as tight as a clam. On the other hand, it will be interesting to see if any reports on his mission leak back to Berlin. We can check this through our double agents."

Martinelli grunted: "Yeah."

Donovan asked: "Who do you think he ought to go and see?"

"Well, it's got to be somebody right on the top level, because it must be of interest to the German High Command, and if Herodsen gives them prior information, they'll know she's on to a good thing and will be even more likely to listen to her in the future. We've simply got to build up both Herodsen and the German interest in Dan Russell."

"Very well, Steve, you had better go ahead on those lines, but make it snappy, there isn't much time to lose."

Two or three days later, Martinelli sent for Russell. He had decided not to mention Hannie Herodsen in the conversation at all, but purely to brief Russell on his coming mission into France.

There was a knock at the door and Russell walked in.

"Morning, Steve."

"Oh hello, Dan. Come right in. Have yourself a seat. Cigarettes in the box over there."

Russell smiled and stretched himself comfortably.

Martinelli looked at him again with renewed interest. Just turned thirty, tall, dark wavy hair, Russell was a nice-looking guy. He was different, too. There was no vanity or brashness about him, although he was very much alive. Always carefully dressed, he had well-kept hands and a perfect set of teeth. His record showed that he had got at least two degrees and had been employed as an executive in an advertising agency in the Middle West. He spoke French well for an American, having been sent by his far-sighted parents to spend a year in France to learn the customs and language; fond of art and music but a man of moderate taste, he made friends easily and well.

"Dan, I've got a most important mission for you to do. Haven't seen you much lately because, as you know, we've been working round the clock. It involves doing a Jedburgh* into France and you'll be picked up five days afterwards. The object of the mission is to talk to two of the most important Maquis leaders—I'll give you their names later.

"As you know, the French Resistance have been preparing for a long time for the day we invade, but naturally we can't disclose the point of our landings until the very last moment. It is more than possible that we will not be making our main thrust at France. It may quite conceivably be a two-pronged assault; but in any case we will rely considerably on the help of the Resistance movements in all the occupied countries.

"Your job will be to contact several groups in order to find out just to what state of preparedness they have managed to reach and to tell them that within the next few months an invasion will be launched from Britain. But, and this is the most important point of all, we cannot, under any circumstances, tell them where we are going to land or in what strength.

"Your job is really a highly diplomatic one. You see, we don't want to disappoint these men who have been waiting for years for this day. We want them to give us every support and assistance. They know how to do it; we've already told them—harassing the German Army, rounding up the collaborators, reporting the movement of troops, paralysing the transport system.

"The difficulty you're going to have to face is the fact that these Frenchmen are obviously impatient of any delay, and naturally each one of them cherishes the hope that the landings will take place in his particular area. What you've got to do is to explain to them that even if we were to come in through Holland or Norway, we would still want them to co-operate as if we were dropping on Paris itself.

"The Germans have planned carefully for our invasion and von Runstedt, against Rommel's opinion, has done the most sensible thing, in view of the fact that he has limited forces at his disposal. He has defended the Atlantic Wall and all the coastal regions right up to Holland, but he has kept his crack reserves quite deep inland so that, wherever the Allies thrust, he will be able to swing panzer divisions into the threatened area with a minimum loss of time. In other words, he's holding back

* A jump behind the lines.

his killer punch until he's certain where our main landings will come. As I've said before, it's the obvious thing to do.

"We've been wondering whether to put you down by Lysander or let you make another parachute drop, but as the moon's in the right quarter I think you can drop on the outward journey and be picked up by Lysander for the return. Naturally, you aren't to tell anybody where you're going and I'll give you the full briefing tomorrow.

"In the meantime, I've had typed out on this sheet of paper the main points that you've got to cover in your conversations with these Frenchmen and their names. You can come into my office at any time and read them, but on no account are you to take the paper outside this room, When you are not reading it, kindly keep it locked in the safe. I've always got the key.

"Naturally, you understand that should you be caught the Krauts would have no mercy in trying to make you talk, so you'd better pick up some cyanide.

"Have you any questions?"

"Not now, but I'll probably have some after the main briefing. Where's the area of the drop?"

"Near a little town called Laval."

Martinelli eyed Dan Russell warily as he left the room.

"And don't forget this is a damned important mission, so watch your step."

The door closed behind him and for a full two or three minutes Martinelli sat motionless, peering ahead with unseeing eyes. This wasn't a pretty business. He was testing to breaking point the loyalty of one of his best men. But he must keep his mind on the prize. Already a plan had begun to germinate, which he wished to discuss with some of the top Morale boys, for if it proved successful there was a good chance of completely hoodwinking the Germans as to where we were going to land.

That night, in Maida Vale, Hannie had invited Dan Russell to dinner at the flat. She had managed, by a stroke of good fortune, to procure a couple of pieces of meat, which were somewhat optimistically described as steaks.

At six-thirty, Dan arrived with a bottle of red wine, obtained she knew not from where. Hannie had lit a coal fire in the grate and the room was warm and cosy. She had managed to buy half a pound of candles and these she placed in various bottles around the room. She put two or three discs on Dan's record player, and turned the volume very low.

When she opened the door to his ring, she accepted a light kiss on her cheek and then danced away.

"I've got a surprise for you; come in." She led him to the sitting-room.

"My, oh my. It might be home," Dan exclaimed appreciatively.

So saying, he took her into his arms and they kissed passionately and long.

Breaking away, Hannie exclaimed happily:

"That's enough for now. I'm very busy in the kitchen and I don't want the meal to spoil."

An hour and a half later, lying back on the sofa, Russell said softly:

"By the way, I haven't told you yet; I'm going out of town for a couple of days, but I shall be back by next week-end."

Hannie's eyes flickered:

"Where are you going?"

Dan laughed: "Never you mind."

Hannie was on to it like a shot, as she said anxiously:

"You . . . you're not leaving the country, are you?"

Dan laughed at her reprovingly.

"You shouldn't ask such awkward questions, but it's possible I may have to brush up my French."

"Oh no, I can't bear you to leave," she said quickly. "Not now."

"Hey, take it easy, it's just a routine call. I told you I'll be back by next week-end."

"But why do they have to pick on you?"

"It's my job. Anyway, we've got to keep them informed on the other side."

"Then . . . then it must be important?"

"No. Just routine. I'm going to look up some old friends of mine."

"Aren't you afraid?"

"Oh yeah, I'm a human, but we've got some pretty good boys over there and they'll look after me real good, I promise you, sweetheart. Now, no more questions, just give me a kiss."

The candles were burning low before they spoke again; the records had stopped playing and the fire was almost out.

The following morning, there were two important briefings in London: one was in Grosvenor Square and the other in St. John's Wood. One was in English, the other in German. The latter was shortest and to the point:

"Top American agent landing France within next thirty-six hours. Please verify. Suspect top-level contact with Maquis."

In the other briefing, Dan Russell was receiving his final instructions.

"You're going to be dropped near a little town called Laval, which lies midway between Rennes and Le Mans. You'll be met by a man called Gaston, leader of the local Maquis. Everything has been laid on so it should be O.K. The moon rises just after midnight and you're due to jump at one forty-five. We'll liaise with Gaston about the return, but I expect we'll pick you up somewhere north of Rennes. And, by the way, don't do anything stupid, because I'm lining up another job for you immediately you return."

So saying, they shook hands and Dan went down to pick up his final stores. These consisted of his papers, all carefully forged, a tiny compass, an automatic, a large sum of money and, finally, a cyanide pill in the shape of a little button.

If he were caught by the Gestapo or the dreaded Milice, all he had to do was to bite on the button, swallow, count five and die.

CHAPTER SIX

THAT night, Russell was a guest of an R.A.F. mess somewhere in Suffolk. It was a heavy bomber station and it had been decided that one of the twelve Lancasters, due to pay a visit to the dockyard installations at St. Nazaire early the following morning, should be diverted from its course in order to fly first to Laval, so that Russell could parachute down to the waiting Maquis.

They were an enthusiastic, light-hearted group of young men, and Russell was able to watch them as they jostled and fought around the bar for their "noggins", as they called them.

Repeatedly he would be tapped on the shoulder and somebody would say:

"I say, old man, it's my turn. What are you having?"

On the whole, he thought, there was little tension. Certainly far less in them than there was in himself. He had never really enjoyed parachuting. It was against all the instincts of self-preservation.

The Squadron Commander couldn't have been much over thirty-five and Russell noticed him go quietly across to one man in a corner, who was sinking pints with considerable rapidity, and have a quiet word in his ear. The chap took the rebuke good-humouredly and that was the end of the matter.

The men obviously had to retain a high level of mental control. The British now had this business of night bombing really worked out to a fine art. Not only were there comparatively few casualties, but the bombers always seemed to reach their targets, lay their eggs with pinpoint accuracy and return safely in the early hours of the dawn.

A mess waiter came in and announced that dinner was served. As they sat down at a long table, beautifully laid, Russell couldn't help looking along the rows of eager faces opposite and wondering what the next hours would hold. It seemed so strange to think that quite possibly at the same time tomorrow night, some of these boys, trained to the peak of physical and mental perfection, could quite easily lie twisted and mangled in the wreckage of their aircraft somewhere in the fields of France. It was a hideous thought and he put it from him.

After dinner they went in for their briefing and Russell took the opportunity to change his clothes, in order to assume the character of his cover story.

Outside on the tarmac, a dozen Lancasters were being finally checked over by their loving ground crew. The night was clear but chilly and, as Russell walked across with the crew of "T" for Tommy, he drank deep the sweet spring air. His parachute harness bit tightly into his legs and made him feel rather like a crab walking along. The ground crew were standing in a little knot beside the aircraft, wishing the skipper and his boys farewell. They always did a wonderful job and it was touching to see the care and pride they had in the aircraft and its crew.

They climbed into the fuselage, a slightly more difficult job for Russell because he already had his parachute on, whereas the others carried them under their arms.

Aircrew used escape-'chutes, which were manually operated, but Russell's was the type in use by the airborne forces and had a static line which was attached to the inside of the aircraft. When Russell jumped it would be the weight of his body, or in other words the force of gravity, that would snap open the nylon ties that held the folds of the parachute fabric and rigging lines meticulously in position within the outer pack. As he plummeted toward the earth, he would still be attached by his static line to the aircraft, but when, finally, all the parachute fabric and rigging lines had been pulled clear of the pack, the weight of his fall would sever the final nylon tie at a breaking strain of seventy-five pounds and then he would be cut off for all time from the Lancaster "T" for Tommy. The descent would be fast, and the final smack, when he hit the surface of mother earth, might be a most unpleasant affair, especially when in the darkness it would be difficult to judge the moment of impact.

The flare path was lit, looking like a highway to heaven, and one by one the aircraft thundered away into the night. Soon it was their turn to taxi out to the far perimeter of the airfield.

For a few moments they waited expectantly until the final clearance came through from the Controller. Then, while the brakes were locked, the engines slowly started roaring to ever-increasing crescendo, while the needles on the rev-counters sped round the dials. Suddenly, the pilot released the brakes and they were speeding on their way, charging down the runway, ever faster and faster into the inky blackness of the night. In a moment, the vibration lessened as the aircraft fought its way into the air, rapidly gaining altitude over the slumbering English countryside.

Soon the pilot had set course for Weymouth, where they were due to pick up a night-fighter escort, and Russell watched the crew mechanically going about their tasks, checking this instrument or that gauge, attentive to every little detail in flying the aircraft.

He chatted to Joe, his despatcher, and then went forward to the pilot's cabin.

"How are you enjoying the ride, Dan?" the skipper enquired.

"Just fine," Russell shouted back.

The cockpit was dark except for a few subdued lights that lit up the maze of dials and, looking down, Russell could just make out the countryside, for, although the moon hadn't yet risen, the night seemed quite bright.

Jack, the second pilot, pointed out the silvery fingers of the Solent, which seemed to infiltrate the dark landmass on the port side.

Shortly after this they could hear the voices of the fighter pilots as they rose unseen from their airfield far below.

Soon they were winging their way south over the English Channel and, on the distant horizon, a rim of light proclaimed the position where the moon would shortly rise.

It wasn't long before they were flying high above the Channel Islands. How strange to think that English people were living down there under the heel of a German garrison.

Russell went back into the fuselage and decided to have a peep through the astrodrome. The sight that met his eyes was one of the utmost beauty; the stars were shining with a clear-cut radiance, but even more beautiful was the sight of the squadron of sleek night fighters flying in close formation 5,000 feet above. The moon struck them with silvery shafts of light that made them look as beautiful as fish taken fresh from the sea.

Already they were passing high above the French coast and penetrating slowly inland. So far, they had received no attention from either flak or enemy fighters.

The navigator thrust a piece of paper into Russell's hand.

"In five minutes we'll be over Rennes. Main force veering southwest, 'H' for Harry and 'S' for Sugar will create diversion by dropping stick of bombs each on the marshalling yards, while we lose height and turn east for Laval."

Suddenly there were a series of whip-cracking noises from outside and the plane began to buck and fret in the disturbed air where ack-ack shells were exploding. Fortunately, the gunners were slightly out of range and soon gave up. The angle of descent seemed to increase and the engines were throttled back as "T" for Tommy sank lower and lower toward the French countryside.

Russell got to his feet and was just making his way to the pilot's cabin when a red light came on, warning him that the time was near. He moved forward and said a hurried "Goodbye." By the time he had returned, Joe had the hatch open. Russell's stomach seemed watery inside. He glanced down but could see nothing but a yawning void. He attached his strop and heaved on it hard to see if it was quite secure.

"Well, Joe, here we go again."

"Good luck, boy," Joe replied, pumping his hand.

Russell sat down on the floor, swinging his legs into position in the aperture. As usual he felt awful but gradually his fear gave way to a cold and remote detachment. He made a final check; strop O.K., legs tight together and position correct.

Somewhere down below a group of the Maquis should be waiting for him and any moment they would be flashing their signals and then the plane would make a circuit before going in for the pinpoint drop.

Suddenly there was a shout from the navigator. Apparently

the signals had been seen and the plane started banking steeply to come into line.

Russell's mouth was dry and he actually found himself whispering a prayer. It was getting very near now and the plane had come on to an even keel. She seemed to be throttled back to the limits of safety and already Joe's hand was raised in silent anticipation. Their altitude was only a thousand feet in order that there was little time for Dan to drift too far away. His eyes were glued to the red light glowing on the roof. At the same instant as the green flashed on, Joe's hand would fall.

The seconds ticked by like an age and Dan levered himself to the very edge of the aperture, which yawned like a bottomless pit. His heart thumped and bumped in his ribs, then suddenly the green light was on, Joe's hand had fallen and with a wrench he slipped through the hole.

The wind tore at his body and clothes, a cold blast of air seemed to suck his very breath away and he was falling down, down, down . . .

His stomach seemed to leap to his throat and then he heard the little clicks high above his head that told him the parachute was unfurling. He seemed cushioned on the velvety night until suddenly there was a loud clap in his ear and, with a jerk, his plummeting fall was arrested as the canopy opened and "breathed" in the cold night air. He pulled himself out of his seat strap, raised his hands high above his head to catch hold of the lift webs.

The plane seemed far away in the distance and, looking down, he could see the pinpoints of light at the reception area. He looked as if he was going to fall a couple of hundred yards away. He felt his body swinging beneath the canopy and so, summoning all his strength, he pulled down hard on the lift webs in order to stop the movement. He kept his feet securely together and was hoping against hope that he wouldn't land in a tree. Suddenly, with a thump and a bang, he found himself head over heels in a field being dragged along the uneven ground with frightening rapidity. He clapped his hand on his quick-release and struggled to get out of the harness. Scrambling to his feet, he ran round in a half circle and thus managed to collapse the canopy.

He was still congratulating himself on his good fortune when he was surrounded by a group of highly excited Frenchmen, all of whom wanted to shake his hand and kiss him at the same time.

After the preliminary greetings were over, and they had buried his parachute, Gaston, the man in command, told him that they would have to make their way to a farmhouse about eight kilometres to the north and nearer Laval. There he was to spend the remainder of the night, so that he would be fresh the following day to make his journey to see the highly important Maurice Camus.

Seemingly completely unaware of any possible danger, they walked across two or three fields until they came to a country lane and there they mounted bicycles in order to complete the journey to the farmhouse.

So far as he could tell, there were approximately fifteen men in the reception committee, and these, after a quick farewell, disappeared in various directions. Soon only Gaston and he were left and, mounting their bicycles, they set off down the road.

Gaston, a middle-aged Frenchman of swarthy build, was hungry for news and, when Russell had answered the barrage of questions put to him, Gaston recited their various victories to date. They were out on forays twice a week, he told him, sometimes more often, and only two nights previously had blown up a signal box at an important main line junction.

They were very pleased with all the arms and equipment that had been sent to them and longed to come out into the open to do battle with the Nazis on equal terms. But their leaders were always counselling caution, begging them to wait for the moment when their combined uprising throughout the country would wreak the utmost havoc on the German High Command.

When would the invasion come, he was most anxious to know. The whole of France was in readiness and the thought that the Allies might come through any other of the occupied countries had never even entered their heads.

At the farmhouse he was given a royal welcome. In spite of the late hour, the whole family were up and waiting to greet him. They sat down before a big fire and drank toast after toast to victory. Finally, as the first streaks of dawn were lighting the sky, they went upstairs to bed, and, as Russell crept between the blankets, he heard one of the farmyard cocks welcoming the new day.

The following morning, he was awakened at nine and, after a quick wash, went down to breakfast.

Gaston had also spent the night at the farmhouse and had been up at seven, making the final arrangements for their departure to meet the chief Resistance leaders.

Russell was to travel many hundreds of miles in the next three days.

He saw Maurice Camus at Chantilly, a mile and a half from the castle and just out of town. German troops occupied the famous castle and it was known that on occasions the Gestapo would come out from Paris to inflict the most inhuman torture on their prisoners, who would seldom, if ever, return.

The house where the meeting took place was one of six in a row, occupied by an old man and wife, and with the houses on either side owned by loyal Frenchmen.

To culminate his series of meetings, he met Colonel Passy just outside Paris. He was, of course, not only one of the heads of the whole Resistance movement in France, but was also General De Gaulle's right hand man.

The meeting took place in the late afternoon. Half an hour after it ended, Russell was on a train for Rennes. There was little time to lose and he hoped that the train would arrive punctually, for at one o'clock that night he was due to be picked up by a Lysander aircraft close to the town of Fougeres. He was accompanied on the journey by a man called Pierre Lamont, but he would be met again at the station by Gaston, who would be responsible for seeing him safely on his way to England. Pierre told him an intriguing story about one of the girls in his group. Apparently, she had been sitting in a railway carriage, which was only occupied by herself and another man, of whom she had taken no notice.

Suddenly the train had started slowing down and, looking out of the window, she had seen dozens of S.S. troops lining the edge of the tracks. It was obviously a snap check on all the travellers. This had not escaped her unknown companion, to whom it must have spelt disaster, for to her astonishment he quickly unbuttoned his overcoat to display an R.A.F. uniform and in excruciating French and English told her he was trying to escape, having been shot down.

She thought for a moment, wondering desperately what to do and then of a sudden a brilliant idea occurred to her. Grabbing him by the hand, she hauled him out into the corridor and, as the train was coming to a jerky halt amid clouds of steam, she pushed him into a toilet and then quickly followed, bolting the door behind her.

As the S.S. troops boarded the train, the cry of "Identity cards" rang down the coaches and German officers moved from compartment to compartment, checking them. In the meantime, Marianne was struggling in the confined space to undress, taking off her coat, cardigan, and finally her jumper.

She then motioned the R.A.F. officer to stay as flat to the wall behind the door as possible.

The inevitable sound of jack-booted footsteps stopped outside the door and a German voice shouted, "Identity card." She waited a moment and when it was repeated answered through the door, "Je me lave, monsieur, mais je vien toute suite." But, naturally enough, the officer wasn't going to wait, so he commanded her in no uncertain terms to open the door immediately.

With a hand clutching her discarded jumper, in a poor attempt to hide her brassiere, she cautiously and modestly opened the door a few inches and handed out her identity card.

With something approaching a smirk, the German glanced at it, bowed slightly and handed it back. "Merci, ma'mselle." Six weeks later, the R.A.F. pilot was back in England.

But their journey was completely uneventful and Gaston told them out in the courtyard that the flight to pick him up had been postponed for twenty-four hours owing to bad weather.

However, it didn't matter very much, for they spent a night in a "safe house" in the centre of Rennes. Conditions for the second attempt were almost ideal; a cloudless night, a good moon and little or no wind. They made their way to the reception area in an old 1937 Citroen belonging to a member of the dreaded Milice. However, this man was in fact working for the Resistance and it was found most helpful to have him in the French counterpart of the Gestapo, run by Collaborationists. Not only was he able to run his car, but he was also able to give timely warning of intended operations against the Maquis and had also on numerous occasions been able to tip off the Resistance that certain people were about to be arrested.

They left the main road and journeyed for some three or four kilometres along narrow winding lanes, until they finally stopped at the entrance to a field with a large five-barred gate.

As they got out of the car, Russell was surprised to see heads popping up from all around and the place seemed fairly bristling with Frenchmen armed to the teeth, with Bren guns, Sten guns, pistols and grenades.

They were in plenty of time and, therefore, Gaston decided to check up on the position of the flares to be used to guide in the pilot. It was a medium sized, flat, grass field with low hedges all around but no large trees. The ground was firm and dry and, as the minutes ticked by, the tension and excitement gradually increased. The Germans were only too well aware that this ferry service existed and were always endeavouring to catch the Maquis red-handed.

The trouble was that the reception committee had to comprise quite a number of men and there was always the danger that a Collaborationist was among them, but it speaks highly for the loyalty and organisation of the Frenchmen that these hazardous journeys were nearly always a success.

The night was cold and very still. At five minutes past one, one of the men shouted and sure enough in the distance could be heard the faint hum from a small-engined aircraft. They waited for several more minutes as the plane steadily approached and then, precisely at the right moment, they lit the flares in order to give the exact location to the pilot. This, of course, was the most dangerous moment of all and of necessity had to be left until the very last second. The lights must have been visible for miles around but, by the time the Germans had located the area, the Frenchmen would have magically melted away in the countryside from whence they came, leaving no trace of their nocturnal meeting.

The sound of the plane grew louder and louder and then for a moment seemed to almost disappear as the pilot dropped down, skimming across the hedges before landing in the field cross-wind. This long-practised feat by the pilots of the ferry service enabled them to also take off cross-wind without turning the aircraft, and thus they could make a very quick getaway. The pilots only ever waited two minutes and, if no one had got into the aircraft within that time, they immediately took off and returned to Britain.

Suddenly, the Lysander was above their heads and touched down almost in front of them, rolling to a stop in the middle of the field. Having already grasped Gaston's hand, Russell raced across the intervening yards, scrambled in behind the pilot and lightly tapped him on the shoulder. He revved the engine and in a matter of moments the plane was bouncing across the field, to become airborne within feet of reaching the hedge on the opposite side.

Up, up they soared and then turning north set course for home.

The second part of Martinelli's plan had worked to perfection.

CHAPTER SEVEN

KALTENBRUNNER sat behind his desk studying two pieces of paper. On one was the brief message received from London five days previously; on the other, which had only just been handed to him, was confirmation from the Gestapo Headquarters in Paris, that an American had been in contact with the Maquis in Chantilly not twenty-four hours previously.

He smiled in triumph and poured himself another drink. Now what would Reichsfuehrer Himmler have to say? It might have taken a little time to establish the contact in London, but their patience was paying handsome dividends. He made a note on his pad to remind him to ask London for the name of the American agent who had been sent to France. It would be interesting to see if they had any record of him. Obviously he would have used a cover name, but there was a good chance that there might be something on the files relating to his past activities. It was essential that they estimate his degree of importance.

Kaltenbrunner was toying with the idea of ringing Himmler, but he decided against it as the evening was already far advanced. Instead, he lifted up the telephone and asked for SS Gruppenfuehrer Mueller, one of his chief subordinates.

However, Mueller was not at home and so Kaltenbrunner had to be content with keeping the information to himself.

He sat morosely at his desk, fretting inwardly that he was unable to share his initial triumph with someone else. If this girl could only keep her head and remain undetected, there was no knowing what information she might not acquire. As his thoughts continued in this vein, he had visions of by-passing Himmler altogether and going direct to the Fuehrer with the date and location of the Allied invasion of Northern Europe.

What a fantastic achievement that would be. If he could only engineer this, he would be far more important to Hitler than even Himmler, Bormann or any of the rest. On second thoughts, perhaps he wouldn't tell Himmler for the time being, of the progress they were making in London.

Kaltenbrunner had yet one further idea. At the moment they were relying on Herodsen's messages being sent by radio through Baber, although she knew that in an emergency she could also call on Kurt Radmin. However, as the British counter-intelligence were becoming extremely active in their efforts to prevent German agents sending news to Germany regarding the military build-up, he thought it might be a good idea to send Herodsen one of their latest radio inventions, which would allow her to send messages direct. The apparatus would be built into a small box of chocolates. They already had specimens of current boxes on sale in English confectionery shops. It was a tiny transmitter, consisting of a small dial, rather like a miniature edition of those found on an ordinary telephone, and also three very small push buttons. It was run on electricity but only had to be plugged into an ordinary light fitting. To operate it, one pushed the first button and then dialled the entire message in code. This was not, in fact, actually transmitting it, but merely transferring it to a magnetised wire tape. The message could be as long as two typewritten pages. Having completed this, the operator would then press the second button and a small bulb would begin to glow. The light from the bulb would fluctuate but when it became at its greatest brilliance, the agent would know that he was directly tuned to one of the powerful receivers somewhere in Germany. He then pushed the third and last button, which would transmit the entire message in three-fifths of a second.

The feat of engineering to accomplish this was quite fantastic and was of the greatest possible benefit to any agent in occupied territory, for it would be virtually impossible for the enemy to monitor such a brief transmission. The only drawback, if drawback it could be called, was the fact that one had to have an aerial of approximately twenty-five feet in length. However, this was not likely to cause very much of a problem and was only a slight disadvantage when weighed against the exceptional merit of the tiny transmitter.

Kaltenbrunner made a further notation on his pad that this should be put in hand immediately.

If anything, Martinelli was even more jubilant than Kaltenbrunner, on the success of Russell's mission to France.

Two days after Russell had been dropped by parachute, a message had reached O.S.S. Headquarters from one of their permanent agents in Cherbourg that apparently all local Gestapo in Northern France had been warned to watch out for the possible landing of an American agent in their area.

To Martinelli, no further verification was required of where the information had originated. He was only astounded that Herodsen had managed to worm her way into Russell's confidence at such an early stage in the proceedings.

Of course, he could not be certain how much she had been told, but whatever it was it had certainly been sufficient to forewarn the Gestapo in at least one area of France.

During the time that Russell was away, Martinelli had had several long meetings with Donovan.

They had discussed for hours on end the various methods of exploiting the situation that they had now firmly established. Their next step would be the most crucial one in the whole operation. It would obviously involve policy at the very highest level and it would be up to General Eisenhower, as Supreme Commander, to either accept or reject their ideas.

They had finally evolved an embryonic plan which, although simple in outline, had many difficult features of a most serious nature and which would obviously have to be carried out in close conjunction with the British. In its broadest terms it amounted to this.

General Donovan knew that we were not, in fact, planning to make a major assault on Holland. Therefore, it stood to reason that if it were possible to get the German General Staff to believe to the contrary it might also be possible to get them to divert additional troops to heavily defend the country. Thus they would be dissipating their strength in an area where they would be completely ineffectual in those vital early days when the Allies would be struggling to establish a bridgehead.

The fact that this German agent was masquerading as a Dutch girl was not only purely fortuitous but fitted excellently into the overall scheme.

The method by which she could be fed false information was a problem over which Martinelli had brooded for many, many weeks. He had finally solved it by objectively considering what sort of organisation would have to be set up should we, in fact, have intended landing in Holland. The answer was simple; they would have had to gain the confidence and support of the Dutch underground movement. This would naturally have meant setting up a special unit in order to obtain and evaluate information from Holland. Within this framework there would also, naturally enough, have been a propaganda section in order to convey to the Dutch populace just how, when and where they would be able to help at the time of the landings.

Working on this theme, it had soon become apparent that the

Americans would never have carried out such an operation alone. Therefore, he had explained to Donovan, any suggested deception would have to include the British. In other words, it would become an Anglo-American exercise.

His next appreciation was the fact that if such a subterfuge were envisaged it would obviously have to be clothed in the utmost secrecy and would, therefore, itself require a cover plan.

Martinelli had racked his brains to think of any occupation in which a group of Dutch nationals could be working without causing undue suspicion. Finally, he had hit upon the almost perfect solution—documentary films. Surely, he had asked himself, what better medium of instruction could there be, to teach an isolated community how to use automatic weapons, for instance, or plastic explosives for sabotage.

It certainly sounded feasible. Herodsen could be used, because of her knowledge of the language; Russell as some sort of a liaison officer from the American forces, and, finally, an Englishman who would ostensibly be given command.

All this appeared not unduly difficult, but the ramifications that would result therefrom were tremendous.

If such a deception were to be put into operation, it was obvious that the Dutch underground would have to believe implicitly that the invasion was coming through their country.

It would probably be necessary to fetch certain Dutch Resistance leaders to London. Conversely, it would be vital to send agents to Holland.

Troop movements in Britain would have to be concentrated in south-east England in order to add credence to the fact that our main assault would be directed at Holland.

It would be necessary to send out a general call for as many Dutch linguists as could be obtained, in order to draft them to various units of the forces to act as interpreters.

All these tiny details, any of which might possibly infiltrate back to the German High Command, would garnish the bait and help convince them that our motives were genuine. After all, a thrust through Holland was the shortest route into Germany.

However, before General Donovan was prepared to put up the scheme for final approval, he wanted it in writing.

The General was well aware how all plans of a similar nature put up to the British were subjected to the most ruthless examination. This was all the more rigid if they were themselves involved in any way. It was also a fact that the British Intelligence were even reluctant to work with the Americans, preferring to rely entirely on their own resources and organisation.

However, there was no doubt that in this case there were exceptional circumstances, and Donovan himself was intrigued with the idea and thought it had good possibilities of success.

Two days later, Martinelli had drafted his proposals in principle and had decided to make the document as short as possible. He entitled it "Operation Stampede".

After a brief résumé of what had taken place since the O.S.S. had been in Algiers and how both Herodsen and Russell had become involved, he outlined his suggestions as follows:

Intention.—To deceive the enemy into believing that the Allies will make a two-pronged assault on Northern Europe, one prong of which would go through Holland and endeavour to make him concentrate additional troops in that country.

Method.—1. Establish a Documentary Film Company in Wardour Street, ostensibly making films in Dutch, and use this as a cover for the organisation.

2. Make immediate contact with Dutch underground movement to request their co-operation for our eventual thrust through the Netherlands.

3. Production of propaganda material to support the intention.

Administrative.—The immediate enrolment of the following personnel in the organisation, which would be called Arista Productions Limited.

(1) English officer (Special Operations Executive) to command. (2) Captain D. Russell (U.S.A.), second in command and i/c Security. (3) Miss H. Herodsen (known German agent)—Translator and general duties. (4) Approximately six Dutch nationals with literary background to prepare propaganda material. (5) Various British personnel and technicians to man the printing machines, provide secretarial services and security guards. (6) Wireless operators (Dutch).

Note.—It is considered necessary that the English officer in command be the only member of the entire organisation to know, firstly, that the operation is a deception on the enemy, and, secondly, that Herodsen is in fact a German agent.

Finally, a space was left for General Donovan to add his remarks and recommendations. In this manner, Martinelli's brain child was finally put up for consideration at the very highest level.

In the meantime, Russell and Herodsen were kept under close

surveillance, the former returning to his general duties at the O.S.S. Headquarters.

In the remarkably short space of a week, Martinelli was summoned to Donovan's office and there he received, almost unbelievingly, carte blanche to go ahead.

He was informed that an English officer would be seconded to him and would be a man who had a working knowledge of the film industry and who was also experienced, to a certain degree, in the preparation of propaganda material. He was attached to Special Operations Executive and was considered an officer of outstanding ability. His name was Major Julian Howard, although to the Americans he was to become known as Colonel Q.

For the next few weeks, Martinelli, assisted by Johnny Sutaro, worked all hours of the day and night on the formation of the organisation.

He decided to call in Howard at the earliest possible moment, not only for them to become acquainted with each other, but also to help with the work in hand.

There were a thousand jobs to be done. Premises to be found and rented, printing machinery to be installed, telephones to be connected and a wireless room to be equipped with the latest short-wave transmitting and receiving sets. They also had to set about selecting their personnel with the able co-operation of the Netherlands Government. But for this, Martinelli had to remain completely in the background and rely entirely on Howard's judgment.

They had decided that, until such time as they had all these initial arrangements completed, they would not introduce Russell. However, Martinelli thought that it might be a good thing for him to pave the way. Consequently, he decided to have a preliminary meeting.

It was essential, and the whole success of the operation probably depended on it, that Russell was completely convinced in the authenticity of the organisation and, indeed, not only Russell but all those who would be working in it.

Martinelli sent for Russell early one afternoon and took him down by car to Virginia Water. He said nothing to Dan on the way, only making desultory conversation and appearing to be completely preoccupied with his own thoughts.

When they reached their destination, he parked his car and took Russell along to the lakeside where he obtained a boat. Rowing himself, Martinelli guided the craft away from the shore and then, resting on his oars, and to a background of spring bird-song from the distant banks, he told Russell of his next and vital mission.

"Dan, I find it hard to convey to you just how important your next mission is going to be. It is so tremendously secret that I have brought you right out here to the middle of this damned lake in order to discuss it without any fear of being overheard. You may think it a little melodramatic but, believe me, the fate of thousands of lives could well depend on it. The fact is, I am going to tell you just where the Allies are going to invade.

"You know as well as I do, Dan, that everyone thinks that the main landings will be in France. That is one of the reasons why the Germans have defended it so heavily—it's the obvious place: very short sea journey and near enough for close air support, excellent beaches, etc., etc. In fact, we still intend landing somewhere in France, but, and this is probably the biggest secret of the war, our main thrust is going to be in through Holland. It's the shortest route to Germany and besides which, it has been suggested that we would prefer to meet the Russians as far to the East as is humanly possible. Now perhaps you will understand why I've brought you here, where there is virtually no possibility of our conversation being overheard."

Russell appeared duly impressed and nodded.

"For this mission you will be under the sole command of a British major, and here I must strongly emphasise two things. Firstly, that you and this major will be the only people to know of our intention to make an assault on Holland, and secondly that after I have effected the introduction you will no longer have any contact with me, or anyone else in the O.S.S. for that matter. It is a lone job and its success will depend almost entirely on security. Your responsibility will be just that—security."

Russell interrupted for the first time.

"Is this going to take place in London, or where?"

"Oh yes, you'll be centred on London; in fact your headquarters will be in Wardour Street. As a matter of fact we are just in the process of setting up the organisation, but there has been a little delay owing to the trouble we've experienced in finding sufficient and reliable Dutch-speaking personnel."

Here Martinelli eyed Russell closely.

"As you can imagine, most Dutch men and women in Britain are engaged on important jobs and can ill be afforded for use on other work. But I guess we'll find them somehow."

Martinelli wondered desperately whether Russell would take the hint and for a moment he feared the worst. But suddenly and quite innocently, Russell said:

"Well, what about Hannie Herodsen?"

"Who?" asked Martinelli, playing his part to perfection.

"Why, you know Hannie Herodsen. She was with us out in Algiers. I'm sure you met her."

"Oh yes, I remember," Martinelli replied slowly. "I didn't know she'd come to England."

"Yes, I met her a couple of months ago at a party. As a matter of fact, I've been seeing her quite a lot recently. She's an interpreter with one of the English Ministries."

"Well, I don't suppose she'd be able to get away then," Martinelli said doubtfully.

"But if this job is that important," said Russell, "surely it's worth asking her?"

At this point Martinelli thought he'd play it down a little.

"Okay, I guess there's no harm in asking. Anyway, I'll leave it up to you."

Russell nodded and seemed to become suddenly lost in his own thoughts. Then softly he murmured:

"So it's Holland, eh? Well, that makes sense I guess. Tell me, Steve, what's our job going to be?"

"A very difficult one," Martinelli replied. "You probably know by now that the British S.O.E. ran into a lot of trouble on their Dutch section and lost nearly forty agents. As a matter of fact I don't really know much about it, but whatever happened, it certainly left us very much out of touch with all that's been going on in Holland. Your job will be to contact the Dutch underground for two important purposes. Firstly, we've got to get a great deal more information about the German military strength, including the size and extent of their coastal defences. And, secondly, it's going to be our job to instruct the Dutch as to how and when they can best help us.

"At the moment they are pretty disorganised, although probably the spirit of resistance is as strong, if not stronger, than in any other country in Europe.

"The Dutch aren't given to violent emotion, but they seem to have a burning hatred and contempt for the Germans, which only needs to be channelled and controlled to forge itself into a most efficient weapon.

"However, the Netherlands will not be an ideal country to

invade. The terrain is very difficult, because there's such a hell of a lot of water, and therefore we'll have to rely on the utmost co-operation from the populace.

"The position on the Continent is roughly as follows. Despite the very heavy coastal defences, the German Army itself is beset with difficulties. As you know, they are taking a hell of a pounding on the Eastern Front, we've got some of them tied down in Italy and they are also dotted all around Europe, trying to keep occupied countries under control. They are also very short of fuel oil for their tanks and aircraft.

"Now the British Intelligence has found out that between the two principal commanders, Field Marshal Gerd von Runstedt and Field Marshal Rommel, there is a wide divergence of opinion.

"Von Runstedt wishes to defend the coastlines only thinly and keep his killer punch in the rear, so that he can first ascertain the main points of our landings and then swing the panzer units straight into the attack.

"Rommel, on the other hand, believes that, as the air superiority will undoubtedly be with the Allies, it will prevent the large-scale movement of troops. So he is in favour of committing the main bulk of their forces to the coastal regions.

"However, Hitler, as Oberkommando der Werhmacht, is uncertain what to do and thus causes a complete stalemate. We must foster his uncertainty.

"Now, if France is too heavily defended, where else could we land? It has finally been decided that our best chance would be in Holland. The Netherlands is, of course, defended but, we believe, with nothing like the strength that we could expect elsewhere. There will also be other diversionary attacks, but our principal landings will be there.

"Naturally enough, the Germans are trying to crack our plans for Operation Overlord. It has become vital for them to know when, and especially where we are going to attack. So your job of security is stupendously important, for they must never have an inkling that it's Holland."

Russell couldn't help interrupting for the second time.

"But, Steve, how the hell are we going to tell the Dutch people and at the same time keep it from the Germans? I should have thought it was almost impossible."

"It's going to be tough, boy," Martinelli said. "But somehow we've got to do it."

"Who's this English major?" Russell asked.

"He's from S.O.E. and apparently a very good man for the job. Of course, our other great difficulty is time—we haven't got any."

"How many people know about this plan?"

Martinelli thought for a moment.

"I guess you could count them on one hand: Churchill, Eisenhower, De Gaulle, and of course the service chiefs, but, other than them, not a soul knows and nobody will know until the invasion fleet has actually put to sea."

Russell was silent for some moments, then he said:

"You know, Steve, I reckon it's darn nigh impossible. It's a hell of a job. If we've got to ask the Dutch for all this information and tell them what to do when we come, how the hell can it be expected that the Krauts won't find out something about it?"

"That's why I told you it was a difficult job. Wherever we land there are going to be problems, someone's got to know about it."

"When do I start?" Russell enquired.

"In two or three days' time."

With that, Martinelli turned the boat about and started rowing for the shore.

In fact, it was two days later that Martinelli thought the time had come for Russell to be introduced to Howard.

He decided to make the meeting as informal as possible and arranged that the following night they should rendezvous in a small pub off Regent Street before going on to supper at Ley On's. He had chosen this particular restaurant because it was right around the corner from 69 Wardour Street and this would give them the opportunity of pointing it out to Russell.

A few minutes after eight o'clock, Russell arrived at the pub. The other two were already there.

Martinelli introduced him to Howard and they shook hands.

Russell looked at him carefully. He was of medium height and build. Probably an Englishman would describe him as dapper, but to an American he was typically English. He had black hair, a prominent nose and sported a thin pencil moustache. He seemed a nice enough man and obviously got on well with Martinelli.

After they had had a couple of drinks, they decided to leave and make their way to Ley On's. When they came to Wardour Street, they turned left and, as they were walking along, Howard said quite quietly to Russell:

"There's your new H.Q., number 69, top two floors."

There was little enough that Russell could see in the blackout.

"I'll meet you there tomorrow morning at nine. Arista Productions Limited."

They passed on to Meard Street, and little did Russell guess that during the time they had been opposite the building they had been under careful surveillance by two of Martinelli's men in a room on the other side of the street. This room was to be manned twenty-four hours a day from that moment onwards and it was equipped with cameras, both cine and still, fitted with telephoto lenses, so that everyone who went in and out of number 69 could be recorded on film.

It had been presumed by Martinelli that if the whole operation worked properly and Herodsen got some news back to Germany, it was virtually certain that the Germans would send other agents to confirm the whole set-up. Martinelli and Howard would naturally wish them to have every facility, but it was vital that we should know when it occurred, in order to gauge how well the deception was working.

It would have been difficult to find three more diverse dining companions. Russell was certainly an intellectual and had the enquiring mind of the student, whereas of the two lawyers, Martinelli probably had the fire and attack, and Howard the dispassionate and logical approach to life. Each of them, in a way, was complementary to the other.

Over supper, the three men talked about everything under the sun other than the job in hand. They discussed such varied topics as the decadence of modern art, world socialism and college life in America. They enjoyed a splendid meal and by the time they had finished were feeling in a mellow and very friendly mood.

Leaving the restaurant, they walked down Wardour Street for the second time that evening, turning right at Shaftesbury Avenue and parted on their separate ways in Piccadilly Circus.

CHAPTER EIGHT

THE following morning at five to nine, Dan Russell was climbing the stairs at number 69. On the third floor he was confronted by a door which obviously led into a suite of offices, outside of which was a small plaque bearing the inscription "Arista Productions Limited". He tried the handle, found the door was unlocked and walked in.

Inside was a somewhat scruffy reception, with a desk standing in one corner, behind which sat a tall young Englishman reading a morning newspaper.

"Good morning, sir, can I help you?"

Russell looked at him warily.

"My name's Russell, I've an appointment to see a Mr. Howard."

"Oh yes, sir, just a moment please."

He dialled a number on the internal 'phone and said:

"A gentleman by the name of Mr. Russell to see Mr. Howard. Okay, thanks. Will you come this way please."

With that he got to his feet and pushed open the door at the side of the desk.

They walked down a short passage and were confronted by yet another door boldly marked "Private".

Russell entered a small office, obviously belonging to Howard's secretary, and at that moment Howard came through from his own room and extended his hand in welcome.

"Good morning, Dan, how are you today?"

"Oh, just fine, thanks."

"Come right in," said Howard, and indicated the chair.

"You're an early bird," Russell quipped.

"On the contrary, a late bird I fear. After I left you at Piccadilly, I decided to come back and work through the night to get up to date on some of the paper work."

"You should have told me. I'd have been glad to come back and lend a hand."

"That's very nice of you, but frankly I don't think there was much you could have done."

In spite of the fact that he had been working all night, Russell noticed that Howard was already washed and shaved and looked none the worse for his nocturnal activities.

"Before I show you over our two floors, I thought you might like to know a little more about the set-up."

"I certainly would," Russell replied.

"Well, Martinelli told me that he had given you the general outline, so perhaps I'd better tell you how I propose we operate. The Dutch section of the S.O.E. have had a most unfortunate experience at the hands of the Germans, which the latter had nicknamed the Englandspiel.* For something like twenty months the Germans actually ran the S.O.E. operations in Holland. They captured forty-odd agents, worked their radios, and it was only in the last few months that we realised just what had happened.

* The England game.

"Not only was this a great catastrophe, but also a big disadvantage for us in another respect. For naturally the Dutch resistance people soon became aware of the treachery, and were very shaken in their confidence. Therefore, we have now somehow got to rekindle their trust in our ability to work successfully against the Germans.

"But, on the overall position, there is one great asset, namely, that during the entire time the Germans were running the Dutch end of S.O.E. there was never any mention that we were interested militarily in the possibilities of an invasion of Holland. Consequently, it is hoped that the Germans may have been lulled into a false sense of security.

"It doesn't mean to say that the country isn't defended. It is, but certainly nothing like as heavily as France or Belgium.

"Now, not only are we going to have to get some people out of Holland, in order to glean as much information as possible, but conversely we're going to have to send those and other agents back again so that all the various isolated resistance groups can be linked and formed into one well organised and effective striking force.

"At this end, we're going to have to use a large number of Dutch nationals who have had no contact with Intelligence before. They are writers, for the most part, and their job will be to prepare and translate instructions which will be distributed in the Netherlands in leaflet form. The trouble is we've got very little time to get all this started.

"But, before we go into it any more thoroughly, what about having a look over the place?"

"Sure, I'd like that very much."

Together they went out and climbed the stairs to the top floor. There were five reasonably large rooms, one of which they found already tightly packed with radio paraphernalia. There were powerful receivers and transmitters and the floor was littered with wire and component parts. Two men were busily engaged on the assembly job and Howard spoke to one of them.

"How's it going, Phillips?"

"Not at all bad, sir. Should have them operational by this evening."

"Excellent. Well, keep at it."

Next door there was a film store, two small offices and quite a large box-room. On the floor beneath, there were four offices in addition to Howard's two. One of them was very spacious and already contained various pieces of printing machinery. These were not printing presses, but were rather large and probably more efficient versions of the ordinary duplicating machines used in general offices.

In a small room adjoining this, a photographic laboratory had been set up, with several stacks of film containers and a small cutting bench along one side of the wall.

The last room was purely an office.

"It's cosy, isn't it?" Howard exclaimed.

"I don't know about cosy, there isn't room to swing a cat."

"Oh, we'll manage, don't you worry. There shouldn't be more than about a dozen of us working here. By the way, the Dutchmen are coming over tomorrow. So perhaps we'd better go into my office and arrange just what they're going to do."

They sat down and discussed in detail how the organisation was expected to operate and, at the end of an hour and a half when Russell got up to leave, he asked Howard if they had a dossier on the names and background of the new Dutch personnel.

"Yes, here you are, Dan. I should take it away and study it. Give you some clue as to the sort of people we're going to be dealing with. They've all been carefully screened but I've no need to tell you that we've still got to be very careful."

"There's only one huge question-mark in my mind," Russell said, "and that is, how these people are going to work on this project and yet not be told that Holland is the point of the invasion?"

Howard smiled. "Well, they'll certainly put two and two together almost immediately. But we're just not going to confirm it for them, that's all. They won't know in which areas we're interested, and they'll certainly never know the date. That's why your job is so particularly difficult, because we will have to maintain the strictest security on our side.

"Anyway, let's just see how it goes. By the way, there's one small point that I've forgotten to mention, and that is that the caretaker in the basement has been supplied by S.O.E. so you had better get to know him."

Russell got up to leave.

"Well, I hope we make out all right."

Howard smiled. "I'm sure we will. Thanks, Dan. See you later."

The following morning, shortly after ten, the Dutch personnel began to arrive. Russell was now quite familiar with their background details, and he was indeed looking forward to meeting them in the flesh.

The first to come in was Max Dikker. He was a short, thick-set man with a mop of blond hair and a very heavy accent. He was pleasant, intelligent and a journalist by profession. Quick on the uptake, always fond of a joke, Russell took to him immediately.

The next to arrive was Piet Kroller, a young man of thirty who had been a sub-editor on a magazine before fleeing to England. He was accompanied by Jan Gucht, a tall, likeable boy of twenty-eight years of age who was to be their radio operator. His assistant was going to be Frans Hendrik, a printer by profession, but who had recently completed a course on radio operation.

In the last little bunch to arrive were Dr. Mulder, Hannie Herodsen and Sarah Bingham. The doctor was a historian and had been a professor at the Hague University for twenty-two years prior to the war. Sarah Bingham was an English girl, whose duties would be purely secretarial.

Dr. Mulder had a young daughter of seventeen to whom he was utterly devoted. He had lost his wife in a German air-raid at the beginning of the war, but fortunately he had been able to bring Gerda with him on his flight from Holland.

At first, the team were formally polite towards one another and a little at a loss as to what to do. But, directly the last of them arrived, Howard asked Russell to get them together in the larger office, so that he could have a word with them.

When he came into the room, he shook hands with each of them in turn and had obviously memorised their names and personal histories. He then addressed them briefly and simply.

"Well, ladies and gentlemen, I bid you welcome. I am sure that you must all be very curious as to the reasons for our gathering together at these offices.

"Each of you has been personally recommended, not only on account of your qualifications for the job in hand, but also because the people for whom you worked in the past have considered your trustworthiness beyond question.

"Now this last factor is of vital importance because we are going to be engaged in direct contact with your homeland. In fact, if I were to tell you that in two days' time one of the leading Dutch resistance men will be coming here from Holland, in order to help us by supplying information, and that he will be returned within a matter of two or three days to Amsterdam, you will realise just how important our strict security must be, for many lives will depend upon it. And here I'd like to introduce to you Mr. Russell, who is an American Army officer responsible for liaison and the security of this organisation.

"Now, about our job. As each of you must be aware, sooner or later we'll be invading Northern Europe and we wish to alert the underground movements in all occupied countries as to the best ways in which they can help us prior to our attacks and indeed during them. We also wish to gain a great deal more information about conditions in your country with regard to defence: the number of German troops, the names of their units and the strength of the resistance groups in each area.

"Unfortunately, we only have very limited time at our disposal in order to get established and to glean the necessary information. We will therefore be working you very hard, but I am sure you won't mind when you realise just how important your job is going to be. Most of you have been associated with the world of literary affairs, either as journalists, writers or historians, and we wish you to immediately get to work under Dr. Mulder in translating and producing leaflets and instructions which we will have distributed in Holland.

"Finally, before asking if you have any questions, I must once again stress the need for the utmost caution and secrecy. You must never discuss your job with any one outside this office. I am warning you that your own personal telephone lines will be tapped and that you personally will be kept under surveillance. This will in no way interfere with your personal freedom but is simply a form of protection and security. As we progress with our work you will realise just how much the Germans would like to know about our activities and our one job in life will be to prevent them doing so.

"Now then, are there any questions?"

For a moment or two nobody said anything. There was a good deal of shuffling of feet and it was obvious that a question was burning on the lips of each of them.

Finally, it was Piet Kroler who spoke the words.

"Mr. Howard, I hope I am not being impertinent by mentioning it, but does this not rather point to the fact that the Allies will be invading Holland?"

Howard smiled: "I knew somebody would ask that question. Well, I'm afraid I can't answer it," he laughed, "I don't even know myself. I have been given a job exactly in the same way as you, but I'm afraid I am not in Mr. Winston Churchill's confidence."

A ripple of laughter went round the room and the meeting dispersed.

It was amazing how quickly the Dutchmen settled in. Under the guidance of Dr. Mulder, who was in fact an expert on psychological warfare, they quickly became organised and by the afternoon were already engaged on various translations, setting up the printing machinery and generally getting the place under control.

Russell noticed that there was a certain reserve within their own ranks, as if they held each other in a certain amount of suspicion. It would wear off, Russell thought to himself. It's probably because they are confounded writers. He was surprised to notice how Hannie became a very efficient member of the staff, saying little but going about her work methodically and with great energy. This was a side of her character he hadn't really suspected.

Excellent, he thought. Howard should be pleased.

At four-thirty that evening, Phillips, the wireless mechanic, reported to Howard that all the sets were now in working order.

Russell was soon able to appreciate how carefully Howard had pre-planned the whole operation.

The radio operators were immediately furnished with code books, wave lengths and the call signs of various clandestine radios in Holland. Later that evening, their first contact was made. Actually, one of the sets required an aerial adjustment, but Phillips waited until darkness had fallen before he went out on to the roof to deal with it.

That evening, as each of the members of Arista Productions left the office to go home, they were photographed from across the street.

When the others had gone, with the exception of the wireless operators, who were continuing to work their sets far into the night, Russell and Howard chatted in the latter's office.

"Well, I must say I'm very pleased with the first day. Everything seems to be going very smoothly."

"Yeah. A funny lot. They don't say very much. By the way, what's that about someone coming over from Holland?"

"Oh, yes," Howard said, "the day after tomorrow. His name is Henk Janssen, a businessman from Amsterdam. He also holds a very important position in one of the main resistance groups. We daren't keep him longer than two days, but we've got to give him a very thorough briefing so that he can contact the other resistance leaders."

"How the hell are we getting him here?" Russell asked.

"By trawler. A rendezvous has been arranged for tomorrow night, when one of our motor torpedo boats will meet the trawler somewhere in the North Sea and take him off. We hope to return him the same way, although it's very tricky because the German E-boats are quite active in the area. If necessary, he may have to be sent back by submarine, but we hope not."

Howard stifled a yawn. "Well, I think I'll go back now and get some sleep. I'm beginning to feel rather tired. Will you hang on for a while?"

"Yes, sure. Do the operators know what to do?"

"Oh yes," Howard said. "They're going to make a number of routine contacts and arrange for regular transmissions. They'll give us full reports in the morning. Anyway, I shouldn't stay too late, you'll need all the sleep you can get. See you tomorrow. Goodnight."

"Goodnight. Sleep well," Russell murmured, and followed Howard out of the office.

Well, they certainly weren't wasting any time. In the short matter of about ten hours the Arista set-up was already in production. They even had a man coming over from Holland. That was quite something. It had probably been arranged by S.O.E., thought Russell.

He wandered through the offices to check that everything had been put away safely, found some papers on a desk and locked them in a drawer. He then went upstairs to see how the operators were getting on.

When Russell left the building an hour later he noticed a man walking slowly past their entrance on the other side of the road. As he had thrown open the street door he had just been in time to catch a glimpse of the man hurriedly turning his head away. That was strange, thought Russell, it must be one of their own men. It certainly couldn't be a German agent. This was only their first day . . . ! His security couldn't be that bad.

The following morning Russell reported the matter to Howard, but he seemed only vaguely interested.

"One of our chaps, old boy," he said. "By the way, I shall want you to go down and meet this Dutchman tonight. We'll book you a room at Harwich, so that you can be on hand to meet him directly he comes ashore. I'll also arrange a car. Don't waste any time in getting him back up here. I'd also appreciate it if you'd give me a ring directly you meet him, so that I'll know when to expect you. I'll give you the address of the naval establishment. Commander Raikes is the chap you'll want to see.

"By the way, Janssen can speak quite good English so you won't have to worry about taking anyone else down with you."

Russell decided to ask Hannie out to lunch and during the meal they chatted gaily about everything other than their job. Over coffee, Russell asked her:

"How are you enjoying it?"

"Oh, fine," she said. "I wonder who this man is, Howard said we were bringing over?"

"I don't know, but we'll see him tomorrow," Russell replied.

"It seems so incredible that with all the Germans around, we are able to spirit him away just for a couple of days and then return him."

"Oh, these things can be arranged, darling," Russell smiled a little patronisingly. Little did he know.

In the meantime, Howard had spoken to Martinelli on the direct line. After discussing several other matters, he asked him:

"By the way, I wonder if you could check up if anyone was watching the building between the hours of seven and eight-thirty last evening. Russell reported to me this morning that somebody was nosing around on the other side of the street. I told him that it was one of our chaps, but I thought I'd just check up. It's a bit early for us to be attracting any attention from the other side, but you never know. If Dan's as quick off the mark as he has been so far, we're going to have the greatest difficulty in allowing any infiltration."

Martinelli replied at the other end:

"He's a good boy in spite of everything."

"Well, I left some papers on one of the desks purposely last night, but when I came in first thing this morning I noticed that he had them locked away in a drawer. Anyway, it creates the right atmosphere. By the way, I'm sending him down to pick up Janssen tomorrow night. We received confirmation of his departure early this morning by radio. I'll telephone you if there's anything fresh to report."

At eight o'clock that evening, Russell was shown into the office of Commander Raikes at his H.Q. in Harwich. He was a tall, heavily built man with a luxuriant growth of beard.

"Oh, hello, I was expecting you. Come right in." He nearly

minced Russell's hand in his handshake. "Take a pew. Can I offer you a drink?"

Russell declined the invitation with as much grace as he could muster. He felt rather like a small boy in the presence of a giant. He certainly wouldn't like to meet this fearsome creature as an enemy.

"Well, everything's laid on, old boy. I'm taking my flotilla most of the way, then I've decided to go ahead myself and pick up Janssen. Wondered if you'd care to come along?"

"Sure, I'd love to," Russell said.

He had never been out on an active patrol with these small craft and it was certainly worth losing a night's sleep for the experience. From all accounts, the British were pretty adept at this type of warfare, although the German E-boat squadrons were also a highly trained and cunning foe.

After an excellent dinner, they went by jeep down to a distant jetty and boarded Commander Raikes' M.T.B. The rest of the flotilla had put off ten minutes before and were waiting to be joined by their commander some half a mile offshore.

With a few crisp commands, the crew cast off and they headed out to sea.

Raikes had a rough and ready personality but was obviously dearly beloved by his crew. He would alternate between a joke and an oath with remarkable rapidity, and appeared to be an excellent seaman, creating an air of great confidence about him which was most infectious.

Russell was quite stirred with the excitement of the occasion.

"My God, what power these boats have got," Russell exclaimed.

The skipper looked down at him with benign condescension. "We aren't on half-throttle, old boy, but we'll show you what we can do later."

They joined the rest of the M.T.B.'s, and, while the radio crackled instructions, they headed out into the North Sea in line astern.

Apparently, the rendezvous was quite near the Dutch coast, because the fishing fleets were strictly controlled by the German naval patrols. Raikes explained that he intended leaving the main flotilla some five miles from the rendezvous while he went inshore to make the pick-up.

The night was very dark, with a long swell running and a light sea breeze.

At precisely one-thirty, after an uneventful passage, the main flotilla dropped behind while they sped on into the night. The crew were all at action stations and there was an air of expectancy as they entered the coastal waters. However, all went according to plan, and as they were throttling back their engines a light flashed, not a quarter of a mile away. Slowly, they nosed towards it, alert, ever on the look-out for any signs of treachery, but all was well. When they got to within about sixty yards they could just make out the dark shape of the trawler, lying hove-to in the trough of the waves. Raikes gently nursed the M.T.B. along the lee side and, as the gap closed between them, Russell could see a tall raincoat-clad figure standing poised ready to jump when the two boats met. The intervening space narrowed to a couple of feet and one of the English seamen shouted "Jump."

With remarkable agility for a tall man, Janssen half jumped, half stepped on to the M.T.B., grasped a stay and was quickly supported by two seamen. With a quick wave to the Dutch fishermen, Raikes nosed the M.T.B. towards the open sea at slow ahead. He didn't want to use his full engines until the last possible moment, because of the noise, which might be picked up on the sound detectors.

Russell introduced himself to Janssen, who was obviously quite thrilled at his escapade. He refused the suggestion that he should go down below and instead wanted to stay up on deck to see all that was going on.

It was virtually impossible to talk and they were still proceeding on half-throttle about twenty minutes later, when, with a shout, a member of the for'ard gun crew pointed to a position on the port bow. They all strained their eyes in that direction.

Raikes gave a sharp command and at the same time grabbed his glasses. The M.T.B. seemed to gather herself together and lurch forward into the night under full throttle. Almost at the same moment a star shell burst over them.

With an oath, Raikes muttered:

"Three E-boats. Get below, you two."

And then followed a battery of commands, while every available gun exploded into action. Fortunately, they had a good start and as bullets started whining above their heads, Raikes was already in contact with the main flotilla lying about two miles further out to sea.

The E-boats obviously thought that this marauding Englishman was alone and they swung quickly into the attack. But the English skipper seemed neither alarmed nor nervous, but was actually chuckling to himself. He was fleeing straight towards his own flotilla, who were now aware that the enemy were closing in. His object was to lure the German craft to well within range of the other M.T.B.'s, who would hold their fire until the very last moment.

The Germans were still holding on hard astern, but gaining very little, and tracer bullets and cannon were lashing the sea all around them, whining over their heads and occasionally pattering the side of the boat.

Raikes suddenly saw the flotilla ahead and steered for the gap between numbers three and four. As he raced through, he turned in a tight circle to starboard, in order to come round and lash the Germans from the rear when they tried to withdraw.

Suddenly the whole flotilla seemed to erupt in a barrage of fire, creating a fantastic firework display. With so many guns brought to bear and with the surprise complete, the Germans didn't stand a chance. The first E-boat suddenly exploded in a welter of flame. And, even as the remaining two turned hard to port in their endeavour to flee, Raikes was already thundering down their flank, his own guns raking the Germans with fire.

In spite of the order to go below, Russell and Janssen were not going to miss the party and were standing at the hatch, their shoulders well above the deck, watching the battle.

Suddenly, a second E-boat seemed to lurch crazily to port and was rapidly losing way. Although its guns hadn't stopped firing, they were obviously in serious difficulties and the flotilla leader had no mercy. Stream upon stream of fire was poured into it, until finally it was left blazing from stem to stern. Raikes yelled the order to cease fire and the flotilla re-formed, racing at full speed toward England.

Janssen could hardly contain his excitement. With tears streaming down his face, he rushed up on deck, grasped Raikes by the arm and shouted at the top of his voice:

"Hurrah! Hurrah! Hurrah!"

Russell was deeply touched by this demonstration of pent-up emotion from a man who had been under the heel of the Germans for too long.

When he could speak again, Janssen shouted:

"Magnificent! Magnificent! Are we all okay?"

Raikes gave a boyish grin.

"Yes, we're okay. That'll teach the bastards to poke their noses where they're not wanted."

It was now almost daylight as they sped toward England. Thank goodness he hadn't stayed in bed, thought Russell. He wouldn't have missed that party for all the world.

After they had enjoyed a huge breakfast, they set out for London by road, and for the first time Russell was able to take stock of his travelling companion. A tall, fair-haired man of nondescript features and a good sense of humour, he was a businessman, living in Amsterdam, and had worked in the resistance movement for the past two years.

It was very difficult, he had explained, for the Germans had been highly successful at liquidating their resistance cells.

Hundreds of Dutchmen had been caught and executed and the nature of the terrain did not offer the ideal countryside for waging a partisan war. He had heard rumours of the Germans capturing many British agents and the Dutch people felt a little lost and afraid, but recently they had become more organised and were now ready and willing to do their utmost to help shorten the war.

Russell had the feeling that in Janssen was reflected the deep and heartfelt hatred that the Dutch people had for the Germans.

Janssen was impatient to know the full implications of his visit, but Russell kept the conversation to generalities and refused to be drawn when closely questioned.

They got out of the car at Shaftesbury Avenue; then walked up Wardour Street and went straight to Howard's office.

As it turned out, Henk Janssen was a veritable hive of information. It was tragic that he was shortly fated to die.

CHAPTER NINE

THAT day, Henk Janssen was questioned closely on conditions in Holland.

He was extremely helpful, for he had memorised details of German military strength, supplied to him by his own resistance group. He also knew a large number of people who were active workers in other underground cells and was able to recommend the name of a man who had intimate knowledge of the coast and dockside installations, both at Rotterdam and other Dutch seaports. Although this contact, by name Jan Bakker, was not, he believed, an active member of a resistance group, yet he felt sure that he could be persuaded to come to England if it were really necessary.

However, after these lengthy conversations, it became quite clear that the Dutch underground as a whole were very nervous at the prospect of being directly linked with London. They had heard rumours of how Colonel H. J. Giskes, of the German military counter-intelligence, had captured many British and Dutch operators and, although they were not aware of the details, they felt that there must have been some treachery.

Howard asked for Bakker's address and Janssen suggested that they should contact him direct. This Howard was only too pleased to do.

At the end of the first evening, Janssen was still not aware of the real purpose of his journey.

Howard had decided that Janssen should spend the night with Max Dikker, who had a small flat in Bayswater. After they had left, he called Russell back into the room and proceeded to give him a dressing down such as Dan had not received since the days when he graduated from his military academy.

"When I sent you down to pick up Janssen I did not either give you permission or suggest that you should go in the M.T.B.s to pick him up. Here you are one of the few people in the country who know, in fact, where the invasion is going to take place, going right out to sea within a few miles of the enemy coast. Just supposing something had gone wrong and your boat had either been sunk or you'd been picked up. Then what would have happened? Not only was it thoughtless, but bloody stupid, and please don't ever do anything like that again."

Russell had murmured his apologies. There was no doubt that Howard was entirely in the right, but more than anything else he was surprised by the fire and venom with which this personal attack had been delivered.

However, as suddenly as the storm had blown up, it equally quickly subsided and in a few minutes Howard was telling him to go home and get some sleep.

Howard stayed back in the office, reading over the notes he had made from all the information that Janssen had supplied. He had one ticklish problem to solve for the next day. He was anxious that Herodsen should actually come in contact with Henk Janssen, but at the same time he wanted to bring this about in a very casual way. After all, Herodsen's duties did not really entitle her to take part in any of these discussions. However,

Howard suddenly hit upon the idea of arranging a little party for the following lunch time at which he would be able to invite the other members of Arista Productions to meet Janssen.

Howard also made enquiries as to which was the nearest reliable contact who could be used to sound out Jan Bakker as to whether he would be prepared to come to England, for he lived on the outskirts of Rotterdam.

Martinelli obtained the necessary information for Howard within an hour, and later that night a message was being beamed to an agent, who worked himself not far from the great port.

From all that Janssen had said, the Germans did not seem unduly alarmed at the prospect of an invasion through Holland. True, they had considerable coastal defences, but there did not seem to be any untoward military activity in the area. This would have to be corrected, Howard mused.

The following morning at nine o'clock, Howard, Russell and Janssen began their final session.

Janssen was utterly incredulous when told the full implication behind his visit. He simply couldn't believe that Holland would be the area of attack. It wasn't a case of his having doubts as to the veracity of Howard's statement, but rather that he was too overjoyed to think it possible. Obviously his thoughts reflected those of the Dutch people and even of the Germans, who must have been entirely convinced that the Allies would land in France.

However, as Howard patiently explained the reasons why the British and Americans had finally decided that the main prong of the assault should be on the Netherlands, so Janssen not only became completely convinced but was also highly enthusiastic.

But, with the innate caution of a businessman, Janssen prodded Howard for further details, and closely questioned him as to what information was required from Holland; whom he was to see and what immediate steps were to be taken.

Howard dealt with the barrage of questions with great fluency, Russell thought, and produced maps and charts of Holland which looked extremely impressive, and gave all the necessary data.

Howard then gave Janssen his final briefing, asking him to make contact with any known resistance leaders with whom he had personal contacts.

He was to explain our desperate need for reliable military information, estimations of the strength of resistance groups, area by area, and finally a request that the Dutch underground as a whole should endeavour to achieve the utmost co-operation between their own groups in order to forge themselves into an effective weapon to be used against the enemy.

That lunch time, Janssen was introduced to the entire group and, at Howard's prompting, both he and Russell allowed him to mix freely amongst the others. Howard had explained to Russell that he wished this in order to foster a spirit of trust and confidence between London and Holland. Naturally, he couldn't tell Russell the two main reasons; first that Hannie should be given the opportunity to meet Janssen, and secondly to try and dispel any particles of doubt that might remain in the minds of his team.

Howard felt quite enthralled to watch Herodsen go about her task. With professional ease, she offered Janssen a drink and a sandwich, and within a few moments was deeply engrossed in conversation.

Howard had always been a little puzzled how the Dutch people had never noticed anything strange in Hannie Herodsen's accent. Presumably she must either speak Dutch so excellently that it was virtually undetectable, or else they assumed that she must come from near the borders of Germany. Anyway, during the entire operation, no mention was ever made of it.

After the party, Janssen was taken upstairs and thoroughly searched. It was just as well. In one pocket they found an English box of matches, and in another some English pennies. While this was going on, Howard and Russell were chatting in the latter's office.

"Well, what do you think?" Russell enquired.

"I am very satisfied," said Howard.

Suddenly a thought struck Russell.

"By the way, are you going to give him any cyanide?"

The question caught Howard off balance. His eyes flickered and then, looking up, he said:

"No, I don't think so. It shouldn't be necessary."

Russell was aghast: "What do you mean, it shouldn't be necessary? Supposing he gets caught?"

Howard was on tricky ground. "He won't be."

"What do you mean, he won't be? I said, supposing he does. You were worried enough when I risked my neck. Now you're proposing to send this man back into Holland with all the information he's been given without the safeguard of a cyanide pill."

Howard's jawline hardened, but he spoke softly, with only the slightest edge to his voice.

"I said it won't be necessary."

"Well, you're in command," Russell flared. "But it seems both stupid and damned unfair to me."

And with that he turned and walked out of the office.

Of course there was a chance that Janssen would be caught. Of course there was a possibility of a sacrifice, but the stakes were high and this was war. Nevertheless, it was a hideous thought, for, if Hannie Herodsen told Berlin, there must be a good chance that Janssen would be picked up. On the other hand, the Germans might prefer to leave him free in order to see what was afoot. It was a hard decision, a soldier's decision, and Howard wished that he could shirk it. But time wasn't on their side. Soon, thousands upon thousands of British, American, French and Dutch soldiers would be storming ashore and his job was to deflect part of the opposing army. This could not be done without sacrifice. However, he rang Martinelli for instructions.

At three-thirty, Janssen came in and said "Goodbye." It had been queried whether he should still return by fishing boat owing to the skirmish when picking him up. But after consultations with the Admiralty, who confirmed that the fight had taken place a good four miles from the point of pick-up, they thought that there was little danger of the enemy having realised the M.T.B.'s mission. After all, two out of three of their boats had been sunk, and as far as Howard was concerned, it couldn't have been better, because it pointed to our having a definite interest in the Dutch coastal waters.

We had also been in contact with the agent who had arranged the Dutch end and he confirmed that the Germans had shown no interest when the trawler returned to harbour.

It was Russell's job to take Janssen down to Harwich, but on this occasion there was no chance of another jaunt at sea.

Two days later, Howard called Russell into his office.

"Sit down, Dan. I'm afraid I've got some bad news."

Russell dropped into the chair and noticed that Howard looked drawn and grey.

"I'm afraid Janssen has been picked up."

Russell could say nothing. He stared at Howard with a mixture of incredulity and venom.

"What happened?" Russell asked.

"We don't know exactly. They certainly didn't arrest him immediately. In fact, it wasn't until the day after he returned."

"Has he . . . has he talked?"

Howard looked straight past Russell and on through the wall. "I don't know."

With that, Dan got to his feet and walked outside.

"Just a minute, Dan," Howard broke in. "I don't want this mentioned to the others for the time being."

Russell nodded grimly and went outside.

Howard didn't tell him that he had contacted Martinelli for instructions and the American had confirmed his order about the cyanide.

It was not until after the war that the full tragedy of Janssen was revealed. He had withstood the torture for eight long and dreadful hours before finally giving in. He talked and the Germans received their first inkling of the Allied intention.*

Four days later, Russell was instructed to go down to a tiny airfield near Crawley Down to meet the Lysander which had been sent to pick up Jan Bakker, the Havenmeester who lived near Rotterdam.

Bakker did not know that he had been contacted because of Janssen's suggestion. As it happened, the approach coincided extremely well with his annual leave and so all that he had to do was to send his wife to some relatives and instead of going on to the seaside resort at which he was going to stay, he booked in at the Hotel Polen in Rokin, Amsterdam, near the Het Paleis. From there one evening he was taken to the Centraal Station, where he was handed over to an unknown member of the Dutch resistance movement. They boarded a train bound for Utrecht.

When they reached their destination, the original contact man returned to Amsterdam after handing him over to yet another member of the underground, a girl, who was waiting in the station courtyard with two bicycles, so that they could cycle out of town. On the outskirts, she handed him over to yet another Dutchman, with whom he journeyed almost twelve miles by various buses, until finally they reached a remote farm at which the pick-up was going to be made.

Without even knowing that Janssen had been to London, Bakker was given a message to tell whoever was in command that Janssen had already been executed.

* It is only fair to record that his family received a monetary settlement from the United States of America.

That night at eleven p.m., a Lysander landed in one of the farmer's distant fields, and, although Bakker was not by any means a young man, he scrambled up the rope ladder dangling from the side of it with tremendous dexterity and tapping the pilot on the shoulder, was soon airborne for the first time in his life.

Russell met him in the early hours of the morning and immediately drove him to London. He was a short, weather-beaten harbour master, not given much to talking and with a rather scant knowledge of the English language but, although not a member of any organised resistance movement, he had nevertheless agreed with alacrity to the suggestion of his going to London.

He was a man whose information would have proved of vital importance had we really intended landing on the Dutch coast. His knowledge was intimate; he knew the areas where the defences were heavy, he knew the beaches that were nothing but quicksand, and you couldn't have had a man better acquainted with the tide, wind and current problems that would beset an invading fleet. He was tired from his journey and dozed fitfully in the car.

When they got to London, Howard was waiting to greet him. After a quarter of an hour's conversation with Bakker, he realised that it would be impossible without the use of an interpreter and so suggested that they should all retire for the night and start fresh the following morning. This was an excellent opportunity to use Hannie Herodsen and so he asked Russell to arrange that she should be available in his office at ten.

When Howard got into bed that night he found that he couldn't sleep for thinking of Janssen's death. What were they going to do in the case of Jan Bakker? Surely he wasn't expected to send another man to his death. What on earth would Russell say? Surely he would become suspicious. He was an intelligent man and he'd soon put two and two together to realise that we were in fact anxious that the Germans should learn of our supposedly secret plans for the invasion of Holland.

Howard was so disturbed that he telephoned Martinelli at his flat and told him that he was coming across.

In spite of the early hour in the morning, a decision had got to be made and he wasn't anxious to make it.

He began to have an implacable hatred of Hannie Herodsen and his disgust almost extended to Russell. He would have to control these emotions or he would find himself giving the game away.

Shortly, if the Germans were really falling for the bait, there should be some sign of military activity which would at least prove that the sacrifices were not in vain.

Martinelli opened the door. He had thoughtfully made a pot of black coffee and as they sat down Howard unburdened his heart.

". . . Not only is it a fearful thing to have to do, but I'm frightened Russell will realise what we're up to," Howard ended.

Martinelli, in spite of just having been dragged from his bed, had the solution almost immediately.

"First, I must check up to see if Bakker has to be sent back without cyanide. If he has, the simple answer to that problem is to get rid of Russell for a few days. I'm sure we could fix that. When he comes back, you must lie to him; tell him that he was given the pill and then he'll never know."

Here was logic, and as much as Howard disliked the whole affair he realised that this was the only solution.

Howard decided to walk back to his flat and enjoy the fresh morning air. The streets were deserted except for the occasional milkman. An early morning mist hung over Hyde Park, obscuring the distant skyline of buildings. He might for all the world have been walking in the country. He made a good breakfast, bathed and shaved and then went straight to the office.

He said good morning to Jenkins, the caretaker, and slowly climbed the stairs.

Well, if Herodsen had been in any doubt, today he hoped would convince her.

At nine-fifteen Russell went to Howard's office.

"Oh, good morning, Dan. Come in."

"I thought I'd better just check up on a couple of things. How long are you keeping Bakker over here?" asked Russell.

"The shortest time possible. We will probably send him back tomorrow. We've got some navy boys coming along to see him, which may take up a little time."

"Right. Do you want me to lay anything on?"

"No, I don't think so, not for the moment."

Russell looked away from Howard.

"I presume that this time he'll be given some cyanide?"

"Naturally," Howard replied in a steady voice. "By the way, has Hannie arrived?"

"Yes," Russell replied. "She's ready."

"Okay then, there's no need to wait until ten o'clock. Directly Bakker arrives, bring him in and we'll get on with it."

At a quarter to ten they started the interrogation, using Hannie Herodsen as their interpreter. They obtained a wealth of detail. Jan Bakker was an observant man. He gave details of German naval strength, the output of various dockyards and considerable information on the strength of the German coastal defences.

They stopped for lunch but immediately afterwards started checking the various information they had recorded on the charts and maps.

Hannie Herodsen discharged her duties most capably and Howard felt convinced, whilst watching her, that there was no doubt in her mind that the whole proceedings were one hundred per cent. genuine. Shortly after they'd finished the afternoon session, Martinelli came through on the direct line.

"I've got some very good news," Martinelli began. "We've just had a report in, that there's a lot of activity in the German headquarters at Leiden and, although we haven't got any information as to what it's all about, it certainly seems very promising. Now, I've also managed to arrange something to get Russell out of the way. In view of this report, which came through this morning, it's been decided to increase the fake build-up of forces in south-east England and on the east coast. The British have already started it for their Pas de Calais deception, so it should all fit in extremely well. In order to keep you informed and also to enable us to use some American troops in the general subterfuge, I have arranged that you send Russell down to a conference at Dover Castle tomorrow. They won't be told what it is all about, just that large scale movement of troops will be starting soon.

"If you can finish with Bakker during the morning, and send him on his way tomorrow night, it should all be completed before Russell returns to London."

"That sounds excellent," said Howard. "Don't forget you're sending me a couple of Naval bods to interrogate Bakker tomorrow morning."

"No, I haven't forgotten," Martinelli said. "And, by the way, I've got a message from General Donovan who wants me to congratulate you on your success so far and hopes that you will be able to bring this to a successful conclusion."

"Thanks," Howard said. "By the way, have you got the details for Russell tomorrow?"

"Hang on, I think I can give them to you right away," Martinelli said at the other end of the line. There was a slight pause, then he came back. "Yes, tell him to report to Colonel Price at ten-thirty tomorrow morning at Dover Castle. They'll be expecting him."

"Thanks very much, Stephen, I'll tell him straight away. Goodbye."

Early the following morning, Russell left for his conference at Dover, travelling down by car.

In Wardour Street two senior American Naval Intelligence officers started their interrogations of Jan Bakker, and Howard made the final arrangements to send him back by Lysander that evening.

As Jan had two or three days left of his holiday, he decided not to go home directly, but to make his way to the house of his relatives at which his wife was staying.

Later that afternoon, Howard himself took Bakker down to the airfield near Crawley Down. He had an intuitive feeling that the fate that had met Janssen was only round the corner for his travelling companion. It was an indescribable way to send a man to his death.

The following Sunday, beforc he had even got back to his work, Jan Bakker was seized by the Gestapo and taken to Mauthausen.

In Berlin, Kaltenbrunner could hardly believe the information he had just received on the telephone from Holland.

On his instruction, they had picked up a certain Havenmeester, Jan Bakker, on his return from a supposed annual holiday. He was a stubborn man but they had eventually succeeded in making him talk. He admitted having just returned from London and virtually confirmed all the details extracted from Janssen.

It was apparent that he had supplied the enemy with considerable information regarding coastal defences. They promised to send Kaltenbrunner a full typescript of the interrogation and, on being assured that no more information would be forthcoming, Kaltenbrunner ordered his summary execution.

There was now no doubt in Kaltenbrunner's mind that he would have to pass on the information he had obtained to both Himmler and if necessary thc Fuehrer. At first, he had intended holding out, demanding to see the Fuehrer personally, but he now decided that in the circumstances he would have to consult Himmler first, for the information was explosive in the extreme.

He had preparcd a small dossier on the recent activities of his brilliant woman agent, and included in it all her reports in full.

Himmler was out at one of the field headquarters and Kaltenbrunner ordered a plane to fly him there immediately.

If Kaltenbrunner hadn't made this important decision it is quite likely that all the effort put into Operation Stampede might have been to no avail, for already it was the first week in May and if the Germans were going to move troops to reinforce Holland they would have to receive their orders very shortly.

For once Himmler was immediately impressed and said that arrangements would have to be made for them to see the Fuehrer straight away. But there was an unavoidable delay of some twenty-four hours, as Hitler was travelling up from Berchtesgaden.

Himmler became impatient in the extreme and together they spent hours discussing the situation from every possible viewpoint and studying the latest maps of Holland.

Himmler was obviously filled with uncertainty and mentioned to Kaltenbrunner the difficulty they had had over the Cicero affair. The evaluation of this type of information was so very difficult, he confided to Kaltenbrunner. The more conclusive the evidence, the more it behove them to be cautious.

"And don't forget," said Himmler, "there was no mention of Holland in Cicero's papers on Operation Overlord."

Kaltenbrunner racked his brain to think of some way to settle the Reichfuehrer's uncertainty.

"But," stressed Kaltenbrunner, "there are two essential differences between the cases. Cicero made the approach to us and required very handsome payment for his pains. He was also a man to be treated with the very utmost suspicion from the word go. But in this operation the situation is entirely the reverse.

"Canaris started it off in Algiers and I took over from there. This girl is German born and has proved herself devoted to the Fatherland. She is not doing it for monetary gain and she's working for the Americans, whose security is not as stringent as that of the British. Besides which, these two men, Janssen and Bakker, took almost eleven hours of persuasion before they finally broke down. Of course, it could be a deception but can we dare risk doing nothing about it?"

"Whatever happens," Himmler answered, "this information has got to be checked. In spite of whatever the Fuehrer may say, I think it is essential for you to arrange for immediate verification by other agents working in London. It it's true, then there must be considerable military evidence to support it. Look at the map;

the ports along the south-east coast of England must surely give some indication. They would have to use an enormous number of landing barges for an assault on Holland. Give me evidence that they are anywhere along the south-east coast of England. I agree, however, that while this is being arranged we must take precautions. We will see the Fuehrer tonight."

Kaltenbrunner made contact with his headquarters and issued the necessary instructions that at least two other agents, preferably Radmin and Baber, be assigned to the task of checking up both on troop movements and, if humanly possible, on the authenticity of the set-up in Wardour Street.

When Hitler was told that night, he was far less uncertain. Already beginning to deteriorate, both physically and mentally, he snatched at any drifting straw and finally remarked that his intuition seemed to confirm that it must be true.

The following day in May 1944, orders were given to send extra troops to Holland. Some of them came from as far away as Novara in Northern Italy. They also drafted a considerable number of Waffen SS, who had only recently come back from the Eastern Front and were in the process of being re-formed.

Finally, instructions were sent to both The Hague and Leiden that defences from Zandvoort south to Hoek van Holland (The Hook) be immediately strengthened and defended in depth.

So operation Stampede began to have effect and the sacrifices were not in vain.

CHAPTER TEN

When the news came through that Jan Bakker had been caught by the Gestapo, a great gloom settled over 69 Wardour Street. Russell naturally thought that Bakker had in all probability committed suicide and he felt very relieved that this time Howard had given him cyanide. Even then, it was not a pleasant death, but infinitely preferable to one chosen by the Gestapo.

During their brief visits to London, both Bakker and Janssen had been accepted as comrades-in-arms and their passing was a heavy blow. It was also generally known among the team about the failure of the Dutch section of S.O.E. and this on top of that helped to create a general air of despondency.

Dr. Mulder asked for an interview with Howard, and during it he voiced his own secret fears.

"Mr. Howard, with the greatest respect, one cannot help wondering if there is a traitor in our midst. How did the Germans find out? Although I didn't know you when I first joined, I now realize that you are a very thorough man and I am certain you must have taken every precaution."

Howard fenced very carefully and decided to create a diversion with a little suggestion, which he felt certain Dr. Mulder would pass on to the others.

"I don't think that the leakage is from our side, Dr. Mulder. I will only say to you, in the greatest confidence, that I suspect one of our contacts in Holland. As you know, we have taken very great pains to screen everyone who has had any connection with us in London and I am quite satisfied that all is well within our group. However, I am a little unhappy about the Dutch side and I have made arrangements that we will no longer use a certain contact in Amsterdam, but I am sure you will appreciate that, in spite of this very tragic loss, we cannot abandon the job we set out to do."

Mulder seemed almost satisfied and then, rather to Howard's surprise, he blurted out another foreboding.

"Mr. Howard, forgive me, but I go about with a dreadful fear. You see, if those two men have talked, and I know the German methods very well, it is quite possible that the Nazis may have learned something of our operations here. I admit that I am not a strong man, and I am worried that possibly one of us might be seized by German agents in London."

Howard immediately endeavoured to reassure him, for his was obviously a very real anxiety for a man with a fertile imagination.

"Dr. Mulder, I will take immediate steps to make sure that you have all the security that we can possibly give you. Please do not be alarmed. Whereas I understand and sympathize with you, yet I must say that I think the chance that anything should happen is very remote indeed."

"Thank you so much, Mr. Howard. You are very kind. I do hope you didn't mind my having mentioned it."

"Not at all, it was quite the right thing to do, and if you are worried at any time in the future just come and see me again."

For a moment, Howard thought Mulder was going to burst into tears, but he managed to control his feelings and left the office full of gratitude.

This was certainly an unexpected turn of events. Russell had reported only a day or two previously that all was not well with the members of the Arista Productions. It was very natural that they should feel a little afraid, for many of them had families in Holland and they were quite well aware what effect an invasion of Holland would have on them.

There was little that Howard could do. In fact, it had now become essential to see this matter through to its bitter conclusion because, if for any reason their operation broke down, the Germans would naturally assume that we had abandoned the idea of an assault on Holland.

The only one who seemed unperturbed was Hannie Herodsen, but even she was beginning to show the occasional sign of nervousness. The strain of long working hours and the responsibility of the secret she carried was beginning to wear her down.

Russell spent many evenings at Hannie Herodsen's flat, but on each occasion that he did so, a report invariably came through to Howard. It appeared that he was genuinely in love with the girl, although Howard was completely unable to assess the feelings that Herodsen had for him. Surely she could not reciprocate his love and at the same time be using him, but he simply couldn't tell.

However, the one and most important bright spot in the darkness was the fact that already several reports were coming through of increasing military activity in Holland.

It became apparent that both Bakker and Janssen had made one or two contacts immediately on their return and prior to their capture, for suddenly there broke out a whole series of incidents in many of the dockyard areas. Wires were cut, acts of sabotage were perpetrated and on one or two occasions direct use of explosive was employed.

The first leaflets had been distributed three days previously and this, combining with all the contacts from London, was obviously having an effect on the Dutch underground as a whole. The Germans were not slow to notice this and, on orders from Berlin, they took ruthless measures to stamp it out.

One afternoon in the third week of May, Howard was requested by Martinelli to attend a top-level meeting. It was a combined Anglo-American conference and had been convened with the express purpose of discussing the deceptive measures to be undertaken in south-east England. It was sensibly decided that, in order to add credence to both the Pas de Calais and the Dutch deceptions, the immediate movement of additional troops of anything between twenty and thirty thousand men to east coast ports should be put in hand without any delay.

Other methods of faking a military build-up were examined

and, within a few days of the conference, very strange happenings were reported on certain tidal creeks round Mersea Island, Burnham-on-Crouch, Brightlingsea, Sheppey and the Isle of Grain.

Strange landing craft that could never have put to sea suddenly appeared, moored side by side in long and efficient-looking rows. Squadrons of tanks and armoured cars could be found massed in dozens of fields.

The odd thing about them was that, upon close inspection, they would appear to undulate slightly, if there was anything like a high wind. This, of course, was because they were made of rubber and had been blown up to make credible likenesses even at the shortest of range.

Guns and lorries also began to appear and, finally, to complete the very thorough and professional job, a machine was brought into use which created fake tank tracks that clearly showed from the air how they had arrived. Other landing craft and amphibious vehicles, all made from the same inflatable rubber, could be seen on the beaches around Rye, Selsey, Angmering and north as far as Sandwich. The phantom invasion fleet and massed supplies were soon scattered all along the east and south-east coast of England.

Additional measures were also taken abroad. Rumours were started in certain neutral countries and veiled hints were relayed to Europe by the new American broadcasting station known as A.B.S.I.E., which commenced transmitting on 30th April.

In a matter of weeks, photographic evidence to support our deceptions was being studied by the German General Staff.

The next incident that occurred was a rather alarming one for Howard.

The day after the conference, Russell came into his room in some agitation.

"Now, I know this probably sounds stupid, but I saw Hannie talking to some strange guy in Leicester Square. Do you think there could be anything in it?"

Howard laughed. "Jealous?"

Russell smiled. "No. But you know what I mean. I could almost suspect my own mother the way I feel."

"I shouldn't give it another thought," Howard said slowly and, he hoped, convincingly.

"Well, I'll keep my eyes skinned anyway: we can never be too careful."

Having got it off his chest, Russell seemed more at ease, and started discussing their other affairs.

"I'm a bit worried about Mulder and his daughter. He seems terribly jumpy. You don't think anyone could have contacted him?"

"Good gracious, no. We've got him under close surveillance and I've already spoken to him. He's a little imaginative. Don't forget he lost his wife in the war."

"Yeah, I know," said Russell. "He's very vulnerable, there's no doubt about that. Anyway, everything seems to be under control at the moment. Have you had any more reports from Holland?"

Howard looked up slowly. "No, not in the last day or two."

But as a matter of fact one had come in about an hour ago. A troop train had apparently gone through Nijmegen the previous day, bound for Rotterdam. There was also a rumour that von Runstedt was expected at the German headquarters in Hilversum, but this hadn't been confirmed. Anyway, it all seemed to point to the fact that the enemy were worried and if troops were being moved in, then it looked as if Arista Productions was beginning to obtain its objective.

Meanwhile, Hannie Herodsen was not without her own troubles. Berlin were apparently extremely pleased with her information but kept asking for further proof. She heard from Bruno Baber that he had been detailed to check up on troop movements in south-east England and also on her work in Wardour Street.

This had thoroughly enraged Hannie and she had sent a strong message to Berlin saying that any interference at this stage might jeopardize the whole affair. If the British had the slightest inkling that their secret had been obtained by the German General Staff, they would obviously abandon all their plans. She explained the tremendous lengths to which they had gone with their security and begged Berlin not to interfere.

So far as Jimmy Foster was concerned, she had gradually allowed him to slip out of the picture, using him as little as possible, as being too great a security risk.

Her main worry was certainly Radmin and Baber. If they made a false move the fat would be in the fire.

One night, as she and Russell were going back to the flat, she suddenly had the feeling that they were being followed and, clinging tightly to Russell's arm, she whispered a quick word of warning.

The night was dark but when Dan turned round he certainly saw a man melt into the shadows. He didn't really know what to do. It could be the British, it could be the O.S.S., it could be the Germans. But, as a precaution, he decided to walk past the flat and turn left at the top of the road. As it happened, a taxi was passing and he hailed it, instructing the driver to go round the block. When they went up Clifton Villas for the second time, there was no sign of anyone, so they stopped the cab and quickly walked into the house.

Everyone's nerves in the outfit seemed to be getting frayed. Even his sweet and dearly loved Hannie was nervous and jumpy at times.

At the office, Max Dikker no longer laughed and joked as of old and Piet Kroller would erupt if you said but a word. The only one to be completely unaffected was Sarah Bingham, who, despite the amount of work given her by Howard and Russell, seemed completely at her ease.

In Holland things seemed to be going extraordinarily well and, in spite of the alertness of the German occupying forces, pamphlets were distributed, military information was obtained and weapons and supplies were dropped to the underground.

Not all of this came within the scope of Operation Stampede, of course, but it all helped to give confidence to the Dutch resistance, who began to actively harass the German Command by disrupting communications and the transport system.

The Germans, for their part, increased the number of their patrols and were constantly on the lookout for any form of resistance. Even now, they had a great number of successes, often capturing underground leaders and breaking up active groups and cells.

Day by day, reports came in of fresh troop movements. The 347th Division were put in to defend the coast between Helder and Alkmaar in Noord Holland; the 719th Division were centred on Haarlem and the 165th Division defended the coast at The Hague. The 19th Panzer Division and the headquarters of the German Air Command were located in the centre of Holland; the 16th G.A.F. were located to the north and west of Amsterdam and still additional troops were being sent in by the German High Command.

The 1st SS Panzer Division was just south of the Dutch border and there was also a strong concentration of troops in the Scheldt Estuary. Besides these active infantry divisions, there were thousands of troops garrisoning the rest of Holland, and the O.K.W. Reserve, consisting of another four panzer divisions, were being re-fitted across the borders in Germany, having been withdrawn from the Eastern Front.

As the last days of May rapidly drew to a close, there were upwards of a hundred thousand troops within the borders of Holland, yet notwithstanding all our deceptions, Hitler was still uncertain from which quarter the attack would eventually come.

He sent "snap and run" flights over Kent and Sussex and the German Air Reconnaissance provided von Runstedt's intelligence branch with more evidence of the build-up of the Allied forces in south-east England.

But Berlin was still far from satisfied, and further orders were issued to both Radmin and Baber to obtain immediate confirmation of Herodsen's reports from Wardour Street.

So it came about that, on the last day of May, Dr. Mulder, returning to his home, was told by his housekeeper that his daughter had not returned from school. He was a little puzzled at first but imagined that she must have gone round to have tea with one of her friends.

However, by six-thirty there was still no word and, beginning to feel the first pangs of anxiety, he rang her school to see if they might have any idea with whom she left, but they were unable to help in any way.

Mulder now became highly alarmed and rang the office. Quite by chance, he was connected with Hannie Herodsen, whom he had always found a most sympathetic listener to his troubles.

"Oh, Hannie," he blurted out. "I am so worried, my little Gerda has not returned from school. She should have been back hours ago, but there is absolutely no sign of her. What am I to do?"

Hannie Herodsen could hardly believe what Mulder was saying at the other end of the phone. She could sense that this time there was something seriously wrong.

At the same moment another thought flashed into her brain. Surely Berlin hadn't been stupid enough to . . .

"Now don't worry, Dr. Mulder. I'm sure she is quite all right. Where are you speaking from?"

"My home."

"Then stay just where you are. I'll have a word with Mr. Russell, but he's out at the moment, so I shan't be able to ring you back for about a quarter of an hour. But please don't worry, she'll be all right, I promise you."

With that, Hannie Herodsen put down the telephone and, grabbing her overcoat, ran downstairs. She had to get to a 'phone box and quickly. She sped up the road and, finding one empty, hastily dialled Baber's number. He answered personally at the other end of the line.

"Bruno, I've just heard . . ."

He cut in almost immediately. "Is that you, Hannie?"

"Yes," she replied.

"Do be careful what you say on the telephone."

"The Doctor's little girl . . .?"

"I know," Baber said quietly.

"Is it you?" Hannie demanded.

"Of course not. But they were instructed."

"Instructed!" Hannie exploded. "Why must they keep interfering?"

"They are getting nervous," Baber replied.

"Where is she?" Hannie demanded furiously.

"I'm afraid I cannot tell you, but in any case I must ask you not to say any more on the 'phone." And with that he cut off.

Hannie left the kiosk and started walking rapidly back to the office. Now what was she to do? British Intelligence would never stand for a thing like that. The idiots, the fools. Couldn't they understand in Berlin that they were hazarding the whole operation? And her life was also at stake, not that that counted for much, she realized. What was she to do? The only course seemed to be to take the most straightforward attitude and immediately get in touch with either Russell or Howard. She felt certain that Radmin was behind it. It was a cunning move to seize the daughter of the most vulnerable man in the organization. She felt certain that he would talk, and then Berlin would really know that her work had not been in vain. But the only reward she would get, if she was not very careful, was a rope round her neck.

Hurrying into the office, Hannie Herodsen went from room to room looking for Russell, but he was not there. Then she must tell Howard immediately, she thought, and walked straight to his office.

Sarah was typing some letters and smiled up at her.

"Do you want to see Mr. Howard?"

"Yes please, Sarah. It's very urgent. I've just had a call from

Dr. Mulder, who seemed frightfully worried because Gerda has disappeared."

"Disappeared," Sarah laughed incredulously. She flicked the intercom. "Hannie would like to see you, Mr. Howard."

"I won't keep her a moment," his voice came over the intercom.

"How did you find this out?" Sarah enquired.

"The Doctor telephoned a few minutes ago. He's terribly upset."

"Oh, I shouldn't worry, you know what he's like. I expect she's just gone home with a friend. After all, she is seventeen."

Hannie smiled weakly. "Yes, I'm sure you're right."

Howard wondered what on earth Hannie Herodsen could want. However, the only way to find out was to have her in and see. He spoke to Sarah.

"Send Hannie in, please."

As she came in through the door, Howard noticed that she was clutching a small handkerchief, but it seemed to be her only sign of nervousness; otherwise she was completely under control.

"Mr. Howard, I felt I ought to tell you. Dr. Mulder's just been on the 'phone. He says his daughter, Gerda, has not returned from school. I've told him not to worry, but you know what he's like. He seems to think she's missing. So I thought it might be a good thing if you had a word with him."

Howard was quite relieved. Poor old Mulder, with his persecution mania. Thank God it wasn't anything worse than that.

"Thanks very much, Hannie. I'll certainly ring him straight away. Leave it to me. I'm sure you're right. She's probably gone to the pictures or something. Thanks for telling me, anyway."

"You're welcome, Mr. Howard. Good night."

Hannie called good night to Sarah, collected her things and left the office.

Although not daring to associate herself too closely with Radmin, she was determined to have a word with him. If he were caught, her life would be in immediate danger. For it was obvious that Berlin had informed all their agents in London to check up on the information she had been sending.

It must have been Kaltenbrunner, the fool, or perhaps the orders came from somewhere higher up. Somehow, she didn't think that Kaltenbrunner would doubt her word. That left Himmler—that's just about what he would do.

In the meantime, Howard rang Mulder and endeavoured to

pacify him. He had just put the telephone down when Russell walked in.

"Oh hello, Dan. Just been speaking to Mulder on the 'phone. His daughter's not returned from the school. Of course, he thinks the Germans have kidnapped her or something."

Russell smiled, but was not entirely reassured.

"Well I hope the kid's okay. You don't think anyone might try . . ."

Howard cut in. "Kidnap her in London? Good Lord, no. Even the Germans wouldn't make a move like that."

"They might be desperate," Russell mused. "Don't forget it's June the 1st tomorrow."

"Well I certainly won't do anything until I've heard from Mulder in a couple of hours' time. But I honestly don't think any harm could have come to her. She's probably gone to the pictures. Anyway, we'll soon see. He's bound to ring back if she doesn't turn up."

But Dr. Mulder did not ring back. Instead, he received the most frightening telephone call of his life.

CHAPTER ELEVEN

DR. MULDER could hardly believe his ears.

"Good evening, Dr. Mulder, I have a message for you from Gerda. She asks you to come to her quickly, but I'm afraid we can only arrange it on condition that you give your word not to speak to anyone. Take a taxi immediately to Regents Park Underground station. You will be met there."

With that the caller rang off and Mulder slumped into a chair in a state of near nervous collapse. His worst fear had been realized, his darling little Gerda was in the hands of the Germans. He knew the Nazis too well not to understand their threat and so, stumbling to his feet, he fetched his hat and overcoat and without saying a word to anyone, went out into the street to find a taxi.

In a very short space of time they had reached their destination. As Mulder leaned forward in the cab in order to step out into the street, a man of medium height, wearing a light raincoat and a trilby hat, walked towards him, raised his hat in greeting and said:

"Dr. Mulder? I am so glad you could come." He then turned

to the driver and said: "Twenty-five Wimpole Street," and scrambling in beside the Doctor he slammed the door.

"My daughter?" Mulder began, but his companion held up his hand in a gesture of silence.

"You will see her shortly," he said. "She is perfectly well."

It was only a matter of three or four minutes before they pulled up outside the address. They got out of the taxi and Mulder waited on the pavement while the stranger paid the fare.

"This way, but don't say a word," he was instructed.

And, with a feeling of great trepidation, Mulder followed. The house, like so many in Wimpole Street, consisted of doctors' consulting rooms. They walked quickly up to the first floor and he was ushered into a waiting-room.

For a few minutes he was left alone and then the stranger came back and beckoned him inside. He had expected to see his little Gerda but, to his dismay, there was another man waiting to see him.

He was well dressed, middle-aged, and immediately came to the point.

"Dr. Mulder, I have probably no need to tell you that we are German agents. We know every detail of your work but we require certain information which I think you may be able to supply. At the moment your daughter is in good health and is waiting to see you, but if she is to remain in that happy state you had better give us very quickly the answers to the questions we want to know."

Mulder began to physically tremble. "I . . . I am not able," he stuttered.

"Please don't be foolish, Dr. Mulder," the man cut in abruptly. "I should hate to have to arrange an extraction of some of your daughter's teeth without any anaesthetic."

Mulder almost collapsed on the floor.

"Where is she? Where is she?" he cried. "I won't say anything until I have seen her."

"If that's the case, we'll have to take you on a little journey because she's now out in the country."

"Then why did you say she was here?"

"My dear Mulder, do you take us for fools? If you don't co-operate you'll never see your daughter again."

Mulder summoned what little courage he had left. "I refuse to say anything until I have seen her."

"Then I'm afraid we'll have to make the journey. But only on this very clear understanding. That when you have seen her, and find that she is in perfect health, you will immediately give us the answers to our questions."

"I'll . . . I'll try," Dr. Mulder groaned.

"Very well, come this way. Hans, you'd better ring Baber and tell him to come over here in our absence."

With this he led Mulder outside.

The following morning at nine-fifteen everyone else had arrived at the office with the exception of Dr. Mulder, and Howard, who had spent the whole previous evening at a top-level conference, told Russell to ring his home.

His housekeeper confirmed that when she arrived there was no sign of him or his daughter and that she had just come downstairs from the bedrooms and had noticed that the beds hadn't been slept in.

Russell told her to stay where she was and to say nothing to anybody. He then rushed through to Howard.

"It looks damned serious. There must have been something in it, after all. His housekeeper has just come in and said that neither Mulder's nor his daughter's beds have been slept in."

"My God, of all the rotten luck. We'll have to get on to this straight away. After last night's conference I can tell you that it is a top priority that Mulder must be found, because D-Day is getting extraordinarily near. But don't say a word to anyone. Wait upstairs until I've had a word with Martinelli."

The latter also cursed his luck when Howard reported the whole affair and said he'd ring back in ten minutes when he'd had a word with M.I.5 and his own S.I. boys. It was obvious they'd have to round up one of the known German agents working in London in order to get a lead, probably the one in Wimpole Street that they had allowed to carry on operating.

Howard waited impatiently. He wondered what on earth he should say to the rest of the team. He certainly couldn't tell them that Mulder was just missing. He wondered desperately if Herodsen knew anything about it. Now he recalled how she was clutching her handkerchief when she had told him the news last evening. But whatever happened they couldn't mention it to her.

He called Russell down.

"Dan, I think you'd better tell everyone that Mulder's been taken ill. Say it's strain through overwork."

"But doesn't Sarah know?" Russell cut in.

"Yes, both she and Hannie know about it. So you had better

say Gerda turned up safely but that her father was taken ill in the night. Tell them that the doctor has ordered him to bed for a week with complete rest and not to be disturbed."

"Yeah, I guess that may do it. What does Steve say?"

"He's ringing back in a few minutes' time."

Martinelli went into action fast. He had a brief word with M.I.5 but didn't tell them what had actually happened. He was only anxious to check Radmin's address in Wimpole Street and on being told that it was definitely No. 25, he called Johnny Sutaro into his office.

"Johnny, we're in trouble. You'll have to get your skates on fast. Both Mulder and his daughter have disappeared. She was obviously snatched late last night. They've got to be found but fast. We must make it appear that we'll turn hell upside down to get him back. In actual fact the more he talks the better, because they're obviously trying to check up on the whole Wardour Street set-up, and he believes it implicitly. But we mustn't let any harm come to either Mulder or his daughter.

"You'll know how to deal with the situation, get on with it and don't come back without them. The only lead I can give you is that Radmin occupies consulting rooms on the first floor of 25 Wimpole Street. You'd better take a girl with you in order to get in without arousing suspicion. I suggest Margaret because she's English but make certain nothing happens to her. You'll need to take a couple of boys and you'd better be armed."

Johnny Sutaro needed no second bidding.

"Right. Leave it to me." And with that he bounded outside.

Martinelli telephoned Howard.

"Jump in a taxi and come right over."

A quarter of an hour later they were talking urgently in Martinelli's room.

"How much do you think Herodsen knows?" Martinelli asked Howard.

"I'm not sure, but I've got my suspicions that she's fully in the picture about snatching Mulder's child."

"Right. Then we'll have to carry out the final phase of our plan a little earlier than I had intended. I haven't told you before, because I didn't know myself. But Donovan informed me this morning that D-Day is on the 5th. That's five days' time. However, there may be some delay because the Met reports aren't too good. Anyway, as you suggested, I have had a complete set of fake plans made out on S.H.A.E.F. paper for our supposed landings in

Holland. They are perfect in every detail. I think it's vital that somehow you arrange for Herodsen to see them, because if she gets any doubts at this late moment, it'll give the whole game away and might even point to the fact that we are going to land in France. I don't know how you're going to arrange it but I should try and have it laid on for tomorrow night. You'll have to try and drop a hint that the big day has arrived, put the cover plans in the safe so that everyone knows they are there, then leave the office vacant for three or four hours. That might give her a chance to get back in again. Do you think she could tackle the safe?"

Howard considered for a moment.

"I'm damned if I know. She's very thorough. I should think that somehow she must have arranged that weeks ago, although I've never seen any evidence that she's been into it."

"Well, that's going to be her problem," said Martinelli. "It wouldn't do to put the plans anywhere else, because obviously you'd never leave them out in a thousand years. So we'll just have to trust to her efficiency. In the meantime we're doing everything we can to find Mulder and his daughter, but when we do get them we'll have to send them somewhere safe until after D-Day has arrived. How's Russell behaving?"

"Perfect. I'm sure he's absolutely sold up the line."

"Okay, Julian, then it's all yours. You've done a wonderful job. All we've got to do now is just to see it through to the end."

With that, Howard returned to his office.

He was certainly nowhere near as confident as Martinelli. So far as he was concerned, things were getting distinctly out of hand.

He decided to call everyone together.

"Well now, I've got some very important news. I know how you've all been working extremely hard, but tomorrow our operation takes on a new phase and I'm going to have to ask you to make even greater sacrifices of your time. We may have to work right into the night every night for the next week or two but I'm sure you will realize how important it is. I've never worked with such a faithful team and I'm truly grateful for all your efforts. We'll lay on meals, so don't worry about food."

Hannie exchanged glances with Russell. It was obvious that things were moving. She wondered what on earth was happening to Mulder and his daughter. She would have been very surprised if she had known.

Within ten minutes, Johnny Sutaro had rounded up his best man, Harry, and Margaret, the English girl, and laid on a car outside. Soon they were racing towards Wimpole Street. As they drove along, Johnny briefly explained to Margaret what she was expected to do.

They had to get inside a consulting-room, he had told her, and it would appear more authentic if she went in first. Directly the door was opened to her, she was to step to one side and then go straight down to the car and await their return.

It took them only a few minutes to reach their destination and Johnny told the driver to stop a hundred yards farther down the road.

The three of them got out and Sutaro told them to relax and not to walk too quickly. He checked off the house numbers as they passed them and then, with heart beating, Margaret pointed to No. 25.

"Yeah, sure, this it is. Let's try our luck, honey."

At that very moment the front door opened and a lady stepped outside. Margaret was as quick as lightning. She smiled pleasantly and put her hand on the door to prevent it closing.

Within seconds they were inside in the hall and Johnny squeezed her arm in appreciation for her quick action.

"Don't be scared," he whispered into her ear. "I'm right behind you. Walk up the stairs and I'll point to the door when we get there."

Fortunately, the whole house seemed to be quiet and they trooped up the stairs in single file. Margaret was so frightened her legs were almost buckling under her and butterflies were doing a war dance in her stomach, but she didn't give way.

At the top of the first flight of stairs there was only one door and, looking at Sutaro for confirmation, she knocked on it boldly.

For a moment or two there was no response and then suddenly they could hear someone walking towards it on the other side. After a slight pause it was opened very slowly and Margaret almost fainted with shock.

"I've come to see the doctor," she said, in something of a trembling voice.

But, before she could get another word out, Sutaro had pushed her to one side and bounded into the room, at the same time pulling out an automatic. He completely bowled the man over who had opened the door and Harry leapt over the two of them, rushing into the other rooms to see if they were all clear. There was no one else in occupation.

In their hurry and excitement, they left the main door open and Margaret rushed down the stairs with her heart in her mouth, out on to the street and along to the waiting car.

They dragged the unfortunate Baber through to the inner office. Johnny Sutaro didn't mince his words.

"Right, we know all about you. Where are they?"

As it happened, Johnny was by no means certain as to whom he was speaking, but the forcefulness of the attack or the confidence with which he had spoken, evoked an immediate reply.

"My name is Hauptmann Baber, and I am an officer in the German Army. My serial number is . . ."

But, before he could say another word, and now knowing with whom he was dealing, Sutaro sank his fist deep into the man's stomach.

"The Geneva Convention doesn't apply to you. Now answer my question. Where is Dr. Mulder and his daughter?"

Baber was stupidly stubborn but not for very long.

"All right, all right," he gasped. "I'll tell you, but promise me I won't die. Promise me . . ."

"Shut up, you rat. Where are they?"

Blood was oozing from the corner of his mouth and his nose.

"Southdown Cottage, in a little village called Bray."

With that, Harry and Johnny started to quickly cast their eye over the room, but unfortunately they had underestimated the staying power of Herr Baber. Johnny looked round just in time to see Baber raising his automatic. If it hadn't been for the fact that he still held his own in his hand, it is doubtful if he would be alive today. He swung round, firing two quick shots. Baber pitched forward on his face and lay writhing on the floor. They rushed over to him, but he was already dead, both bullets having entered his body through the chest.

In the next moment, they could hear various doors being opened upon the floors above.

"Get down to the car, Harry, I've got to ring Steve."

He grabbed the 'phone and dialled the number, waiting impatiently for the operator to answer.

"Get me Martinelli and make it fast."

A few more moments delay and then he heard his chief's voice on the other end of the line.

"Johnny here. We're in trouble. The address you want is Southdown Cottage, Bray. We've just shot one of them here and it's created quite a disturbance. I'm going to try and get out and make my way straight down to Bray. Can you fix it with the police?"

"Leave it to me," Martinelli snapped. "Get down there as fast as you can. I'll also send another car."

As he rushed out of the door, he almost knocked over a man coming down the stairs.

"There's a guy been shot in there. Call the police." And with that he leapt down the stairs three at a time and doubled to the car, which already had its engine running.

Harry had the door opened and he leapt inside.

"Okay, beat it," he snapped, and with that the car sped away.

"Have we got a map?" Johnny asked.

"Yes, there's one in the locker," the driver answered.

"Okay, give it to me. We've got to find the quickest way to Bray."

Suddenly, Sutaro remembered that he'd still got Margaret in the car.

"Here just a moment. Pull up."

The car came to a halt just as they were about to cross Baker Street.

"Thanks, Margaret, you did a great job. You'd better get back and report to Martinelli and tell him we're on our way."

With that, she jumped out of the car and waved them goodbye.

Back in the office, Hannie Herodsen was trying hard to concentrate on her work and conceal the anxiety that was gnawing at her heart. She felt desperately frightened that if either Radmin or Baber were caught, they would somehow implicate her. She was too old a hand at the game to expect any mercy, especially when they found her right within their own organization. And it also seemed from what Howard had said, that the day of the invasion was getting near.

As it was just on lunchtime, she decided to go back to the flat and at least warn Berlin. She would also need to make tentative arrangements for getting out, because when the landings took place and the Allies learned that their plans had been betrayed, she felt they would leave no stone unturned in their efforts to find their betrayer.

Hannie took a taxi to Maida Vale and when she got into the flat, briefly scribbled her message on a sheet of paper, coded it and then took out the small box of chocolates that had been sent to her from Germany. She plugged it into a little table light and quickly scribbled her message.

"Have strong suspicion day of invasion imminent. Stand by for verification within thirty-six hours—Stop—Please make arrangements my withdrawal any time from June third at shortest possible notice—Stop—Other agents' activities in London causing acute embarrassment—Stop—Could lead to complete failure of mission—Stop—Have seen two new maps which confirm landings probable along coast north of Hague. Should also expect airborne landings area of Utrecht—Stop."

She coded the message and then, pressing the first button, recorded it into the machine. Next she tuned into the most powerful transmitter by pressing button number two and waited until the light became at its most brilliant. Finally, at exactly one-thirty, she pushed button number three and sent out the message.

It was astounding to think that one second later it had been picked up in her homeland.

Howard, waiting for news from Martinelli, was checking the last lot of reports from Holland when he came through on direct line.

"I thought I'd let you know that we've found out where they are, and I've sent two cars to pick them up. Unfortunately, we've had a spot of trouble in Wimpole Street. One of their men has been killed. I only pray that they don't withdraw Herodsen, although somehow I don't think they will. Everything all right at your end?"

"Not too bad," said Howard. "I don't think anyone was very suspicious about Mulder being taken ill. He's been acting so strangely recently that I think it's almost been expected. However, I feel convinced from the look of relief that came over Hannie's face that she knows about the Mulder affair. I've got a feeling that she must have expected the possibility of our picking her up and now that we've said he's ill she obviously thinks we are going to keep quiet. Anyway, I will keep you in touch if there are any developments."

"Fine," said Martinelli. "I hope to give you a buzz any time now. By the way, I don't think I told you, they've taken them out to a little village called Bray."

"Good God, I know it well," said Howard. "I hope they're all right."

"Yeah, so do I. Goodbye for now."

Johnny had raced through Staines and was fast approaching Maidenhead. The map told them that Bray was just inside the Berkshire border, being a very tiny Thames-side village. They had no idea where the cottage was situated but Johnny was banking on the fact that it would probably be well known to the local inhabitants.

Unbeknown to the authorities at that time, there was a German agent living in Staines and it was he who finally sent Radmin's confirmation to Berlin, that at least one prong of the Allied assault would be launched on Holland.

Radmin had no doubt that every word that Mulder had spoken was true and this only confirmed the reports of Herodsen.

Turning left over the bridge at Maidenhead, the car raced the last few miles.

As they approached the village, they saw an old lady walking along and, stopping the car, Johnny got out and asked her if she knew the cottage.

"Oh yes," she said, and gave them quite explicit instructions.

They would have to be very careful on this occasion and extraordinarily quick, for they couldn't be certain what the Germans might do. They would virtually have to take the cottage by storm.

Sutaro was just wishing that he had a little more support when they heard the toot of a car behind. The second car must have driven even faster than they had done.

Johnny was very glad and told his driver to stop. There were four men inside, two of whom he knew, and quickly he explained the position.

Directly they reached the cottage they must lose no time in getting out of their cars and surrounding the place to cover the routes of escape and also stand by in case they needed any assistance inside.

In spite of the careful directions, it took them a few moments to find Southdown Cottage. All seemed very quiet as Johnny and Harry raced up the path and the others pelted round behind. Suddenly they heard a door being slammed and almost at the same moment a shot rang out from the rear. Radmin fell to the ground mortally wounded.

He had obviously heard them coming and was trying desperately to escape.

The front door was open and as he stepped inside the first thing that Sutaro heard was the sound of a man sobbing. He tried the first door on his left and there in a corner sat Mulder on a chair, broken-hearted.

"You're too late," he wailed. "You're too late. She's upstairs."

For a second, Johnny and Harry hesitated, stunned by the words Mulder had spoken.

Then, climbing the narrow stairs, they went into a bedroom where, lying on an old iron bedstead, was the body of Gerda, tied down by the hands and feet.

Sutaro gave it a cursory examination but he couldn't decide quite how she could have died, for there were no visible signs of violence. In fact, it was later established at a post-mortem that she died of a weak heart accelerated by shock.

Downstairs, Radmin had been brought inside and, although not dead, was obviously dying.

Poor Dr. Mulder was completely broken and utterly inconsolable. He had now lost not only everyone he had in the world but also his pride, for he had betrayed the supposed secret of the D-Day landings and thereby in his own eyes he was a traitor to his country and all that he held dear.

Sutaro wasn't quite sure what to do with Mulder. He tried to get him into the car outside, but he wouldn't be moved, wishing to remain behind, like a dog beside the body of its dead master.

Johnny decided to go down to the village and ring Martinelli.

There were no signs of any other occupants at the cottage and he told Harry to look in the larder and see if he could make a pot of tea for Mulder.

He had to walk some way to the telephone and tried to employ his brain in thinking of what he was going to say to Martinelli. It had been a bad day in many ways and the death of this girl, he knew not from how, was not going to put Martinelli in a pleasant frame of mind.

It didn't take him long to get through and he was connected almost immediately to his chief.

"Well, how did you make out, Johnny?"

"Not too good, I'm afraid, Steve. The girl's dead, but we shot the Kraut trying to escape. Mulder's in a bad state of crack-up."

There was no answer from the other end of the line. And for a moment he thought they were cut off.

"Are you still there, Steve?"

"Yes, I'm here," the voice said at the other end wearily. "What happened to the girl?"

"I don't know. As a matter of fact I couldn't see any sign of violence at all. We'll have a doctor look her over. As far as the other chap was concerned, he tried to get away and one of the boys pinged him."

"My God," muttered Martinelli. "What a hell of a day. Well, anyway, you certainly can't bring Mulder back to London. We'll have to keep him underground for the time being. How's he making out?"

"Just terrible."

"Well you'd better take him cross-country to your old headquarters and tell them to fix him up there. In fact, I'll ring them myself. He's not to be left alone on any account. I'm very sorry for the poor old boy. Of all the goddamned luck. By the way, did anyone hear the shooting?"

"No, not as far as I know," Sutaro answered. "Hardly seen a soul."

"Okay, I'll arrange to have the two bodies picked up and also send down a doctor to have a look at the girl. Naturally, we'll have to keep it hushed up. We've had a whale of a row about your little show in Wimpole Street this morning. Anyway, it's all under control. I suppose you haven't been able to get anything out of Mulder?"

"No, I'm afraid not."

"Okay. Well I suggest that you take him to the place I told you and explain that it's safest down there for the time being. You'd better also tell him that Mr. Howard will come down for details. Take it easy on the guy, he's had a pretty rough time."

"Sure."

"Once you've got there, come straight back."

"Right, Steve."

When he got back to the cottage Mulder was far calmer and he gave him Martinelli's message.

He didn't say very much, but meekly agreed to do whatever was suggested. At first he wanted to go upstairs again, but Johnny advised him not to.

Leaving the two men behind, as he had been instructed, they set off in the car to make the cross-country journey to Oxfordshire.

While they were driving along, Mulder told them what had happened. He explained that when they had arrived down at the cottage he was taken into the room downstairs and Radmin said that unless he was prepared to answer all his questions on the spot, he would never see his daughter alive again.

"I'm afraid I told them everything I know," he said in a misery of despair. "And now what will happen? Oh, what will happen when we go to invade?"

He lapsed into silence for a moment or two before continuing.

"When I had answered all his questions, Radmin agreed that I could go upstairs, but he went first and it must have been as my little Gerda heard me coming up that she . . . that she simply died . . . I cannot understand it. Radmin promised me that he had done nothing to her other than tie her hands and I believe him, but when I got up there she was already dead. Now she has joined her mother. God rest them both. Oh, I wish I were dead," and with that the poor old doctor burst into tears again.

When he had calmed down, Johnny Sutaro gently asked him a vital question.

"Did Radmin communicate with anyone?"

"Yes, I'm afraid he did. He had a little wireless set in a tiny box and he actually made me sit and wait while he sent the message before he would let me go upstairs."

"What time was that?"

"I can't remember. It must have been sometime in the early morning."

"But what have you been doing all the time?"

"Waiting. He was waiting for someone to come. I do believe he would have killed me. I don't think he was ever going to go back to the cottage because he burnt a lot of things. Anyway, I didn't really understand, I was too upset."

"And you've been downstairs there ever since?"

"Yes. Just sitting and thinking of my little Gerda."

Johnny didn't ask him any more questions.

When he got back to London in the evening, he went straight to Martinelli's office. Howard was also in the room and Martinelli introduced them.

"Well, what's happened, Johnny?"

He explained briefly all that Mulder had told him, and Martinelli confirmed that they had found the little radio set, when they had gone down to fetch the bodies.

"Okay, Johnny, you did a good day's work and we're grateful to you. Now perhaps you'd kindly leave me with Major Howard."

"Sure," Johnny replied. "Goodnight, Major, nice to have met you."

When the door closed behind him, Martinelli looked across at Howard.

"Well, it could have been more disastrous I suppose. It's a real tragedy about the poor old doctor. I don't know what we're going to do about him, but as far as Operation Stampede is concerned, if they don't believe it now, they never will."

"That's true," Howard replied.

"Now it only remains for the final phase. I've laid it on for tomorrow night. That's provided all the plans are ready."

"Yes, I've got them here," Martinelli said. "Have a look at them." He opened a drawer and pulled them out.

They were a complete set of detailed plans for the invasion of the Dutch coast, drawn up by S.H.A.E.F.

"We've got to keep the pressure up right until the very last moment because not only will it add to the general confusion but even after we've landed in France they may still think that it is only a diversionary attack and that we still intend coming in through Holland. The only way to finally convince them is to let them see a copy of these plans."

"The only thing that worries me," said Howard, "is how she is going to get into the safe. I've done everything I could to facilitate her getting a copy of the key. On three separate occasions, I've left the bunch lying on my desk at night, but I've always had the feeling that they've never been touched. I also lent them to Russell twice so that he would take them home, hoping that she would be quick enough off the mark to try and get a wax imprint or something. Anyway, we'll just have to wait and see."

"I'll tell you what," said Martinelli. "When you put the envelope in the safe, lay it flat and somehow see if you can place something like a little paper clip right on the edge so that if the envelope is moved it's bound to fall off. Then we'll know whether or not they've managed to get in."

"That's a good idea," said Howard. "Anyway, I'd better be getting on my way. I've got a tremendous amount to do. Our radios, at this time of night, are never out of contact, and I shall have a stack of information to evaluate and pass on."

Martinelli nodded.

"By the way, that was an interesting report yesterday about the new issue of arms and tanks to the 19th Panzer."

"I don't think there's any doubt that, even if they aren't entirely sure, they're certainly taking every precaution. Anyway, every single tank that goes to Holland is one less available for Normandy. Well, I'd better not keep you."

Howard got up. "Good night, Stephen. Thanks for all your help today."

He went straight back to the office. Everyone was working late in Arista Productions. Information seemed to be pouring in and they had stepped up their leaflet production from ten to fifteen thousand sheets a day. These were sent, in many cases, with the containers of supply which were being dropped with clockwork regularity.

The atmosphere of urgency, probably coupled with the absence of Mulder, had worked quite a remarkable change in the morale of Howard's team. They were getting on with the job so well that they had little time to worry or fret. Most of them were working twelve and fifteen hours a day, but they did it with a good spirit and Howard found himself becoming more and more attached to them.

He cast his eye over the reports and noted that there were several fresh troop movements. These he carefully entered on his map. The gamble seemed to be paying off in a very big way.

Now it was time for them to have their final throw. He told everyone that he had been to see Mulder and that he had sent them his greetings and was already feeling very much better. This also seemed welcome news because they all had a soft spot for the dear old doctor in spite of the fact that he sometimes got on their nerves.

That night, Howard noticed that Russell and Hannie Herodsen left together as usual. They had certainly been living together on and off for months now. It was going to be a fateful day when Russell learned the truth about his mistress.

In Berlin they were still unaware of the fate that had befallen two of their best agents in London.

It was Himmler's turn to get in touch with Kaltenbrunner, which he did, to advise him that Radmin had confirmed every detail that they wished to know. It only remained for him to congratulate Kaltenbrunner on behalf of the Fuehrer for the great success that he had achieved.

"If your agents can only get us the date of the attack, whether it be for their assault on Holland, or on France or on both, whichever it might be."

Kaltenbrunner promised to see what he could do.

It was an ambitious scheme of the Allies to attack the Continent on both the Dutch coast and the Pas de Calais. Kaltenbrunner was very surprised that they could muster sufficient forces, for, in spite of their very considerable strength, it would require dozens and dozens of divisions to mount two major assaults so far apart. Anyway, with luck, both attacks would be hurled into the sea.

Now all they wanted was the date.

CHAPTER TWELVE

On the following afternoon, June 2nd, 1944, Howard called everyone into his office. He had learnt a few tricks at the Bar and he wanted to make this little meeting as effective as possible.

He sat on the edge of his desk as everyone crowded into the room. In his hand he held a big buff envelope containing the plans for the invasion of Holland.

He suggested that they should sit on the floor and then, smiling confidently, he told them why he had gathered them together.

"Firstly, I'd like to thank you all for the wonderful way in which you have carried out your duties during these last few weeks. It has been a very great strain but the end is now in sight." He paused. "I haven't really been able to explain to you before, because for the last two or three weeks I have been waiting for some very important information. It has now come into my hands and it will enable us to complete our operation.

"Naturally, to a great extent we have had to work in the dark because obviously it would have been far too great a risk to indicate with any exactitude the area of our landings. But the time has come to prepare our final leaflets, all of which will have to be printed within the next twenty-four hours. Now, this will mean, I'm afraid, that I shall have to ask you to forgo your night's rest. So I suggest," and here Howard moved to the safe, "that we all go out and get a meal so that we can start work in about three hours' time. Let me see, that will make it about nine o'clock."

With that he turned the key in the lock of the safe and smiled their dismissal, and in order that Hannie Herodsen should clearly hear, he called to Dan Russell.

"By the way, Dan, I've got one or two things to discuss with you, so may I suggest that we have dinner together?"

"Sure," Dan called. "I'll be glad to. I must just go upstairs and lock everything away."

"Fine," Howard called after him. He had already spoken to Jenkins, the caretaker, and told him to keep out of the way for the next three hours. Now it only remained to ring up Martinelli to warn his men on the other side of the street to watch the building as carefully as never before.

"Well, this is it," said Martinelli on the other end of the line. "Good luck, Julian. I shan't leave my office until I've heard from you."

"Righto," Howard replied. "I'll get in touch directly I've got any news." And with that he replaced the telephone receiver. Moving over to the safe, he re-opened it and adjusted the envelope inside, carefully placing the paper clip in position, and then shut the door.

Upstairs, Dan had just finished putting his papers away, and as he walked along the passage and passed Hannie's little room he glanced in and saw her taking several things from the drawers of her desk and putting them into her bag. He stood for a second smiling at her and then whispered.

"Packing, darling?"

She looked up, startled, and then laughed. "I wish I were. No, I'm only clearing up. I'll see you later, Dan. Goodbye."

"Okay," Dan laughed. "I've got to have supper with the boss-man, otherwise I'd take you. Where are you going to eat?"

"Oh, I'm . . ." She hesitated. "I'm going to go back to the flat to have a quick bath. I think I've just got time, but I may go round the corner and get a snack first."

"Okay, sweetheart. See you soon."

She smiled at him and then Russell ran down the stairs and into Howard's office.

"Ready when you are."

"Fine, let's go."

They walked down the passage and when they reached the reception were just in time to see Hannie going down the stairs in front of them.

Howard watched her go, not without a feeling of misgiving. She looked very purposeful. He only prayed that she would shortly return.

Russell called after her: "Be good."

She turned round briefly, waved, and then disappeared out into the street.

"I thought we might go up and have a meal in a little restaurant I know in Percy Street; it's just off Tottenham Court Road."

"Sure, anywhere you say," Russell replied.

Howard wanted to put as much distance between themselves and Wardour Street as they could possibly manage, because, whatever happened, he didn't want Russell to return too soon.

"How are you feeling? Shall we walk and get a spot of exercise?"

"Yeah, sure. Why not? It's been a lovely day."

"It certainly has," Howard agreed.

They set off up Old Compton Street and, by way of conversation, Russell said:

"You know, in many ways I wish I were taking a more active part in this bit of the war. I feel my place is over on the other side."

Howard laughed. "Oh, I expect we all feel like that, but we're really doing a far more important job than scrapping this time."

He tried to keep the sarcasm out of his voice. If only Russell had realised that the whole operation had pivoted on his unreliability. It was a tragedy because he was a very nice boy. He had just fallen for the wrong girl and the old tricks, that was all.

"You know, Julian. I've had a funny hunch for some while now."

"What's that?" Howard asked.

"I don't think we're going to land in Holland."

Howard could have dropped dead in his tracks.

"What on earth gave you that idea?"

"I don't know. I've often tried to analyse my feelings during these last ten days. Somehow it's just a little too obvious. Maybe not for the Germans, but it is for me. And when I think of the sacrifices we've made, boy I hope it's been worthwhile!"

Howard was almost unnerved by this little speech. It seemed almost prophetic, but laughingly he said:

"Well, you'll see very soon just how wrong you can be." And with that he promptly changed the subject.

As they were passing a pub, Howard suggested that they should pop in and have a drink, and Russell readily agreed.

Hannie Herodsen went into a snack bar just around the corner and ordered a sandwich. She was beginning to feel very nervous now. This was her one and only chance. She had the key to the safe, that had been manufactured in Berlin from a wax cast with which they had provided her.

As she sat sipping her coffee and eating her sandwich, she glanced into her bag to see that everything she required was there; the safe key, a box of matches which disguised a tiny Minox camera and also the small box of chocolates which would connect her direct to Berlin.

Everything had been arranged for her journey. It was imperative for her to return immediately so that she could take the roll of film. She looked at the clock on the wall, only a quarter of an hour had gone by. How slowly time seemed to drag on occasions like this.

It was strange that at lunchtime when she had rung both Baber and Radmin, that there had been no reply. It was a blessing that she was working independently of them.

After half an hour she decided that a reasonable amount of time had elapsed and that it was safe to return to the office. She knew that the operators would still be there on the floor above, but she hoped and prayed that they would remain at their task and not be aware of what was happening in the office below.

Hannie walked up the street for the last time and hurriedly climbed the stairs, every nerve tingling in her body. She glanced in all the rooms on the third floor and then decided to have a quick look upstairs without disturbing the radio room. Nobody was in and, taking her courage in both hands, she walked along the corridor into Howard's office. She took out the key from her handbag, but was trembling so much that she could hardly get it into the lock. However, taking a firm control of her nerves, she slipped it in through the keyhole and twisted it to the right. It moved with the utmost ease. Turning the handle she swung the safe door towards her and then stopped for a moment or two to listen. She could hear the faint noises from the radio room above. Next, she reached inside and took out the envelope.

The flap was open, thank goodness, and she slipped the sheets of paper on to Howard's desk. Then she took out the camera, having already pre-set the exposure and focus, and hastily photographed, page by page, the official plans from S.H.A.E.F. for the invasion of Holland.

Suddenly Hannie stiffened; she could hear someone coming down from the floor above. It could only be one of the operators. She remained frozen by Howard's desk, not daring to breathe, but to her utter relief, the man walked straight on down the stairs and obviously out into the street.

Hannie had taken the precaution of slipping on a pair of silk gloves and now she hurriedly replaced the documents inside the envelope and then slipped it back into the safe.

All well so far. Next, she pushed the safe door to, turned the handle and then the key. She then picked up her matchbox camera and put it into her bag.

Finally, she looked round to check that everything was exactly as she had found it and, walking quickly down the passage, went through the reception out on to the stairs.

She was just walking down the first flight when she heard the street door open. Too late to go back now, so she continued on her way, praying that it was neither Howard nor Russell.

As she turned the corner Hannie saw Jan Gucht coming up the stairs.

"Oh, you are just off, Hannie?" he said.

"Yes, I'm going home for a meal."

"Oh, that's just fine. I had to slip out for a packet of cigarettes. I'm afraid we'll be on duty all night, but so will you for a change," he smiled.

"Yes, indeed. I'll see you later."

"Cheerio."

With that she had passed him and was soon out in the street. She hailed a passing taxi and gave him her address in Maida Vale.

From now onwards, time was essential for her to escape. Hannie had to return to the flat in order to send her final message to Berlin to tell them she had started her journey. She had to do this at the flat because of the aerial, which Foster had fixed outside her bedroom window, for without it her little chocolate box wireless set would be out of range.

Otherwise everything had been prepared for her departure. She was leaving all her clothes behind, but any other incriminating evidence had been carefully destroyed.

She paid off the taxi and rushed upstairs. In a fever of anxiety, she plugged in her wireless set and sent off the agreed signal to alert them for her return. Unplugging the set, she put it in her bag, and quickly went from room to room, checking that there was nothing important that she had left behind.

Hannie Herodsen then put the keys to the flat on the kitchen table and went out, slamming the front door behind her.

She was soon hurrying down Clifton Villas and was lucky enough to pick up a passing taxi, which took her straight to Liverpool Street Station, from where she would start on the first leg of her journey home.

CHAPTER THIRTEEN

At nine o'clock precisely, Russell and Howard returned to find that nearly everyone else had reassembled before them. All, that is, with the exception of Hannie Herodsen.

Russell went upstairs into his room and Howard walked swiftly into his office. He shut the door and, in a fever of excitement, took out the key to his safe and, trembling almost as much as Hannie had done, turned the key in the lock and swung the door open. Very carefully he looked inside and to his utter joy could see that there was no sign of a paper clip lying on the edge of the envelope. He snatched it out and looked at it carefully. There was certainly no indication that it had been touched and he was just about to replace it when the very slightest aroma of perfume assailed his nostrils. Lifting the envelope close to his nose, he could distinctly smell the trace of Hannie's perfume. She had probably used gloves, he thought, and these she might have carried in her handbag. Hence, they must have become impregnated with a trace of her perfume.

He quickly lifted up the telephone to speak to Martinelli. He tried very hard to keep the excitement out of his voice.

"Hello, is that you, Steve? Julian here. I've got some good news for you. The trap was sprung. Not only had the paper clip slipped off the envelope, but there was the very slightest suspicion of perfume, so I am convinced we're home and dry."

Martinelli didn't try to conceal his overwhelming joy. There was a piercing "Yippee" which almost burst Howard's ear drum. He assumed that the American on the other end of the line was satisfied with the results that they had achieved!

When Martinelli could talk coherently again, he enquired if Herodsen was still there.

"Well, she certainly hasn't come back yet."

"And she never will," he called down the 'phone.

"Now what do we do?" enquired Howard.

"We'll give her a couple of hours and, of course, make no attempt to catch up with her. If she only but knew it, we would give her every assistance to get safely away."

"Very well then, I'll ring you again in an hour or so's time."

"Right, you do that," said Martinelli. "And in any case by that time I should have a report from the man who has been tailing her. We'll then know at least how she's left London, for I'm convinced she won't stay around a minute longer than necessary."

"Righto. Goodbye for now." And with that Howard replaced the receiver.

It was just a question of routine now, keeping the organization at work until D-Day had safely arrived.

Howard went up to the radio room and just as he was returning down the stairs he caught sight of Russell, who said:

"I say, Hannie hasn't returned yet. I don't know what's keeping her, she's not usually unpunctual."

"Oh, she'll be along soon enough."

"Well, I rang her flat but there was no reply."

"I expect she's already on her way."

"Yeah, I guess so."

And with that they passed each other on the stairs. Howard went straight to his office.

An hour later, after he had set the copy for the latest leaflets, he was sitting at his desk when Russell tapped at the door and walked in.

"Say, I'm very worried about Hannie. She still hasn't come in. I've got a feeling that something must have happened. I think I'll slip back to the flat and have a look-see."

It seemed pointless to let him carry on.

"You'd better sit down, Dan," Howard said quietly.

"What do you mean? I'm trying to find Hannie."

"Yes, I know. It's about Hannie that I want to speak to you. Why don't you sit down."

Russell immediately sensed that something was very much amiss and, with a look of complete bewilderment, he sat down in the chair.

"What's this all about, Julian? I don't get it."

Howard swallowed hard.

"Dan, I just really don't know how to tell you, but the fact is I don't think you'll ever see Hannie Herodsen again."

For a moment he sat completely dumbfounded.

"What! What do you mean?"

Howard felt that it was no time to mince words.

"Hannie Herodsen was a top German spy and you've been living with her for the last three or four months."

He didn't expect quite the explosive reaction that Russell would make to his remark.

"Are you crazy or something?" He jumped to his feet and made toward the desk. "What the hell are you talking about?"

"Do I have to repeat myself, Dan? I should have thought that it was abundantly clear. I said that Hannie Herodsen was a German spy." He enunciated each word with crystal precision.

"You're a bloody liar, I don't believe it. I'm going out to find her." And with that he made for the door.

Howard stood up and shouted at him hard. "Dan, just a minute."

Russell stopped and turned round. "Well?"

"Here's a 'phone direct to Martinelli. Why don't you ring him?"

"Steve?" Russell said in puzzlement.

"Yes, Martinelli. He's known about this all the time."

Again Russell was struck speechless. "Do you mean . . . do you mean you fellows have been taking me for a ride?"

"I suppose that is the expression," Howard said grimly. This was quite the most unpleasant conversation he had ever held.

"Here's the phone. Why don't you ring him?"

"Hell, I don't want to ring him. I'll go round and see him, God damn it."

"You do that, but before you go I would just like to have a word with you quietly and sensibly."

In his heart Russell now realized that what Howard was saying was obviously true. He didn't know whether to lose his temper, to shout with rage or to burst into tears.

Howard spoke very quietly. "I shan't pretend that I've enjoyed this mission. I think it's been one of the most distasteful and one of the hardest that I've ever had to work on. You were a fool, you broke your security, but if it's any consolation we aided and abetted you. I'm afraid in years to come you'll probably look back and remember that a lot of men were fated to die on this operation, but before you start blaming yourself you can also remember that you probably helped to save thousands of Allied lives. Every single German, every single tank and every single gun that, through our efforts, have found their way to Holland will make our task just that much easier when we finally land in France. I don't suppose we'll even be able to judge its success until after the war. But here's just one more final thought. At least you've got out of this with your life, which is more than Janssen or Bakker or Mulder's daughter. Even the poor old doctor is a broken man, and you might as well know that I consider myself as responsible as you for the way in which events have worked out. But it's war and we're dealing with a very ruthless foe. I'm afraid one can't use kid gloves, much as one would like to. Well, Dan, I've no more to say. I suggest you go along and see Martinelli."

"But . . . but Hannie, was she a German?"

"Yes, I'm afraid so."

"Oh, my God." Russell buried his head in his hands. "And I loved her. Now what am I going to do?"

"You're going to take the sensible approach," Howard said softly. "You're going to forget her and remember you've done a great job."

With that, Russell got to his feet, looked at Howard for two or three long moments and, without saying a word, turned and walked out of the office.

Howard picked up the 'phone and rang through to Martinelli.

"I've just been through the worst interview of my life. You'd better take over from here. I sent Russell over to you."

Howard put on his hat and went downstairs to the nearest pub and bought himself a large brandy.

Had the operation been worthwhile? It would seem so from the reports that came flowing in. And the men who had died? What of their families? How were they going to manage? And poor Dr. Mulder with no family at all?

Howard wandered back to the office. He felt utterly weary and dejected and yet in a way he felt slightly elated too. They had achieved something. In fact, they had achieved all they set out to do. Holland now contained a hundred thousand German men. Munitions and supplies had been diverted there too, and as for Herodsen, well he wouldn't give much for her chances by the time she arrived back with her precious films. For when the Germans realized to what extent they had been duped, it was obvious that someone would have a price to pay.

And finally, what about the Dutch people? Those honourable and gallant patriots that had helped in every conceivable way. Well, they would have to be patient for just a little longer. Their struggle had not been in vain.

Howard suddenly remembered that he had almost forgotten the one man who brought the whole thing about. Stephen Martinelli.

He had done a magnificent job. Shrewd, logical and always determined, the success was rightly his.

POSTSCRIPT

HANNIE HERODSEN did get back to Berlin. How, nobody knows, but by the time she arrived the invasion of Europe was just about to begin and it wasn't in Holland! It was probably grossly unfair that she had to pay for her failure with her life, for she was a truly great spy. She was executed three weeks after her arrival home on the personal orders of Kaltenbrunner, the man she had been working for and the man who had been made to look a fool.

Dr. Mulder was given a liberal pension and returned to Holland after the war, but he never got over the loss of his wife and daughter. One day, in a fit of despair, he hanged himself in a country barn.

As for the families of Janssen and Bakker, they were compensated to a generous degree by the United States of America. Some may say that monetary settlement could in no way offset the loss of a husband or a father, and that, of course, is true. But many gallant men had to die in order that Holland and the rest of Europe could be free again.

Captain Dan Russell? Well, he returned to America, having been awarded a decoration for his part in Operation Stampede. Before being too hasty in judging him, might it not be as well to imagine ourselves in his shoes? If, faced with a similar set of circumstances, might we not have acted in just the same way?

And what of the two men who controlled every facet of this skilful deception, Stephen Martinelli and Major Julian Howard? They were both lawyers by profession and to their professions they returned, and it might be added in closing that they both returned very successfully.

Finally let us consider the O.S.S. It had started as an eager, if somewhat inexperienced, group of young men who had embarked on the precarious art of international espionage. But through their industry and ability to learn from their mistakes, they created the first-class Secret Service which President Roosevelt envisaged way back in the dark days of Pearl Harbour.

There is little else to record. A wartime operation successfully carried out: some failures, some successes, and a price that had to be paid.

As Sir Winston Churchill said:

"Our deception measures both before and after D-Day had aimed at confused thinking. Their success was admirable and had far-reaching results on the battle."

THE MOST DANGEROUS GAME

Richard Connell

"The Most Dangerous Game" is published by arrangement with A. M. Heath and Co. Ltd.

"OFF there to the right—somewhere—is a large island," said Whitney. "It's rather a mystery——"

"What island is it?" Rainsford asked.

"The old charts call it 'Ship-Trap Island'," Whitney replied. "A suggestive name, isn't it? Sailors have a curious dread of the place. I don't know why. Some superstition——"

"Can't see it," remarked Rainsford, trying to peer through the dank tropical night that was palpable as it pressed its thick warm blackness in upon the yacht.

"You've good eyes," said Whitney, with a laugh, "and I've seen you pick off a moose moving in the brown fall bush at four hundred yards, but even you can't see four miles or so through a moonless Caribbean night."

"Nor four yards," admitted Rainsford. "Ugh! It's like moist velvet."

"It will be light enough in Rio," promised Whitney. "We should make it in a few days. I hope the jaguar guns have come from Purdey's. We should have some good hunting up the Amazon. Great sport, hunting."

"The best sport in the world," agreed Rainsford.

"For the hunter," amended Whitney. "Not for the jaguar."

"Don't talk rot, Whitney," said Rainsford. "You're a big-game hunter, not a philosopher. Who cares how a jaguar feels?"

"Perhaps the jaguar does," observed Whitney.

"Bah! They've no understanding."

"Even so, I rather think they understand one thing at least—fear. The fear of pain and the fear of death."

"Nonsense," laughed Rainsford. "This hot weather is making you soft, Whitney. Be a realist. The world is made up of two classes—the hunters and the hunted. Luckily, you and I are hunters. Do you think we've passed that island yet?"

"I can't tell in the dark. I hope so."

"Why?" asked Rainsford.

"The place has a reputation—a bad one."

"Cannibals?" suggested Rainsford.

"Hardly. Even cannibals wouldn't live in such a God-forsaken place. But it's got into sailor lore, somehow. Didn't you notice that the crew's nerves seem a bit jumpy today?"

"They were a bit strange, now you mention it. Even Captain Nielsen——"

"Yes, even that tough-minded old Swede, who'd go up to the devil himself and ask him for a light. Those fishy blue eyes held a look I never saw there before. All I could get out of him was, 'This place has an evil name among seafaring men, sir'. Then he said to me, very gravely, 'Don't you feel anything?'—as if the air about us was actually poisonous. Now, you mustn't laugh when I tell you this—I did feel something like a sudden chill.

"There was no breeze. The sea was as flat as a plate-glass window. We were drawing near the island then. What I felt was a—a mental chill—a sort of sudden dread."

"Pure imagination," said Rainsford. "One superstitious sailor can taint the whole ship's company with his fear."

"Maybe. But sometimes I think sailors have an extra sense that tells them when they are in danger. Sometimes I think evil is a tangible thing—with wave lengths, just as sound and light have. An evil place can, so to speak, broadcast vibrations of evil. Anyhow, I'm glad we're getting out of this zone. Well, I think I'll turn in now, Rainsford."

"I'm not sleepy," said Rainsford. "I'm going to smoke another pipe up on the after deck."

"Good night, then, Rainsford. See you at breakfast."

"Right. Good night, Whitney."

There was no sound in the night as Rainsford sat there, but the muffled throb of the engine that drove the yacht swiftly through the darkness, and the swish and ripple of the wash of the propeller.

Rainsford, reclining in a steamer chair, indolently puffed on his favourite briar. The sensuous drowsiness of the night was on him. "It's so dark," he thought, "that I could sleep without closing my eyes; the night would be my eyelids——"

An abrupt sound startled him. Off to the right he heard it, and his ears, expert in such matters, could not be mistaken. Again he heard the sound, and again. Somewhere, off in the blackness, someone had fired a gun three times.

Rainsford sprang up and moved quickly to the rail, mystified. He strained his eyes in the direction from which the reports had come, but it was like trying to see through a blanket. He leaped upon the rail and balanced himself there, to get greater elevation; his pipe, striking a rope, was knocked from his mouth. He lunged for it; a short, hoarse cry came from his lips as he realized he had reached too far and had lost his balance. The cry was pinched off short as the blood-warm waters of the Caribbean Sea closed over his head.

He struggled up to the surface and tried to cry out, but the wash from the speeding yacht slapped him in the face and the salt water in his open mouth made him gag and strangle. Desperately he struck out with strong strokes after the receding lights of the yacht, but he stopped before he had swum fifty feet. A certain cool-headedness had come to him; it was not the first time he had been in a tight place. There was a chance that his cries could be heard by someone aboard the yacht, but that chance was slender, and grew more slender as the yacht raced on. He wrestled himself out of his clothes, and shouted with all his power. The lights of the yacht became faint and ever-vanishing fireflies; then they were blotted out entirely by the night.

Rainsford remembered the shots. They had come from the right, and doggedly he swam in that direction, swimming with slow, deliberate strokes, conserving his strength. For a seemingly endless time he fought the sea. He began to count his strokes desperately; he could do possibly a hundred more and then——

Rainsford heard a sound. It came out of the darkness, a high, screaming sound, the sound of an animal in an extremity of anguish and terror.

He did not recognize the animal that made the sound; he did not try to; with fresh vitality he swam toward the sound. He heard it again; then it was cut short by another noise, crisp, staccato.

"Pistol shot," muttered Rainsford, swimming on.

Ten minutes of determined effort brought another sound to his ears—the most welcome he had ever heard—the muttering and growling of the sea breaking on a rocky shore. He was almost on the rocks before he saw them; on a night less calm he would have been shattered against them. With his remaining strength he dragged himself from the swirling waters. Jagged crags appeared to jut up into the opaqueness; he forced himself upward, hand over hand. Gasping, his hands raw, he reached a flat place at the top. Dense jungle came down to the very edge of the cliffs. What perils that tangle of trees and underbrush might hold for him did not concern Rainsford just then. All he knew was that he was safe from his enemy, the sea, and that utter weariness was on him.

He flung himself down at the jungle edge and tumbled headlong into the deepest sleep of his life.

When he opened his eyes he knew from the position of the sun that it was late in the afternoon. Sleep had given him new vigour; a sharp hunger was picking at him. He looked about him, almost cheerfully.

"Where there are pistol shots, there are men. Where there are men, there is food," he thought. But what kind of men, he wondered, in so forbidding a place? An unbroken front of snarled and jagged jungle fringed the shore.

He saw no sign of a trail through the closely knit web of weeds and trees; it was easier to go along the shore, and Rainsford floundered along by the water. Not far from where he had landed, he stopped.

Some wounded thing, by the evidence a large animal, had thrashed about in the underbrush; the jungle weeds were crushed down and the moss was lacerated; one patch of weeds was stained crimson. A small, glittering object not far away caught Rainsford's eye and he picked it up. It was an empty cartridge.

"A twenty-two," he remarked. "That's odd. It must have been a fairly large animal, too. The hunter had his nerve to tackle it with a light gun. It's clear that the brute put up a fight. I suppose the first three shots I heard was when the hunter flushed his quarry and wounded it. The last shot was when he trailed it here and finished it."

He examined the ground closely and found what he had hoped to find—the print of hunting boots. They pointed along the cliff in the direction he had been going. Eagerly he hurried along, now slipping on a rotten log or a loose stone, but making headway; night was beginning to settle down on the island.

Bleak darkness was blacking out the sea and jungle when Rainsford sighted the lights. He came upon them as he turned a crook in the coast line, and his first thought was that he had come upon a village, for there were many lights. But as he forged along he saw to his great astonishment that all the lights were in one enormous building—a lofty structure with pointed towers plunging upward into the gloom. His eyes made out the shadowy outlines of a palatial château; it was set on a high bluff, and on three sides of it cliffs dived down to where the sea licked greedy lips in the shadows.

"Mirage," thought Rainsford. But it was no mirage, he found, when he opened the tall spiked iron gate. The stone steps were real enough; the massive door with a leering gargoyle for a knocker was real enough; yet about it all hung an air of unreality.

He lifted the knocker, and it creaked up stiffly, as if it had never before been used. He let it fall, and it startled him with its booming loudness. He thought he heard footsteps within; the door remained closed. Again Rainsford lifted the heavy knocker, and let it fall. The door opened then, opened as suddenly as if it were on a spring, and Rainsford stood blinking in the river of glaring gold light that poured out. The first thing Rainsford's eyes discerned was the largest man Rainsford had ever seen—a gigantic creature, solidly made and black-bearded to the waist. In his hand the man held a long-barrel revolver, and he was pointing it straight at Rainsford's heart.

Out of the snarl of beard two small eyes regarded Rainsford.

"Don't be alarmed," said Rainsford, with a smile which he hoped was disarming. "I'm no robber. I fell off a yacht. My name is Sanger Rainsford of New York City."

The menacing look in the eyes did not change. The revolver pointed as rigidly as if the giant were a statue. He gave no sign that he understood Rainsford's words, or that he had even heard them. He was dressed in uniform, a black uniform trimmed with grey astrakhan.

"I'm Sanger Rainsford of New York," Rainsford began again. "I fell off a yacht. I am hungry."

The man's only answer was to raise with his thumb the hammer of his revolver. Then Rainsford saw the man's free hand go to his forehead in a military salute, and he saw him click his heels together and stand at attention. Another man was coming down the broad marble steps, an erect slender man in evening clothes. He advanced to Rainsford and held out his hand.

In a cultivated voice marked by a slight accent that gave it added precision and deliberateness, he said, "It is a very great pleasure and honour to welcome Mr. Sanger Rainsford, the celebrated hunter, to my home."

Automatically Rainsford shook the man's hand.

"I've read your book about hunting snow leopards in Tibet, you see," explained the man. "I am General Zaroff."

Rainsford's first impression was that the man was singularly handsome; his second was that there was an original, almost bizarre, quality about the general's face. He was a tall man past middle age, for his hair was a vivid white; but his thick eyebrows and pointed military moustache were as black as the night from which Rainsford had come. His eyes, too, were black and very bright. He had high cheekbones, a sharp-cut nose, a spare, dark face, the face of a man used to giving orders, the face of an aristocrat. Turning to the giant in uniform, the general made a sign. The giant put away his pistol, saluted, withdrew.

"Ivan is an incredibly strong fellow," remarked the general, "but he has the misfortune to be deaf and dumb. A simple fellow, but I'm afraid, like all his race, a bit of a savage."

"Is he Russian?"

"He is a Cossack," said the general, and his smile showed red lips and pointed teeth. "So am I.

"Come," he said, "we shouldn't be chatting here. We can talk later. Now you want clothes, food, rest. You shall have them. This is a most restful spot."

Ivan had reappeared, and the general spoke to him with lips that moved but gave forth no sound.

"Follow Ivan, if you please, Mr. Rainsford," said the general. "I was about to have my dinner when you came. I'll wait for you. You'll find that my clothes will fit you, I think."

It was to a huge, beam-ceilinged bedroom with a canopied bed big enough for six men that Rainsford followed the silent giant. Ivan laid out an evening suit, and Rainsford, as he put it on, noticed that it came from a London tailor who ordinarily cut and sewed for none below the rank of duke.

The dining room to which Ivan conducted him was in many ways remarkable. There was a medieval magnificence about it; it suggested a baronial hall of feudal times with its oaken panels, its high ceiling, its vast refectory table where twoscore men could sit down to eat. About the hall were the mounted heads of many animals—lions, tigers, elephants, moose, bears; larger or more perfect specimens Rainsford had never seen. At the great table the general was sitting, alone.

"You'll have a cocktail, Mr. Rainsford," he suggested. The cocktail was surpassingly good; and, Rainsford noted, the table appointments were of the finest, the linen, the crystal, the silver, the china.

They were eating *borsch,* the rich, red soup with sour cream so dear to Russian palates. Half apologetically General Zaroff said, "We do our best to preserve the amenities of civilization here. Please forgive any lapses. We are well off the beaten track, you know. Do you think the champagne has suffered from its long ocean trip?"

"Not in the least," declared Rainsford. He was finding the general a most thoughtful and affable host, a true cosmopolite. But there was one small trait of the general's that made Rainsford uncomfortable. Whenever he looked up from his plate he found the general studying him, appraising him narrowly.

"Perhaps," said General Zaroff, "you were surprised that I recognized your name. You see, I read all books on hunting published in English, French, and Russian. I have but one passion in my life, Mr. Rainsford, and it is the hunt."

"You have some wonderful heads here," said Rainsford as he ate a particularly well cooked filet mignon. "That Cape buffalo is the largest I ever saw."

"Oh, that fellow. Yes, he was a monster."

"Did he charge you?"

"Hurled me against a tree," said the general. "Fractured my skull. But I got the brute."

"I've always thought," said Rainsford, "that the Cape buffalo is the most dangerous of all big game."

For a moment the general did not reply; he was smiling his curious red-lipped smile. Then he said slowly, "No. You are wrong, sir. The Cape buffalo is not the most dangerous big game." He sipped his wine. "Here in my preserve on this island," he said in the same slow tone, "I hunt more dangerous game."

Rainsford expressed his surprise. "Is there big game on this island?"

The general nodded. "The biggest."

"Really?"

"Oh, it isn't here naturally, of course. I have to stock the island."

"What have you imported, General?" Rainsford asked. "Tigers?"

The general smiled. "No," he said. "Hunting tigers ceased to interest me some years ago. I exhausted their possibilities, you see. No thrill left in tigers, no real danger. I live for danger, Mr. Rainsford."

The general took from his pocket a gold cigarette case and offered his guest a long black cigarette with a silver tip; it was perfumed and gave off a smell like incense.

"We will have some capital hunting, you and I," said the general. "I shall be most glad to have your society."

"But what game——" began Rainsford.

"I'll tell you," said the general. "You will be amused, I know. I think I may say, in all modesty, that I have done a rare thing. I have invented a new sensation. May I pour you another glass of port, Mr. Rainsford?"

"Thank you, General."

The general filled both glasses, and said, "God makes some men poets. Some He makes kings, some beggars. Me He made a hunter. My hand was made for the trigger, my father said. He was a very rich man with a quarter of a million acres in the Crimea, and he was an ardent sportsman. When I was only five years old he gave me a little gun, specially made in Moscow for me, to shoot sparrows with. When I shot some of his prize turkeys with it, he did not punish me; he complimented me on my marksmanship. I killed my first bear in the Caucasus when I was ten. My whole life has been one prolonged hunt. I went into the army—it was expected of noblemen's sons—and for a time commanded a division of Cossack cavalry, but my real interest was always the hunt. I have hunted every kind of game in every land. It would be impossible for me to tell you how many animals I have killed."

The general puffed at his cigarette.

"After the débâcle in Russia I left the country, for it was imprudent for an officer of the Czar to stay there. Many noble Russians lost everything. I, luckily, had invested heavily in American securities, so I shall never have to open a tearoom in Monte Carlo or drive a taxi in Paris. Naturally, I continued to hunt—grizzlies in your Rockies, crocodiles in the Ganges, rhinoceroses in East Africa. It was in Africa that the Cape buffalo hit me and laid me up for six months. As soon as I recovered I started for the Amazon to hunt jaguars, for I had heard they were unusally cunning. They weren't." The Cossack sighed. "They were no match at all for a hunter with his wits about him, and a high-powered rifle. I was bitterly disappointed. I was lying in my tent with a splitting headache one night when a terrible thought pushed its way into my mind. Hunting was beginning to bore me! And hunting, remember, had been my life. I have heard that in America businessmen often go to pieces when they give up the business that has been their life."

"Yes, that's so," said Rainsford.

The general smiled. "I had no wish to go to pieces," he said. "I must do something. Now, mine is an analytical mind, Mr. Rainsford. Doubtless that is why I enjoy the problems of the chase."

"No doubt, General Zaroff."

"So," continued the general, "I asked myself why the hunt no longer fascinated me. You are much younger than I am, Mr. Rainsford, and have not hunted as much, but you perhaps can guess the answer."

"What was it?"

"Simply this: hunting had ceased to be what you call a 'sporting proposition'. It had become too easy. I always got my quarry. Always. There is no greater bore than perfection."

The general lit a fresh cigarette.

"No animal had a chance with me any more. That is no boast; it is a mathematical certainty. The animal had nothing but his legs and his instinct. Instinct is no match for reason. When I thought of this it was a tragic moment for me, I can tell you."

Rainsford leaned across the table, absorbed in what his host was saying.

"It came to me as an inspiration what I must do," the general went on.

"And that was?"

The general smiled the quiet smile of one who has faced an obstacle and surmounted it with success. "I had to invent a new animal to hunt," he said.

"A new animal? You are joking."

"Not at all," said the general. "I never joke about hunting. I needed a new animal. I found one. So I bought this island, built this house, and here I do my hunting. The island is perfect for my purposes—there are jungles with a maze of trails in them, hills, swamps——"

"But the animal, General Zaroff?"

"Oh," said the general, "it supplies me with the most exciting hunting in the world. No other hunting compares with it for an instant. Every day I hunt, and I never grow bored now, for I have a quarry with which I can match my wits."

Rainsford's bewilderment showed in his face.

"I wanted the ideal animal to hunt," explained the general. "So I said, 'What are the attributes of an ideal quarry?' And the answer was, of course: 'It must have courage, cunning, and above all, it must be able to reason'."

"But no animal can reason," objected Rainsford.

"My dear fellow," said the general, "there is one that can."

"But you can't mean——" gasped Rainsford.

"And why not?"

"I can't believe you are serious, General Zaroff. This is a grisly joke."

"Why should I not be serious? I am speaking of hunting."

"Hunting? Good God, General Zaroff, what you speak of is murder."

The general laughed with entire good nature. He regarded Rainsford quizzically. "I refuse to believe that so modern and civilized a young man as you seem to be harbours romantic ideas about the value of human life. Surely your experiences in the war——" He stopped.

"Did not make me condone cold-blooded murder," finished Rainsford stiffly.

Laughter shook the general. "How extraordinary droll you are!" he said. "One does not expect nowadays to find a young man of the educated class, even in America, with such a naïve, and, if I may say so, mid-Victorian point of view. It's like finding a snuffbox in a limousine. Ah, well, doubtless you had Puritan ancestors. So many Americans appear to have had. I'll wager you'll forget your notions when you go hunting with me. You've a genuine new thrill in store for you, Mr. Rainsford."

"Thank you, I'm a hunter, not a murderer."

"Dear me," said the general, quite unruffled, "again that unpleasant word. But I think I can show you that your scruples are quite ill founded."

"Yes?"

"Life is for the strong, to be lived by the strong, and, if needs be, taken by the strong. The weak of the world were put here to give the strong pleasure. I am strong. Why should I not use my gift? If I wish to hunt, why should I not? I hunt the scum of the earth—sailors from tramp ships—lascars, blacks, Chinese, whites, mongrels—a thoroughbred horse or hound is worth more than a score of them."

"But they are men," said Rainsford hotly.

"Precisely," said the general. "That is why I use them. It gives me pleasure. They can reason, after a fashion. So they are dangerous."

"But where do you get them?"

The general's left eyelid fluttered down in a wink. "This island is called Ship-Trap," he answered. "Sometimes an angry god of the high seas sends them to me. Sometimes, when Providence is not so kind, I help Providence a bit. Come to the window with me."

Rainsford went to the window and looked out towards the sea.

"Watch! Out there!" exclaimed the general, pointing into the night. Rainsford's eyes saw only blackness, and then, as the general pressed a button, far out to sea Rainsford saw the flash of lights.

The general chuckled. "They indicate a channel," he said, "where there's none: giant rocks with razor edges crouch like a sea monster with wide-open jaws. They can crush a ship as easily as I crush this nut." He dropped a walnut on the hardwood floor and brought his heel grinding down on it. "Oh, yes," he said casually, as if in answer to a question, "I have electricity. We try to be civilized here."

"Civilized? And you shoot down men?"

A trace of anger was in the general's black eyes, but it was there for but a second, and he said, in his most pleasant manner: "Dear me, what a righteous young man you are! I assure you I do not do the thing you suggest. That would be barbarous. I treat these visitors with every consideration. They get plenty of good food and exercise. They get into splendid physical condition. You shall see for yourself tomorrow."

"What do you mean?"

"We'll visit my training school," smiled the general. "It's in the cellar. I have about a dozen pupils down there now. They're from the Spanish bark *San Lucar* that had the bad luck to go on the rocks out there. A very inferior lot, I regret to say. Poor specimens and more accustomed to the deck than to the jungle."

He raised his hand, and Ivan, who served as waiter, brought thick Turkish coffee. Rainsford, with an effort, held his tongue in check.

"It's a game, you see," pursued the general blandly. "I suggest to one of them that we go hunting. I give him a supply of food and an excellent hunting knife. I give him three hours' start. I am to follow, armed only with a pistol of the smallest calibre and range. If my quarry eludes me for three whole days, he wins the game. If I find him—" the general smiled—"he loses."

"Suppose he refuses to be hunted?"

"Oh," said the general, "I give him his option, of course. He need not play that game if he doesn't wish to. If he does not wish to hunt, I turn him over to Ivan. Ivan once had the honour of serving as official knouter to the Great White Czar, and he has his own ideas of sport. Invariably, Mr. Rainsford, invariably they choose the hunt."

"And if they win?"

The smile on the general's face widened. "To date I have not lost," he said.

Then he added, hastily, "I don't wish you to think me a braggart, Mr. Rainsford. Many of them afford only the most elementary sort of problem. Occasionally I strike a tartar. One almost did win. I eventually had to use the dogs."

"The dogs?"

"This way, please. I'll show you."

The general steered Rainsford to a window. The lights from the windows sent a flickering illumination that made grotesque patterns on the courtyard below, and Rainsford could see moving about there a dozen or so huge black shapes; as they turned towards him, their eyes glittered greenly.

"A rather good lot, I think," observed the general. "They are let out at seven every night. If anyone should try to get into my house—or out of it—something extremely regrettable would occur to him." He hummed a snatch of song from the Folies Bergère.

"And now," said the general, "I want to show you my new collection of heads. Will you come with me to the library?"

"I hope," said Rainsford, "that you will excuse me tonight, General Zaroff. I'm really not feeling at all well."

"Ah, indeed?" the general inquired solicitously. "Well, I suppose that's only natural, after your long swim. You need a good, restful night's sleep. Tomorrow you'll feel like a new man, I'll wager. Then we'll hunt, eh? I've one rather promising prospect——"

Rainsford was hurrying from the room.

"Sorry you can't go with me tonight," called the general. "I expect rather fair sport—a big, strong black. He looks resourceful—Well, good night, Mr. Rainsford; I hope that you have a good night's rest."

The bed was good and the pyjamas of the softest silk, and he was tired in every fibre of his being, but nevertheless Rainsford could not quiet his brain with the opiate of sleep. He lay, eyes wide open. Once he thought he heard stealthy steps in the corridor outside his room. He sought to throw open the door; it would not open. He went to the window and looked out. His room was high up in one of the towers. The lights of the château were out now, and it was dark and silent, but there was a fragment of sallow moon, and by its wan light he could see, dimly, the courtyard; there, weaving in and out in the pattern of shadow, were black, noiseless forms; the hounds heard him at the window and looked up, expectantly, with their green eyes. Rainsford went back to the bed and lay down. By many methods he tried to put himself to sleep. He had achieved a doze when, just as morning began to come, he heard, far off in the jungle, the faint report of a pistol.

General Zaroff did not appear until luncheon. He was dressed faultlessly in the tweeds of a country squire. He was solicitous about the state of Rainsford's health.

"As for me," sighed the general, "I do not feel so well. I am worried, Mr. Rainsford. Last night, I detected traces of my old complaint."

To Rainsford's questioning glance the general said, "Ennui. Boredom."

Then, taking a second helping of crêpe suzette, the general explained, "The hunting was not good last night. The fellow lost his head. He made a straight trail that offered no problems at all. That's the trouble with these sailors; they have dull brains to begin with, and they do not know how to get about in the woods. They do excessively stupid and obvious things. It's most annoying. Will you have another glass of Chablis, Mr. Rainsford?"

"General," said Rainsford firmly, "I wish to leave this island at once."

The general raised his thickets of eyebrows; he seemed hurt. "But my dear fellow," the general protested, "you've only just come. You've had no hunting——"

"I wish to go today," said Rainsford. He saw the dead black eyes of the general on him, studying him. General Zaroff's face suddenly brightened.

He filled Rainsford's glass with venerable Chablis from a dusty bottle.

"Tonight," said the general, "we will hunt—you and I."

Rainsford shook his head. "No, General," he said. "I will not hunt."

The general shrugged his shoulders and delicately ate a hothouse grape. "As you wish, my friend," he said. "The choice rests entirely with you. But may I not venture to suggest that you will find my idea of sport more diverting than Ivan's?"

He nodded towards the corner to where the giant stood scowling, his thick arms crossed on his hogshead of chest.

"You don't mean——" cried Rainsford.

"My dear fellow," said the general, "have I not told you I always mean what I say about hunting? This is really an inspiration. I drink to a foeman worthy of my steel—at last."

The general raised his glass, but Rainsford sat staring at him.

"You'll find this game worth playing," the general said enthusiastically. "Your brain against mine. Your woodcraft against mine. Your strength and stamina against mine. Outdoor chess! And the stake is not without value, eh?"

"And if I win——" began Rainsford huskily.

"I'll cheerfully acknowledge myself defeated if I do not find you by midnight of the third day," said General Zaroff. "My sloop will place you on the mainland near a town."

The general read what Rainsford was thinking.

"Oh, you can trust me," said the Cossack. "I will give you my word as a gentleman and a sportsman. Of course you, in turn, must agree to say nothing of your visit here."

"I'll agree to nothing of the kind," said Rainsford.

"Oh," said the general, "in that case—— But why discuss it now? Three days hence we can discuss it over a bottle of Veuve Clicquot, unless——"

The general sipped his wine.

Then a businesslike air animated him. "Ivan," he said to Rainsford, "will supply you with hunting clothes, food, a knife. I suggest you wear moccasins; they leave a poorer trail. I suggest too that you avoid the big swamp in the southeast corner of the island. We call it Death Swamp. There's quicksand there. One foolish fellow tried it. The deplorable part of it was that Lazarus followed him. You can imagine my feelings, Mr. Rainsford. I loved Lazarus; he was the finest hound in my pack. Well, I must beg you to excuse me now. I always take a siesta after lunch. You'll hardly have time for a nap, I fear. You'll want to start, no doubt. I shall not follow till dusk. Hunting at night is so much more exciting than by day, don't you think? *Au revoir,* Mr. Rainsford, *au revoir.*"

General Zaroff, with a deep, courtly bow, strolled from the room.

From another door came Ivan. Under one arm he carried khaki hunting clothes, a haversack of food, a leather sheath containing a long-bladed hunting knife; his right hand rested on a cocked revolver thrust in the crimson sash about his waist. . . .

Rainsford had fought his way through the bush for two hours.

"I must keep my nerve. I must keep my nerve," he said through tight teeth.

He had not been entirely clear-headed when the château gates snapped shut behind him. His whole idea at first was to put distance between himself and General Zaroff, and, to this end, he had plunged along, spurred on by the sharp rowels of something very like panic. Now he had got a grip on himself, had stopped, and was taking stock of himself and the situation.

He saw that straight flight was futile; inevitably it would bring him face to face with the sea. He was in a picture with a frame of water, and his operations, clearly, must take place within that frame.

"I'll give him a trail to follow," muttered Rainsford, and he struck off from the rude path he had been following into the trackless wilderness. He executed a series of intricate loops; he doubled on his trail again and again, recalling all the lore of the fox hunt, and all the dodges of the fox. Night found him leg-weary, with hands and face lashed by the branches, on a thickly wooded ridge. He knew it would be insane to blunder on through the dark, even if he had the strength. His need for rest was imperative and he thought, "I have played the fox, now I must play the cat of the fable." A big tree with a thick trunk and outspread branches was nearby, and, taking care to leave not the slightest mark, he climbed up into the crotch, and stretching out on one of the broad limbs, after a fashion, rested. Rest brought him new confidence and almost a feeling of security. Even so zealous a hunter as General Zaroff could not trace him there, he told himself; only the devil himself could follow that complicated trail through the jungle after dark. But, perhaps, the general was a devil——

An apprehensive night crawled slowly by like a wounded snake, and sleep did not visit Rainsford, although the silence of a dead world was on the jungle. Towards morning when a dingy grey was varnishing the sky, the cry of some startled bird focused Rainsford's attention in that direction. Something was coming through the bush, coming slowly, carefully, coming by the same winding way Rainsford had come. He flattened himself down on the limb, and through a screen of leaves almost as thick as tapestry, he watched. The thing that was approaching him was a man.

It was General Zaroff. He made his way along with his eyes fixed in utmost concentration on the ground before him. He paused, almost beneath the tree, dropped to his knees and studied the ground. Rainsford's impulse was to hurl himself down like a panther, but he saw that the general's right hand held something small and metallic—an automatic pistol.

The hunter shook his head several times, as if he were puzzled. Then he straightened up and took from his case one of his black cigarettes; its pungent incense-like smoke floated up to Rainsford's nostrils. Rainsford held his breath. The general's eyes had left the ground and were travelling inch by inch up the tree. Rainsford froze there, every muscle tensed for a spring. But the sharp eyes of the hunter stopped before they reached the limb where Rainsford lay; a smile spread over his brown face. Very deliberately he blew a smoke ring into the air; then he turned his back on the tree and walked carelessly away, back along the trail he had come. The swish of the underbrush against his hunting boots grew fainter and fainter.

The pent-up air burst hotly from Rainsford's lungs. His first thought made him feel sick and numb. The general could follow a trail through the woods at night; he could follow an extremely difficult trail; he must have uncanny powers; only by the merest chance had the Cossack failed to see his quarry.

Rainsford's second thought was even more terrible. It sent a shudder of cold horror through his whole being. Why had the general smiled? Why had he turned back?

Rainsford did not want to believe what his reason told him was true, but the truth was as evident as the sun that had by now pushed through the morning mists. The general was playing with him! The general was saving him for another day's sport! The Cossack was the cat; he was the mouse. Then it was that Rainsford knew the full meaning of terror.

"I will not lose my nerve. I will not."

He slid down from the tree, and struck off again into the woods. His face was set and he forced the machinery of his mind to function. Three hundred yards from his hiding place he stopped where a huge dead tree leaned precariously on a smaller living one. Throwing off his sack of food, Rainsford took his knife from its sheath and began to work with all his energy.

The job was finished at last, and he threw himself down behind a fallen log a hundred feet away. He did not have to wait long. The cat was coming again to play with the mouse.

Following the trail with the sureness of a bloodhound came General Zaroff. Nothing escaped those searching black eyes, no crushed blade of grass, no bent twig, no mark, no matter how faint, in the moss. So intent was the Cossack on his stalking that he was upon the thing Rainsford had made before he saw it. His foot touched the protruding bough that was the trigger. Even as he touched it, the general sensed his danger and leaped back with the agility of an ape. But he was not quite quick enough; the dead tree, delicately adjusted to rest on the cut living one, crashed down and struck the general a glancing blow on the shoulder as it fell; but for his alertness, he must have been smashed beneath it. He staggered, but he did not fall; nor did he drop his revolver. He stood there, rubbing his injured shoulder, and Rainsford, with fear again gripping his heart, heard the general's mocking laugh ring through the jungle.

"Rainsford," called the general, "if you are within sound of my voice, as I suppose you are, let me congratulate you. Not many men know how to make a Malay man-catcher. Luckily for me, I too have hunted in Malacca. You are proving interesting, Mr. Rainsford. I am going now to have my wound dressed; it's only a slight one. But I shall be back. I shall be back."

When the general, nursing his bruised shoulder, had gone, Rainsford took up his flight again. It was flight now, a desperate, hopeless flight, that carried him on for some hours. Dusk came, then darkness, and still he pressed on. The ground grew softer under his moccasins; the vegetation grew ranker, denser; insects bit him savagely. Then, as he stepped forward, his foot sank into the ooze. He tried to wrench it back, but the muck sucked viciously at his foot as if it were a giant leech. With a violent effort, he tore his foot loose. He knew where he was now. Death Swamp and its quicksand.

His hands were tight closed as if his nerve were something tangible that someone in the darkness was trying to tear from his grip. The softness of the earth had given him an idea. He stepped back from the quicksand a dozen feet or so and, like some huge prehistoric beaver, he began to dig.

Rainsford had dug himself in in France when a second's delay meant death. That had been a placid pastime compared to his digging now. The pit grew deeper; when it was above his shoulders, he climbed out and from some hard saplings cut stakes and sharpened them to a fine point. These stakes he planted in the bottom of the pit with the points sticking up. With flying fingers he wove a rough carpet of weeds and branches and with it he covered the mouth of the pit. Then, wet with sweat and aching with tiredness, he crouched behind the stump of a lightning-charred tree.

He knew his pursuer was coming; he heard the padding sound of feet on the soft earth, and the night breeze brought him the perfume of the general's cigarette. It seemed to Rainsford that the general was coming with unusual swiftness; he was not feeling his way along, foot by foot. Rainsford, crouching there, could not see the general, nor could he see the pit. He lived a year in a minute. Then he felt an impulse to cry aloud with joy, for he heard the sharp crackle of the breaking branches as the cover of the pit gave way; he heard the sharp scream of pain as the pointed stakes found their mark. He leaped up from his place of concealment. Then he cowered back. Three feet from the pit a man was standing, with an electric torch in his hand.

"You've done well, Rainsford," the voice of the general called. "Your Burmese tiger pit has claimed one of my best dogs. Again you score, I think, Mr. Rainsford, I'll see what you can do against my whole pack. I'm going home for a rest now. Thank you for a most amusing evening."

At daybreak Rainsford, lying near the swamp, was awakened by a sound that made him know that he had new things to learn about fear. It was a distant sound, faint and wavering, but he knew it. It was the baying of a pack of hounds.

Rainsford knew he could do one of two things. He could stay where he was and wait. That was suicide. He could flee. That was postponing the inevitable. For a moment he stood there, thinking. An idea that held a wild chance came to him, and, tightening his belt, he headed away from the swamp.

The baying of the hounds drew nearer, then still nearer, nearer, ever nearer. On a ridge Rainsford climbed a tree. Down a water-course, not a quarter of a mile away, he could see the bush moving. Straining his eyes, he saw the lean figure of General Zaroff; just ahead of him Rainsford made out another figure whose wide shoulders surged through the tall jungle weeds; it was the giant Ivan, and he seemed pulled forward by some unseen force; Rainsford knew that Ivan must be holding the pack in leash.

They would be on him any minute now. His mind worked frantically. He thought of a native trick he had learned in Uganda. He slid down the tree. He caught hold of a springy young sapling and to it he fastened his hunting knife, with the blade pointing down the trail; with a bit of wild grapevine he tied back the sapling. Then he ran for his life. The hounds raised their voices as they hit the fresh scent. Rainsford knew now how an animal at bay feels.

He had to stop to get his breath. The baying of the hounds stopped abruptly, and Rainsford's heart stopped too. They must have reached the knife.

He shinned excitedly up a tree and looked back. His pursuers had stopped. But the hope that was in Rainsford's brain when he climbed died, for he saw in the shadow valley that General Zaroff was still on his feet. But Ivan was not. The knife, driven by the recoil of the spring tree, had not wholly failed.

Rainsford had hardly tumbled to the ground when the pack took up the cry again.

"Nerve, nerve, nerve!" he panted, as he dashed along. A blue gap showed between the trees dead ahead. Ever nearer drew the hounds. Rainsford forced himself on towards the gap. He reached it. It was the shore of the sea. Across a cove he could see the gloomy grey stone of the château. Twenty feet below him the sea rumbled and hissed. Rainsford hesitated. He heard the hounds. Then he leaped far out into the sea. . . .

When the general and his pack reached the place by the sea, the Cossack stopped. For some minutes he stood regarding the blue-green expanse of water. He shrugged his shoulders. Then he sat down, took a drink of brandy from a silver flask, lit a perfumed cigarette, and hummed a bit from *Madame Butterfly*.

General Zaroff had an exceedingly good dinner in his great panelled dining hall that evening. With it he had a bottle of Pol Roger and half a bottle of Chambertin. Two slight annoyances kept him from perfect enjoyment. One was the thought that it would be difficult to replace Ivan; the other was that his quarry had escaped him; of course, the American hadn't played the game —so thought the general as he tasted his after-dinner liqueur. In his library he read, to soothe himself, from the works of Marcus Aurelius. At ten he went up to his bedroom. He was deliciously tired, he said to himself, as he locked himself in. There was a little moonlight, so, before turning on his light, he went to the window and looked down at the courtyard. He could see the great hounds, and he called, "Better luck another time," to them. Then he switched on the light.

A man, who had been hiding in the curtains of the bed, was standing there.

"Rainsford!" screamed the general. "How in God's name did you get here?"

"Swam," said Rainsford. "I found it quicker than walking through the jungle."

The general sucked in his breath and smiled. "I congratulate you," he said. "You have won the game."

Rainsford did not smile. "I am still a beast at bay," he said, in a low, hoarse voice. "Get ready, General Zaroff."

The general made one of his deepest bows. "I see," he said. "Splendid! One of us is to furnish a repast for the hounds. The other will sleep in this very excellent bed. On guard, Rainsford. . . ."

He had never slept in a better bed, Rainsford decided.

THE BIG BITE

Charles Williams

"The Big Bite" is published by
Cassell & Co.

The Author

Before his first book was published, in 1951, Charles Williams spent ten years at sea as a radio operator in merchant ships and as an ordinary seaman. Since then he has written seven more novels, and now lives in Florida where he enjoys duck shooting, reading, swimming, fishing and "peering at marine wild life through a mask".

CHAPTER ONE

THEY said it was going to be as good as ever, but it wasn't. You could see that by the end of the first week of practice. They'd stuck it back on, all right, and it looked like a leg, but something was gone. McGilvray, who's probably the best T-formation quarterback that ever lived, was handing the ball off a half-stride ahead of me. We'd played together two years in college and five in the pros, so he knew where I was supposed to be. I did too, but I wasn't getting there. About the tenth time they unpiled the beef off us after the fumble he spat out some topsoil and said, "We're just a little rusty yet, Harlan. Maybe I'm leading you too much."

"It could be, dear," I said. I knew better.

The next time he handed the ball off to me where I was instead of where I was supposed to be, and two rookies smeared me back off the line. Not the Cleveland Browns; just rookies trying out. It went on that way. When they ran off the pictures looking for the missed blocking assignments, you could see it wasn't that at all. They open it up for you, but they don't guarantee to keep it dredged out all summer like a ship channel. When you're a half-stride slow in the National Football League you're an old lady trying to walk up Niagara Falls with a crutch; they run down your throat faster than you can spit out your teeth. The old man gave me every chance in the world, and even tried me out in a defensive spot before he let me go, but it was no use. I couldn't pivot and swing fast enough to go with the play even when I saw it coming, and they ran through me like B-girls through a sailor's bankroll. I'd racked up a lot of yardage for him in five seasons and he didn't like it any better than I did, but in the pros when you haven't got it any more you're out of anything to sell. He came in when I was cleaning out my locker the last afternoon and even became emotional to the extent of lighting the cold cigar they said he'd had in his mouth since the flying wedge went out of style.

"Rough," he said. "Like a cob."

"Yeah," I said. "But cheer up. That coloured boy can carry it for you. He runs pretty good."

"In three years he'll run pretty good. And then maybe some goddam drunk'll knock *his* leg off. But I meant you. You got any plans?"

"No," I said.

"Ever think of coaching?"

"I've already got a crock leg," I said. "What do I want with ulcers?"

"You'd have had five more years. At least."

"Yes," I said. "At fifteen thousand a year."

He grunted. "Maybe." He took the cigar out of his mouth and threw it fifteen feet across the room, where it hit the wall and bounced into the urinal. "Drunks," he said.

I went back to the hotel to pack and check out. Four or five sports writers were hanging around the lobby. They slapped me on the back and told me how I'd be back next season and the leg would be fine and I'd rack up a six-yard average. I said, "Sure, sure," and after a while I got away from them and went up to the room. I undressed for a shower, and looked at it. It had knitted all right; I didn't even limp. It didn't feel awkward or look any different from the other one except for some scar tissue. It was just great, except that it wasn't worth a damn any more. The only thing I'd ever owned in my life was a mechanism that ran like something bathed in oil and now it had been smashed and when they put it back together something was gone. Maybe there isn't any name for it, actually. The medics will give you a song and dance about co-ordination and instantaneous response and frammis on the updike, but I don't think they know either. The nearest you can come to it is that it's a smooth surge of power from dead stand still to full speed in about three strides, and you either have it or you don't. If you have it, you can sell it—or at least you can until you get past thirty or thirty-two and it begins to slow down on you. I'd taken a short-cut. A drunk sideswiped me and knocked me off the highway and when I quit rolling I was sitting in a ditch holding a Buick convertible in my lap. I thought of five more years and sixty to seventy thousand dollars doing the only thing I had ever liked or was any good at, and my hands knotted. I swung my fist at the leg and knocked it off the luggage stand where it was propped. The big lump of muscle on the calf ridged up and hurt as I walked into the shower. I stared bleakly at the white tile wall while the water poured over me. The dirty, sad, drunken son—— There wasn't even any use cursing him. He was dead. He'd been killed in the same wreck.

I checked out before the squad came in from practice, caught a bus into Los Angeles, and sat around the airport until I could get on a plane going east. I didn't really know where I was going, and didn't care. I got off in New Orleans and for one of the few times in my life I went on a binge myself. It was a honey and lasted a week; when I began to come out of it I was in a motel somewhere on U.S. 90 out toward the Mississippi line with a girl named Frances. I never did know her last name and couldn't figure out where she'd come from or how we'd got away out there unless they'd put us off a bus, but it didn't seem to matter. She knew nothing about football and cared less and had never heard of me, which was fine, but she drank like somebody trying to finish a highball while a cab was waiting outside with the meter running. She seemed to think something terrible was going to happen to her if she ever sobered up. The third morning I got up while she was still asleep and caught a bus back to town. I didn't know what the answer was yet, but drinking wasn't it. I went over to Galveston and swam in the surf and lay in the sun on the beach until I'd cooked the booze out of my system. The fourth day I was there Purvis caught up with me.

I was staying at one of the beach hotels and was just coming in through the lobby in swim trunks and a terry cloth robe late in the afternoon when a man reading a paper in one of the chairs got up and came toward me. He caught me just as I stepped into the elevator.

"John Harlan?" he asked.

"That's right," I said. "What can I do for you?"

"Purvis," he said. "Old Colony Insurance."

"Save yourself a trip," I cut him off. "I don't need any." But the elevator boy had already closed the door and we were going up.

Purvis shook his head. "I don't sell it. I'd just like to talk to you a few minutes, if you don't mind."

I shrugged. "You an adjuster?" I couldn't see why they'd be pawing through it now. The whole thing had been settled five months ago.

"Investigator," he said.

I looked at him then, for the first time, and knew I'd seen him somewhere before. He was about five-ten, and slender, with a built-in slouch, and appeared to be around forty although the hair showing under the beat-up old felt hat was completely grey. His clothes looked as if he dressed by jumping into them from the top of a stepladder. You wouldn't have given him a second glance, unless the first one had been at his face. It was thin and grey and a little tired, but there was a deadly efficiency about it you couldn't miss even if you were half asleep. The eyes were grey too, and as impersonal as outer space. I remembered then where I'd seen him before.

"You came to the hospital," I said.

He nodded.

The elevator stopped and the doors opened. I led the way down the corridor, unlocked the door, and stood back for him to go in. The room was on the south side, with a window looking out over the Gulf, but there was little breeze and it was breathless and hot. It was just at sunset and the piled masses of cloud to seaward were fired with red and orange, some of which was reflected back into the room to give it a strange, wine-coloured light. He sat down in the armchair near the door, took off his hat and dropped it on the carpet, and fished a pack of cigarettes from the side pocket of his coat. I tossed the robe over the bed and when I turned he was watching me. I walked over to the dresser beyond the foot of the bed and picked up my own cigarettes. As I lit one and dropped the match in a tray I caught sight of him again, in the mirror, and he was still staring at me. It was obvious and deliberate, and he didn't seem to care at all. I felt like a girl on a runway, and began to get hacked.

He blew out smoke and leaned back in the chair. "Stacked," he said. "Walk back here again."

"You that way?" I said. "Beat it."

He shook his head indifferently. "I'm not trying to make you. Just want to see how you walk."

"Why?" I asked.

"It's professional."

I came back and sat down on the bed with the cigarette. He watched me utterly without expression, and then he shook his head again. "You're a screwed duck."

"That's news?" I asked.

"No jury in the world would give you a nickel, even if you hadn't already signed a waiver. Take a look at yourself. You got any idea how far you'd get trying to look smashed-up and pathetic to twelve average Joes with pots and fallen arches? They'd laugh like it was a vaudeville show."

"You just came over to cheer me up, is that it?" I said. "I know all that. And I have signed the release, or waiver, or whatever you call it——"

"What did they give you?"

"Five thousand," I said. "And the hospital bills."

"You took the short end, pal."

"In another year or two I might have figured that out myself. Look. The leg had healed perfectly. I was up and walking. Not even a limp. The medics said it was as good as ever——"

"And when you reported for practice, it wasn't? You'd slowed down?"

"It's not measurable," I said. "The only way you can tell it is by trying to run through eleven pros who haven't slowed down. You can figure it out then while they're walking around on your face five yards back of where you should have been. It's nothing you could prove to anybody. X-rays wouldn't show it."

He nodded, and moved his hands. "Motion is a thousand signals, and a thousand movements, linked. One square corner anywhere and you break it up and the flow is gone. You're not a professional athlete any more; you're just another taxpayer with two arms and legs. There's no shortage."

"So why keep kicking it around?" I asked. "The whole thing was settled months ago." Then I thought of something. "What's the name of your outfit again?"

"Old Colony Life."

"Hell, that wasn't the company——"

"No. Of course not. I thought you understood that. We didn't have anything to do with the liability he carried on the car. That was some California company."

"Then what's the angle? How'd you get in the act?"

"Life insurance. About a hundred thousand worth."

I stared at him, puzzled. "I don't get it."

He sighed. "Cannon was insured with Old Colony——"

"I read you," I said. "That far. But what about it? He was insured. He's dead. You pick up the tab. Looks cut and dried to me. I figure he cost me fifty to seventy-five thousand, depending on when and if I might have got hurt in the natural course of events, playing. And now he's cost you a hundred grand. That's a pretty good night's work for one souse, but I don't see what either of us can do about it now unless maybe we send out for a box of Kleenex and have a good cry."

"I'd just like to ask you a few questions. If you don't mind."

I shrugged. "Go ahead. But I don't see how there can be much room for doubt he's dead. He was buried while I was there in the hospital."

"I know. Just say we're still a little curious as to how he died."

I stared at him. "Don't you read the papers?"

"Only the funnies. And today's horoscope."

"Everybody knows how he died. He was killed in the wreck when he sideswiped me and knocked me off the road."

"Sure. I know. I read the Highway Patrol report. I talked to the officers. I talked to the doctor. I talked to the other witnesses that were there when they untangled him from the wreck. I talked to you in the hospital. Now I'm talking to you again. It's a living."

"You don't believe he was killed in the wreck?"

"I didn't say that, did I?"

"Why else?"

"Routine, Harlan. Any time a policy-holder dies violently, without witnesses right at the scene——"

"Bat sweat," I said. "Five months after it happened, and you're still poking around in it. Why?"

"We never close a case until we're sure."

"Well, look. He must have been alive when he passed me. I never heard of a corpse driving a car, even the way he was driving it. And when they took him out of it he was dead, with his head caved in. What else do you want?"

"I don't know," he said. "Suppose you tell me the whole thing again, the way you did at the hospital?"

"Sure," I said. "You figure maybe I walked over and knocked his roof in while I was pinned down with a crushed leg under a four-thousand-pound convertible? I'll admit I was a little put out about it——"

He shook his head. "The whole thing, as nearly as you can remember it."

I sighed and lit another cigarette. "All right. It was just after dark. I was coming into town from that fishing cabin where I was camping, to see a movie. A mile or so after I got out on the highway, from the dirt road coming out of the swamp, a car came up behind me, going very fast. I was doing fifty, so he must have been clipping it off around sixty-five. There was no other traffic on the road, nobody in sight at all, so he had all the room in the world to pass me and then pull back into the right-hand lane, but instead he cut right in across my left front fender and knocked me off into the ditch. The car rolled a couple of times with me on the floorboards, but on the last one I fell out—the top was down—and then it teetered on two wheels and fell back on top of me. He crashed, too. Just as I was going up and over the first time—while

I was diving for the bottom—I saw his headlights swing in a big circle like somebody waving a flashlight around with his arm. Not that I was particularly interested in what happened to the sad bastard at the moment, but it's just one of those things that register on your mind in the middle of everything, for some reason. I don't know how long it was before they got there with the wrecker and pulled the car off me, but it seemed like about two average life-times. I was out cold, at least part of the time."

"But not all of it?"

"No."

"And his car had come to rest against a culvert about a hundred yards ahead of you?"

"So they told me later."

"Did you hear anything during the time you were conscious?"

"Such as what for instance?"

"Cars going by, people talking, anybody moving——"

"No. Believe me, pal. I was never lonelier in my life."

"Nothing at all? You didn't hear anything?"

"Just night sounds. You know—frogs, things like that. And something dripping. I remember hoping it wasn't gasoline."

I could see the disappointment in his face. "That's all?"

"That's all I remem—— No. Wait. Once I thought I heard him moaning or trying to call for help, from the other car."

He made a little gesture with his hand, and something in his eyes told me that was what he'd been fishing for all the time. "You said the same thing before. You really think you heard him moan, or cry out?"

"I think so."

"You can't be any more positive than that?"

"You ever been knocked out?" I asked.

He nodded.

"Then you know how it is. It's all fuzzy afterward, especially if you were in and out several times. You don't know how much of it you might have dreamed."

He nodded. "But there is a chance you did hear him? Remember, you've told me twice, just the same way."

"Sure," I said. "But what of it? What difference does it make if he did groan or something?"

"You see the pictures of his head?"

"I didn't want to see any pictures of his head. I had pictures of my own."

"I thought not," he said. "I saw them. He didn't make any noise, believe me."

"Then I must have imagined it."

He grunted. "Maybe."

I got it then, but before I could say anything he abruptly changed the subject. "You ever meet his wife? Widow, I mean."

"No."

"She never did come to see you in the hospital?"

"No. Her lawyer, and the insurance joker. That's all."

He looked thoughtful. "Did that ever strike you as a little odd? I mean, her husband crashes into you and lays you up in the hospital for weeks and she doesn't even bring you a bunch of violets. They established the fact the wreck was entirely Cannon's fault, she didn't know but what you might sue the estate for sixteen million dollars, and still she wouldn't waste half an hour going out to the hospital to butter you up a little."

"As I said, her lawyer did."

"Not the same thing at all. This babe's a looker." He moved his hands again. He could say a lot of things with his hands. "A dish like that can pour more oil on the troubled waters in five minutes than a lawyer can in a month. And they know it. All of them."

"Well, after all," I said, "her husband was killed in the wreck——"

"She didn't take to bed about it."

"What do you mean by that?"

He shrugged. "Nothing in particular. How long had you been out there at that cabin before the accident?"

"About six days, I think. Let's see, I got there on Saturday, and it was the following Thursday night he creamed me. Why?"

"I just wondered. How'd you happen to be there, anyway? You don't come from that part of the country."

"I like to fish. Do about a month of it each spring when I'm not working at some off-season job. A lot of bass in that lake and the cabin belongs to an old friend, a guy I knew in college."

He nodded. "I see. Ever been there before this year?"

"Once. About three years ago. Just over the week-end."

"And you never did meet the Cannons? I thought maybe—that is, he had a camp out there too, not far from your friend's."

"Well, you might say I met *him*," I said wearily. "Or have we mentioned that? But as far as I know I've never seen her in my life. I don't even know what she looks like."

"One of those very rich brunettes, blue-black hair, brown eyes, fairly tall, around thirty. Lovely woman. Not classic, but what they call striking. Coloration—you know what I mean."

"Oh? Sure. I——" I started to say something else, but for some reason I bit it off and waited.

"If you'd ever seen her you'd remember her," he went on. "Here, I've got a picture of her." He took it out of the inside pocket of his coat and handed it to me. "What'd you say?"

I looked at it, "Nothing," I said.

She was a dream, all right, and she was the same one. I was almost positive of that. The light had been pretty poor, there under the trees, but as he said himself if you'd ever seen her once you'd remember her.

"Well?" he asked.

It was just a hunch, but I played it. "Toothsome," I said. "But I never saw her before."

CHAPTER TWO

He picked his hat off the floor and stood up. "Well, that's about it. Thanks for sparing the time."

"Not at all," I said.

When he was gone I took a quick shower and lay down on the bed with a cigarette. It burned down to the end and I lit another as the sun went down and twilight thickened inside the room. It was all crazy, but several things stood out like moles on a bubble-dancer. The first was that for some reason he didn't think Cannon had been killed in that wreck. Not in the wreck itself, or as a result of it. Why? A man goes off the road and crashes at sixty miles an hour and when they sift him out of the wreckage with his head knocked in you wonder if he died of gastric ulcers? No. Purvis believed he had been murdered after the crash. But still he wouldn't admit it.

Maybe, though, the latter was understandable, if you looked at it correctly. He had somebody in mind, but you didn't go around making irresponsible statements like that until you had some proof to back them up. The police had already written it off as a traffic fatality, so he'd have his neck out a mile. The slandered party could sue the insurance company.

The next thing that stuck out was that it wouldn't make any difference at all as far as the insurance company was concerned whether he'd died in the wreck or been murdered by somebody after the wreck—unless the beneficiary of the insurance policy was involved in the murder. If somebody else tagged him out they still had to pick up the tab, as far as I knew. The beneficiary would no doubt be his widow. Therefore, he had his eye on Mrs. Cannon. That tied in perfectly, because it was Mrs. Cannon he kept asking about. He couldn't understand why I'd never seen her the whole time I was there, why she'd never come to the hospital. I was one up on him in that department. After looking at the picture, I was pretty sure I knew why she hadn't. She didn't want to come anywhere near me because she was afraid I might recognize her.

No, I thought; at best it was just a guess. That might be it, or it might not. I'd never thought about it particularly while I was in the hospital, and just assumed she was overcome with grief and didn't want to be reminded of the wreck any more than she had to. It didn't matter to me; as far as I was concerned I'd already seen enough of the Cannon family. And there was no reason, actually, that she had to; she had no connection with the accident. She wasn't even in the car with him when he rode me off the highway. Her lawyer and the insurance adjuster had taken care of smoothing down my hackles and working out a settlement that looked fair to me at the time. So why should she show up?

But then, again, when you thought about it, why shouldn't she? Purvis had intimated she wasn't grief-stricken quite to the point of throwing herself on the funeral pyre. And in five weeks she might have dropped around for a couple of minutes some afternoon between the first and second cocktails and said, "I'm sorry my husband knocked your leg off. Here's a roll of Scotch tape."

So maybe she had avoided me deliberately. She knew I'd seen her out there near the lake less than fifteen minutes before the wreck and would probably recognize her if I saw her again. But I'd never mentioned the fact to anybody, so presumably I didn't know just who it was I'd seen. If it were just any woman, it was of no importance; if it were Mrs. Cannon maybe it became highly significant. Why? Was she supposed to have been somewhere else at the time? I didn't know, but one thing was certain as hell. If she *didn't* want anybody to know she'd been out there, she would have been very careful to stay away from me.

But why was Purvis digging into it after all this time? It had been five months. Surely they must have had to pay off on the insurance policy before this, and when they paid you'd think they would write it off and close it. It didn't make sense.

There was one more thing that didn't make a lot of sense, and that was why I'd told Purvis I'd never seen her. It was just a hunch, and I still wasn't sure why I'd done it. Well, I thought, I wasn't Purvis's mother, was I? Let him dig up his own information; he sure as hell hadn't dislocated his jaw telling me anything. There was another angle, too. Suppose something a little funny had been going on out there that evening; the chump on the side-lines that got run over wasn't Purvis. It was John Harlan.

I got up and dressed, and went out to dinner. It was a little after nine when I came back to the room with a copy of *Field and Stream* and tried to read it. It was no use. I kept seeing a picture of a very lovely and very wealthy brunette who became widowed and even richer while I lay there with a Buick in my lap. Toss that seal a fish, Jeeves, so he'll stop barking. Five thousand will do. The telephone rang. I reached over to the table beside the bed and picked it up.

"Harlan?" a man's voice said. "This is Purvis again——"

"You still in town?" I asked.

"No. At home. I work out of the Houston office, or did I tell you? But what I called about—there was something else I wanted to ask you. That convertible top was down? Right?"

"Sure," I said, frowning. "Why?"

"You were alone, of course; but do you remember whether you had anything on the seat beside you?"

"On the seat? Not that I remember. But what difference——?"

"Just something I got to wondering about," he said easily. "Not important at all. But you know how it is; you get to working on one of these things and you keep trying to get the whole picture——"

He went on. It was a pretty fair snow job, but it would take a better one to make you stop wondering why he'd asked a crazy question like that.

"—so the seat *was* empty?" he wound up.

"Of course," I said. "That is, except for some dirty clothes."

"Clothes?"

"A bag of laundry I was taking into town."

"Laundry?" There was the faintest hint of excitement in his voice. Then he said, "Wait a minute. I don't get it. I thought you said you were going to town to see a movie. It was after eight p.m., and all the laundries would be closed——"

I sighed. "You paying for this call?"

"Sure. But——"

"All right. As long as I'm not being nicked for the toll charges, I don't mind going into a long-winded song and dance about some goofy thing that doesn't amount to a damn. There's a kid, see, at a filling station there in town. Just finished high school, and has an athletic scholarship at S.M.U. or T.C.U. or one of those South-western Conference schools. He knows who I am. Or used to be, I should say. He's a football maniac, so if I asked him he'd wash the clothes himself with soapflakes and dry 'em by blowing his breath on 'em. I intended to leave the bundle there at the station and have him call a laundry route man to pick it up the next morning. Save me a trip into town during the day when I could be fishing. That wrap it up?"

"Sure, I didn't quite catch his uncle's name, and when he was baptized, but you can call me collect from Omaha——"

"Well, you asked."

"So I did. It was a pretty good-sized bundle, huh?"

"I'm afraid I've lost the check list," I said wearily. "If it makes any difference how many dirty socks I had on hand in March——"

"I mean, it wasn't just a couple of shirts?"

"No. It was a whole bunch of stuff in a white laundry bag. Some sheets, blankets, and so on, from the cabin——"

"Uh-uh," he said slowly.

"I don't scan you," I said. "What difference——?"

"Just an angle," he said casually. "As you say, it doesn't amount to a damn. Thanks a lot, Harlan. See you——"

"Hey, hold it," I said. It was too late. I heard the phone click as he hung up.

I sat on the side of the bed and lit a cigarette. Reading was out of the question now, and sleep was impossible. A bundle of laundry on the seat beside me—why the hell had he been interested in a stupid thing like that? Something about the way he had said, "Uh-uh," told me that was exactly what he'd been hoping to learn.

Try again, I thought. Go back over the whole thing. Everybody's missed it so far—everybody but Purvis. Look. Secondary road, with practically no traffic on it, this joker comes up behind you going very fast, drunk as a skunk, passes, cuts in—— Why?

Well, obviously, because he was too drunk to drive. But if he was that drunk and driving that fast, why hadn't he crashed before? It would be thirty miles back to any place he could have got that kind of a bun on, unless he was carrying his supplies with him. No. That wasn't an answer. It was luck. Coincidence. A drunk can smash up anywhere. It was just the bounce of the ball that it happened to be me he'd leaned on.

You're still missing it, I told myself. That's exactly the way everybody else has figured it from the beginning, but Purvis is looking at it from a different angle altogether. He's got a bundle of laundry mixed up in it. Why? Because it was lying in the seat. It was in a white bag—— I stopped then and sat very still on the side of the bed. Was that where we'd all gone off the track? Taking it for granted Cannon was drunk? Maybe he hadn't been. Suppose he'd crashed me deliberately? And then somebody had killed him, caved his head in while he was lying unconscious in the wreck?

No, hell, I thought. *It was too fantastic.* But was it? I knew something that even Purvis didn't know—but probably suspected. Mrs. Cannon was out there at the lake that evening. Suppose Cannon had been looking for her, believing she was out there with somebody. Maybe he came out of the swamp road behind me, trying to get a look at who was in the car. He caught up with me, with his headlights splashing against the back of the car, and saw I was alone. The top was down; it would be obvious there was nobody with me. Then, just as he was passing, for a fraction of a second he caught a glimpse of somebody bent over or crouched down in the seat beside me, hiding from the lights. So he blew his stack completely.

But nobody could be that crazy. He'd be taking a chance of crashing himself—which he did. A man would have to be absolutely berserk to do a thing like that. Well, how did I know he wasn't? I didn't even know him, to say nothing of having any idea of what was sloshing around in his mind as he came up behind me. Maybe he thought I was somebody else. Maybe he didn't care if he did kill himself along with her. Maybe—— There were a dozen possibilities.

But still it was moonshine—unless you had more to go on than that. Purvis had, or he'd never have started digging into it. I had to talk to him again. But what good would that do? He wouldn't give you the time of day; he was too cagey. Yes, but he didn't have to *tell* me anything; I could find out a lot by watching the direction his questions took. That had worked pretty well so far. I could call him and tell him I'd just remembered some goofy thing that might have a bearing on it, and get him started again. Then I stopped. I couldn't call him tonight; I didn't even know his first name, and there were probably dozens of Purvises in the Houston telephone directory.

I threw some clothes on and went out to get a cup of coffee. When I came back it was hours before I got to sleep. It wasn't the coffee, however; coffee never bothers me that way. I was thinking of Mrs. Cannon again, and of a hundred thousand dollars, and a lot of things were growing clearer in my mind as I tossed and turned on the sweaty sheet. I was finished, wasn't I? Football was the only thing I knew or was any good at, and they'd taken that away from me. What was left? Coaching? High school character-building? Getting shoved around by Monday morning quarterbacks for peanuts? The hell with that. Selling? Nuts. I liked violence and rough body contact and money and excitement and then money again, and I hated failure in the way you can hate it only if you grew up with it. I'd seen enough ineffectual futility by the time I was twelve to last me the rest of my life, and I was a pro making them put it on the line when I was a junior in high school. I was big and fast and I was good —and I knew it. They called me a cold-blooded savage and Whore Harlan and What's-in-it-for-me Harlan, but they paid me. Not openly, and not the school itself, but I got it. In college I got more. So now it was all over. They'd stopped the train and put me off because some guy had crashed into me with a car. Maybe he'd even done it deliberately. I cursed and sat up in bed, groping for cigarettes in the hot darkness. I wanted to get my hands on something or somebody and have an accounting. He was dead and beyond reach. But she wasn't, and maybe she was at the bottom of the whole thing. I thought of the way she looked in that picture, and of the money she or somebody had cheated me of. I lit a cigarette and stared coldly at the match as I blew it out. *You should have done it to somebody else, baby,* I thought; *I don't like having it done to me. . . .*

In the morning, after I'd had some breakfast, I came back to the room and put in a call to Houston. In a moment a girl's voice trilled, "Good-morning-Old-Colony-Life-Insurance-Company."

"I'd like to speak to Mr. Purvis," I said.

"I beg your pardon. What was the name again?"

"Purvis."

"I'm sorry, but there's no one here by that name. Are you sure you have the right number?"

"Of course," I said impatiently. "He's an investigator. Works out of the Houston office. This *is* Houston, isn't it?"

"Yes, sir. But we have no Mr. Purvis. Just a moment, please——"

I waited irritably. What was the matter with her? Didn't she even know who worked there? She came back on. "Hello, I'm sorry to keep you waiting. I just checked with one of the other girls who's been here longer. There *used* to be a Mr. Purvis, but he left the company several months ago."

"Oh," I said. "I see——" It was a little fast, and it took me a moment to catch up. "Well, look," I went on hurriedly, before she could hang up, "could you give me his last telephone number or address, off the old personnel records?"

"Just a minute, please."

I dug up an old envelope and uncapped my pen. "Hello," she said when she came back on. "This is four months old, but he might still be there."

I wrote it down. "Thanks a million," I said.

I hung up and lit a cigarette. So that's the way it was. It explained a number of things, such as why the company was still pawing around in the mess months after they should have paid off on the policy. The company wasn't. They'd probably paid long ago and written it off as closed, but Purvis had gone into business for himself. Blackmail, extortion—call it whatever you liked. Something had made him suspicious when he'd gone up there to investigate, while he was still on the payroll. Maybe he'd never reported any of it, and now he was getting ready to put the squeeze on somebody. He'd hoped to get a little more ammunition, so he'd come down to pump me again. I was just the chump in the middle. Maybe I should rent myself out as a battleground so they could go on walking back and forth across my face with their tug-of-war for the rest of my life. If Cannon had crashed me deliberately, somebody in that mess had short-changed me about fifty thousand dollars, the way I saw it, and it was about time I found out who it was. Purvis knew, so what better place to start? I reached for the telephone again and put in a call to the number the girl had given me.

There was no answer. "Shall I try again in about ten minutes?" the operator asked.

"Please," I said.

There was still no answer then, and I came up with the same

empty ringing when I tried twice more during the morning. Well, maybe he had another job; he wouldn't be home perhaps until around five or six in the afternoon. I went out on the beach and tried to swim, but I was wild with impatience and kept thinking of Purvis. At a few minutes to six I came back to the room and tried the number again.

A man's voice answered, a tired and irritable voice.

"I'd like to speak to Mr. Purvis," I said. "Is he there?"

"Mr. who?" he rasped.

"Purvis. P-u-r-v-i-s. Does he live there?"

"Nah. Yah got the wrong nummer, mate. He moved away from here a long time ago."

"Well, do you know where I can get hold of him? Did he leave a forwarding——?"

"Nah, nah. Got no idea where he is."

He hung up.

I stood looking at the phone. What now? Get hold of a Houston directory and start calling all the Purvises until I found him? Not on toll charges, anyway; if I were going to do that I'd better go up there. And what if he lived in a boarding house? The phone wouldn't even be listed under his name. Well, hell, I had to do something; sitting here wondering about it would drive me crazy. I grabbed my clothes and started dressing. Just as I was buttoning down the tabs on my shirt collar the telephone rang stridently. I reached it in one leap.

"Hello."

"Harlan?"

My pulse quickened as I recognized the smooth, persuasive wise-guy voice. "Oh, hello, is that you again?" I asked casually. "What is it now?"

"Been having any trouble trying to get hold of me?" he asked innocently.

"Trying to get hold of you? What the hell would I be trying to call you for?"

"Oh, I didn't know," he replied easily. "It just occurred to me that if you'd called Old Colony they would give you an address, but I've moved from there. But since you didn't——"

He let it trail off almost derisively and I knew he was fully aware I had talked to the girl at Old Colony. He probably still had a pipeline in there. So now he'd got in touch with me again even though he knew I was wise to the fact he no longer worked there and that any investigating he was doing now was strictly off the record and probably for the purposes of blackmail. As a way of sounding me out, it was pretty smooth. I wouldn't have tried to call him if I hadn't been interested in the thing myself.

"Not bad," I said.

He chuckled. "I didn't think it would take you over twenty-four hours to decide that five grand settlement was a bag of peanuts you'd toss to a squirrel. You did recognize the babe, didn't you? You covered pretty well with the picture, but you'd already given it away when I described her."

"Well, it might be pretty hard to remember just where I saw her before," I said. "You know how it is. Babes here. Babes there——"

"Oh, sure," he replied. "I didn't think it would be any cinch."

"But you might know of some way of making it easier?"

"I wouldn't have called you if I didn't. I've got a little proposition in mind, if you think you'd be interested."

"I wouldn't know until I've heard it, would I? Suppose you come down and we look into it."

He hesitated. "I'm expecting a phone call; if I go out I might miss it. Would you mind coming up here?"

"No," I said. "Give me your address."

He told me and I wrote it down. "See you in a couple of hours," I said, and hung up.

CHAPTER THREE

I HAD to wait for a bus, so it was after nine when I arrived in Houston. The night was still and darkly overcast above the lights of the city, and a scattering of fat raindrops splashed against the walk as I came out of the bus station to hail a cab. I read off the address Purvis had given me. The ride took about ten minutes; I sat impatiently on the edge of the seat, smoking and trying to think. I had no plan of action and wasn't sure of anything except that this time Purvis was going to do some talking himself. He was committed now; it was understood he knew something specific about what had happened that night, and he'd put a few facts on the line or wish he had.

It was a narrow street in an older section given over to second-hand stores and hole-in-the-wall markets and a few old apartment buildings. The driver pulled up before a three-storey brick with a small vestibule in which a light was burning. I got out and paid him. The street was deserted except for two men talking beneath a bar sign down at the other end of the block. Purvis's apartment was on the third floor. I pressed the buzzer. In a moment the door clicked and I went in.

There was no elevator. I went up two steps at a time, meeting no one in the halls or on the stairs, but hearing snatches of what sounded like the same television programme on all three floors. Number 303 was the first one on the right at the head of the stairs. I touched the bell and Purvis opened the door almost immediately. He nodded, but said nothing until I had come inside and the door was closed.

It was a small living-room. Directly across from the door was a window which presumably looked out on the street, but the blind was drawn all the way down. At the left was an open door going into the bedroom, while on the right, just opposite it, another opened into a small dinette. The living-room was fitted with the usual landlord-tan wallpaper and the beat-up odds and ends of shabby furniture that would come with a furnished flat in this neighbourhood, so dreary and like a thousand others that Purvis's things stood out and hit you right in the eye the moment you walked in. There were five or six framed copies of paintings of girls in ballet costumes, the same pictures you sometimes see in the anterooms of doctors' offices. Some arty, horse-faced girl I got stuck with once at a party told me who the painter was that did them, but I couldn't remember now. Dago was all I could think of, but that wasn't it. There were some more pictures in one big frame over a desk at the right, beside the doorway going into the dinette, but these were photographs. They were all signed, and they were all of ballet dancers. There must have been a dozen of them. An *aficionado,* I thought, remembering that way he had of describing things with his hands and what he had said about motion. In a corner across the room near the window was a high-fidelity sound system that blended into the other furnishings like a thousand-dollar bill among the nickels on a Salvation Army tambourine. It was playing something longhair.

"Sit down, Harlan," he said, nodding to the old sofa at my left. He went over and turned off the music, and then folded his lank frame into a chair near the desk. *"Les Sylphides,"* he murmured.

"Meyer," I said.

His eyebrows raised. "How's that?"

"A gag," I said. "Skip it. You had something to tell me."

He was dressed in a pair of grey slacks and a dark sports shirt with long sleeves. It was hot in the room in spite of the little fan whirring away on top of the desk, but he didn't sweat. The cynical, young-old face was fine-boned and pale and very tired, but that deadly efficiency was still there in the eyes. There wasn't much to him inside the clothes; you felt that if you put a hand on his chest and pushed he'd fold up around your arm like a wet towel. He lit a cigarette and regarded me through the smoke.

"Her husband crashed you deliberately," he said casually. "But I suppose you know that by now."

"Yes," I said. "Or maybe I was just supposed to be a by-product. He could have been trying to kill her."

"Both of you, I think."

I remembered what she had done when I saw her out there by the lake and knew he was probably right, but I didn't say anything. He was going to do the talking this time.

"What was it tipped you in the first place?" I asked. "There's nothing suspicious about a guy being found dead in a bad car smash-up."

He shrugged. "Be corny, and call it a sixth sense. I don't know what it is, but you get it after a while if you keep going to these things long enough. You pull a hundred packages out of the file and they're all just about alike, but one of 'em will start you ringing like a burglar alarm. The first thing was the way his head was pushed in——"

"Well," I interrupted, "he did roll a car at sixty-five miles an hour. He figured to get bruised a little——"

"Sure," he said. "But when reliable witnesses got there he was still under the wheel. He had four broken ribs to prove it. His skull had been crushed by some terrific blow, and the wound was a little to the rear and slightly to the right of the top of his head. So what did he hit it on? The dash? That was in his lap. Granted the top of the car was caved in until it was practically sitting on his haircut, but what he was hit with wasn't flat——"

"Freaks happen all the time in bad wrecks. Nobody's ever explained just how you can get knocked out of a pair of shoes that are laced up tight, but it's been done."

He nodded. "That's right. But there were too many freaks in this one. For one thing, he wasn't drunk. At least, not nearly as drunk as everybody thought. So the only other alternative theory is that he deliberately tried to kill you. And if the people he really meant to kill were still out there at the lake——" He stopped and gave me a cold grin. "That's where you saw her, of course. Anyway, if they were still out there, which way would they have to go to get back to town?"

"Right past where we crashed," I said.

He spread his hands. "You see?"

"What makes you so sure he wasn't drunk?"

"I didn't say that. I said I didn't think he was *that* drunk. Nobody ever established it. No laboratory tests were made. Look at it this way. He was a prominent citizen; he was dead; there was a smell of alcohol about his body, and a pint bottle, about one-third full, in the glove compartment of the car—which didn't break, incidentally, because the highway maps and papers in it cushioned the shock of the crash. But still the real reason he was assumed to be blotto drunk was the fact that *only a blotto drunk would have cut in like that*. You see? They just reversed cause and effect, and didn't even bother to look for any other explanation."

"Why didn't they make the lab tests?" I asked.

"To prove what? Liability for the accident? It was his, from start to finish. They told you that as soon as you came around. The skid marks and the positions of the cars proved that, and what you told them only confirmed it. And what's the percentage in building a drunk-driving case against a dead man? You going to take him to court?"

"What about your outfit?"

"What difference did proof of drunkenness make to us? He was dead. We had to pay off on his life insurance, whether he was crocked or sober. By the time I got up there it would have been impossible, anyway. They'd already buried him. I was just making a routine investigation, until I began to see there could have been another reason for his driving you off the road. I backtracked down the highway until I found the place he bought the bottle——"

"The same one? How do you know?"

He shrugged wearily. "Jesus, I *don't* know. All that's certain is that it was a pint, and that it was the same brand. Sure, he could have had three more in the meantime and thrown the bottles out. But in the insurance business you get in the habit of playing the percentages, and the percentages say that was the same bottle. He appeared to be sober when he bought it, and I doubt very much that two-thirds of it would have made him so drunk he couldn't see something as big as a Buick convertible. Now, can we drop that for the moment?"

"Sure," I said. "Go on."

He leaned back in his chair and studied me thoughtfully. "I gather from the fact you're here you might be interested in re-negotiating your settlement with Mrs. Cannon?"

"Right," I said.

"It'll be a little extra-legal, if you follow me."

"So it's extra-legal. It's money. Did she collect the insurance?"

He nodded. "And she's loaded, besides. Cannon left an estate that'll add up to somewhere around three hundred thousand, after taxes. No other heirs."

I leaned forward on the sofa. "All right. Go on."

"Say a hundred grand. Split seventy-five, twenty-five."

"Seventy-five for me?"

He shook his head with a pained kind of smile on his face. "Seventy-five for me, chum."

"Back off and look again," I said. "The wind's whistling through your head."

"How's that?"

"Who got run over out there that night? You or me?"

He shrugged. "That doesn't enter into it. Who dug up the evidence, after everybody else had sloughed it off as a traffic fatality?"

"You've got more?"

"More what?"

"Evidence."

"Some," he said. "But maybe not quite enough. That's where you come in."

"Where I come in is when somebody says sixty grand. That's my cue line."

He sighed. "Fifty."

I knew that was what he'd planned on from the first. Try to chisel me, would he?

"Sixty," I said. "Take it or leave it. You wouldn't have called me in if you hadn't needed me."

"I need you like I need the gon. It just happens you're in a very good position to put on the pressure. It's a psychological twist that'd make it easy, but I can do it alone if I have to."

I grinned at him very coldly. "Then do it alone."

"You think I can't?"

"That's right. You need somebody who was right there when

he was murdered and who might or might not have been completely unconscious all the time under that other car. It's a highly specialized field, and not many applicants could qualify."

He exhaled a lungful of smoke and watched it moodily. I knew I'd hit him where it hurt. "Well, let's table that discussion for the moment," he said. "How about a cold beer?"

"Sure," I said. I had him on the run now and all I had to do was keep the heat on him. Let him drop his guard and then jump him again. And I'd let him have it, but good.

We went out through the door at the right. It led into the dinette and kitchen, which were divided by the refrigerator and a serving bar about chest high. You had to go around the end of the bar to reach the refrigerator, which opened from the kitchen side. He flicked on the light. The kitchen part was just a cubbyhole with a sink and a two-burner gas stove next to the wall. You couldn't see into the living-room from here. He opened the reefer and took out two bottles of imported beer. I think it was Danish. He uncapped them and set them on the drainboard of the sink. There was no window, and it was very hot under the light.

"You had more to go on than what you've told me so far, didn't you?" I asked casually. "I mean, beside that hole in his head and the fact he wasn't drunk."

"What makes you think so?"

"You must have."

He stared at me very coolly. "So? So maybe there is more."

"Such as?" I asked. Now was as good a time as any.

"Such as nothing, at the moment."

I reached out with my left and caught the front of his shirt. Pulling him to me, I gave him the open right hand across the side of the face. "Let's have it now," I said. It was a mistake.

There was no resistance in him at all. He came right on up against me like a couple of old inner tubes hanging off my arm and when he got there he exploded. I had Purvis all over me. Fragments of flying Purvis hit me in the solar plexus and Adam's apple at the same time, and then something chopped me just under the left ear and I was through. I didn't even fall; he eased me to the floor like somebody putting down an old mattress he'd been carrying around. I was sick and I couldn't get my breath. My whole body felt paralysed. I tried to turn over. It was no use.

A convention of Purvises stood in a circle, looking down at me. "I wouldn't try that again," they said, all speaking at once. They sounded a long way off.

I retched and gagged, trying to get air through my throat again. The kitchen tilted and went on spinning slowly like a carousel. I opened my mouth and tried to bite a mouthful of air before I died of suffocation. Just before the room went completely black I started breathing again, but I still couldn't move.

There was a sound somewhere like that of a buzzer, and I thought it was just another of the ringing noises in my head until he stepped over me and started around the serving bar. "Don't go away," he said and flicked off the light. I lay in darkness and in agony.

If I could hit him just once I'd break him in two. The next time I'd have better sense than to pull him toward me. I'd take him apart. But I had to get up first. I tried again, and this time I managed to roll over. Sweat ran off my face and I had to fight against vomiting on the floor. I heard a door chime and then the door opening, and voices. The door closed. Purvis had company. It was a man. I could hear snatches of what he was saying.

"Federal radio inspector . . . complaints of television interference . . . amateur transmitter in the neighbourhood . . ."

"No, I haven't got a television set," Purvis said.

"Oh. Well, thanks."

"Not at——" Purvis began. His voice cut off with a shaky inward sucking of breath as if he had started to pull it in to scream, and then I heard the impact itself as if somebody had hurled a green watermelon against the wall. It was sickening. I froze up tight, forgetting my pain, and waited. Something slid softly to the floor, as if being helped, the way Purvis had eased me down. Then nothing happened at all. There was no sound. I slowly exhaled, beginning to feel the pain in my throat again. He moved. I heard footsteps coming toward the dinette. Something blocked off the light coming in from the living-room, and I knew he was standing in the doorway. He seemed to fill it. I couldn't see him, because I was lying behind the serving bar and refrigerator. I waited, sweating with suspense. Would he come on in and look around into the kitchen side? I was helpless; he'd kick my head in like someone killing a snake. He stood there for a moment, and then I heard him turn and go away. It sounded as if he was going into the bedroom. He came out again and I heard the desk drawer being pulled open. There was a rustling of papers. I tried to breathe quietly, but air seemed to gasp and hiss through the agony in my throat like steam through old radiator pipes.

I could move a little now, and managed to push myself up to

my hands and knees. If he did come out here and find me I wanted at least to be on my feet. I heard him shut the desk drawer and then the sound of his footsteps again. They appeared to be going toward the front door. He was leaving. I crawled silently around the end of the bar and came forward until I could see most of the living-room. Purvis's feet and legs were in view, near the sofa. I slipped along the linoleum another two or three feet and peered around the edge of the doorway. He was standing in the front door. I saw his feet and legs first and then my glance went on up, and up. He was as big as a house. His back was turned toward me as he peered out into the hall, and he seemed to fill the doorway. He was bareheaded, and his hair was dark and brush-cut. He went out softly, pulling the door shut. I never had seen his face. I sighed weakly and pushed myself to my feet. I had to hold on to the refrigerator. My clothes were soaked with sweat.

I didn't know whether I'd ever be able to speak again. My throat felt as if I had a logging chain doubled around it with a tractor pulling on each end. I wheezed as I staggered into the living-room and stood looking down at Purvis. He lay on his back with his eyes open, staring blankly up at the ceiling. His left forearm was broken, bent grotesquely across the rug as if he had another elbow inside the dark blue sleeve. He'd shoved it up instinctively, in that last thousandth of a second he was alive, trying to ward off the blow, and the impact had been so terrible it had broken it and then had enough power left over to make that kind of a mess of his head. I looked around to see what he had been hit with. There was nothing. The big guy must have brought it with him and then taken it away.

The whole thing had happened so suddenly I was having a little trouble catching up. The only thing I was sure of was that I had to get out of there, and fast. I was still groggy from that judo manhandling Purvis had given me, but this didn't look like the safest place in the world to lie around and recover. Somebody else might come up. I'd have a sweet time explaining what I was doing here alone in the apartment with a man who was spilling the contents of his head on to a threadbare rug. "I was just sitting in the kitchen having a beer, officer. Sure, I heard this guy kill him, but I didn't think anything about it; you know how it is, just figured it was some friend of his . . ." *Cut it out,* I thought. *Get the hell out of here.*

I walked softly to the door and had sense enough to take my handkerchief in my hand as I turned the knob. I looked out. The corridor was deserted. Slipping out, I transferred the handkerchief to the outer knob, turned it, and silently closed the door. I put the handkerchief back in my pocket and went down the stairs. The hallway on the second floor was empty. I could hear snatches of a television programme and someone laughing. Then I was out in the street, weak and shaking a little as I turned the corner and went on. Nobody had seen me. *But what about that taxi driver?* I thought uneasily. He'd remember bringing me here. He'd recall he picked me up at the bus station. But, hell, he'd never actually looked at me. He couldn't describe me, except to say that I was pretty big. It didn't mean anything.

I started walking. It was a block before I met anyone, and then it was a coloured girl who went on past without looking at me. When she was gone and I was alone again I felt my throat and tried to say something. I made a croaking noise. I cleared it painfully and tried again. "Mrs. Cannon," I said hoarsely. It sounded like gravel being forced through a pipe. "Rich bitch. Testing. Rich bitch." My voice cleared up slightly, but I wondered if I wasn't still a little punchy.

When I was out of the area, a good ten blocks away, I ducked into a dimly lit bar where a jukebox was wailing and ordered a bottle of beer. Sitting on a stool between a big blonde who was yakking six thousand feet to the mile to her escort and a pint-sized redhead who was crocked to the eyeballs and singing something under her breath, I sipped the beer and tried to sort it out. If that taxi driver remembered me, or if the police happened to think of looking into Purvis's long-distance calls, I was in a bad spot. I hadn't been seen leaving the building, but maybe the other guy had. We were about the same size, and the cops could probably make out with whichever of us they caught first. But assume I never was even connected with it? What next? Where did I go from here? Purvis was dead; I'd never find out anything from him now. Was I going to have to give it up, just because some big ox had knocked his roof in?

Who was the big joker, anyway? Purvis had obviously gone into the shakedown racket on a full-time basis, so maybe the guy was one of his victims or intended victims—but in that case, why hadn't Purvis recognized him. Wouldn't he know him? He obviously hadn't, because he'd been sucked out of position by that wheeze about investigating complaints of something lousing up television reception in the neighbourhood. He hadn't been expecting trouble, because if he had the guy wouldn't have been able to hit him with a handful of rice. I knew that from what had happened to me. He could move faster than any human being I'd ever seen in my life. But maybe that big guy was a little fast, too. He'd probably had the pipe or loaded club up his sleeve. I sure as hell wouldn't want to tangle with him in a dark alley. He was about my size, and if he could match speed with Purvis——I stopped.

I'd had to say it twice before it soaked in. I got it now, and it all matched perfectly. I was in business, if I didn't let him get behind me with that piece of pipe.

CHAPTER FOUR

I CALLED a cab and went on into town and caught the next bus to Galveston. It was a little after midnight when I got back to my room in the hotel. I stripped off my sweat-soaked clothing, took a shower, and lay down on the bed with a cigarette.

There were a lot of angles to figure, and it was going to be dangerous as hell. Assuming I was right so far, he had already killed two men; there was no reason to believe he'd be bashful about running up his score if he suspected I was moving in on him. Of course, I had an idea now of what he looked like, which cut his chances of being able to catch me off guard as he had Purvis and brain me with that club, but I still had to sleep sometimes, and there was nothing in the by-laws said he couldn't switch to a gun if he wanted. Once I knew his name and was sure I had the right man I knew how to tie his hands so he couldn't do anything to me, but until I did I was wide open for the same kind of pay-off Purvis had got. And I had to go back there to be sure.

It was odd Purvis hadn't recognized him; he was the first to grasp the fact Mrs. Cannon must have a boy friend and that he should be a big man somewhere around my size but still he'd goofed off and let the big joker walk right in on him. That indicated the guy had been keeping himself as well covered as she had. Purvis must have been up there several times, snooping around trying to find out who he was, and all he'd accomplished was to set himself up like a duck in a shooting gallery. There were a couple of factors in my favour, however. The first, of course, was that I had seen him once, even if only from the back. And the second was that he might come out a little more into the open now that—as far as he knew—the only person left who suspected him was dead. The police had written the thing off as a traffic fatality, so he had nothing to fear from them. Purvis had been the only killjoy spoiling his fun, and now that Purvis had been eliminated he could relax. Unless——

I lit another cigarette off the old one, and thought about that. He'd had his eye on Purvis, obviously. So maybe he knew Purvis had been to see me. There wouldn't be much doubt as to what we'd talked about, and when I showed up around there a couple of days later there'd be even less. My name would go right on to his list. Dangerous? Dangerous was hardly the word.

Bat sweat. Since when was I this impressed by a thug with a piece of pipe? Let him scare me off? This was big. This was once-in-a-lifetime stuff. So maybe I could just tell the police about it and they'd give me a cigar and a parking ticket, and I could go to work selling aluminium pots to housewives. I could be a big shot like my old man and live in a stinking dark apartment over a dry-cleaning shop, lying in bed with a bottle of muscatel while the termites ate the frilling place out from under him a two-by-four at a time and the crazy short-order cook in the next apartment chased cockroaches up the walls with a cleaver. Sure. Be a big operator like that just because some meatball drives a Cadillac up your leg trying to kill his wife and her boy friend and you don't like to send them a bill. This is Whore Harlan? The boy who can see a loose buck farther than most people can see the Washington Monument? Turn the knob, children; you must have the wrong channel.

Of course, the whole thing could still be only a pipe dream, just a bunch of coincidences strung together. The big guy who killed Purvis might be a visiting brother from some other lodge altogether; Purvis probably had more than one iron in the fire. But it looked good this way, no matter how you shook it up; there were too many interlocking pieces that matched.

Cannon was doing about sixty-five. At best, all he had was a brief glimpse of the silhouette of some big guy in his headlights and then an even briefer glimpse of somebody else apparently trying to hide from the lights by crouching down in the seat. To make up his mind that fast, provided he did crash me deliberately, he must have had a preconceived idea of who those people were. The chances were he was actually looking for them. I knew Mrs. Cannon was out there by the lake; so maybe the big guy was out there too. She had been waiting beside the swamp road for somebody in a car, because when she saw me coming she stepped out into the road for an instant, and then realized her mistake and stepped back. It was still only twilight and I didn't have my lights on, so she could see the car all right. Therefore, the car she was waiting for could have looked something like mine. She couldn't have been expecting Cannon, because his was a grey Cadillac sedan. So suppose it was a convertible with the top down. That tied in with the theory Cannon had smashed me deliberately; I was the same size as this big joker and presumably even our cars were similar.

Say they *were* both out there. To get back to town they had to come right past where we had crashed. They stopped and investigated when they saw Cannon's car. He was in it, unconscious or helpless. He'd wanted to kill them, apparently; maybe the feeling was mutual. At any rate, they'd never have a better opportunity. Nobody would ever suspect. And nobody had, except Purvis. He kept getting in their hair, sniffing around, so they stepped on him too. They'd also step on me in a minute if they suspected me, but I should have seen enough of the game by this time to know how it was played. Swing first and never turn your back on anybody.

So far, I didn't have any actual proof of this, except that I knew Mrs. Cannon had been out there at the lake and I'd been in the next room when Purvis was killed, but I didn't need too much in the way of evidence. The threat was enough if I backed it up with some real pressure, and I was beginning to have an idea about that.

I crushed out the cigarette and lay back on the pillow. It was a little while before I got to sleep because the thought of that taxi driver began to nag me again. A lot depended on how much publicity there was when Purvis's body was found. If he came forward, a little heads-up police work would put the finger on me without too much trouble. They'd know he picked me up at the bus station, and the approximate time. Check that against bus arrivals and Galveston wouldn't be too difficult to arrive at. A record of his telephone calls would show he had talked to somebody down here twice in the past two days, to somebody in this hotel. From then on a kid could do it. Of course, I hadn't killed Purvis and I was pretty sure I could tell them where to find the guy who had if they started leaning on me too hard, but it would be a damned expensive speech if I did have to tell them.

When I awoke the next morning, my throat still felt as if a horse had stepped on it. *That judo,* I thought; *they could keep it.*

Just give me good, clean, bone-crunching professional football where you could tell by looking at a guy about how hard he'd be able to hit you. I thought of Purvis before I got out of bed, but there was no particular feeling about him one way or another aside from the fact I'd just as soon forget what his head had looked like if it was all right with everybody. It was something about the combination of dark blood and grey hair. He was an odd-ball, all right. I wondered what he would have done with the money if he'd got it. Probably spent the rest of his life following a ballet troupe around like a baseball filbert following the Giants. He must have been dreaming of that one big score for years, and then when he was near enough to put out his hand and touch it he wound up looking like something somebody had stepped on.

I turned Purvis off like closing a tap and rolled out of bed. There was a lot to be done to get the show on the road, and if I didn't want *my* head pushed in, it had to be planned and executed with a hell of a lot of precision. I shaved, took a hurried shower, and went down to the coffee shop for breakfast, picking up a Houston *Post* on the way. There was nothing in it about Purvis's murder. I hadn't expected there would be, this soon. This edition probably went to press about the time he was killed. It wouldn't break before the afternoon papers at the earliest, and maybe not until tomorrow morning. Hell, it might be days before anybody found him. The longer the better, I thought; let that cabby forget the address.

I stopped at the cashier's desk on the way back up to the room and asked them to get my bill ready, saying there would be one more long-distance call they'd have to get the charges on. It was to George Grey in Fort Worth. I was lucky and caught him just as he was coming into his office in the oil-well supply outfit he and his father owned.

"Who is calling?" his secretary asked.

"John Harlan," I said.

He came on. "Hey, you big ape, why haven't you been to see us? Where are you?"

"Galveston," I said, "right at the moment."

"Well, look——" He hesitated slightly. "I mean, I read about it in the papers. It's a rotten shame. What are you planning to do, John?"

"I haven't decided yet," I said. "But that's what I called about——"

"Well, come on up and let's talk it over. I think we can use you. We need another salesman, and you worked in the fields a couple of summers, long enough to know something about the business. That is, unless you figure on trying it again next year."

"No," I said. "I'm washed up for good. That next year stuff is newspaper talk. I haven't settled on anything yet, and want to get off by myself for a couple of weeks and sort it out a little. I thought I'd go back and finish that fishing trip, provided nobody's using the cabin."

"Say, that's fine. You're as welcome as the flowers in May, boy. Nobody up there at all, and the way it looks now I won't be able to get away till duck season. Have yourself a trip, and keep what I told you in mind. You got a key to the place?"

"No," I replied. "I mailed it back to you. Or rather, one of the nurses did, while I was in the hospital."

"Sure. I remember now. Well, get a hacksaw and saw the lock off. You can buy a new one and send me the keys when you leave. No. Wait—— That'd mean I'd have to replace all the duplicates I've scattered around among my friends. Why don't I just mail you a key?"

"That's what I was going to suggest," I said. "Mail it up there to Wayles, care of General Delivery. I can pick it up when I get in town."

"I'll get it off today. Jesus, I wish I was going with you. Catch a four-pounder for me. Guess all your duffle and tackle is still up there, isn't it?"

"That's right."

"Well, I hope you have better luck this time than you did the other. That was rugged."

"It's the breaks," I said. I stared at the cigarette burning in the ash tray. "By the way, did you ever meet this Cannon? The drunk that clobbered me?"

"Yes. As a matter of fact, I did, once. Why?"

"Just wondering," I said. "I thought somebody said he had a camp out there too."

"He did. However, that wasn't where I met him. Just happened to run into him clear over in Mississippi one time, hunting quail. Struck me as something of a creep; I didn't care much for him."

"How's that?" I asked.

"A lush, for one thing. Wonder he didn't kill himself long

before he did. And he had a highly specialized sense of humour; the things he'd do for kicks. Liked to shoot birds to watch 'em blow up, or something."

"Quail?"

"Not quail. Sparrows, cardinals, anything that was handy. You ever seen a cardinal shot from twenty feet with the full-choke side of a twelve-gauge double?"

"I don't think so," I said. "But it sounds like something that would have to grow on you."

We yakked a minute or two about old times in school. I wanted to ask him if he knew anything about Mrs. Cannon, but decided against it. I was supposed to be merely going fishing; there was no use starting anyone wondering. When I had hung up I took an inventory of the money situation. I'd cashed a draft in New Orleans, and still had a little over nine hundred dollars in traveller's checks. That would have to do. I could get by with making a down payment on a car. I had sold the Buick after it was repaired following the wreck, and deposited the money along with the insurance company settlement in the bank in Oklahoma City, but it would take too long to cash another draft now. I was in a hurry. I packed the two bags and checked out and caught the next bus to Houston.

It was a little after eleven when I arrived. I left the bags in two lockers in the station and went out. White sunlight blasted into the streets and traffic fumes and the stink of diesel buses hung heavy in the air. Early editions of the afternoon papers were on the street now. I bought one and ducked into an air-conditioned coffee shop to order a hamburger and a glass of iced tea. There was no mention of Purvis. I went through the paper from front to back, hurrying up one column and down the next, scanning the leads. Somebody had been run over by a loaded ten-ton truck. A man was dead of knife wounds in a brawl out near the turning basin. The body of a young girl had been found in some weeds on a vacant lot. All of a city's twenty-four-hour output of violence had been run down and checked out and put into print, but Purvis was still waiting. I thought of him lying there in the hot living-room with his head smashed open like a dropped piggy-bank and the blood dried now and black, with all the poised and graceful ballet girls looking down at his body from the walls. I shrugged irritably and pushed the hamburger away. It was tasteless. So Purvis had leaned out too far after the brass ring and fallen off. They wouldn't get me. By the time they realized I was moving in on them they'd already be in the cage and all I had to do was drop the lid on them.

Maybe, I thought uneasily. Then I brushed it aside. There was too much to do, and I was itching to get started. Turning hurriedly to the back of the paper, I took a quick look at the used car ads. The nearest lot was only a few blocks away. I walked. The place was overflowing with cars; salesmen climbed into my arms and made little cooing sounds in my ears, but the tune changed after I'd picked out a '54 Olds and we started to make out the papers for financing. The out-of-state address was bad, and so was the fact I didn't have a job at the moment, here or anywhere else. I cursed, thinking of the delay in cashing a draft. It would take another whole day, anyway. All the bright salesmen cried a little and assured me if things were different they would like nothing better than to adopt me and let me dribble leopard-upholstered Cadillacs through my fingers all day and lie naked among Lincoln Capris all night, but you knew how those nasty bastards in the finance companies were.

I said, "Sure, sure," and on the way out I saw a 1950 Chevrolet tagged at $595. I looked at it once, kicked the right front tyre, and went on toward the sidewalk. They hauled me back, rubbed the Chevy up against me with a lingering, hot-bellied caress and said we could do business for five and a quarter. I fumbled in my pockets and dropped the folder of hundred-dollar traveller's checks on the ground, and said I guessed I'd look around. I got almost to the sidewalk again. I drove the Chevy around the block while a salesman pointed out how they'd just refurbished the frammistan and put new whirtles in the springerwarp, and I said sure, but maybe his sister was diseased. Very young, he said; first time piece, she don't catch nothing from sailors. It was a one-owner car used by an elderly clergyman just to go back and forth from the parsonage to the church on Sundays when it was raining. I said, sure, you could see that; he'd only rung up 76,000 miles on it and had the fenders ironed out so often you could read Braille through them. But, hell. It ran, and the motor sounded all right. I offered $425. They said $500. We all cried some more. I came in on the second chorus with an offer of $450, and started for the street again. We closed at $475, with a free tankful of gas and an offer to clean the windshield.

"Never mind," I said. "Just kiss me, and help me up."

I drove it around to a parking lot not too far from the bus station, and put the bags in. It was one thirty. The next stop was a pawnshop. I picked up a second-hand portable typewriter, a pair of 7-by-50 binoculars, and a Colt ·45 automatic. Then I stopped at a sporting goods store, after thinking it over, and bought a box of ammunition for the gun. I didn't like the idea, but this wasn't a child's game now. Stowing all this in the car, I looked up the biggest store in town that specialized in sound and recording equipment. I was there nearly two hours getting a thorough fill-in on tape recorders and trying out the different models. When I left I had a good one with a sensitive microphone designed for wide-angle pickup. I caught a cab and went back to the lot with it. After putting it in the trunk of the Chev I walked out to the corner again. A boy was calling the final edition of one of the afternoon papers. I bought one and sat behind the wheel as I shuffled through it. They had found Purvis. The second page story led off.

Private Investigator Slain. The body of Winton L. Purvis, 38, *private detective and former insurance investigator, was discovered early this afternoon in his apartment at* 10325 *Caroline Street. He was apparently struck on the head with terrific force by some heavy object, though no trace of the murder weapon was found at the scene. Police are as yet without clue as to the identity of the assailant, but are convinced he is a large man of great physical strength.*

There wasn't much more. Apparently it had broken just in time to get the bare essential facts in the last edition; there'd be more tomorrow. But there was enough here to start it rolling —the address and the fact they were looking for a big man. I hoped that cabby wasn't sitting behind his wheel somewhere in the city as I was, leafing through the paper.

Well, the ball had to bounce—one way or the other. But I couldn't sit here and waste time. I switched on the ignition and rolled out into the river of traffic. Mrs. Cannon, here I come.

CHAPTER FIVE

WAYLES . . .

I tried to remember it as I drove. It was a small town, a county seat, built in the old style around a square and a brick courthouse where pigeons cooed in the early mornings and made a mess of the red walls with bird-lime at all times of the day. I'd lived in several just like it when I was a kid growing up; there are a thousand of them in the south. Just driving through, you wouldn't think there'd be anybody in one of them who'd be worth

$300,000, but it would fool you. There are always a few, the second and third generations of the business families who made it in cotton and timber and sometimes in oil or banks or real estate. I shook my head impatiently, watching the headlights bore a tunnel in the darkness. That didn't matter. I knew she had it. I was trying to remember something about the town. I thought there was a hotel at one end of the square. I hoped there was, for it was important.

It was odd now, to think I had been there for nearly five weeks and was still this vague about the actual layout of the square, but I hadn't lingered after I got out of the hospital. As soon as I was able to drive I'd just got into the repaired Buick and shoved for Oklahoma City. Wayles? I've had Wayles, buster, and I give it to you. In Oklahoma City I'd had some more medics proof-read the leg for typographical errors and they said the local talent had done a good job and that it was as good as ever. It was there I'd finally signed clear with the insurance company.

There were two or three likely-looking motels with vacancy signs out on the edge of town, but I passed them up. If I had to, I could come back, but I wanted that hotel if it was where I thought it was. The highway from Houston came in the south-west corner of the square, ran along the south side, and then went on straight east. It was after ten p.m. and few cars were on the street. I passed the courthouse and slowed, and then I saw it on the east side of the square, just where I vaguely remembered it and hoped it would be. The sign said Hotel Enders.

It was near the middle of the block. I turned and went up the east side and slid into the loading zone. The entrance was through a screen door between a dress shop and a jewellery store, both closed now but throwing light out on to the walk from their display windows. I went down a narrow corridor on coco-nut matting. There was a small lobby at the end and some stairs beyond the desk. A bridge lamp was burning near the cigarette machine and to the left was a wire rack of paperback books. An airplane type fan on a standard was droning away in a corner, keeping the stale air in circulation even if it didn't cool anything. A fat woman with short grey hair and jowls like a bulldog was reading a magazine at the desk. A coloured boy about eight feet long was folded up and stacked in one of the armchairs against the other wall, asleep, with sections of arms and legs dangling out on to the floor. He wore an old maroon jacket with an R.O.T.C. type collar, and shoes like overnight bags. The woman looked up at me from her magazine with the unwinking stare of one of the more haughty types of turtles.

"Yes?" she asked.

"You got a single with bath?" I asked. "In front?"

She nodded. I signed the register. She looked around the edge of me, and snapped, "Raymond!"

Nothing happened. I put the pen back in the holder and turned just as she let him have the other barrel. "*Ray*-mond!"

He whimpered a little, and moved one of his feet, which was a neat trick in itself without a dolly. "Don't get him up," I said. "He might fall on somebody. I'll bring in the bags."

"Parking behind the hotel," she said. "Turn in at the alley two doors down." She nodded her head toward the corridor going on through to the rear of the building. "Just bring your bags in through the back."

I drove the car around and unloaded. It was very dark. Two other cars were parked in the area. I had already put the gun and the binoculars in one of the bags. Locking the typewriter in the trunk because I didn't need it tonight, I took the two bags and the recorder—which was in a case that looked like any other piece of luggage when it was closed—and walked toward the oblong of light where the rear door of the hotel had opened. Raymond shuffled out and took the bags; I held on to the recorder. He led the way through the lobby and up a flight of stairs. The room was near the end of the corridor on the second floor. He unlocked the door and we went in. He snapped on the light. It was any third-rate hotel room anywhere, iron bedstead, dingy spread, worn carpet, and a dresser covered with a pane of glass under which was the card that would tell you about the Bonton Cleaners and the Black Cat Café. The only thing I actually saw in it was the window. The blind was pulled all the way down so I couldn't see out now, but I had a hunch the location was just right. Raymond goofed around, opening the closet and then the bathroom door as if he half expected bats to fly out of them. Maybe he'd leave in the next day or two and I could get a look out that window.

"Anything else, Cap'n?" he asked.

"No," I said. I handed him a dollar. "Go buy your feet a bowl of chili."

He drifted out and closed the door. I threw the bolt, snapped off the light, and stepped quickly across to the window. Raising the blind, I looked out. It was good. It was like a sniper's nest, covering a pass. The whole square was spread out in front of and below me. I could see everything except the area directly beyond the courthouse and the section of the sidewalk just under me. If he lived in Wayles, I'd see him. Even if he worked in one of the outlying side streets and lived in the edge of town he'd come around the square sooner or later because all the principal business section was here.

People were coming out of a movie on the north side. Some more were stooging around the front of a drug-store on the corner beyond it. A few went past along the sidewalks on the south side, mostly couples with the women looking in the lighted store windows. I stepped back and unsnapped one of the bags, groping in it for the binoculars. Sliding them out of the case, I hunkered down by the window and adjusted the focus. Their faces leaped up at me. Pretty girls, teenagers, housewives, men of all sizes and ages. I saw no one who looked anything like Mrs. Cannon, but there were several men well over six feet. It wasn't going to be easy. The population of the town would probably be between six and eight thousand, and this was Texas, where they grow tall. There'd be a lot of men the size of the one I was looking for. I could see a little of what Purvis had been up against and why that big goon had been able to move in on him like that. He couldn't have remembered the faces and descriptions of *all* the oversized men in a town this size.

I swept the glasses on around the square. On the west side, partly cut off by the dark bulk of the courthouse, a sign caught my eye—NNON MOTORS. That would be it. I knew that—in addition to other things—he had owned an automobile agency. Most of the showroom was in view behind its plate glass window. I readjusted the focus slightly and it all leaped into hard, sharp detail. I could see the white sidewalls of the tyres on the display models, the door opening off the showroom floor which presumably led into an office, and the counter farther to the right where the parts department was. I could even see some gaskets hanging on hooks behind the counter. This was luck. There was always a good chance he was somebody who worked there, and if he were he had as much privacy now as a goldfish.

There was no use looking any more tonight. I pulled the blind down and switched on the light. It was fine so far. The success of the whole thing depended on my finding him before he knew

I was here looking for him, and I was in a good spot to do it. *Success, hell,* I thought, lighting a cigarette. It was more than that If I didn't find out who he was before he found out who I was, I'd wind up where Purvis had. I had to spot him fast, or he'd be stalking me from behind while I was still looking.

I put the glasses back in their case and opened the recorder. I hadn't been able to try it out thoroughly and test it under operating conditions in the store because naturally I couldn't explain what I wanted to do with it. Finding a wall outlet behind the writing desk, I plugged it in, turned it on, and cranked up the gain. There was a long cord on the microphone. Pulling back the sheet and bedspread, I shoved the mike under them and then threw my jacket over it, covering it completely. It wouldn't have to be that muffled under actual operating conditions, but the room would probably be larger. Going into the bathroom, I turned on one of the taps in the wash basin. I turned it off. I whistled a few bars of some popular tune, very softly. Coming back into the room, I picked up the telephone.

When the lady bulldog at the desk answered, I said, "I'd like to leave a call for six o'clock."

"Six o'clock. Thank you," she said.

"Thank *you,*" I said.

I took the change out of my pocket and placed it on the glass top of the dresser. Through the open window floated the sounds on the street below. A car went past, its tyres squealing a little as it made the turn at the corner. A horn beeped, and a kid's voice said, "Hi, beautiful."

That was enough, I thought. I wondered how much of it I'd got. Re-rolling the tape, I switched in on play-back and cut the gain way down. Water ran out of the tap and I could even hear my shoes squeaking on the linoleum in the bathroom. I whistled. The telephone knocked against its cradle. It all came through. I let it run out to the end. "Hi, beautiful," the speaker said softly, just above the level of the tube hiss and background noise. Perfect, I thought. I coiled the power cord and mike cable and put them back in the case and locked it.

I undressed and turned out the light. It was very hot and the sheet stuck to me with sweat. I got up and turned on the overhead fan, which helped a little. Fifty thousand. Seventy-five. A hundred thousand. After taxes, I thought, grinning coldly. The gasoline tax, driving up here.

But the figures were too big to have any actual meaning. You couldn't imagine that much. Sure, over a period of five years, or ten, working for it. But not in an afternoon. Not by just walking in and telling her, "I'll take a hundred grand off the top. Slip it in my hip pocket, honey." It was a dream. It was too simple and easy to be real.

The hell it was. She had it, didn't she? She had it and plenty more, and where was the percentage in being rich in Death Row? She'd be able to see that, without any trouble. There was plenty for both of us. Hell, at a hundred thousand I was the biggest bargain since free lunch and the nickel beer.

I awoke before six and almost by the time my eyes were open excitement began to take hold of me. This was the day, I could feel it. I rolled out of bed and stepped to the window. Pulling the blind back a little, I peered out. The square lay peaceful and almost deserted in the growing light. There was no breeze, but the air was faintly cool and there was a fresh, early-morning-in-summer look about the scene that reminded me of when I was a boy in other towns like this, of riding my bike out in the dawn to go fishing for crappies and goggle-eyes in some creek in the country where everything would still be wet with the dew. *Jesus, you're a lyrical bastard,* I thought. Go ahead and remember the rest of it, like how it was stepping over the old man where he'd passed out in his own vomit in the middle of the bedroom floor. And don't forget that old sow he used to bring home with him when he was crocked to the eyeballs. There was a dewy sight in the dawn.

On the north side of the square, a few doors this side of the movie house, an all-night café was open. The only cars in evidence in the whole square were parked in front of it. While I was watching, two men wearing hard hats and carrying lunch boxes came out, got in one of the cars, and drove off. Pipeline workers, probably. *Get in gear,* I thought. If I wanted any coffee or breakfast, I'd better get it now. I took a quick shower. While I was rubbing down with the towel, the telephone rang. It was the six-o'clock call, a man's voice. I dressed and went downstairs. The grey-haired woman and Raymond were gone. The man behind the desk was pleasant looking and middle-aged, with brown eyes and steel-rimmed glasses. I dropped the key on the desk.

"Good morning," he said. "Are you staying over?"

"I may," I said. "I'm headed for a fishing trip out at Swanson

Lake, but I might wait over and go tomorrow. Don't feel too well, for some reason. Something I ate late night, I guess."

"Stomach cramps?" he asked sympathetically.

I shook my head. "Just a little upset. Think I'll try some coffee and orange juice, and maybe a couple of aspirin, and see what happens."

I cut across the corner of the square. There were five or six people in the restaurant, mostly hard hats and a truck driver or two. A blonde with a Georgian accent brought me some toast and a cup of coffee. I bought two packs of cigarettes and came back to the hotel. The square was still quiet, except for the pigeons flapping around under the eaves of the courthouse.

"Any better?" the brown-eyed man asked.

"Not much," I replied. I grabbed a couple of the paper-backed books off the stand and dropped fifty cents on the desk as I picked up the key. "Think I'll stay in the sack for a while. Tell the maid just to pass up my room."

"Sure thing," he said. Then he added, "We can get you a doctor, if you like."

"It's not that bad," I said. "Thanks just the same." I went up to the room. Stripping down to my shorts because it was going to be hot, I slid the binoculars out of their case and put them on the carpet under the window. I placed an ash tray beside them, and a pack of cigarettes and some matches. I sat down on the floor and raised the blind about three inches. By putting my face up close I could see nearly all the square. There was practically no chance anybody down there would notice me; this side of the building would be in shadow until noon. Whoever looked up at the second floor anyway?

Hardly anything was moving yet. A bakery truck stopped before the café on the north side and a man went in carrying a tray of rolls. About halfway down the block on the south side a man on a stepladder was cleaning the windows of the J. C. Penney Store. Yellow sunlight hit the gables of the courthouse, inched down the slopes of the red tile roof, and began to shatter into hot sprays of colour against the third floor windows. The cool freshness of early morning was wilting a little. It was going to be a scorcher. I got up and turned on the fan, and brought a towel from the bathroom to mop the sweat from my face.

I lit a cigarette, smoked it out to the end, and fired up another. Time went on. Sunlight was hitting the big plate glass window of the Cannon Motors showroom on the west side of the square now. A few cars were beginning to slide into the rows of angle parking spaces. I studied the drivers carefully as they got out and fished in their pockets for nickels for the meters, and if they were big men I put the glasses on them. None of them resembled him at all. If they were tall enough they were thin, or if heavily built they were shorter or had sandy hair or long hair or damned little hair of any kind.

I was growing uncomfortable. I shifted around, trying to stretch my legs. The gimp one ached a little. I looked at the scar tissue around the knee and cursed under my breath. The meat-headed, punch-drunk bastard—— Who? Cannon? Mrs. Cannon? Or this big goon I thought I was looking for? I must have gravel in my head. What did I think I was proving with this Grade-B movie routine? Just before some big guy had killed Purvis I'd strung together a chain of improbable coincidences and come up with a pearl necklace. What the hell—the chances were he'd never heard of Mrs. Cannon. He might be from Kokomo, or Tucson, Arizona. He could be anybody. Maybe people were standing in line to kill Purvis. Maybe he'd won a contest, or something, to get first crack at him. Send in six new subscriptions and kill Purvis at our expense.

I grabbed suddenly for the glasses and trained them on the doorway of the Cannon Motors showroom. A girl had stopped there, her hand on the knob. It wasn't Mrs. Cannon, however. This was a blonde. She was wearing a blue dress and white shoes, carrying a white handbag with long straps. She seemed to be waiting for somebody to open the door for her. I swung the glasses the way she was looking and sucked in my breath sharply, but then let it ease out again in disappointment. The man coming along the walk was the right size, but his hair was longer and it was the colour of cotton. He unlocked the door and they went in. I watched her trip across the tile floor of the showroom and go into the office. She had nice legs.

Well, there'd be others working in the place. I turned the glasses on it every few minutes, in the meantime keeping a sharp lookout over the nearer end of the square. Most of the stores were open now. More people were on the walks, and it was becoming more difficult to look them all over as they moved along.

My sweeping gaze stopped abruptly, and I came to sharp attention. What I had seen was a Chevrolet convertible coming along the street on the south side of the square. There was a man in it, a man who had wide shoulders and was bareheaded. His hair was dark, or so it seemed in the brief instant he was in view. I snatched at the glasses, but in the time I was putting them up to my eyes he swung into an alley and disappeared. I watched the mouth of the alley, very alert now. No one came out. He could have been the one, I thought. The convertible was significant. I waited while minutes dragged by, but there was no sign of him.

Maybe there was parking back there for employees of the stores along that side of the square. I studied the area. The alley was in the middle of the block, with the J. C. Penney store on one side of it and a shoe repair shop on the other. Adjoining the Penney store on the east, toward me, was a barber's shop and then a small jewellery store. On the west side of the alley, beyond the shoe place, was a sporting goods store and next to that a dry-cleaner's. I went up the line, glancing at the doorways. They were all open now except the dry-cleaning place and the sporting goods store. I couldn't see anybody inside, however, except some girls in Penney's. I swung back, watching the sidewalk. Then I stopped suddenly. The door of the sporting goods store was open now. Somebody must have come in from the rear. I grabbed the glasses and focused on it.

There was no one visible, but I could see for several feet back inside the doorway with every detail hard and clear. There was a showcase on the right and I could even make out the rows of bass bugs on a glass shelf inside. The glasses shook a little. I steadied them on the window sill and looked again. Behind the showcase were some shelves of stock, among which I could make out boxes that probably contained reels and some flatter ones which looked like the type flylines came in. Nobody came in sight.

I muttered impatiently and looked away. I couldn't waste all day on a wild guess; I had the rest of the square to cover. I gave it a good going-over and saw no likely-looking prospects. In a moment I was back staring at the front of the sporting goods store again. Something on the glass showcase caught my eye. It was rounded and black, and partly cut off by the door frame. I looked at it again and grunted softly to myself. It was the end of a telephone handset.

Well, I could eliminate this bird and quit worrying about him. Taking the glasses down, I looked at the sign above the door. TALLANT'S, it said. I stood up and reached for the telephone book on the little stand in the corner. Looking up the number, I lifted the telephone down and got into position again with the glasses propped across the window sill. The phone cord was just long enough to reach.

"Would you get me 2279?" I said, when the man at the desk answered.

"Just a minute, please."

I heard him dialling, and then the phone ringing at the other end. I waited, keeping the glasses zeroed in on the area above the showcase. He came into view and lifted the handset. He was a tall man with tremendous shoulders, and he had short-cropped dark hair. I exhaled softly.

"Hello. Tallant's Sporting Goods," he said.

It was an odd sensation, watching his lips move at the same time I was listening to his voice on the receiver.

"Hope you weren't busy," I said. "I just wondered if you had any reports on how the bass are hitting out at Swanson Lake."

"Been pretty good the last few days, I hear," he replied. "But mostly on live bait. Who's calling?"

"You wouldn't know me," I said. "I just came up from Beaumont. A friend of mine down there said I could probably get a report on the lake at your place. George Tallant, I think he said. That's you, isn't it?"

"*Dan* Tallant," he corrected.

"Oh sure. That's right. So it's been pretty good, huh?" I was staring intently, very excited now. He was the one, all right. I was almost positive of it, in spite of the fact he was leaning over the showcase, fore-shortened, as he talked, and it was hard to fit him into the pose as I'd seen him before, erect and facing the other way.

He said something else, just as the idea hit me. "By the way," I broke in, "you don't happen to have a GBF torpedo-head fly-line, do you? For a six-ounce rod——"

"No-o. I don't think so," he replied. "I don't carry much of a selection, because nearly everybody around here uses spinning gear. But just a minute; I'll look——"

I saw him straighten and turn, looking at that section of stock right behind the phone where I thought I had seen the flyline boxes. I got him dead to rights in the glasses, the same picture exactly as before, the height and the tremendous spread of shoulders, the small ears in close to the head, the short, crisp black hair, and that impression he was young and as strong as a fighting bull. There was no doubt of it at all. I was talking to the man who had killed Purvis.

CHAPTER SIX

WHEN he had hung up he moved back to the rear of the store again and I couldn't see him any more. I lowered the glasses, dropped the phone back on its cradle, and sat for a moment staring at it. Right into the end zone on the first play; this was better than I'd even dared hope for. I'd proved I was right, located him, and identified him—all in the first two or three hours. Improbable, was it? A dream? Hell, it was turning into reality faster than I could keep up with it.

All right, all right, I warned myself, *don't dislocate your shoulder patting yourself on the back.* There was plenty to do yet, and the tricky and dangerous part was just beginning. Mrs. Cannon was next. I stood up and went into the bathroom to shave. Here I come, you brown-eyed Fort Knox.

Nine-thirty was a little early to go calling on a woman, especially unannounced, but that's the way it had to be. If I waited until later she might not be home, and if I phoned first I never would see her. I was the last person in the world she wanted to meet face to face. I grinned at my reflection in the mirror, a little coldly. That was all right. So maybe she wouldn't like me. I was going to be a hell of a lot more unpopular with her in about twenty-four hours if things went off as scheduled.

I dressed in a fresh pair of grey slacks and a subdued sports shirt, combed my hair, and took a last gander at myself in the mirror. I'd do. I looked as scrubbed and wholesome as a freshly-laundered moose, and about half as subtle. She'd never suspect me of anything.

I looked up her address in the telephone book. Three-twenty-four Cherrywood Drive, it said. Putting the binoculars in the bag with the gun, I locked it, and then checked the recorder to be sure its case was locked too. I went downstairs, did the how-you-feeling-now-much-better-thanks routine with the solicitous type at the desk, and on out the rear door to the car. Coming out of the alley, I turned north, avoiding the square. At the first filling station I pulled in and gassed up. The attendant told me how to find Cherrywood Drive.

It was south-west of the square, near the crest of a sloping hill overlooking the town. Near the bottom the bungalows had a housing-development look about them, but farther up they were bigger, on large, landscaped lots. Cherrywood Drive was only four blocks long and there were just three houses in the last block, two of them on the left, or downhill side. I slowed looking at the numbers. The Cannon place would be the second one on the left, the last house on the street. It was near the corner where Cherrywood terminated in an intersecting street going downhill. Beyond the intersecting street was a wooded area, still undeveloped. I liked the whole layout but I didn't want to take too much time now in looking it over. If I goofed around out here until she got a look at me out the window she probably wouldn't be "in" when I rang the buzzer.

The other two houses were white Colonial types with columns and wide lawns and driveways. Directly across from the Cannon house was a vacant lot, grown up with pines, however, rather than weeds. I pulled the old Chevy to the kerb on that side and walked across the street. The Cannon house was newer, a long, low ranch style built of light-coloured brick with a sweeping, low-angled white roof covered with broken quartz. It looked very western and a little out of place among all these pines. It sat back from the street in a large expanse of well-tended lawn, but there was no circular drive. A flagstone walk bordered with some kind of low shrubs led to the front door, and beyond it a wide concrete driveway went straight back to the two-car garage adjoining the house on the far end. Both doors of the garage were closed. That should mean she was home.

It was hot now and I could feel perspiration beginning to break out on my face. I went quickly up the walk. A coloured man in a straw hat was digging in the flower bed under the big picture window in front. His shirt was plastered to his back with sweat. Curtains were drawn across the window and I couldn't see in. *Remember,* I told myself, *you've never seen her before in your life. Sell her on it.*

I rang the bell. The gardener straightened and brushed his wet face with a hand, looking up at me. "You know if Mrs. Cannon's home?" I asked.

"Yassuh, I think so," he said. He went back to his work.

I'd just started to reach for the bell again when the door opened. A young coloured girl looked out at me indifferently. She was chewing gum and held a broom in her left hand.

"Is Mrs. Cannon in?" I asked.

"I'll find out," she said. "Who I say it is?"

"Mr. Warren," I said, mumbling a little.

"Just a minute."

She disappeared, leaving the door ajar. It opened into a small entry hall. There was a door at the left of that, going into the living-room apparently, but I couldn't see much of it. I waited. Maybe I shouldn't have said Warren, I thought. It might still sound too much like Harlan. O'Toole or Schutzbank or something would have done better. But still it had to be within shooting distance; I didn't want her to get the idea I was aware I might have to pitch her a phoney name to get in. That would ruin it all. *Oh, hell,* I thought; *it's been five months and she doesn't know I'm within two thousand miles.*

The girl came back. Mrs. Cannon was in. I could wait in the parlour. I followed her in through the entry hall and stood in the living-room. "She'll be heah in a minute," she said, and went on out through a door at the right rear, which seemed to lead into the dining-room. As soon as she was gone, I looked swiftly around, trying to get as good a picture of the layout as I could before Mrs. Cannon got here.

Apparently there was no dog. That had been worrying me, but I didn't see any signs of one. Certainly there wasn't one in the house, or he'd have been around to investigate me by this time, and I couldn't see any kennel in the patio behind the house. There was another plate glass window at the rear of the living-room, fitted with a gauzy curtain which was closed now but was fairly transparent with the bright sunlight behind it. The patio was enclosed with a white-painted cinder block wall about four feet high. Below it down the hillside was another wooded vacant lot. Approaching the house from the rear would be a cinch. Getting in, however, was going to be another matter.

I'd noticed something when I first stepped into the entry hall, but it hadn't actually registered until now. The house was air-conditioned. I could feel the coolness penetrating my sweaty shirt. It was fine after the sticky heat outside, but there was another angle to it I didn't like at all. The doors and windows would be tightly closed all the time it was turned on, so it wasn't going to be merely a matter of unlatching a screen. It wasn't good. I glanced swiftly around, studying the room.

It was a long one. At the far end was a raised fireplace with a copper hood. To the left of it was an open doorway which apparently led into a study or library because I could see rows of books along the wall and the front end of a mounted sailfish. At the right was the hallway which went on through to the rest of the house. Some chairs and a small sectional sofa were scattered about that end, before the fireplace, but the focal point of the room was nearer the centre where a long sofa was backed up against the curtains of the front window. A coffee table and three large chairs faced it in a rough semicircle, and it was probable this was the part of the room generally used when only a few people were present because it faced the large rear window overlooking the patio. It looked good to me. At each end of the sofa there was a table with a big, red-shaded lamp on it. The lamp cords disappeared behind the sofa. I made a mental note I'd probably need a three-way outlet plug. There was a whispering sound like that of slippers on carpet. I turned just as Mrs. Cannon came into the room from the hallway.

When she saw me, she stopped. Her eyes widened a little, and I knew she recognized me. I didn't care now, because I was in, and I was too busy anyway trying to keep from staring at her to worry about it.

Striking, Purvis had said. She was, but he hadn't scratched the surface.

The other time had been just a flashing glimpse at dusk, and that photograph hadn't amounted to much more than an inventory. She was wearing bullfighter's pants and a white shirt with the sleeves rolled up; the blue-black hair was cut rather short and it swirled carelessly about a slender oval face the colour of honey or good pale vermouth. She was a construction job from the ground up without being overdone about it anywhere —just medium height and rather slim with only a touch of that overblown calendar-girl effect above the sucked-in waist— but if you had to look twice to be sure that wasn't Manolete inside those pants you were in bad shape and ought to see an optometrist or psychiatrist before you got any worse. The pants themselves were black and very smooth, and what they did to her thighs—or vice-versa—should happen more often. Below them her legs were bare and honey-coloured and she wore bullfighter's slippers. *Break it up,* I thought; *in another two seconds you won't know whether to say hello or charge.*

It was her eyes, however, that could throw the match in the gasoline. They were large and very lovely, fringed with long dark lashes, and they were brown—not soft or fawn-like, but self-possessed and cool with a hint of the devil in them, a devil not too well tied up and only half asleep. You had an impression that if she ever really turned them on you with that sidelong come-hither out of the corners and from under the lashes she could roll your shirt up your back like a window-blind. Mrs. Cannon was a large order of girl; she may have killed her husband, but I was willing to bet he'd never been bored when he was alive.

She recognized me; she was off guard for just an instant and I saw the sudden wariness in her eyes. Then she recovered and murmured politely, "Good morning, Mr.—ah——"

"Harlan," I said. "John Harlan."

"Oh," she said. "I thought Geraldine said a Mr. Warren. I couldn't imagine—— Won't you sit down, Mr. Harlan?"

She flowed forward like warm honey poured out of a jug and took one of the big chairs facing the sofa. I remained standing until she was seated and then sat down on the sofa. She leaned forward to take a cigarette from the box on the coffee table. I sprang up again to light it for her. She looked up at me over the flame of the match, smiling a little, and said, "Thank you."

I lit one for myself and sat down again. "I want to apologize for coming so early in the morning," I said, "but I'm on my way out to the lake to go fishing and didn't want to miss you."

"That's quite all right," she replied smoothly. "I've been up for hours."

I had to hand it to her; she was as cool as they come. I knew she was raging inside at that maid for not getting my name straight and at the same time she was probably going crazy trying to figure out—now that I had got in—whether I recognized her as the woman I'd seen out there at the lake, but none of it showed on her face.

"You know, I expected somebody much older," I said. "I don't know where I got the impression, but I thought you'd be thirty or thirty-five." It was an old gag, of course, and she'd recognize it as such, but still it was the truth in a way. Purvis'd said she was thirty, but she didn't look it.

She gave me a faint smile and nodded. "You're very flattering, Mr. Harlan," she murmured. "And so early in the morning, too."

I wasn't sure, but I thought I could see that amused devil looking out of her eyes for just a second. It was beginning to appear to her that I didn't know I'd ever seen her before, and the tension was easing. Two-hundred-and-thirty pounds of ham-handed athlete trying to be a smoothie probably tickled her, too. She'd heard all the compliments, by experts; and with those eyes she'd probably been using men for throw-rugs since she was three. Well, that was all right. I'd be something new for her; I'd be the first one that ever cost her a hundred thousand dollars. She'd probably sleep with a lock of my hair under her pillow.

I pitched my voice down a little and looked at my hands. "I—uh——" I said. Then I glanced up at her, ill at ease and awkward, but sincere as hell. "There isn't anything, really, that I can say, is there?" I asked.

"I don't think there's anything that *has* to be said," she replied quietly. "It wasn't your fault."

"Well, it isn't a question of blame," I said haltingly. "It's just that—well, there *was* a wreck, and I was involved in it. I wanted to come and see you after I got out of the hospital, but didn't know what there was I could say if I did come. I knew how badly you were torn up about it, too, and realized you didn't want to see me and be reminded of it——"

That ought to get her off the hook, I thought, *so she could relax.* I was just a big simple muscle-head who didn't have the faintest idea why she'd avoided me. There was nothing for her to be afraid of any more. All I had to do now was ease her mind as to why I'd come back here, and I'd be in.

It was as if we were working off the same script. "It's quite all right," she said. "I'm glad you came. And I'm very sorry I didn't come to see you in the hospital, but it's nice to know that you understood. However, I'll admit I was a little surprised at seeing you now. I didn't know you were back in this part of the country."

"I came back to finish that fishing trip," I explained. "Going to work on a new job in September. I won't get a vacation for a year, so I thought I'd better do my fishing now while I could."

The big eyes became very grave and sympathetic. This baby was good. "I was so very sorry to read that you had been—I mean, that you weren't going to play any more. Do you think the accident had anything to do with it?"

I shrugged. "No way to tell, actually. It was just one of those things."

She ran the rheostats up a little and brushed my face with a lingering glance that would melt butter at fifteen feet. "I hated to hear it," she said simply.

Not half as much as you're going to hate it this time tomorrow, baby, I thought. I took my eyes away from her face. Looking at her was too damned distracting, and I still had plenty to do. Part of what I'd come for had been accomplished, but the big item still remained. How was I going to get in? The front door was out of the question; that was probably locked all the time. How about windows? They'd all be closed because of the air-conditioning. But maybe they wouldn't be latched. There weren't any windows in the living-room, however, except the big plate glass ones, and of course they didn't open at all. I couldn't think of any excuse to get into another part of the house to look for some. Maybe I'd been too optimistic.

Then I saw two windows, and knew I was worse off than ever. Looking out through that filmy curtain, I could see a little of the two wings of the house that formed the sides of the U plan. On both sides there were windows, smaller ones, looking out over the patio. They were the casement type. I'd never tried it, but I knew they couldn't be opened from outside except by stripping and wrecking the gear and crank mechanism that operated them. It was a worm type gear, which can be driven from only one end. They'd all be the same. Windows were out; it had to be a door.

Suddenly I was conscious she was saying something. "Oh?" I asked, "I beg your pardon?"

She smiled. "Would you like some coffee?"

"Sure," I said. "Uh—thanks."

"Geraldine!" she called.

There was no answer. She looked at me and lifted her shoulders with a graceful shrugging motion, spreading her hands. "Would you excuse me for a moment?"

"Surely," I said. I stood up. She went out toward the dining-room I watched the rear of those bullfighter pants out of sight, and then turned, and while I was still turning and saying, "*Holy* hell!" very softly under my breath I saw the answer to the thing I was looking for. It was a glass door opening on to the patio. I'd been looking at it all the time but hadn't noticed it because it was behind that semi-transparent curtain. It was just to the left of the end of the big picture window and I'd thought it was a part of it. The curtain had been made wide enough to cover the door in addition to the window when it was closed, apparently so as to give an unbroken line clear across that side of the room.

I could hear her talking to Esmeralda or whatever her name was out in the kitchen. I stepped swiftly across to the door and pulled back the end of the curtain. Opening it, I tried the knob from the outside. It didn't turn; the night latch was on. Looking quickly around to be sure I was still alone, I reversed the push-button plungers in the edge of the door to unlatch it, closed it softly, and let the curtain fall back in position. The door apparently wasn't used much, so the chances were she didn't bother to check it every night.

I walked back and sat down. In a moment she came in from the dining-room with two cups of coffee and some cream and sugar on a tray. I did some more of the earnest young man about how sorry I was for the accident, even if it wasn't my fault, and while I talked I tried to keep my eyes off her long enough to get the exact layout of that patio. She regretted some more that I was washed up in football. I shoved the silken weight of her off the edge of my mind and told her how brave she was. She told me I was nice and that it was considerate of me to call this way, and I knew she was just waiting for me to get the hell out of here so she could call Tallant. They were going to have one hot conference about this, but I thought I had her fooled. I was just a goof who'd come back to go fishing. I wondered if the maid slept in, and decided she probably didn't. They'd had to stay under cover all this time, so Tallant was probably coming here late at night. They were too cagey to be seen together for probably another six months, even with Purvis out of the way. So that's the way it was. She'd be waiting for him—waiting—— *Damn it,* I thought. *Cut it out and attend to business. Get that look off your pan; don't think she won't recognize it—she's been seeing it since she was twelve. Be sorry about something.*

About what?

Hell, anything.

"Are you going to be here very long, Mr. Harlan?" she asked.

"Two weeks," I replied. "Maybe a little less."

"And you're out at that same cabin where you were before?"

"I will be," I said. "Right now I'm at the Enders Hotel. The friend of mine that owns the shack is mailing me a key. It'll probably be here today."

"Well, I do hope I'll see you again while you're here," she said.

I stood up on cue. "It's been nice meeting you," I said earnestly. "I probably won't come to town much, but if you're out that way drop in and go fishing with me. Heh, heh."

She smiled, the way you would at a meat-head who wasn't too bright, and came to the door with me. She held out her hand very graciously. I took it. The brown eyes looked up at me from about the level of my shoulder. *Brother!* I thought. I simpered like a clown and said good-bye three times, standing on one foot and then the other, gave her another poor-but-honest pitch about how nice it was of her to let me call, and finally backed out the door like a high school kid escaping from the stage after winning a scholarship in the essay contest. She'd call Tallant all right the minute the door was closed, but they'd just have a good laugh. I was utterly harmless.

I drove on around the corner and down the hill, casing the terrain, and went back to the hotel. I parked the car behind it and went shopping. I bought a small pencil flash-light in a drugstore, and in Woolworth's I picked up a three-way outlet plug for a wall receptacle, some typewriter paper, a pad of yellow second sheets, and a few sheets of carbon paper. What else? I already had the cardboard box. Oh, yes. Wrapping paper, twine, and some address stickers.

I walked back to the hotel, avoiding the south side of the square and keeping a lookout for Tallant. I didn't see him anywhere.

CHAPTER SEVEN

It was almost noon now; blazing sunlight fell straight into the square, and it was very hot inside the room. I put down all the stuff I'd bought, turned on the fan, and lit a cigarette. The minute I stopped moving and planning I started thinking about her again. I could see the sleeping devil inside those cool brown eyes and that slender figure packed into those bullfighter pants and the way she moved. I became uncomfortable, and cursed her, trying to drive her out of my mind. The hell with Mrs. Cannon. Stick to business. There'd be plenty of that later. With a hundred thousand dollars I'd be using types like Mrs. Cannon to strike matches on.

I pushed her off me and got back on the track. Now. The typewriter was down in the car, the recorder was up here, and for the next two moves I had to switch them. But I didn't want to go lugging stuff back and forth past that desk down there like an ant at a picnic; there was no use starting people wondering what I was doing. I was supposed to be on my way to a fishing camp. Then why not go on out there now? But maybe the key hadn't arrived. Everything had broken so smoothly and so fast I was way ahead of schedule. Still, it could be. If George had mailed it yesterday——

Well, hell, one way of finding out would be to go around there and ask. I went down in the street again and one of the locals told me how to find the post-office. It was on a side street north of the square.

"Harlan?" The man at the General Delivery window looked in his pigeonholes and shook his head at me. "Nothing today."

"Any more mail coming in from the west in the next few hours?" I asked. "From Fort Worth?"

"Putting up some now," he said. "Try in half an hour."

I went over to the coffee shop that's across the street from every Federal office building in the country and ordered a coke. There was a wire rack near the entrance with a stack of Houston *Posts* on it. I grabbed one off and shuffled through it while I drank the coke. Purvis was there, near the bottom of the second page, but it was about the same story as last night with no new developments. Then I remembered this was the out-of-town edition and probably went to press about the time I left Houston last evening. It was still hard to realize I'd accomplished so much in such a short time. God, this time tomorrow—— Easy, pal, easy. It's a long time till tomorrow, and a thousand things could happen.

A whistle blew somewhere and it was twelve o'clock. The coffee shop began to fill up with government stenographer types, Honey Chile division, wearing cotton prints and ordering lettuce and tomato sandwiches. I ordered a sandwich myself but got to thinking of Mrs. Cannon and choked on it. I paid the bill, went back across the street, and stooged around the post-office for another ten minutes, looking at the mug-shots of the wanted men stuck up on the wall next to last year's duck hunting regulations. Then suddenly while I was staring at them and thinking of what some psychology prof had told a class of us in college about there being no such thing as a criminal type of face, a little chill ran up my back. I was breaking the law, and they could blow the whistle on *me*. But, hell, who'd tell them? Mrs. Cannon? She'd go to the chair just to get me sent up for a couple of years? That was a yak. But still——

I shrugged it off impatiently. What the hell, it wouldn't be the Federals, anyway. It was nothing to them. Then I stopped suddenly. Wasn't it? The way I had it planned I had to send something through the mail, didn't I? The fact I was sending it in the other direction and to nobody in particular didn't make any difference; I was still using Uncle Sugar's mails for something illegal, and there was hardly anything that'd cause him any quicker to take a good, long look down your throat. No, I'd have to fake that part. Uncle I'd just as soon leave alone.

Well, that could be done easily enough, I thought. All I had to do was mail something else, something legitimate that looked like the same package. No sweat there.

I went back to the General Delivery window again. This time the key was there. It was stuck to a piece of cardboard with Scotch tape and mailed in a brown Manila envelope. On the way back to the hotel I went past a hardware store that had a display of sporting goods in the window. One of the items was a big card full of cork-bodied bass bugs, the kind you use with a flyrod. I went in and bought six of them. George would appreciate them, and I had to mail something to somebody.

I packed everything, checked out of the hotel, and loaded the car. On the way out of town I stopped at a small grocery store and bought some eggs, bacon, bread, and coffee. The road going out toward the lake ran south from the square, a little-travelled secondary road that connected with an east-west highway about thirty miles beyond at a town named Breward. Some people contended it was a short cut in coming up from Houston, or had been until they'd widened and speeded-up the other highway, and that Cannon had been coming from Houston when he'd hit me. He'd been down there on a business trip. Purvis, apparently, had found out he had come into town on the main highway and then gone out to the lake. How, I didn't know, but it didn't matter now because I was using a different approach to the matter of proving the whole thing.

It was a narrow blacktop highway not too well kept up, winding over rolling, red clay hills with rural mail-boxes here and there and ramshackle farmhouses sitting back from the road behind them. The road shimmered with heat and the fields looked withered and brown as if it hadn't rained for a long time. Eight miles out I came down into the river bottom where he had wrecked me. The road went straight across on a long fill about six feet high. I crossed the bridge over the river first, steel girders with wooden planking that rattled under the tyres. About two hundred yards beyond it was the concrete culvert where he had crashed. There were no other cars in sight. I slowed, looking at it.

They had repaired the place where he'd knocked a chunk off the wing of the culvert, and the weeds and shredded bushes were beginning to grow back again. I looked ahead to where I had spun in myself. The scars were still visible on the side of the fill where the wrecker had dragged the Buick back on to the road. It wasn't as far from Cannon's car as I had thought. I'd said a hundred yards, but I could see now it was considerably less, not much more than a good booming punt. Call it sixty. Mrs. Cannon and Tallant were bound to have seen it; it hadn't gone any further off the road than Cannon's had. So they must have come back to have a look at me and be sure I was unconscious or dead before they slugged him. Maybe they'd even checked again, before they shoved off, to make certain I was still out. A little chill chased itself up my back. Suppose I'd come around about that time and said something to them, or groaned. I'd have probably got the same treatment. These two characters played a rough brand of ball, and they made up their own rules as they went along. I thought of what I had to do tonight and tomorrow morning. For a little while it was going to be like juggling dynamite caps, and if I didn't have control of the situation every second it could blow up right in my face.

I drove on. The road in to the lake turned off to the right about two miles ahead. An arrow-shaped sign that read *Pete's Live Bait Skiffs,* had fallen down and was propped against a stump in some dead grass. The road itself was just a pair of ruts wandering over a sand-hill through some cut-over pine. A mile or so ahead there were some fields and an abandoned farmhouse, and then it dropped back into the river bottom again. The air was a little cooler under the big timber, but the sloughs were mostly dried up now in late summer and the mud had dried and cracked in geometric patterns. In about fifteen minutes I came to a fork in the road with Pete's sign pointing to the left. I'd never been down there, and presumably the Cannon camp was in that direction. The other fork was just a dim trace. It went nowhere except to George's camp, around the upper end of another narrow arm of the lake.

In another few minutes I came abruptly into the clearing. The grey, weather-beaten little two-room shack with its shake roof stood under a couple of big oaks near the water. Beyond it I could see the inlet extending straight ahead, the water flat and glaring in the sun like a sheet of metal between the dark walls of timber. I stopped the car in the shade before the front porch and got out. It was intensely silent; there was a feeling of isolation about the place as if it were a thousand miles to the nearest road instead of only six.

I unlocked the door and went in. Everything was just as I had left it. A deputy-sheriff had come out and locked it after the wreck. The front room held a cook-stove and a home-made pine table covered with oilcloth. Cooking utensils hung from nails in the wall behind the stove and there were some shelves of staple groceries. I unlatched and opened the small windows at each end of the room and went into the back one. It was a little larger and held two single beds and an army cot. Some more cots were folded and stacked in a corner and my two flyrods in their aluminium cases lay on one of the beds. Hunting and fishing clothes hung on nails all around the room. The trapped, dead air was stiflingly hot. I opened the windows, feeling my shirt sticking to me with sweat.

I looked at my watch. It was a little after two. Leaving the recorder in the car, I brought in the bags and the typewriter. Putting the bags in the back room, I set the typewriter on the table in the front and took the cover off. I opened one of the bags and got out the yellow typing paper and carbons. Then I remembered I hadn't bought an eraser. Must have had a lot of confidence in myself, I thought sourly; I hadn't used a typewriter since I'd got out of college. I scouted around the cabin and finally scared up the stub of a pencil that had a little eraser left on the end of it.

It was still intensely hot in the cabin, and I was thirsty. I stripped off my shirt and slacks, hung them draped over hangers on the front porch so the perspiration would dry, took the water pail, and walked up the trail to the spring in my shorts. I dipped up a pail full with the small aluminium saucepan hanging from a nail driven into a sweetgum tree beside the spring, took a good, long drink of it, and came back.

I arranged the paper beside the typewriter, got a pack of cigarettes and some matches out of one of the bags, and located an ash tray. I dragged up a chair and sat down before the typewriter. It was deathly silent. I had this whole end of the world to myself and I was about to put down on paper the highest-priced short piece of prose ever written. I grinned. All it took to be a successful writer was a guaranteed audience; Hitler had proved that.

Never mind the gags, I thought impatiently; *get to work.* I rolled a sheet of the yellow paper into the machine for a rough first draft and began. I made a lot of mistakes at first because I wasn't familiar with the machine and hadn't used one for a long time. I didn't like the way it began, and after I'd wadded it up I didn't like the next version either. The pile of discarded yellow pages grew higher on the floor beside me. Sweat ran down my body and I got a towel to mop it off. It was an hour and a half before I had it all down the way I wanted, a little more than a full page, single spaced.

I read it over:

To the District Attorneys at Houston, Texas, and Wayles, Texas.

My name is John Gallagher Harlan. I was born in Tulsa, Oklahoma, July 10th, 1927, the son of Patrick and Marianne Harlan, both now deceased. I am a graduate of—— University, class of 1949, and a former professional football player. I am six feet three inches tall, and weigh two hundred and thirty pounds. There is a hirsute mole under my left shoulder-blade, and considerable scar tissue around and below my left knee. An examination of the bones of my left leg will show it was badly broken in two places, not very long ago. The bridgework, the result of teeth lost in football scrimmages, was done by Paul J. Scarff, D.D.S., Medical-Dental Building, San Francisco, California.

The above data is unimportant except for purposes of possible identification and verification of the fact I actually existed, because if you receive this at all it will only be because I am dead. I will have been killed by Daniel R. Tallant and/or Mrs. Howard L. Cannon, both of Wayles, Texas.

I do not know whether you will be able to find my body, or, in the event that you do, whether you will ever be able to gather sufficient evidence to convict them, but this will assist you to the extent of explaining their motive. I was killed to prevent my disclosure of the following information:

Both Mrs. Cannon and Mr. Tallant are already guilty of murder. Mrs. Cannon's husband did not die as the result of an automobile accident on the night of March 4th, 1956, as was believed, but was bludgeoned to death by Mr. Tallant, with Mrs. Cannon's connivance and/or assistance, shortly afterwards as he lay unconscious in the wreckage of his car. I was present at the time, pinned under the side of my own automobile some sixty yards away. I heard voices, followed by the sound of a blow, but feigned unconsciousness to keep from being killed myself.

I went on to explain how I had seen her out there near the lake a few minutes before and how Cannon had driven me off the road because he believed I was Tallant and that she was in the car with me.

I wound it up:

This will also clear up the death of Mr. Wilton L. Purvis of 10325 Caroline Street, Houston, Texas, on the night of August 8, 1956. He was attempting to blackmail the aforesaid two murderers on the strength of the evidence he had collected against them, and was himself killed by a single powerful blow on the head delivered by Mr. Tallant. I was present in the apartment at the time, in the kitchen where I could not be seen from the living-room or the doorway to the dining-room. Mr. Tallant gained access to the Purvis apartment by posing as a Federal radio inspector investigating complaints of neighbourhood television interference. In corroboration of the fact that I was there, I offer the following: Mr. Purvis was wearing a dark blue sports shirt and grey flannel slacks. His left arm was broken by the blow. There were two bottles of imported beer on the drainboard in the kitchen, opened but untouched.

I am aware that none of the above is acceptable as evidence in a court of law, but I believe that, given the facts, you can eventually get a confession from them or enough evidence of your own to convict.

Your inference as to why I withheld this information is correct. I am *using it for extortion, to the extent of $100,000. This disclosure I realize, will tend greatly to discredit my story on the ground that I am a criminal myself, even if a first offender. There is another, and slightly more subtle, side to this, however, if you will consider it closely. I freely admit the attempted extortion; the mere fact that you are reading this guarantees I am dead. Therefore it is, in effect, a deathbed confession, and should carry some weight.*

Signed: JOHN GALLAGHER HARLAN.

I rolled in two fresh sheets of paper with a carbon between, and copied it very neatly, going slowly and making no mistakes. When I had finished I tore the originals into strips, wadded them up with all the discarded versions and the carbon paper, and burned them in the cookstove, later using the poker to reduce the ashes to powder. The two pages of the carbon copy I folded and left on the table. I closed the typewriter and put it away. So much for that.

There were two rolls of spare recorder tape in one of the bags. Removing them from the flat cardboard boxes they were packed in, I took them down to the edge of the lake and threw them far out into the water. They sank. Coming back to the kitchen, I put the six bass bugs I'd bought in one of the boxes, wrapped it with some of the brown paper, tied it with twine, and put on an address sticker. The other box was identical, and would look just the same when it was wrapped. I took both of them out to the car and put them in the glove compartment, along with the wrapping paper, address labels, twine, and a book of stamps.

I took the .45 automatic out of the bag, loaded the clip and inserted it, and put it in the car. It was late in the afternoon now. I walked out on the little pier where the skiff was tied up with a padlock and chain and went for a swim. When I came out I built up a fire in the stove, made some coffee, and fried a couple of eggs. Afterward I washed the dishes and sat on the front porch in the gathering dusk, smoking a cigarette. This time tomorrow I'd be well on my way to becoming rich, or any one or all three of us might be dead. I wasn't too nervous. I felt about the same way I always did standing in my own end zone on opening kick-off while I watched the ball come sailing down toward me.

When it was completely dark I dressed in a charcoal flannel suit, crepe-soled shoes, and a blue shirt. I made sure I had the flashlight and my pen, locked the windows and doors, and went out and got in the car. I was as ready now as I was ever going to be.

CHAPTER EIGHT

Just before I came out on the highway I pulled off the road among the pines far enough to be out of range of any passing headlights, and waited. No car came out behind me. I lit a cigarette, and looked at my watch. It was a little after eight. I still had lots of time to put in, and this was a good place to find out if he was checking up on me. An hour dragged by, and then another. Mosquitoes buzzed around my ears and an owl went *who-who-who-ah-who* somewhere out in the timber. Now and then a car went past on the road beyond, but none of them turned in. I pulled back on to the road and went on. About halfway to town, headlights showed up behind me. I slowed deliberately to see if he would pass. He did. It was an old pickup truck. It went on and out of sight.

When I came into town I turned left, taking to the side streets. There were big trees on both sides, with street lights only at the intersections. It was after eleven now and few cars were about. Some six blocks on I turned north again until I hit the street that went up the hill past the Cannon house. I followed it for several blocks, until I came to the playing field which was on the left. The street began to rise here, going up the hill. There were four or five houses on the right. I pulled to the kerb in dense shadow under the trees and cut the lights. There was no one in sight; no cars went past. I waited a few minutes, letting my eyes become accustomed to the darkness. There was no sound except a radio playing faintly somewhere inside one of the houses. I got out and lifted out the recorder, checking to be sure I had the three-way outlet plug, the ball of twine, and my pocket-knife.

Stars shone brilliantly in a clear sky, but there was no moon. I crossed the street and went up past the playing field. There were no street lights ahead now. The pavement stopped and I stayed near the edge of the road, ready to fade into the darkness away from the road if a car appeared. None did. I went on up the hill. When I reached the wooded area behind and below the Cannon house I crossed the street again and stepped in among the pines. The dense shadows were like velvet. I stepped softly on pine needles, moving on up toward the light I could see briefly at intervals through the trees. I came out at last in a narrow open strip just behind the patio wall. There were a number of long poles stuck into the ground. Standing beside one of the poles, I looked at the rear of the house.

Lights were on in the living-room. The curtain was still drawn across the big plate glass window, but I could see through it well enough to make out four people seated around a card table. It looked like two men and two women. I wondered if one of them could be Tallant, but didn't see any silhouette that appeared to be large enough. It was going to be a long wait, though, because even after these people went home I had to be sure he wasn't going to show.

Half an hour crept past. I began to want a cigarette very badly, but I couldn't light one here in the open. I put the recorder down near the pole and walked back among the pines. When I was screened by them on all sides I squatted down and lit one with a brief flare of a match. I smoked it slowly and ground the stub out against the ground. When I returned to the house the bridge game was breaking up. They all disappeared into the hallway at the left end of the living-room, and in a moment one person came back. Presumably that was Mrs. Cannon. I could hear two cars driving away from the front of the house. Lights began to go out in the room. Then one came on at the rear of the right wing of the house. That would be her bedroom. The curtains over the windows were opaque here, but I could see the glow of illumination around the edges. In about twenty minutes these lights clicked off too and the whole house was in darkness. She had gone to bed. Alone? So far, I thought. If Tallant had been one of the bridge players, he would have left to come back later. I looked at the luminous hands of my watch again. It was ten minutes past midnight.

I settled down for the monotonous wait. Mosquitoes swarmed about my ears and bit me on the backs of the hands. Then suddenly a light came on behind a small ground-glass window just forward of the bedroom. Bath, I thought. Did that mean Tallant was there? No. It went off again almost immediately. She was probably after a sleeping-pill or glass of water. If Cannon's head had looked anything like Purvis's after they hit him, I thought, she probably bought sleeping-pills by the quart.

The minutes dragged on. It was one o'clock. Then one-thirty.

There were no signs of Tallant. He must not be coming, or he'd have been here by this time. Some Tallant, I thought. I'd have been in there before the light bulb got cold. I thought of her in that room alone and wondered if she slept in one of those shortie nightgowns or maybe just in the raw. Then I wrenched my mind away from her and cursed under my breath. Thinking about her always made me uncomfortable. Well, maybe she'd told him not to come. That happened, too.

The house was dark and silent and the others in the neighbourhood had long since put out their lights. I began to grow impatient, and a little nervous, wanting to get it over with, but I made myself wait. Being caught in there would ruin everything. Give her until three o'clock, anyway. She should be asleep then if she was going to sleep at all. I began to worry about the door again. Suppose she had discovered the night latch was off? But I'd seen her leave the living-room to go to bed, and she hadn't checked it. Stop stewing about it. Mosquitoes sang about my face. I flailed at them with my hands. It was a long, long hour.

When the hands of the watch came up to three I was tense and eager. I set the recorder on top of the wall and climbed over, landing softly on the grass on the other side. Going slowly and avoiding the lawn furniture from memory, I eased up to the flagstone terrace outside the living-room door. The soft-soled shoes made no sound on it. I located the door and reached for the screen. It didn't open.

I stood for a moment, cursing silently. I'd been right there at the door and hadn't had brains enough to check the screen to see if it was unlatched. But maybe it had been latched since then. That would mean the door was locked again. Well, there was no way to tell until I got the screen open. I set down the recorder and took out my pocket-knife.

Switching on the little flashlight, I ran the beam along the edge of the frame inside until I located the hook. It took only a few seconds to work the knife blade through the mesh, place it under the hook, and pry upward. It came free with a little rattle as it bounced up and fell back against the wood. I switched off the light and waited, holding my breath. The night was silent all around me. It was all right, I thought; she couldn't have heard it inside with all the doors and windows closed. The door, damn it, the door! I eased the screen open and took hold of the knob. It turned. I breathed softly.

I stepped inside, gently closed the door, and pushed around the end of the curtain. It was cool after the heat outside. The blackness was impenetrable. I stood motionless for a long minute, listening intently. There was utter silence except for a faint whirring noise somewhere in the house from the blower mechanism of the air-conditioner. I switched on the flashlight and stepped across the room to the long sofa. Lifting the red-shaded lamp off the end table, I placed it on the sofa, and moved the table out of the way. Nothing made any sound on the carpet. Squatting, I looked behind the sofa. It was fine. There was plenty of room for the recorder, between the back of the sofa and the wall. I set the light down on the table, picked up the end of the sofa and moved it out from the wall until I could get behind it.

I was working fast now, and silently, with all the moves worked out and memorized in advance. Taking out my knife, I cut away a section of the fabric of the sofa back, near the centre, and stuffed it in one of the pockets of my coat. I could see the coil springs now, and the padding in front of them. I opened the case of the recorder, took out the microphone, and put it in position between two of the springs, facing the front. I lashed it securely in place with some of the twine. Feeling around with my fingers, I was satisfied. It wasn't quite touching the padding.

I turned and located the electrical point in the skirting under the drapery of the window. Just as I had thought, it was a dual receptacle with both circuits in use by the big lamps at each end of the sofa. I pulled out one of the lamp cords, inserted the multiple plug in its place, and then plugged in the lamp and the recorder in two of its outlets. I put the recorder on the floor against the wall and set the controls, all except the on-off switch. Moving the sofa back to its original position very carefully, I replaced the end table, and put the lamp back on it. Sitting on the end of the sofa, I reached back with my right hand. I could just touch the switch. I turned it on and brushed my finger-tips against one of the spools. It was turning. The curtain wasn't fouling it anywhere; everything should be all right. I turned it off again and stood up. Moving away a little, I swung the light around the end of the sofa to see if there was anything visible that would give it away. It was all right. The end table cut off any view behind the sofa.

I straightened and wiped my face with my handkerchief, suddenly conscious that in spite of the air-conditioning I was soaked with sweat. I had been oblivious to everything, working under pressure with tremendous concentration. It was all set now; the only thing that remained was getting out of here. I swept the light around once more to be sure I hadn't left anything, and eased over to the door. Pulling back the curtain, I slipped out, closed the door gently, eased the screen back into position, and was outside on the terrace. I exhaled a long breath and felt the tension unwind inside me. I went back down the hill and looked at my watch as I unlocked the door and got in the car. It was twenty minutes past three.

I rolled down the windows and lit a cigarette. I had four and a half hours to wait, and then came the tricky and dangerous part of it. I wondered if I'd be able to sleep if I stretched out somewhere. No. There wasn't a chance. I was still keyed too high. It would be better not to go back to the cabin, anyway. I didn't know where Tallant was, and as long as I didn't it would be a good idea to stay away from anywhere he could find *me*. The best thing to do right now was stay out of sight and keep moving. I drove back through the quiet streets and hit the road going south, but when I came to the turnoff I went on past. It was twenty miles down to Breward. I drove slowly. When I got down there I found an all-night café open on the highway and had some breakfast.

I took my time eating it and read yesterday's paper as if I hadn't heard any news since Hitler marched into Poland. Dawn was breaking when I started back. A few miles out of Breward I found a place to pull off the road at an old abandoned sawmill. There was a huge pile of sawdust and a pond with pads growing in it. I got out of the car and sat on a big timber, smoking cigarettes and thinking while it grew light and the sun came up. The air was intensely still. I looked at my watch every few minutes, growing tighter now.

Timing was very important. I wanted to hit them early in the morning while they still had sleep in their eyes, and it was vital I get there before the maid showed up and started work. But it also had to be within shooting distance of 8.30 so the post office would be open when I was ready for it.

It was time to go. I flipped the last cigarette into the pond and stood up. I took the .45 out of the glove compartment and slid it into the right-hand pocket of my jacket, wondering how easily people bluffed who had already committed two murders. Probably not too readily, I thought. I wheeled the car on to the road and started back to town.

It was ten minutes to eight when I pulled to the kerb in front of the Cannon house. The sun was higher now and growing hot;

nothing stirred along the street except a dog making his morning rounds. I hurried up the walk. A rolled newspaper lay on the concrete slab of the porch. I picked it up and leaned on the buzzer. I could hear it somewhere inside the house. I waited a moment and jabbed it again, long and impatiently. Standing there in the sun, I was roasting inside the flannel suit. Somewhere down the block I heard a garage door fall, and a car backed out into the street. I was just reaching for the buzzer when the door opened.

I'd got her out of bed, all right. The dark hair was tousled, and she was wearing a blue robe tied tightly about the slender waist. The big eyes were still a little sleepy and the irritation in them came into focus as she looked out and saw me. She made a half-hearted attempt to mask it, but it didn't quite come off.

"Oh. It's you, Mr. Harlan. Aren't you up a little early?"

"I've got to talk to you," I said curtly. I pushed on in. She stepped back, a little startled. I reached back to close the door behind me, and as I did I slid my fingers down the edge, found the two push-buttons of the night latch, and reversed them. She was watching my face and didn't see it.

You could see she thought all this was a little high-handed. "I *beg* your pardon——"

"Shut up," I said.

She took another step backward and her eyes went round with amazement. In another second she recovered, and the surprise gave way to blazing anger. "Would you mind telling me——"

I cut her off. "Is the maid here yet?"

"Mr. Harlan, will you please leave this house? Before I call the police."

I caught the front of her robe. "Shut up. And listen. If the maid's here, get rid of her. If she's due within the next half hour, call her and tell her not to come. You wouldn't want her to hear this."

She was scared now, but trying not to show it.

"Don't worry," I said. "I'm not a sex maniac that's flipped his lid, if that's bothering you. This is strictly business. Now, how about that maid?"

She moistened her lips. "She comes at nine."

"Good," I said. I let go her robe and grinned at her a little coldly. "Let's go into the living-room, shall we? What kind of hostess are you, anyway?"

She was still having a little trouble trying to catch up. She'd typed me yesterday as a harmless yokel with two left feet, and now I'd crossed her up. I had to give her credit, though; by the time we'd walked on into the living-room and sat down facing each other across the coffee table she had recovered. I was just something she had to endure until I decided to leave.

"Cigarette?" I asked, holding out the pack.

She shook her head.

"Better have one," I said. "Good for the nerves. This is going to be a little rugged."

"Would you mind just saying whatever it was you forced your way in here to say——"

"Right," I answered. "I've got something here I'd like you to read."

She stared at me as I took the folded yellow pages of the carbon copy from the breast pocket of my jacket. I held them while I finished lighting the cigarette and dropped the match in a tray. "Here," I said.

She unfolded them. I studied her face as she started to read. There was a hint of shock right at first, and I knew that was when she saw the thing was addressed to the two District Attorneys. From then on her face was a mask—a very lovely honey-coloured mask dominated by two brown eyes that were completely inscrutable. She finished, folded it up, and dropped it on the coffee table.

I leaned back on the sofa with my hands behind my head and the cigarette hanging out of the side of my mouth. "Well?" I asked.

She took one of the cigarettes from the pack I had left lying on the table. She lit it with the table lighter. Her hands were steady. "Mr. Harlan," she asked quietly, "do you mind if I ask a rather personal question? Have you ever been confined in a mental institution?"

"Pretty good act," I said. "But you're wasting time."

"I mean it."

I sighed. "This is a nice routine, but we can skip the rest of it, if it's all right with you, and get on with the negotiations. I want a hundred thousand dollars. Do I get it?"

She stared at me. "You couldn't be serious."

I nodded toward the letter. "You read that, didn't you?"

"Yes. And a more fantastic——"

I cut her off. "Save the arguments for the jury. If this goes to trial you're going to need them. The two of you killed your husband while he was unconscious, and if you think you can get that reduced from murder in the first degree, you're crazy as hell. The jury wouldn't be out long enough to finish their cigarettes. Now, listen——"

"Of all the utterly fantastic, insane——"

I leaned forward across the table. "Shut up, and I'll read the score to you. You and Tallant and your husband can go around killing each other every day of the week and twice on Sundays, and I couldn't care less. But when you rope me in on it it's a different story. Your husband deliberately tried to kill me because he thought I was Tallant, and he wound up by putting a permanent wave in one of my legs. They may not look like much, compared to Grable's, but I made a damn good living with them, and now I don't any more. He left you a hundred thousand dollars in insurance, but that was just a clerical error. He should have left it to me. I've come after it. Do I get it, or don't I?"

She stared at me. "You have a wonderful imagination, Mr. Harlan, even if it is slightly deranged. My husband was drinking. He lost control of his car——"

I cut her off. "We've wasted enough time. Get Tallant on the phone. I'll tell you what to say."

"You mean the Mr. Tallant who runs the sporting goods shop?"

"Among other things, that's the Mr. Tallant. Now get with it."

Her eyebrows raised. "And if I don't?"

I reached across the table, caught her by the front of the robe, and hauled her to her feet. "You're not big enough to tell me whether you will or won't. Where's the phone?"

The brown eyes were full of contempt. "You're looking right at it." She half turned her head and nodded. The telephone was on a stand in the corner of the room between the rear window and the dining-room door.

"Come on," I said. I took her arm and propelled her ahead of me. The directory was on a shelf under the instrument. I handed it to her opened to the first page inside the cover.

"There are the numbers," I said. "The local police, and the Sheriff's office. If you think I'm bluffing, or crazy, here's your chance to call me. Dial either one. Tell them a man has forced his way into your house and is threatening you. They'll have a car here in less than three minutes."

She eyed me coolly. "And in less than two I would be disfigured for life."

"I won't touch you. I've got a gun, but I won't resist arrest, either. I'm not that silly. Add it up. Carrying a gun without a permit, illegal entry, assault, attempted extortion—say five to ten years for a package deal. Go ahead."

She looked at me and then at the telephone. I picked up the

instrument and held it out toward her. "Call the police. Or call Tallant. It's up to you."

She tried to bluff it out. For an instant her eyes locked with mine, but then they dropped. She lifted the receiver and dialled.

It wasn't one of the emergency numbers. She was calling Tallant.

CHAPTER NINE

"JUST say something's come up," I ordered, "and that he's to get over here as fast as he can. Not another word."

She stared coldly. In the dead silence of the room I could hear the phone ringing at the other end. It stopped.

"Mr. Tallant?" she asked. "This is Mrs. Cannon. Something has come up, and I wonder if you could drive over here right away——"

I pressed down the plunger on the cradle to break the connection and took the receiver away from her, but the damage was already done.

"Smart," I said. "But that's all right. He can't do anything."

"What do you mean?" she asked coldly.

"Skip it," I said. I put the phone back on the stand. This girl was sharp. If Tallant had come on cold, without knowing how much she might have already said, I'd have had the advantage. But she'd outfoxed me, and tipped him. She'd told him as plainly as if she'd drawn him a picture that I was here—or somebody was here—putting the pressure on her, but that she hadn't admitted a thing. *Mr.* Tallant—— Hah!

But suppose? For just a moment uncertainty took hold of me. Maybe she really didn't know him. I knew he had killed Purvis, all right, because I'd seen him, but the rest of it was just a lot of logical surmises strung together. And if she *hadn't* had anything to do with Cannon's death, I was as far up the creek as you could get without a helicopter.

No, I thought suddenly. *The hell she wasn't implicated. Use your head.* She's given herself away twice in the past three minutes. She chickened out when you threw that bluff at her about calling the police. And she made an even bigger boo-boo.

"You're pretty smooth," I said, "but you goofed on that one."

"I beg your pardon?"

"It's *Mister* Tallant and *Mrs.* Cannon, but you dialled his number without looking it up."

We were still facing each other by the telephone. "Really?" she said, raising her eyebrows. "Is that so remarkable? We happen to be on a committee together."

"What kind of committee?"

"We're trying to form a Little Theatre group."

"Very interesting," I said. I went back and sat down on the end of the sofa. He'd be here any minute now, and I was beginning to grow tense again. The two of them together were going to be something to handle. She remained across the room looking at me as if I were something that had crawled out of a shower drain. We waited. Nobody said anything. The silence went on building up so that when the door chime tinkled out in the kitchen it was like a hand-grenade going off.

She turned and started toward the entrance hallway. The instant she was through the door I reached down behind the sofa and flipped on the switch of the recorder. Then I sprang up and followed her. I was leaning against the door frame between the living-room and the entry hall when she opened the outer door. Tallant was standing on the porch.

We were almost the same size exactly, but he could have been a year or so younger and you had to admit he was a handsome devil. It was obvious he'd never ploughed up as many stadiums with his face as I had, but nobody except a chump would have ever called his good looks girlish. The eyes were blue-grey and rather hard, and the cleft chin didn't detract at all from the tough competence of the jaw. The short-cropped dark hair had a tendency to be curly. *A smooth hunk of cookie,* I thought. Whether you were after the same girl or the same fumble, he'd give you a bad time either way.

"Come in, Mr. Tallant," she said. I didn't have any idea what kind of message she was passing along to him with her eyes, but I watched his. I also cased him for a gun, but didn't see any place he could be carrying one. He was wearing a sports shirt and no jacket.

He stepped inside the entry hall. As she closed the door he inclined his head a little in my direction and said, "Who's this?" It wasn't too convincing. He knew who I was, all right.

I lounged against the door frame and watched his face. "I'm a Federal radio inspector," I said. "Checking up on television interference in the neighbourhood."

He was good, all right, and he'd been prepared, but that was a little too hot to field without showing it. I saw it hit him for a fraction of a second before he covered.

He frowned then. "What's this?" he asked quietly. "A gag?"

"Never mind," I said. "You've already answered your own question. Come on in and sit down. I've got something I want you to read."

I stepped aside and let them come through the doorway. I was careful not to let him get too near, and he was just as careful not to turn his back, though it was all too well covered to be obvious. Nobody said anything for a moment, but tension was like smoke in the room.

I'd left the letter on the coffee table intentionally. He'd have to go there to pick it up, so the logical place to sit down would be the handiest—the sofa or one of the chairs facing it. I nodded in that direction. "Mrs. Cannon's already read the good news," I said. "I think she missed one angle of it, but you'll probably catch on. If you'll notice, it's a carbon copy."

"Say, what the hell is this?" he asked roughly. "Who are you? And what do you want?"

I waved a hand. "The letter, Tallant. Why don't you just pick it up and read it? It'll explain everything."

He shrugged indifferently and walked over to the coffee table, picked up the folded yellow sheets and sat down on the end of the sofa where I'd been. She lit a cigarette with studied arrogance and perched on the arm of one of the big chairs. I watched his face as he read. The mouth grew ugly. When he finished he looked up at me, his eyes hard.

I stood back out of reach and gave them the pitch, straight down the middle and smoking. "All right. I told you it was a carbon copy. You can see that for yourselves. A friend of mine has two originals, both signed. If anything happens to me, they go in the mail, one to the District Attorney at Houston and the other to the D.A. here. They'll have three murders to work on, and you can figure out for yourselves what the odds are that they'll be able to burn you for at least one. Don't think you can hide me well enough, either. If they don't find me for ten years they'll still be able to identify what's left with that dope on the broken leg and the dental work.

"Everybody knows I was under my own car there at the wreck, and if the police get this letter they'll know I was in the next room when Purvis was killed because there's never been anything in the papers about those two bottles of beer. You haven't got a chance in the world.

"Hold still and you won't get hurt. All I want is a hundred thousand dollars, which is exactly what you collected from the insurance company. There's plenty more, and none of it would do you any good in Death Row. So how's it going to be?"

While I was talking Tallant had got hold of himself again, and now there was only a nasty smile on his face as he looked at me. "You mean you've got the guts to try to shake Mrs. Cannon down with a pipe dream like this?"

"Come off it Jocko," I said. "I was standing in the next room when you killed Purvis. You want to deny it on the stand?"

He picked up the letter again and made a big deal of looking for something in it. "Here it is. '*—in the kitchen, where I could not be seen from the living-room——*' I assume from the way you put it that Purvis—whoever he was—was killed in the living-room. Now, this man couldn't see you, but you could see him. You have X-ray eyes, or something?"

"I didn't say I saw you kill him," I replied. "I said I was in the next room. But you were the only person in there with him, and I don't think he could hit himself over the head hard enough to break his own arm and split his head open at the same time. Little far-fetched, wouldn't you think?"

He snorted. "So you didn't *see* the man, but you say it was me. It just came to you, like that? A revelation, or something?"

"I saw you go out," I said wearily.

"Oh, you saw the man go out the door? He backed out, is that it?"

"No, he didn't back out."

"Then you saw him from the rear?"

"That's right."

"You never did see his face?"

"No," I said. I was beginning to get a little tired of it, but if it made him feel any better to think he was making a monkey of me it was all right.

"Did this man have his name stencilled on his clothes somewhere in the back?"

"Oh, knock it off, Tallant. You can play Mr. District Attorney some other time."

He looked at Mrs. Cannon and spread his hands. He smiled. "The defence rests."

"Never mind the hokum," I said. "The question is, do you want the police to have this? So far, you're covered from every angle. Nobody suspects you. But they get one look at this, and everything hits the fan. They'll come at you from a thousand angles at once. They'll question you separately for thirty-six hours at a time and it's going to be hard to remember what the other one's supposed to be saying and what you're supposed to be saying and what you *did* say fourteen hours ago when you had your last cigarette, and then they'll tell you the other one has cracked wide open and is trying to turn State's evidence to get off with life. You want to try it and see how you hold up?"

He lit a cigarette and shrugged. "If you think the police will take the word of a blackmailing creep like you against a woman of her standing, go ahead and stick your neck out. They'll make it plenty rough for you."

"When you get tired of bluffing," I said, "we'll start to talk business."

"We've already talked it. She's not going to pay you a nickel for any framed-up mess of lies like this, and I'd advise you to fade while you still can."

"How about letting her answer for herself, chum? It's her neck."

I turned and glanced at her; she was still perched on the arm of the chair, smoking. Her eyes met mine coolly. "I never heard anything as fantastic in my life."

He gestured with the hand holding the cigarette. "So, scram."

"That's your answer, is it?" I said, making it come up tough.

"That's our answer."

It was time for a little bluster. "All right, friend, I see you want to do it the hard way. Go ahead and stew about it for a while. Start wondering just where Purvis got his information. Purvis was a cop, and a good one, and he didn't look in a crystal ball to find out she had a boy friend and that Cannon learned about it and that Cannon *wasn't* that drunk when he drove me off the road. You want to know where he got his information? He got it the same way the police'll get it when they start checking—by talking to people, a little bit here and a little bit there. Purvis did it alone; so go ahead and start wondering just how much a dozen men working on it can dig up.

"Just simmer for a while. I'll be around, and when you start making sense you can get in touch with me. I'm a bargain, but you'd better hurry and make up your minds before the price starts going up."

I picked up the letter and let myself out the front door. As I got in the car and pulled away from the kerb I saw the curtains over the front window twitch just slightly. They were making sure I was gone. I went straight ahead for three blocks and then turned downhill. At the corner I turned right again and was on the parallel street behind the Cannon house. I pulled to the kerb and stopped. It was 8.25.

So far, so good, I thought. It had gone off about as I had expected. It had hit him hard at first, until he'd had time to recover and think a little. That friend-with-a-copy gag was so old it had whiskers, and he knew it, but there was just enough possibility I might be telling the truth to make him hold off and bluff while he stalled for time. When he finally convinced himself I was working alone he'd come out there to the cabin and blow my head off while I was asleep. I lit a cigarette and took a couple of puffs on it. Everything depended on the next few minutes.

Suppose they had moved, gone into the bedroom or somewhere? *Oh, hell,* I thought; *quit stewing about it. You set them up like Arruza putting a bull into position; there's no reason they should move.* I looked at my watch again. It was time.

I pulled away from the kerb and drove straight ahead until I hit the street going uphill past the side of the Cannon house. I turned and went up. When I swung around the next corner I saw Tallant's convertible still parked at the kerb. I cut the motor and eased to a stop. There was no movement at the front window curtains; they wouldn't be expecting me now. I went silently up the walk, carefully turned the knob on the front door, pulled it open, and went in fast.

I could hear Tallant's voice sounding angry in the living-room. It chopped off abruptly, and I knew they had heard the front door open. As I came striding through the doorway from the entry hall they whirled and stared at me. He was lighting a cigarette by the coffee table and she was across by the rear window as if she had been staring out into the patio.

Tallant recovered first. His face hardened and he took a step toward me. "We told you once, Harlan——"

I took the .45 out of my pocket and pointed it at him. "Turn around," I ordered. "Go to the other end of the room and sit down on that hearth."

He stopped, cautious but not too scared. You could almost read his thought. I couldn't be very sure of my ground if I had to resort to throwing my weight around and trying to scare them with a gun. He turned and shot a glance at her. *Get a load of this character,* it seemed to say.

"Move," I snapped at him.

"Knock it off, you silly bastard——"

"*Move!*"

He moved then. Maybe he thought I'd gone crazy and it would be a good thing to humour me. He backed across the room and sat down on the hearth, smiled wearily at her, and shrugged. I shot a quick glance at her myself. She had remained where she was, near the window. She was still outwardly cool and arrogant, but I thought I saw the beginnings of apprehension in her eyes. Maybe she was quicker than he was, and was already beginning to wonder if something hadn't gone wrong with the script.

I stepped forward, still holding the gun in my right hand. With the left I picked up the red-shaded lamp on the end table and dropped it on the sofa. Sliding the table out of the way, I pushed the end of the sofa away from the wall and reached behind it. They froze dead still now and stared as if hypnotized. I watched them as I lifted the recorder into view.

She gasped, and I thought for a second she was going to fall. In the sudden, taut silence that followed, he began to get up slowly from the hearth with deadliness quite naked in his eyes. I had them. I had them, that is, if I got out of here alive with that tape.

I pointed the gun at him. "Sit down," I said.

He stopped, just half erect, and hesitated. For a second it hung in the balance, ready to go either way. I hoped he didn't have sense enough at the moment to realize I couldn't shoot without ruining it all. A bullet through the leg would stop him without killing him, but anything that brought the police into it now would put me right up the creek with them.

I had sense enough myself not to keep talking and making threats. I just held the gun and waited while the silence stretched out. He sat back down, very slowly, his face white and greasy with sweat. I sighed, but didn't relax too much. The whole situation was still explosive, and it would take only one bad move to set it off.

"Stand over there near him," I told her.

She moved like someone in a trance.

"Just stay where you are, both of you, and nobody'll get hurt," I said. "What the hell, relax. It's only money."

I set the recorder on the end table and flipped the controls to rewind. When I had most of the tape back on the spool I set it for playback and adjusted the gain. They stared while that tense silence fell over the room again.

The first voice issuing from the loudspeaker was my own.

"—wondering where Purvis got his information. Purvis was a cop——" I'd rolled it back a little too far, but it didn't matter. I let it run.

The voices came through fine. I did the threatening act, and then there was the sound of the front door opening and closing. A moment of silence followed. They would be watching out the front window to be sure I was gone.

I waited, holding the gun ready. It was coming now.

CHAPTER TEN

THERE was tension in the room like an electric charge. The first voice to come out of the loudspeaker was Tallant's:

"He's gone!"

MRS. CANNON: "Dan! I'm scared! What are we going to do?"

TALLANT: "Julia, for Christ's sake, relax! There's nothing to get excited about. He's just bluffing——"

MRS. CANNON: "*I told you!* I told you to go back and see if he was still unconscious under that other car. Why didn't you listen——?"

TALLANT: "Will you shut up for a minute? I tell you, he was out the whole time. He's guessing, and making it up. He got the idea from Purvis. Purvis must have described you, and he realized it was you he saw out there on the road in the swamp——"

MRS. CANNON: "And why in the name of God didn't you make sure there was nobody else in the apartment before——?"

TALLANT: "Listen! He has to be lying about that too. I tell you I looked. There wasn't anybody in that kitchen."

MRS. CANNON: "What about those two bottles of beer?"

TALLANT: "I didn't see any bottles of beer."

MRS. CANNON: "Can't you see, you fool, he has to be telling the truth? The police would know. And there hasn't been anything about them in the paper. And where did he get that thing about the radio inspector, if he wasn't there?"

TALLANT: "All right! All right! Maybe he was there. But it's just his word against mine——"

MRS. CANNON: "*Word!* For the love of heaven, can't you see that if the police even suspect for a minute you were there they'll see the whole thing?"

TALLANT: "Look, he won't go to the police. How can he?"

MRS. CANNON: "Of course he's not going to the police, because we're going to pay him off. There's no other way. If there's even a hint that it wasn't an accident, we haven't a chance in the world."

TALLANT: "Are you crazy? Pay him off? Don't you know any better than to give in to a blackmailer? Once you give him a nickel, he'll bleed you for the rest of your life."

MRS. CANNON: "Maybe you have a better suggestion."

TALLANT: "You're damn' right I do."

MRS. CANNON: "No! *We can't!*"

TALLANT: "The hell we can't. He's asking for it, the same as Purvis."

MRS. CANNON: "But suppose he's telling the truth about the other copy of that letter?"

TALLANT: "He's not. It's an old dodge."

MRS. CANNON: "But, Dan! We don't *know*. We can't take the chance."

TALLANT: "There's no other way, I tell you! The thing to do is bluff him and stall for time until we're sure. Then get rid of him. We're in this too deep to be squeamish or turn chicken now. Jesus Christ, I wish we'd never been out there that day! If only——Oh, hell, there's no use crying about it now. We've got to go ahead."

MRS. CANNON: "Purvis. And now this one. Will we ever be able to stop?"

TALLANT: "We'll never be safe as long as he's alive. You know that."

MRS. CANNON: "Yes. You're right. But we've got to be sure, first, I mean, that he's the only one. And we've got to be careful. We can't let anything go wrong this time."

TALLANT: "Don't worry. If he's stupid enough to think we'd fall for an old gag like that, he's too stupid to worry us. Let him think we believe it."

MRS. CANNON: "But suppose he *is* telling the truth?"

TALLANT: "He's not! Good God, can't you see that? Do you think a pig like Harlan would divide anything with anybody? He's in it alone. He wouldn't trust anybody else."

MRS. CANNON: "It's so dangerous. If we guess wrong——"

TALLANT: "Stop it! Stop it! Leave it to me. I can out-guess a thug like that——Shhhhhh!"

There was the sound of the front door opening and closing, and then Tallant's voice saying, "We told you once, Harlan——"

That was all of it.

Brother, I thought, *it's enough.* Once that was out of their reach I could write my own ticket.

Tallant had started to get up. He stared at her, his eyes hard. "How did he get that in here? Don't you even know what goes on in your own house?"

"Sit down," I said. "I planted it last night after she'd gone to bed. Now. Both of you stay right where you are. This is not going to cost you anything but money, and you've got plenty of that, so play it safe, and don't take any chances."

"I'll get you, Harlan," he said.

I nodded toward the machine. "I heard you the first time."

He remained crouched, estimating his chances.

"Sit down," I said again. He slowly settled back on the hearth.

The room fell silent again. I flipped the machine on to rewind and put all the tape back on one spool. Lifting it off, I backed across to the opposite end of the room, near the doorway to the entrance hall. There was a big chair here, with a table beside it. I slid the table around a little so I could sit on the arm of the chair, facing them, with its surface in front of me. They were twenty-five feet away, at least. I put the gun down on the table, still watching them, and pulled the empty cardboard box from my pocket. Slipping the roll of tape inside it, I took out the wrapping paper and what was left of the ball of twine and made a shipping parcel of it. They continued to watch me like two big cats. I stuck on an address label, but left it blank. Finally I put on some stamps and shoved it into the breast pocket of my jacket alongside the other package containing the bass bugs. They were identical except for weight. I stood up with the gun in my hand again. "Toss me your car keys," I said to Tallant.

He shook his head. "You'll have to take 'em away from me."

I wondered if he thought I was that stupid. "Doesn't matter," I said. "I'll just rip the ignition wiring out of your car."

He slowly drew the keys from his pocket and threw them across the room near my feet. I picked them up.

I switched my gaze to her. "Where are yours?"

She made no answer.

"Come on," I said. "A little co-operation."

"They're in the dining-hall. On the sideboard."

"Get 'em," I ordered.

"Get them yourself, if you want them. They're behind you."

I motioned with the gun like somebody in a western movie. "The keys, honey. You're driving me to town."

Her face was white as chalk, but she defied me. "Do you think I'd go out of the house dressed this way?"

Women, I thought. "Never mind the way you're dressed. You won't have to get out of the car. Is there a door from the kitchen into the garage?"

She nodded.

"All right. Lead the way."

She hesitated. I stared at her without saying anything. In a moment the defiance wilted and she came toward me. I stepped aside to let her go through the doorway. They ganged me then, but I had been expecting it and was ready.

As she passed me she swayed slightly and then fell, as if she had fainted. She came over against me and tried to get her arms around my neck. I peeled her off with one arm and dropped her across the chair, turning at the same time to meet him. He had come too far and was moving too fast to stop or change direction by the time he saw I'd got rid of her. I sidestepped and gave him the stiff-arm with the flat side of the gun just above his ear. He ploughed on into the table and chair and came to rest with the wreckage of the table settling down on top of him.

She opened her eyes and began pushing herself out of the chair. "*You ape——*"

"Sure, sure," I said.

"You've killed him!"

"He's all right," I said. "Just take your feet out of his face and he'll get up."

He climbed unsteadily to his knees with a trickle of blood running down the side of his neck, too groggy to stand yet. All the fight was gone out of both of them for the moment. I jerked my head for her to go ahead into the dining-room. She went through the doorway.

"We'll be back in a few minutes," I said to Tallant. "Make yourself at home. Go ahead and call the police if you want me to be picked up with this roll of tape on me."

He put a hand up to the side of his head and stared at the blood on his fingers as he brought it away. "Some day," he said softly.

I said nothing. I went on into the dining-room and motioned for her to pick up the keys. She led the way. The kitchen door opened into a two-car garage. The stall next to the kitchen was vacant; a new Buick sedan stood in the other. I stepped out and stood where I could watch her and the doorway at the same time.

"Open the garage door and get in the car," I told her.

She pressed a button on the wall and there was a whirring sound of an electric motor. The door behind the Buick came up. She got in behind the wheel. I crossed over and climbed into the rear seat.

"Post office," I said.

There was no sign of Tallant. We backed out into the street. I put the gun on safety and shoved it into the right-hand pocket of my jacket, breathing softly in relief now that the pressure was off. We rolled down the hill, saying nothing. I looked at her face in the mirror. It was white and still, the brown eyes enormous but devoid of any expression at all, as if she were beyond caring.

We were several blocks from the house now. "Pull to the kerb for a minute," I said.

We stopped. I took out the box containing the bass bugs. It was much lighter than the other, so there was no chance of mixing them up. When I'd packed it I had put wadded paper inside so they wouldn't rattle around. Taking out my pen, I printed George Gray's address on the sticker. She could see what I was doing by glancing into the mirror, but she couldn't see the address. I placed it upside down in my lap and recapped the pen.

"All right," I said.

We went on. I leaned back in the seat and lit a cigarette. Traffic was fairly heavy this time of the morning. "There's a drive-in box in front," I said. "Just pull up at that and we won't have to go inside."

We came into the square and across the west side, past the Cannon Motors showroom. I could see the new models shining beyond the glass. "Nice," I said.

She made no reply.

We turned right at the next corner. When we got to the post office there was another car in front of the drive-in box and we had to wait a minute. I held the parcel so she couldn't see the address. The other car pulled away and she moved up. She turned her head a little and watched without expression as I reached out and dropped it into the slot sticking out over the kerb.

"There it goes, honey," I said. "You've had it."

She said nothing. We pulled away from the kerb and went on. When we came up the hill and made the turn into the street before the house, I told her, "Pull back into the garage." Tallant's car was still standing at the kerb. Apparently he hadn't felt up to bridging the ignition switch and taking it on the lam. Or maybe he'd wanted to hear just what had become of the tape. It would be understandable, I thought.

She closed the garage door and we went in through the kitchen. Tallant was on the sofa in the living-room holding a towel to the cut place over his ear. His face was savage as he looked up at us. I left the gun in my pocket and leaned against the doorway.

"Tell him, honey," I said.

"He mailed it," she said woodenly. She walked across to one of the big chairs by the coffee table, sat down, and reached wearily for a cigarette.

"You see?" I asked.

He stared and said nothing.

I lit a cigarette and waved the match at them. "Anybody want me to draw him a picture? If not, let's get on with the business."

He started to open his mouth, but was interrupted by the sound of the door chime. I motioned for them to remain where they were, and went to the front door. No one was there. When I came back she nodded coldly in the direction of the dining-room. I went through and opened the rear door, which opened on the patio. It was the coloured girl. She was chewing gum.

I dug a dollar out of my pocket. "How's to duck over to the store and buy a dozen eggs? Mrs. Cannon needs them for breakfast."

She dropped the gum into neutral and considered this. "Long way to the sto'."

"Well, be sure they're fresh, then," I said, and closed the door. I started back into the living-room, but heard it open again behind me. She stuck her head inside.

"'Miz Cannon all right?" she asked. "She don't nevah eat eggs."

"She does now," I said. "She's on a diet."

Her eyes grew big. "You a doctah?"

"Yes," I said.

"She ain't got nothin' bad, is she?"

"No. Just a touch of caisson disease," I said. "All she needs is rest. And eggs, if she ever gets any."

"Oh." She pulled her head back out of the door.

I went back into the living-room. They hadn't moved. Tallant looked up at me. "You don't think you're going to get away with this?"

I sighed and went over by them to crush out the cigarette. "You're a hard man to convince, pal. But if you insist, I'll make the spiel. Here goes.

"You're dead, both of you. You had two ways out; you could pay me off, or if you were sure there wasn't anybody else with another copy of that letter you could kill me. That last has just been answered for you. The whole thing is on the tape, in your own words, and she just now saw me put it in the mail. If anything happens to me, it goes to the police, along with a copy of the letter. There's no way you can get it back except by buying it. The man I sent it to has orders to pay no attention to a telephone call from me asking to have it mailed back or given to some other person. He'll give it to me only, in person, and he names the place and time. So you can see jumping up and down on my face isn't going to do you any good. If you did force me to call him, he'd only tell me where to meet him. And if I didn't show up alone and in one piece he wouldn't show at all. So you can scratch that.

"Which just leaves the easy way. I can't see what the hell you're crying about. He left over a quarter of a million, plus the insurance. What do you want, anyway? Give me mine, I kiss you both for luck, and fade. Nobody else knows about it, so you settle down, join the P.T.A., and spend the rest of your lives bitching about what the younger generation's coming to. Looks simple to me. How about it?"

She was recovering faster than he was. "And what guarantee do we have you'll keep your word?" she asked coldly.

"None," I said. "But what else can you do?"

"I see what you mean. We're completely at the mercy of a conscienceless thug who'd betray his own mother."

"Sure, sure," I said.

"And you wouldn't even return the tape——"

"Of course I'd return it. What the hell, you think I want it for a souvenir? Look, use your head. This is a simple business proposition. I don't give a damn what you do or what becomes of you, or whether you kill everybody in this end of the state, as long as I get paid for being run over out there that night. Why get hot under the collar like a bunch of emotional types? You're a couple of tough cookies looking out for yourselves;

I'm another cookie looking out for John Harlan. What's to blow your stack about? It's just merchandise——"

Tallant leaned forward with his fingers gripping the edge of the coffee table so tightly the knuckles were white. "You dirty bastard——"

I walked over and dropped his car keys on the table. "Why don't you get lost? I'm talking to the chairman of the board, and we can probably work out a deal without any static from you. You're getting a free ride, so what are you kicking about anyway?"

He stared up at me. "You think I'm going to hold still for this?"

"You kidding? What the hell are you holding still for? She's paying the freight, isn't she?"

"Who said she was?"

"She did, as I recall. But we can ask her again." I turned and looked at her. "How about it, baby?"

She stared coldly for an instant, but then she nodded. She was a realist, that girl.

"You'll get it," she said.

It was as easy as that.

CHAPTER ELEVEN

"THAT'S using the old head," I told her. I sat down on the chair at the end of the coffee table, between them. "You and I are going to get along fine, honey."

"I *am* flattered," she said.

"Now, let's work it out."

"What do you mean?"

"Julia, I tell you——" Tallant interrupted.

I waved a hand at him. "Shut up. I'm talking to one of the men."

He started to rise, his face ugly. For an instant I was afraid I'd pushed him too far; after all, I still had that tape on me, even if they didn't suspect it. If he went crazy and lost his head enough to jump me they might find it. I had to be more careful.

But I couldn't let him know he had me worried. "Why don't you scram, Tallant? You're just getting in the way."

"And leave her here alone with you?"

"Cut it out, will you? I'm not going to hurt her. We're just talking business, and we need you like we need a fourth for bridge."

"You might as well go, Dan," she said. "There's no use starting a fight."

"But, damn it, Julia——"

"Let me handle it, please."

"Don't you understand? Listen, if you give in to him, you'll never get him off your back——"

"Do you have any other suggestion?" she asked coldly. "It would seem to me you've bungled enough already."

"*Bungled!* Listen, who let him plant that recorder in here?"

"Will you go?" she asked.

"Make up your minds, will you?" I said. "That maid will be back here in a few minutes."

"All right! All right!" Tallant stood up, his face dark with rage. "If you're going to let yourself be pushed around by this thug——"

"You don't catch on very fast, do you?" I asked. "There's nothing else you can do."

"He's right," she said wearily. "Can't you see it?"

"I'd never pay blackmail——"

"Who's asking you to?" I said. "Hell, you couldn't pay for a drink. Beat it."

He stared down at me for an instant, and then turned silently and went out. The front door slammed. I breathed a little easier. He'd been on the ragged edge of losing his head.

She picked up a cigarette from the box on the table. I held a match across to her, and then lit one for myself. She stood up, walked slowly across to the rear window, and then came back to perch on the arm of the sofa, diagonally across the table from me. She was a smooth-looking dish.

I leaned back in the chair. "With your looks you could have done better."

She raised her eyebrows and said coldly, "I beg your pardon?"

"You're a tough number, and a smooth one. A realist, and you've got a head on you. But why'd you go for that character? He's acting like an overgrown kid."

She regarded me coolly. "I believe you wanted to discuss something with me. Would you mind coming to the point?"

"Sure," I said. "Money."

"Precisely. And what about it?"

"Just this. We've been tossing a lot of big words around, but let's take a closer look. A hundred thousand dollars in cash makes a nice musical sound when you say it, but when you start to break it down it gets complicated. First, nobody keeps anything like that in a checking account, no matter how much he has. Second, even if he did he'd still cause a hell of a lot of talk when he started drawing it out in cash. So let's hear something specific. How, where, when, and so on."

She leaned forward and knocked ash into a tray. "I can raise it."

"Fill me in."

"Is it any of your business, as long as I do it?"

"Sure. Take a look. I can get in the wringer, too, if we're not careful. I've been here to see you a couple of times. Then you go to your bank and say you want to raise a hundred grand in cash. What for? To pay the light bill, you say. This is a small town. Talk gets started."

The brown eyes regarded me with level speculation. "Well, perhaps if you named some more reasonable figure, say ten thousand, it might be easier——"

I shook my head. "Unh-unh."

"Twenty?"

"Come off it, baby. I've been around, too. We understand each other better than that."

She shrugged. "I was afraid we did."

"Well, nice try, anyway. But now, let's get on. How are you going to raise it, and how long will it take?"

She thought for a moment. Then she said, "It'll take about a week, and it can all be handled in Houston, which should be safe enough as far as gossip is concerned. I have securities—mostly common stocks and railroad bonds—sufficient to cover it. They can be converted easily. I'll place a sell order with the brokerage firm down there, and they'll give me a cheque for the proceeds. I deposit the cheque in a Houston bank, and when it clears, draw out the cash and give it to you. They may wonder at it, but not seriously. Banks deal with eccentrics all the time."

I had to admire her coolness. She could have been merely figuring out her share of a luncheon tab. "You're an unflustered tomato," I said.

She shrugged again. "What would you like? Hysterics? I learned to face facts very early in life. If there were any way out I'd fight you right down to the ground, but when there isn't, why not accept it?"

"Good for you." I stood up. "It's a pleasure doing business with you."

"I can assure you it's no pleasure as far as I'm concerned. I wish you'd never been born."

"It's just the breaks, Brown Eyes. Some days you can't murder a soul without getting caught at it." I yanked the microphone cord out of the back of the sofa and pulled out the power plug. She watched me.

"You unlatched one of the doors when you were here yesterday?" It was more a statement than a question.

I nodded toward the door in back of the curtain. "That one."

"Clever. And I thought you were an utter idiot."

"Well, better luck next time, honey." I closed the recorder. "Just so we don't start anybody thinking, I won't come around here any more, but I'll be in touch with you by phone to see how you're coming along raising the geetus."

"Where will you be? Here in town?"

"No. Out there at the fishing camp. It'll look better that way. Now, let's see. This is Thursday, right?"

She nodded.

"Well, how about a week from today, in Houston? Think you can do it by then?"

"Yes. And can you have the tape back from your fellow thug by that time?"

"I think so." I started for the door, and then turned. "Anyway, we'll be in touch. And just one more thing. Better caution Tallant about flipping his lid and trying something silly. Remember, if anything happens to me you'll both land in Death Row."

She said nothing. I went on out and got in the car. On the way out of town I stopped at a small grocery and bought a dozen cans of beer and some more supplies for the kitchen. I picked up a roll of the plastic film they use to wrap things in a refrigerator with, and two rolls of Scotch tape. I bought fifty pounds of ice, wrapped it in an old blanket, and shoved off for the lake.

It was a little before ten when I swung off on to the road going into the swamp. I met no one. About four miles in, where the road wound through a heavy stand of pine on a hillside dropping away to the bottom, I slowed. In a moment I found it, a faint trace of an old logging road leading off to the left. It had been unused for years and the ruts were sifted over with dead pine needles. I pulled off on to it and went ahead until the car was out of sight of anyone going by. When I stopped and cut the engine there was dead silence except for a faint whisper of breeze through the tops of the pines. I took the roll of tape out of my pocket and began wrapping it in the plastic, stretching the film tightly for a good waterproof seal. I used the whole roll, and then bound it solidly with the Scotch tape. When I had finished I got out, took the jack handle from the trunk, and looked about for a likely spot. Off to the left some fifteen or twenty yards, vines grew around an old stump. I parted them, scooped out a hole with the jack handle and buried the package, tamping the soil down neatly and carefully rearranging the pine needles and leaves over it. Nobody would ever find it. I turned the car about and drove back on the road. After I was back in the ruts, I backed up and then came forward again to erase the tracks leading in.

The cabin lay in mottled shade from the big oaks around it as I drove into the clearing. I unlocked the front door and went inside. Starting a fire in the cook-stove, I burned the carbon copy of the letter and the rest of the typing paper, along with the carton the plastic wrap had come in. Then I took the typewriter outside and locked it in the trunk of the car with the recorder.

I brought in the ice and put it in the box, and piled the beer cans on it. After I had arranged the groceries on the shelves, I opened some pork and beans and ate them out of the can to save dishwashing. Punching one of the cans of beer, I took it out on to the porch and lit a cigarette. I was tired from being up all night, but too excited to be sleepy. It was wonderful. I had it made; in one stroke I'd tied them up and left them with no way out except to pay me. A week from today I'd meet her in Houston, she'd hand me a fortune in good, hard cash, and I'd be on my way. Nobody would ever know.

After I had finished the beer I put on swim trunks and went down to the pier. The skiff, moored to it with a padlock and chain, was half full of rainwater. I bailed it out and then went for a swim. The water was warm and fairly clear now in late summer. I climbed out and lay down on the pier in the shade of the big oaks overhanging it, conscious of the drowsy hush of midday. Four days' tension unwound inside me like a breaking clock spring, and I went to sleep.

I didn't know what woke me. I opened my eyes and Julia Cannon was standing beside my legs looking down at me.

"Hello," I said.

She nodded. "Hello."

I rubbed a hand across my face. "How long have you been here?"

"Just a few minutes."

I couldn't see anyone else, either here on the pier or up by her car in front of the cabin. "Where's the moose?"

"Moose?"

"Tallant."

"I don't know," she said.

It was late afternoon, and shadows were reaching out across the clearing. She wore a dark pleated skirt and a soft, white, long-sleeved blouse with French cuffs. I turned my head slightly and completed the survey. She had on nylons in that area, and sling pumps.

"Nice," I said.

She made no reply.

"Don't mind me," I said. "I always wake up this way."

She was carrying a pack of cigarettes in her hand, and a paper book of matches, because women never have pockets in anything. She fumbled with them now, lighting one.

I reached up a hand for it. "Thanks," I said. She lit another for herself.

"Quite neat," she said. "An entire philosophy in one gesture."

I propped myself on an elbow. "Don't be an egg-head, honey. You're stacked all wrong."

She shrugged.

"What's on your mind?" I asked.

"Nothing." She sat down with her back against one of the upright poles to which the pier was secured. Raising her legs, she tucked the skirt in under them.

"What progress with the money?" I asked.

"I called the broker in Houston and gave him a list of securities to sell. The proceeds will be deposited to my account in the bank down there next Tuesday."

"Nice going," I said. "I'll meet you Thursday morning. Right?"

She nodded. "I'll be at the Rice Hotel."

"Alone?"

"Is that your concern?"

I took a drag on the cigarette. "You can bet it is. I don't want Tallant around when I give that tape back to you. I've seen some of his work."

"You think of everything, don't you?"

"Take a look at the hole you're in and you can answer your own question. We work it this way. Tallant is to be up here in his store on Thursday morning. Just before I meet you with the tape, I call him long distance. If I don't hear his voice, I don't show."

She nodded coolly. "That sounds all right. You'll have the recorder with you? I shall want to hear the tape, naturally."

"Of course. I'll come to your room at the hotel. We play it back, you put the money in my warm little hand, and I fade."

"Very well," she said. She looked musingly at my face. "Tough, aren't you?"

"I try to get along."

"You should go far. Is blackmail a new field for you?"

"Maiden voyage."

"I must say you have a masterly grasp of its intricacies, for a beginner."

"Thank you. I like your legs."

"You don't have any trouble with the moral aspects?"

"Why should I? I'm just a press agent in reverse. You're paying me to keep you off the front page."

The brown eyes met mine probingly. "Never mind the comic rationalization. It doesn't bother you in the slightest, does it?"

"No. I'm a bastard. I admit it."

"Frank, to say the least."

"Look. It's a jungle. They throw you into it naked, and sixty years later they carry you off in a box. You just do the best you can."

She smiled a little mockingly. "Ah. The beginnings of thought. You're a nihilist."

"That's out of style," I said. "Nobody's been one for years."

"You *are* surprising. I didn't think you'd know what it meant."

"Duh," I said. "I saw it in a comic book."

She shrugged. "Never mind." Her glance crawled up me from toes to shoulders and back again. "Just don't be an egg-head. You're stacked all wrong."

I looked at her face. It was completely expressionless. "How about a beer?" I asked. "I've got some on ice."

"Love one," she said. "How about helping me up? These high heels——"

I stood up and reached a hand down for her. She took it and I lifted. She came erect, teetered a little, and braced herself with a hand on my shoulder. I took her arm as she walked ahead of me down the pier.

"Thank you," she said when we were on solid ground, and

pulled her arm away. I was listening for something in her voice, and thought I heard it.

She led the way toward the car instead of the front porch of the cabin. I stood behind her as she opened the right front door. "Something I wanted to get," she said, reaching into the glove compartment.

There was an overnight bag on the floor in back. She turned and saw me looking at it.

"I was—I mean, I'm going to Dallas to visit friends over the week-end," she said.

"Hot there, this time of year," I said.

"Yes. Isn't it?"

The sun was far down now, below the wall of timber around the clearing, and there was something about the light that played up her flamboyant colouring—warm red, honey, deep brown, and the jet shadow of her hair. She had taken something from the glove compartment, but at the moment I wouldn't have noticed if she'd been carrying a lighted neon sign in each hand.

"You promised me a beer," she said.

"Sure," I replied. We went up on the porch. "Make yourself at home. I'll change out of these trunks and open a couple of cans."

I went through into the back room, took off the swim trunks, and put on shorts and a pair of flannel slacks. Just as I was shoving my feet into sandals she came in. She leaned against the door frame, holding a cigarette in her fingers, and swept an amused glance around the room at the beds and the duck-hunting clothes hanging along the walls.

"Very cosy," she said. "A little crude—but masculine."

I tossed the trunks across a chair and stepped toward her. She didn't move out of the doorway. I leaned an arm against the frame above her head and stood looking down at her.

"Long drive," I said.

She tilted her head back. "Yes. Isn't it?"

She put a hand up on my arm. "No shirt. Characteristic."

I said nothing.

"Like oak."

"Yes," I said. "Isn't it?"

She stared musingly at the gold cuff link on her wrist as the hand slid downward, across my shoulder. The cigarette slipped from the fingers of her other hand and fell to the floor. She didn't appear to notice it.

"You dropped your cigarette," I said.

She glanced down. "Oh. So I did."

It was lying near her feet. She placed the toe of one of the pumps on it and ground it slowly into the floor.

She looked back up at my face.

"I was finished with it," she said.

CHAPTER TWELVE

It was dark in the room. She stirred languidly beside me on the narrow bed and sat up, groping on the table for a cigarette. The big match flared, revealing her nakedness. She couldn't have cared less. She was a cool devil in most ways, but when she was after fun she took it fervently and unbuttoned.

"Oh," she said. The hand carrying the match stopped its movement a little short of the end of the cigarette.

"What is it?" I asked.

"I almost forgot the thing I came out here for."

"Like hell you did," I said.

She turned her head slightly and smiled at me in the light of the match. It was a large assortment of smile wanton and go-to-hell at the same time, with just a trace of well-fed cat. "No," she said. "I brought you something."

"Not really?"

"Shut up." She lit the cigarette and waved the match to put it out. "It's on the table in the other room."

"What is?" Then I remembered she had taken something from the glove compartment of the car.

"The envelope. With the money in it."

"Money?"

"Really. I'm not that distracting, am I?"

"How much money?"

"That's more like it. You should stay in character."

"The hell with that. How much?"

"Eight thousand."

"Why?"

"Partial payment. What else? I happened to have that much available, and since I had to give it to you sooner or later——"

"You're a relaxed type."

"Not relaxed. Realistic. Don't misunderstand me; I'm not soft. If you'd left yourself open anywhere, you'd never have extorted a nickel from me. But you didn't—so what's the use stalling or crying about it?"

"How about this? Not that I'm kicking, you understand, but you did surprise me a little——"

"Women can surprise you? At your age?"

"So I'm stupid."

"Just say you intrigued me."

"That's good."

"You're quite interesting. You have daring, imagination, and no more moral restraint than a cobra. I don't like dull men."

"So you like me. Crap."

"I didn't say I like you. I said you interested me."

"That's nice," I said. I got up and went into the other room. Striking a match, I located the envelope on the table and opened it. It was a big nine by twelve Manila type, and inside were a lot of loose bills plus two blocks of fifties. The match burned down and scorched my fingers while I stared. I tried to imagine what a hundred thousand would look like. It would be a little over twelve times as much. I struck another match and carried it into the back room. When I put the envelope on the table beside the bed some of the money slid out. I looked from it to her in the flickering light.

"What is it?" she asked.

"Colour scheme," I said. "Make a great painting. *Nude brunette with eight thousand dollars."*

She smiled mockingly. "Ah, your aesthetic side."

"I'm a sensitive type," I said. "I live for beauty."

"But, really, you're more complex than that. Shouldn't your great painting also include a broiled T-bone steak and a bottle of cheap bourbon?"

"Leave out the bourbon," I said. "I don't drink." The match went out and I dropped it on the floor. I sat on the side of the bed and struck another to light a cigarette.

"You see now why you interest me?" she asked.

"No," I said.

"You're an odd mixture. All your tastes are elemental; you operate right at the instinctive level. And yet you demonstrate great imagination and some intelligence in your campaigns to satisfy these primitive urges."

"Sure, sure," I said. "Why don't you write a book?"

"You're a magnificent brute."

The match went out and I tried to remember in the dark what the money looked like.

"You just take what you want."

"Sure, sure," I said.

Her voice went on. "I think we're a lot more alike in some ways than either of us would care to admit."

Women, I thought. They yakked all the time except when they were being laid or asleep. They could make a federal case out of as simple a thing as a jump in the hay, and then afterward they had to analyse it like a bridge hand. Well, what the hell, maybe she wasn't as bad as a lot of them, at that. At least she didn't require three days' conversation to get into bed; all she had to do was see one handy and have room to throw her clothes. She had talent, too, once she got there. I began to think about that again, stretched out beside her, and shut her up with the old classic method of turning off the yak. It was all right with her.

We stooged around the cabin all the next day, and late in the afternoon we went for a swim. She didn't have a suit in her over-night bag, but that didn't bother her to any extent. Afterward she dressed in white shorts and a knit pullover thing with short sleeves and we sat on the front porch drinking beer. She was something to see, even after nearly twenty-four hours of her.

"You're a good-looking dish," I said.

She smiled lazily and stretched out a leg, looking at her red toe-nails. "Why, thank you, Cyrano. You overwhelm me."

"What about Tallant?" I asked.

"Very well. What about Tallant?"

"Does he think you're in Dallas?"

"I suppose so. But does it matter?"

"No. Except he might blow his stack if he found out where you really were."

"Well, he can't do anything."

I lit a cigarette. "No. Of course not—as long as he's in his right mind. But I don't think he's as tough as you are, and he might flip. He's close enough to the edge now; why push him over the line?"

She smiled mockingly. "Ah, there speaks the ardent lover——"

"Nuts. This thing is tricky enough now without getting it loused up with a lot of personal angles. If you want to put the harpoon in Tallant, do it after I get out of the country."

"He doesn't own me."

"Well, he's tried hard enough," I said, thinking of Cannon and Purvis. "Aren't you going to get married?"

"I don't know."

"Wasn't that the idea?"

"What do you mean?"

"You know what I mean. You were running around with him, but Cannon got wise to it. He'd have divorced you, but the property settlement wouldn't have been very big, with the evidence he had. So when he came uncorked and tried to drive you off the road and left himself set up like a duck in a shooting gallery, you blew the whistle on him."

"I see no point in discussing it. Emotion of any kind would be beyond your comprehension."

"Hell, it's nothing to me. But what'd you do—get tired of him? Tallant, I mean."

She leaned back on her elbows and regarded me thoughtfully. "He does tend to get a little intense and possessive. And maybe I could like you better."

"Sure, sure," I said. "Have all the fun you want, but let's don't get too careless, shall we? Not till I get mine and get out of here. This is a big deal, and I don't want it screwed up by some jealous type going off his rocker. One false move and we'll have the cops around here like cats at a fish fry."

"Are you trying to get rid of me?" she asked coldly.

"Of course not. I'm just trying to use common sense."

"Use all you want. But I'm going to stay."

"Sure, sure. Stick around. What the hell!"

She smiled. "After all, I'm supposed to have gone somewhere for the week-end. And I like it here."

"That's an old gag," I said.

She laughed.

I gave up. Women never made any sense, anyway. And there really wasn't any reason Tallant would come out here and find her; I was just jittery because there was so much at stake. *Relax,* I thought; *quit worrying and join the party.*

That was Friday afternoon. Saturday morning at ten, while we were drinking coffee in the front room, he walked in on us. He was carrying a gun in his right hand, and he was wired and set to go off.

For some reason—probably just dumb luck—she was dressed, for a change. For the best part of two days she'd been lying around like an oyster on the half shell, but this morning when she climbed out of the sack she'd put the pleated skirt and the blouse back on. Maybe that helped; I didn't know. On the face of it, it wouldn't seem to make a great deal of difference; there couldn't be much chance she'd been out here two days and nights just to give me her recipe for pineapple fritters, but you can never tell for sure about a joker who's beginning to lose his marbles. If he'd happened to walk in on us in the sack or while she was lying around in nothing but her nail polish he might have killed us both before we could open our mouths. As it was, it was bad enough.

She was sitting at the table facing the open front door and I was at the stove pouring another cup of coffee when I heard her say, "*Well!*" I wheeled, and he was standing in the door. He was so big it looked as if it had been stretched around him. His mouth twitched, he hadn't shaved for two or three days, and his eyes had the wild, staring look of a man who was going to swing at the next cockroach that laughed at him.

My gun was in the back room in a duffle bag and I was ten feet from him, at least, with nothing in my hand but a coffee pot. Gooseflesh prickled across my shoulders. She was all right, though. He didn't scare her a nickel's worth, and she was just the girl to show him. She smiled at him with exactly the right shade of contempt to push him over the line, and said, "My, aren't we dramatic?" I couldn't think of anything helpful except to pray he'd use the whole clip on her before he remembered me.

He took a slow step into the room and turned just enough to watch us both. He was wearing dark slacks and a white shirt with the cuffs rolled halfway up his rope-muscled forearms. The shirt was stained down the front with something he'd spilled on it, and he looked like a man on the wrong end of a two-day binge. If he'd been drunk, though, he wasn't now. He was just unstable and dangerous as hell.

"So you went to Dallas," he said harshly.

She rested her chin in one cupped palm and regarded him with faint amusement. "Are you asking me, dear?"

"Why did you even bother to lie about it, you lousy little chippy?"

She shrugged. "I didn't. I started to Dallas, but you might say I changed my mind. It looked as if it might be more fun to stay here." She smiled sweetly. "And do you know, it was. I've been having a wonderful time."

I took a chance and breathed, hoping he wouldn't notice I was still alive. Maybe he'd just kill her and go away. I wanted to kill her myself.

He walked slowly over to the table and stood looking down at her with the veins standing out on his temples. The gun lined up with her face. "Look up here," he said. "Look up at me, you round-heeled bitch——"

She glanced up calmly. "Yes, dear? And what are you going to do?"

If she'd only shut up—— He was still talking, so maybe there was a chance. But, oh, for the love of God, couldn't she keep her stupid mouth shut for a minute?

I was careful not to move. "Tallant," I said softly.

He didn't even hear me. His face twitched. "I wish to God I'd never seen you. Or even heard of you. Why couldn't you have died when you were born? Look at you! You're what I went through it for——"

"Tallant," I said again, a little louder this time.

He turned then. "Don't get in a hurry," he said. "I'm coming to you."

"Listen," I said. "Don't be a fool, Tallant. You haven't got a chance in the world. If you kill us the police will get that tape. You want to commit suicide?"

"Shut up!" he shouted. "I don't care! It'll be worth it——"

"Cut it out," I went on, trying to keep my voice calm. "Use your head. Go on and get out of here, and you're in the clear. Nobody'll ever know, and she's the one who has to pick up the tab. She's paying off for you. Stop acting like a kid."

"I'll kill both of you!"

Gently, I thought. *Don't move. Don't set him off.* He was making threats, having to prime himself to keep going. He was beginning to waver, and the moment to use the gun was slipping away. We might make it—if she didn't open her fat mouth again.

She did. And she put both feet in it this time. "You haven't been following me, have you, dear? You know I don't like that."

He started to turn. *Throw the coffee pot,* I thought bitterly; *that always works fine in the movies.* Then, without any warning, he cracked. He looked around helplessly, like some big, tortured kid, and said, "*Why?* Why did you do it?"

"Get out," she said contemptuously.

"Julia——" He dropped the gun to the floor and stood with his chin on his chest. "Julia——" Turning, he ran out the door.

I picked up the gun and went out on the porch. He was stumbling along the road and in a moment he entered the wall of timber at the edge of the clearing and was out of sight. His car would be back up there somewhere.

She came up beside me and put an arm across my shoulders. I

turned, caught the front of her blouse, and slapped her across the face with the back of my hand. It made a sharp sound in the stillness. She cried out and stepped back.

I wiped the sweat off my face with a hand that was still shaking, and walked past her into the back room. Throwing the big suitcase on the bed, I began tossing clothes into it. She came back and stood in the doorway. Her face was white except for the angry red splotch on her cheek, and she stared at me with amazement.

"What did you do that for?" she asked.

"For being an idiot."

"What do you mean?"

I straightened with a shirt in my hand. "Go ahead. Get yourself killed. But you can leave me out of it."

She shrugged. "He's harmless."

"Sure, sure," I said. He was harmless. He'd only killed two men so far.

"What's the matter?" she asked, with just a shade of the same contempt she'd used on him. "Are you afraid of him?"

"Don't try to ride me," I said. "I'll slap your face around under your ear."

She sniffed. "What's wrong with you, anyway? He can't do anything to you, and you know it."

I walked over and stood looking down at her. "Try to get this through your fat head. Maybe you can't, but try it, anyway. He can't do anything to me as long as he cares what happens to him. That's what the whole thing was based on. The minute he quits caring, threatening him with that tape is about as bright as trying to put out hell with a water pistol. He's half nuts, and you're pushing him over the line. He's already killed two men because of you—God knows why, when he could have laid you for a bar of soap—but he did, and now that he's got himself into a jam that can put him in the electric chair, you start giving him the treatment. You don't think he'll be back. I do. And the next time he probably won't do so much talking first; he'll be smoking up the place when he comes through the door——"

"You have his gun."

"I've got news for you," I said. "They made two guns last year."

"Well, what are you going to do?" she asked, leaning against the door frame.

"I'm going to get the hell out of here while I'm in one piece. I don't want any punchy maniac blowing my head off from behind, or while I'm asleep."

Her eyebrows arched. "Well! And what about me?"

"The hell with what about you. You meet me in Houston Thursday at noon with that money, the way you're supposed to. In the meantime, try the Marine Corps."

She flared up. "Don't talk to me that way!"

"Beat it," I said. I turned back to my packing.

"Why, you arrogant muscle-brain——"

I collected my shaving gear off a shelf and dropped it in the bag.

"John——"

There was something plaintive about it. I turned. She leaned her head back against the door frame and the big eyes were contrite. "I'm sorry," she said.

It was a smooth routine, from blazing hellcat to appealing little girl in one breath, and I was about to tell her what she could do with it when something else occurred to me. Tallant might flip his lid and kill her, even after she'd gone back home. What was I thinking about, going off and leaving her? That was stupid; the thing to do was take her with me so I'd know damn well she would still be alive Thursday morning.

I walked over to her. "I'm sorry, too," I said. "I guess he scared me a little."

She looked up at me with an eager smile. "Why don't we go away somewhere, if you don't want to stay here?"

You're reading my mail, I thought. I put my hand under her chin, tilted her face up, and kissed her. "That's the ticket. Just the two of us, like a honeymoon."

Her eyes were shining. "Wonderful. Where shall we go?"

"Anywhere, baby."

"Houston?"

"We'll go there Thursday." I didn't want to be around Houston any longer than I had to. There was always a chance that taxi driver had spilled my description to the cops.

She laughed. "Well, what does it matter? Who cares where he is, on a honeymoon?"

"Sure," I said. I put the envelope with the eight thousand on top of the other stuff in the bag, and after she'd packed hers I carried the two of them outside and locked the cabin.

"There's no use taking both cars," she said. "Why don't we go in mine?"

"No," I said. "You go ahead. Turn right when you get out on the highway. I'll follow you and leave my car in Breward. I can pick it up again when we start down to Houston."

She frowned slightly. "But why not just leave it here? Nobody'll bother it."

"Save having to come back in and get it," I replied. Naturally, I couldn't tell her I wanted her to go out first so I could stop and dig up that tape. I'd leave it in the car, of course, and she'd never know. When we came back through Breward and I drove it on down to Houston I could leave it on a lot and while she was at the bank I'd get the tape out of it, still carrying out the illusion somebody else had it all the time.

She shrugged. "All right."

I put the bags in her Buick and got in my car. When I stepped on the starter, nothing happened. I tried again. The battery was dead.

That was odd. The generator had been charging all right. Maybe it was just a bad connection. I tried the lights. They came on dimly, and then died. Well, so you buy an old clunk——

She got out of the Buick. "What's the matter?"

"Dead battery," I said.

"Why do you suppose that is? Did you leave the radio on?"

"It hasn't got a radio. Well, you can push me to get it started."

"Oh, let's go," she said impatiently. "Leave it here."

"Push it," I said. I climbed back in. She manœuvred up behind me and came up against the bumper. I managed to swing around and we started out the road. After a quarter of a mile there still hadn't been a cough out of the motor. She stopped and got out.

"What do you suppose is the matter?"

"Maybe the battery's shorted out inside; not enough juice even for the ignition."

"Well, leave the silly thing here, John. Let's go."

"I can't leave it here in the road."

"Oh, all right."

She got back in the Buick, went past me, and turned around. We manœuvred the Chevy back to the cabin and left it in the yard. I started to lift the hood to have a look under it, but shrugged. All it needed was another battery. We could bring one in when we came back. I didn't like the idea of coming back in here, but it would be safe enough. All I'd have to do would be call Tallant's shop beforehand and make sure he was there instead of down here looking for us.

I got in the car with her and we drove out of the bottom. Before we came out on the highway it occurred to me it was damned strange the car hadn't started. With her pushing it, there should have been enough spark from the generator to fire it.

Oh, well, I thought, and dropped it. It was a mistake, but I was making them one after another by that time.

CHAPTER THIRTEEN

We drove to Shreveport. When we checked in at the hotel, she waited impatiently until the bellhop got his tip and left; then she came close to me, put her hands up behind my neck, smiled delightfully, and said, "Isn't this nice?"

"Sure, sure," I said. I'd intended to ask the desk to send up the Houston papers, but I'd forgotten.

She leaned against me a little. "Riding in a car always does something funny to me. Maybe it's the vibration."

"Could be," I said.

"Being on a ship does the same thing."

So does breathing, I thought.

She brushed her hand through my hair, whirled away from me, and spun herself on to the bed. She doubled up her legs and lit a cigarette, smiling roguishly at me above the match. "Air-conditioning, no mosquitoes, tiled bath, clean sheets—this is much better, don't you think?"

"Who's got a one-track mind?" I asked.

She made a face. "All right. But is that so bad?"

"It's fine with me," I said.

"Well! Couldn't you be just a *little* more ardent?"

I lit a cigarette and sat down on the other bed, facing her. "I don't always get your message," I said. "Seems to me you should be sore as a boil."

"So I should."

"But you're not?"

She shrugged. "What good would it do?"

"I see what you mean. If you can't whip 'em, join 'em."

"That's part of it. But maybe I like you."

"Sure, sure."

She looked at me thoughtfully. "It's odd, I know. But there's something fascinating about you. You're exciting."

"Why?" I asked.

"I don't know, really. It's a lot of things, I guess. You're big, and hard, and utterly ruthless. You're so completely a male animal from every angle——"

"And you like 'em male?"

She glanced up at me from under those long lashes. "Haven't you formed any opinion about that yet?"

We didn't leave the room for twenty-four hours. We had our meals sent up, and I got hold of all the Houston papers. There was nothing in them about Purvis, which could mean anything. The police would still be actively working on it, even if it didn't rate any space. There was no love-nest angle and no way they could work in some pictures of a half-dressed babe; he was just another sleazy character with his roof shoved in. They're a dime a dozen in any large city and have to have a real homey angle somewhere to stay in the papers more than a couple of days. That taxi driver could have come forward and given my description to the cops without anyone's bothering to get out an extra about it. That was the scarey part of it; I wouldn't know, and I had to go back down there.

I thought about it. Why go down there at all? She could go draw out the money and meet me in San Antonio or Dallas or somewhere else. No, that wasn't so hot. She'd be wandering around over the state alone with over ninety thousand in cash, and there was no telling what'd happen. The way she was bothered, she was just as likely to take off up an alley after a telephone lineman. I wasn't so sure now but what she might be a little whacky, at least when she was troubled with ants in the pants, which seemed to be most of the time. There was no doubt she was one of the smoothest-looking dishes I'd ever seen, but she was beginning to strike me as a character. They both were, as a matter of fact, and they didn't look half as dangerous as they had at first. It was just dumb luck they'd fooled the police the way they had, and Purvis had been merely stupid. Hell, I'd made them look silly, right from the start.

We went to a movie Sunday afternoon and out to dinner afterward. Men turned and looked at her everywhere she went. She was in a good mood when we came back, and didn't seem to mind whether I listened to her yakking or not. When you've reached the saturation point in love-making, there's nothing you can get as sick of as being shut up for any length of time in a hotel room with a woman, but I had to hand it to her. She was good-natured all the time, and if I just grunted occasionally when she was beating her gums fourteen to the dozen while brushing her hair or washing out her stockings with the bathroom door open it was all right with her. She just didn't want me to be out of reach for a minute.

On Monday she wanted to go shopping, and nothing would do but that I go with her. She had three or four hundred dollars beside what she'd given me, and I wandered through shops and sat around bored stiff while she bought stockings and another nightgown and some perfume and looked at ten times as much more she didn't buy.

"You don't mind, do you, John?" she said, smiling happily at me. "After all, I'm doing it for you."

"Sure, go ahead," I said. What the hell, I had to keep her pacified and contented until Thursday morning, and wandering around in stores was as easy a way to do it as any. She was beginning to wear me out.

She kept me up most of the night, yakking and being very sweet and chummy and giving me the old build-up, so it was late when I awoke on Tuesday morning, some time after ten o'clock. She was still asleep beside me, wearing the new shortie nightgown she'd bought. I raised up on one elbow and looked at her, and all sorts of bells began to go off in my mind. She was beautiful as hell, and even asleep she didn't look stupid. What kind of an act was she putting on, and why was she doing it?

So maybe she did need men the way an alcoholic needs booze—she still had too much in the way of equipment to have to knock herself out chasing them. They'd be falling all over her. Why break a leg trying to scramble into the sack with a guy who was putting the bite on her for a hundred grand? I wasn't that good. I'd never had any illusions about anything since I was eleven, and that included myself. I was no particular great-lover type. In two hours on any public beach she could pick up a half dozen big hard-shouldered jokers who'd give her just as good a run for her money in the hay and even throw in the old moonlight-and-roses pitch at no extra charge. So what was the gag?

Was it a stall? But why? What did she hope to gain by it? It didn't make any sense. I had the goods on them, and there was no way on earth they could squirm out of it. But this whole thing was too easy; it didn't ring true. My first impression of the two of them was that they were sharp, brainy, and dangerous as hell. Then he'd acted like some punchy adolescent out there at the cabin. And now she was a happy-go-lucky roundheel with nothing on her mind but a place to fall. Was the whole thing an act for my benefit? Did they think they could con me, string me along with a measly eight thousand and a lot of empty promises? Well, we'd see about that. I reached over and shook her.

Her eyes opened. She looked at me rather coldly for an instant until she was fully awake, and then she smiled. "What is it, John?"

"I just wanted some information," I said shortly. "What's the name of that brokerage firm in Houston? The one that's selling the stocks for you?"

With no hesitation at all, she replied, "Harley and Bryson. Why?"

"And who handles your account?"

"George Harley, Jr." She looked puzzled. "But why, John?"

I ignored her. Picking up the phone from the table beside the bed, I told the operator, "I want to put in a long-distance call to Houston. Person-to-person to Mr. George Harley, Jr., at the brokerage firm of Harley and Bryson. Got it?"

"Yes, sir," she replied. "Just a moment, please."

I passed the phone over to her. She stared. "Ask Harley how he's coming along unloading your stocks. Hold the receiver out a little from your ear, and pray you've been telling me the truth."

She took it and held it as I told her. I slid over, holding her tightly with my cheek against her head and my own ear touching the outer rim of the receiver. I could hear the long-lines operators talking.

The receptionist answered. "Just a moment, please."

After a short pause, a man came on. "Harley speaking."

I squeezed her arm. If she'd been lying, she was in a bad spot.

"Oh, Mr. Harley," she said calmly. "Julia Cannon."

"Oh, good morning, Mrs. Cannon."

"I just called to ask if you had executed the order I phoned in the other day——"

"Oh, yes. I was just about to send through a statement. Let's see. . . . Have it right here somewhere, I think . . . Just a moment . . . Yes . . . Here it is . . . Hmmmmmm. General Motors . . . Boeing . . . Anaconda . . . Hmmmmmm . . . yesterday's market . . . cheque . . . be deposited your account bank here as instructed . . . total proceeds, less commission, ninety-seven thousand, six hundred, forty-four dollars, eighty-one cents . . . apparently all in order . . . Hmmm . . ."

I sat up on the bed and reached for a cigarette. She looked at me. I nodded and waved a hand. She said, "Thank you, Mr. Harley. Good-bye." She hung up.

I handed her a lighted cigarette.

"What was that all about?" she asked.

"Just checking, honey. Just checking."

"You thought I was lying?"

"It just occurred to me I didn't have anybody's word for it but yours."

"You think I'd dare? Under the circumstances?"

"Relax," I said. I felt like a million.

Of course she hadn't been trying anything funny. How could she? They were absolutely helpless, and their staying alive depended on their doing exactly what I told them. Of course she was knocking herself out to be nice to me. If anybody had me where the wool was that short I'd be an eager beaver myself. I thought about it. The stocks were already sold; I'd heard the man say so myself. All I had to do now was go down there Thursday and pick up that big, fat bundle of folding money.

"You must think I'm insane," she said petulantly.

"Honey, I think you're terrific."

"Do you like me? Just a little?"

"Sure, sure," I said. Like her? She was Fort Knox, with legs. I was just reaching for a cigarette when the bells began to ring again.

My hand hung there halfway to the cigarette pack while the whole thing raced through my mind at once. Was that it? Was that the angle? Sure. It figured from every direction. Look at it, you fool. You underestimated them and got yourself sucked out of position, but good. They almost had you.

I grinned coldly. Almost. But not quite. There was still time.

It had been close, though, if I were right. This was Tuesday. I had been with her since Thursday afternoon, been with her every minute. She'd seen to that. She knew every move I'd made and she knew definitely I hadn't been in contact with anybody. So suppose they were feeling me out, stretching out the time I was incommunicado, testing me a little at a time? That would account for the fact the car wouldn't start—he'd butchered it some way that first night to make sure that if I went anywhere it would only be with her—and it would explain this whole lovey-dovey routine on her part. They simply didn't believe there was anybody else in this thing with me, and when they had finally proved it to their own satisfaction they'd knock me off. Like that.

I hadn't quite sold them with that piece of razzle-dazzle that morning. They weren't sure I had mailed the tape, or if I had, that I had mailed it to an accomplice. And every hour that went by without my getting in contact with *somebody* to assure him I was still alive was making my position more dangerous. The deadly efficiency of it made me shiver.

Well, we'll see about it, I thought. *Thank God I'd caught it in time.*

She gave me a provocative, sidelong glance and then made a face at me. "Well, if *that's* all you woke me up for——" She sat up in bed, stripped off the nightgown with casual unconcern and strode naked into the bathroom. She left the door just partly open, as she always did, and started yakking as she turned on the shower.

I lit the cigarette.

"—don't you think so, John?"

Smart baby, I thought. I didn't say anything.

"John?"

"Yes," I said. "What is it?"

"You brute," she protested above the noise of the shower, "you're not even listening to me. I said, aren't we having a good time?"

"Sure, sure," I said. "A wonderful time."

She went on chattering. I reached out for the telephone, lifting it carefully off the cradle. When the operator answered, I said quietly, "I want to make another long-distance call."

"Yes, sir," she replied. "Just one moment."

The yakking went on from the shower. It paused momentarily on a questioning note.

"Sure, sure," I answered, holding my hand over the mouthpiece.

"Well, that's better. I think you're sweet, too."

"Aren't we both," I said. That'll hold you for a minute, you sweet, deadly bitch. It did. She started humming in the shower.

"All right, sir," the operator said.

I took my hand off the transmitter and spoke directly into it, very quietly. "Fort Worth. Person-to-person to George Gray at the Gray Midcontinent Equipment Company."

"Yes, sir. Will you hold on, please?"

The humming continued from the bathroom. I breathed softly; she couldn't possibly have heard me. *All right, baby,* I thought; *I've got you.*

I could hear Information in Fort Worth giving the number, and then the telephone ringing.

The humming stopped. "Oh, John?"

I grinned coldly. Putting my hand back over the transmitter, I said, "Stop the yakking for a minute, will you? I'm trying to make a telephone call. And turn off that shower."

The shower stopped abruptly. The door opened and she came out, naked, beautiful, and dripping, with a big towel in her hand. "A telephone call?" she asked with big-eyed innocence. "To whom, John?"

I smiled. "Long distance. To a friend of mine. You may have heard me speak of him."

"Oh," she said, with no surprise in her voice and no change of expression. The world lost a great actress, I thought. After six days she must have figured they about had it made, but no disappointment showed on her face at all.

Just then George's voice sounded in the receiver. "Hello? Gray speaking."

"John," I said. "How are you, boy?"

I held the receiver tightly against my ear. She'd be able to hear there was a voice on the other end and to recognize it as a man's, probably, but unable to catch a word of what it said.

"Well, you old son-of-a-gun," George said. "It's good to hear from you. How's fishing?"

I looked at her. "Fine," I said. "It's been very good. I just thought I'd let you know everything's under control here, and that the trip has been very successful. We've made ourselves a deal, boy."

"Then you will go to work for us——?"

"Sure," I said. "Right away. Next Thursday, in fact. Oh, say, you got the package all right, I guess?"

"Sure. Thanks a lot, John. You say——"

"I knew you'd appreciate it," I chuckled. "Thought they were tied up pretty neatly, myself. And hooked, what I mean. Well, I just didn't want to let too much time go by without letting you know I was okay and that the deal was set. Here's the scoop. I'm going down to Houston Thursday morning and I'll be at the Rice Hotel by about eleven. I'll get in touch with you from there about the details of the deal. I won't take up any more of your time right now. See you, George."

"Fine," he replied. "Good-bye."

I hung up and looked at her again. She merely glanced at me questioningly and went on drying herself. Her breasts swung gently under the towel. "Then he'll have the tape there by Thursday morning?" she asked in a matter-of-fact tone. "That *was* your fellow thug, wasn't it?"

I stared at her, partly in admiration and partly in amazement at her coolness, and then I caught on and just managed to restrain the impulse to laugh. She wasn't acting at all. I'd just put on all that show for nothing; it had never occurred to her to doubt I was telling the truth about an accomplice.

I grinned at her. "Honey," I said. "You're cute. And you're stacked."

She smiled, and dropped the towel across the back of a chair as she looked down at herself. "How did you ever guess?" she asked.

We checked out of the hotel late Wednesday afternoon and started back. I drove. She sat rather quietly beside me for a long time. "I've had a wonderful time, John," she said after a while.

"Good," I said. "So have I." I felt wonderful. We were on the last lap. The whole thing had been so easy it was ridiculous and now all that remained was picking up the money.

"After we've finished the business in Houston, wouldn't you like to go down to Galveston?" she asked. "For just a few days?"

Women never seemed to realize they defeat their own purpose. There's nothing on earth you can need worse when you do and need less when you don't. I was caught up. I started to open my mouth to tell her to get herself a new boy when it occurred to me there was no sense antagonizing her at this stage of the game.

"Sure," I said. "That would be wonderful. We'll spend the week-end down there." After all, as soon as I got my hands on that money I could fade and there was nothing she could do about it. I'd drive the car as far as Dallas, sell it, and take a plane to the Coast. I was already making plans.

Mazatlan, on the west coast of Mexico, had been buzzing around in my head for a long time. A couple of years ago I'd made a trip down there with another guy on the squad after the season was over. We'd had a fine time, catching sails, and I could see the place was going to grow. They were putting a highway through all the way from the border and the tourists and fishermen were going to flock in. It might never be another Acapulco, but if an operator with a bank-roll and a good eye for a buck moved in now he could get in on the ground floor. The thing to do was drift down there, shack up with some babe to learn the language, and keep an eye open all the time for the good thing.

She was saying something again. "What?" I asked. I pulled out to pass a truck, and came back in the lane again.

"I said I'll have to stop at the house when we go through town and pack another bag. I'll need beach things."

"Oh," I thought about it. Well, why not? It'd be dark; nobody would see me with her if she pulled right into the garage. And while we were at the house she could use the phone to get a line on Tallant's whereabouts before we went out to the camp to get my car started with the new battery I'd picked up. I didn't like the idea of going out there at night without knowing where he was. He'd realize I was coming back sooner or later to get the car, and if he'd gone completely off his rocker by this time he might be waiting for me with a gun.

"Sure," I said.

We stopped to have dinner on the way, and it was a little after nine p.m. when we came into Wayles. She was driving then. She skirted the square, keeping to the darker streets. When we came up past the side of the Cannon house it was dark and the whole area was quiet except for the sound of a radio or television set coming from a house farther up the street. She stopped in front of the garage door, and got out to open it herself just in case one of the neighbours might be watching. She got back in and drove inside. I waited until she'd shut the door before I got out. We stood in the hot, airless garage with the headlight glaring against a white concrete wall. When she unlocked the door going into the kitchen I cut the car lights and felt my way along after her.

When we were inside the kitchen, I closed the door and latched it. She clicked on a light and smiled at me. "You know, we could stay here and go on down to Houston early in the morning. Nobody knows you're in here."

I shook my head. "Let's get going."

"All right," she said.

"Wait," I told her. "Don't turn on a light in the living-room. You can see through that curtain if there's enough light behind it."

"There's nothing back of the house but a vacant lot," she protested. Then she shrugged. "But you already know that, don't you?"

"That's right. So just turn on one in the dining-room. That'll give you enough to use the phone. I want you to call Tallant's number."

She frowned. "Why?"

"I want to know for sure where he is before we go out there to pick up my car."

"Oh, for heaven's sake, John. Are you still making a fuss about him?"

"Never mind," I said. I took her arm and shoved her through the door ahead of me. "Call him."

There was enough illumination in this end of the room for her to dial. I sat on the arm of the big chair on the other side of the doorway. The air-conditioning was turned off and it was hot in the room and intensely silent. When she finished dialling I could hear the telephone ringing at the other end. *No, it's not really the phone ringing,* I thought. *It's just an illusion the telephone company throws in to keep subscribers pacified.* It went on. There was no answer. She dropped the instrument back in its cradle and looked around at me.

I didn't like it at all. "Try his shop."

"He closes at six."

I took a cigarette from my pocket. "Never mind. Try it."

She shrugged. "All right, but he wouldn't be there this time of night."

"Don't give me so much static. What the hell, he does gunsmithing, doesn't he? And keeps his books."

She dialled the number. "Is there any particular message you'd like me to give him?"

"No. As soon as you hear his voice, hang up."

There was no answer.

I lit the cigarette while she hung up and stood looking at me. "You know his habits. You got any idea where he could be?"

"No."

"How about lodges? Pool halls? Where does he hang out when he's not pawing up the shrubbery after somebody's wife?"

She shrugged. "He's an amateur astronomer, he plays chess with a number of other men around town, and he goes away on two and three day fishing trips. He could be anywhere. What does it matter?"

I waved a hand at her to cut out the yakking. I still didn't like the idea of going out there at night not knowing where he was. Still, there were a lot of other places he could be. Maybe his nerve had broken and he'd left the country. *Hell,* I thought, *it had been four days. He couldn't have been out there waiting for us all that time.* We'd take a chance on it.

"Pack your bag," I said. "Let's get rolling."

"Are we going by to pick up your car?"

"Sure. Shake it up, will you?"

"I'd like to change before we go."

"All right, all right. Just don't take all night."

"You sound nervous——"

"Get the lead out, will you?"

She started across the living-room toward the hallway leading to the other wing of the house. Then she stopped and turned. "You'll have to reach down the bag for me," she said. "It's on a shelf in one of the bedroom closets."

"Okay," I said. I followed her.

The hallway turned at right angles. Beyond that it was very dark. I stayed close behind her, holding her arm so I wouldn't bump into the walls. "Where's the light?" I asked impatiently.

We went through a doorway. I felt it brush my arm. "Here by the bed," she said. "Just a minute."

She was standing close in front of me and I could tell she was groping around for the lamp. Suddenly she turned and put her hand on my arm. It slid upward, along my shoulder.

"John," she said softly, "let's stay here tonight. We could go out there early in the morning and still be in Houston by noon."

"No."

"Please!" Her arms came up around my neck. She pulled my head down and her lips were against mine.

I suppose it's pure reflex. You're whipped, but never completely defeated; if you were dying on your feet your reaction to that piece of business would always be the same. My arms tightened around her.

"Don't let me fall," she whispered. All her weight seemed to be hanging around my neck.

A light switch clicked and the room was full of sudden light. I whirled, taking her with me part of the way until she pushed hard against my chest, spun outward, and fell. Tallant was sitting crosswise in an overstuffed chair near the door we'd come in. His legs were hanging over the arm, and a pump shotgun was balanced across his knees.

His eyes didn't look crazy at all; they were just cold and very hard. He gestured slightly with one hand. "Nice work, Julia. Move to your left and stay down."

CHAPTER FOURTEEN

SHE moved across the shaggy white rug on her hands and knees, toward the dressing table beyond the foot of the bed.

"Sit down, Harlan," he ordered.

"Look——"

"This is a twelve-gauge, loaded with fours. It'll cut you in two."

I sat down on the side of the bed. It was a big king-sized affair with a blond oak headboard and green chenille spread. There were three windows in the room, their curtains all tightly closed.

It had all happened a little too suddenly for me. One thing was obvious, though. He wasn't crazy; the whole thing had been planned by both of them, and that business out at the cabin was an act.

I was careful not to make any abrupt moves. "Listen Tallant, I don't know what you're trying to prove, but haven't you forgotten something?"

He shook his head. "I don't think so." His gaze shifted just slightly toward her, still keeping me in his field of vision. "We're all right, I'm pretty sure," he told her. "Checks out fine, so far."

She got off the rug and sat down on the upholstered bench before the dressing table. She sighed as she reached around for a pack of cigarettes lying among the cosmetics, and shook her head. "Believe me, I was glad to get your message."

I stared at her. Message? For a moment I even forgot him and his gun.

She glanced at him and smiled. "Mr. Harlan appears to be a little at sea about it all."

He shrugged. "He'll catch on pretty soon."

"What the hell is all this?" I asked roughly.

She lit a cigarette and regarded me coolly. "A simple enough message, Mr. Harlan. Merely a lone coffee cup sitting on the drain-board of the sink, out in the kitchen. Would you care for a translation?"

"Look," I said, "I'm getting a little tired of this——"

"It said, quite simply: bring the gentleman on back to the bedroom; everything is as planned."

"So we're here," I said. "So what of it?"

I reached in my pocket for a cigarette, not remembering until I'd already started the movement that it could be a dangerous thing to do if he was at all trigger-happy with that shotgun. He merely watched me boredly. So she'd already given him the high-sign I didn't have the gun with me. They were cute. They were just full of cloak-and-dagger routines.

"You ought to be on television," I said.

They merely stared at me, saying nothing.

I lit the cigarette. None of this business made any sense, but

I wasn't scared, even as deadly as he looked with that shotgun. Nothing could change the fact I still had them where I wanted them and they couldn't touch me. I'd only been afraid of him when I thought he was about to flip his lid.

"You were with him every minute he was out of the hotel room?" Tallant asked her.

"Every second," she replied. "He was never out of my sight. But he made one call from the room."

"Two," he said.

She nodded. "That's what I meant. One beside the call to Harley and Bryson." She paused, and then went on, "I gather, from the fact we're all here, that you think it's all right."

"I think so," he said.

"What's all this flap about telephone calls?" I asked.

"We're trying to find out something," Tallant replied coolly.

"What? Or is it any of my business?" I asked. Then a little feeling of uneasiness took hold of me. How had he known I'd made two calls from the room?

"We'll get to it in a minute," Tallant replied. "You came here to sell us a story. We're just looking it over before we buy it. You don't mind?"

"No. It's all right with me," I said. "But suppose you fill me in. I gather that cuddly routine of hers and that punchy act of yours was supposed to get me out of there so you could shake down the cabin?"

He nodded. "Partly."

I didn't catch exactly what he meant by that, but I let it pass. "So what were you looking for? Maybe I could help you."

"A roll of recorder tape."

I glanced across at her. "Maybe you'd better tell him again."

"Why?" she asked.

"Apparently he didn't get the word. You saw me drop it in the mailbox."

She shrugged. "I saw you drop *something* in the box. Let's put it that way."

"Are you crazy——?"

Tallant broke in on me. He shifted a little in his chair, and said, "It's hot in here, Julia. How about turning on the air-conditioner?"

"Excuse me," she said, and went out the doorway into the hall. In a moment I heard the unit begin humming. She came back.

"I don't know but what I've acquired an aversion to air-conditioned bedrooms that may stay with me for the rest of my life," she said calmly as she sat down. "Four days and nights of Mr. Harlan's lordly condescension could leave their mark on any girl."

There was a passing shadow of expression on Tallant's face for the first time. His mouth grew hard, but he said nothing.

"Look, what the hell is this?" I asked. "You saw me mail that roll of tape——"

She leaned forward a little with her chin in the palm of her hand. "Of course you mailed something. I saw you, as you so obviously intended. It might or might not have been the roll of tape. My impression of it afterward was that when it fell into the box it didn't sound heavy enough to be the real package. That's just an impression, of course, and I'll admit I could be wrong. However, whether you mailed it or not still isn't the major consideration. You could very easily have put it in the mail addressed to yourself somewhere, or addressed to nowhere in particular. Illusion was your object, naturally, and it was quite effective, at least from a short range point of view. In football I believe you call it a fake handoff——" She broke off and studied me thoughtfully. "You're still with me, Mr. Harlan?"

I was with her, all right. I felt the uneasiness again. I was sunk, though, if I let them see it. "Cut it out," I said curtly. "You mean you think I've still got it?"

She smiled. "You're following the wrong rabbit, Mr. Harlan."

"What do you mean?"

"Frankly, there's no way we could know whether you still have it or not. There are too many places you could have hidden it. But that's not the issue at hand. What we've been trying to establish is that *no one else has it*. There's a subtle and very important difference. You see?"

"Look! Have you gone crazy? You heard me talking to the man I mailed it to——"

"Did I?" she asked softly. She glanced at Tallant then, and said, "Or perhaps I should ask Dan."

I stared at one and then the other. "What in hell are you talking about?"

She smiled. "I think perhaps we are confusing Mr. Harlan. He may not be able to keep up."

"You'll have to judge that," Tallant replied. "Appraising him was your job and, naturally, I haven't had your opportunities."

I shot a quick look at him. On the outside, he was as calm and efficient as ever, but this was the second time I'd had the impression he was being ridden hard by something he was trying to keep under control.

She caught it too. "Really, Dan." Then she went on coolly. "Of course appraising him was my job, and I think I've done it. Mr. Harlan is what he himself would call a tough guy, but he's not an utter fool. He's almost completely insulated against every human emotion except greed, and he mistakes insensitivity for courage. He has imagination and daring of a sort, enough to conceive a plan like this and to attempt to carry it through alone, but not enough to recognize the flaws in it, and subtlety is not his dish of tea."

He grunted. "Well, maybe we'd better bring him up to date." He shifted the gun just slightly and went on in a level, cold voice, "You'll recall, Harlan, you told us we had two possible ways out. We could pay you, or, if we were convinced you were working alone, we could kill you. It was nice of you to point that out, even if a little unnecessary. So then you proceeded to prove to us that you were *not* working alone. The only trouble with it is we're still not convinced you proved your point. And since neither of us is stupid enough to place himself at the mercy of a blackmailer for the rest of his life if there's any other way out, we're going to insist on a little more proof before we buy——"

I broke in on him. "Skip the diagram," I said. "You think I'm bluffing, so you're going to call me. But have you stopped to think that could be just a little dangerous? You'd never know you were wrong until the police knocked on the door."

He nodded. "We know that. Or rather, let's say we realize we're supposed to be aware of it, as part of the rules. But there's another and slightly more subtle angle to it I don't think you've considered yet.

"However, let's take all the aspects in their proper order so we're sure we understand each other. First, if something happens to you, your accomplice is going to turn that tape and your letter over to the police. Right?"

"Of course."

"Very well. Now. That raises an interesting question. Just *how* does he know something has happened to you?"

I grinned coldly. So that *was* their angle, all along. Catching it back there in the hotel room that morning had saved my life.

"How does he know?" I asked. "Why, when he quits hearing from me, of course."

He nodded. "I see. And just when was the last time he did hear from you?"

I looked at her and grinned. "Tell him, honey."

She returned my glance with an enigmatic smile, and said, "No. You tell him."

I shrugged. "Sure, if you insist. Don't you want him to know you were standing there at the foot of the bed, naked, while you listened to me talking to him?" I turned to Tallant. "It was around ten-fifteen yesterday morning."

His eyebrows raised. "You're sure of this?"

"Ask your lady friend," I said. "That was what she was there for, wasn't it?"

"Oh, we know you made the call, all right. The thing I'm questioning is whether the man you talked to even knew anything about this."

I felt the little shiver go up my back again. It was unaccountable, because I knew there was no way on earth they could have checked the call. She couldn't have heard me give the name to the operator, and I'd kept my eye on her from then on, to be sure she hadn't tried to get it out of the hotel operator. She had never been out of my sight a minute.

"Nuts," I said. "Now you're beginning to talk like an idiot. Why don't you ask her to repeat the conversation?"

He shook his head. "I don't have to. I know who the man was you talked to, and I don't think he's in the blackmail business, or about to go in it. His name is George Gray. He's vice-president and second largest stockholder in the Gray Midcontinent Equipment Company of Fort Worth, son of the founder, worth around three-quarters of a million dollars, married, has two children, member of the Chamber of Commerce, and the best country club, and he's quite active in his church, in Community Chest and hospital drives, and in several civic organizations. That sound like a blackmailer to you?"

My mouth dropped open. I could only stare at him.

"Now, Harlan," he went on coldly, "what we're interested in finding out from you is whether you're going to insist Gray is your accomplice, which is ridiculous, or if not, why you called him instead of the real accomplice—*if you even have one*."

I couldn't say anything. My tongue was stuck to the roof of my mouth.

He smiled coldly. Still holding the gun across his knee with his right hand, he reached into his jacket pocket with his left and brought something out. I stared. It was a roll of recorder tape.

"Great machine, the recorder," he said. "Private detectives use them, too. Your telephone in that hotel room was bugged after the first day."

Then he had *both* sides of the conversation.

He must have seen it in my face. "You're so right, Harlan. Gray didn't even know what you were talking about, as near as I can gather. He thought you were referring to the job he offered you. I don't know what was actually in the package you sent him, but obviously it wasn't recorder tape. So let's hear your story, and you'd better make it good."

I tried to pull myself together and get my mind to work. They were deadly as hell, and they were closing in on me. Only one thing was clear, and that was the moment they were absolutely certain I was alone in this thing they'd kill me like erasing a mistake in a letter. Maybe I was done for now, but the only thing left was to go on bluffing. They hadn't *quite* made up their minds yet, or I wouldn't be alive now.

I leaned forward and tried to make my voice sound tough. "My story? It's exactly the same thing I told you from the first. You know that roll of recorder tape will hang you. She saw me put it in the mail. You know I haven't got it, because you searched the cabin and the car. Therefore, somebody else's got it. You don't know who, and there's no way you can find out. Now, if you want to take a chance I'm lying about it, go ahead. There's only one way you can lose, and that's to lose all the way. The first time you'll know you were wrong is when the cops knock on the door. You're tough, but not that tough. Nobody is."

"Why not?" she asked innocently.

"Look at it yourself. You can see what the odds are. And if you're wrong you go to the chair. That's a rough dose."

She turned toward him and smiled fleetingly. "You see, Dan? Psychological fine points are not Mr. Harlan's forte."

"Put it away," I said. "You're not even making sense."

"I think we are," he said. "Remember, I told you there was another angle you hadn't considered?"

"Sure. More double-talk."

"Not at all. It's quite real, and it has a definite bearing on the validity of the threat. We're not in as much immediate danger as you think."

"Bat sweat."

"I'm serious. Just listen for a moment. Let's say for the sake of argument, that you're telling the truth. We grant you an accomplice."

"That's nice of you."

"Let's be very original and call him X. And now we stipulate further that you've come up here to do something that could be highly dangerous, and that you have vanished."

"Go on," I said.

"The specified time has run out with no word from you. He assumes, correctly enough, that something has happened to you. So what does he do?"

"Now, that's a bright question. What do you think he does? He turns the tape and the letter over to the police."

Tallant shook his head with a faint smile. "No."

"Don't be stupid. Of course he does."

"I don't think so, and right there is the point you overlooked. Your whole threat is just a threat on paper, an arbitrary rule set up in an imaginary game. He doesn't turn it over the police, for the simple reason that he would have everything to lose and nothing whatever to gain."

"Oh, for Christ's sake——"

The smile became a little colder. "You don't see it yet? What, specifically, does he stand to gain? Revenge? Don't be stupid yourself. What the hell does he care about you, or what happened to you? He's not a relative, because you have none. We checked."

"He's a friend of mine——"

"Don't be ridiculous. In your business, friends are expendable."

"So what does he stand to lose? Eight cents' worth of stamps."

They exchanged glances. "What does he stand to lose?" he asked. "Really, Harlan. He stands to lose a hundred thousand dollars."

I saw what he was driving at, and I could feel the walls move a little closer around me.

He went on like a professor giving a lecture. "This tape you have is worth nothing in itself. It has only what we will call potential value, or value solely as a threat. The minute you carry out the threat, it's value drops to zero. You understand that, I suppose? The police would give him nothing for it, obviously. All they'd do, if they found out who he was, would be to put him in jail for not giving it to them sooner. So there we come right to the heart of the matter.

"X has something that has a potential value of—to use your own figure—a hundred thousand dollars. That is, as long as he hangs on to it and threatens us with it. So why would he turn it over to an ungrateful bunch of slobs like the police and have its value drop to zero when he can retain it himself and keep the value alive? Is he insane?"

I tried to say something. I couldn't.

He continued. "So what happens? Nothing, in our opinion. Except that some time in the future, after you have disappeared completely, friend X comes sidling up to us with the same old sad story."

I got myself started at last. "So what have you accomplished? You have to pay him off."

He shrugged. "Perhaps. If you do have an accomplice, we're probably ruined, because the thing becomes an endless chain and could go on for ever. You'll bleed us white, or we'd have to try to escape. But we're almost certain now you haven't got one."

He stopped, and the room was silent except for the faint humming of the air-conditioner somewhere in the house. I tried to estimate my chances of getting to him without being cut in two by that shotgun, and came up with an even zero.

He apparently read my thoughts. He shook his head. "Not now. We're going to wait you out."

"What do you mean?"

"We're going to see if X does show up. We don't think he will, but if he does we haven't got any more to lose by waiting for him than we have by being suckers and paying you now. We're going to keep you here. Nobody saw you come in. Nobody knows where you are. As far as the rest of the world is concerned, you've already disappeared, and could be dead."

I felt cold all over. "You can't get away with it."

"I think so," he replied calmly. "Do you know what a trial balloon is?"

I just stared at him.

"It's a political dodge. A politician deliberately lets something leak to sample public reaction before he commits himself. If he gets the wrong reaction, he can deny the whole thing. That's your status at the moment. You're a trial balloon."

The room was silent. Nobody moved. "You see?" he went on. "It's an unusual sort of thing. We're going to find out exactly what would happen if you turned up missing. Before you actually do, that is."

CHAPTER FIFTEEN

I DIDN'T have a chance; they had me cut off from every direction. Now that it was too late I could see why Purvis had approached me. He'd had sense enough to know he couldn't bluff it through alone; they were too hard and dangerous for that. They had to know positively there were two people in it—and one of them for ever out of reach—before they could be handled. He'd studied Cannon's death for a long time and he'd studied her; even without knowing for sure who the man was in the case he'd been aware of the kind of people he was up against. And still they'd managed to kill him.

They'd kill me the same way. It wasn't a mere matter of getting that tape back; as long as anybody on earth knew they'd killed Cannon they were in danger. They were pretty sure right now I was the only one, and as soon as they were convinced of it they'd get rid of me. Every hour that passed without someone else's showing up was making them more certain. And nobody else was going to show up.

The cold voice went on. "Your car has been abandoned in New Orleans. The cabin is closed; your gear and fishing tackle are gone——"

I leaned forward. "Listen. Somebody's bound to know she was out there. Or that you were out there. You've been seen driving my car. Maybe driving it out. You say there's been nobody looking for me, but you were gone long enough to drive the car to New Orleans. I was seen in Shreveport by God knows how many people. I was registered at a hotel there——" I stopped.

He smiled "As Mr. John Abernathy, of Kansas City."

"Listen! I called George Gray from there——"

"Gray didn't know where you were calling from. He probably just assumed it was from here." He paused for a moment, and then went on. "Nobody knew she was down there at that cabin. Nobody saw you leave there with her. That end of the lake is the most isolated place in the country. I drove your car out at night—after I'd searched it and put it in running order again. As far as knowing nobody had come out there while I was gone to New Orleans with your heap—that was easy. I piled up a little mound of dirt in each rut near the edge of the clearing. When I came back they were still there; no car had been across them. They're there yet, or were four hours ago. Harlan, you've disappeared. You didn't even leave a ripple. And nobody gives a damn."

"George Gray——"

"So you won't call him Thursday. He'll ask the Governor to order out the National Guard, won't he? He offered you a job; you accepted it, and then changed your mind. He's going to get excited about that?"

The room fell silent again as they glanced at each other. I tried to think. I couldn't come up with anything. There had to be a way. But where was it?

"You can't get away with it," I said. "Look. You were gone from town long enough to drive a car to New Orleans. They're going to wonder why your shop's closed. The whole thing's screwy. You give yourself away in a dozen places——"

He shook his head. "I drove your car to New Orleans Saturday night and came back Sunday on a bus, while I was supposed to be on a fishing trip to Caddo Lake, and when the shop was closed anyway. I've checked the cabin out there at night coming in from a different road farther down the lake and walking up about two miles. I'm in the shop every day; I come in through the back way here at night. Everything's perfectly normal on the surface; there's nothing suspicious at all. Nobody saw you come in here, and nobody'll ever see you go out. The maid has a week off to visit her family in Louisiana."

A week. Some time within a week.

I fought down an impulse to cry out at him. "Good God," I said, "do you mean you'd go through all this just to keep from paying me off and getting the tape back?"

"It isn't merely a question of the tape. We think you hid that somewhere. I've looked for it, and can't find it. The chances are, nobody'll ever find it. It's you. We're in this too deep to have anyone running around loose who knows about it. You must have realized the chances you were taking when you walked into it; I don't see that you've got any kick coming now that it's backfired on you. Get up."

There was nothing else to do. I stood up. He got out of the chair, holding the gun, and began backing out the doorway into the hall. "Follow me, and don't get any closer."

In the hallway he clicked on a light switch. I passed the open door to the bath and came abreast another door on the left. He stopped and nodded curtly.

"Open that."

I opened it.

"Turn around and stand in the doorway. Don't try to jump in and slam it, because I'll cut you in two. That's right. Go on in slowly."

They both followed me in, Tallant first with the shotgun in my back. The light was already on in here. It was another bedroom, smaller than the other. It had one window opposite the door, facing the patio, but there were heavy curtains over it and they were drawn. There was a single bed with its head up against the wall under the window, and a night table stood beside it. The floor was covered with a grey carpet, and there was an armchair and a bridge lamp against the wall to the left.

"Lie down on the bed," he commanded.

I turned and looked at him. He was near the door, at least eight feet away, with the gun pointing right at my chest.

"Go on," he said flatly. "I won't take any chances with you."

I lay down. She came past him and around to my left side. Reaching down, she picked up something dangling from the side of the bed. I saw what it was. It was a pair of handcuffs made fast to the steel frame of the bed with a short length of chain.

"Don't try to grab her," he warned me.

She caught my left hand and snapped the cuff over the wrist. Then she came around to the other side of the bed and made my right hand fast with another on that side. I could move my hands, but there wasn't enough slack in the chains to bring them together. He put down the gun, tied my feet together with a piece of rope that had been lying in the chair, and then secured them to the foot of the bed. Forcing my mouth open, he shoved a wadded handkerchief in it and plastered adhesive tape across my face to keep it in. She had gone back to the doorway and was silently watching. There was no expression on her face at all—no pity, no regret, not even any hate. It was just something that had to be done, and they did it. They'd kill me the same way.

No, I thought. *She would, perhaps, but he'd make it a personal thing.* He wasn't quite as tough, and he had the spurs in him. That business of her having to shack up with me for the past six days was riding him hard, and every time he thought about it it dug him a little more. They'd had to do it that way, and it had meant nothing to her, but he wasn't liking it a bit. I'd seen it twice in the past half hour, and wondered about it. He was going to make it rough on me, as rough as he could, but there was another side to it, too. If you get emotional you can always lose your head, and if you do you're never quite as dangerous as a cold type who's just doing a job.

He stepped back, took out a handkerchief, and wiped the sweat from his face. He'd been under a strain too, in spite of the calm way he looked outside.

Suddenly he caught her in his arms. "Julia——!"

She broke it up after the first wild clinch. "Please, Dan. Not in front of this vermin."

He turned his face and looked at me for an instant, his eyes savage. They went out and closed the door. *It was an act out there at the cabin,* I thought, *but it wasn't quite all an act.*

They didn't come back; there was dead silence in the house. They were probably in her bedroom. I thought about it, trying to keep from getting panicky. It couldn't happen, not here in the quiet upper-middle-class residential district of a small town where a dented fender in the Cadillac was a big deal. Next door they'd be playing bridge; up the street they were watching television or waiting for a daughter to get home from a date. Murder? *Here?* That was a pipe dream. Murder never happened in a place like this.

I was simply being erased. I'd tried to move in on them without having a good look at them first, and now I was lying here watching myself disappear like a ripple dying out on a pond. Nobody would ever know it. Who'd miss me? Who'd raise an alarm? The police would impound my car in New Orleans, and after a long time they'd sell it for storage charges. George Gray would mutter into his soft-boiled eggs some morning that he couldn't see why that sad bastard of a Harlan couldn't at least have mailed back the key to the cabin. You wouldn't expect the big moose to tell anybody he'd changed his mind about the job, but, by God, he could have sent back the key. The bank would keep sending statements to my apartment in Oklahoma City until the landlord closed it and sold my stuff for the rent. Three years from now some sports writer covering the pro football circuit would say to somebody in a bar that that guy out there this afternoon reminded him a little of Harlan. Wonder what ever happened to him; make mine a Martini on the rocks—

That was it. That was the thing that scared you till you felt cold right down in the guts. They could get away with it so easily. They'd done it before, and they'd do it again. One traffic fatality, one unsolved and forgotten murder two hundred miles away, and one disappearance nobody ever even noticed, and not once did they slip up. Six months from now there'd be a blurb in the local paper: *Mrs. Julia Cannon and Mr. Daniel R. Tallant were married today in a simple ceremony at the bride's lovely home on Cherrywood Drive. Mrs. Cannon, widow of the late Howard L. Cannon, Wayles automobile dealer, is prominent in social and civic activities, being vice-president of the Women's Club and one of the founders of the Little Theatre group.*

I lay there looking up at the ceiling and watching myself disappear. Sweat collected on my forehead. The only way I could get it off was by turning my head and rubbing my face against the pillow.

Some time just before dawn he came in again, unshackled me, and let me go to the john. The gun was covering me every second. They fastened me down again and left. It grew light in the room. I knew he was gone for the day. She'd probably turned in again. I could hear cars out in the street once in a while, very faintly because with the air-conditioning turned on all the doors and windows were closed. I lay staring at nothing, trying not to think. After a while I must have gone to sleep. It didn't seem possible, but the next thing I knew she was standing beside the bed yanking the adhesive tape off my mouth.

She was wearing a cotton house dress and a handerchief tied around her hair. A vacuum sweeper was whirring behind her and she had the hose and one of the brush attachments in her hand. She smiled, looking like any very attractive housewife in the world. *Maybe it's deliberate,* I thought, trying to keep my stomach from turning over. The whole thing was calculated, in an attempt to break me down.

The tape gave way, bringing the handkerchief out of my mouth. A power lawn mower was making a racket in the patio, and I realized that was the reason she felt it was safe enough to remove the gag. There was hardly any chance I'd be heard if I yelled my head off anyway, even without the mower. There was nothing on the east side of the house but a deserted street and some woods.

"Housework!" she said. She shrugged good-naturedly, and reached out with the toe of one shoe to press down the switch of the vacuum sweeper. It stopped whining. She sat down in the armchair near the bed and took a cigarette from a pocket of the dress.

I said nothing. She lit the cigarette. "Do you want one?"

"Keep it," I said.

"Very well, if you're going to be surly. Oh, incidentally, just in case you should manage to grab me with one of those brutal looking hands, the keys to these handcuffs are in another room."

"Your luck's going to run out on you some day," I said.

She blew out some smoke and looked at it thoughtfully. "It already has," she replied quietly. "But I wouldn't expect you to see that."

"What time is it?" I asked.

"About one p.m."

I thought about it. This was Thursday; if I hadn't let them booby-trap me I'd have been on my way out of Houston right this minute with a fortune in my luggage and nothing to worry about. And now I was lying here waiting for the two of them to get around to murdering me.

It must have shown on my face. Her eyebrows raised. "Really, where's the treasured toughness?"

"Shut up," I said.

She leaned back in the chair and studied me reflectively. "You're not really hard, you know. You're merely insulated. And you're a fool, in spite of that bit of sleight of hand the other day. You walked into this thing without even taking the trouble to learn something about the people you were going to try to blackmail. I wonder how long that veneer of toughness would have lasted if you'd ever had the intelligence to see, just once, how many ways there are in this world you can be utterly destroyed by random little sequences of events that look as harmless as marshmallows. If I hadn't stepped out of the shadows in front of your car on a road down there in the swamp that evening five months ago, neither of us would be here in this position. That's obvious, isn't it? Dan Tallant's car was down there too, and I thought you were Dan. But that's also obvious. Even you saw it, so it must be, because you never see anything but the obvious."

"Why don't you write it down?" I said. "Maybe somebody'll publish it."

She went on as if she hadn't even heard me. "I don't think you even know what I'm talking about. I don't mean you alone. I mean all of us. We're all destroyed, destroyed for wanting too many things and not caring how we get them. If you really want to preen yourself as a tough guy, Mr. Harlan, you should wait and be tough after there's no longer any hope of winning. It's easy till then. It's also very bad to have any intelligence along with it but, fortunately, I think you have been spared that."

"Turn it off," I said. "You're not even making sense. I don't read you at all."

"Oh, I'm aware of that. Perhaps I just felt like talking. And there is some satisfaction in the spectacle of the lordly Mr. Harlan in the role of captive audience. Imagine your having to listen to the inane babblings of a woman, and not only that but to the babblings of a woman you don't even have any hope of bedding with—which is obviously the only thing women are any good for.

"But to get back to the harmless little chains of events—where should we begin? With a boy going fishing, and liking it? Or a girl encountering cruelty for the first time, being laughed at at a children's party because her shoes were half-soled? Ridiculous? Certainly. Thousands of children have been skewered by their contemporaries at parties, millions of men like to go on fishing trips. You have to fit in a horde of other harmless little things and match them up to get the right combination. But there are so many of them and so many combinations that will pay off in annihilation, sooner or later you can almost count on blowing yourself up. Add the fact that nowadays Chevrolets and Buicks look considerably alike, at least in the dusk and seen only in one quick glance. Add a man deciding to take a bag of laundry into town. Not any time, you understand, but this particular time."

She paused and smiled faintly, as if she were thinking of something a long way off. "Try this on your toughness, Mr. Harlan. None of this could have happened if those three cars had come out of that bottom in any other sequence at all. Mathematically, there are six possibilities, of course, if you merely shook them up in a dice cup. Consider that. On top of all the other interlocking little events that fell into their pattern to set up disaster, the odds were still six to one that they'd remain harmless, and pass unnoticed. And yet the right number came up, and here we are."

"*We* are?"

She nodded. "I realize the futility of trying to make you understand, Mr. Harlan. I'm merely talking. I don't usually rattle on this way, but this afternoon for some reason I just felt in the mood. Here we are, as I say. Destroyed. And yet never once have you even stopped to wonder why those cars came out of the bottom in that particular sequence. Even aside from the laws of chance, there was every reason in the world my husband's should have been the last. But it wasn't. It was next to last, and that set up the disaster."

I couldn't see what difference it made, now that it had happened and I was as good as dead, but I asked anyway. I could see she was going to go on talking, and there was no way I could shut her up.

"Why should he have been last?"

She shook her head. "You surprise me at times. You show flashes of intelligence, and then you go dead again. Purvis knew, and he didn't even see me out there. He did it by sheer deduction. I was unfaithful to my husband. I realize you have already grasped this, at least as far as its surface aspects are concerned, and there would be no point in attempting to explore it to any depth because eventually we'd run into language connected with emotion, which obviously would have no meaning to you. How would you describe a sunset to a blind mole living on the dark side of the moon?

"But I'm digressing. To get back to why the three cars came out of the bottom in that particular sequence—my husband, as you probably guessed, came out there to the Cannon summer cottage looking for us. He had been in Houston, but had returned ahead of schedule, probably for that very reason. And he found us. Or rather, I should say, he found Dan. I had wanted to be alone for a little while to think, and I'd taken a walk a short distance around the lake. Mr. Cannon, while he was not drunk, had had enough to be ugly. He became very abusive—he could be quite violent on occasion. Dan denied that I was with him. Of course, it was more or less obvious somebody must have been with him for he would hardly have come out there alone, and there was a good chance I was the one because Dan had no key to the place. Dan did the best he could, however, and insisted he had borrowed a key—several hunting and fishing cronies of Mr. Cannon's had duplicates. This was a flimsy thing at best, because it could be easily checked, but Dan was desperate and was hoping I would hear the row and stay out of sight. I did. I circled the clearing the cabin was in and started out the road, knowing Dan would come along and pick me up. It is a little over a quarter mile out to where the two roads join—that one and the one going on around to George Gray's cabin, where you were staying. I passed this juncture—you will recall the place where you saw me was about two hundred yards this side of it. I was waiting there for Dan to drive by. When I saw your car coming, of course, I thought it was he. When I realized my mistake, I stepped back off the road again. Then it occurred to me Dan might have some difficulty picking me up. Obviously, Mr. Cannon, being suspicious, would not leave first. Dan would have to. And Mr. Cannon would be following him very closely to see if he did meet someone along the road. This is precisely what happened. When Dan came by, only a few minutes after you did, he caught sight of me but did not stop. He motioned for me to stay out of sight. My husband's Cadillac was right behind him. Surely it must have occurred to you there was something strange in the fact my husband's car wasn't the last one in the procession?"

I hadn't even thought about it. And I didn't care. What difference did it make now?

"Turn it off," I said. "I knew the two of you'd killed him, and that was all I was interested in."

"Really?"

"Of course."

"I told you I felt like talking, so even at the risk of boring you I'll proceed. What happened, naturally, was that Dan speeded up going around some turns in the road, and got far enough ahead to pull off and out of sight. My husband went on past, and when he caught up with you just after you got out on the highway, it was perfectly natural that he thought you were Dan. Dan came back and got me. So there you have the marching order for disaster. What you didn't know, and what I don't think Purvis even guessed, was that we actually saw the crash."

"You did? I didn't think you were that close behind."

"We were about a mile back, but if you'll recall the road drops off a long hill into that river bottom where you crashed. It isn't straightaway, but from the brow of the hill you can see the road going across that straight section of fill and the bridge itself. We happened to be right there when it happened. Of course you both had your headlights on then and we didn't know for sure it was your car my husband had driven off the road—not until we got there, that is—but it was perfectly obvious the whole thing was deliberate. He had at least another mile of straight road ahead of him, and there were no other cars in sight at all. The inference was inescapable."

"So you're going to get away with it?" I said.

Her eyes were moody as she studied the end of her cigarette, and it was a moment before she answered. "Do you ever?" she asked.

CHAPTER SIXTEEN

"WHAT do you mean?"

"Getting away with it, as you put it, is perhaps only an illusion. You go on delaying the ultimate disaster, but you never eliminate it."

I jumped at this. "Well, get wise to yourself. Turn me loose——"

She smiled coldly. "Really, you are a child. I assure you we have every intention of going on. We began it, and now we can't ever go back. Neither, I might add, can you."

"Then why do it? Why get yourself in any deeper?"

Her eyebrows raised. "Deeper?"

"Certainly."

"Really. Don't be absurd. There's only one depth, and that's absolute. You wouldn't say something was more dead, would you, or more pregnant?"

"So you'd do it just because you've got nothing more to lose?"

"Not at all. We'll do it because we have to. Removing you and your threat is another bulkhead shored up, another finger in the dike, another postponing of the inevitable. Futile? Perhaps. But what do you do when you see the bulkhead crumpling? You shore it up, even while you're watching the next one start to buckle. But perhaps I'm tiring you."

I stared at her. "Well, what in the name of God did you do it for if you didn't think you could win?"

"Well, obviously, because we thought we could—then. Five months have changed that—for me, at least. You have too much time to think. Too much time to—as you put it—look at the odds. Incidentally, that is a very good parallel. Imagine a roulette wheel that ran for five months, or a year, or ten years, before it stopped. With all your money bet on just one number, and with that much time to examine the laws of probability, you must inevitably come to doubt the wisdom of it. Add to that the fact that you never really know for sure when the roulette wheel *has* stopped. It may be an illusion, a very deliberate illusion fostered by the people who are operating it, if you follow me.

"There are too many possibilities inherent in any situation like this, too many factors completely out of your control and utterly unpredictable. Purvis shouldn't have become suspicious, but he did. The possibility of your paths ever crossing again was mathematically negligible, but it happened. The odds were astronomical against your being in Purvis's apartment at the precise moment he was killed, and even laughably impossible that you could have been there without being seen, and yet——" She shrugged and crushed out the cigarette.

"You think the police will catch up with you some day, then?"

"I think it quite likely," she said.

"Then I don't see why you keep on."

Her eyebrows raised. "You don't? I thought I had just told you." She stood up and looked down at me. "But there is another facet to it which you may be able to understand. I should hate very much to be defeated by you. I underestimated you once and let you make a fool of me. It won't happen again."

I started to say something. She shoved the handkerchief back in my mouth and plastered the tape over it. She started out, but turned in the doorway. "Oh, I forgot to ask if you wanted anything to eat."

I stared at her, not even bothering to shake my head.

She went out. I lay there thinking about her and trying to think of something. I was as good as dead unless I could get to one of them, and you didn't have to be very bright to see she wasn't the one. I didn't read her too well, but she was undoubtedly the smoothest, hardest specimen I'd ever run into. She didn't think they had a chance of winning any more, but she was going right on as calmly as a woman picking up a bridge hand. There was no use looking for the soft spot in her, because she was armour all the way through.

What about him? He wasn't what you would call one of the softer type of citizens, but at least he looked a little more promising than she did. For one thing, he was badly gone on her, and intensely jealous. Maybe I could make him lose his head by giving him the needle, but what good would that do as long as he had the gun? He'd just kill me that much quicker. It was hopeless.

As soon as it was dark he came in. He had another gun with him this time, a hand gun that looked like a Luger. He held it and watched with deadly efficiency while she unlocked the handcuffs and untied my feet. I went to the bathroom with him right behind me. There wasn't a flaw in his procedure anywhere. One false move, and I'd have my spine shattered. They fastened me down again.

He stood looking at me. "Nobody's shown up yet," he said.

I stared at him. I still had the gag in my mouth and couldn't have spoken if there'd been anything to say.

"I'm going out to see if anybody's been to the cabin," he said. "Better hope so, pal." They went out and closed the door.

After a while I began to hear voices very faintly, coming from the direction of the living-room. I tried to see what time it was, but my watch had stopped because I hadn't been able to wind it. The sound of voices increased and I could hear laughter now and then, and music. She was giving a party—*Mrs. Julia Cannon entertained a small group of her friends last night at an informal gathering at her lovely home on Cherrywood Drive*——The cold-blooded deadliness of it got to me for a moment and I felt sick. The only thing she'd forgotten was to use me for a cloak room. She should have brought the mink stoles and evening wraps and thrown them on my face.

It went on for hours, or so it seemed. It must have been after midnight when it began to quiet down. I wondered if he had been at the party. Apparently he had, for when he came back his face was slightly flushed as if he had been drinking. The house had been silent for about an hour then, so I supposed he had left with the other guests and then sneaked back. They played a smooth game, and they never made a mistake or left themselves open anywhere.

She was still dressed in an evening gown and he had on a dark suit. She stood in the doorway behind him as he came in.

"Your friend must have forgotten you," he said. "Nobody's been out there."

I looked at him. He was feeling his drinks, all right, and he was looking for trouble.

He stepped forward and ripped the adhesive off my mouth. It was stuck to the beard stubble on my face and made a tearing sound as it came away.

He looked over his shoulder at her. "Maybe this would be a good time to find out where he hid that tape."

"Somebody might hear him if he shouts," she warned.

He took the gun out of his pocket again. "If he makes any noise he'll get this across his face."

I hadn't had any water for twenty-four hours. My mouth was so dry I couldn't speak even after the handkerchief was gone from it. I tried to moisten it with saliva. It wasn't too successful.

"How about it?" he asked roughly.

My jaw felt as if it had been broken when I tried to move it. My voice cracked. "I told you, you simple bastard. I mailed it."

"Funny he hasn't shown up around here, isn't it?"

I didn't care any more what he did. If I had to go through another twenty-four hours of lying here I'd go crazy. It was better to provoke something now and take my chances than to go out of my mind.

"Well, why worry about him?" I asked. "When he does show up she can always lay him for you. She doesn't mind."

It got to him so fast he didn't even think to swing at me with the gun. He dropped it into his left hand and smashed me on the jaw with the right. It made my head ring, but I thought I heard a finger break.

"Don't be a fool, Dan," she said with exasperation. "Can't you see he's deliberately trying to make you lose your head?"

"Maybe he's in a hurry. Why keep him waiting?"

She shook her head. "It's been only one day."

"Seven altogether."

"I liked the first six," I said. "Fun, wasn't it, honey?"

He looked down at me with the veins beginning to stand out on his temples. He was half drunk, half crazy from thinking about just that, and wide open for the needle.

"Dan! Don't be juvenile. Are you going to let this stupid thug make a fool of you?"

He didn't even hear her. He was just staring at me, his eyes going wilder and more savage every second. He shifted the gun back to his right hand and started to chop at my face with it. She sprang forward and caught his arm.

"Not in here, you fool!" she said in a furious whisper. "Do you want to have to carry him two blocks to your car?" She didn't say anything about making a sloppy mess in her beautiful home, but the thought was there.

"Maybe you'd just like me to turn him loose?" he asked savagely.

"Oh, don't be an idiot! But if you're going to do it tonight, at least—for the love of heaven—do it right. Don't start behaving like a madman. You've got to get him out of here, the way we planned it."

"You want to be sure you don't have anything to do with it? Is that it?"

"Of course not! Listen, Dan!" she said urgently. "Please don't lose your head now. This is dangerous."

He appeared to be getting a grip on himself and becoming rational enough again to realize she was right. He straightened and backed away a step.

"You just don't know how to handle her," I said. "When she starts throwing her weight around, get rough with her. She loves it."

He wheeled and lunged at me, his hands reaching for my throat as he fell across the bed. She sprang forward and began tugging at his arm. "Stop it! Dan, stop it!"

He sat up. His face was white and glistening with sweat. "All right, all right," he said, fighting for breath. He swung around and began tearing at the rope holding my legs. "I'll take the precious son of a bitch out there where you won't have to see it, if that's what's worrying you. I'll take care of it. Just keep out of my way——"

The rope came free. He hurried around to the left side of the bed, groping in the pocket of his trousers. His hand came out, holding a pair of small keys tied together with twine. I watched him, hardly daring to breathe now. If I didn't get a chance within the next few seconds I'd never have one again. He unlocked the handcuff on the left side and slid the loop of the chain out of the other half of it. I saw what he was going to do. He'd shackle my hands together with that pair before he broke the other one loose.

She was standing below the foot of the bed, silently watching. Suddenly she gestured impatiently. "Put the gag back in his mouth. You can't take him out of here that way."

"All right!" he said furiously. He grabbed the handkerchief and began wadding it back in my mouth. He stuck the tape back over it. Most of the adhesive was gone from it now and it didn't hold very well. I lay perfectly still, as if I had forgotten as well as he had that my left wrist was free now and that the handcuff was lying beside my hand.

He pushed down hard against my mouth with his hand to fasten the tape. "There, you son of a bitch."

I drew the left arm back a little. My fingers closed over one loop of the handcuffs.

"Dan!" she shrieked. "Look out!"

I swung it as hard as I could. The cuff hit him over the right temple, but even as it landed I knew I hadn't had enough swing on it to knock him out. He jerked and grunted and fell over on top of me. I tried to pull the arm free to swing again, but I could get only the forearm out. He was across my upper arm and shoulder. I put the hand against his throat and strained, trying to pull him to the right so I could reach him with that one too. His body rolled a little. I could get my right hand on his shirt collar. I locked my fingers on it and pulled, but he was coming around now and beginning to struggle. I let go with the left and shoved it downward, toward his right-hand coat pocket where the gun was.

Then she was on us both. He rolled back a little when she landed, and all his weight was on my left arm. I was still short of the pocket a good six inches when her hand flashed into it and came out with the gun. She tried to back off us. I grabbed for her and caught the upper edge of the strapless gown. A seam ripped. She slashed downward at my arm with the gun, and it went numb up to the shoulder.

She slid back and stood up, still holding the gun. Her hair was dishevelled and her eyes wild, and the torn gown was threatening to slide down on to her hips. She looked deadly enough to give you nightmares for the rest of your life. He put a hand on my chest and pushed upward, swinging the other one at my face. I turned, heaving my shoulders, and he lost his balance and fell on me again. I got both hands on his throat once more. There was no strength at all in the left one, but I managed to hold on. He was still weak from the blow on the head, and I was cutting off his wind now. In all the wildness I looked at her again and saw her trying to find the safety on the gun. It was pointed right at my face.

He gave one last effort and jerked free and then the gun went off. It was like a hand-grenade exploding in a cistern. The wave of sound rolled over me, reverberated around the walls, and then rolled back like thunder. He jerked and went limp in my arms and his face dropped on to my chest. The sound chopped off, and there was dead silence except for the ringing in my ears.

I looked at her, still too numb to move. She was standing very still, staring with horror at the back of his head. The gun slipped from her fingers and thudded gently on the carpet. Her mouth opened and she put the flat side of three closed fingers up over it, like some genteel type patting back a yawn, while her eyes went wider and wider with shock. There was a greenish tinge to the pallor of her face just as she collapsed slowly to her knees and then fell forward, out of sight below the foot of the bed. She had killed him. He was lying across me, I was still handcuffed to the bed, and everybody in this end of town would have heard the shot. And then she had capped everything by fainting.

What had he done with the keys? He'd had them. Were they

in the bed, or had he put them back in one of his pockets? I couldn't get my mind to work at all. It was as if it had been shocked into numbness by all the violence and sound and now that they were gone I was lying here in utter silence trying to kick it awake. Somebody would call the police. If they didn't get any answer when they came they'd break in. I had to get her awake so she could go to the door if they did come, and I couldn't even reach her.

I rolled him off me and sat up. The keys were nowhere in sight on the bed. Where were they? *Where? Hurry,* I thought. For the love of God, find them before they start pounding on the door. I slid off the bed. I couldn't stand erect because of the shortness of the chain between the handcuff and the bed frame. I couldn't reach the foot of the bed, where she was. Wildness began to take possession of me. *Stop it, for Christ's sake,* I said aloud, like a man in delirium. *Get hold of yourself. He had the keys here; he hasn't been anywhere else, so they're still here.*

I caught him by a shoulder and pushed. He moved over a little. The keys weren't under him. He was lying on his back now. I plunged my left hand into his right-hand trousers pocket and yanked it wrong side out. There was nothing in it but some change and a pocket-knife. I reached across and turned the left one out. There was a folded handkerchief in it. I threw it aside, and then stared. The keys dropped out, falling on to the sheet right at the far edge of the bed. I lunged for them and my finger-tips brushed them off on to the floor on the other side.

It was a nightmare now. I reached across as far as I could, and then downward. My extended fingertips just brushed the carpet. There was no telling where they had landed. I pushed backward and slid off the bed on the near side, sprawling on the floor. There they were. They were lying on the carpet just under the far side of the bed, near the foot. Rolling on to my back, I slid under as far as my shackled right arm would let me. In this position I couldn't see them any more because my body was cutting off too much of the light, but I remembered about where they had been. My left hand frenziedly patted the carpet. Nothing. They *had* to be there. I was pawing like a madman and lunging against the restraining chain. How long had it been now? *Stop it,* I thought wildly. If you go to pieces now you're dead. Suppose it was just a parlour game; you'd figure out the answer to it in five seconds.

They had to be further down toward the foot, but I was

reaching as far as I could now. Move the bed, you fool. *Move the bed.* I caught the underside of it with my left hand, and heaved. Nothing happened except that I slid myself along the carpet. He was on it and he was too heavy. Moving it without something to brace myself against was impossible. I swung my legs around wildly, reversing my position so my feet were against the wall under the headboard. Grasping the underside of the board with the fingers of my left hand, I heaved backward. The bed slid a couple of inches and then stopped. I heaved again. Nothing gave. The foot of it had come up against her. That was where she had fallen. In this awkward position I couldn't move it against the weight of both of them.

Well, maybe it was far enough. I swung back the way I had been at first and began wildly sweeping my left hand around. There they were! My outstretched finger-tips touched metal. They slid off. I strained, pulling against the chain. The end of the middle finger brushed against them again. I tried to press down and pull them toward me. The finger slid off. They were a fraction of an inch out of reach.

Maybe I was already going crazy. I could hear myself cursing endlessly and idiotically in a kind of chant like a phonograph somebody had turned on and then forgotten. I clamped my mouth shut, wondering if I would explode from the pressure inside me.

There was absolute silence for a second or two, and then the telephone began ringing.

CHAPTER SEVENTEEN

They had left the bedroom door open when they came in, and I could hear it quite plainly out in the living-room. It went on and on with that insistent and angry sound an unanswered telephone has. It was probably one of the neighbourhood busy-bodies who had heard the shot. *"Oh, Mrs. Cannon, I'm sorry I disturbed you, but I thought I heard something that sounded like a gun and it seemed to come from over there and I wondered if you were all right——"* Stop it, I thought. For Christ's sake, turn it off! You're beginning to gibber. Do something. When the old biddy doesn't raise somebody she's going to call the cops. They'll get an answer. They'll push the door in. I lunged against the chain like an animal in a steel trap. I couldn't even touch the keys now. I stopped and lay perfectly still in the calm that is beyond frenzy.

Then suddenly the perfectly obvious answer to the whole thing occurred to me. I could reach them with my foot. Cursing myself for a fool, I slid my body around until I was lying crosswise under the bed. I could see them, now that I wasn't cutting off the light. They were lying almost under the foot of the bed. I shoved my left foot forward and got the toe of the shoe behind them. I dragged them slowly toward me. They pressed down into the nap of the carpet once and I had to go back and pick them up again. In a moment I could reach them with my hand.

The telephone stopped ringing just as I picked them up.

Now whoever it was would call the cops. Maybe somebody already had. I was sweating, and my hands shook. She hadn't stirred. I juggled the keys frantically in my hand and slid out from under the bed. The first one was right. The handcuffs clicked open and I came erect, lunging toward her. She lay on her back behind the footboard of the bed, her eyes closed and one arm stretched out beyond her head. Her face was dead white and the long lashes made shadows on her cheek. I fell to the floor beside her and grabbed her bare shoulder, shaking it furiously. There was no response.

I sprang up and ran through the hallway to the bath. Wetting the end of a towel in the wash basin, I hurried back. Kneeling beside her, I began rubbing her face roughly with the wet cloth. She made a little gasping sound but did not move. Her eyes remained closed. The house was utterly silent now that the telephone had stopped. I could feel time rushing past me like water over the spillway of a dam.

Why didn't I run and leave her here? Get out, before the police came. No, I thought savagely; there was still a chance. God, if I could only get her awake—— She moved her head a little and her eyes opened. She stared blankly up at me. Her mouth started to open. I put a hand over it.

I put my face down close to hers and whispered furiously, "Listen. Can you hear me?"

There was no response, nothing but that same blank stare.

I grabbed her shoulder with my other hand and shook her. "Don't scream! Don't make any noise at all. Understand?"

Comprehension began to dawn in her eyes. She was still in shock, but maybe I could get through to her. I took my hand away from her mouth. "Listen! You've got to snap out of it. Somebody may have called the cops."

The telephone began ringing again.

Tyres screamed out on the street somewhere as a car slid to a stop.

Her lips moved. *"Dan——"*

The doorbell chimed.

"Oh, Jesus!"

I grabbed her by both shoulders. "They're here. The cops. You've got to go to the door or they'll break in. Somebody reported the shot."

"Dan! I killed him——"

I hauled her up to a sitting position and put my mouth against her ear. "Shut up! You've got to go to that door. Can you stand up?"

She stared at me. "There's nothing we can do now."

I fought down a crazy impulse to scream at her. "Listen, you little fool——" I broke off, staring at the torn evening gown. She couldn't go to the door in that. She was supposed to have been asleep. "Where is your robe?"

The doorbell chimed again. The telephone went on ringing.

I shook her. "Get out of that dress!"

There must be a robe of some kind in the clothes closet of her bedroom. I sprang up and ran in there. A blue dressing gown was thrown across the back of a chair and some slippers were on the floor beside it. When I got back in the other room she was still sitting in the same place with her hands up against her temples.

I knelt beside her and slapped her across the side of the face. "Get out of that dress! Look! They're going to break in here in about one more minute, and when they do you're going to the chair for murder."

She seemed to understand me at last. She began fumbling with the top of the dress. It would take her an hour the way she was going at it. I grabbed it and tried to help. We weren't getting anywhere. How did they get in the goddamned things—from the top or bottom? I caught it and tried to rip it. It was some kind of strong net material that was stiff to the touch and didn't tear straight. It bunched up and was strong as screen wire. I cursed. Snatching my pocket-knife from the pocket of my trousers, I put the blade inside the dress, petticoat, and everything, and sawed it all the way to the hem. I hauled her erect in nothing but her pants and bra and garter belt, and grabbed the robe. Somehow she managed to stand. We got the robe about her shoulders and belted it.

"Lean on me." I snapped. I knelt and yanked off the high-heeled shoes one at a time and slid her feet into the mules.

I shoved her ahead of me toward the door into the hall. "All right," I hissed at her. "You're on your own. Answer the door, and the hell with the telephone. You've been asleep. Something woke you, but you don't know what it was. Make it good, or they've got you."

She swayed once and put out a hand to free herself. Then she was gone down the hall. I eased along after her until I reached the L, and flattened myself against the wall still out of sight of the living-room. Her mules made no sound against the carpet, so I couldn't tell whether she was still going or not. At least, I hadn't heard her fall. Then the front door opened. I breathed a ragged sigh of relief.

I could hear them. "Mrs. Cannon?" It was a man's voice.

"Yes," she said. "What is it?"

"Sorry to trouble you. I'm Charlie Lane, from the Sheriff's office. Somebody reported a disturbance of some sort in the neighbourhood. Thought it was a gunshot——"

She said just what I'd told her, and she said it correctly, with just the right amount of sleepiness in her voice. She was good.

"You didn't hear a shot then?" he asked.

"I don't know," she said. "I'm not sure what woke me."

"Probably the telephone," he answered. "Mrs. Ives said she tried to call you before she phoned us. Said the sound seemed to come from over here."

"Probably a car backfiring," she said wearily. It sounded as if she had yawned. *What an actress,* I thought.

"Could have been," he agreed. "But she insisted it was a gun. Said she was awake, reading and she never did hear any car. Well, sorry I troubled you, Mrs. Cannon. We'll look around the neighbourhood. Don't worry about it."

"Thank you," she said. The door closed. The telephone had already stopped ringing. My knees felt rubbery as I leaned against the wall and wiped sweat from my face.

She was returning. I hurried down the hall and into the room where he was. Scooping up the gun, I put it on safety and shoved it in my pocket. I looked at him and came back out into the hall.

"You'd better come on down to your own bedroom," I said, taking her arm.

She stopped and looked at me. Her face was intensely still and her eyes were cold as ice. "Thank you," she said softly. "Thank you so very much for everything, Mr. Harlan."

She brushed past me and walked as erect as a ramrod into her own room and collapsed slowly across the bed. Her face was in her arms, but there was no sound of crying.

I went back in and stood looking down at him, trying to think. We'd thrown them off the track for the moment, but what now? I could still save it if we could get him out of here. But how? They were still prowling the neighbourhood; a car leaving here now would make them suspicious as hell.

Well, I could walk out and get away. Leave her here and keep going. The hell with her. It was her problem, wasn't it?

No. The hell it was. I was tied to her. If they caught her she'd talk. I was implicated in murder now as well as blackmail. There was something else too. I wasn't going to quit and just throw it away after I was in it this far. I wanted that money, and I was going to get it. There had to be a way. All we had to do was get him out of here——

Sure. It started to come to me. He'd set the whole thing up himself. Nobody knew I was here, and nobody knew he was here. It was made to order. As far as anyone was aware, she was the only one in the house; the police had just been here and had seen she was all right. She'd been asleep. If they were still suspicious about that shot, at least they had to assume it hadn't come from here. And if her car were to leave here—not tonight, but tomorrow, in a perfectly routine manner—with nobody in it except her, what could possibly be suspicious about that? Hell, it was perfect.

But how much time did we have? I had to be out of here before daybreak, and there was a lot to do. I glanced at my watch, and then remembered it had stopped. Stepping hurriedly over to the bed, I looked at his. 2.55. It was going to be close.

I heard a sound in the bathroom next door. She was begining to snap out of it. That was fine, because she was going to have to come out of her spin and give me a hand if she wanted to save her neck. I started into the bath to give her the word.

The door was open. She was standing before the medicine cabinet, shaking capsules out of a brown bottle. There were at least a dozen of them in the palm of her left hand and a tumbler of water was standing on the back rim of the basin. I jumped for her. She heard me and whirled. I caught her wrist, forced her hand open, and dropped the capsules into the john. Taking the bottle from her other hand, I shook the remaining ones out, threw them into the can, and flushed it.

"Look, you little fool!" I hissed at her. "Have you gone crazy? There's nothing to it. All we have to do is get him out of here. I know a way to do it——"

She held herself erect with both hands on the wash basin. Her face was white as chalk, and she spoke as if all the breath had been squeezed out of her. "Aren't you ever going to be through with me and leave me alone? Couldn't you even let me die with a little dignity?"

"Die, hell. Who wants to die?"

"I've had those for months. I've been saving them, because I knew there was a good chance I'd have to use them some day——"

"Shut up!"

"—I won't be taken alive. I have no intention of becoming the feature attraction at a Roman carnival——"

I caught her shoulders. "Listen," I whispered furiously. "They won't catch you. Use your head, you little idiot. Nobody knows he's even been here. All we have to do is get him out, and you'll never be suspected."

She stared with hopeless bitterness. "Shore up another bulkhead. Plug another leak in the dike. Keep watching the roulette wheel to see if it's really stopped or whether they're just pretending it has, to fool you. Why? I've had enough. I'm through."

I shook her. "I thought you were tough. Why, you little punk, are you going to fold up and quit now? Stand there like a nitwit and let 'em burn you?"

"Are you suggesting there is anything else to do?"

"Of course. Shut up for a minute and listen to me." I told her the idea. "It'll work fine."

"Will it?" she asked.

"What the hell's the matter with you?"

"Don't you see?" she said wearily. "You never win in the end. You can't. You merely postpone defeat."

"You won't even make an effort to save yourself?"

"What good would it do?"

I wanted to swing at her. I was beginning to feel crazy. Catching her by both shoulders again, I put my face right down in hers and snarled at her. "Tough? Why, you runny-nosed little cry-baby, you haven't got the guts of a louse. Go ahead. Quit. Stand here and let 'em take you. Have your picture all over the front page of every paper in the country. Have sob-sisters pawing over you, photographers flashing bulbs in your face every time they take you from the jail to the court-room, people staring at you. Look, by the second day they'll have a name for you. The Black Widow."

"What do you think I was saving those pills for?"

"They're gone now. I doubt if you'd have had the guts to swallow 'em, anyway. You're a punk. Why don't you face it?"

Anger was beginning to show in her eyes now. That was what I wanted to see.

"And just what do you want?" she asked coldly.

"The same thing I've been after all the time. I can save your neck, but you haven't brains enough to see it. Look. You can't bring Tallant back, but at least you can keep from having your name smeared all over every paper in the country and winding up in the chair for killing him. How do you want it?"

"What makes you think you can do it?"

"I'll show you if you'll stop acting like a crippled chicken."

"What do you want me to do?"

"Nothing right now. Just give me your car keys and go lie down."

Her eyes widened. "Are you going to try to—to take him away?"

"Not tonight. Of course not. If they saw your car leaving here now they might stop it. Even if the police didn't see it, one of the old busybodies around here'd notice. Just get out of my way, and I'll tell you everything to do before I shove off."

She went in her bedroom and gave me the car keys out of her purse and lay down on the bed. I went back and looked at him The top of his head was a mess, but he hadn't bled too much. The bullet had entered just at the base of his skull and come out on top. That was bad; I had to find it. It took me about five minutes. All that was necessary was to stand about where she had been and line it up. It had gone into the pillow my own head had been on, not more than about three inches from my face, and was still inside. I could feel it with my fingers. There'd be a lot of bloodstained feathers inside; it wouldn't do to leave it around here even if I got the bullet out. I took it out through the kitchen, opened the trunk of the car, and put it inside. That was the beauty of the whole thing. It wasn't necessary to go outside at all. I went back.

The other pillow was all right. There was no blood on it. The sheet was badly bloodstained, and the top of the mattress pad, but the mattress itself was all right. I rolled the sheet and pad around him and then wrapped a folded blanket around the upper half of his body and tied him up with the rope he'd had around my legs. This was the hard part now.

He was heavy. I was puffing and wet with sweat by the time I dragged and carried him as far as the garage. I had to rest before I could boost him up into the trunk. When I had him folded into it I went back into her bedroom.

"What'd you do with my suitcase?" I asked.

"It's in the closet there," she replied without looking up.

"What about the money? I guess you took that out?"

"No. It's still in there."

"Good," I said. I had bloodstains on the sports shirt I was wearing. I brought the suitcase out, shaved, and changed into a new one. The one I had taken off I rolled into a newspaper and stuck in the car trunk, first cutting out the laundry mark with a razor blade and flushing it down the john. The whole thing was beginning to make me sick now, and I was glad it was about over. I took the two handcuffs and the chains off the bed and threw them in the suitcase and put it in her car. That was it.

I went back. "All right," I told her. "Everything's set except for remaking that bed. You can do that."

She got up without saying anything, took some fresh sheets out of a closet, and made the bed. She put the spread over it. I looked around. The cops could paw through here a week and never find anything to indicate I'd ever been here, or Tallant either. We went back in her bedroom. I looked at her watch on the dresser and wound and reset my own. It was 4.15.

"Sit down," I said.

She sat down on the bed, staring at me without any expression at all. I tossed her the keys and lit a cigarette.

"You've got it made," I said. "It's a cinch from here on. Here's what you do, and be sure you get it all straight. Call any one of the local biddies on some excuse in the morning and just mention you're going to Galveston to visit friends over the week-end. Back the car out of the garage and leave it at the kerb while you come back and get your suitcase. Throw it in the back. Stop at some service station where you're known—or even at Cannon Motors—and have the car gassed up. Everything's perfectly natural and aboveboard, see? You even let them sweep out the car, but for Christ's sake if they start checking the tyres be sure you don't let go your keys. If anybody ever opens that trunk, you're dead.

"Drive on out that road to Breward. Time it so you get to that road turning off to the lake at about a quarter to ten. I'll be waiting for you in the trees just off the road, and I'll have that tape with me——"

She interrupted me. Her eyes were very cold. "So you did have it all the time?"

"Of course. But that's a dead issue now. I don't even have to give it to you, but I might as well. I don't want it. Anyway, get to that turn-off about a quarter to ten, the way I told you. If there are any other cars in sight, just pull off and pretend to be looking at a road map. I don't want anybody to see me. When it's clear, I'll hop in.

"This is Friday, and I'm not sure the banks down there are open tomorrow, but we can make it in three hours. I'll drop you off at the Carson Hotel. You get a room and then take a taxi to the bank. Draw out ninety-two thousand in cash. Have you got a briefcase?"

She nodded.

"All right. Bring it." I looked at my watch again and stood up. "But never mind now. I'd better get going. I can tell you the rest of it after you pick me up."

"What about——"

"I'll take care of him. All you do is drive the car from here to the turn-off and from then on the whole thing is my baby. You're paying me; I'll do it."

"All right," she said.

"You're convinced now it can be done, and that it's easy?" I asked. "No more of this flipping your lid and trying to kill yourself?"

"I'm all right now," she said coldly. "I'll meet you."

"Fine," I said. I went in the bath and drew a big drink of water from the tap and then threw the cigarette in the john. "I'll see you. Put your light out in here as if you'd gone back to bed." I waved a hand and went down the hall.

I let myself out into the patio through the door behind the curtain and stood for a moment letting my eyes become accustomed to the darkness. When I could see a little I eased back to the wall and climbed it. The whole neighbourhood was silent and the houses were dark. I slipped along the road and stood for a minute looking up and down the street before I crossed it. When I was in the woods on the other side I breathed more freely and walked faster.

I circled downhill and came out on a deserted street four blocks away. In another ten minutes I was on the Breward road going out of town. Twice I met cars, but I saw their lights a long way ahead and got off the road until they had gone by. By daybreak I had passed the river bottom where we had crashed, and was going up the hill on the other side. I left the road then and cut across. In about fifteen minutes I came out on the dirt road going in to the lake. Just at sunrise I was digging up the tape where I had buried it under the old stump. I slipped it in a pocket and sat down to rest while I smoked a cigarette. There was plenty of time. It was still a few minutes to nine when I got back out to the Breward road again. I sat down out of sight in the timber and waited. I was tired and hungry and almost numb now from this rat-race that seemed to have been going on for ever, but excitement was strong inside. In just a few more hours it would all be over and I'd have it made for good. They'd almost beaten me, but I had whipped them in the end.

By nine-thirty I was beginning to stare anxiously down the road, starting to worry again. A thousand things could have gone wrong. Suppose she had flipped again and killed herself? Suppose the police had come back and searched the place? She could be right; they could still be working on the case, keeping it under cover until they had the evidence they needed. Suppose they picked her up? My bag was in the car with Tallant's body. Probably a half dozen things in it had my name on them.

Right on the button at 9.45 she came by and picked me up. Everything was going beautifully.

CHAPTER EIGHTEEN

I PUSHED it hard, but took no chances, remembering the cargo we had in the trunk and what would happen if we had a wreck. It was a little before one when we came into down-town Houston.

"I'll drop you at the hotel," I said. "Register, and then grab a cab for the bank. Draw out the money, come back to the hotel, and wait for me to call. I'll register at the Magill Hotel. It'll be some time after midnight by the time I get back, and when I do the car'll be empty and you won't have anything to worry about. I'll turn the tape over to you when I meet you and you've got it made."

"Simple, isn't it?" she said coldly.

"Like shooting fish," I said.

I pulled up in front of the hotel loading zone. Some uniformed types helped her out and took her luggage. I wheeled it on out and caught the Galveston highway. When I got down there I bought a shovel at a hardware store and put it in the car. There were several hours to kill. When it was dark I started out for West beach. I drove for miles, until I was all alone along a vast stretch of empty dunes and scrub salt cedars. Parking the car well off the road, I went back in the edge of the cedars, found a sandy spot, and started to dig. It took over an hour to scoop out a place long enough and a little over four feet deep. A few cars went past, down near the edge of the water, but they could only see the car.

When I had finished I lit a cigarette and waited until there were no headlights in sight anywhere before I opened the trunk and dragged him out. I dropped him in the hole, threw in the pillow, the bloodstained clothes, and the handcuffs, and began pushing the sand back in with the shovel. When it was pretty well smoothed off I threw loose sand across the whole area with a swinging motion of the shovel, and turned on the headlights for an instant to see how it looked. It was fine. It might be a year before anybody even happened to stop at this particular spot. Nobody would ever see Tallant again.

I drove back toward town. After two or three miles I stopped and threw the shovel back among some cedars. It was 12.30 a.m. when I came into the outskirts of Houston, hot, tired, and thirsty. I pulled into the white glare of light of a drive-in and ordered a lemonade. While I was drinking it in the car I saw the telephone booth inside. The urge to know, to hear her say she had it and was waiting for me, became overpowering. I could even go right to the Carson and get it, take a cab to the airport, and be on my way tonight if I could catch a no-show on some plane going west. I didn't want to sleep; I wanted to be on a plane with that money under my arm at last. I went into the booth, looked up the number of the Carson, and dialled.

It was very hot inside the booth. The little fan whirled. When the girl at the switchboard answered, I said, "Mrs. Cannon, please."

"One moment, sir."

I could hear her ringing the room. It went on. There was no answer.

"I'm sorry, sir," the girl said. "She doesn't answer, but perhaps she is asleep. I'll keep trying."

"If you would," I said. "It's very important."

She rang some more. Nothing happened. I began to worry. What the hell was the matter with her, anyway? She surely couldn't have gone out.

"She must not be in her room," the girl said. "Just a moment and I'll have her paged in the lobby and in the restaurant."

"Never mind," I said. "I'll call back."

"Oh, it'll be no trouble," she interrupted. "It will take only a minute——"

"I'll try later," I said. I started to hang up.

"Is there any message?" she asked quickly. "Would you like to leave a number? Uh—I could try her room again, also, if you would like. It's just possible she might have taken a sleeping pill and be a little slow waking——"

I put the receiver back on the hook and went back outside, thinking about sleeping pills. She was crazy—there was no telling. But I had thrown them away. That didn't mean anything; she could have had a trunkful of the damned things. I paid for the lemonade and drove off.

The streets were almost deserted now. I heard a siren wailing somewhere in the distance behind me. When I was downtown I parked the car about a block away from the Carson, took my bag out, and walked around to the Magill. I was tight now with worry and uneasiness. *Oh, hell,* I thought; *she just went out somewhere; I'll call again after I register.* But the picture persisted; suppose she had drawn out the money and it was *lying there beside her in a locked hotel room while she drifted down and down into sleep with a bottle of those capsules inside her?* I shook my head and walked on. No, I told myself. That was too whacky even for her.

The small lobby of the Magill was deserted except for the clerk half asleep behind his desk. I registered. He turned the card around and glanced at the name.

"Oh, Mr. Harlan," he said. "Just a minute. Someone left a message." He reached for a pad lying on a shelf beside the small switchboard, and studied it for a moment with his lips pursed.

Maybe it's in Sanskrit, I thought, and he has to translate it. I wanted to strangle him. "Yes?" I asked.

"Hmmmm. It was a lady. She didn't leave any name. She called twice. Said she would be out until late, but that she would call you again and try to catch you as soon as you checked in."

I breathed softly. "Thanks," I said.

He clanged the bell on the desk and a coloured boy appeared from somewhere. When I was up in the room and he had departed with his tip I took off my coat and stared at the telephone. Should I try the Carson again? No. She was probably still out, and she'd said she would call again. She already had, twice, so she apparently wasn't trying to run out on me or anything. I unpacked my bag, and checked the envelope containing the eight thousand. Just for something to do, I counted it again. It was all there, to the last five-dollar bill. I forced myself to sit down, and lit a cigarette. I stared at the telephone, trying to force it to ring. Five minutes went by. Ten minutes.

It rang. I grabbed it.

"Mr. Harlan?" It was her voice, all right. I could hear music in the background. Where in the name of God was she? In some honkytonk?

"Yes," I said. "Where are you? Have you got it?"

"I'm in a bar on Fannin," she replied.

I took a slow breath and drew my left hand across my face. "*Have—you—got—it?*"

"Of course," she replied coolly. "It's right here in the booth with me."

I could feel nerves uncoiling all over my body. "All right. Good. Do you want me to meet you at the Carson?"

"No. I'll come there."

"For God's sake, hurry it up. You're sober, aren't you?"

"Of course." She hung up.

They never made any sense, I thought. Wandering around in bars at one in the morning with $92,000 in cash. I got up and began pacing up and down the room. I'd have gone crazy trying to sit still. I thought of all I had gone through for that money. It seemed a lifetime since that afternoon Purvis had walked up to me in the lobby of the hotel in Galveston. And now in a few minutes I'd get my hands on it at last. She had it. She was bringing it here. I lit a cigarette, took two puffs on it, and crushed it out. It suddenly occurred to me I hadn't eaten anything in over two days. Who cared? I wanted to sing, or shout, or climb up the walls.

There was a light tap on the door. I sprang forward to open it.

She was very smooth looking in a light skirt and straw-coloured blouse with a bunch of violets pinned to one shoulder. She was carrying a briefcase and her purse, and she had a folded newspaper under her arm.

"Come in," I said. "Come in."

I closed the door and started to reach for the briefcase. She tossed it carelessly on the bed and sat down in the armchair near the desk and telephone stand. I forgot her. I sat down on the bed and sliced open the zipper of the briefcase. My hands shook a little. God, it was wonderful. It was in bundles, tied with paper bands with the denomination stamped on them. I let them fall out on the bed. They fell in little stacks.

"Quite an interesting sight," she said.

I turned. She wasn't looking at the money. The brown eyes were on my face with a cool and faintly mocking expression in them.

"You're satisfied now?" she asked.

"Sure, sure," I said.

She reached out a hand and knocked cigarette ash into a tray. The sleeves of the straw-coloured blouse were long and full, tapering in closely at her wrists. "Everything is all right? The roulette wheel has stopped at last, and you've won? You're happy?"

"What do you think?" I said. "This is what I started out to get, and I got it."

"You're a success story. You are to be congratulated, Mr. Harlan. I assume you have carried out your end of the bargain?"

"Sure," I said.

"You are a man of honour. Knowing you has been one of the high points of my life."

"Write me about it," I said. "Every other Christmas."

"Sure, sure. Call me up. I'm in the book. So who has to like it? So write me about it. So what else is new? Learn the patter of the insulated and be a real tough guy. It's easy."

"Excuse me for living."

"I'm sorry. I forgot that one."

I said nothing. She was silent for a moment.

Then, without looking at me, she asked, "I won't ask any of the details, but—it was on Galveston Island?"

"Yes," I said. "Does it matter?"

She shook her head slowly, still looking down at the end of her cigarette. "I guess not."

"The tape's there on the dresser," I said.

"Thank you." She looked toward it without interest, and made no move to pick it up.

"Don't you want it?"

"Not particularly."

I stared at her. "I don't get you."

"It isn't important, is it? I mean, it has no actual value except as a hockey puck or a ball has value as long as a game of some kind is in progress. The game is over, so it is no longer something to be pursued. And, obviously, you could have made twenty copies of it by this time."

"You're an odd-ball," I said.

"No doubt. You make a great effort to understand people, don't you?"

"Not often."

"Couldn't that be a little dangerous, in your profession?"

"I don't know," I said. "But listen. Why were you wandering around in bars with all that money on you? I thought you'd be at the hotel."

"Oh, I haven't been back to the hotel since the morning papers hit the street."

I stared at her puzzled. "Why not?"

The paper she had brought in was lying folded in her lap. She tossed it to me. "Perhaps that will clear it up for you."

I unfolded it. In the centre of the front page a two-column picture of Julia Cannon hit me right in the eye. SOUGHT, the caption read.

I stared, feeling cold in the centre of my back. There were two columns of the story. Headlines and sub-heads sprang up at me. WIDOW SOUGHT IN "PERFECT-CRIME" SLAYING . . . REPORTED IN HOUSTON . . . TIE-UP WITH PURVIS SLAYING HINTED . . . NEW MYSTERY ADDED . . .

A story of five months' dogged but unpublicized police work was revealed today in the announcement by the Lucerne County Sheriff's office that it is believed to be almost certain now that Howard L. Cannon, Wayles automobile dealer, was murdered last March instead of meeting his death in an automobile crash as was supposed. The dead man's widow, Mrs. Julia Cannon, is being sought for questioning in connection with the crime, as is Daniel R. Tallant, Wayles sporting goods dealer. Both are missing. It is further suspected that Tallant himself may have met with foul play.

Both new light and fresh mystery were added to the case in the past twenty-four hours with the announcement that Tallant is wanted for questioning in connection with the death of Wilton L. Purvis, former insurance investigator of Houston, who figured prominently in the investigation of the supposedly accidental death of Cannon last March, and by the announcement that Tallant has disappeared, following a mysterious gunshot heard in the vicinity of the Cannon home last night and that his car was later found parked near a wooded area some two blocks away.

Following a search of the Cannon home by police yesterday, it was announced that definite traces of blood were found on the floor of the garage——

That was where I had put him down.

—and that an empty cartridge case was found in one of the bedrooms of the house——

Oh, Jesus, I hadn't even thought of that.

She was saying something.

"Shut up!" I said. I felt as if my head would fly off. "I've got to see what it says——"

She shook her head. "It's not really necessary. I can tell you what it says. It says, quite simply and beautifully, that the roulette wheel has stopped at last. They have been working on it for five months, and since Purvis's death they have been working with the Houston police. A picture of Dan has been identified by three people as the man they saw in the vicinity of Purvis's apartment house that night. You see? They don't stop the wheel; they just let you think it's stopped. I tried to tell you that.

"They know I'm in Houston. The bank has reported I cashed that cheque for ninety-two thousand this afternoon. They think I'm trying to escape, using the money, and every exit has been blocked off. I shall be picked up in a matter of hours, if not minutes. If I had stayed in the hotel I would be in custody now——"

"Shut up!" I fought to keep my voice down. I wanted to scream at her. "Let me read——"

She shook her head. "You are so obvious. There is no mention of you anywhere in the story. Apparently nobody has any idea you have been connected with it at all."

I sighed weakly. I was all right. I was still free. They'd been there at the Carson when I called, and all the time the girl had been stalling me so they could trace it. I shuddered, thinking of how it would have been if I'd called from here instead of that pay phone. I was in the clear. They couldn't do anything to me because they didn't even know about me. Nobody did. Except——

She smiled. "Nobody except me, Mr. Harlan."

I stared at her.

She shook her head. "You can't kill me. You are registered in this room, under your own name. And you might have some difficulty in getting my body out of here."

"Wh—what are you going to do? Why did you come here?"

She took a puff of the cigarette and slowly tapped the ash into a tray. "I'm not going to do anything. In another half hour I shall be dead. I told you I have no taste for Roman carnival."

"Where——?"

"Not here. Obviously, that would be in very bad taste because it would embarrass you. I shall check in at some other hotel, under another name. By the time my description registers, I shall be beyond their reach. Naturally, I had the prescription refilled before I left town yesterday."

I shook my head helplessly. "I don't dig you."

"Is that surprising? You never make any effort to understand anybody. You never listen. And I've told you it could be dangerous in a profession such as yours."

I leaned forward. "Look. You mean you're going to walk out of here, and say nothing to anybody? And you'll be dead when they find you?"

"Precisely."

"How about the room clerk? Did you ask him the number of this room?"

She shook her head. "He gave it to me when I called you from the bar. I didn't stop at the desk on the way up, and he barely glanced at me. He probably thinks I'm a call girl somebody ordered."

I went on staring at her. "It throws me. What did you come here for?"

"Why, to say good-bye. And to give you that money."

She would never make sense to me. "Why? I—I mean, why the money?"

Her eyebrows raised. "I promised it to you, didn't I? And what else could I do with it? I had already cashed the cheque before I learned I was trapped with no further place to run."

I shook my head. It was unbelievable. But there it was. I had the money, and as soon as she walked out of this hotel I was free to run and nobody would even be looking for me.

"As a matter of fact," she said, "I offered part of it to an old friend of mine tonight, but she didn't want it. She doesn't expect to live much longer, and she said it was of no value to her. Another odd-ball, no doubt. So what remained but to bring it to you?"

I sighed, feeling weak all over. "Thanks," I said. "Thanks a million."

"Not at all, Mr. Harlan." She smiled, and stirred as if to get up. "You are entirely welcome. I thought you would appreciate it."

CHAPTER NINETEEN

I LOOKED at my watch. I could probably catch one of the early flights to the Coast. "Well, I won't keep you. And hadn't you better shove right along? You wouldn't want to stooge around too long and let them pick you up."

She smiled again. "And certainly not in your room? I was wondering if you would actually say that."

"So I've said it."

"The so beautifully consistent Mr. Harlan." She gathered up her purse. "But there was one other thing."

"What's that?"

"The good-bye," she said quietly.

"All right. So good-bye."

She studied me thoughtfully. "The farewell carries a legacy with it."

"What?"

"I wanted to leave you something."

Without thinking, I glanced around at the money piled on the bed.

She shook her head. "Not that. That's yours, free and clear, to enjoy as you wish. You might even say you earned it; at least you worked hard enough for it. No. The legacy is something else entirely."

She still had the purse in her hands. I lunged forward and grabbed it. I opened it and looked inside.

She smiled. "There is no weapon in it. Unless a bottle of capsules is a weapon."

I shook my head. She reached out and retrieved the purse.

I began to get it then. She had blown her stack completely. She was crazy.

"So what is this big deal you're going to leave me?" I asked. Maybe I'd better humour her so she'd shove before the cops found her here.

"It's quite simple, Mr. Harlan," she said. "What I am going to bequeath to you is an emotion."

I was right. She had flipped.

"You lead a very barren life, insulated as you are against everything. I have just done what I could to rectify that, by arrangeing for you to have one with you rather consistently in the future, the only emotion—besides greed—that I believe you are capable of feeling. Fear."

"What?"

She leaned back in her chair. "I'm not very fond of you, Mr. Harlan. That may have escaped your attention up to this time, since hypersensitivity to the feelings of others is not a weakness of yours, but I assure you it is quite true. But I *have* studied you. And one of the things I found intriguing was your predilection for the letter-to-be-opened-after-my-death sort of threat you like to hold over people. So I thought you might appreciate this thing I have arranged for you."

"What in hell are you talking about?"

She stood up and crushed out her cigarette. "I have a friend here in town who is a very old woman in very ill-health. She is the one I just spoke of as refusing the money because she doesn't expect to live much longer. She used to be one of my teachers years ago. I am quite fond of her, and I am glad to be able to say that for some perverse reason she likes me. Like a great many very old women she has grown to be unimpressed by lots of things and she has a somewhat irreverent sense of humour. She also happens to have a notary's commission.

"I spent about two hours out at her home today, after the morning papers came out. I wrote out a rather full account of all this thing, particularly in reference to your participation in it, and signed it in her presence. She put her seal on it. She doesn't know what is in the document, but she witnessed the signature. It has been sealed, and will be placed in her lawyer's safe, to be opened when she dies. That may be next month, next year, or three years from now——"

I stared at her. I couldn't even open my mouth to speak.

"There is no statute of limitations on murder, Mr. Harlan," she went on. "You are guilty of withholding evidence of two murders, and of being not only an accessory but an active participant in a third."

I finally got my mouth open. Nothing came out.

She turned and started toward the door. Then she paused with her hand on the knob.

"Of course, I could have merely had it notarized and then left it beside me tonight so the police would find it in the morning, but it seeemed to me to lack finesse. That way, you wouldn't have time to enjoy your wealth, or to savour your emotion to its fullest. Emotion can grow, you see. Or at least, that particular one can. The passage of time and the night-and-day uncertainty somehow mature it and give it a certain poignant quality I am sure you will appreciate."

I grabbed her arm. "You can't do it! No——"

She smiled and opened the door. Gently disengaging her arm, she said. "Good night, Mr. Harlan. And think of me from time to time, will you?"

She lifted her hand in a little gesture of farewell and went down the hall towards the stairs. I leaned against the door and watched her. It was an erect and unhurried walk, as if she didn't have a care in the world.

I went back inside and closed the door. A month . . . a year . . . three years. . . . I sat down on the bed. It was lumpy and uncomfortable. I looked around and saw I was sitting on the pile of money. I pushed it off on to the floor. I'd never know. The first inkling I'd ever have of it was when they came knocking on the door to pick me up. Run? Run where? They always found you.

I tried to light a cigarette. My hands shook so badly I let it fall to the floor. I didn't even try to pick it up. I went on staring at the wall.

That was the horrible part of it.

I'd never know when——

Mr. Harlan?

A Mr. John Harlan. He live here?

A fat man, a thin man, a man with one gold tooth, a tall man, a man with tufts of hair in his ears, a smiling man, a man with one drooping eyelid——

A man with a Panama hat pushed back on his head, a man with a cigar in his mouth——

A man with spring sunlight in his face, a man wearing a raincoat against the November rain——

Mr. Harlan?

Is this Mr. Joseph N. Carraday, whose real name is John Harlan?

A man sweating in the Florida sun, a man with Chicago snow on the shoulders of his overcoat——

He looks at you through the narrow opening of the doorway.

Mr. Harlan?

I've come to read the water meter. To collect for the *Times-Picayune-Mirror-Sun-Post-Dispatch-Examiner-Herald-Tribune* To sell you an aluminium pot. To tell you about our new hospitalization plan.

To arrest you for murder.

No!

I lunged to my feet. It was here. Here in this city. Look. All I had to do was find her so I could get it away from her and destroy it. Hell, finding her would be easy. She was a Notary Public. She was an old woman. She was ill. How many old-women-ill-Notaries-Public were there in a city of maybe less than a million?

I grabbed up the telephone directory and flipped wildly through the yellow pages.

Naturopathic Physicians . . . Newspaper Dealers . . . Night Clubs . . .

Notaries Public . . .

Column after column of Notaries Public.

Most of them weren't even listed by name. They were listed by the places they worked: insurance agencies, attorney's offices, banks, real estate offices.

I was shaking. I stared at the yellow columns. Hell, I could do it. Hire private detectives. That was it. Look, I had lots of money. Hire all the private detectives in town. They'd find her. They'd find her before——

Before what?

Why, before she died, of course.

And so what was I going to find her for? To kill her? If she wouldn't tell me where the statement was, I'd have to threaten to kill her to make her talk, and if I killed her they would get me just that much quicker——

And she didn't have it, anyway. Her attorney had it.

So I had to find her, and then find out who her attorney was. And if she wouldn't tell me who her attorney was, I had to threaten to kill her to make her talk, and if I killed her——

How many attorneys were there in a city of maybe less than a million? The yellow pages flew by in a blur.

Attorneys. (See Lawyers.)

Lapidaries . . . Lawn Mowers . . . Lawn Mowers, Rental . . .

Lawyers.

I stared. Page after page of lawyers. Entire races of lawyers. A torrent of lawyers, a waterfall of lawyers, a whole river of lawyers overflowing from the bottomless springs of a thousand law schools and spreading across the pages faster than I could turn them. I put my head down in my hands.

No. Don't go to pieces. You can do it. You've got money. Look at all the money you've got. Hire detectives. Find her. Find her lawyer. Find her lawyer's safe. Open the safe. How? Hire somebody to open the safe. A safe-cracker.

Safe-crackers . . .

Saddlery . . . Safe Depositories . . . Safes . . . Safety Equipment . . . Scales . . . *What?*

Get hold of yourself. Look, it doesn't mean anything.

It was just a momentary aberration. You've been looking for all those other things in the yellow pages, so naturally——

I sat down then, and picked up the cigarette. It was all right. It's just a problem, see. Find her, find the attorney—lawyer, that is —get somebody to open the safe. She'll live that long. Sure she will.

Hell, it's nothing, compared to what they were up against.

Suddenly, I thought of Tallant. He was dead. And by now she was probably dropping off to sleep, for the last time. The roulette wheel had stopped for them and they were at peace. They were resting.

And why shouldn't they be? They had got up and given me their seats in front of the wheel.

No, by God, I thought. *I'll beat 'em. I'll show 'em. All I have to do is find her, and then find the lawyer*——But first I'd better get out of here. This place wasn't safe any more. Maybe the clerk had recognized her. Maybe he had called the police. That was it; pack up and move somewhere else, and then I would be able to think.

Hurry.